THE fate SERIES

COMPLETE SERIES BOXSET

HEIDI LIS

Defying Fate—Copyright © 2015 by Heidi Lis
Sealing My Fate—Copyright © 2016 by Heidi Lis
Cruel Twist of Fate—Copyright © 2018 by Heidi Lis

The Fate Series Boxset
Copyright © 2018 by Heidi Lis

No part of this publication may be reproduced or transmitted in any form or by any means, electronic or mechanical, including photocopying, recording, or by any information storage and retrieval system without the written permission of the author, except for the use of brief quotations in a book review.

This book is a work of fiction. Names, characters, places, and incidents either are products of the author's imagination or are used fictitiously. Any resemblance to actual persons, living or dead, events, or locales is entirely coincidental.

Defying Fate—
Editing by Joanna Villalongo
Editing by Emma Mack of Tink's Typos

Sealing My Fate—
Editing by Joanna V at Precision Freelance
Proofreading by Emma at Ultra Editing Company

Cruel Twist Of Fate—
Editing by Joanna at Precision Freelance
Proofreading by Emma at Ultra Editing Company

The Fate Series Boxset—
Cover Design—Jay Aheer at Simply Defined Art
Interior Design & Formatting by T.E. Black Designs; www.teblackdesigns.com

Defying *fate*

BOOK ONE IN THE FATE SERIES

HEIDI LIS

prologue

I'VE BEEN ON EDGE ALL day. The opportunity I've waited so long for has finally presented itself and tonight, I'm taking it. All is in order, I've planned my escape, and my best friend, Kara, has my car hiding down the street, fully gassed and waiting. The keys to my future are tucked safely in my duffle bag under my bed. Sitting in the dark, I'm barely breathing. I know he'll be home soon. Trying to calm my nerves, I take several deep breaths, knowing if he suspects anything I'm in trouble. I need this plan to work.

Hearing his car pull up, I can only pray he is alone, like I've anticipated. It's typical for him to come home with an associate or two, but Thursday nights is his weekly meeting night. The one night he meets with his colleagues and then returns home alone. Yet another reason I picked tonight to plan my escape. I would have left earlier, but he had one of his guys hanging around the house until he returned home. Evil bastard that he is.

"Izzabella," He calls searching for me.

It's the first thing he says whenever he gets home. And every day, it's like a spike to my heart. Little did I know his angel eyes hid the demon that lurks inside. Counting to ten, I'm waiting... quietly. Slipping under the bed, I hang onto my bag, silently praying I can pull this off. He keeps calling my name, his footsteps are becoming louder and more frantic. The more manic he becomes, the more terrified I feel. *Please God, just let him get in his car and leave to go looking for me.* This is what I've counted on, him home alone and not finding me. He'll have no choice but to get in his car and go looking for me. The instant he pulls out of the driveway, I'll run like hell. I'll only have a few minutes before one of his guys shows up here at the house. As soon as I hear the garage door open, I take my first real breath even though I can still hear him yelling out my name. I feel nauseous. I'm cold and hot, sweating and shaking, fighting back the urge to cry. I can't though, I simply can't break down now.

To steady my breathing, I slowly count backward from one hundred.

As soon as I hear his car pull away, I bolt from under the bed, dragging my bag as it gets tangled in one of the bed legs. Shouting, I'm damn near frantic knowing I have to be quick. One last pull and my bag comes flying out, knocking over the things on my nightstand. I don't waste the time to straighten things up, I head straight for the back door instead.

Running toward my car down the darkened path, I'm trembling with fear and excitement. Fear, because I know what I'm about to do and the consequences I will face if he catches me. A rush of adrenaline in the dark night makes searching for my keys in my bag damn near impossible. Why the hell I didn't have them already in my hand, I'll never know. By the time I find them, I'm so worked up it takes both of my hands for my car to roar to life. With no sight of any cars, I catch my breath and glance at the belongings of what's left of my life. I notice Kara made sure I had all that I needed for now.

With that, I wipe away the few stray tears that are left of my sorrows. It's time for me to leave. To search for my new beginning and find my way in life. A life without fear. A life without hurting. A life without him. Driving away from his house, I only look ahead. I'll never look back.

chapter ONE

Waking up this morning, I feel refreshed even though I, once again, slept on the hard floor. The little two-bedroom house I'm renting is filled only with whatever I could fit in my car. I left the rest back in Iowa. No furniture, no bedroom set, no television. I only needed the essentials.

I guess leaving the way I did is both a blessing and a curse. All I can say in my defense is, leaving on bad terms was not what I'd wanted, but I needed a fresh start.

I knew that my new beginning needed to be far away from all the things that reminded me of my past and my failures. I sure as hell didn't need to stay there just for my many mistakes to be rubbed in my face on a daily basis. My family, who now hates me, are only one small part of the things better left behind. The stories and the gossip about me were spreading like wildfire, and I couldn't take it anymore. Fucking rumor mill. So yes, the only answer was to leave.

I headed as far West as I could go and ended up in Washington State. I suppose a number of reasons had me coming this far. For one, I couldn't get any farther. Secondly, it turned out to be beyond beautiful. Like God's country. The pretty, evergreen trees that line the streets and nearby mountains just took my breath away. The moment I arrived and basked in my new surroundings I thought yes, Monroe is a good place to start afresh.

It's a small town, with a great feel to it. Only thirty short minutes from Seattle, enough distance to stay out of the big city limelight.

Taking in a big breath of the pure country air, it just feels right. The peace that I'm feeling right now is the most peace I have felt for quite some time.

Upon entering this beautiful town, the first thing I needed to look for was a place to live. I had saved some money, but not enough to get by for very long. That meant I also needed a job. Slowly I could buy some furniture to furnish my new home. None of my new things would be brand-new or designer. Nope. They would be second hand, and they would be the best things I have ever bought because I would have done it all on my own.

Yesterday, while driving around with the newspaper, I found a few possibilities and made some phone calls. I was hoping I could find a place right away so I could stop wasting money on hotels and takeout food. *God*, I thought, *to sleep in a bed that was my own and even to cook a meal, would feel like heaven*. A week on the road, staying in motels and living on fast food was getting old fast.

It didn't take me long. By my third phone call, I had found the one. It was a small two-bedroom house in need of repairs, but it had a homey feel to it and was located on a quiet street. The homeowner, a little old lady named Evelyn Kennedy, was even willing to let me plant some flowers out front if I wanted to. Yep, it just got better and better. I knew I was going to love Evelyn.

The little blue house had a wrap-around porch and shutters that needed painting due to wear and tear. The rest of the house was pretty much the same, in need of a few repairs and some love. The living room did have a wood burning fireplace and that alone could have sold it to me. I planned on doing some reading in front of it while eating late-night snacks. There is nothing better than the smell of a fire. The kitchen, although small, was lovely. Its outdated appliances were on the brink of dying, but they managed to put a tiny smile on my face. The bathroom needed a deep cleaning, and I decided that would be my top priority, once I got some cleaning supplies. The good news is the one and only bathroom was tiny. The pink porcelain sink to the flowered wall paper was a site to take in, but for some reason, it fit. Looking at this sweet old lady, you would understand.

As I walked around the place, Mrs. Kennedy watched me. A little too closely for my liking. I figured she was wondering why I did not have much to my name and even more likely why I was alone. She could wonder all she liked. If she thought I was going to repeat my sad story, she was mistaken. Evelyn Kennedy could wonder all she liked because that wasn't likely to happen any time soon.

At the end of the tour she touched my cheek, giving me a warm smile. "My dear, I want you to rent my house. I think you could brighten up this old place. Paint, plant and make it your home. Maybe you could cheer each other up."

I had no idea how to respond, so I just stared at her.

Thankfully, she seemed to understand the reason for my silence. "No worries, my dear. Anytime you need anything you just give me a call."

Finally finding my voice, I thanked her. I took out the exact amount of cash that would cover my first rent payment, and practically shoved it in her hands. For a second she looked stunned, but she recovered fast and repeated her offer that I could call her anytime I needed anything, and with that, she went on her merry way.

By the time I'd unpacked and gotten over the fact that I actually had a home, I laid out my blankets and pillow and crashed. My time on the road knocked the hell out of me. The added mental stress of my escape from hell was weighing heavily on my shoulders, as well. Being alone felt great. I knew that I had found peace, a new beginning, so why did I feel so unsure of myself? Life could be so fucking confusing at times. I had given up trying to figure it out long ago, but for a few moments, as I drifted into sleep, I wondered if I would ever feel sure of anything again.

That was last night. Today, I'm feeling a bit refreshed and I'm ready to make a go of things. Even so, I jumped when my phone rings. Luckily, it's just Kara calling to check up on me.

She's my best friend back in Iowa, and it sucked to leave her, but she understood. She always did when it came to me. Hell, she even encouraged me to get away. She once told me to run for the hills and find some hot biker to ride into the wind with. That's my Kara, the ever loving, hot biker chick who I happen to share a love of hot biker guys with. It all started when we discovered them in the sex-filled books we liked reading. Damn girl made me laugh out loud with the way she went on about them. I miss her like crazy.

After we finish our chat, I take notice of my empty cupboards. Ah hell, I need to get showered and get some groceries. I need to get today's newspaper as well, so that I can start job hunting. The rent has set me back some, and unless I plan on starving by the end of my third month out here, I need to find a job.

As soon as I've showered, I pile my hair on top of my head and throw on some makeup. Next, I get my jeans and tank top on, and then

I'm out the door, smiling as I walk down the walkway to my car. This is the first time I have smiled a genuine smile in what feels like forever.

While driving down the street, I take a good look at my new neighbors' houses. All seems well and quiet, until I get to the corner. I come to a stop because I see four Harley-Davidsons parked in the driveway. This makes me smile even wider because Kara would totally love the sight of all these bikes. Shaking my head, I laugh as I notice three huge men coming out of the house. Oh, Sweet Jesus! I try not to look obvious, but seeing gigantic, delicious male specimens walking out of a house will stop traffic any day of the week.

Oh yeah. Bikers. Damn, not only do they look like a stereotypical biker should look, they are hot as holy hell. I make a mental note to call Kara later. She will have me bringing my new neighbors hot meals to introduce myself. Better yet, she might move out here too. It wouldn't be for me either; it would be for the Harleys down the street from me. All this smiling is making my cheeks hurt.

Driving away, I hear the rumbling of the bikes as they start to life. Damn! I will have to keep driving by here and checking out my new neighbors.

Welcome to the neighborhood, Izzy.

chapter TWO

THE NEXT FEW DAYS GO by fast. I'm slowly getting some furniture in the house and some food to stock my cupboards. I have yet to find a job, but that's okay, I'm getting a chance at getting settled into my new life.

While I was out, I found some awesome flowers at the store, so I headed out to plant them in the front yard, like my lovely landlord suggested. I can honestly say that Mrs. Kennedy is the sweetest old lady I have ever met; all four feet seven inches of her. I just wanted to hug her to death but, my display of gratitude would probably crush that sweet woman.

Knee deep in dirt and flowers I hum along to Muse, my favorite band in my library. It's a beautiful day, and the morning rain shower has been just what the ground needed.

I'm so absorbed in my planting that I don't realize I have company, until a slight movement catches my eye and startles the hell out of me. I calm down when I see that I have been snuck up on by a sweet-faced little girl of maybe six or seven. She's wearing black jeans with a cute pink blouse and black boots up to her knees. Her look is adorable, but eye-raising. It's like she's trying to look older than she is.

I give her a smile.
She smiles right back.

Okay, I guess I'm going to need to talk first. Keeping my tone friendly and non-threatening, I greet her. "Hi, I'm sorry I didn't see anyone standing there."

"Hi, I like your flowers." She is eyeing my planted flowers, smiling from ear to ear.

"Thank you," I reply, getting a little dazzled by her big and happy brown eyes. "I think they will brighten up the yard. Do you live around here?"

"Yes, I live down the street."

"Oh, my name is Izzy. What's yours?" I raised my eyes to look at her. *'Down the street huh?'*

"My name is Eve." She sways back and forth in her boots and looks down at them like she's suddenly shy. "Can I help you plant your flowers? I don't get to do plant stuff at home. My daddy doesn't get into flowers and stuff."

My curiosity piques. "What about your momma?"

Her smile drops away, as she winces like it's a sore subject. I want to take my question back.

Shit. What do I say? Great, Izzy, you make this cute, little girl sad and you have no idea how to fix it. Say something. "I'm sorry, I didn't mean to make you sad."

"No, it's okay. My momma isn't around much. I live with my daddy. I... I should go. Nice meeting you, Izzy."

I can't stand the sight of her apparent sadness, her smile replaced with a frown, so I blurt out. "Eve, maybe tomorrow you can stop by and help me? Ask your dad first, and see if it's alright?" The last thing I need is a dad angry at me right now. And, just in case her daddy is one of those Harley riding men, I really don't need to piss him off.

Her eyes get wide with excitement. "Awesome! I'd love to! My daddy will be happy to hear a pretty lady moved down the street from us."

I burst out laughing.

Okay, that last part is not quite what I was expecting. I force back another chuckle.

"I sure will. Bye Izzy, it was nice to meet you." She waves her hand and starts walking away.

Gosh, what a cute and sweet little girl. I wipe my hands on my jeans and wave right back. "Bye Eve. See you after school." I assume she's coming from school based on her having a backpack hanging off her shoulder.

Suddenly she stops and turns. "Please don't plant anymore. Wait for me, okay?" She eyes the unplanted flowers on the ground by my feet.

"No problem sweetheart, I'll save you plenty of flowers and dirt to dig up."

She strolls down the street, and I watch her. I am making sure she gets home okay. Yep, that's all. I'm not waiting to see which house she goes to. Okay, that's a lie. I'm totally watching to see which house it is.

As she passes house after house, I can feel my heart start to race. Sure enough, she walks right to the end of the street and enters the house that had the Harleys parked in its driveway earlier today. "Oh, Shit." Huh, well that is interesting.

JUST LIKE CLOCKWORK, THE NEXT day a jubilant and excited Eve comes skipping along into my yard. I timed it so that I'd be out here at the exact same time as yesterday.

"Oh my gosh, I'm so excited to help you," she gushes with that radiant smile of hers back in place. "This is awesome. I told my daddy all about you and how I was helping you make your yard beautiful."

She carries on, talking a mile a minute and I can't help wonder when she last saw her mother. Eve's so excited, it's like she never gets any fun girl-time. I wonder if she ever spends time with any females. I find it sad and unnerving.

Finally, she stops to catch her breath and I finally get a chance to speak. "Eve, I'm so glad you're here and eager to help me. How did I get so lucky to get such a great helper and neighbor?" I wink down at her smiling face.

Nodding back at me, she's smiling from ear to ear. "That's me. I am a good helper, my daddy says so."

Gosh, what a *sweetheart*. It warms my heart to hear her talking about her daddy with such happiness. He seems like a great dad. I can't help myself; I move the hair from her face and tuck it behind her ear.

"I bet he does, let's get to work." Her smile is infectious.

We spend the better part of the next two hours working as a team. I dig the holes, Eve plants the flowers and we cover them back up. We laugh and chat as we work, getting to know each other.

Finding out her mom is hardly a presence in her life makes me sad. This little girl is like the daughter I never got to have. Hell, from what I had learned, the possibility of my body carrying a child is close to zero. He took that from me.

Eve pulls me out of my dark thoughts with her excitement. "Izzy, I'm all dirty, but hey, look at our flower garden! We put together the nicest yard on the street. My daddy said he would drive by later and look at our hard work."

I focus my attention on the patch of the garden we've been working on. She's right, it does look fantastic. Her dad driving by, now that has my attention.

"What does your dad do?" I ask while removing a few yellowed leaves from the otherwise perfect flowers. *Don't sound too interested, Izzy.*

Wiping her face with the back of her hand, she smudges a dirt streak up her cheek. It's adorable. "He owns a shop in town."

"What kind of shop does he have?" Okay, I am quizzing this poor little girl about her Harley loving daddy. It feels wrong and creepy. But I still do it.

"They work on cars and bikes. My daddy's the boss. The guys all look up to him." The pride in her words warms me. When she talks about her daddy, she glows.

Smiling, I add. "I bet they do."

We finish up, and Eve strolls down the street towards her house. Once I've made sure that she reached it, I go inside to wash my hands in the sink. Moments later I hear the rumbling of a motorcycle as it drives up the street. It seems to slow down as it passes my house and then revs up once again.

Shit. I guess he did drive by to check out the yard. Why do I care? Why should I let this excite me? Just the thought that some big, burly, probably incredibly hot looking guy is driving by my house is insane.

Oh God, get a grip Izzy. He is driving by to see the flowers that his daughter helped plant.

I need a life. Better yet, a sex life.

After my shower I lie in bed, letting my thoughts return to the rumbling of that motorcycle as it passed by my house. Damn, all of those sexy romance books have me thinking that every biker is big, burly and hot. A man who would know just what a girl like me needed. He would take me over. His dominance would seduce me and I would submit to him willingly. I would surrender all of my insecurities, my fears, and he would take me in his big arms and never let me go. He would possess my body and own my soul in very splendid ways.

Yeah, drifting off to sleep, I picture myself in the arms of a broad-shouldered man with pythons for arms, and tattoos that weave intricate designs as they lace themselves around my small body. In my fantasies, his smell and dark and sexy voice are a complete turn on. His hands are rough with calloused fingertips, but man, I bet they'd feel like heaven against my skin. I can only imagine how incredible his hard body would feel against mine. It has me getting all kinds of turned on, and my last naughty thought puts a smile on my face. Okay, more like an enormous smile.

Yeah, tonight I would not worry.

Tonight I would not think about my past.

CHAPTER THREE

SATURDAY MORNING CAME AND I was sleeping soundly, until a constant knocking at my door had me wiping the sleep out of my eyes. "Jesus H. Christ, who the hell is at my door this early?" I am like the walking dead, stumbling in the direction of that annoying knock. The floors are cold on my bare feet. *Oh man, I need socks.*

Opening the door, I find my sweet little helper staring up at me, looking uneasy. Her shy smile alone wakes me from my sleepy haze. Even though I'm surprised to see her here so early, it makes me really happy.

Grinning at her, I say. "Hey Eve, how are you sweetie?"

"Hey, Izzy." Her big brown eyes light up like liquid honey. *So pretty.* "I didn't mean to wake you up. My daddy said it was okay to come over."

Really? It's odd he let his daughter spend a Saturday morning with some strange woman he's never even met. I could be about to throw a wild party for all he knows. Then again, it's odd that he allowed her to visit me on a weekday. Shit, maybe he doesn't care. Maybe all my dreams of him are totally off base, and he is actually some asshole; a lousy excuse for a dad. *Great, there goes my dream of a sexy, Harley riding man with a heart of gold.* Dammit, all to hell and back. My dreams were just starting to get good, too.

I open my door wider and try to shake off my less than subtle thoughts of a big, hot biker doing all sorts of naughty things to me. I'm better off concentrating on the little girl looking at me with a huge frigging smile on her face. "Come in honey, I just need to get dressed." When she doesn't move fast enough, I put my arm around her shoulder and bring her inside. I don't need my neighbors to get an eyeful of me in my sleepy state.

Eve came and sat in the living room. I feel bad that my living room is sparsely decorated at best. I only had time to buy a few things so far. I picked up the television at a thrift store just yesterday. It's sitting on a 'falling apart' stand, but it was only twenty bucks.

I wish I could afford nicer things, especially now that it looks like Eve is going to be spending time in more than just my garden.

Why I care what a little girl thinks about my place is beyond me, but I am nervous for the first time in forever.

When I'm dressed, I invite Eve to have breakfast with me. It's nice to have someone to share a meal with again, and I start to feel a little less uncomfortable about my almost empty house. We spend most of the morning laughing and talking like we've known each other forever. Having her with me is so natural, it's like she belongs here. Eventually, we head outside to take in our flower garden.

We're sitting on the porch and talking about what she's learning at school when I hear the roar of a motorcycle approaching. My stomach tightens and I am nervous for some strange damn reason. The very loud bike comes down the street and then stops in front of my house.

Holy Hell! I immediately notice how large his frame is. *Wow.* Every cell in my body is suddenly on high alert. This guy could be trouble, so I jump up and stand in front of Eve.

Now if you were looking at us and you didn't know us, you would think I am a mother protecting her daughter. Why? Who the hell knows?

Staring at him, his looks both excite and terrify me. Handsome here, has a killer body. Oh yeah, this man works out. His white t-shirt shows off all his manly tattoos that sleeve his muscular arm. 'Mouthwatering' comes to mind, even though I don't want to see him that way. His leather vest has some intricate emblems on it. I don't waste my time looking at those when I can look at his smoking hot body. Moving my gaze downward, I take in his faded blue jeans and chain belt. The black biker boots hanging open at the bottom are just as hot. Not one thing is wrong with this man.

When I finally look at eye-candy's face my insides do somersaults, my core burns up, and my legs turn to jelly. This man is T.R.O.U.B.L.E. Fuck-Me-Eyes, a strong jaw, dreamy black hair that screams 'pull on me while I make you scream.' Jesus, can a guy get any sexier than this man in front of me now?

Then he smiles. Holy shit, perfection. My books never prepared me for this. He gets off his bike and struts over to us. Even though he has fogged my brain, I immediately place my arm around Eve. Mr.-Sexy-Bad-Ass-Biker-Dude could knock me out with just a slap. I know this, but I don't budge. Besides, he might not even be Eve's dad.

Eve says something along the lines of 'that's my dad' and tries to pull free of my hold, but I don't let go of her.

It's weird how protective I feel. Almost motherly. Downright weird since I am sure Eve is his daughter. Can never be too sure, though. Truth be known, I am using Eve so I won't fall. My jellied legs are starting to tremble.

Now only a few feet from us, the biker lets out a slight chuckle. "Protecting my daughter from me, are we?" He raises an eyebrow as if questioning me. The smirk on his lips is my undoing. He says something else, but I'm too lost in those eyes, lips, everything.

Shit. What did this god of a man just say? Hell.

"I...um."

"You..."

"Um, I mean you're Eve's daddy?" I shudder and rock back and forth on my feet.

"Well, since she is my daughter, yeah, I'm her daddy." He raises that eyebrow at me again. He seems to like doing that. Now he's clearly aware of what it's doing to me because his smirk turns lopsided, showing off the deep dimple on his left cheek. Oh, Mother of Pearl, he just gets better looking.

Eve interrupts the heated stare between her daddy and me with a giggle. "Stop it, daddy." She then grabs my hand in hers, smiling from ear to ear. "Don't let him scare you, he likes to do that."

His deep chuckle lets me know how true this statement is. "Do I now?"

"Yep and you know it. Look at all the lovely flowers we planted." Her eyes and voice beaming with excitement as she walks over to the last row of flowers we finished that wrap around the porch.

A look of happiness and awe comes across his face as he looks at his little girl and me. Damn, he still makes me nervous. And why is he eyeing me like I am a piece of meat? For that matter, why am I eyeing him like a piece of meat?

"So what do you think, Daddy?"

Smiling and shaking his head, he adds. "Real beautiful baby, it looks like you both have been really busy." He crosses his arms over his massive chest and gives me a bright grin.

I need to say something.

"Eve has been a lot of help and it has been great having her around. It's nice to know someone in this town, and she is such a great little girl." I stumbled over to her and put my arm around her shoulder again, pulling her against my side.

Her dad eyes me with a smile, "Eve, why don't you get on home? I want to talk to Izzy for a minute. I'll be there real soon. Tell Izzy bye and thank you." Even though he is speaking to Eve his eyes never once leave mine.

She looks between her father and me before giving me a hug, telling me thanks and walking away.

Somewhat sad to see her go, I sigh. "Bye, Eve."

She pauses, then turns and walks back to me. Looking slightly unsure, she asks me with wide eyes. "Can I stop by again, you know, just to talk?"

Smiling big, I can't help but adore her. "Honey you can stop any time you want. I will be out looking for a job next week, so if I'm not home, you know why." Then for some strange reason, I bend down and kiss her head.

"Cool Izzy, bye for now." She gives me another hug, then skips down the sidewalk before stopping suddenly. "You know, I think the purple ones you chose are prettier than the ones I picked out."

"Oh, I'm not so sure. I may have to go and get some of those yellow ones you like so much. Maybe you can help me plant those too?" I like having her around and if planting flowers is her thing, we'll fill this whole yard with them.

"Sure. Awesome." Then she waves and takes off toward her house.

I am nervous and playing with the hem on my t-shirt as I watch her go. I am a mess, no makeup, and I just threw on some shorts and a t-shirt. *Great.*

Crossing his arms, he eyes my body from head to toe and back up to meet my eyes. I gulp in a nervous response to being mentally eye-fucked by handsome here. Okay, maybe he doesn't mind that I'm a mess. Nope, he definitely doesn't care.

With a smirk and one eyebrow lifted, he says to me. "So, I am glad to meet the person my daughter won't stop talking about."

Blushing and nervous, I respond. "She is amazing. I love spending time with her. I know you don't know me and it must be strange letting her be with a complete stranger, but she has been a huge help." I know I am blushing because my ears feel hot as hell.

"I was unsure when she told me she was spending time with our new neighbor down the street. But, I have been keeping an eye on you. I would never just let my baby spend time at a stranger's house and not make sure she was safe." His hand is on his hip looping in his front pocket.

"Oh, she is totally safe with me. I would never harm her." I realize that I'm now giving him an annoyed look. The idea of anyone hurting such a sweet child pisses me off. And I am obviously nervous, so I keep talking.

Holding his hands up, he tries to calm me. "I know, I know. You don't need to explain. I can see why she's so in awe of you." Then he looks me up and down again and lets out a low whistle. "I must say, you are a pleasant surprise."

What! "What do you mean by surprise?" I'm slightly curious and not sure I want to know the answer. Okay, maybe I do. Yep, I definitely do.

"You're not what I was expecting, let's just say that." His smile curves on one side, revealing that dimple again, and his dark eyes sizzle as if daring me. *Oh, Shit.*

"Okay, is that good or bad?" Matching his smile.

Amused, he cocks his head to the side. "Not sure yet." Then he's voice turns low and sexy. "I will let you know when I figure it out."

"Okay." The word is barely a whisper. Everything about him, everything he's saying, is taking me by complete surprise.

"You're new to town?" His voice returns to normal as he asks the question.

"Yep." I get the feeling that he's trying to size me up. *Probably because you're spending time with his daughter, stupid!*

"Okay." A few wrinkles appear on his forehead.

What's with the frown?

"You said you were looking for a job?" He slowly strolls closer to me as he talks.

Biting my lip, I try to hold my ground. I'm torn between running away and jumping into his arms. No man has ever affected me like this before. "Ah yeah. I need to find something pretty soon, so I'll probably be looking around most of the week." I anxiously wrap my hands in my shirt again. I am feeling uneasy that he is slowly getting closer to me. On the one hand, it is precisely what I want. On the other hand, his proximity scares me shitless. The closer he gets, the more my senses come to life. It's the way he looks. The way his lips move when he speaks. The sound of his voice as it washes over me. And *Good Lord*, don't get me started on how great he smells. I swear every hair on my body is now standing at attention. Escaping my hellish past, one would think I'd be hesitant to let another man stand this close to me, but this man...I'm drawn to him. I'm not scared of him. In fact, I'm the exact opposite.

"I might have something for you." He says as he comes to a stop right in front of me. He is so close I can touch him. I am hyper aware of everything about him and it's all yummy.

Shit, did I just think yummy? Yep, I sure did!

"What?" It's the only thing I can think to say. I'm getting lost in his eyes. They are sparkling with mischief and I can tell he is trying not to laugh. My mind is all over the place. He not only confuses the hell out of me, his hotness makes me weak in the knees.

"Look, Izzy, I own a shop nearby and we need a new front office girl. Are you interested?" His stare is masking his apparent smile he is hiding. I'm sure he realizes how sexy he is, and I am like a drooling idiot, staring at him.

I drop my gaze so I can clear my head enough to answer him. "Um, are you sure? You don't even know if I have any experience." Although his offer sounds perfect, my lack of know-how could be a serious problem.

When I glance up, he's squinting slightly, head off to the side. Then he lets out a chuckle. "Oh, I'm so hoping you don't. You see, I would like to be the one to teach you more things than just one, babe." He is licking his lip and holding back a smile as he shakes his head back and forth.

Oh my! What in the world is he saying to me? The look in his eyes and the roughness of his voice tells me it's not just work he's thinking about. Clearing the lust-filled fog from my mind, I stutter, "I'm not sure. You make me nervous. Eve's right, you do like to make people nervous."

Laughing openly now, he moves, so he's standing next to me and puts his arm loosely around my shoulder. "Nah, babe. I just like to be in control."

No Shit! My sigh gives way to mentally rolling my eyes at him. "I bet you do." Witty responses just keep coming right out of my mouth. Damn.

"So are you interested? I am in need of someone, and you need a job. Great fit if you ask me." Arm still around my shoulder, his smile widens as his eyes dip lower. No need for me to look myself to figure out where his eyes are centered on now.

Oh, I bet he would be a great fit. I shake my head and give in. "Okay, why not?" Then remembering my sweet new friend, I ask, "Does Eve ever stop by the shop?" The thought of spending more time with her makes my heart swell.

He pulls me tight against his side and smiles nice and wide, like he's glad that I like Eve so much. "Sure does."

"Even better." I smile back, too anxious to do anything else. I love the way I feel against him.

"It seems like you want this job to be closer to my daughter than to me." The twinkle in his eyes confirms my suspicion that he loves the idea of his daughter and me spending time together. To be honest, I like it, as well.

"I don't know you. But seeing her is the highlight of my day. She seems to brighten me up, and I could use that in my life right now." I say without taking a breath.

This causes him to tense up. "You okay? You're not in some trouble are you?" He tips my chin up to search my eyes, and the look he is giving me, makes me tense up as well.

When I don't answer fast enough, he frowns. "Tell me, are you in some trouble?"

"What? Hell no. I'm just saying life has not been kind to me. That's why I'm here."

"Eve said it's just you?"

"Yep, just me. Alone." I admit nervously.

He quietly says. "Maybe not for long."

That totally catches me off guard, even though it probably shouldn't. "What? Gosh, you say the most open-ended things?"

"Yep." He says with a slight shake of his head. "Keeps you guessing, doesn't it?" The cheeky bastard then winks at me.

"Why should I do that?" I question his cheeky side.

"That way I am always on your mind." He says in a smooth, sexy voice. Desire pools in those deep brown eyes of his.

I merely moan. "Oh God, you like to play mind games don't you?"

"No babe, I don't play games. As I said, I just think you would be an excellent fit." There he goes using that word again. Only this time he says it with a wickedly delicious grin on his face.

The sexual innuendo is not lost on me. "Fit for what?" I question, playing innocent. I'm sure it won't work because the look he is giving me is not innocent at all.

"Now who is asking openly ended questions?" Cheeky, damn cheeky.

"I can't help it. You are so, so, I don't know what you are." Flabbergasted is what I am.

"Work for me and find out." He looks at me with a more serious expression.

"Where and when?" I ask, eyeing him with a slight smile on my blushing face. It just slips out of my lips.

"Monday 8 a.m. at Ryles Custom Shop on Riley Avenue." He whispers while staring at my lips.

The way he's looking at me, is seriously making it hard to breathe. "Um, okay. I'll see you then."

"You most definitely will, Izzy. By the way, love the name. It suits you. Your name just rolls off the tip of my tongue." He winks and smirks with that damn sexy look. Oh, Sweet Jesus.

"Smooth aren't you?" Then it dawns on me. "Wait. What is your name?"

Leaning into me with his shoulder bumping mine, he raises that sexy eyebrow. "Oh, darlin' asking for my name so soon?"

Breathe Izzy slowly. "If I am going to work for you, I think I need a name to call you by."

"You can call me whatever you like." His eyes jet wide, then he says, "Braxton Ryles, but you can call me Brax. All my friends do."

Oh, of course, makes sense. Braxton Ryles of Ryles Custom Shop. *Duh!*

"Brax. I like it." I let his name sink into my brain. Like I could forget it; his name, his body, and even his manly smell are forever ingrained in my mind.

"Oh, I know how much you will." His grin is full of the devil. Wait. What the hell is he talking about *now*?

"See ya Monday, pretty lady," he says as he starts to stroll down the walkway toward his bike.

Pretty lady. Wow, now that makes me laugh. I've never thought of myself as much of a lady. He keeps surprising me so much I am out of my element. "You know I'm not sure what I am getting myself into with you, big guy."

"Well, you got one thing right." He says, swinging his leg over the beast of a machine.

"What's that?"

"I am a big guy." Yep, there he goes and blows my mind yet again.

He dazzles me with that megawatt smile, but his wink is my undoing. I swear, my heart skips a few beats before sweat beads my forehead. *This guy is driving me crazy!*

"Monday Iz, I'm looking forward to it." He tells me while putting on his navigator sunglasses and bringing his bike to roaring life.

It is impossible not to gawk at him as he pulls away. I'm sure I look like a total idiot but what the hell ever. Braxton is like a tornado ready to knock me on my ass. He just blew into my life, and I feel like he has somehow changed it forever. What's it going to be like to work for this smooth-talking, sexy-as-hell, badass biker?

Seriously Izzy, you might have hit the hot guy lottery.

chapter FOUR

MONDAY CAME FAST AND HERE I am, sitting in my car outside Ryles Custom Shop. It is an impressive building with five bay doors and plenty of parking. The big bay windows house a pleasant, open reception area, and I can see the big desk in the front where I assume I will be sitting answering phone calls and helping customers with God knows what. I know nothing about bikes or cars.

This is such a bad idea. Saturday night, I had an unexpected visitor bring me dinner. Braxton showed up with a plate of food in hand. He grilled chicken and as he put it, *"Didn't want you going hungry."* That was it. Well, I did get a sexy wink before he turned around and walked back home. Left me speechless, I'm not used to this type of kindness. He has a heart…a big one.

I am going to be around Braxton all the time. Shit, he's going to be my boss. I slam my head against my steering wheel, trying to convince myself that working here is a good idea. I know my libido is going to be running overtime, I just hope I can keep up.

Oh, who am I kidding? My inexperience and hormones are going to be my undoing and I'm going to make a mess of things. Why the hell did I think I could do this? My head already hurts. I rub it with my fingers to try and pry the stress away, but it's not helping. I don't need one of my major migraines on my first day on the job. It will be a miracle if I make it one week, let alone one day.

I should probably get out of my car and get inside. No need to be late, too. I hope I don't embarrass myself. I get so tongue-tied when I even think about Brax, let alone having to work beside him all day. Ooh, tongue-tied. That delicious image in my mind is just... Oh shit! There goes my libido again.

Braxton is most likely going to have to fire me on my first day. Ogling my neighbor is bad enough. Ogling my boss is a big no-no. It's making my stomach churn and my head starts to pound. I can't do this.

A sudden rapping on my window makes my heart jump out of my chest as my eyes snap open. I look up and lean forward so I can make out who the hell is tapping so annoyingly. My glance travels up a body until I meet the most incredible, big brown eyes.

Ah hell, of course it's him. Braxton.

I forgot how breathtakingly beautiful his eyes were. The instant my brown eyes meet his chocolate ones, I get a sudden chill all the way down my spine. Remembering the hot dreams I had last night of this hot son-of-a-gun makes my toes curl. Those memories alone make my core start to ache *for him*. Oh my, this is not good!

This is never going to work. I am going to spend my days drooling over him and mentally eye-fucking him every chance I get. So not good! I should just go home now and make up some shit excuse, so he can find somebody who knows what they are doing.

I roll down my window and force a smile as I feel my face heat up and turn bright red. His smile gets a little wider, and his eyes dance with amusement. Oh man, I wish I could read his mind right now. His eyes are telling me something. I just wish I could pinpoint what.

"Right on time, Iz. You are making me happy already." He says as he leans into my car door.

"You told me to be here at eight and here I am. But you may want to reconsider hiring me." I say smiling back, hoping that I don't throw up on him. My past insecurities are screaming at me, saying, *"You're not good enough!"* As much as I need a job, I don't want to look like an idiot. Not in front of him. I wonder if he can tell I'm scared shitless right now.

"Why?" His eyebrows furrow together as in trying to process why I said this.

"Well, I... I don't know a lot about bikes or cars," I say in a nervous whisper. He makes me nervous and it is unnerving me.

"Did I ask you if you had experience with bikes or cars? I believe I told you I had hoped you didn't have any experience. You recall that conversation?"

Oh Jesus, stop looking at me like that, *please*.

Trying to get up the courage, I tilt my chin challengingly. "Yeah, but I thought you were talking about something else. Not the job." Oh shit. What if I misread him? What if he's just a guy who likes to flirt with girls because he's a flirty guy?

"Izzy, Izzy, Izzy. You are too damned cute, you know that?" He says with a slight chuckle. As he leans into my open window, I can smell his cologne, and it burns a path through every cell in my body. And by burn, I mean an exquisite burn. The fierce kind of burn that slowly starts a fire in the pit of your stomach and then radiates until you're completely consumed by it.

Smug bastard. He knows what he is doing, and the maddening thing is, it's working.

"Oh, you are so messing with my head. I'm not even sure how to take you." Let alone right now, my head has been swimming since I met him. What a major flirt.

"Hmmm." He says as he pulls his lips tightly together and shakes his head. "Let's just say there is only one way to take me, you can be assured of that."

Ugh! "Braxton you are so confusing, maybe this was a bad idea. I left a bad situation, and you are like jumping from the frying pan into the fire." Christ, what did I walk into here? Moaning and laying my head back against my seat, I huff out a gigantic breath.

He seems to process what I have just told him for a few seconds, and then he says. "Darlin', you have nothing to worry about. Looks to me like whatever situation you left behind, you may need protecting. I'll keep you safe. You need me for anything else, I'm here, as well. As far as the frying pan, I can only imagine how good it would be to sizzle with you."

Oh My God! Seriously?

"Braxton I'm serious. What is this?" I say with my hand gesturing a movement from me to him.

He leans down, so he is close to my face. Like nose-to-nose close. "Time will tell but for right now, I need an office girl. A beautiful and sweet office girl. You fit the bill just right."

My insides do somersaults, and my panties instantly get wet. *What am I getting myself into?*

"Come on, darlin'. Let's get to work." Braxton gives me a wink, then opens my door for me and stands back so I can climb out.

He walks ahead of me as we head into the office area. It looks like I will have a small office where I will do most of my work, but I will be trained to help work the counter in the reception area, as well.

Braxton walks me through the duties of ordering parts as well as processing and organizing service calls and tickets. I will oversee billing and collecting money owed. All seems pretty straightforward.

I gradually meet the mechanics who are also Braxton's best friends. They are like a bunch of buddies who seriously know what the hell they are doing. The shop has five bay areas that are all full and then there are bikes and cars parked outside waiting to be fixed.

Taking it all in, I let out a big whistle, then look up at Braxton. "Man, you have a great business going here."

"Thanks," he says with a mixture of sexy authority and pride. "We like to have fun, but we also like to earn money. The guys know the difference between play time and get-shit-done time."

"I see, so you don't have to yell at your buddies too much?" I playfully jab him with my shoulder.

"Nope. They do not like to have a pissed-off Brax in their faces." He says this as he is looking straight ahead.

"I wouldn't want a pissed-off Braxton in my face either," I say, glancing back at the guys.

Suddenly he stops and turns right to me.

He eyes me with curiosity. "Why do you call me Braxton instead of Brax?"

I shrug my shoulders. "It's your name. It's unique, and I like it. Should I call you Brax instead?" Maybe I have offended him or something. I like Braxton, I might be the only one calling him it, but so be it. I've never been one to follow others, usually I do the polar opposite. Most likely why I ended up the way I did. Shaking off those bad memories, I need to concentrate on the here and now.

A large smile plays across his face.

"I just find it curious. Everyone calls me Brax, and yet you call me by my given name. I hate it when people call me that, but for some reason when you say it, it sounds kind of nice."

He is deep in thought, and his look is somewhat sad. "Do you need some nice in your life Braxton?" I say with as much sincerity as I can.

My comment seems to strike a nerve because he stands dead still and stares at me. His look of wonder gives way to a deeper emotion. I'm not sure what he is thinking, but as I gaze into his eyes, things became crystal clear to me. Braxton may be complex and a master at mind games, but he also looks vulnerable. He's a man in need of something special. I always wanted to be something special or at least someone's special.

Maybe we could be something special to each other. If only. All I need is a little love in my life, so I know I'm not falling apart.

Braxton may need something special, but my kind of special is dark, broken and bruised.

chapter FIVE

Surviving my first month at Ryles wasn't as bad as I first thought. It has been a hell of a lot harder than I ever imagined. The Parts Orders have me so screwed up, my brain is fried. Having zero knowledge of bike and car parts has seriously impaired my ability to do my job. I have explained to Braxton this is exactly 1why he should have hired someone with experience. To this, he just laughs and makes some joke about 'fuck experience.' Braxton has been amazing, though. He is always there for me to ask questions and takes time answering each and every one. Most of the time, he laughs as he corrects my many feeble attempts. I have never felt so valued while feeling like a complete screw-up. I have to say, this is an awesome place to work. Any other job, I would have been fired ten times over by now.

I've gotten to know his best friends/co-workers, Knox and Brody. They are a riot and enjoy teasing the new girl to the point my cheeks hurt from smiling. Alex and Cage are more standoffish and rarely acknowledge me. Not sure if they don't like me, or they just don't talk much. Jag and Minter are the newest mechanics and are a riot as well. They joke more than they should, and they tend to get most of the cleanup duties because the shop gets pretty dirty. That leaves me, the only female in the shop, and the odd man out. Most of the time, they tend to embarrass my ass, making sure to point out my many mistakes. They dish it out, but I tend to dish it back. God knows they are growing on me.

Eve has yet to come by the shop, and it makes me sad. I have been anxiously waiting to see her with each passing week. By the time I finally get home, she has already walked by after school. I had no idea I would miss a seven-year-old girl as much as I do. I have seen her a few times on the weekends, she would stop by and we would catch up on what's happening at school. I found myself several times during the weekdays pausing, looking at my computer screen and wondering how she is doing.

"Hey Braxton, when is Eve going to stop by? I miss her," I say looking at him as he sits at my desk trying to teach me how to fill out the end of week reports.

His body tenses when he speaks, "Oh, yeah, that. She is with her mom for a few days then she will be home again."

I pause and am stunned, I had no idea her mother was in the picture. From what I had gathered, it sounded like a momma bear was not a constant in their lives.

I admit, somewhat stunned. "Oh, I didn't know she had a relationship with her mother. She seemed sad one time when I mentioned her mom. I never brought it up again."

With shoulders pulled back, Braxton deeply sighs. "Let's just say she is trying to make up for her lack of mothering. I'm not all confident she can pull off the whole mothering thing. I just want my little girl happy." I just nod and get back to figuring out the newest Parts Order.

Braxton is now standing in the door to my office like he is deep in thought. Looking at the floor like he is studying it for some answer, I watch him being, what, vulnerable maybe? Uncomfortable, perhaps? Never thought I would see a man like him helpless. My big, smooth-talking, confident Braxton looks more like an awkward big ole' teddy bear right now.

"You know in the seven years Eve has been in my life, I can count on one hand the times her momma has acted like a momma. Bitch is all fucked up; should have never got messed up with her. But she gave me Eve, and that is the greatest gift anyone could have given me."

His eyes looked pained and soulful. As if deep in thought, the distant gaze that settles in his face saddens me. I would rather have the egomaniac, smooth, flirty Braxton than this version of him. Flirty Braxton, I can deal with. I'm not sure how the hell to handle this side of him. If I knew him better, maybe I would know how to respond.

I instantly feel the need to comfort him.

Getting up from my chair, I walk over to him and peer up into those damn beautiful brown eyes. Damn, it's like God blessed this man with great looks and a big heart.

"Come here." I pull his hands out of his pockets and tug so I can wrap my petite arms around his shoulders.

Smiling wide, I warmly say. "This might be inappropriate, but you need a hug, and I am the world's best hugger."

His chuckle vibrates through me as he engulfs me into the biggest bear hug.

I have to admit it! Best Teddy Bear Hug Ever!

His warm breath on my skin sends shock waves down my spine.

"Damn Iz, you're so fuckin' sweet." He murmurs as he nuzzles his face in my neck.

I know I'm blushing, so I hold on to him tighter. "Bet your ass, big guy."

"What the hell is going on?" A bitchy screech comes from behind me.

Braxton's body instantly tenses, and my eyes go wide in shock. My gut screams at me not to turn around, but I do it anyway.

Turning around still holding onto Braxton, I see a stunning blonde. Tall, curvy, bitchy and all sorts of pissed off. I instantly know who this is, Eve looks just like her.

Well damn, she is like the picture-perfect Barbie.

"What the fuck do you mean?" Braxton's voice is tense. He's holding onto me tightly with my back pressed against his chest. The chain of his belt and the hardness of his chest is molded against my backside. Oh man, he is rock hard and tense.

With one hand on her slender waist, she points her finger like a dagger directly my way. "Who in the hell does she think she is, hanging onto you?" Spitting pure venom directed at lucky me.

Her words make me wince and I...snap. I have a big mouth, and she has insulted me. Not going to happen, Braxton's baby momma or not, I am not backing down to cower from this two-bit blonde witch.

Standing tall, I snap back at her. "Hey, I am standing right here. Just ask me who I am. Better yet, don't. I'm Izzy and what is your problem anyway?"

Hip hitched off to her side, her blood red nail polish on her long ass nails is a bit much. Her dress is more like a napkin. Barely covering her noticeably fake, enormous, watermelons she has for breasts. Her bleached blonde hair, long ass nails, and her larger than life boobs, has me shaking my head. Is there anything real on this chick?

I'll go with NO!

"Brax, she's a scrawny little girl. Or better yet, isn't she a bit old for your liking? Never had to slum when you had me."

I can hear the growl coming from Braxton. "What the fuck do you want, Tiffany?"

Staring me down, she looks like she wants to strike me down. "For starters, I want your new office twit's hands off of you."

How the hell does she know I work here? Where is Kara when I need her most? My girl would chew Tiffany up and spit her out like a bad habit. This bitch is begging to be knocked out.

Breathing slowly, Braxton grimly looks at blondie. "First of all, where is Eve? Secondly, who gives a fuck who has their hands on me? You lost that privilege."

As he angrily talks to his baby momma, his fingers dig into my shoulders. *OUCH!*

Tiffany has stepped forward while I step back into a colossal hard body. Okay, this is beyond awkward.

Braxton pulls me tighter into him. Enveloping me protectively in his massive arms does ease some of my anxiousness.

Trying to pull away, I sharply spit out. "Look, I am not a part of whatever you two have going on. Excuse me while I go back to work."

Tiffany runs her red, long nails down Braxton's chest. Horrified, I wiggle to the side the best I can. That bitch is not touching me.

Not being able to bite my tongue any longer, I am beyond pissed off. "Keep your long ass, red daggers away from me."

"Ah baby don't worry, you're not my type. I like big, hard men. See, Brax is mine. Always has been and always will be." Like the wicked witch she is, she then laughs. "He might fuck you, but you? You'll never be me, honey." Her nasty words are harsh and bitchy, just like her.

Coughing, I am utterly disgusted. "I don't want to be a damn thing like you." Gesturing with my hands, I point out. "You're all fake. Starting with your nails to your gigantic boobs, I mean, Jesus did you actually think they look good? Damn."

She's laughing louder than necessary. "You don't know men do you, honey? Brax here paid for these babies. He likes big, mouthwatering tits." Rolling her eyes, she sizes my chest up and laughs again. She may have the larger chest, but I'm all real.

In a rather snickering tone, she then adds. "Too bad for you, you don't have what he likes." Licking her finger, she cups her breasts as if showing those suckers off. Like anyone could miss them. She is proud of those ugly suckers!

Angrily, I shrug off Braxton's hand gripping my shoulder. I have had my limit with this chick, and I let her know it.

"You're right about one thing; I'm not fake. There's not a damn fake thing about me. The only thing I am, is real. Real feels great; real keeps things solid. Real doesn't need to be something it's not." With that, I stormed off. Braxton's laugh is easily heard as I make my escape. Even though I'm no longer in the room with them, I can hear Braxton talking.

"Tiffany, at one time, I thought you were everything. All these years, popping in and out of my life, but fuck, I was wrong. It took Izzy to come into our lives, to make me see what 'real' is. That woman is as real as it gets. You could learn a few things from her. The problem is, you just made an enemy out of her."

Rather loudly, Tiffany screeches. "What the hell do you mean ours? Has she been around Eve? My daughter will not be around that whore!"

"Bitch, what did you say? Listen, you do not say who the fuck Eve, or I for that matter, can see. Izzy's been more of a mom than you have, and she's only been around for a short time. In that time, Eve has planted flowers, ate breakfast and gone shopping with her. Sounds like a good woman to me." His deep growl is enough to make me nervous. Good thing he is talking to her and not me.

"What the fuck does that mean?" There's no mistaking the hostility in her voice. She is so loud, I'm sure the guys can now hear her.

"Eve likes her, and so do I. She is doing great at taking over the job you once had." His venomous words hit her where it counted. I wince as I'm sure this is just going to make her hate me even more.

Listening to them, I want to throw up. Leaning against the wall down the hall from them, I just want to get the hell out of here.

"Hey, pretty girl, what the hell are you doing?"

I jump and start to yelp, but manage to cover my mouth in time, so I don't embarrass myself any more than I already have. Looking over my shoulder, I see a tall man with a broad smirk. His eyes dance with mischief, and my goodness, he is handsome.

"Jesus, do all of Braxton's friends look hot as hell, or what?" Realizing my mistake, I said that out loud.

Handsome here, must get a kick out of it because he throws his head back, laughing. I'm totally busted.

Raising an eyebrow, snickering with a wicked laugh he replies. "You have got to be Izzy. I've heard all about you."

What!

My mouth is hanging open and I am still wondering who he is. "Do I know you? Wait. Of course, I don't. If I had met you, I would have remembered your name, that's for sure."

Standing with his hand against the wall, his eyes dance with amusement. "Ah honey, flattery will get you everywhere with me. So, tell me, what are you doing out here? Just who are you eavesdropping on?"

Hearing the rather loud voices down the hall, he has to realize what's going on. It does not take a detective to figure out that I'm hiding. It's as if a light bulb has gone off in his head, he nods in response.

Running a hand over his forehead, he huffs out loud. "Oh, I see you have met the lovely Tiffany? She's nothing but trouble I'm afraid." His look is one of regret, he solemnly adds. "The only real thing she did was give Brax little Eve. The rest is just bad. She puts Brax through hell all of the time. I have no clue why he puts up with her games. She whirls into town and like clockwork, he comes running. In a blink of an eye, she goes up and disappears. Fucks with his head and leaves Eve in tears. Shit's bad." His look is as if his mind is a million miles away.

Hearing that pisses me off to no end. Thinking of what Eve must feel every time her mother leaves makes my heart ache for this sweet little girl. It's like Tiffany only comes back to get her fill of Braxton. Damn shame. What I wouldn't give to have a little girl like Eve. No, my chance was taken away from me.

Interrupting my thoughts, sexy here speaks. "Name is Liam Talbot, honey. It's weird, but it seems like I already know you. Brax talks a lot. Needed to meet you for myself, so I can put a face to that sweet name he won't shut up about."

"What!" I say with nervous energy. My damn lip is quivering so bad I bite my lip to stop it. "Why does he talk about me? He barely knows me."

The smile he gives me is so warm and, well, pleasant. It's weird, I've never got so many warm welcomes in my life. Since I got here, it seems like there's a welcome crew wherever I go. My family treats me like shit, yet these strangers, who don't know me from a hole in the ground, treat me with kindness. Oh my, what a pleasant and welcome change.

"So Izzy, huh? Got to say, that's a kick ass name." His face is so close to mine. I am rather dazzled with his big, bright, blue eyes. The bluest damn eyes I have ever seen. The slight wrinkles around his eyes tell me we might be around the same age. At the moment, his eyes are filled with sincerity.

His closeness throws me off kilter. "It's short for Izzabella, and I tend to agree, it is pretty kick ass." I ramble.

Nodding his head, he then points his finger towards the shouting in the next room. "Honey, the time you spent with Eve has put a big smile on her face. She won't stop talking about you. You are more like a mother to her than her own. It seems Brax taking a liking to you has ruffled her feathers. Hence, why she has decided now is a good time to show up."

Raising my voice a few octaves, I ask baffled. "Me?" Pressing my thumb against my chest, "She is here all wound up, because of me? I didn't do shit to her."

Understanding and agreeing with me, he simply confirms.

"Nope, it's just you replaced her in Eve's eyes. That shit has her all upset. That and taking Brax's attention away from her, of course."

Oh, my god! "The hell I did. I've spent some time planting flowers with Eve. What, I'm not supposed to hang out with her?" How did I get myself into this situation? Being a good neighbor has turned into some clusterfuck of a situation.

Backing up, he holds up his hands and smiles at me.

"Listen, here's a word of advice. You like Eve she adores you. Just keep on doing what you're doing because that little girl is on cloud nine. Plus, Brax likes you. He needs a good woman in his life, and you seem to fit the bill."

"I just work here. I happen to be his neighbor, and he offered me a job. I am not his woman. Right now, I have no idea what the hell I am doing. *Shit*. I need to get the hell out of here." Wanting nothing more than to leave, I realize my purse is in the office where all the drama is unfolding. Shit! Shit! Shit!

"So you're going to leave. Shit gets tough, and you're going to hightail it out of here? If you do that, you're no better than Tiffany. Brax and Eve need a woman who is going to stay when shit gets tough."

"Liam," Trying to contain my anger, I say rather grimly. "I am *not* his woman."

Just then I hear a loud roar from Braxton, followed by Tiffany coming down the hall toward us. She pauses when she notices Liam is standing next to me. Her eyes slant thin, giving him a death glare.

"Great Liam, don't tell me you're here getting Brax's sloppy seconds."

"Oh my god. Bitch, I am nobody's sloppy seconds. I don't belong to Braxton, and I just met Liam. You're UN-FUCK-ING-BELIEVABLE! You don't know me and I sure as hell don't want to know you."

Towering inferno struts over to me and slaps me hard right across the face; as my head whips to the side. I don't know what came over me, but in a flash, one of my hands is in the mop she calls hair while the other grips her throat. I bend her backwards on the desk and say, "That was your freebie. Believe me when I tell you, if you ever think about touching me again, I will beat the living hell out of you. Eve's mother or not! Are we clear?" Not waiting for an answer, I give her a hard shove that makes her stumble in the stilts she calls shoes. Damn, that hurt! My face feels like it's on fire. Braxton stands there trying to hide his smile while Liam bends over with his hands on his knees and laughs his ass off. I'll admit, if I wasn't so pissed, it would have been funny. But it's not. I'm tired of people thinking it's okay to put their hands on me because they want to throw a tantrum like some child. Rubbing my cheek, I'm not only pissed as hell, I'm disgusted…

Braxton walks over to me, caressing my redden cheek with his thumb. I notice Liam having a firm hold on Tiffany. Braxton attempts to speak, but I cut him off raising my hand.

"Listen, I don't know you. I'm sickened by the way you act. You're Eve's mother, and yet you walk around like a crazy lady. Maybe you are. I don't know, nor do I care." It's a shame; this woman is beyond beautiful, but her personality makes her ugly as sin.

Having said my peace, I feel more relaxed. Braxton's eyes have a surprised look to them, maybe a bit in awe. Liam is still laughing. And Tiffany, well, she just looks outplayed.

Standing stiff, Braxton's attention is directed towards Tiffany. "Tiff, you ever lay a hand on Izzy again, you will answer to me. Bitch, I'm not kidding. You are the mother of my child, but you act like some crazy bitch. You're upset because you had me, and now you don't. Izzy is far too good for me, but she's my friend and now an employee. Eve loves her and for once she has a good role model. Shit doesn't get better than that." Wow, now I'm the one in awe. God almighty, he can be so damn sweet, and, really cute.

With tears rolling down her cheeks, she wipes them away. She turns out of Liam's arms and strolls for the door. Before she leaves, she mumbles something, I am sure it's directed at me.

Suddenly, she stops turning her attention our way. "Liam, you're my brother. Are going to let Brax talk to me like this?"

The room starts to spin. What? Her brother, you have got to be kidding me?

Acknowledging her, Liam explains. "Tiff, you did all of this on your own. Fucked with Brax most of his life. Thinking about my niece and the way you treat her drives me crazy. You're no good little sister, fucking truth stings like a bitch doesn't it?" Liam says, not skipping a beat.

On her way out the door, again she turns giving us an angry look. "Fuck off, Liam."

Okay. Now that the tornado known as 'Tiffany' is long gone, I fall back against the wall. Holding my head in my hands, I suddenly find it hard to breathe. Braxton walks over to me and caresses my cheek.

With my eyes closed, I can sense Braxton is near me. "Izzy. Babe I'm sorry about all of that. She's pissed at me, not you."

Oh My God, he can't be serious.

Irritated and slightly pissed at what he said, my look quickly lets him know I'm not stupid. "Really! You? No, I don't think so. She believes I screwed your brains out, and not just yours, but Liam's, too! She hates *me*; she slapped *me*. She threatened me on her way out. I would say she is pissed at *me*. I didn't do a damn thing. This shit between you and her is none of my damn business. What the hell?" The only thing my mind can process is, what he was thinking getting involved with an unstable bitch like her in the first place? Then it becomes apparent to me. She's blonde, long-legged and has a hot curvy body. *Duh!*

"She's jealous, Izzy. Plain, straight up jealous. She sees how much you mean to Eve and now you are here working her old job. Putting a smile on my face, I might add." He smiles as big as he can to prove his point.

Oh, my God! I don't need this shit. "It was nice working for you, but this obviously is not going to work. Find a new girl you can screw six ways to Sunday and piss her off with *that* new girl. I have had my share of shit. Hot or not Braxton, reality is a bitch, and she likes to slap the shit out of me now and then." No need for me to explain all of that to him, so I shut it.

I walk to my office to grab my purse. And in an instant, all I feel is a strong arm around my waist. The next thing I know, is I'm pressed up against a very hard-bodied Braxton.

He's heaving as he leans in closer to my ear. "Izzy, if you think I am letting you out of my sight, think the fuck again." His anger is evident by the tight hold he has on me. I'm not afraid. No, I'm slightly turned on. The idea someone wants me, well, it's something sweet. Unfortunately, this situation is not a good one.

Struggling with him, I beg. "Let me go."

With an even tighter grip, I feel his hard body tense up. "Stop it, Izzy." So sweet, and so demanding.

Braxton then hauls me up against the wall in my tiny office. Our eyes lock as if in a sudden standstill. Hearing the door close, I assume Liam has left us alone.

His heavy stare just confirms to me just how hot he is.

My moan comes out as barely a whisper. "Braxton."

"Babe. Shh." He whispers back.

He leans into me, his lips barely touching mine. I am yearning to feel the softness of them as he teases me with a slow lick to his lower lip. My eyes are entranced. His wet, velvety tongue glistens, as if inviting me in. I'm visibly shaken and every ounce of my body feels like it's on fire. Braxton is intoxicating. Whimpering, I lick my parched lips in response. His eyes are blazing with lust, and I ache to touch him. A part of me wants to stop this madness, the other part has me mentally stripping him naked. God, shut my brain off, please.

Braxton moans as his lips graze my jaw. "Sweet, sweet, Izzy. You drive me crazy." He stops moving to gaze into my eyes. "Seeing Tiff slap you had me wanting to rip her head off. No one is going to touch you. Only me. Jesus, when it comes to you, I can't think straight." The slight chuckle, he lets out only has me shaking with need.

I can't help but moan. "Braxton, why? Why do you want me?" I need to know what he sees in me. Before this goes any further, I need to know why?

Pulling back, he just looks at me with an odd expression. "You can't be serious?"

"Well yeah, I am. Your baby momma is hot, just saying. I, on the other hand, let's just say nothing special. So, I ask again, why me?"

The slit in his eyes tells me he is not amused. "Fuck, Izzy! She doesn't hold a candle to you. You glow so much brighter. Your goodness and sweetness are a fucking wet dream, baby." I can sense his demeanor shift as his look is now more mischievous. "Bet you feel like heaven, too. Been dreaming about having you under me since I met you," he says with that mega smile of his.

Trying to block out that damn smirk of his, I am still in disbelief. "What? Oh, my god. You can't be serious." Forcing the back of my head against the wall, he just keeps saying all the right things. *This can't be happening?*

His dark voice snaps my attention back to him. "Done talking, babe. Give me those sweet lips."

I don't have a second to ponder this as he crashes his lips against mine. Instant fireworks go off in my mind. His lips are soft, warm, and the wetness of them take hold of my trembling ones. He is in control, and I fucking love it. My head swims. I am so lost in his arms, I let him devour me. His tongue sweeps across my lower lip, begging entrance into my mouth. I open wide to welcome him in. Gently, I suck on his tongue, drawing him in deeper. Each passing second, my desire grows and every nerve in my body is set on fire. My nails draw blood as I dig them into his shoulders. My passion is being unleashed. The grinding of his hips allows his belt buckle to hit me in just the right spot. Instantly a moan escapes my quivering lips. With his hands on my ass, Braxton grinds his larger than life erection against my heated core. Sweet Jesus, this feels so damn good.

"Braxton." I muster a whisper.

"Feel me, Izzy. I want you so fucking bad, I can almost taste it. I want to crawl up deep inside you." His voice is trembling as his hands, lips and erection are doing such things to my needy body.

Yes...please!

Losing all self-control, I let my desire absorb every delectable inch of him. "Braxton. You feel so good." Even though this feels out of this world, I'm afraid to allow it to happen. "This is still wrong."

"No babe, there isn't a damn thing wrong here. Feels like heaven; feeling you grind on me. My dick has never been so hard in my life. I've never wanted a woman like I fucking want you. I need you, Izzy. Need some sweetness in my life like you said earlier. You didn't know it, but you were spot on. Never had such sweetness before in my life. Now that I got a taste of it, I got to have it."

I'm suddenly finding myself hauled in his strong arms over to my tiny desk and laid out flat on top of it. Papers were now scattered, half on the floor and the other half under my body.

I am under him and, oh my world, the full weight of his muscular body feels so damn good. I know I have died and gone to heaven. There are no words to describe the feeling between us right now. His hot breath on my face has me in his trance. Drawing out moans from down deep inside my soul, I swear I let the words slip out of my mouth I have no control over. We fit so well that the bulge between his legs is rubbing my oh so sweet spot perfectly. He's rubbing up and down, round and round with the perfect amount of friction. Never in my life has anyone made me feel like this. I could explode from just rubbing against me, fully clothed. Jesus, Mary and Joseph.

Nuzzling my neck, he bites and licks his way to my ear. "Are you ready for me, Izzy?"

Moaning and sighing, I can only gasp. "Oh Braxton, ahhhh…"

His stiff arms wrap around my whole body. I have never felt so cherished in my life. Hell, at the moment, I'll surrender just to have this man manipulate my body into submission.

He pauses momentarily as a look of seriousness seems to wash over his face. Sweetly kissing my nose, he asks, "Remember what I said about us sizzling, baby? Your body is on fire for me. Please tell me you want this?" Running his hand down the side of my body, he hitches my leg up over his hip. I end up running my fingers through his unruly hair, yanking it to let him know I understand him perfectly. *Hell to yes, I want you, Braxton.*

Pushing his head away from my neck, I look into his big brown eyes. What I see surprises me? His eyes are now midnight black full of lust and raw heat. "The only thing I know is, how I wish we were naked and I had you wrapped up inside of me. I want to feel that dick of yours throbbing and knocking on my cervix like it's a damn door. I want it. Hard and fast, then slow and steady. Need you to rock my damn world, Braxton. Does that answer your question, *Baby*?" I figured it was my turn to shock him speechless.

Moaning, he starts to say something when we both stop and stare at his vibrating…*dick*. 'What the hell?'

"Ah, Braxton is it me or is your dick vibrating?" I say as I cannot contain my laughter.

Standing up, he pulls his phone out of his front pocket. Glancing at the screen, he swears under his breath as he answers it. "What the fuck now?"

I have never hated phones as much as I do right this minute. My impending explosion has now left me sexually frustrated and ready to blow.

He nods his head to get my attention. "Sorry babe, it's Eve. Need to take this." Of course he does, it's his daughter for goodness sake.

His once frustrated look has now transformed into a heart-warming smile. "Hey, sweet girl. What's up?" An unintentional moan escapes my mouth listening how sweet he is with his daughter. In response to hearing me moan, he tightly closes his eyes and rubs his very hard bulge in his pants. I slightly chuckle, which earns me a scowl. It seems like I'm not the only one left sexually frustrated.

"Okay listen, you do not have to go back to your mother. She is bringing you *where?* Here, at the shop? No kidding." He takes about five big breaths before answering again.

I can only imagine what is going on. From the one-sided conversation I can hear, it sounds like Tiffany is bringing Eve here to the shop. The witch does not give up. *Izzy breathe and get the fuck out of here.*

I'm slow to get up off of my desk. Getting my bearings, I straighten out my clothes in an attempt to calm my raging libido. Just hearing the name Tiffany is like taking an ice-cold shower. Leaving my office looking like I just hosed the boss would not look good. Braxton's sudden voice change causes me to jump. Ah, it seems he is now talking to his baby momma. Time to escape, I head for the door.

Holding the phone to his chin, I get a very stern glare.

"Don't even think about it, Iz." Not only his glare but the tone of his voice is tense and rather seething.

I whisper to him for some damn reason, like I care if Tiffany can hear me or not. "I'm out of here. Once is enough of a run in with her. Not in the mood to get slapped again. Especially in front of Eve. You settle with her." As I turn toward the door, Braxton stops me for the second time today. This time, his huge hand catches my arm. Alarmed, I stomp my foot down on his, and it has no effect on him whatsoever.

"Not happening, Izzy. You and I are going to talk quick, before my daughter gets here with her bitch of a mother." Braxton ended his call and now has me pulled against him. Kissing the top of my head, he breathes me in as I do the same with him. For such a new thing between us, this feels right. It feels like we have done this a million times.

"Braxton, I need to get lost. Nothing good will come of this if I am here." Looking up at him, I can see his internal struggle. He knows it's the right thing to do.

"Don't like it, but I can't argue with you about it either. Bitch is doing this to piss me and you off. The only thing she is going to do is, play the 'pity me' card, and I don't need you to witness it. But damn honey, I want to finish what we started here. Things were just getting good."

"Um. Yes, it was nice; still unsure if it is wise though. Maybe it was a good thing we got interrupted. I'm sure once you get your head straight, you might change your mind about me." Sensing my insecurity, he tenses.

"What the hell are you talking about? You have got to be shitting me right now." His look of aggravation gives into my madness.

"No, I am not shitting you. Who the hell says that?" My annoyance with him comes across as bitchy.

"I do. Now, will you care to explain yourself? Me wanting you is not a heat of the moment thing. I've wanted you since I saw you on the porch with Eve. Never seen a woman so sweet and fuckin' hot in my life. That is no lie either."

To my utter surprise, I can see the truth behind his words. The only question is can I trust them?

"Oh, for Christ's sake, now you're lying to me. I can't even come close to your baby momma. I am sure all your leading ladies look more like her than me." I know I'm putting myself down, but it helps me to put things into perspective. I guess it's just easier this way.

Braxton leans in close so we're inches from one another. "I know what you're doing and it won't work, either. Already told you, she does not hold a candle to you. Now, enough with putting yourself down just to run away from me, or I will smack your cute ass."

"Pfft, seriously, are you blind now in your old age?" Oh, crap, that did it. His look is daring, eyebrows raised even his lips were stretched thin.

"Who are you calling old, Izzy? I know it's not me, but if it is, you're just begging to have my hand across your ass. Honey, if I had you around when I was getting my dick wet with Tiff' I would've jumped on you in a heartbeat. Would have grabbed your innocent little body and never looked back."

I start laughing, and this is my first mistake. Braxton looks like I just slapped him right across the face. He not so gently grabs me and whips me around across his broad shoulders and smacks my ass with a very hard and loud slap. His hands are so damn big; it covers my entire ass with his one palm. Fuck that hurts.

I struggle to get out of his bear-hold as he puts me down with a smirk on his face. He enjoyed that. The ass is hiding his smile, but I can see traces of it.

"Not flipping funny, Braxton," I tell him while rubbing my backside.

Body bent backward; he laughs at me. "Sure the hell is, honey."

Hand on my hip, I protest. "Is not."

"Fuck yeah, it was!"

The voices coming from reception tells me Eve has arrived. Damn it, now I'm stuck. Sensing my worry, Braxton leans in to kiss my lips ever so sweetly. I instantly melt holding onto him. The only thing I want is to lose myself into those big strong arms. Snapping back to reality, Braxton is talking against my lips.

"Babe, stay in here, yeah?" Having lost any rational thoughts, I nod in agreement.

"I'll be back soon, keep the door closed. She won't get back here, I swear." Finding it hard to swallow I just nod at his sweetness once again.

"Promise?" I whisper to him.

"Yeah, babe." He said kissing me one last time, mumbling.

"Damn kissable lips. Fuckin' dick is throbbing. See what you do to me?" He says, rubbing his cock in an attempt to calm it down. Good luck with that, buddy. My mental high-five, knowing I caused that raises an eyebrow at him as he walks out the door.

Sitting back in my chair, I try to come back down to earth. This man has me spinning in circles. His scent, his eyes, his body is all so consuming, it's over-fucking-whelming. I lose myself when I'm around him. It's like my mind shuts down, and my body takes over. My body just happens to scream for his touch and melts under his stare. The more I'm around him, I know I don't stand a chance. What the heck do I do? I suppose nothing, for now.

Feels like an eternity, the longer I am in my office. Having time to knock some sense back into my mind, I decide. No way am I staying in this room just waiting for him to tend to his baby momma. I adore Eve, but her mother is, well, no words begin to describe what I think of her.

Waiting until I hear the conversation flowing, I grab my purse and quietly open the door and peek out to see if the coast is clear. Not seeing anyone, I quietly close my door and go down the hallway toward the garage. I hope I can escape without being seen.

Making my way into the garage, surprisingly, I don't see any of the guys. I hurry myself to my car. Once inside, I see the coast is clear. I start my little Accord up and high-tail it out of the parking lot. The only thing is, I didn't notice there was a bike following me until I was a few streets away from the shop.

Damn it, I know it has to be one of the guys because he is staying very close behind me. I know it's not Braxton because this bike is very different from his. Braxton's bike is definitely cool as shit; all black and sleek, chrome always polished and pretty. Asking me, who knows nothing about them in the first place, I would describe it as a very manly bike. I think he called it a Sportster, or something. Hell, I have no idea. The only thing is it's pretty damn hot when I see Braxton riding it. Hell, he could make anything look sexy just by sitting on it.

This bike is black as well, just not as big. The person driving is not as big and burly as my hot biker, either. Well shit, peeking closer in my rearview mirror, it looks like the guy on the bike is Liam. Now, why the hell would Liam be following me? Fuck. Fuck. Shit. Braxton must have told him to follow me, which means he is most likely pissed off. Great a pissed off Braxton is never a good thing. One thing for sure is Liam is the bitch's brother, and I don't know if I can trust him.

Driving in circles, I'm trying to see if Liam or whoever it may be following me will give up and go back to the shop. My phone alerts me to an incoming text message. Blowing out a breath before I glance at it, shit, yep, it's who I thought it was. A pissed-off Braxton, from what I can gather. Yikes!

Braxton: Where the hell are you?

Great, I am not answering him. Better yet, the more I think about it, why should I be forced to hang out in my office just to avoid Tiffany? The witch is trying to piss me off, why should I give her the satisfaction of knowing she is getting to me? Braxton or no Braxton, I am not cowering away with my tail in-between my legs. If Kara were here, she would slap the shit out of me, kind of like Tiffany did earlier, but only to get me to wake up. Kara had seen me at my worst; she was the only one who never wavered. She stayed by my side when everyone else turned their backs. Being forced to live through some pretty dark things is never easy. Even worse, is when your flesh and blood turns on you. Sadly, when you need them the most is when they aren't there. Heartache and pain, that's what I knew.

Hell, I did not move here to be reminded of things better off forgotten. I would be calling my best friend later for some much-needed advice on how to handle this messy situation. Why do I always find myself in these types of situations? What I need is to live carefree. Just to fucking live without fear and worry.

Just then a new message beeps at me.

Braxton: Izzy pickup and call me NOW!!

Followed by:

Braxton: Pull the fucking car over and let Liam talk to you!

Shit.....
Another message from Braxton:

Braxton: So help me Izzy when I get my hands on u. Why did u leave? I wanted u here with ME!

Great, so do I pull over or go home? Yeah, I am going home.

Pulling into my driveway, I have a bike up my ass, and he pulls up right next to my car door. Jesus. What is his issue?

Pulling off his helmet, he holds it on his lap. A smile appears to be itching to get out. "Izzy girl, what are you up to?"

Getting out of my car, I say innocently, "What's going on? Why are you following me?" I sound cool, calm and collected.

Smirking, Liam attempts to control his chuckle. "Shit girl, you have a very pissed off Brax breathing down my neck. I was sent to find you and make sure you're okay. He saw you sneak off and went apeshit. He told me, and I quote, "Get her ass back here, now." Got to say, not real happy because I was trying to make sure my sister is not up to something.

Irritated, I enlighten him. "What are you talking about? I was not about to sit in my office like a dog." Hell no, is that happening.

Getting off his bike, Liam walks with me up to my porch. "Listen, he is worried about you. He is not comfortable with Tiff having her claws aimed at you. He wants you safe and out of her sight. Plain and simple, he wants you." The grin he throws my way is mischievous as hell.

Shit, the pit of my heart loves to hear this. The idea that my splendid looking biker boss wants me, little old me, fills my eyes with tears. If Liam only knew how much my heart aches for someone, especially someone like Braxton. My heart may be doing somersaults, but my head is weary. My insecurities creep in, telling me I will never be good enough for a man like Braxton. I've been told, more times than not, that I am not worthy of love.

"He doesn't even know me, Liam. I am not in the mood to be involved in some drama. I left shit to move here. I don't need to find new shit to get myself tangled in. Like him or not, I can't do this." As much as this hurt, it's the truth. Makes it worse Braxton has a daughter with her. It's like an eighteen- year sentence of them being together, in one way or another. Eighteen years of me being the other woman.

I'm struggling to control the tears that are filling my eyes. "Liam, thank you for seeing me home, I'm not going back to the shop. Tell Braxton I am staying here, and he can deal with his daughter and her momma. That is what he should be concerned with, not me. Tell him I am going to find another job, so he should look for another office girl, as well." Feeling dejected I say, "It's for the best."

Sighing heavily. "Jesus Izzy girl, why are you doing this to him? He just found you?"

"Pretty obvious, isn't it? She's your sister. She will be involved with him until Eve turns eighteen years old. I am not looking to be the other woman for that long. He might decide I'm not worth the trouble." My damn eyes won't stop watering.

"Are you trying to piss him off, or me? I see the way you two look at each other. It's damn hot. Listen, my sister is nothing but trouble. I know she may be Eve's mother, but she is not her mom. Damn shame, the only reason she is in her life now, is because she heard about you, and it's pissed her off."

"Exactly and the only ones who will suffer, are Eve and Braxton. I will not be the cause of it. Tell him I like him enough to step back."

"He is not going to like this."

"It doesn't matter if he does or not, this is my life. I don't like it, but it is for the best when a little girl is involved." With shaky hands, I unlock my door. With barely a whisper, I look over my shoulder. "Later Liam." I then walk inside.

Before closing my door, I watch Liam walk back to his bike muttering so loudly I can hear him. He rants on about how much shit he was going to hear from Brax, but then the words 'damn women' had drawn a chuckle from me before closing my front door.

Walking straight to my bedroom, I'm like a zombie. Stripping down to my bra and undies, I cover up in bed. Staring at my phone, I read all of his text messages. I know he is pissed, but too damn bad. I need to stay strong. Why is this so hard?

Wiping the tears that have fallen, I go to call Kara, she will, no doubt, give me a much-needed pep talk. I can start looking for a new job tomorrow.

As I begin to type her number, my phone beeps, causing me to jump. Shit, it's him.

Braxton: If you think for one minute, I am letting you go! Think again. This shit will blow over, and I will make sure Tiff is not a problem. I would be at your place right fuckin' now if it weren't for the fact I have my daughter crying her eyes out. Seems her momma talked shit, and now my baby is upset. You will hear from me Iz, count on it!

Reading his text has me crying into my pillow. Same old story with me, with a glimpse of happiness, comes heartache.

With a heavy heart, I text him back.

Izzy: Let it go, Braxton. I know you will find in the long run, I am not worth the trouble. Give Eve a hug from me! Take care.

Not being able to take any more, I turn my phone off. I would cry myself asleep once again as I have done so many nights before. It's becoming a nightly ritual for me. Life is just so damn hard; I wish I could be numb to it all. Moving here was to get away from my heartache, not to find more of it.

Chapter Six

IT'S IN THE MIDDLE OF the night, and I feel like I am being squeezed to death. Not being able to move very well, I start to panic. *Why can't I move my arms*? Within seconds, I realize I have vast arms wrapped around me. I begin to scream until I hear *him*. His words are so gruff, but sweet at the same time. It's soothing to my storm, it's tender when all I feel is utter turmoil. Turning my head to look behind me, I see Braxton. To my surprise, he looks terrible. His eyes are bloodshot, and all I see is tension. My only thought is to wrap my hands around him but instead, I ask him how he broke into my house? I wasn't really surprised to learn he had easily picked the lock. We shared a few good laughs before I had to wonder *why* he was here.

"Braxton, honey," I whisper to him. "Why are you in bed with me?" Pushing aside all rational thoughts, I should be upset he broke into my house. Instead, all I want to do is enjoy the fact he is in my bed…with me.

A warm smile spreads across his weary face, but I can't help but notice the visible tension. Eyes swathed with worry lines and lips stretched thin, it's easy to see he is distraught. "I couldn't bear to stay away. I knew you were hurting. You being upset is not a feeling I like, especially when you tell Liam you are quitting your damn job. Not to mention, in your last text you told me to forget about you. Not one thing I like about any of those things. I'm here to tell you I'm not letting you go."

His words mean so much to me, I wish I could curl up in them and embrace all that is Braxton, but I can't. The simple truth is he has a baby momma, and all I see is trouble brewing.

"Braxton, this just isn't going to work." My words are filled with regret and I'm trying desperately for him to see my point. It has nothing to do with him or me, it all has to do with a tall fake blonde.

"Babe shh, you give up way too easy. Honestly, do you think I'm going to let that bitch decide if I can be with you? I will deal with her one way or another. I will also make sure you are safe. Get it straight. You are not quitting, and you are not leaving me." His words are strong and so are his arms as they wrap me up like a boa constrictor.

Why is he making this so damn hard?

"Braxton, there is no 'us' to give up on or leave. We let things go too far today, that's it," I say while wiping away stray tears that have fallen. I need for him to see how this thing between us will only end badly.

Biting his lower lip, Brax growls out as if to warn me. "Who are you trying to kid? You damn well know there is something going on between us. You are lying to yourself if you think otherwise."

I face away from him as I rest my head on my pillow, feeling somewhat lost and sad. Maybe if we had met each other under different circumstances, things could be different.

Needing him to understand, I take a deep breath to calm myself so I can explain it to him. "Honey, I don't know what to do here. Do you realize until Eve is eighteen, she will be involved in your life, whether you like it or not?" I feel his body stiffen as I say it. I'm not sure he even realizes how long he will be forced to have her in his life. The thought of long-legged, fake-tits Tiffany makes me sick to my stomach, and I'm not the one who shares a kid with her. Fuck. Eve. This sweet girl is stuck in the middle of a shit storm. Poor baby.

I can feel his head move as he leans in close to my ear. "No. She may be involved with Eve, but she has no involvement with me. I live my life for me, not her." He's telling me this, but I'm not so sure he believes it.

Frustrated, I continue to argue my point. "Yes, I know that, but you are lying to yourself if you think she is going to let you have a normal relationship. With any woman! She will work her ass off trying to get you back into her life." I turn my head to look into those sad red-rimmed brown eyes. He needs to hear what I'm saying.

"Not...Gonna...Happen!" Instantly, he is grabbing my shoulders to yield my undivided attention.

"Delusional!" I huff out in response.

"Realist, Izzy. She has no say in my personal life. Not anymore. I may have made mistakes in the past, going back to her now and again, thinking I wanted her, but it ended all the same. She screwed up over and again. I can't live like that. Not anymore. Not now that I've met you." Running his nose in my hair; his movements are smooth, sweet and sexy.

"*Me?*" *I must be dreaming, did he just say 'me'? Oh, my God.*

"You, Izzy." Braxton yawns fatigued, then sleepily says, "I'm tired as hell. Let's sleep and talk later."

He snuggles in closer to me, and I can feel he has no shirt on. His chest is rubbing against my bare shoulders. I have my bra on and feeling skin on skin with him is like a fire smoldering before it ignites into flames. His touch is the most amazing thing I have ever felt. No man has ever made me feel this with one touch alone. Between his hot smoldering body and his very sexy face that does all sorts of naughty things to me, his touch is just too much. Sleep? Who the hell does he think is going to get some rest?

Intrigued, I have to ask. "Are you naked, Braxton?"

I feel his hot breath on the back of my neck. His intense growl is just plain sexy, and it's making my body sizzle to life.

"Feel me and find out, Iz."

I hate to moan, but my body has its own ideas. Not being able to contain myself, I roll my hips against him. I seriously love spooning.

I'm losing my ability to think, and speaking is getting increasingly difficult. "Seriously, are you trying to kill me? I mean, how much do you think I am going to be able to take? From the moment I saw you, I have been changing my underwear faster than I can wash them. I use my rabbit daily and thanks to you, it has forced me to change batteries faster than I can buy them. Jesus H. Christ, what you do to me." I let it all slip out without my damn mouth filter. *Argh. Shit, did I just say that to him...Seriously?*

Braxton chokes and then starts to laugh as if it's the funniest thing he has ever heard.

"Oh, hell. Damn, Izzy, the things you say never cease to amaze me. I have never had a woman be honest enough to say those things without either being embarrassed or not gutsy enough to admit it. Girl, you just jumped up by ten fucking points with your very flattering remarks." He nuzzles my neck once again and turns it up a notch by nibbling on my ear with hot, heavy breaths. Oh, his breaths are warm and wet and sending shivers all the way to my toes.

"Oh really, did I impress big bad Braxton? Must be the first girl to do that, huh?" I should have known if I dared his playful side, he'd play along.

"Damn straight baby, you intrigue me to the point I might go bat shit crazy." His erection pressing into my backside is undoing my resolve. Moans escape from the both of us.

"Hmmm. Oh my. Seriously Braxton, this is unfair. I've been sexually frustrated since I met you. This is killing me."

His hip grinding and hot breaths on my neck only emphasizes how much he wants me. He'd better watch it, or else I might jump his damn bones. Bastard would like that though. To torture me even more, his hardened shaft is pressed against me moving in an up and down motion. Shit, I swear I can feel everything down to the pulse of blood pumping to his growing erection.

Jokingly, Braxton says, "Show me. Get your little rabbit friend and show me what I do to you. I think I need a visual. The visual of you getting off just thinking about me turns me the fuck on."

Using my sexiest voice, I reply, "Oh, you would like that wouldn't you?"

"Bet your ass I would and right now, your ass feels fucking incredible pressed up against my cock." Circling his hips harder this time.

We both moan as I rotate my hips to meet his. When our bodies come together, it's that little bit of friction that ignites into passion. Braxton reaches around the front of me slowly, taking his time. His fingers snake around and find my panties soaked. He presses his thumb against my clit at the same time his cock continuously makes contact with my ass. Oh, sweet mother.

I can't help myself. Needing to feel him more of him, I snake my hand around his neck to pull him closer to me. The more he rocks, the harder he rubs my sweet spot. That makes me yank on him even harder. I dig my fingers through his hair, pulling it as I try to smash his face into my back. I realize I am building, and my insides tighten to the point of no return. Oh, my god, I don't want him to stop. I want more; I need more.

"Oh, sweet Jesus, Braxton don't stop touching me." Moaning, groaning and digging my fingernails into his scalp. Shit, I might have drawn blood as he winces and lets out a groan himself. Not sure if it was from pain or pleasure, or maybe both.

"Don't plan on it babe, the harder you pull my hair only makes me rock into you that much more. Let go, baby. Come apart for me. I want to see how beautiful you look when you come apart. Show me what I do to you. Fuck Izzy, your body feels like fucking heaven."

His teeth nip a bit harder this time. *Yeah, bite met. Mark me.* At least this time, I want a mark on me. *His mark.* Braxton's mark would be a welcomed one. The others are just a disgusting reminder. Maybe I need some of Braxton's marks to help me forget the other ones.

Breathing harder I grind my core against his hand. Moaning and pulling and rubbing and losing all sense of rationality, I fall apart. I cry out and I'm trembling. Fuck! I can't stop the feelings, I need him. No! I. Fucking. Want. Him. My orgasm is drawn out with the feeling of his palm on my clit and the rubbing of his dick against my backside. I ride it out with not an ounce of embarrassment.

"That's it Izzy, fucking ride my hand. Feel me baby, rock hard against your sweet ass. Jesus, I feel like I'm seventeen again. If it's this damn good now, wait till I have you naked and riding my cock baby. I might not live through that. I want you Iz, like I need the air to breathe."

Collapsing into him, he wraps me up to kiss my head. To say that was one of the most powerful orgasms I ever had would be an understatement. *Good Lord*, I never knew how good it could be. My orgasms to-date have been okay, I seem to have better ones with my hand than the lackluster lovers I have had in my past. Some guys know what they are doing better than others. Most men are selfish and only think about their own needs. They could give a fuck if the girl they are with getting off or not.

With Braxton, it's different. He sets my body on fire with his eyes alone. When his voice comes into play with his rocking body, it's just over the top fuck-a-licious.

Smiling like a school girl, I chuckle a bit too loudly. "Braxton, that was fucking-amazing. Jesus, did you take a class in all the ways to please a woman or am I just damn lucky?"

Holding me tighter, he whispers in my ear. "Iz, you're like a drug and I'm addicted. I can't get enough when I am around you, girl." His laughter stops as he says, "Shit, you lit up and turned into a sex kitten, ready to eat me alive. Hmmm. Sparkplug. My new nickname for you is Sparkplug."

"What the hell does that mean?" Turning my head so I can look in his eyes, all I see is mischief. "What does 'Sparkplug' mean?" Taking in his wild array of emotions dancing across his face, I'm not sure what he is going to tell me.

"One minute you are sweet and innocent and then you turn it on and watch out, you spark and ignite. Sparkplug baby, my own personal sparkplug." Kissing the tip of my nose, oh so sweetly.

With our bodies now aligned, I wrap my arms around his strong shoulders. I take my time running my hands all over his body and all I feel are muscles. He is very muscular, his tattoos are on display, and I am in awe. A man with tattoos always looked good to me, but the way Braxton sports them, damn, it's mouth-watering. So I run my fingertips over them. I start at his right shoulder and trace the tribal looking design all the way down his arm. It's a full arm tattoo, and I have no idea the meaning, but it is massive and beautiful. Just like him.

"Braxton, your tattoos are fabulous. Especially this one, I love the way it goes down your arm and wraps around your wrist. I could get lost in all of them. Spend all day tracing them with my tongue." So I do, I lean over and run my tongue along his wrist and up his arm. It's sensual and a turn-on, not gross in any way. I moan and watch his face with my eyes. With his eyes locked on me, he lays back and lets me explore.

Once I am up his arm, I trace my fingers across his chest to his other side. He has a big eagle with its wings spanned across his chest. It's intricate and very detailed. The artist did a kick-ass job as far as I can see. I spend some time running my fingers around his nipples and lick them lightly. I bite one hard enough to feel Braxton wince. He smiles. The lick I give it draws out a moan from his very luscious lips.

"Iz." My name escapes his soft lips gingerly.

His other arm is sporting a dragon that wraps down his arm. It's just as intricate as the rest. I return my gaze to his stomach, and my insides flutter with excitement. Hot damn, the design that outlines his taut muscles is incredible. I notice, upon closer inspection, he has a name above his heart.

Lightly tracing it, a smile spreads across my face. I notice the letters that are scripted in the eagle's wing, right above his heart.

"Eve. I can see it here. If you didn't look closely, you would never see it. It's beautiful Braxton." I never let my eyes wander, they are entranced in his daughter's name.

Softly he replies, "Yeah, she is my heart. It seemed only right to have her mark on me. Do you really like it?"

"Hmm, I love it. What a beautiful thing to do. Mine are not as beautiful as yours." I accidently let this slip.

That seems to get his attention.

"You got tats, sweetheart? Damn, how the hell did I not notice them?" He's still trying to peer at my half naked body, even though I'm still half covered by the blanket.

Slightly embarrassed, I only nod. I know he is going to ask me where and I will have to show him. Shit should have kept my mouth shut.

"Oh Izzy, don't hold out on me now. It's only fair. You licked mine so I should get to return the favor." Smiling, he gives me the look of the devil.

Shit. Damn. Oh, my God.

"Wouldn't you like to know?" I give him my best glare before I blurt out with a laugh.

"Bet your ass, now fess up Sparkplug." He says, slapping my thigh.

My newfound nickname is pretty funny, but Braxton calling me that makes it sweet. Braxton giving me a nickname is, hot as sin.

I give him a serious look now because, what I've got to say is not funny in any way. "I got my first one several years back and then just kept adding some here and there. Some I wanted and some not so much." I get quieter as I mention them to him without him knowing what I mean by 'marks' on my body. My mistake. He was never supposed to find out about my sordid past. *Great Izzy, open mouth and insert foot.*

Sitting up some, Braxton gives me a look of 'what the hell does that mean?'

"Izzy, what the hell do you mean 'some not so much?' Don't tell me you let some dick mark you when you didn't want it?" His sweet voice and body language is now a little frightening.

Rolling my eyes with a shake of my head, I am now pissed at myself for saying anything. *Seriously Izzy, what the hell? Major buzz kill.*

I sigh with regret. "Doesn't matter now, does it? What happened to me was then, not now. Someday I want to have a few of my marks covered up."

He pauses and shakes his head as if he did not just hear me right. His nostrils flare with anger. "Iz, spill it. Now. Not fuckin' liking what is coming out of your mouth."

Shit. "Braxton, leave it alone. If you're nice, I will show you my butterflies." Wanting to distract his anger, I try to plaster a fake ass smile on my face. This is not a can of worms I want to be opened.

His glare is seeking entrance into my soul. Or maybe just trying to figure me out, either way he is searching.

He relaxes a bit. "Yeah babe, show me some skin. First the butterflies then I want to see the others. It's Showtime, baby doll." He just cracks me up, but underneath his smile, I can see his nervousness. He can't hide it from me.

Turning around, I go to stand. "Here, see how the butterflies span my entire back." I showcase my back by the moonlight coming in the window. I turn slightly to my side so he can see how my butterflies span up my side. It's quite beautiful. This is my only piece that is truly me. Life imitating art and all.

Braxton instantly sits up and turns on the nightstand light to get a better look. The moon shining through the window did not give him enough light, I guess. Hey, at least the light will let me take in his tattoos better. I drink the sight of him in as soon as the light fills the room. Losing myself in his body art, I raise an eyebrow and have to pick up my mouth up off of the floor.

"Izzy," he says in his sexy voice. "These are hot as hell." He reaches out to trace them. They start at my right hip and curve around my side and end up on my shoulder. I have no idea what I was thinking at the time, but they are beautiful. Delicate designs with blues, yellows and mostly black.

As his eyes dance across my back, his genuine smile warms my heart. "Alright Sparkplug, let's continue."

"I got a tramp stamp; people thought I was one, so why disappoint them, right?" I shove my panties down and reveal my lower back tattoo. It's a tribal design, and it spans from hip to hip dipping low into my ass crack. Yeah, this one hurt like hell. I did it to piss him off, the dick from my past who acted like he owned me. It was silly but I did it, and I paid the price for it.

"Holy Fuck! That's hot babe. Damn, taking you from behind is going to be sexy as hell."

Braxton is just too sexy for words, lying against my headboard in black boxer briefs. Sweet God, I could just eat him up.

He smirks and smacks his forehead with the palm of his hand when I shake my ass at him. "Keep going Sparkplug. Life is good." Excitement radiates from him as he claps his hands together.

"That's enough show and tell for one night there, big guy," I say smiling.

With a devil's grin, I start crawling to meet him in the middle of my bed. Braxton reaches out for me and pulls me to his chest. Our noses touch as he lays his forehead against mine.

"You don't have to look at me, but you will tell me what happened with those marks you didn't want. As much as I loved the show, your distraction is not going to make me forget what you told me earlier."

Closing my eyes, I whisper "Braxton, I can't. So much pain and suffering. I left to get away. I don't want you to know a thing about what I have lived with." Grabbing his shoulders, I pull him tighter to me. Our foreheads still resting against one another as we stay like this.

"Not moving, so you need to spill it. Part of me getting to know you is finding out about your life. Not a damn thing you can tell me will make me feel any different. Shit happens to all of us. Some good and some downright bad, but that's life, Iz. I know it better than anyone."

Whispering, I silently beg. "I can't Braxton, I just need time. Time for me to heal myself, I'm not ready for you to judge me just yet."

Shaking his head, he blows out a big breath.

"Izzy, my sweet girl, you know I would never judge you. I'm no choir boy. I have done shit and seen shit that would make you second guess being in this bed with me, but I have no worries about you judging me. I'm not proud of all the things I did, but I can't change my past. This is who I am. Only move forward and do better with what you got." Holding my hand in his, he is confident and self-assured. I stare at him in bewilderment.

"Putting it that way makes sense Braxton. Thank you for saying that." I like the way he just explained that. Life can be shitty, and it can be great. Like right now, I'm in bed with an almost naked, sexy as hell Braxton. Life before, with Dominic, was horrid and downright terrifying.

I unintentionally start rubbing my left thigh. I did it as if remembering what I have survived; times best forgotten.

Watching me, Braxton pulls me to his knees, and I come sliding up the bed flat on my back. He places my knees aside, so I'm straddling his body exposing my thighs. He strokes his fingers and freezes. Holding my breath, I realize he's found it. The mark. His mark. The one *he* said would always remind me of *him*. Together or not, I would always remember him. Sick fucking bastard.

"What in holy hell is this?" He pulls me closer to him so he can see the mark more clearly. I always wore long shorts for this reason alone. No one needs to see this ugly ass scar. One of the reasons I don't spread my legs for just anyone.

Running his fingers over the red, raised mark outlining my scar, he huffs out a breath like he's been kicked in the gut. His grip is biting into me like a death grip. It's time to come clean or just give him enough, so he leaves it alone. I think the second option is the way to go for now.

"What the fuck is this? Just who the hell did this to you? Goddammit, Izzy. This pisses me off."

"No need to get pissed, Braxton. It happened, and now it's over. This mark was meant to always remind me of him. He made sure the mark was in a spot that would stop me from wanting ever to sleep with any other man. He got his wish, I've never shown anyone. Until just now."

"He as in *whom*? Who the fuck thought this would be okay to do to his girl?" Braxton's eyes were piercing into my soul with the look he was giving me.

I have to laugh at his reference to 'his girl'.

"I was only a possession to him, not a girl or his woman. Just a person to possess and ruin. The sick part is while everyone liked him, they hated me. They thought he was a nice guy, took good care of the sick, broken and messed up Izzy."

Braxton is shaking and controlling his breathing as best he can. He pinches the bridge of his nose with his fingers, I am assuming to help settle him down.

"One night, I disobeyed him..." I whisper as tears start to fill my eyes to the point Braxton is beginning to look fuzzy.

He cuts me off.

Braxton's look is murderous. "What?! You *disobeyed*? Who the fuck does he thinks he is? You're not a dog, Izzy."

I must look scared because I can feel a shift in his demeanor. He rubs his hand up and down my arm.

"I was not at home when he wanted me to be. I got home thirty minutes later and that was all it took for him to go bat-shit crazy on me. He slapped me around, he punched me in the gut and then things got worse." Shaking, I can feel the tears as they fall freely down my cheeks.

Nervously, I look into his troubled eyes. My insecurity is at an all-time high. I take a few deep breaths to gain some much-needed courage. "He took a knife and ripped off my shorts. While taking me as roughly as he could, he took a knife and as he got off, he pierced my thigh with it. Every time he got pissed at me, he took his knife to me somewhere hidden, but meant for me to see every time I was naked." Revealing this to Braxton has drained all of my energy.

"Motherfucking twisted bastard. Please tell me you had his ass hauled to jail." Not even taking a breath in between words he keeps on going. "What about your family? Who the hell did you tell?"

Holding my shaking hands up I silently beg him to slow down. "There was no one to tell, only my best friend, Kara. She saved me from taking the same knife and slitting my wrists. Figured I might as well take my life with his favorite tool. The sad thing is, he would have probably liked that." Lowering my eyes, I try to wipe the remaining tears that slide down my cheeks. Remembering all the horrible things Dominic said to me, they all come back screaming in my head. I never let myself grieve for the sad girl who just took his beatings. I just pushed everything down, and buried it as deep as I could. It was the only way I survived this long.

Grabbing me tight, he is 'hushing me' and rocking me against him. Jesus, when Braxton hugs you, you just get lost in those big ass arms.

"Babe, never again. You don't have to be scared. Not anymore. I will never let anyone hurt you. Fuck that, I need to know who this guy is. Iz, you need to let me kick his ass for you. This fucker needs to feel my pain, let me show him what it means to put the fear of God into someone. Fuck. Fuck. Fuck. I need a damn drink."

Now I'm trying to hush him, I turn and look into his eyes, honest to God, he needs to understand my pain and my fear. Fear is an emotion I know all too well and I need Braxton to understand that I can't live with that fear anymore. It almost killed me once. It might do me in this time around. No more. I can take no more.

Pleading with only my eyes, I warmly say, "No honey, you don't ever get to see him. If he knows where I am, he will come for me and then I'm as good as dead. He will torture me and then I might as well be dead."

"Not. Fucking. Happening." Seething mad are the only words to describe Braxton right now.

Braxton then spins me around. He is inspecting my body for other marks. I am suddenly shy and start to fight him from looking. He is much stronger than I, so it's a losing battle for me.

"Show me. All of them. Right the fuck now." Great.

Rolling my eyes, I proceed to show him my marks. Nine in all, in different areas all over my small body. Four are on my thighs, three on the inside of my arms by my armpits and two on my chest; one for each breast. Yeah, just great for some potential guy in my bed. Who the hell wants to look at a woman who has knife marks that scar me both physically and better yet, emotionally? I look like 'Jack the fucking Ripper' had a party with me.

Braxton kisses each and every one. Taking his time, he gently caresses them before placing a very soft kiss over every scar. Not missing a one. Feeling his touch does some weird things to me. I am embarrassed for him to see them, but he never flinches when he comes face to face with one. It's sweet, and I realize I am crying so hard I can't keep them from spilling down my near naked chest.

"Baby, I am so fucking sorry for each and every time he took a knife to you. A *real* man doesn't do this shit. Bad enough he put his hands on you. But the fucker used a knife on you. He made sure they were where you had to see them everyday. You and any guy who wanted to sleep with you. Fucker needs his ass beat, and he needs a knife to cut his dick off. Let him see what it feels like."

He looks into my eyes as he grazes his lips over my shaking frame. I can feel myself trembling as I cry. Braxton is rubbing my back, trying to calm me. Skin to skin, his touch does just that. Crying still, I am cradled in his arms in a fetal position.

"Name, Izzy. I want the motherfucker's name. Not messing around here." His words firm and intense, like his body.

My pleading stare seems to have little effect on him. "Forget it, Braxton, let it go."

"Fuck, Izzy, not going to happen!"

"Name, Izzy?" Impatient, his hold on my arms tightens.

I jump, biting back the bile in my throat. "Dominic Santos."

Several things happen when I let his vile name escape my tortured lips. I swore to myself I would never say his name again. But fuck me, I am telling Braxton his name. I have lost my ever-loving mind. The last thing I need is for Dominic to find me. What if I am with Eve and Dominic finds me? The thought of it sickens me, and I gasp.

"What's wrong, Izzy?" Braxton senses my body tensing, and it puts him on alarm.

"Oh my god, you can't find him. Promise me, please." Anxiety rises in my voice, and I flap my hands around like I'm a crazy person.

"Nope." He holds my arms down.

"Shit Braxton. What if I am with Eve and he finds me? He might hurt her. I don't care about me, but I will not let him hurt her because of me. Braxton listen to me." Panic spreads throughout my body.

"Fuck that, Izzy, that piece of shit isn't ever going to touch my girls."

What? Wait? What did he say?

"Girls?" I ask in a soft voice questioning him.

"Yeah, my two girls. Eve and you. He is never going to lay a finger on either one." He eyes me with a stern 'don't mess with me' look.

"Please Braxton, let it go. Kara is watching him for me back home when she can." Damn! I didn't mean to say that out loud, either. I just need to shut my damned mouth.

"Who? Wait one fucking minute? He is back where you came from, and your friend is watching over him? Like doing what? What is she going to do about it?" He looks at me like I have lost my mind.

"You don't understand," I groan and roll my eyes. "He is my best friend's brother." I cringe when I let this slip out as well.

Standing up in a flash, Braxton is pacing the room. He is ranting questioning me a mile a minute. How can I be friends with her? Why didn't Kara stop this from happening? I let him rant, it's what he does. After he processes it, hopefully he will let it go.

Drowning out his words, I sit back and watch him strut around in his black boxers. His muscles are hard to ignore. I'm snapped from watching eye-candy when my phone starts ringing. Oh hell, who can that be?

Leaning over to my nightstand, I see the name lit up, and the name on it freezes me to my spot. My eyes grow wide when I see that Braxton is eyeing my phone as well.

We look at each other and before I can get to it he grabs it and pushes the talk button.

Oh shit......

"Kara!" He says in a very dark and dangerous tone.

Chapter Seven

I LISTENED TO BRAXTON TALK to Kara for over twenty long minutes. He wanted to know all about Dominic, the dick. It was a long and very sordid story. Kara has been my best friend since junior high where we had hit if off instantly. She had my back, and I had hers.

I remember that day when the 'popular' clique of girls was talking smack about me. I was an easy shot for them. I never talked back, I just went along with my day like they did not exist. It was hard, and I usually hid in the bathroom, crying and shit. One day in particular, it was bad. I had attended a party the night before with some friends of mine. A very popular kid in our class was eyeing me, and I'd noticed he'd been watching me at school for some time. I didn't hide the way I would watch him. He was hot and like most of the girls in school, he knew he was admired.

At times, he would say 'hi' to me in the halls, I melted each and every time. I was stupid not to notice that it was always when none of the popular girls were around, he made sure of it. I never noticed it then because my only thought was he was acknowledging me. Little ole me, I was lucky.

Luckily, I found myself at that party. Erik was there and asked me to dance. His buddies were there and some of the popular girls, as well. I was floored he asked me to dance in front of them, but I was not going to pass this chance up. No way.

We were slow dancing. While most eyes were on us, he leaned in and kissed me. Lost in his touch and his arms, I was on cloud nine. I never kissed with tongue before, so the french kiss was all new to me. My friends told me how to do it. They would show me in the mirror how to swirl my tongue around. Yeah, I could do this.

His kiss was soft and when I felt his tongue slide across my lips I opened them and invited him in. Nervously, I swirled my tongue with his. I was nervous, so I was tentative at first. He gently told me to relax. I was a goner. Yep, Erik Landz had me hook, line and sinker. The night ended with him getting my number, and I was on top of the freaking world. Little did I know that would end the next day.

Going to school the next day, I was nervous, but excited to see him. Since he kissed me the night before and asked for my number, I assumed he liked me, and I was his girlfriend. Walking the halls, I got nervous as I was rounding the corner to our lockers. His was down the row from mine. The minute I rounded the corner, there he was. A blonde, preppy dressed Erik is leaning against his locker. He had Amber, the bitch from hell, and some other girls around him. I looked down and went to my locker. The giggles and the 'Oh my God' were all I could hear. I never looked their way. Getting my stuff for my first class, I was about to close my locker when the girls were walking by me.

Amber the bitch, walked up to me and flat out asked me where I learned to kiss. Seriously, she flat out asked me that. She laughed, and the other's then followed her lead.

"Oh my God, Erik just told us you have no clue how to french kiss. How embarrassing. He is so disgusted he put his lips on you, he had to bleach out his mouth when he got home. You're pathetic, maybe you should take lessons, Izzy." Saying my name, she let it linger; yep, pretty pathetic.

The day passed with the whole school hearing about this, and I was pretty much the laughing stock for the day. After the fifth period, I ran to the restroom and threw up. Disgusted and sickened, I wanted to run the fuck away. A girl came into the bathroom and banged on my stall door. Shocked and scared, I thought she was going to make fun of me, too. She didn't, but she looked at me with such a pissed off look. She told me that she had heard it was Jason, Erik's best friend, who had made fun of him all night after our kiss. He made this shit up so Erik would not be associated with me.

Before going home, two things happened. First, Amber got a fat lip, all courtesy of my new friend Kara. Second, Erik and Jason got an earful. Poor Erik got his ass handed to him in front of his buddies. She called him out on liking me but did not have the balls to stand up to his friends. I had to hand it to her, she had me convinced before the day ended. The newest gossip was Amber's fat lip and Eric acting like a dick.

From that day forward, she was my best friend. I started hanging with her all the time and spent a lot of time around her house. I met her brother, Dominic, a few times and each time he spent more and more time watching me and talking to me. He was older and in college when we were in just the 9th grade.

I'll never forget that one night at her house when Dominic's girlfriend had gone home early. He was hanging out with us in the kitchen and was spending a lot of time next to me. He made me nervous. He was tall, dark and handsome and he dated the popular girls. They flocked to him.

Even in college, he dated girls in high school. They loved dating an older guy, and he liked to dominate the younger girls. I fully understand that now. That night, we spent watching a movie when Kara decided to go to her room and talk to her boyfriend. Dominic told me to stay with him and keep him company while his sister spoke to Chris. Kara dated Chris off and on, tonight they were on.

We laughed, and he kept sliding closer to me on the couch. Having his arm across the back of the sofa, he would slide his fingers across my shoulder, back and forth. Talk about nervous, I was deathly scared. First I had some 9th-grade dick tell the school I couldn't french kiss, now I had a college guy hitting on me.

He ended up walking me to his room. I thought we would just talk, like Kara and her boyfriend were doing. I had no clue what I was doing. He sat on his bed, and I sat next to him with one leg on the floor. My leg was shaking so badly; it was jumping up and down. Dominic kept telling me not to be nervous, while he kept running his hands up and down my leg.

The next thing I know I am naked and under him in, like, minutes. Hell, I am not even sure how the fuck it happened. To this day, it is a blur. I was naked in bed with a college guy who had plenty of experience, while here I am, a virgin who can't kiss very well.

After that night I not only knew how to french kiss, I was no longer a virgin. The guy dominated me. He was gentle though, and I survived. That was the only thing on my mind. I could not live with the embarrassment of being awful with him, too.

Dominic finished and cuddled with me for some time. He was attentive and friendly. He knew it was my first time. I knew he had a girlfriend, I was just easy prey.

The next morning, I saw him. I'd left him the night before as he was drifting off to sleep. I was in the kitchen with Kara. She laughed and thought it was funny. Her brother was a man whore, her words not mine. I was nervous to see him, would he make fun of me? Would he be nice to me or would he ignore me? All variations of the questions that had me up all night, trying to figure out what would play out.

I didn't have to wait long. In strolls a sleepy Dominic. No shirt, just black board shorts. Damn he had a beautiful body, and I had that for my first time. Maybe I was lucky after all.

He noticed me and smiled. Walking over to me, he ran his hands up my legs and stepped in for a kiss. It was brief, it was soft, and it was nice. I smiled and blushed red as a tomato. I know this because I could feel my face. It was on fire and my hands were sweating.

While he's looking at me, he acknowledges his sister with a 'hi'. He then grabs water and leaves the room. That's it. No other words said. He goes back to his room, and I am shocked. What the hell is with that? He walks back in, smiles and kisses me. I look at Kara, and she shrugs her shoulders before making us pancakes.

An hour later, we are laughing in the living room when Dominic's girlfriend strolls by. She walks right in, smirking at us and proceeds to his bedroom. I'm frozen in my seat and I know I'm as pale as a ghost. What the fuck?

Kara laughs so hard that she doubles over before falling out of her chair.

"Bitch doesn't know his dick was up in my friend last night. Let's hope he takes a shower before she blows him."

I choke, did she seriously just say that. Shrugging her shoulders again, I melt into my chair. I needed to get home, and fast.

I did not see Dominic again for a month or so, but the next time he is not dating anyone. He sees me and I don't fight him, I go willingly. That is how it all started. Things were really good between us.

Kara warned me that Dominic was into some wild things and I should be careful. But it was casual, and it was fun. I never took it too seriously, he was good for my ego. I went from being a girl who was laughed at because she could not kiss right, to being laid, by a hot college guy. Not bad, if I say so myself.

The next couple of years was much the same. I saw him whenever and when I did, he took what he wanted. It did not matter if I was dating someone or not. He wanted me, so he had me.

Like most things in life, all good things come to an end. My personal favorite, the old saying 'if it's too good to be true' yeah, that one should have been a big red flag for me. But no, common sense did not come into play when it came to Dominic.

I learned in the years to come, Dominic was seriously into some dark shit. He was involved with a local gang, and it was his way or the highway. I tried to take the highway, but there was no escaping him. Dominic possessed what he wanted, and it would be his decision to end things if he wanted. I wanted to stop things, but he did not feel the same. I was to obey. To submit. To give it all to him.

I never realized he was grooming me. He took a young, naïve girl, and shaped her into a person she hardly recognized. My once hot hookup saw me as nothing but a warm body for him to abuse how he saw fit.

Izzy no longer existed. The only thing that remained was a shell of a girl I used to be. Kara knew enough to keep her shit intact. She knew what would happen to me if she didn't. It came to a point where Kara and Dominic were like strangers to each other. She hated him and wanted me to be free of him, but she also knew there was not a fucking thing she could do about it. It killed her, and her guilt over how we hooked up that night years before was my death sentence.

Sticks and stones may break my bones, but chains and whips excite me. Yeah, that should be Dominic's motto. I learned more than I wanted from him. Escaping him took me a long time of waiting for just the right moment. I found my chance, and I took it. Leaving everything behind. My family, who had grown to hate me over some bullshit, was the least of my concerns. Being the family disappointment was one thing, but dying at the hands of Dominic was a whole lot worse. He was the monster I needed to get away from. I could never go far enough, but Seattle seemed like an excellent start.

One night, I did something unspeakable. I took off. With Kara's help I did it. I took control for once.

chapter EIGHT

WAKING UP, I EXPECTED TO find a sexy body next to me, but instead my hand felt around and there was nothing but a cold bed. My hand kept reaching and feeling out for a hand, a leg but nothing. Just my luck. Sitting up wiping the sleep from my eyes, I look around feeling frustrated. Recalling our conversation last night has left me feeling bare. I did not hold anything back from him either, at least not before I couldn't take anymore and I nodded off to sleep. I vaguely remember him holding me as we talked about Kara. Mostly it was about Dominic. Dominic this and Dominic that. I did, however, keep one secret from him; it was just too personal, and I still haven't fully recovered from it myself. When and if he ever finds out, he would need to understand my feelings.

Shivers run down my spine just thinking about my past. To think about telling my worst nightmare stories to Braxton makes me sick to my stomach. A man I just met. A man I like. A man I am trying to impress. Ugh. Why can't I ever learn just to shut my mouth? My mind is still somewhat foggy, so I'm not sure how much I've even said to him about that sick bastard. Rubbing my forehead in disgust, it most likely is the reason he is not in bed with me this morning. *There's nothing like running him off, Iz. Great. What a way to have him running for the hills, then to tell him about your sordid past.*

Showering and dressed for the day, I am cleaning when a soft knock at my door catches my attention. Opening it, I see the sweet little face I have grown to love. Eve is dressed like a biker chick. She is going to grow up to be one, I am confident about that. She has on a t-shirt, jeans and knee high flat black boots. The girl is so damn cute. She's going to be a knockout when she is older. The thought of Braxton keeping the boys away brings a smile to my face. Looking at her, it is easy to see her mother. She looks a lot like her, with her blonde hair with long natural curls. Eve is tall and slender for a young girl. She is beautiful, stunning even. To make her even more likable, she is sweet as sugar.

"Hey honey, what are you doing looking so cute today?" I can't hide my smile from her. She just brightens up my damn day. That's not something she gets from her mother. Nope, she definitely got it all from her dad. Dimples and all, boy oh boy.

Twirling her hair with her hand, she smiles and tilts her head to the side.

"I was missing you, and I just took off to come and see you." I could sense she was not telling me something.

"Hey," I use my finger to tilt her chin up so her eyes can meet mine. I could understand most people just by looking into their eyes. Most people don't use the eyes to read what they are feeling and thinking, but I do. I have always had it and it has saved me many nights of pain and suffering. Sensing what the other person was thinking or feeling, I used this talent to help defuse a confrontation or easily flirt my way out of it. It's helped my ass out several times.

"Izzy, my mom stopped by and now she is yelling at my dad. She had gotten so mad at me before I went into the house. Dad doesn't know the half of it." She blew out a breath trying to hide the tears welling in her beautiful eyes.

I hated seeing this sweet girl so sad. It was a déjà vu moment as if I was listening to myself not so long ago. I was as lost and hurt as she is now. It struck a chord in my heart and shattered it. Her eyes said it all.

I grabbed her and crushed her to my chest. I cradled her and took her into my house. We walked over to the couch and sat down. She started to cry instantly, again breaking my heart even more. I remember feeling like I had no one, I was left to face pain and despair all by myself; just like she's feeling now. They say it takes one to know one but dang, it hurts to see the pain in her eyes. The pain I endured and lived with scarred me; deeply. I refuse to let someone I know feel that kind of pain. To be bullied by the hands and words of another person is its own kind of hell. I'll be damned if I'm going to sit by and let Eve be hurt like this. Not with me around. She may have shit for a mother, but I am her friend.

"Honey, I am so sorry, did you tell your dad?" I say looking down at her as she lay against my chest. Kissing the top of her head, I rock her and just listen. She needed to talk to someone and I can imagine she can't with her bitch of a mother. Braxton is too gruff most of the time. His only care is to protect Eve, he is just not always gentle about it.

"She yells at me, mostly over stupid stuff. I don't think she likes me very much." Her words trail off as she weeps. It guts me to see her like this. Eve is like a flower ready to bloom but before she can get the chance, she gets crushed by the one person who should love her the most. I let her continue with the story of a girl tormented by a mother who would rather not be held down by a child. Eve feels like she cramps her style, and the only reason she has anything to do with her, is because she is hot after Braxton.

It not only pisses me off, it makes me sick. Tiffany has this perfect gift in front of her who looks up at her with those puppy dog eyes. Eve only wants attention and the love of her mother. Only she is not going to get it. The only way she will get it is if Braxton stays with her. That thought only makes me want to throw-up in my mouth. I freeze when I hear my name mentioned.

She looks up at me and wipes her nose with the back of her hand. I can tell right away she doesn't want to say, she's all hushed as she lowers her head to speak.

"My momma hates you. She says you just want to tear my family apart. She told me you didn't even like me. The only reason you hang out with me, is to get closer to my dad."

She stops speaking and I am trembling. Holding my shit together is almost becoming impossible. How can a woman tell her daughter all of these lies and have no conscience? I am suddenly panicked.

Does Eve believe her? Does this sweet child harbor ill feelings for me? If she did, would she be with me right now crying in my arms? I don't think so, I believe she was lost and needed someone. She needed me. The thought breaks a smile on my face. I smile as I grab and kiss her head.

"Baby girl, that is so not true do you understand that? None of what she said is right. I love hanging out with you and it has nothing to do with your dad. Eve, I'm not sure what to say here. I don't have any kids, but I do know what it is like to be hurt by people you love.

People who should always protect you and make you feel safe. I am not one of those people who want to hurt you Eve. I care about you." Closing my eyes, the tears gently fall on my cheeks as I silently pray for this sweet, sweet girl.

With my eyes still closed, I jump when my front door swings open and in strides a very not happy looking Braxton. Still absolutely beautiful, his nose flares and he looks like he is going to tear someone's head off. Tense, his muscles taut, he is on a mission. He notices me with his daughter sitting on the couch. Eve straddled in my lap, my arms cradling her. You could see the look of wonderment as Braxton wrinkles his forehead. The moment he realizes his little girl is sniffling and wiping her eyes, he softens. He groans and comes over and kneels down in front of us, his eyes never leaving Eve. He gently rubs his hands up and down her arms trying to comfort her.

"Hey, baby girl, what's going on? You had me scared. Not sure where you ran off to at first, then it hit me. You wanted to be with your best buddy, Iz. Came running when I got done with your mother." Acid laced in his words.

"Is...is she gone?" The poor thing was shuddering in her crying state.

"Yeah honey, when she got done yelling and hollering, she took off. I told her I was done listening to it." He finally lets his gaze go from Eve to me. I can tell he likes what he sees so far. He likes me holding his baby girl, and he likes that she has someone who treats her with care and love.

His expression changes when he can see the tears streaming down my face, not having much make-up on I know I can't have mascara running down my cheeks, but, I bet I look dandy.

"What the hell? Iz, why are you and my daughter both crying?" He wasn't mad, I could tell by the soulful look in his amazing, trance setting eyes of his. He was concerned and trying not to get upset. You could tell Braxton did not do well with the crying ladies.

"Nothing that a good ole' ass kicking wouldn't fix. Sorry, Eve honey, I didn't mean to say that out loud and in front of you." I say shaking my head and wiping my eyes, I realized my mistake by once again not filtering my mouth, and just airing whatever comes to my mind.

His smile is as soft as his words. "Nothing worse than she has heard her whole life, Iz. She doesn't get sheltered too much, as I am sure you know by now. Want to fill me in why you are both crying?"

"It's momma. She hates me just as much as she hates Izzy, daddy. Why does momma hate me so much?" The honesty in this child is so pure and innocent, it just takes my breath away. She was one hundred percent truthful with her dad, asking why her mother hates her. Seriously, this situation is so fucked up.

"No baby, she doesn't hate you. She just doesn't know how to love you. It's not in her to love a child, like she damn well should. As far as Izzy, she's jealous. She sees how much you look up to her, and it drives your momma crazy. It's not you, honey." Braxton has tears in his eyes as he caresses her cheek. I think he finally realizes how hard this is on Eve.

"You mean this is all Izzy's fault? She hates me because of Izzy?" Her voice raised an octave, and I can feel how tense her body is. She straightened up and looked at me with hurt and uncertainty.

The way Braxton's body tensed up, I honestly wanted to crawl in a hole. When did this become all about me?

"Not at all. Come on Eve, honestly do you believe that? Listen to me and listen to me real good. Your momma has always been flighty with you and you damn well know it. She is in this fit because I am spending time with Izzy. She hates it, and she can see you like her, so it makes her madder. Not Izzy's fault. The only thing Izzy has done, is like you a whole damn lot. The reason she came to work for me was because of you. It was so she could see you more. She took the job to be closer to you. Now tell me that is not a woman you should like and look up to. This woman is here on the couch, listening to you and holding you. She is damn sure crying with you, as well. Tell me when that thing you call 'mother' ever did that with you?" Braxton was proving a point, but halfway through his sermon he was getting a tiny bit louder and terse.

He realized what he was saying was the truth, and it pissed him off. He was sticking up for me. Not only did it bring a smile to my face, it warmed the hell out of my heart. Big damn teddy bear, I just wanted to haul off and hug the shit out of him. And maybe kiss him some, and then maybe stroke his chest with my fingertips. That would lead to heavy petting and some much-needed licking, Shit. Shit. Shit. I need to get my head back on straight and back to the moment at hand. I have to say something.

"Eve, I am so sorry if you think this is all because of me. I never want you to hurt in any way. If I am to blame for any part of it, I will take myself out of the equation. You understand that?" My eyes are pleading with hers; I want her to understand I would put her feelings above my own.

"Like *hell* you are, woman! There's no way I'm letting you go anywhere! The only thing you have done, is treat my daughter like she was your own. Hell, you two are like best friends, and I'm the third wheel. I want to be in this equation, and I think you know that Izzy, don't you?" His voice and matches his eyes so sweet and tender.

Closing my eyes momentarily, I whimper as his words mean so much to me. Sighing, I say, "Ah you are cute when you pout those lips of yours, big guy."

"Okay, but my momma is really mad, Izzy. She told me to stop hanging around you. I heard her say to some man on the phone she was going to find some dirt out on you. What does that mean, daddy? Izzy's not dirt. Daddy, will momma hurt Izzy because I like her?" The rising panic in her shaky little voice is so sad.

Crying again, she sank into her father's big arms. He held her close and kept his eyes on mine. His eyes were telling me a story of hurt for his daughter and anger with the woman who helped him create this little girl. Confusion maybe, but I also saw a person who wanted to let me know he would protect me, his Izzy. Damn it, those eyes of his. They could tell a story all on their own.

Grabbing his phone, he asked Liam to come and get his niece so he could spend some time talking to me. He explained to his daughter none of this is her fault, and he would protect both of his girls, Eve and me. There he goes again 'his two girls'. It never gets old to hear, though.

Moments later Liam strolls through my front door, smiling from ear to ear.

"Hey there, Izzy girl. Eve sweetheart, why don't you come with your Uncle Liam and let's go get some ice cream. I need my girl so we can pick up the chick at the ice cream parlor." He snickers and laughs when Eve runs to him to give him a big hug.

Braxton makes such a noise we all look his way. "Easy man, my girl is not some pawn to use for your personal pleasure. No picking up chicks with my girl."

"Hey, just giving everyone a laugh here, it's way too damn serious in this room." Walking into the living room, Liam looks over at me.

"Izzy honey, stay strong. We got your back girl, don't worry." Liam winks and gives me a panty melting smile.

Oh my. "Ummm... Liam, my back thanks you for watching it."

He's laughing about how 'he loves my sense of humor.'

Before walking out the door with Eve, he glances back one more time smirking.

"Don't do anything I wouldn't do now you two." Seriously, I just stare at him. Not only good looking his sense of humor is funny as hell. I really like him.

Clearing his throat, Braxton must have seen my eyes linger on Liam longer than necessary. My cheeks instantly feel like they are on fire.

"What?" Baffled and trying to ease his consciousness. "Hey, I was just thinking my friend Kara would be all over Liam in a heartbeat."

"Sure you were. Now, I had something I wanted to talk to you about, but right now, I need to make a point and stake my claim," He says while his eyes scan my body. Following the path his eyes, my body comes to life.

Breathlessly, I ask, "What point do you need to make and how do you plan to claim me?" I try to act innocent but I know what he meant and why. I put my hand on my hip and give him a glance like I was waiting for his response.

Closing the distance, he hauls me in his arms before laying us down on the couch. Nose to nose and lips to lips, our breathing becomes labored. Our hearts are pounding and the temperature in the room is steadily rising. The humor of this fades as our basic instincts take over.

"Talk later honey. I need to remind you who your eyes should be looking at. Don't like you looking at Liam like that, babe. Seriously, I hated it. Those sweet, big brown eyes need to be undressing me, not Liam."

"I was not undressing him," I argued but was failing.

"Was so. Liar." His sexy as sin smile leaves me damn near speechless.

Biting my lip, I whisper saying, "Not."

"You are a shit liar and for that little stunt, you need to be reminded whose fucking body makes you scream in pleasure. It's my hands you were coming on so hard in your bed honey, not Liam's. Never will it be anyone other than me." His whisper gingerly touches my lips. His tongue wets my bottom lip, making me moan as I arch my body into his.

I come clean. "Okay, I was checking him out. I think you need to remind me again and again how my eyes are only for you. Make me remember how I came so fucking hard with your hand. Only this time, I want you naked." My forward words seem to have caused Braxton to stop breathing. He has a dumbstruck look on his face that is quickly replaced by an evil grin.

Barely able to contain my laugh, I say in a sexy voice. "I think I need you to remind me often, no very often, just how much I belong to you." Whispering in his ear while he is slowly pulling my shirt over my head, he whistles. Eyeing my red lacy bra, his eyes squint with approval.

Breathing heavily, Braxton says, "I love the color red. I think it's going to be my favorite fucking color." He continues to groan. "You in this little red number have ruined me, only red, and only ever with you." He repeats 'only with you' a few more times.

"It's a good thing you like the color red because I'm wearing the matching thong." Thanking my lucky stars, I put on a matching set.

The deep growl, which escapes his throat is followed by the rubbing of his very hard cock against my molten hot center. The wicked gleam in his eyes travels to my chest. He chases the seam of my bra until he reaches the front clasp. Deftly, he pops the clasp. I hate how proficient he is at unhooking it. I eye him with a less than happy glare. He got my drift.

"Easy Izzy, I'm no saint. Just really good at unhooking bras."

"Yeah, don't remind me, okay." I can't help but think of all the women he has pleased before me.

With his eyebrow raised, he darts his tongue out to wet his lower lip as if ready to eat me alive. "You have nothing to worry about, baby. No woman has ever looked this good to me. Ever."

Pfft, who the hell is he kidding? He probably said that to whomever he was screwing for the night.

Slightly irritated, I say with displeasure. "Yeah right. Let me guess, you said that to every warm body you slid into just to make them feel special." I used my fingers to emphasise the word special.

Shaking his head, he stopped tracing my body with his very skilled fingers. No. No. No.

"No lie babe, I don't say sappy shit to whores who spread their legs for me." His eyes told me he was telling me the truth. Not easy to hear, but honesty is honesty.

"Great timing Braxton! Tell me about how many women spread their legs for you while you undress me! As a matter of fact, why don't you name them?!" My resentment of this whole conversation has me running my mouth again.

Did he seriously think I wanted to know this shit? My moment of passion has now passed.

"No Iz, no names necessary. I don't remember half of them anyway. I was just making a point. They meant nothing, you mean everything." He's dead serious, his eyes say it all. He is looking deep into my soul. I knew it. He knew it. The look between is heavy and my passion ignites once again.

"What?" I lost my breath as I could not believe he just said I meant everything to him. How can this happen, so fast? I know how I feel about him, and it scares me shitless. But to have him say the same back to me is just un-fucking-believable.

It's all I could say. He was serious, and I was definitely caught off guard. I had no idea what was happening, but his tone and his words were more serious than I expected from a guy like Braxton. He slept with whoever he wanted and the girls who would come into the shop hung on his every word. A few came in half naked to flirt their asses off. Others wanted to sleep with him or blow him as payment for fixing their cars. I'm not lying either, the shit was unreal to me. It's a different kind of world. I wonder how many times he took them up on their offers. The more I think about it, the more it pisses me off.

Snapping me out of my mental distaste Braxton caresses my cheek with his thumb.

"I mean it when I say you mean something here. Shit, don't know why or how, but you are inside my head, and you are not leaving it. You were made for me honey; I know it and so do you. You may have been the last thing I was looking for, but, you were exactly what I needed. Oh Iz." His soft voice lingers like a whisper.

It's all he says as he slowly takes my shorts off of my heels and stares at my naked chest and bright red, little lacy thong. He is memorizing every inch of me, and I am panting hard. My chest heaves in and out in an attempt to catch my breath. Oh my god, his eyes so full of raw lust. His lips plump and firm, the minute he took the tip of his tongue and ran it across his lower lip I felt a jolt through my body. I lean up and slammed my lips on his. I needed him like he was my next breath.

Taking control, Braxton traced his tongue along my bottom lip, biting it gently. That ignited a deep growl and the next thing I knew his shirt was off. Next, he was unbuttoning his jeans, yanking them off as fast as he could. Standing before me in his black boxers, he looked mouthwatering.

Here we are both nearly naked, me in my red, lacy thong and him in his sexy black boxers. Leaning down Braxton is licking up the back side of my leg, towards the spot where I ache for him the most. He takes his time, gently stroking his wet, very hot tongue along the elastic of my thong. He continues licking a path toward my belly button. He displays his affection by gently tracing each one of my scars, softly kissing each one before moving to the next. He sends shivers down my spine and goosebumps cover my body as he loves each of my scars. I am withering under his hot, hard body as he covers me. The weight of him on top of me feels like heaven. With a feather-like touch, he strokes my chest. He trails a blaze of fire as his hands cover and cradle my breasts. Rolling my nipples with his fingers, he bends then takes one breast in his mouth. His tongue swirls around it, pulling my nipple into his mouth. He growls as he sucks harder and more vigorously. The intense feeling of each suck has me nearly coming apart.

"Jesus Braxton. Oh, yes. Honey, that's it. Make me yours, baby." My eyes are rolling in the back of my head from all the pleasure he's giving me. I begin to arch my body, trying to gain friction where I desperately need it.

With a possessive voice, he says, "Izzy doll, I need inside you so fuckin' bad. Baby, when I get inside your tight little body, I am going to own it. Iz, this body belongs to me. Mine." He commands with such authority.

It feels so good, I feel like I'm losing control. Hell, he can have anything, just as long as he keeps doing what he's doing.

"You want me? Show me, show me why you want this hot little body." I would have laughed if I could have. It was meant to be funny, but the feeling and the look he was giving me was sober and brutally honest. Our intense gaze locked onto one another as we get ready to unleash our built up sexual tension.

"Fuck me. Iz, you're so hot. You're fucking incredible, baby. You know that? Don't worry darlin' I will not only show you what you mean to me, I will mark you, so no other asshole ever dares take what's mine. You are perfect for me, and I will be goddamned if anyone tries."

Each word, he spoke, was followed up with a hard grind of his dick against my very wet heat. My want and need for him begs for him to claim, mark, stamp and fuck me into submission.

I'm not sure what I'm in for, but it's a ride I'm definitely wiling to taking. As long as he keeps caring for me like this, I can face anything. Even his trifling baby momma. At least I hope so. Right now though, I need to feel him deep inside me.

Taking my lips, Braxton loses his control. The onslaught of his desire is finally being unleashed. Our tongues are dueling and our teeth clashing. He has me under his submission with his lips, alone. Pleasure and pain is a combination I have learned to shy away from, but with Braxton it feels marvelous. To prove his dominance, he grips my hair and pulls. My head snaps back and our eyes lock. After holding my gaze for a few seconds, he's back to punishing my lips with his deliciously plump, wet ones.

"Oh my God Braxton, I am going to explode. You feel so fucking good." I stop saying another word as tears well in my eyes and spill down over my cheeks. I can't stop them once they start. Braxton makes me feel cherished and loved. How the hell I can feel love from a guy I barely know is bizarre.

"Baby, no. Why the tears?" Braxton takes his finger and wipes the flowing river coming down my cheeks hitting the pillow. Failing in his attempt at stopping them, he bends down and kisses my cheeks instead. If he was hoping to prevent them from coming, his tenderness only makes them flow harder.

"Oh Braxton, I'm no good for you. You deserve someone better, someone not damaged or broken." I cry out the words that I don't want to believe myself, but deep down, how can I not? All movement on his part stops.

"Baby, not going there. You're too good for me. You may not believe it, but it's true. Not another word of not being good enough, got it?" His look is now stern but loving at the same time.

"I can't believe that I want this so fucking bad. I just want to be enough for you but...I...I," unable to reply as my sobs take over.

"Izzy. Izzy. Izzy. You don't need words, honey. Let me love you. Let me show you what you make me feel. No one has ever made me feel this fuckin' good, Iz. No one. I can't explain it, but feel my words in my touch. Fuck babe, I need you. No more interruptions, nothing going to stop me from rocking into your tight body. That pussy has been screaming for my dick for a while now, and it's time that he has it."

Sobbing, I struggle to form words. "Only you would make a dick joke right now."

His silence only unsettles me more. He is touching every inch of my body, fire blazing in his touches. I am very close to losing it.

"Braxton, if you don't give him what he wants, my pussy will take over and swallow him whole." There. I told him. The fucker wants to play around, and I'm frustrated and ready to blow.

He lets out a wicked laugh. "Ah, babe, do not threaten my dick. Although, I have to admit, the thought of your pussy swallowing me whole does sound like a dream. Either way I see it, I win."

No longer wanting to play, I take control.

"Fuck. Me. Braxton, please baby. I can't stand it any longer." Trying to pull him on top of me so I can wrap my legs around him is increasingly challenging as a light sheen of sweat has slicked our bodies. Yummy. Sweat, slick, sex. Oh yes.

Braxton grunts out his response. "Oh babe, my fuckin' pleasure."

No more words, tearing my sexy red thong off in about two seconds flat, I am clawing at his boxers. They come off in another two seconds, and now we are bare to each other. Braxton cradles my head in his hands and kisses along my jaw to my neck.

Arching my hips up, I want his mouth between my thighs. I ache for him, and before my mind can go off for too long, I can feel his hot breaths bearing down on my wet center. He must approve of my happy trail that leads to my wetness because he mumbles under his breath.

"Oh, fuck me, how I love a shaved pussy. Iz, you are my fuckin' dream." He followed it by the hot sweep of his tongue that starts at my happy trail and then all the way down till he reaches my glistening channel. Sliding my lips apart with his fingers, Braxton uses his other arm under my ass to prop me up higher in line with his smoldering mouth. With the help of me arching higher, Braxton takes advantage our new position and covers my pussy with his entire mouth. It's hot and wet. Oh, Sweet Jesus, it's nirvana. I tremble as he brings me closer to my impending explosion. Flicking my bundle of nerves with his tongue, he makes a figure eight that has me on the brink. Sucking my clit into his mouth felt like pure heaven but when he closes his teeth around it, I am lost in the world of pleasure like I have never known before.

"Oh. Oh. Oh my god. Braxton…Holy shit."

Braxton moans as he slides his tongue up into my wet center and his tongue lashing is all consuming. Closing my eyes, I enjoy every moment. Words are coming out of my mouth, but my moans drown them out.

Pulling away, Braxton kisses my juices along his journey up my body until we are face to face once again. "All of your sweetness on my tongue, out of this fucking world."

Crashing his lips down on me, I can taste myself. It's a heady combination.

Losing himself, Braxton rolls back so his dick lines up with me. He presses forward until his cock finds his home. Only pressing in an inch or so, he pauses to look into my lust-filled eyes.

"This is the moment I've been waiting for all of my fucking life. The instant I feel you wrapped around my cock, you're mine. Do you hear me, babe?"

Breathing heavily, I nod my head.

"Say it, Iz. I need to hear you tell me you're mine. Tell me, baby."

"I...I'm yours," I say.

With barely a nod, he slams home. I moan and cry out as I try to adjust to his larger than most man muscle. My god, he is stretching me so tightly I swear I can feel the pulse of blood pumping into his cock. He fits that snug inside of me.

"Oh baby, you feel like heaven. I knew it would be this good with you." He left the rest of the sentence off as he lays his head in the crook of my neck and starts thrusting. Gentle at first. Then he picks up speed, the faster he pumps into me, the harder he makes it. It's so good, I want it harder.

Wrapping my arms around his shoulders and my legs around his waist, I hang on for dear life. I wrap my legs around his waist. I can't get enough of him, I want him to crawl up inside me and never leave. He feels so good, he feels so different. He feels like home.

"Oh God Braxton, you feel so amazing." My body is jerking from his hard thrusts. I know I won't be able to walk right tomorrow and that idea alone has me yearning for more.

Picking up his pace, he wraps an arm around my leg. Not getting close enough or deep enough, Braxton pulls both of my legs over his shoulders as I am swept up almost in his lap. He bends his body back some and wraps his hands around my shoulders, and I can only gasp. He is so deep I can feel him in my throat, I swear to God.

Droplets of sweat drip down his face and holding onto my shoulders, he pounds into me tirelessly. His eyes never leave mine and mine are polarized by his neither of us blinking.

"I'm going to come so damn hard. Never felt this good before, not like this...ever." It's all he gets out as I can feel his release shoot out like a flame. I explode at the same time. My cervix feels like it has been penetrated, and I do as I told him I would; I swallow him whole.

Both of us are finding it hard to catch our breaths. Sweat is dripping down both our bodies. I marvel at the sensation of him as collapses his weight upon mine.

"Oh Braxton!" I whisper as I lick the bead of sweat running down his neck. He is just too yummy for words.

"Trying to catch my breath here darlin'." We both force out a laugh with what energy we have left at the moment. We sound like we both just ran a marathon. Water, I need a drink of water.

I'm drowning in all things Braxton as he trails soft wet kisses against my damp skin. Goosebumps line my body in response.

Chapter Nine

I CAN'T TAKE IT! THE BITCH known as Tiffany has been hanging around the office for days! I can see her trying to worm her way back into Braxton's heart, and most likely wants in his bed, again. He tells me not to worry but I'm a jealous woman, and that green-eyed monster is rearing its ugly head. Sitting in my office, I hide out and close my door. I can hear her with him, and it's fucking killing me as to why he doesn't tell her just to piss off. Sure she is Eve's mother, but he said on numerous occasions that she did not have anything to do with his life. I tried to tell him he is in denial if he thinks for one second she is going to leave him alone for the next thirteen years or so.

Our first official fight was over her and our first official night of sleeping away from each other was over her. Now, I am forced to sit in my office and hear her. She is laughing at something that Braxton has said. If I didn't know any better, I would say this is her plan. Get closer to him and then, when she has him where she wants him, she would turn him against me.

They have a connection I can't compare with. She is after all his baby momma. Something I will never be able to give him. My choice was taken from me a long time ago. My shot at motherhood was cut short, by the hands of a monster. My daughter was the one thing I knew I did right even though it was under so much stress. She was the light at the end of a very dark tunnel.

I can still see her beautiful face, her hair just the same shade of brown as mine. Irish blood running through our veins. Her facial features were a mirror of my own. Big eyes, light skin and a petite narrow button nose. Her tiny hands are so sweet. I didn't think her fingers would be so long. When I held her for the first time, she gripped my finger so tightly, I marveled at it. It was the single best moment of my entire life. I had no idea my time with her would be so limited. Holding her was my escape from pain and anguish. When I looked into her eyes, it was as if staring back at myself. She had such big, brown, beautiful, soulful eyes. Eyes like mine and, I swear I could read her thoughts.

My eyes sting with tears as I recall her beautiful face. She's such a pretty girl with so much love in her. She may have had a bastard of a father, but she was just like me, innocent! I was taken advantage of by a monster. He's a gorgeous man whose smile could make you melt. He was the voice of an archangel, but underneath it all was a heart that was as black as coal. The angel turned into the devil by the time I realized it, it was too late. Too late for me to get out unscathed.

My opportunity to leave was an accident. My weak broken soul turned into heartbreak, then hatred and I finally just snapped. I used all my hurt and loss and turned it into anger. My anger, fueled by the desire to kill him, allowed me to find my escape. I never got the chance to kill him, but never say 'never'. The time might present itself again someday, and then I would not hesitate. I would kill him at the drop of a hat. He took something from me. He killed a part of me. It's time I did the same to him. He needed to feel pain and suffering at the hands of another. I was his biggest conquest, it's only fair he should suffer by my hands.

Only I wish that could happen. I escaped him so I could live another day. What I did was like signing my death sentence in his eyes. The only peace I will ever have will be if he is no longer on this earth torturing people. I will not be able to live without looking over my shoulder as long as he is still out there, lurking in the shadows.

Wiping my tears as I sit at my desk, my mood is anything less than great. I can still hear Braxton laughing with her. Trifling trick. What the hell? He knows I am in here. He honestly can't believe I would be okay with him hanging out with her, laughing his ass off while I am stuck in my damn office. What the fuck?

"Penny for your thoughts?" My eyes look up, and I see Liam is leaning his head into my office with the door slightly ajar.

He must sense my mood and judging that I was just crying my eyes out. I am sure he wants to turn the fuck around and pretend like he did not just find me like this.

"Hey Izzy girl, what the hell?" Shutting the door behind him, he comes over and pulls me into a hug.

I stay quiet. Surely he is not so stupid as to not know what the hell is wrong with me. Why isn't he out there telling his sister to leave?

Clearing his throat, Liam's eyes happen to look weary. "Izzy, what is going on with you?"

My stare back at him is less than friendly. "Seriously, are you that flipping dumb?"

"Ouch! Okay, that one hurt. No, I am not. I came in here because I know you're hiding out. I know my bitch of a sister is doing everything she can to piss you off. It's working, right?" He tightens his lips and raises his eyebrows as if he knows he is right.

Pulling out of his hug, I sigh. "What do you think?" I'm beyond agitated, I'm pissed off. "What is the deal with her and Braxton in there acting like old friends catching up?"

Liam has a habit of rubbing the back of his neck when he is uncomfortable. Just like he's doing now. I'm not going to like what he is about to say.

"Listen Izzy, Brax and Tiffany are beyond complicated." He is dancing around with his words. Yeah, not liking the way he is approaching this.

With a slight roll of my eyes, I simply sigh. "Yeah, no shit."

"No, it's like he knows she is bad news. But he has a soft spot for her, she gave him Eve." My heart just stopped. Great. Thanks, Liam. Like I did not already know this fact.

"She's a master of mind games, sounds like to me."

"The best, I'm afraid. But now let me tell you," he sits down in the chair opposite my desk and leans his elbows on his knees trying to get comfortable. "They are like a train wreck; together they just don't work. The problem is, Brax has a hard time every time she comes back for a visit. She somehow worms her way back into his heart and his bed." The way he says 'bed' tells me how uncomfortable he is admitting this.

"What?" I yell it as loud as I can, not only does it disgust me, it pisses me off.

"It's like he hates her one minute and the next she's spread eagle for him."

I'm not sure why I'm surprised by this, but Braxton is not a guy who is hard up to find a date if he wanted one.

"Yeah, I guess that is one way to put it." Rubbing his neck yet again, I think he is as confused as I am.

"When was the last time he slept with her?" He had to know I was going to ask him this question.

"What? Izzy that is not going to..." now he looks terrified, his eyes are telling me a story I am most likely not going to like.

Interrupting him, I say, "When, Liam?"

"Shit Izzy," he huffs out, gritting his teeth. "About the time he met you." He looks a little green as he admits Braxton had slept with his sister around the same time he met me.

My resolve is slipping. "Liam. Has he slept with her since he has been seeing me? You need to tell me the damn truth. I know she is your sister and Eve is your niece, but I am the one getting hurt here."

Swearing under his breath is not making me feel any better. "I'm not sure, Izzy girl. I don't snoop around Brax and his latest conquests. You would need to ask him." Bet your ass I am going to do that after I slap the shit out of him first.

"Wuss."

Rolling my eyes, I think 'fuck that' and grab my purse and head for the door. It's pretty quiet so I have no idea where the former, or not so old, love birds are at the moment. I refuse to sit around and take this crap anymore. What the hell does he think he is doing with me? With her? I stomp down the hall and go by his office. His door is ajar, I just happen to peak in to see her sitting on his desk and leaning her chest into him as he sits in his chair. He is smiling, at her. Not a stupid smile either, it's a broad happy smile.

He must sense my presence as I storm by his door. "Yo, Izzy, come back here," He yells from his desk. Fuck him, I am so out of here.

Primarily running towards the front door, he catches me by my arm with his hand. Yanked back hard I'm pressed to his side, as he looks like nothing is wrong.

"Fuck off, Braxton. Let me go." I say through clenched teeth, in an attempt not to rip his fucking head off.

He looks at me a bit shocked I'd say as I had just slapped him across the face. Deep down, I want to.

"What the hell is wrong with you?" His eyes crazed as he assesses what is up with me.

"Seriously? You need even to ask me? You are more delusional than I thought." Trembling and angry, I am shaking I'm so pissed.

"Izzy, you need to calm the fuck down and talk to me."

The only thought, I have, is 'NO' I don't. Not a second later the source of my mood is leaning against the wall smirking like she one happy woman.

"HER. That's my problem." I'm seething while look at the bitch.

Braxton turns his head and looks at Tiffany, who now has a sad look on her face. Shit. She is playing him. Is he this caught up with her that he can't see it? I make sure to point this out to him.

"Oh my God. She is playing you. You are playing into her hands, and you're too blind to see it." Screaming my words at him with all I got.

"I am not being played by anyone and that means you, as well." He says. What the hell does that mean?

Now I look at him like I was just the one slapped. Me?

"What the hell are you talking about?" I whip my head at him as I am utterly shocked.

"Listen Iz, Tiff was just talking with me about our daughter." Holding up his hands as if to settle me down, yeah, like that is going to fucking work. Wrong.

Ouch, like I need to be reminded that he has a daughter with her.

"Is that so? Well it sounded like a damn good conversation. Let me go, so you can get back to it as she sits and offers up her fake-as-shit tits to you on a silver fucking platter."

Well, that did it. Braxton looks pissed off, Tiffany looks pleased when Braxton is facing away from her, only to put on the poor innocent as he turns back to her. It's fucking brilliant on her part.

I huff out a breath and start to laugh, this is just too fucking funny not to. Clapping my hands together to prove my point further, I have to hand it to her.

Directing my attention towards the now wide-eyed Tiffany, she looks at me like I'm plain crazy. "You are good, got to tell you. Well played. Let me get this straight, you come to town and see your perfect little girl? No, you use her just to get closer to Braxton. Let me clarify that. You get more intimate with Braxton by playing your act just to get him into bed. Now, I happen to enter the picture, and it threatens your plans to bed him again for the umpteenth number of times. Shit, I admit, he is a man. You're easy and pretty, but your ace in the hole is a sweet little girl. You sick bitch, you use her to get your orgasms with her daddy."

Tiffany stands taller as she strolls over my way. "You have no idea what the hell you are talking about. I love my daughter and her daddy. Brax belongs to me and I was just reminding him of that fact. You are just a warm body for him to use and then throw away. He does it a lot. Then I return home, and it's me that his dick claims." I swear I vomit in my mouth.

"You're sick," I scantly eye her and Braxton, "both of you."

"Shut the fuck up, both of you. Where are you going, Izzy?" Braxton now realizes just how fucked this is, I can see the nervousness in his eyes when he sees me leaving.

"I quit, let your baby momma have my job. It was hers to begin with, now you can screw *her* against the wall instead of me." Admitting my feelings hurts a little, but I have to protect what little heart I have left. I gave it to him and that was a stupid move on my part. I know this, but I believed in him. I stopped telling myself not to get close. My heart aches as the last of it was just now crushed into pieces.

"Izzy, we are not doing this again." Braxton then looks over at the blonde bitch. "Tiffany head on back to my office and wait for me."

Her voice purrs like a kitten. "Sure thing honey, don't keep me waiting long."

I stare at her mentally and throw daggers before saying my peace.

"Oh, he won't be long. I am walking out that fucking door and out of your lives. All of you; you both deserve each other. Both fucking liars and players who'd do anything to get what you want. Pretty pathetic."

Trying to walk away, his hand returns to my arm, and I am being led down into the garage. Practically being pushed into the shop, all heads turn our way. Tears welling in my eyes, heartbroken, I am suddenly tired. I'm so exhausted. All the years I've had to fight to just to live, and this is where I end up. I'm sick of the bullshit, really I am.

"Leave us the fuck alone, get OUT." He roars like a mighty lion. Frustrated and angry Braxton wipes his hand across his forehead before he starts in on me.

"Jesus Christ Izzy, I have no idea what a fucking game you are playing, but you're letting her come between us. We were just talking and for the first time in forever, we were getting along. She was having a normal fucking conversation. We were talking about our daughter." Shit he is actually buying her bullshit. How damn clouded is he with this woman?

Angrily, I yell right back. "Yeah, I know you have a daughter. She is using Eve to get to you. Why do you think she is so fucking nice to you now? Has she ever been this way with you?"

Silence is all I get.

"I take it the answer is no, of course not. Jesus, it's me, she doesn't want you to be with me so now she is playing the mommy card. You just happen to take it hook, line and sinker. I know her kind.

Her type of person has used me in the past. The mind fucking tricks they use. They are nice to get us to lower our guard and then they use it to blindside us." My anger is at an all-time high and always like when I get angry. I cry.

"That fucker Dominic might have been that way with you, but Tiffany does not play mind games with me," Braxton says as he is shaking his head. Seriously? God, he is delusional.

"You're just blind to it, you want to see the good in her because she is Eve's mother. You're whipped by her. By the way, when was the last time you slept with her?" As I say the words, I am gauging his reaction. Watching his eye movements, any 'tell' and I will pick up on it.

His head snaps and worry lines crease his flawless face.

"What the fuck Izzy, what kind of question is that?"

Pointing my finger at his chest, I say, "One that deserves an honest fucking answer from you."

Grabbing my hand rather forcefully, I can tell just how angry he is. "Stop it, just stop it right the fuck now."

"Denial, I just knew it. You're such a fucking liar, you sweet talk me and take me to bed and get what you want. Then seconds later you're in bed with your dick so far up in that bitch you can't see straight. Must be some lay, huh *Brax*?" I make sure the emphasis is in his name.

His voice sounds hurt. "Brax-you never call me that."

Yeah and I don't like being played a fool either. "I see you in a whole new light, Braxton to me is gentle and nice, and the kind of man I would kill to have. This man before me now is not. You're the man whore they all said you were. They call you Brax, the bitch who gets your dick wet, calls you Brax. Might as well call you what you are." My raised voice is cracking as my body quakes with nervous energy; my tears are sure to follow.

"My fucking Braxton, the one who held me tight, the one that whispered sweet things to me as he made love to me; that man is everything *you aren't*." My honest tears must resonate with him as his whole body language changes.

"Izzy, look. This shit is fucked up. I'm screwed no matter what I do here. She is the mother to my fucking daughter; I can't just ignore that. Eve wants to love her, she wants me to try to do the same."

What the fuck did he just say? Oh my god, Eve. It all becomes clear. His little girl wants him to be with her mother. I can't win this fight; I won't hurt Eve like that. I just wish I hadn't given my heart to him. Should have stayed my ground and not come to work for him. Should not have let him claim my body for his own and I should not have enjoyed every minute of it as well. Shoulda', woulda', coulda'.

Not an ounce of fight left in me, and I have to laugh it out so I won't break down in hysterics. "Now the truth comes out, how long has Eve wanted for you and her mother to get back together?" I channel down my anger.

"Seems like forever, I tried over and again. Shit's not good, but I can't stand to see my girl hurting like she is. I love my daughter and would do anything for her. You understand what I mean?"

Choking back my tears, I contain my voice to a whisper. "Loud and fucking clear. I won't hurt Eve, she is too sweet. In the end, I think you are smart enough to realize how this turns out, right?"

"Yeah, that's the fucked up part. I finally found a good woman, a woman who is perfect for me." Getting angry, he finds a wrench and throws it across the room, swearing while he does it.

"Fuck! Fuck! Shit!" The howl that escapes his throat is filled with anger, regret and something much deeper.

Wincing at the very loud clank as the wrench hits the wall, I stumble back some.

"Goodbye, Braxton." I'm walking back towards the door.

"Fucking wait Izzy, I can't lose you." His words and worrisome eyes break me.

With tears spilling down my face, I whisper out. "You already have."

Walking out to my car shoulders down, crying and hurting with a kind of loss I have never known. Losing my daughter destroyed me; losing Braxton might just do me in. Getting in my car all, I can hear is yelling swearing and chairs being thrown around. I don't turnaround; I can't look. I simply drive away. Away from my heart. Away from Braxton.

Chapter Ten

'GIMME THREE STEPS' BY LYNYRD Skynyrd is blaring in the bar as I set my tray down to order my next round of drinks. Swaying my hips to the music, I call out what I need to Sam, our bartender. A week after my blow-out with Braxton I found a job at a local pub and eatery called Fireside Bar and Grill. It's in Maltby, a smaller town next to Monroe. The local pub is the main hangout. A friendly crowd, usually a handful of bikers, head in around dinner time and stay until close. Most likely one of the reasons I love it here. At first I was nervous, but for the most part, they are cool. Most of them are friendly and flirtatious I have to admit it's a welcome distraction. I just happened to stumble on the job opening and took it.

I still cry every night when I dream about him. I wonder all the fucking time how he and Eve are doing. It's killing me, but I had to move on. This job came along at the right time. I was sitting here one night having too many drinks, just drowning my sorrows and minding my own business. By the end of the evening, I had a new job lined up. It worked out well for both of us. Sam desperately needed a barmaid, and I needed a job.

Tonight is a slow night. Everything was great until the door opens and in strolls a few of the guys who work for Braxton. I immediately roll my eyes and silently pray he won't walk in next. My shift is finished and now I wish I had just gone home.

Of course I ignored them, but Cage was on the phone at the drop of a hat. It didn't take a genius to guess who he was calling. Not ten minutes later, in strolls Braxton and he's walking straight over to me.

His look is all serious, a bit perplexed even. "Izzy let's get out of here. What the hell are you doing anyway?"

My mouth is hanging open as I feel I'm in the twilight zone. "What the hell are you doing here? You have no say in what I do. Not anymore." I turn my head and take another sip of my drink. Numbing my brain is my goal of late. Sometimes I stay after my shift to have a few beers like I am now. Well, at least I was until I was so rudely interrupted.

My arm is suddenly being tugged on as if on instinct, I pull away harder than I intended to and stumble off my stool. Finding myself on my butt, I am not only pissed off, I'm embarrassed as all eyes are now on me.

"Braxton what the hell are you doing harassing my customers?" Sam says as he gets out from behind the bar and strides towards me.

There is no mistaking the death glare Braxton is sending Sam. "Mind your own business, Sam she's with me." Sam inches his way closer next to me. I am now between these two men who are both ready to throw down or have a pissing contest.

I'm shocked speechless, and I need to correct Braxton on his mistake. "I am *not* with you. What the hell, Braxton?" I say holding my hands up as if to say 'ah duh!' Between his odd behavior and the current spin of the room, I realize I'm slightly intoxicated.

I'm so ticked and embarrassed getting my ass up off the floor I dust off my pants and realize my tank top has slipped. Now my chest is spilling out for all to see. I don't give it another thought. "Leave me alone. Jesus, Braxton."

Braxton's laughing so hard he tilts his head back. The only thing, I'm thinking, is how thrilled I am that I can entertain him to the point he is in hysterics.

His laughing alone sets me off, gritting my teeth, I say, "Not funny."

"So fuckin' funny, babe. Now that the girls are back in place, let's get you home before you embarrass yourself even more."

I start to talk and then stumble slightly. "Don't think so *babe*."

Pulling me closer to him, Braxton grasps my arm and gets right into my face. "Iz, are you trying to piss me off?"

I stare at him dumbfounded, yeah the twilight zone. "Let me check. Nope!" I pop my lips together.

Braxton sighs deeply rolling his eyes directly at me. "You're pissing me off, Iz!"

"Don't care, *Braxton*." I hiss back as I try to lean away from him damn near falling off the stool on the other side. God, seriously, can I stop looking like an idiot?

Ignoring the heavy breathing on my right, I let my gaze swing back to Sam, who is now back behind the bar, leaning back with his arms crossed and watching this sideshow play out. Huh, looking at Sam right now I notice how handsome he is. I'm not sure why I have not noticed this before, and then it dawns on me. My minds been occupied with a tall, muscular piece of eye candy whose name starts with a letter B.

My fog filled mind just won't shut down. "Sam, you're a beautiful man." In my defense, I thought my mind was saying it not my mouth. I realize my mistake when Sam snickers and Braxton lets out a 'what the hell' under his breath.

The sparkle in Sam's eyes should have let me know what was to come. "Izzy, you're more than beautiful." He says softly with a big flirty smile. Not a Braxton smile, granted, but a great smile. Smiling back, I marvel at his sweet words forgetting I have a big guy next to me.

"Knock it off, *Izzy*! I swear I am going to lose my shit right now." The anger emanating from Braxton is a bit scary, but I'm not one bit bothered. The fact I'm not feeling much due to my drinking is helping my courage.

Swiping my hand as if to dismiss him, I say, "Sam, don't you listen to him. He's too busy screwing his ex to worry about little ole me." Drunk and running my mouth off, not a great idea.

I find myself in a headlock, Braxton's arms feel like pythons crushing me to him.

"Cut it out Iz, I am not screwing her." Yep, he is totally annoyed with me. Good, now he knows how it feels.

"Pffft. Not my business anymore. Go on and get your dick wet all you want. Tell me Sam, are you currently getting your dick wet or are you lonely and broken-hearted just like me?" I slur out my words as confidently as I can.

I ignore Braxton and his posse, who are all surrounding us. Sam looks at them and just laughs them off. Braxton seems to be daring Sam to back the fuck off, but he does not seem one bit intimated.

"Yeah Izzy, seems like both of our hearts have been broken by the same two people. They just seem to leave a trail of destruction everywhere they go." Sam is talking to me, but his eyes never leave, Braxton.

"What?" Mouth hanging open, I stare at Sam. No Way!

"Tell her Brax. Tell her how Tiffany broke my fucking heart because I caught you screwing her out in my damn parking lot."

"Jesus Christ," Braxton swears loudly rubbing his jaw.

"Holy Shit." That comes from Liam, who I just notice has joined in on our little party that is slowly growing.

The other three Cage, Jagger, and Brody are slightly laughing, drinking their beers like they are enjoying this freak show.

My mind is blown; this is beyond bizarre. I gasp, directing my disgust at Braxton. "You didn't. Jesus Christ, you're a pig, Braxton. A fucking pig."

I can sense the sudden worry that crosses his face. "Iz, it's not what you think. It was a while ago."

The realization of their sordid history makes me ill. "Oh my God. So you two have been doing this cat and mouse shit for how many years now? All the while screwing with people's lives. You make me sick." I try to push him away from me.

"Baby, that's old news. I told you about it, how it happened with me and her. I told you all of it, yeah?" He looks at me with an 'I told you so look.'

"Oh, you told me some things. Then I had to sit in my office like a mouse and hide out while you laughed and got all smiley with your baby momma." Shit, I feel sick.

Getting off the bar stool, I stumble yet again. Braxton grabs a hold of me by my arm and pulls me up tight to his side. His grip is tight, and the feel of his arms around me make me suddenly very sad. I want his arms holding me, but I also want him to want me enough to stand up to his ex. I would die to have Braxton standing up to her and making me that special one. Too bad dreams are just nightmares in disguise.

Obsessing over my thoughts, I need to distance myself from him as his eyes are mentally judging me. Great, here come the waterworks.

"Get your hands off of me!" I cry out as tears start to escape and spill over. "*I fucking want you, I* was ready to fight for you. It's *you* that was not willing to fight for *me*. It hurts Braxton, you crushed my heart. Every dream I have ever had in my life has turned into a nightmare. My life is a living nightmare!" I'm yelling in hysterics.

Braxton is speechless, stumbling out of his grasp. His worry lines are well defined in his forehead. It's the first time tonight I notice how horrible he looks, almost like he has not slept in days. Well, join the sleepless club buddy.

It's Sam now who breaks the sudden silence. "Izzy, let me take you to the back room. You can rest and use the restroom if you feel like getting sick because, to tell you the truth, I am ready to vomit myself."

Liam instantly pulls me against him in a protective kind of way. Not sure why he is all of a sudden acting like a big brother.

"Liam, let me go. You want to help someone, go help your sister. Or maybe Braxton has been tending to her every need. Hell, I'm sure his bed wasn't cold for long."

I turn to glare toward, Braxton. Slightly proud I zinged him like I did. But my small victory is short lived when I see his expression change and now has tears filling his eyes. *Oh Braxton!* My heart takes a nose dive.

"Izzy, I guess you'll never know how I feel about you. I'm dying here, I fucking want you like I have never wanted anyone before. I'm screwed no matter what I do." He steps closer to me and then squats down, so we are eye to eye.

"I want you. I always will. And the answer to your question, I have not slept with her. How could I sleep with her? When you have wrecked me, no one will *ever* compare to you." Leaning his forehead, he rests it on mine. He is killing me once again with sweetness.

I let my hurt give way to fuel my anger. I'm mad, not for what he said, not for what he did, but for saying it and then not following it through with his actions. He let me walk away because of her, only now he is here telling me I'll never know how he feels. What the *Hell*? I lash out and slap him hard across the face.

"Piss off, Braxton. Damn you for making me fall in love with you. For showing me that I was good enough before you ripped my goddamned heart out. You say I have wrecked you, but why are you with her and not me? I'll tell you why, you're a fucking coward when it comes to her."

I carelessly sway my walk from him to find Sam come around the bar, and I crash my body against his chest. His arms enveloped me as he tenderly kisses the top of my head.

"Come on, Izzy. Let's get you to rest for a while. When I close, I can take you home." Sam, is so sweet and apparently not caring he is in a room full of Braxton's friends, either.

The growl that comes from Braxton makes me jumpy. "The FUCK you are Sam! I am not letting any man near my woman."

"*Your* woman? Don't you mean, Tiffany?! You chose your woman the minute you told me how Eve wants you to be with her. I'm not good enough and I sure as hell won't be your mistress."

"You were never my mistress. Wait…" he pauses as he looks like he's just realized something. "Did you just say you have fallen in love with me?"

Oh, my god, he studies my face as I am bewildered by his question. Did I tell him I fell in love with him? Shit. Shit. Shit. That was for my ears only. Not drinking ever again! Oh my god, why did I say that? With a shrug of my shoulders, I try to play it off so I don't to let him know my insides are in turmoil. "Doesn't matter, it doesn't change a damn thing."

Sensing his jubilant admiration with the fact he indeed knows I have fallen in love with him, his eyes sparkle with desire. "It changes everything."

Chapter Eleven

MY HEAD HURTS LIKE HELL. I need Advil and water. Stumbling out of bed, I run my hand through my hair that feels a bit like a rat's nest. Fumbling with the cap, I finally get the bottle of Advil open and pop a few in my dry mouth. Swallowing my water, I realize how parched I am. I only made it to the couch. Screw walking back to bed, I feel like shit. My aching body needs to sleep off the hangover from hell.

Last night was like a fog in my mind. I vaguely recall Braxton yelling at Sam, only to have Sam shout back to Braxton. I remember Liam trying to get me home, but I ended up staying with Sam, instead. Hell, we had something in common; we have both been victims of Braxton and Tiffany. I still can't believe I admitted I was falling for him. How dumb can I be? I was hurt, I was mad and I let my emotions get the best of me. The look in Braxton's eyes told me he was, without a doubt, shocked by my admission but they also told me how much he approves of them.

My confusion with this is the part that hurts the most. He can't have it both ways. It's either her or me, plain and simple. If only. She will be in his life in one way or another until Eve is eighteen. That fact sends shivers down my spine.

My phone starts vibrating on the near side of my coffee table. I don't even remember leaving it there. What bugs me more is, I haven't turned it back on since my breakup with Braxton. That's strange.

Clearing my throat, I don't give it another thought as I stretch my hand searching for it since it hurts to open my eyes.

"Hello." I don't even look at who is calling me. I only have a few people I consider friends, so my options are slim on who it might be.

A friendly voice greets me, "Izzy, it's me honey."

Pleasantly surprised by my friend; my voice comes out like I've been smoking for the last thirty years. "Kara, god what time is it?"

After a slight pause, she bursts out laughing. "You got company to go along with that sexy voice you got going on?"

"Pfft. Not after the night I had. I had an interesting conversation with Braxton after drinking more than I should have. Luckily Sam got me home, somehow."

It dawns on me, I don't remember any of it. Looking at what I am wearing I realize I am in a tank top and underwear. Shit, did Sam undress me and put me to bed? Oh my God, my already pounding head starts to hurt worse.

"What? How did Braxton come into play again? Last I heard you left his ass and was working for, Sam."

"Oh, well. It's a long, story. I'll fill you in later. My head is pounding, and I feel like I am going to vomit any minute."

"Okay, babe. Um, Izzy, girl I got some news for you." She sounds nervous, and Kara has *never* been nervous. Not unless it is about her brother.

I can feel the blood draining from my face as I slowly sit up. "Shit Kara, what is it?" I almost hate to ask.

"It's Dominic, he is on the warpath. He's going nuts as to why he can't find you. Paid me a visit last night and threatened me if I didn't give you up." Her voice is off. There's something she is not telling me.

I hold my breath, and then say softly, "What aren't you telling me, Kara?"

She takes a minute to answer me. It seems Dominic is uncovering every stone to try and find me. She spends the next few minutes going on about my safety, and no doubt she is also scared for herself. Dominic is not at all stupid to think she never talks to me. He knows us better than that.

I'm in full blown panic mode, now. "Get out of there! Come here and stay with me! Pack up your shit and get here, like yesterday. I mean it Kara, I will not let that bastard hurt you again."

"Izzy." Her voice shakes as she says my name.

"Listen to me Kara, get your shit and get here as soon as you can. We can figure it all out once you're here and safe."

After a moment of silence, I know she has to process all of this before she acts. She works for herself doing freelance work, so it's not like she can't work from here.

"Oh, all right. I will call you later and let you know when I will be getting a flight." Her voice returns to herself as I can tell she has been nervous having to face her brother alone. Lying to Dominic never ends well.

Sighing with relief, I sag back into my comfy couch. "Love you girl, stay safe and get your butt here."

"You too," her voice laced with excitement as she says, "by the way don't forget to hook me up with that hot biker, Liam?"

"Kara, you are obsessed with anyone who rides a motorcycle." Now I know why she is suddenly excited to come here, and it has nothing to do with seeing me.

Clearing her voice, Kara is acting out some pretty hot scenes she wanted to have with sexy, Liam. "Listen, Izzy you're the one who told me how hot he was."

I burst out laughing as I recall the conversation we had over Braxton and, hotter than sin, Liam. All this easy going conversation has my head pounding so I end our phone call and go back to nursing my hangover from hell. The serene moment has me drifting back to sleep.

Then...

KNOCK-KNOCK-KNOCK

Seriously, you have got to be kidding me. I stumble to my front door having some serious trouble with the lock. I have no clue who this could be, but I sure did not expect who greets me as I open the door. *Great!*

"What the hell to do you want, Braxton? I don't have the time or energy to deal with you right now. Or anytime in the foreseeable future, for that matter," I say as I attempt to slam the door in his face. Shit, he's the reason I have the hangover I have.

Turning, I walk painstakingly slow back to my couch as the room starts to spin, and my head wants to explode. I knew he would most likely follow me, so I don't bother closing the door.

"Ah, does someone have a hangover today?" His teasing tone does nothing but irk me.

Gingerly, I lie down on my couch and cover my head with my blanket. "Pfft, don't be a smart-ass, Braxton."

"Oh honey, don't say ass to me when yours is hanging out for me to look at." I lift my head out of my cover to give him my most deadly glare. He is so infuriating and yet so damn sexy giving me his signature smirk.

"I am covered up with my blanket so you can't see my ass." I want to be pissed at him, but I almost laugh instead.

"Saw it lots last night, and I approve of the black thong you are sporting." Turning his head sideways, he tries to steal a glance at my leg that is peeking out from under the blanket.

I just groan in frustration.

"Don't give me that look. You brought it all on yourself, started spouting off about letting that fucker Sam take you home. Not my girl."

I huff out quite loudly. Headache or no headache, he needs to understand. "Braxton, what part of I'm not your girl do you not get?"

His raised eyebrow and bottom lip wedged between his teeth shows me he is deep in thought. "You love me, right?"

"What?" I'm not able to focus on his words because my head is cradle in my arms, and I'm begging the basketball team who took up, a full court game to please go elsewhere.

"Do. You. Love. Me?" He says, easing down into my personal space.

I knew my little slip up last night would not get missed, but this is just not the time for this conversation. "You can't be serious right now, Braxton. My head hurts and I feel like I may vomit, now my best friend is being hounded by her brother, who's looking for me. I don't have time for your bullshit right now."

Backing away quickly his stance is stiff. "What do you mean the fucker is looking for you?" One minute he is all jokes and smiles, now he's tense and pissed off.

I close my eyes, realizing my mistake. I reveal way too much information when I should just learn to keep my mouth shut! With a calm voice, I continue, "Just what I said. I asked Kara to get out of there and come here to stay with me. When she gets here, we can figure out what to do next."

"Iz, you need to be careful. Get your girl here safely, then we can make a plan."

My eyes are fully raised and directed right at him. He can't be serious because nothing has changed. He is still with *her*. Rubbing my temples, I am too drained to think straight. Hands covering my face, my muffled words sound more like a cry. "What are *you* going to do? You have your life, and I have mine." I am still trying to understand why he is even here with me. "Braxton, go home and leave me alone."

"Do you remember last night at all darlin'?" He asks so sweetly.

I question him, saying, "The part where I slapped you silly or the part where I left with, Sam?"

He throws his head back and laughs, but his chuckle lets me know I've missed something. What the hell did I miss? I was drunk, Sam brought me home, that's it. "Oh honey, you never left with, Sam. You were drunk as hell by the end of the night, and I was sitting outside waiting for you. Sam, got a welcome crew outside, and he handed you over to me. Told you, no one is taking my woman anywhere."

Oh no, the images flashing in my mind make me nervous as hell. I don't remember any of this, I knew continuing to drink would be a bad idea. At the time, I wanted to forget Braxton was in the bar with me. But holy hell, what happened in the parking lot when Sam realized Braxton was still there? "Shit, Braxton what did you say to, Sam? He was kind to me, and he is my boss. If you get me fired, I will shoot you myself."

"Yeah honey, see how that works out for you. Not going to get you fired, I did tell Sam, however, if he valued his life he would not touch you ever again. Let's just say he understands where I am coming from." Finally making himself comfortable, he relaxes at the end of the couch and is pulling my legs into his lap rubbing my feet. Hearing me sigh to the amazing foot job I'm getting, Braxton smirks at me with his dreamy 'sexy' eyes. On one hand, I'm pissed off at him but then he touches me and, I no longer want to be mad at him. I've lived with evil and hurt and I know I should shy away from him...but I don't want to. Something about him speaks to soul. He calms me with his looks alone. *I know I'm safe.* I know he would never treat me like Dominic did. I may not be able to explain it when all logic tells me stay away from him. Sometimes you need to take a leap of faith. I'm taking my leap, I just hope he doesn't make me regret it.

I am putty when it comes to this man. He may be gruff at times, but then he is sweet as he is now. Right now he's caressing my legs looking at me with nothing but love in his big warm eyes. Beautiful, sexy and hot. No words match how good looking Braxton is to me. Leaning my head against my couch, I exhale gazing at his sweet smiling face. Gosh, he is beautiful.

My smile is mixed with some confusion about what transpired last night. "You brought me home last night?"

With no hesitation, he says, "Yep brought you back in your car. Undressed you, and I must admit, I took my time enjoying every delicious minute, as I tucked you under the covers. I waited most of the night to make sure you didn't puke all over yourself before I left. You can never be too sure." His lips curl up as if he is hiding something.

Huh. "What aren't you telling me?" I hate the smug look on his face.

"Let's just say, last night sealed the deal for me, sweetheart. Hearing you lay your heart out there like that. I'm happy to report I'm a gentleman, and did not do all of the wicked things, you wanted me to do to you. But," he pauses and whistles. "I have to tell you, sex with you when you're sober is fantastic. You drunk? Well let's just say I can't wait till I'm balls deep in you. You get a dirty mouth on you when you're liquored up." He says jokingly, stroking his bottom lip with his thumb.

I'm caught off guard by his declaration, so I just laugh. "You can't hold me responsible when I don't know what I am saying. That's crap, and you know it."

Disagreeing with me Braxton is shaking his head. "No. I think you're more honest when you have no inhibitions. Last night you knew what you were saying. You were honest and open and I got to tell you sweetheart, my dick left here hard and throbbing." Rubbing his crotch to make his point, I'm tempted to kick him there. It would serve him right.

"Oh, did you go home so Tiffany could help you out with it?" Ouch! That was not nice. I regretted it the minute I said it. But, I'm still hurt. He looks slightly shocked and worried.

"Hell, no! I did not let her touch me. Iz, I have not been with her since I have known you." His voice and eyes tell me this is true, but Liam said another story. I hinted I knew differently, and then he demanded who would dare open his mouth.

"Never mind who, Braxton. When was the last time you slept with that trifling trick?!" I challenge raising my eyebrows.

"Oh, Iz, you are so far from the truth. I was playing her game mostly. I don't want to spend a minute more than I need to with her. She is up to something, I know it. What's the old saying? Keep your friends close but your enemies closer. Yeah, you get my drift now?"

Sitting up, I lean closer to him. "What?" I whisper as I'm confused and relieved to hear he doesn't want her.

Tucking a piece of my hair behind my ear, he sighs.

"Sweetheart, you got all bent out of shape and I could not tell you what I was doing. I needed her to see us argue and fight. That is the only way I am going to find out what she is doing. I hated to do this, but I knew I would never give you up. So I went with it, hoping you would understand when the time was right." He is gazing at me intently waiting for my reaction. He seems nervous as he keeps taking deep powerful breaths. I should make him grovel but I melt under his intense stare.

I'm stunned, to say the least. "You don't want her? Are you telling me you still want *ME*?" I'm suddenly nervous forgetting all about my current aches and pains. He needs to prove to me that he wants me though. That means hands off of that bitch, once and for all.

"Yeah, babe, that is exactly what I'm saying. I was never going to let you slip through my fingers." He leans in and pulls me onto his lap.

My heart wins out over my brain. "Oh Braxton, you have no idea how happy I am to hear that." Pulling back some, I admit to him my fears and how angry I am at him for not trusting me enough to tell me what was going on. He has been playing this game with Tiffany for so long now I'm not convinced he is totally over her. In my attempt to get him to understand, I halt my conversation mid-sentence. "Wait a minute, what about, Eve?"

Showcasing that damn dimple, his smile widens. "What can I say? Eve knows deep down how her mother is. Besides, she likes you. She is confused, but she also knows how happy you make her daddy. Eve wants to see her old man with a smile, instead of being so damn grumpy all of the time."

That damn dimple is my undoing. I reach for his face, pressing my lips against his. It doesn't take him long before his hands fist in my hair. I suddenly halt all actions. Forgetting all about my headache, the fact I have not brushed my teeth, has me heading to the bathroom. I not only brush them twice, I use mouthwash. I want to enjoy this moment to the fullest. Slowly sauntering back to the couch, I marvel at his sexy grin he is giving me. Opening his arms I fall into them straddling his lap. Realizing I've brushed my teeth, he lets out a chuckle and remarks I'm minty fresh. Grasping my hips, he brings me closer making sure to rock his cock between my thighs. He smiles with a wicked grin then pulls my face to his. He is claiming my lips with mild aggression like he is making up for lost time. Lost in the moment at how incredible he feels, I respond by sucking on his tongue.

Today is my turn to claim him. Dropping my gaze to meet his lust filled eyes, I'm eagerly rubbing against his chest. "You claim me, Braxton?" I'm hoping he plays along.

His tongue darts out to wet his lips. "Yeah babe, claimed you a long time ago."

Perfect! "That's good to know because I'm claiming you right now."

I reach and undo his zipper so I can palm his already hard erection. Running my hands down inside his jeans, I find him commando. His flesh is so velvety soft as his shaft pulses hot, tracing my finger along his thick vein. The more I rub, the more he moans, pressing his hardness into my hand. Begging me to continue, we work together to lower his jeans.

My other hand pulls my panties to the side as I straddle him. Looking into his eyes, I waste no time lining us up so I can slam down on him in one fast motion. I instantly cry out with a combination of pain, and plenty of juicy passion.

The instant our bodies make contact, Braxton moans. "Fuck me, Iz, never wanted to be claimed by a woman before. Glad it's you, cause the way you're riding my cock. Damn girl, I've died and gone to heaven."

"No talking honey, time for me to rock your world." My head hurts like hell, but my need to fuck Braxton is drowning that out, it's the throbbing pain in-between my legs that's winning out at the moment.

"Yes, Ma'am." That's all he whispers as a wave of desire rush throughout his body.

No more words are said as he rips off my tank top to kiss my breast. My nipples are so hard, I swear I could cut glass with them or maybe poke his eye out.

I marvel at the techniques of him sucking and biting my nipples. Arching my back, I grab his shoulders, and thrust down on him. We both cry out in pleasure as we let our emotions get the best of us. With my feet balanced on the couch, I lower myself again all the way. Slowly I glide up, allowing just enough of his cock still inside so he won't slip out entirely then slam back down with as much force as I can. Holy hell, Braxton is built like an *Iron Horse* or is it a *Stallion*? Either way, his body was made for sin.

My body is inching closer to orgasm as I lean forward, resting my head on his shoulder. Braxton grasps my hips as I rock meeting his hard motions, making sure to hit that one sweet spot. My orgasm is power packed, and I come so hard I see stars. Biting his shoulder, my body quivers as I try to calm my breathing. The instant my teeth pierce his skin, it detonates his impending release. His final thrust spills his seed like a stream of hot lava setting my uterus on fire.

Screaming out in utter pleasure, I enjoy the ride. "Oh. Oh. Braxton!"

"Jesus Christ. Every time with you just gets better and better. Swear to God Izzy, no one has ever claimed my dick so hard in my life."

He kisses my head holding me tight against his chest, as we both try to calm our racing heartbeats. I realize this incredible experience did nothing to help my hangover.

"Oh Braxton, my head hurts."

I must amuse him because I can feel his chest rise against my cheek. "Yeah, babe my head down below is hurting too."

Oh my god, he never stops. "Not funny, I mean it."

His hands slide up and down my sides. "I would say I'm sorry, but that would be a lie. That was beyond hot babe. You are mine sweetheart, and you just rocked my fucking world."

I love hearing Braxton saying these things. What woman wouldn't love to hear those words after the fantastic sex we just had?

I kiss his chest and snuggle into him; he leans back on the couch, puts his feet up and pulls me down on him and covers us with a blanket. We sit like this, in complete silence, just enjoying one another. We fit so freaking perfectly together like this.

Rubbing his fingers up and down my arms Braxton sighs, and then says, "Babe, when is your friend Kara coming out?"

I know he asked me a question, but I'm so sated and comfortable I'm drifting off to sleepy land. Hearing Kara's name, I can only assume what he asked me, so I just mumble, saying, "Mmmm, she is getting a flight out soon." Kissing my bare shoulder, he seems content.

"Good babe, when she gets here we are all going to have a talk."

Opening my eyes for a second before I close them from exhaustion, I ask him, "Oh that reminds me, can Liam have that talk with us?"

Braxton leans his head back to look down at me with a frown on his face, and an eyebrow rose to question me.

Oh goodness, Braxton. "Oh please, Kara wants me to set her up with him. She has a thing for bikers and I told her how hot he was, she is like a moth to a flame."

"Sure darlin', anything for you." Kissing the top of my head while laughing. Then he drops it for a more serious look. "But I got to tell ya, I'm not excited to hear that you think Liam is hot. That kind of pisses me off actually."

"Hmmm, no one is as hot as you, honey."

Tightening his hands around me, he says, "That's nice to hear and I love it when you call me honey. I also know how you feel about me because you told me all night in your drunken state." Lowering his eyes, he tilts my chin with his finger. "It warmed my heart to hear you talk with no filters."

I act shocked. "I never filter my mouth, I think it and it just spills out."

"I like that as well."

"I'm sure you do. Maybe I can show you what else my mouth is good for some time."

"I like that even better, honey." His smile is ear to ear.

This flirty side is great, but I do need to address a particular person of interest. "I'm sure you do, but we still need to talk about us and your ex. I'm too tired right now because I just spent what energy I had riding your big cock."

Grabbing onto my ass with his big hands, he says, "Oh Iz, how I like your dirty talk, keep it up and you will be riding it again."

I can't help but yawn. "I'm too tired. Sorry, big fella." I say with my palm on his chest as I notice a twinkle of mischief in his eyes.

"You know, speaking of Liam, if Kara is anything like you, he will be in a constant state of bliss. Fucker will be smiling from ear to ear." He laughs as he kisses my head again, running his nose through my damp hair.

"You smell great even after your drunken state last night."

I marvel at his sweet touches, saying, "Glad you think so, is Liam seeing anyone?"

"Not that I am aware of, not that it would stop him." He laughs out letting me know a bit more about Liam than I want to know.

I can't help but laugh because it sounds like he is describing my girl Kara. "Same goes for her, if she wants him, she'll have him. I get a lot of my courage from just being around her." It's no lie; she has taught me how to survive over the years.

"If she's anything like you; that bastard is in trouble."

"Oh Braxton, you have no idea."

Chapter Twelve

"SHUT UP! YOU ARE SO bad, Kara." I choke, laughing as my best friend is eyeing some guy at the bar talking with his friend. Her one-sided conversation with herself is mentally stripping the clothes off this poor guy; it's beyond hilarious. I have missed spending time with my best friend. Her 'I don't give a fuck' attitude is just what I need to keep my mind off my problems, life is just good.

Kara showed up yesterday, and tonight, we are at the Pub drinking way more than we should. Sam gave me the night off to spend with her to have some much-needed fun. I told him we might stop in and to be honest, with the way he is watching me, I would say he is enjoying himself. I wink and nod my beer as to thank him for being so great. He didn't pry about what happened with Braxton the other night and for that I am grateful. Hell, I'm not even sure I know what is going on between Braxton and me. It's a beautiful disaster in the making.

Braxton and I decided I was going to continue to work for, Sam. Coming back to the shop was not a good idea since Tiffany stops in a lot. He is still trying to figure out what she is up to, so I am keeping my distance. My safety is his primary concern; his second is to spend time with her to find out what she wants. Either way, it sucks for me. I would love to go back and work with the man that is growing on me by the minute but for now, this is the way it has to be. I just want to live my life with Braxton. No more Tiffany, no more Dominic, just us. If only.

Kara takes a sip of her drink before holding up her finger. "So Izzy, you know what tomorrow night is, right? Or is living out here in the Pacific Northwest got you all screwed up?"

Eyeing her, I have no clue what she means, half of the time she says things out of left field. I'm clueless. She doesn't wait; she blurts out.

"Duh! Kane, Toews, Saad, Crawford. Do I need to go on?" The way she curls her tongue when she says the name Crawford can only mean one thing. She has my attention, and fast like, it means Hockey and the Blackhawks. Once she said the name Toews, I knew what she meant.

I spill my beer down my chin. "Holy shit, the playoffs. Damn, how the hell could I have forgotten? God, I swear living here has screwed with my time. Everything is on so early here for me to watch, this time zone takes some getting used to." Note to self, tape them, so I can watch them later.

"Well, it's a good thing I am here to remind you then. It's tradition for you to make your game day feast and I am here with you so what could be better than that? Give me a high five, sister!" She says, rubbing her hands together as if getting ready for a party.

We have this tradition; game nights I make barbeque ribs, coleslaw, and baked potatoes. The picture perfect night. We drink too much beer, eat ribs and watch our dear Blackhawks. We're from the Midwest, so naturally, Chicago is our home team. I am a huge Jonathan Toews groupie but Kara is all Cory Crawford. When we won the Stanley Cup last year, we were in the streets in Chicago drunk and partying by Wrigley Field. It was awesome until Dominic caught up with us. It was fun while it lasted, and as usual, he killed our good time.

Drowning out those bad memories, I raise my beer to her as if to cheer to better times. "Hell yeah, tomorrow we can go to the store and get what we need and gear up to watch our boys kill it. Who the hell are we playing?"

Dropping her head, she looks at me if disgusted. "Oh my God, what has happened to you? Duh, we play the damn Kings, again!" We played them last year in the playoffs, too.

Raising our glasses, we toast our beloved team. We both hate the Kings and for good reason. Last year they played dirty, and Toews took some serious hits. I am so looking forward to some payback hits on them.

"Cheers to that, baby."

Close to an hour later, in walks the man of my current naughty dreams. I just happen to look over at the door the minute he enters, and a big gust of the wind follows him. He truly is a sight to take in. My insides twist, my breath seizes and my eyes nearly fall from their sockets.

Hot damn, his swag alone demands your undivided attention. His eyes scan the bar and eventually, they find what they are looking for as he spots us. The instant our eyes connect, my world is once again flipped upside down, and I want to devour every inch of him. Eyeing the both of us, he smiles and dips his chin at me. I bump Kara on the shoulder to let her know Braxton is here. Kara only knows Braxton from what I have told her, but seeing him in person is a whole other experience. Swear to God, that man takes my breath away. As my nerves take notice, my heart rate speeds up. Hot as sin Liam is right behind him. Even better. The slight huff of breath that escapes my friend lets me know she sees them, as well. I don't even need to look at her face to know her mouth is hanging open, ogling the hotness walking our way.

Her hand grabs my shoulder. "Holy shit, did we just hit the lottery of hot men, or what? Which one is, Braxton? I sure don't want to hit on him," she says, never once looking at me. Nice.

Reaching our table, Braxton kisses me and pulls me into an affectionate embrace. The minute his tender lips graze my cheek, I am hit with his cologne. I don't know what kind he wears, but if he changes it, I'll shoot him.

Liam strolls over to Kara, winks and hits her with a killer smile. Wrapped in Braxton's big arms, I can see Kara turn red as she leans her body into Liam. Yeah, she likes him. I can imagine she is mentally stripping his clothes off. He's not the first guy she's done that to tonight.

Braxton sits next to me and pulls me toward his lap, all the while rubbing my arms. "Hey baby, how are you girls?" He looks at our half empty glasses.

I'm momentarily lost in my thought. *Keep rubbing me like this Braxton, and my slight ache down below might need your attention.* I can't help it, every time I'm around him, my libido revs to life. I'll keep my naughty thoughts to myself for now.

"Great, better now that you're here," I say, looking over my shoulder to gaze into his playful eyes.

His darting glance is laced with mischief. "Is that right?" He says with his arm around my shoulder.

I'm not only weak in the knees, his mere presence has my pulse racing.

Clearing her throat, Kara is throwing daggers at me. Probably because I have yet to introduce everyone properly. With a roll of my own eyes, I mentally tell her to 'keep your damn clothes on.' Goodness, impatient much?

"Liam, Braxton, this is my best friend, Kara. Kara, this is my Braxton." I'm lost in his big brown eyes yet again. Clearing my throat, I look over at Kara saying, "The hot one next to you is, Liam." I can't help but laugh.

"Cute, Iz." Braxton grips me a little tighter, as his jealous side emerges.

"Sweet Jesus," A flush creeps across her cheeks. "First of all, Braxton, you are every bit as hot as Izzy has said you were. I see why she can't think straight around you, *Good Lord.*"

Her ears are now bright red and the poor thing is squirming in her seat. I love every minute of it.

She whistles rather loudly, looking at Liam. Liam's eyes were trained on Kara. No matter how hard she tried, she couldn't hide how attracted to him she really was. Fidgeting with her hair, she looks down at the table. "Did she tell you I wanted to meet you?"

"She might have forgotten to mention it to me, but Brax did say she had a friend who was coming into town."

She turns her head so her hair flares out, which is her way of flirting. "I'm new to town and looking for a good time while I'm here. Are you up for a good time, Liam?"

Liam is the one now whistling loudly. "I like a girl who likes to have fun and I have been known to be an excellent host." He eyes her body saying, "I think you and I could have a lot of fun together."

Pounding my hand on the table, I'm laughing so hard, I might fall off my stool. "*Good Lord,* you two are like two horn dogs waiting to hump the other's leg."

Kara immediately responds. "Now Izzy, you know it won't be a leg I'm humping."

Liam is smiling like the cat that ate the canary. Giving Braxton a slight nod, he says, "Damn, liking this woman already. Izzy girl, so glad you introduced us. I might have to kiss your cheek just to thank you."

"Lips on your girl, leave mine alone." Braxton offers up his witty comment.

Sam brings us a round of beers but the way Liam and Kara are into each other, we might need to leave sooner rather than later. Their light-hearted teasing is heating up the room rather quickly.

Interrupting the stare down between her and Liam, Kara holds up her finger taking a drink. "Are you guys coming over to Izzy's tomorrow night for dinner and the game?"

"What game? If it includes eating count us in," Braxton says in an easygoing manner.

Kara look confused. "Um, well, has Izzy not told you about our obsessions with the Blackhawks? Damn, she makes the same pre-game spread every game. I'm shocked she hasn't told you about it." Knowing the answer is no, she shakes her head with a disgusted look on her face. "Christ, my girl moves out here and forgets all about the Hawks." Directing her evil glare at me, she says, "Tazer, would be ashamed."

Braxton *hears* a guy's name and gets irritated. Jeez, jealous much?!

Wrinkling his nose, Braxton asks, "Who the hell is Tazer?"

Oh, just shoot me now. "Ugh, she is talking about my favorite hockey player. Jonathan Toews, aka Tazer, number 19. Yeah, I'm sort of obsessed with him." What can I say, watching him on the ice is so damn hot.

"Obsessed is putting it mildly, the girl has his jerseys, shirts, socks, hats and let's not forget my favorite... panties." She says with a wicked eyebrow rise.

"Panties?" Braxton pulls his body in, then slowly releases a deep breath.

"Gotta' like panties." Liam chuckles, before finishing off his beer and slamming it on the table.

"Iz," Braxton, whispers in my ear almost laughing. "Tell me about your Tazer panties."

My ears are on fire, so I know I'm red as a beet. "*Good Lord*! I only have a few pairs and on game day, well, you know. I do my part so they can win." Taking a gigantic sip of my beer does nothing to hide my embarrassment as all sets of eyes are on me.

Kara pounds her fist on the table. "Oh Shit! Tell them what you told the guy at the sporting goods store that one time! No...better yet, let me." Not even taking a breath, she doesn't miss a beat.

"So, we're shopping at this store and sweet little Izzy here, goes up to the sales guy, smiling and looking all innocent as she asks him if they have any Toews panties. Now, this poor kid starts choking and turns all sorts of red because he's embarrassed. So, she decides to play with him some more and tells him she wants him on her ass! I know what she means, she wants 'Toews' on the ass of her panties but by the look on his face, he's totally out of his element. Damn, I wish I took a picture of his face!" Kara, is laughing so hard she has to hang on to Liam's shoulder for support. "Imagine if you told him you wanted 'Kane' on your ass instead? We could have played it off as Izzy wanted him to *cane* her ass. Now, *that* would have been priceless!"

Braxton, just snickers under his breath and says, "You are shameless. How about I *cane* your ass instead?"

"Well now, that just won't do since your last name is not Kane, and your first name is not Patrick. But I might consider it, if you can handle the puck like he does." I've definitely had too many beers because challenging Braxton to do anything sexual is like playing with fire. I have to admit though, I would love any form of fire coming from him.

His throaty growl gives way to his slow smile. "Oh sweetheart, I am going out to buy you some panties that say 'Property of Brax.' How does that sound?" He then bites my earlobe, hard!

Feeling his teeth clamp down on my ear has me moaning. It felt so darn good, I almost begged for more.

"That might be okay, but on game day? Toews will be on my ass. It's tradition. Can't change it because that would be bad luck."

Liam has Kara in a sideways hug laughing as if this is the funniest thing he has ever heard.

I'm going to have to wipe that shit-eating grin off of his face. "Hey, I wouldn't laugh too hard. Kara has "Crawford" on her ass on game days."

Liam holds back his laugh eyeing me as he knocks Braxton on his shoulder with his fist. "We have our hands full with these two. You realize this, right?"

"No, Shit." Braxton huffs.

With his hands clenching briefly, then releasing, Braxton asks, "Hey Izzy, what kind of snacks are we having for the big game?"

Smiling, I say, "BBQ ribs, coleslaw, baked potatoes, a relish tray, nachos, and of course, beer. Lot and lots of beer."

With a nod of his head, Liam seems excited. "Hell to the yes, count me in. Izzy girl, you had me with beer and the panties, but ribs added to the mix? Hell, sounds like heaven to me. Might even cheer for your Blackhawks, even though I am a Kings fan. Maybe, if you modeled those panties for me, I could change that." His eyes squint with the challenge.

Braxton gives a soft head shake. "Easy there, buddy. Kara, can show her panties all she wants, but Iz's ass is for my viewing pleasure only."

I mutter out a 'hum' noise. "No way honey, its tradition. We get down to our panties by the end of the third if they are winning. Just the way it goes down with us."

"Say what? So you both get down to your panties and strut around? Just the two of you? Is there something you want to tell me about you two? Just how close are you?" Braxton asks looking at Kara and then back at me puzzled.

We both laugh. Kara and I are fun and crazy but we're not into women.

"I hate to ruin your wildest dreams, honey. We may party hard, but we don't party that hard. Sorry," I say as I quickly kiss his lips and try not to laugh.

"Shit, just when I thought I might get a show with my ribs tomorrow night. Well, I like vaginas, so we are all good. Dick's don't do much for me." Liam says with giddiness.

"I got a vagina!" Exclaims Kara.

Oh my, my girl is drunk and horny. Liam is in for a wild night with this hard to control woman.

"Kara's vagina is up for your viewing pleasure." I can't believe I just said that. All this talk of vagina's and dicks is getting to me. Lord help me.

"Yes it is! Liam, just let me know, my Crawford panties can say Liam, instead." Kara, just throws this out there like they have known each other forever, instead of five minutes. The shit is funny though.

"Damn straight," Liam says shaking his head emphatically. He mouths 'like her' over her shoulder with a broad grin.

Braxton's head is moving like he is watching a Ping-Pong match. Between my one-liners, Kara's lines, and now Liam's one-liners, he is lost somewhere in between.

"Okay, you crazy bunch. You two keep your dick and vagina to yourselves. Iz's vagina is the only one I'm interested in." Braxton's wide-eyed look has us all laughing our asses off.

With a playful tone, Braxton exchanges a look with Liam and Kara. "You two go crazy. Didn't realize how fucking perfect you two were going to be for each other. God, I need a drink. A strong fucking drink." Braxton, nods over at Sam to bring us another round of beers.

"You a good cook, sweetheart?" Braxton whispers in my ear.

"Not too bad, I like my ribs. Cook those suckers all day in beer. Ribs fall right off the bone and melt in your mouth. Beer, hockey and ribs, damn good time."

"I know something else that could melt in your mouth," Braxton says as he licks my ear.

I let out a satisfied sigh.

"Izzy girl, you seriously cook your ribs in beer girl?" Liam asks with a look of amazement.

"Sure do."

"Damn girl, you sold me. What time should I be there?"

"Oh, six I think. Kara is staying with me and by the looks of you two, you might be spending the night there, too," I say as I wink at him and raise my mug to Kara, who is dazzled with him. I can't blame her, though.

Not to be left out, Braxton whispers, "Can I have a sleepover as well?"

"Why Braxton Ryles, do you want to sleep in me, I mean with me?" No one misses my little slip-up. I have to admit, it was funny.

"Yeah, babe. I sure do. Unfortunately, I have to get home to Eve. My mom is with her now and Tiffany is bugging me about seeing her tomorrow. So, I got to go home. But I will be taking you and tucking you in first." Gazing at his face, his eyes dance with mischief and the panty melting smile he shows me has me dripping wet. Geez, I can't keep my panties dry when he is around.

Hearing this causes me to pout out my lips. "You better make it good so I can dream about it all night long. Without you."

"You know it," he says. Those strong demanding lips of his are begging me to take them, and who the hell am I to displease? In a proactive move, I seize his lips, as I beg for more. To my pleasure, he growls into my mouth as he grinds against me with his growing erection.

"Well, well, well, what do we have here? Looks like Brax has his whore back." The voice is screeching and plain old bitchy. I should have known with Braxton here with me, she would not be far behind.

I can feel his body tense on hearing her voice. He pulls back, whipping his head in her direction. "What the fuck are you doing here?" His voice is not welcoming at all. Note to self, do not interrupt him when he is devouring my mouth.

"Oh please. It's a free country, Brax. I knew you were lying to me about seeing this worthless bitch, so I followed your ass."

Wow, she is such a nasty witch. I find it uncomfortable to swallow and have a compulsion to flee right about now.

It's Kara who has her hands up, backing away with a shudder. "Bitch, who the fuck are you? Wait! Hold on, you must be the bitch that's making my best friend miserable!" Not staying still, Kara is over to the blonde bitch faster than lightening.

"Oh Shit," Liam says as he wasn't fast enough to grab Kara's arm.

"Fuck." Braxton huffs out.

Dry washing my hands, I only say, "Jesus, there goes my sleepover dreams."

It's Tiffany's daunting scowl at Kara that holds everyone's attention. "Oh, how sweet, are you here to fight her battles? You don't scare me."

"You should be fucking scared of me, bitch. You have no idea what I'm capable of." Kara is dead serious. It was Dominic who taught her how to fight and fight dirty if necessary.

"Please, just go away. My God, Brax what have you got yourself into with these two? Liam, you seriously like her? I mean shit brother, your standards have sunk." She uses her hand to scan Kara's body.

"Brother?" Kara is startled and looks over at him and then me.

Holding up my drink, I tell her, "Yep! That raving, blonde bitch is hot-as-sin Liam's sister. Welcome to my world." Taking a long drink of my beer, I say with a shrug of my shoulder.

Kara shows the palm of her hand, "Shit. Well hopefully, her brother won't mind if I kick her ass!"

"I might pay to see it." Liam responds.

All sets of eyes turn toward him. Wow, can't believe he just said that.

"Tiffany, get the fuck out of here. Now! I'll see you tomorrow, with Eve. Don't make me fuckin' repeat myself, either!" Braxton gets up and walks so he is right in her face, hands on his hips.

"Pfft, this little stunt is going to cost you." She's pointing her nasty finger toward me. What the hell? I'm just sitting here.

"Just be warned Brax, I will make sure your latest whore knows where her place is. Enjoy her while you can," Tiffany says, as she turns to strut away.

Liam is now standing up to his sister. "Jesus Christ, Tiffany! Get the fuck out of here before I let Kara kick your ass and don't you even think about threatening Izzy again, you hear me? Oh, one more thing, your days of fucking with Brax are over! Now get the fuck out of here before I forget you're my sister and treat you like the bitch you are!"

"Fucking come near my friend again, and I will do more than kick your ass. Don't push me because, you won't like the results." Kara says in a cold, calculating voice.

I like the entertainment, but I'm suddenly bored and ready to leave.

"Thanks Tiffany, for ruining our night. The sooner you leave, the sooner Braxton can take me home and put me to bed." I say with a wink and a smile. Fuck her. I take one last drink of my beer and it's warm as hell. Yuck!

Tiffany shouts as she heads for the door.

She then looks over her shoulder, yelling this time. "Time's ticking Izzabella, I know your secret!" All I hear is her laughing, as she walks out the door.

What the fuck did she just call me?

Izzabella!

Fuck! Only one person called me that.

God, what has she done?

Kara goes white and I turn green as our eyes lock in utter shock.

Tiffany

"TIME'S TICKING IZZABELLA." I LOVED wiping that smug smile from her damn face the minute my words registered with her. Bitch wasn't so smug then. Hell no. She turned white as a ghost. Fucking priceless.

Walking in that damn bar and seeing her hands all over Brax, had me seeing red. I followed him hoping he had not lied to me about not seeing her anymore. He misled me on purpose. He fucking played me. Well played Brax, but I'm far from done. I'm about to unleash hell on that bitch. Only then will I have Brax's attention again. He may have her now but soon enough the devil will be coming for her. Good riddance.

Walking to my car, I'm shaking so bad I drop my keys. Shit. Picking them up, I fumble with the buttons and accidently hit the damn panic button. Now, I'm not only really pissed but my ear drums are ringing. I aggressively take my anger out on my car window. I slap it not once, not twice but three damn times. Each hard slap stings my hand. It's painful but it feels so good to feel something other than the pain left by Brax's new whore.

"Who the FUCK do you think you are?" I scream hitting my window a few more times. This woman comes out of nowhere and my world is set upside down. My kid and my man had the perfect relationship. It fucking worked. Now, it doesn't. I'm like an afterthought. I'm not important. Well they have no fucking clue how important I am. Looking around the dirt parking, it's dark and pitch quiet. Not a sole walking around. I'm totally alone out here but I'll be damned if I will let her take my daughter and my man from me.

To get my life back and make sure Brax's new office twit takes a hike, I needed a plan. I've never needed a plan before. I would stroll into town to see my daughter for a few days and end up in bed with Brax. I love my daughter but I'm a free spirit. She is in a good place with Brax. He takes care of her and loves that girl to no end. I never wanted kids. I heard that Brax thinks I got pregnant on purpose. Truth be told, I may have helped my chances of getting pregnant by putting holes in his condom a few times, but it was more of a joke. Like playing Russian roulette. I played and nine months later Eve joined us. Only my introduction to motherhood was more of a nightmare. I had no role model.

I spent my earlier years hanging around my brother Liam and his buddies. At the time Liam was not involved in the Lost Souls MC, yet. My uncle, Marty, that was his life. I was a wild child in the making. Knowing if I ever got in trouble or needed anything, I could count on him to help me out. Uncle Marty would make sure of that since he was my mother's brother. My mother died when I was around Eve's age. Liam's a few years older. He took the news better than I did when she passed. From that point forward, my life, revolved around men. My father was a selfish bastard. Mick was drinking more than watching out for me. Sadly, Liam had taken over the job of taking care of me.

When I started getting interested in boys, it was Brax who looked like a walking sex god. He was built back then but nothing like he is now. We fought more than we were friendly. Both of us liked to spar with words. I never took it too serious. He would always end our talks with a smile and a wink. Liam would cringe anytime we would spend time together. In the end, he saw the writing on the wall. After his repeated threats to stay away from one another, he finally gave up.

In my early twenties, I was drinking and partying whenever the hell I wanted. My father could give a fuck and now Liam was involved with the Lost Souls MC. He wasn't around much at all. That left me with a lot of time to get into trouble. I did a pretty good job at it until Brax showed up one night bitching me out. When he got angry, you listened. His muscles would flare and he commanded your attention. He told me, "One day you are going to seriously get hurt." I listened all the while having a wild sex scene play out in my mind. In that moment I played out all the ways he would bend me over and fuck me till I begged him to stop. After my wild romp played, I shrugged off his warning. I played it off until one night it actually happened.

I was with Derek a local bad boy who hung out at this particular bar I visited. Henley's was a great hangout. Local bikers were the usual clientele. It was not the kind of place you wouldn't go unless you could handle it. I was a bad ass and I sure thought I could handle it. I ended up in the bathroom with Derek, my panties around my ankles and he was ready to take what he wanted. My drunken stupor had me wanting him one minute only to fight him off the second. He took it as a challenge and I ended up with more than a few bruises. The prick then thought it was okay to share me with his buddy. Hell to no. I sobered up real fast. I fought him off and drew blood on his face. Got to love fake nails, perfect fucking weapon when needed. I scratched his face till I had skin and blood under my nails. I was about to get my damn head bashed in bathroom mirror but a very pissed off Brax walked in and halted his plan. Derek about shit himself and his buddy backed up with his hands high. Fucking prick.

I have no idea how Brax found me, but my head sure as hell thanked god. Leaving the bar with glass in my head did not sound like fun.

"You have two fucking seconds to let her go or else I fuck you up." Brax had said breathing heavy looking like he was ready to kill. Derek and his prick of a friend, whoever he was took off as fast as they could. Brax stood frozen and I could tell was disgusted. His eyes glared into mine and I fucked hated what I saw. He was disgusted with me.

I slumped into his protective arms and cried. Fucking cried. I don't cry. I fight. I don't let anyone see me hurting. I've learned to live in a man's world and that meant being strong and never letting anyone take what was mine.

That was the first night I felt Brax's possessive nature. I knew I had to have him. Not only that but I knew I could manipulate. When he looked at me it was easy to see he was attracted to me. Why the hell not. I was a blonde beauty with decent tits and a nice body. My long ass legs could straddle a man like Brax and hang on for the ride of my life.

That night started the Tiffany-Brax love affair. We kept it secret for a while. Sneaking around until Liam caught us and all hell broke loose. Liam and I weren't close by any means but I was his sister. Brax was a member of the Lost Souls MC. My absent father, Mick, could care less what I did or who. He stayed out of my business as long as I cleaned of the house. I worked during the days at a local diner and at night I was in Brax's bed. It was easy. I wasn't clingy. I wanted what I wanted and as long as Brax gave it to me, I was satisfied.

One night Mick and I had a major falling out and I decided to up and leave town. I had met Bo at the diner and finally took him up on his offer to take care of me. He came in several times a week, he said just to see me. I found out he lived in a town about an hour away. It was perfect. Bo was looking for a lost girl to take care off. It would have been creepy if not for the fact he was hot. Not sure why a tall, dark haired, green eyed guy was lonely...but he was. Took a liking to me right away. I had his number and instead of calling Brax after my fight with my father, I called Bo. He was new and exciting. Always looking for my next thrill, I took it. He picked me up and with only a suitcase filled with some clothes, I left without a word. It worked for a few months but I slowly missed Brax. That started my many long weekends I spent back at home to get my fill of Brax. He didn't question too much. I told him I needed my space. Using sex to get what I needed from Brax worked. Once I got my fill I went back to Bo. Both men never really knew what I was doing with my time apart from them but hell it's my life and what they don't know won't kill them.

I was as happy as I could get. Never one to feel really happy, I always wanted more. I wasn't really happy with my tits so I wormed my way and Brax paid for my boob job. I needed new clothes, Bo paid for them. No need for a job when I got two men taking care of me. All they wanted out of the deal was sex. I was good at sex. That's the one thing I knew.

On more than one occasion Brax did beg me to stay with him. He said he would take care of me. Something about me not having a mother figure and he felt obligated to help Liam's sister out. That fucking pissed me off. I never asked for him to take care of me like that. I stupidly mentioned to him about my fantasy about becoming a mother one day. Would I be a good mother? Fuck if I knew. I never had one growing up. He assured me I could.

Eve came about a year later. It was a royal mess. Bo could not have kids so he knew it wasn't him. That got me kicked out of his house and a one-way trip back home to Brax and my father's house. My motherly never took hold, I ached to leave. I never wanted to be stuck in one place. Brax may have been the best guy and best daddy in the world but I needed to fly. I needed to be free.

I stayed till Eve was a few years old and I slowly began take trips. Each time leaving for more than a week until it was a few. It was our routine. Eve stayed with Brax full time. She looked like me but acted like him. It hurt to see me in her. I wanted to be motherly but it just didn't happen for me...until this bitch Izzy showed up trying to take what was always mine.

I never had to fight for Brax's attention. I came back into town saw Eve and would end up fucking the only man who probably cares about me. Deep down he wants to hate me but he just can't do it. I'm the teenager he grew up having a love/hate relationship with. I'm the girl he rescued and I'm the girl he cared for. Love, hell, I'm not sure it was ever love but it was hot.

Now for some reason, I feel beyond threatened. What if Eve or Brax are no longer available to me anymore? What if they replace me? I may be Eve's biological mother but the way she talked about Izzy made me sick. The way her eyes would go big and her smile would glow. I lost it.

Liam tolerated me at best but I'd be damned if I was going to let him stop me. I asked my father and he called uncle Marty with what few things I knew about Izzy which wasn't much. Seems the Lost Souls MC had members back in Izzy's hometown. Damn, that was easy and I had a lead. That damn lead turned out to be golden. I found this asshole Dominic who acted like he owned this woman. Music to my damn ears. The sooner he came to get this bitch the better. I could not believe the shit I slowly learned. Between this guy Dominic and my uncle Marty, I did learn some things about Izzy and some not so great things about Dominic. That bastard is downright scary. This bitch was in for a rude awakening. I'd stay close until Dominic would come and get her. Little by little I'd play along with this psycho. I was the only one with inside information. It was me who could set this plan into action. Once again, I'm needed and this time it's fucking sweet as sugar. We talked and he explained he would be in touch.

Sitting in my car outside the fucking bar where Brax is with Izzy, I realize Dominic better hurry the fuck up or else I might take matters in my own hands. I knew I had to be careful. My uncle was distant with me since the Lost Souls lost Brax a few years back. With me leaving all the damn time, Brax pulled back. He needed to be home for Eve. He started up his own mechanic business with my uncle's blessing. I did one better and worked there for a time with one of my many failed attempts to be home longer than a month. I know Brax hired me thinking I would stick around but like usual one day I up and left.

Which brings to me now, I can't pull away from this fucking bar. I'm waiting for Brax to leave with that bitch. The more I see them together the better for my rage. When I'm angry I feel alive.

All of a sudden my phone rings in my lap.

"Hello." My voice is cold as the ice in my veins.

"Tiffany, Dominic here. Things are set in motion. You'll be seeing me soon. How is my Izzabella?" His voice is the exact opposite of mine. He sounds fucking excited and cheery.

"Pfft. I'm sitting outside a bar where your bitch is digging her claws in my man."

"Tsk-tsk. I told you already never use that tone or word to describe my Izzabella."

"Well then I suggest you come and pry her fucking fingers off my man's dick!" I scream it back at him. How dare he tsk-tsk me?

"My patients running thin with you Tiffany. Don't you worry about *my* girl, her fingers won't be around any man. Not when I get to her. She's mine."

"You better hurry then because from what I just walked in on her fingers are going to be busy tonight." I said it to piss him off. The more pissed he gets the faster he'll get his ass here and get this bitch out of my life.

He ended the call. Surprise. Surprise.

After his call I felt a bit more relaxed. Soon enough he will be here and then I can get back to my life. My routine. Come into town, see Eve and fuck Brax. That is what I know and that is what I want. Driving away from the bar I look in my rear view mirror back at my brother's and Brax's bikes. An odd sensation washes over me. Is it regret? Maybe. More likely it's anger. When I come around I get all of their attentions. As soon as Izzy came into town I lost it. I want it back. I'll do whatever I have to make sure I am the center of their fucking world again.

chapter THIRTEEN

I CAN HARDLY BELIEVE SHE got up and left the way she did. Fucking Izzabella. After all I have done for her. Trying to release my pent up anger, I throw my glass against the wall and watch it shatter. The shards of glass are reminiscent of what my heart feels like. This strange sense of abandonment is new to me. It's not a welcome feeling, either. Never thought I would have to drop everything just to find my girl. This bitch is forcing me to do things I don't want to do to her. Hanging my head, my extremities are shaking with rage. Punching a wall might curb my desire to seek vengeance. No, I doubt it. My workouts don't even help anymore. There was a time when a great workout could calm me when I was at the highest level of pissed off. Now my aggressive workouts, since she has left, have done nothing to ease my real feelings for Izzabella. One side of me wants to cherish her sensual body, the other side of me wants nothing more than to punish her. Either way, she is not going to like what I do to her once she returns home to me. And she will return home to me. I will be forced to discipline her and for once in my life, I am struggling with that fact. It's never been an issue before, I craved her punishments. My sadistic desire, as fucked up as it may be, is all I've ever known.

Her ungrateful excuse of a family has been all over my shit, asking me how she is. Fuckers never liked the girl, especially after she got her brother killed. They need to leave me be.

Little did they know, it was me who killed the bastard. How dare he come and try to take what's mine?! Killing him was easy, my job required me to show no mercy, and that's exactly who I am. It was easy for me. Izzabella, not so much. But she needed to see first-hand, what happens when they try to take away what belongs to me. Make no mistake, Izzabella belongs to *me*.

Her family thinks I was the one to save their damaged and troubled daughter after they wrote her off for being a bad seed. It makes me sick, how can they just turn their backs on their family? Their own blood? But in a way, Kara being Izzabella's best friend was a huge inconvenience. I don't like to share my girl, even if it is with my own sister. Kara liked to challenge me, though. She has pushed me more times than I'd like to admit. Always questioning me on how I treated, Izzabella. Demanding I change my ways or else I'd be alone. I would admire her for that, if it weren't for her trying to take Izzabella away from me, too. Let's face it, families are messy, they love to interfere when they shouldn't. But, Izzabella Parker's family was notorious for it! Diffusing fires with them over the years was fucking exhausting, and that's putting it mildly. What they don't realize is, I'm the fucking devil in all of this, yet they see me as their daughter's savior.

Pretty fucked up, if you ask me. But hey, if they want to see me as Prince Charming, who the fuck am I to argue with them? In the beginning, it was so easy with, Izzabella. She was sweet and innocent. It didn't turn into something more until she graduated high school. My beautiful, Izzabella always was so quiet and shy, but I took hold of her, and turned her into this sexy creature. Her inhibitions and insecurities held her back. But after training her, she became exactly what I wanted when I wanted it, and how I wanted it. She became the woman I desired, the girl I cherished. Only my way of showing it was...unconventional. Some call me a sadistic fuck, if I need a label to describe me.

Sitting at my desk while spinning my pen, my thoughts drift back to simpler times. I can honestly say I love her in my own sick way, I guess. Feelings and emotions never came into play with anyone I've ever been with. I fucked whoever I wanted to fuck, whenever I wanted to fuck them and Izzabella knew better than to say anything about it. If she did, she knew the consequences.

Two punishments were all it had taken from my hands and knife before she got the idea. Yeah, those times when it was all punishment, were the fucking best. *It was her.* There was something about punishing *her* that made it more enjoyable than anyone else I've ever punished. No one got me off like my Izzabella did. Seeing the fear in her eyes, and knowing it was me she was afraid of, gave me power like

I'd never felt. Knowing she was so afraid of me she would do whatever I told her to do, whenever I told her to do it, rocked my fucking world!

I added in the knife when my threats became futile. Never believing I was going to use it was her first mistake. Izzabella, disobeyed me by going out with my sister of all people, pissed me off beyond belief. I never realized how breathtakingly beautiful she was until I tied her hands to the bed. Seeing her completely helpless and under my control made my dick harder than it had ever been. She mocked me and dared me to 'get on with it.' Yeah, she took my punishment fucks like a champ. That night though, her drunken state had her mouth running a little too freely.

I couldn't let that stand, so I turned up my punishment by grabbing my favorite knife and sliding it along her naked chest. With the blade barely caressing her pale skin, I ran it between her firm, yet plump breasts. Her breathing hitched. Panicking, her body began to tremble like a leaf. I loved seeing her like this. I ran my knife down until it reached her center, and split her panties off her body. She jerked abruptly with a stifled cry. Seeing her so afraid was a glorious sight to behold.

Grabbing her hip with my free hand, I forced myself into her in one swift, merciless thrust. The tears that ran down her face as I took her hard and fast only fueled the intensity of my fucking. A scared Izzabella turned me on. Her fear fed my darkest, most depraved passions, making me crave more. Feeding my soul, I craved more. That was the first night I introduced my knife to her trembling body. The pinch of her skin, giving way to the drops of blood that appeared, made my climax tear through my body like a tornado tears through a house. Her scream, followed by the stream of blood running down her thigh, gave me what I had been craving my whole life: Total domination. My new found love of her cry, followed by her tears, her blood and the blade of my knife proved to be useful with my sweet little Izzabella.

Over time, seeing my marks on her proved to me, and everyone else, that she belonged to me, and only me. Marking that beautiful body so only I would appreciate it was, in part, for my own pure enjoyment. I placed my marks in areas that would clearly be seen by any asshole who dared to sleep with what was already mine.

Izzabella would never want to take another man to her bed knowing her scars would show. How would she explain them? Any normal guy would think twice about fucking a woman who had knife scars on her most sensitive areas. I even made sure they were easily seen by her whenever she looked in the mirror. Fucking brilliant, if you ask me.

Things were great until she ended up pregnant. She was scared shitless, but I also saw happiness behind her eyes. She thought she was masking her real feelings, but I can read that woman better than anyone. I had to do something. What the fuck was I going to do with kid? Growing up, I was a major disappointment in my parent's eyes. Always in trouble, hanging out with the wrong crowds growing up helped me later on in life. Learning how to survive the rough streets of Chicago was not only important, it meant life or death for someone like me. Once I got into college things all changed for me. Tall, dark and handsome, learning to use my looks to my advantage was pretty fucking easy. I may have looked like a pretty boy, but the man underneath was lethal. If need be.

My allegiance to the Lost Souls MC was my first and only priority in my life. I never fucking wanted kids, but the little fucker would be an excellent bargaining tool to use with, Izzabella. I had to find a way to make this shit work. What I had not expected was to see her start to glow as the months went by. The first few months were hard on her. She was throwing up all the time but fuck, she still looked amazing. No more punishments were needed. She changed but so did I. For nine long months I hardly touched her. Fucking longest nine months in my life but I found ways to satisfy my needs and cravings. None of them were my Izzabella though.

When the baby came, Izzabella named her 'Willow.' What the fuck? Her attachment to the little girl was immediate. I allowed them to be together until she started putting *Willow* ahead of me. Whenever I wanted to fuck, she had too many excuses as to why she couldn't. Fuck that! I am not a patient man by any means. I let that shit fly for weeks, then I had to remind her just how sharp my knife skills were.

Only this time, I had a baby. One time, Izzabella tried to take the kid and run from me. After I figured out what she had planned, I made sure to punish her in the worst possible way. I took the one thing she loved the most: Willow. Once I found a family for her, I snatched her right out of Izzabella's arms. Didn't even let her kiss her goodbye. From there, shit just got worse. Izzabella got her brother involved. He showed up one night to confront me. Me! Stupid bastard!

The bastard died by my hands and I made sure Izzabella saw it all. Fucker came to *my* house to take *my* property, and then get the kid back. I have no idea how she got word to her brother, but I do know where she got the information. My sister, Kara.

Kara and I have a very strained relationship. Once she got older and realized just how deadly my 'brothers' and I were, she quickly learned her place. It took one of my brothers to show her exactly what would happen to her if she ever got involved in my shit, again. That shit included her best friend, my Izzabella, and her offspring.

Turned that shit around and made it look like Izzabella got in a fight with her sick brother, and in a heated argument, she killed him. I made it look like Izzabella had lost her mind by doing drugs and whoring around town. She sounded like a messed up girl who was on a road of destruction. Such a blessing I came into the picture and looked after the weak, damaged girl. I was the White Knight that saved her from the path of drugs and uncertainty. Worked like a fucking charm. Her family disowned her when they found out about what she did to her brother. Her fucking father turned her over to me and told me she was no longer their problem. Fuck, that was easy.

Except now, after all the planning and time I had invested in this girl, she up and left. Bitch knew what she was doing this time, planned it well. If I didn't want to kill her, I just might admire the way she did it. She used my own fucking tricks on me and like a pussy-whipped motherfucker, I took the bait. Hook, line and fucking sinker. I admire her skills, but the bitch stills needs to be punished. Reliving this shit has me aggravated and pissed the fuck off. This little petite woman has me all sorts of fucked up.

My ringing phone breaks my mental stroll down memory lane. "Yo," I answer my phone with little or no welcome in my tone.

"Is this Dominic Santos?" A rather sharp voice asks.

"Depends on who the fuck is asking and what the fuck you want!" I hate playing mind games and how the hell did this bitch get my number? Who the fuck could this possibly be? I pulled the phone from my ear to look at the caller I.D. display. Huh, not a number I recognize.

"My name is Tiffany. Let's just say, I know what you're looking for and where you can find it."

This bitch must not know who the fuck she's talking to because no bitch in their right mind would ever come at me like this. Not unless they're prepared for the punishment that comes along with having a smart fucking mouth.

But she does have my attention, "Go on."

"Does the name *Izzy* mean anything to you?" She lets her name roll off her tongue like it has a nasty aftertaste. This bitch is about to piss me off if she doesn't calm the fuck down. But she seems to know my Izzabella, so I'll have to hold off on putting this trick in her place.

Looks like my night just got a whole lot better. I don't even have to look for Izzabella, she was handed to me by a bitch named Tiffany.

"*Izzabella* is her name. *My Izzabella.* How do you know her?" I shouted. Jesus, I hated when people called her Izzy. Her name is Izzabella, and just the thought of holding her close to me again. Well, wow.

"Sorry, *Izzabella*. Do you want the wench, or not?" She spits her venom like my girl is some disgusting low life. Well, that shit just won't fly with me.

"Bitch, you ever call her a wench again, me and you are going to have problems. Understand?" Bitch better fucking hear me.

"L-look, I want her to disappear. She took something of mine and I want it back." Bitch now is talking in a tone more suitable when speaking to Dominic Santos the 'Enforcer of the Lost Souls MC.'

"What did she take of yours? A fucking puppy?" I'm getting pissed now. Why would Izzabella want anything from this bitch?

"No, asshole. My man," she says grinding her teeth.

"The fuck you say? The only man for Izzabella is me!" I stand and want to punch something, or better yet, someone. My violent streak shows up with a vengeance.

"Seems that she has replaced you with my old man. So tell me, when are you are going to come and take her back to wherever you call home?"

I'm seething, but I'm trying to rein in my desire to kill someone. "Where are you, exactly?"

"In the Seattle area, a small town named Monroe. My man owns a repair shop here and until recently, she worked for him. I got her fired and out of my man's life, or so I thought. But it seems they're on again and that's a huge problem for me. He and my daughter are all I got. I want them ready and waiting on *me*, not her!"

Bitch seems to be threatened by my girl. The idea that my Izzabella is with any man pisses me off. But the idea that my girl has put this bitch in her place? Well, that puts a fucking smile on my face. "A repair shop-huh? Might have an idea on how to get all the information I need before I surprise my sweet Izzabella again. Ready to work on a little surprise reunion with me so I can surprise my girl?" I ask her, but my mind is already planning ways to get my girl back.

"Fuck, whatever. Just get here and get this bitch's claws out of my man."

"Listen, bitch. This is the second time I've told about calling my girl names. Disrespect her again, and it's going to be you I deal with when I come to the Seattle area. Am I clear? Now I got some plans to make, wait for my call." Ending the call with this yapping cunt, I call my brothers at the 'Lost Souls MC' for some help.

I started hanging out with them when I first got to college. They were a badass MC and no one messed with them. Ever. I met them through a friend of mine named Marcus. I prospected for them for a year and did some trial runs with them before I patched in. I earned my mark because I had a talent for torturing people. We found this out on my second run with them. Some asshole was not paying the agreed price for his shipment of cocaine. Annoying the shit out of me, I took control of the situation and within record time, he gave us the money he owed, plus interest. Not only did I like what I did to this scumbag drug dealer, I fucking loved it. It was a rush beyond my wildest fantasies.

Chicago was our home turf, but we had members spread across the country. Whenever a brother needed help or needed anything, they were ready to help. We ran drugs and weapons for many different cartels in the United States and Mexico. Over time, I paid my dues. Now, I was the one they feared. No one wanted to get on my bad side. My particular skills spoke for themselves. Money, drugs, women - none of it held much interest to me. My status in the ranks was the only thing I wanted, the only thing I needed. All women were all the same to me, a warm body to get off with. Only one woman has ever held my interest, the only one I could not tame; my Izzabella.

Having no idea if her appeal was due to her indifference to me, or if she was just that desirable. Either way, I wanted that petite sassy mouthed girl. Only my love came at a different price, my love was rough. My love hurt. My love came at the end of a knife, a price too high for most. Izzabella was the only one who could take my love, who could take my knife. Marking her the way I did was selfish, but that's how I roll.

Don't mistake me for some lovesick bitch, because I'm not. I enjoy hurting people and I love hurting Izzabella. Her cries from the pain I inflict on her turns me on, but it's an act of hurting her that's the ultimate foreplay. As much as I want to spend my life dominating her, she needs to be taught a very serious lesson for this latest stunt. Fuck, just *thinking* about what I'm going to do to her is making my dick hard.

Would she have to die at my hands for her ultimate betrayal? She left me, and no one leaves me. *EVER*! I just don't know if I want her to be permanently gone from my side.

"Yo Marcus," blowing out puff rings of my cigar, "seems I have found my girl." I could not contain my excitement.

"No shit? Well, what's the plan?" Marcus seemed intrigued by what was going on in my head. He is the only one that understood what my real feelings for her were.

"Not sure, so I need to plan this carefully. The bitch already ran on me once. This woman told me she was hanging with her man. If she touched this motherfucker..." trying to control my temper, I say, "that may speed up my plans." The thought of her not being around for me, bothered me. I wanted her so much, I fucking ached. But I don't know if I can let her live after this. She may be my weakness, but I can't let my brothers see that shit. I'll cover the feelings I have for Izzabella just like I covered my real feelings for our daughter, Willow. Willow looked just like my Izzabella and every time I looked at those little eyes, it killed me all over again. The only thing I saw was her mother's betrayal. I gave her all of me, and in the end, she chose to leave me. I'm drowning in my need to be with her and my need to hurt her. The pain it's causing me feels like my head is being squeezed in a vice, and it's gripping me tighter and tighter. Fuck, it's killing me! I quickly end my call with Marcus and squeeze my eyes closed.

"It's time my sweet, sweet Izzabella. Maybe our little reunion will have to include our daughter!" Izzabella thinks she's gone for good. Showing her Willow is alive and well will fuck with her mind, for sure. If coming home with me included being with our daughter, how could she refuse me? Mindfucking her is what I do best.

Sitting at my desk, I plan out our reunion. Thinking over all the years of living with her and without her, a part of me wants to be good for her. A part of me wants to be the man she always wanted me to be, a man who deserves her. Blowing smoke from my cigar, I puff out more ringlets. Thinking about her has me rubbing my dick. I ache to take her hard and fast. Lowering my zipper, I begin stroking my growing cock. Closing my eyes, I can see the fear in her brown ones. Hearing her cries and seeing the blood run down her thighs makes me stroke my cock faster and harder. But it's the sound my Izzabella makes when she climaxes that is my undoing. I come harder than I ever have by my own hand and it's the hot, wet come running down my hand that has me whisper out to my girl.

"Izzabella. Oh, my sweetness. Look what you do to me...I'm coming for you baby. God, I can't fucking wait to have your legs wrapped around me, milking my cock with your tight pussy. I need to be buried inside of you, owing you. Owning all of you. Tell me you miss me, Izzabella. Say you'll stay with me. Stay with me and maybe I won't hurt you …that bad.

Chapter Fourteen

A WEEK HAD PASSED SINCE that fucked up night at the bar when Tiffany came in and blew it all to hell. How did she know my actual name? I never told her. I don't recall ever talking to Braxton about it, either. He calls me Iz, never Izzabella. The only person, who knows my given name, other than Kara, is Liam. The first day I met him, he had me so flustered, I accidentally let it slip. The idea of her finding Dominic is unrealistic and downright frightening. She would have no idea where to look. Would she? A lucky guess, most likely. This bitch is playing with my head, and I'm letting her.

    Kara refused to let Tiffany spoil our plans for the game. My ribs were mouthwatering, the beer was cold and, Kara and we got down to our Toews and Crawford panties by the 3rd period. Ignoring the stares and sexy comments from Braxton, we paraded around the house to the tunes of Chelsea Dagger. Of course, I needed to explain who The Fratellis were, and the song, Chelsea Dagger. Any real Blackhawks fan knows this is our goal song. It rocks so much I have it in my music library. Most of my night was spent cheering my team on. The rest was spent ignoring Braxton's comments about my favorite player, Jonathan Toews whenever he was on the ice. Liam and Kara sat and enjoyed the sideshow as much as the food and hockey. The idea of me wearing another man's name on my ass, upset him. That is, until I told him I would provide him with a certain sexual favor if my favorite player scored before the game ended. His whole attitude changed immediately. He went from being pissed off, to screaming at the tv cheering for #19.

"Yo' man, get that puck in the damn net! My woman promised me a fuckin' blowjob if you do." Braxton shouting at the television and being mindful not to spill his beer was comical.

When it happened, he jumped up so fast, his beer did spill all down his chest. To top off the night, in the last 45 seconds of the 3rd period, my man caught a pass from Brandon Saad, and shot the puck top-shelf, right past the goalies head. He scored the winning goal. I had to explain 'top-shelf' to Braxton, telling him it is a term to describe when the puck is hit in the high part of the net. It was exhausting, if I was completely honest, because I never needed to explain hockey to any guy before. It was kind of cute.

"Yes. Yes. Yes," pumping his fists in the air, Braxton hollers, "my new favorite player. Got to like the man that helps me get my dick sucked."

Oh, my God, he acted like he won some lottery or something. I've got to say, seeing Braxton so excited had my heart beating out of my chest. He has no idea how much pleasing him pleases me. Knowing I am good enough to for a man like Braxton means everything to me.

I went to bed with a smile on my face and Braxton went to bed satisfied.

Liam and Kara were like two horny teenagers, swear to God. I think Kara was panty-less by the end of the game. Thankfully, she had a very long shirt on that covered her ass. Life was good, fantastic company, excellent food, and I had a hot sexy man by my side. I passed out between the soft kisses and the sweet nothings Braxton whispered in my ear. Panty melting and heart pounding, if I were not so worn out from my man's loving, it would have kept me up. I swear my heartbeat races with each sound of his voice.

Today, Braxton phoned to let me know he was working late. A new customer at the shop was bringing in a couple of the higher end cars for him to fix. He was excited because it was going to bring in some serious cash. Liam was hanging around more because Tiffany was becoming a permanent fixture. This bitch was becoming a bigger and more irritating pain in my ass! I swear, if I didn't know any better, I'd say she was in major cock-block mode. My rabbit and I have reacquainted ourselves with each other a lot as of late because her presence alone is putting up some walls between Braxton and me. We both avoid the topic of her when we are together, but in doing so, the tension is beyond awkward.

Kara stayed at my house while I worked my shifts at the Pub. The nights I worked late, she came in and sat at a table talking with Sam, or Liam, who would make an appearance and drink with her. The two made a great couple, all cute eyes and sweet laughs between them. Watching them for the past few nights, I noticed the gentle caresses of their touches. With stolen kisses here and there, they laughed and carried on like they had not a care in the world. It made me envious and sad. I wanted that. I wanted a carefree life with a man who showered me with kisses and spent all his free time holding my hand. I thought I would have all of that with Braxton but it seems like Tiffany has all of his attention these days. Seems that bitch has everyone's attention.

Braxton's daily calls to me have dwindled over the past few days. It's either he is busy, or he is trying to figure out what Tiffany is up to. And at the end of the day, he is spending time with Eve. How can I complain about him spending time at work or with his daughter? It's the time he spends with Tiffany that gets under my skin. The more time he spends with her, the less time I get to spend with him. She wants time to remind him of the good times they had. Trifling trick!

Having time off from work, I decide I am going to go and surprise Braxton at the shop. I can't stay long, but I need to see him. I miss the hell out of him. I miss the way he looks at me, the way he kisses me, and the way he just melts my insides when he smiles at me. Jesus!

Pulling into the parking lot, I find it to be pretty empty. Not many bikes or cars around. I do, however, see two very flashy red sports cars in the customer parking area. *WOW*. Those must be the cars Braxton is fixing for his new client. Damn, after a closer look, I notice that they are Audi R8's. These cars are stunning when I see them up close and personal. I can't help but imagine what it would be like to drive one of these babies.

With a shake of my head, I skip up to the door. The idea of seeing those damn sexy eyes of Braxton's has my insides all twisted into knots. Opening the door I notice the lights are on, but the place is deserted. It wouldn't be so weird if it wasn't in the middle of the day. What the hell? Walking to the garage, I peer inside. It, too, is dimly lit and empty. Must be lunchtime, the guys tend to dim the lights when no one was in the shop. Just as I am about to head back to his office, I hear some soft voices.

Hearing a female voice, I instantly tense up. This bitch is here, again? She spends more time with Braxton than I do these days. I slump down by the wall near the door where the voices are coming from. I'm eavesdropping because I'm fucking angry and jealous. This bitch is the reason I don't see Braxton as much as I'd like anymore. With shaking hands, I take out my phone. After muting it, I decide to text Kara because I need some advice on how to handle this shit. My anxiety is at an all-time high, I'm dizzy and I feel like I'm going to throw up at any moment.

Izzy: Okay, at the shop hiding outside his office door. Tiffany is here with him. I can hear her sick voice all sweet and cunning. WHAT THE HELL DO I DO?

Seconds later:

Kara: Slap the BITCH silly. No, seriously, barge in there and put her in her place. She is messing with YOUR MAN.

Shit, Kara....

Izzy: What the hell am I doing? I am spying on him like some school girl. He will be pissed if he finds me here, hiding out like some jealous bitch.

Kara: Come get me, I'LL kick her ass...Please ;-)

Izzy: Funny. LOL. I'll let you know. I should leave and call him later. Seems he is too busy with her to call me or come and see me. Sucks!

Kara: KICK HIS ASS. Better yet. I'LL KICK HIS ASS.

Laughing, I put my phone back in my purse and decide to leave. Before I can walk away, I hear soft voices coming from Braxton's office. The instant I hear *her* voice, my body stiffens and when I hear my name, my blood runs cold. Peering inside the slightly ajar door, her back may be facing me, but her words I can make out pretty clear.

"I mean it, I know all about her and she is bad news. My daddy helped me find out about her past. She fucking *killed* her brother! The guy she was with? He literally owns her and from what I heard, he's into some real sick shit. All the 'horrible' things he did to her, she wanted. The fucked up thing is, she got pregnant and told the guy she didn't want it. Even after she found out she was having a girl, she still called it an 'it.' Can you believe that shit? She had a daughter that she never wanted, and she calls *me* a worthless mother! Isn't *that* the pot calling the kettle black!

The way she's twisting and spitting out lies about me sounds so vile and disgusting. Shit, if I didn't know who she was talking about, I wouldn't like me, either. Listening to her lie about me just about kills me. I'm finding it hard to breathe and my chest feels like it's caving. What does Braxton think about me? Does he believe her? Will he listen to me when I try to tell him the truth? Does it even matter anymore?! I'm gasping for air, as the tears stream down my face. I can't even hear words anymore, all I hear is his muffled voice but that bitch just keeps talking. I clamp my hand over my mouth so I don't make any noise. I don't want them to know I've been out here, listening.

This fucking bitch just keeps talking. "Dominic, the man that claims her or what the fuck ever it is, had to take the baby so she wouldn't hurt her. I still can't believe she killed her own brother! All he wanted to do was get her help, but she refused. Her family won't have anything to do with her. Her father told Dominic to take her. What a fucking mess."

Oh no, no, no she has it all wrong!

It's the clearing of Braxton's throat that causes my heart to stop.

"How the fuck did you find all of this out? How do you know you can trust this dick? For all I know, he is telling you this to make me turn against her." Braxton's voice is void of any emotion.

Tiffany tries to hush him. "Baby, I talked to my uncle. He knows this Dominic guy and told me straight up, if Dominic is saying this shit about her, then it could to be true, and you should steer clear. I did this for you, Brax."

Feeling more confident in her words and wielding them like a dagger, she goes in for the kill. When she starts leaking again, I try and brace myself for the blow that I know is about to come.

"He's done so much to help her, makes him look like some kind of saint. Even though he was providing her with all that she needed, she didn't want it. It seems she has some sort of metal breakdown and left."

That's all I need to hear. *What the fuck?* Lies! All fucking lies! She found Dominic and he brainwashed the bitch into believing I'm some sick, twisted druggie. How the hell did he get to her?

Wait. Willow. How does she know about my daughter? Willow was literally snatched from my arms when I refused to sleep with him. He made me pay the ultimate sacrifice. My little girl was stolen from me and this bitch is saying I'm the one who's fucked up? Oh god, too much. I can't live through this shit again. He always wins. Fucker made sure I can never have any more kids. Whatever he had that doctor do to me, I'll never know. The truth is, in itself, some distorted lie. I'm drowning once again, my chest aches. I can't breathe; the walls are collapsing down on me. What the fuck? I need to get the hell out of here. I can't...I can't deal with this.

Heavy tears are now flowing, and I can't believe the train wreck of my past has collided with my present. I should have known Dominic would find me. He has ruined me, forever.

I brush my legs off; once I can stand up straight. I stumble down the hall toward the door to my car. My mind; I have no answer for what my mind is thinking. The one thing I did catch was, my daughter was still alive. How the hell? I never knew if she was alive or not. Dominic was the ultimate game player messing with my mind too many times to count, it was just better to die on the inside. No feelings meant I could no longer feel hurt. My heart has been broken so many times at the hands of Dominic that it's a wonder I am sane.

My sobs give way to more tears as I stumble to my car like a zombie. I'm so distraught I don't even register Liam, who is running my way.

"Wow, what the hell is going on sweetheart?" His eyes travel over my face and body for any signs as to what the hell is going on.

Shaking my head, my fingers touch my parted lips. "It's over. It's over. It's over." I just keep saying it over and again. My gaze lingers not focusing on anything. I can't even concentrate on Liam's worried expression.

"Honey, you're scaring me." Pulling me in for a much-needed hug, he rubs my back as if to comfort me.

My uncontrolled shivering has my body silently begging for help. In an attempt to hold back my whimpers, my fingernails grip his back tighter as I have difficulty thinking rationally. "Liam, I need to go, I have to get out of here." My words are barely audible as I begin to hyperventilate. If he only knew these words meant more than just leave the parking lot, they say I need to move away from here.

Liam is looking at me, blinking his eyes quickly like he's confused. "Izzy Girl, slowly tell me what is going on? Are you okay? Is Kara okay? Where the fuck is Brax?" He looks around the parking lot like he expects Braxton to appear.

Weak in the legs, I have a sudden need to sit down. I'm numb as indecisiveness over take my mind. "Don't know, don't care; doesn't matter, not now. Not ever again." My arms limp because I don't have the strength to hang on to him anymore. My heart is aching for me to fix this. Fix what damage Tiffany has created. To tell Braxton the truth, but the truth comes at a price. I could do all of this but Dominic is still coming for me. I'm sure of this. Tiffany is still going to be around, and with Dominic and Tiffany around, there will *never* be an Izzy and Braxton.

"Lies. She told Braxton all the lies that Dominic wanted her to say. The bastard found me, used your sister to spread the knockout punch to Braxton. How fucking dumb am I? Did I honestly believe I could live any life away from Dominic? Maybe? And maybe I just hoped I would be able to live a life on my own. Find a path that I could be proud of because my life the last several years did not leave me much to be proud. But being here, I found friends and a purpose. I felt the best I had felt in years and found a man worth fighting for." Leaning over with my hands on my knees, I shake my head repeatedly. My fate revolves around a bunch of lies.

"Talk some sense to me Izzy, what the hell is going on?" Liam is spouting inane and irrational thoughts about his sister. Backing away with raised hands, he keeps looking over his shoulder like he is looking for Braxton to come running.

Trying to forget my past and the feeling that I deserve to be judged, my voice loses its courage. "Somehow Tiffany found Dominic. I just got to listen in to her rejoicing in telling Braxton all about it; her version of course or should I say, Dominic's. He won't talk to me after that load of crap." The knot in my belly makes me nauseous and my eyes feel like a swollen mess.

Liam sighs swearing under his breath. "Izzy, he won't believe what my sister tells him, sweetheart. He knows better."

I pinch the bridge of my nose knowing Liam is only trying to console me, but I just don't buy it. "It doesn't matter." I pull my gaze to his concerned eyes, "Not anymore. The damage is done."

"The hell if it doesn't. You are not letting this fucker and my sister do this to the two of you. You hear me, Izzy? I'm serious."

Pulling out his phone, I assume Liam is calling Braxton. I grab for it, but it's no use.

"Liam put the phone away. From the scene I just walked in on, I've already lost him. I can see the writing on the wall. She won and got what she wanted, so just let it go." I tell him as I unlock my car door. As I try to escape he pulls me and stands in between me and the door, effectively stopping me from closing it.

He then leans down, nose flaring with anger and says, "Izzy, you listen to me and hear me well. I fucking know my sister, and I also know my best friend. Brax does not want the bitch. She is trying her damnedest to get her claws into him but honey, she won't do it." The struggle I see in him makes this even harder. After all, we are talking about his sister.

"Sweet Liam, this is too much shit to set straight. Take care of him for me and take care of your niece. God help her with a moth..., never mind." I was going to say mother but shit, she is still his sister.

I try to start my car but Liam is not moving. When he started fumbling with his phone, I should have known what he was doing. Not two seconds later, who comes strolling out of the door is Braxton with a skimpily dressed Tiffany. My stomach rolled at the sight, but I could not contain it. I leaned on the door and tossed my cookies. This day just gets better and better.

"Izzy?" He appears shocked to see me. With his eyes wide, he strides over to us.

I recoil at the sharpness coming from Braxton, shit the bitch got to him. She must be so fucking proud of herself.

Liam's body goes rigid as he starts to verbalizing his disappointment in a infuriated looking Braxton. "What the fuck, buddy? Jesus, I found her coming out of the goddamn shop white as a fucking ghost and by the looks of you two, I can see why. Are you this goddamned stupid? Listening to my sister's bullshit?" He yells, pointing a finger at his evil, smiling sister.

"Shut the hell up brother! Brax needed to know the truth about his low-life whore." She says while running up behind Braxton. Looking at them side-by-side hurts like hell. They make a stunning couple standing there. *What the hell?*

I throw up again then look up to see Braxton eyeing me with such an intense glare. Chills run down my spine and I gag yet again.

With a strong hand pressed across Braxton's chest, Liam is stopping him from advancing to me.

"Liam, get away from Izzy, I need a word with her." Braxton's words are so cold, not one ounce of empathy in them.

"*First*, why don't you tell me what's my sister been telling you?"

"Not your concern Liam, why are you protecting her?" They are both chest to chest, like two pissing bulls.

"Are you fucking serious right now?! You let that bitch get her claws into you while your girl is listening outside your damn door. It seems my sister was telling you all sorts of bullshit to make your girl look bad." Liam says while puffing out his chest toward Braxton. I have no idea who would win in a showdown between these two because Liam, may be slightly taller, but Braxton is more muscular.

"Whatever. You have no idea what you're talking about. Izzy wasn't in there." Braxton sounds so sure of himself. *Oh my God, does he think I have no idea what he was doing with her.*

I hold my head up and try to stand but my protector, Liam, is not moving a muscle. Struggling to stand next to him, I dare a pained look at Braxton.

In an emotion filled voice, I say, "I was in there and was about to come into your office when I heard you both. I happened to see her sitting on your desk facing you. I then overheard a twisted rundown of my screwed up life." I'm wildly shaking my head side to side. "The icing on the cake was how fucking backwards she had my story. I got to tell you, I pictured this day going a lot better than it has." I'm rocking in place and trembling while I face them with tears that refuse to stop. I have nothing else to lose, so I have to know.

"How did you do it, how did you find, Dominic?" I don't yell or scream at her, I just only ask her.

Always one for being dramatic, she has one hand on her hip and the other resting on Braxton's shoulder. I want to poke her eyeballs out.

"Oh, little Izzabella…"

Oh hell no! "*No one calls me Izzabella!* not anymore," I yell, cutting her off.

"Seems like your man, Dominic, does." She is enjoying this.

I look over at Braxton, who has a face made of stone. Liam has his arms crossed over his chest. When he notices my body shaking, Liam hooks an arm around me and pulls me closer to him. I look at him almost shocked. I'm speechless, taking in the scene before me. The man with a sister who is ruining my life has his arm around me, protecting me. My Braxton, or so I thought was my man, is standing next to the other man's sister, her arm around his shoulder, like she is protecting him. Yep, this is not only awkward, it's uncomfortable.

I shake my head at her knowing what she has done. "You have no fucking clue what you have done, what life sentence you have handed me. Answer my question first, how did you find him?" I ask this time with more intensity.

"Lost Souls, ring a bell?" Tiffany says confidently.

Of course, it does.

"The fuck you say?" Braxton says puzzled looking at her disgustedly.

Liam's hold on me turns slightly painful. *Ouch!*

"What the fuck, Tiffany? What have you done?" Liam barely gets the words out before he is seething mad, and his body starts to shake uncontrollably.

"Uncle Marty is a member of the Lost Souls MC. I asked daddy to help me, and he turned to Uncle Marty. Come to find out, it didn't take much to find some things out about Little Miss Happy Pants. It was just luck this Dominic happened to be a 'Lost Soul', himself. By the sounds of it I did you all a favor, this girl is all sorts of messed up." Her witty comments match her mischievous twinkle in her eyes.

I say nothing, I am just connecting all of the dots. Braxton's watching me with a close and uncomfortable eye but has yet to say anything.

I have nothing left, so I let her know what she has done to me. "Do you understand he will most likely kill me? The shit you said earlier, it was all lies. You got it all twisted up. Some of what you said had some truth, but it was the other way around. Dominic hurt me so many times I lost count years ago. Yes, I have a daughter. He took her out of my goddamned arms to teach me a fucking lesson about what would happen to me if I tried to leave him again. He killed my brother in front of me to prove another point." I am hoarse, exhausted and just want to disappear. If going to the authorities would help me, I would have gone years ago, but there is no escaping Dominic. I realize that now more than ever.

I look over at the silent Braxton and still, he says nothing. It pisses me off.

"*Say something!* Don't stand there just looking at me like you don't know me. You fucking know me."

Braxton just closes his eyes shutting out the world. He pauses taking several deep breaths. When he opens his eyes, they are brimming with tears. "I'm not sure. A *daughter,* Izzy? *Do I know you? What else are you hiding?*"

That question cut me so deep, I doubled over with grief. I let out such a loud cry because, once again, I feel like I've lost everything. There is only so much a person can take before they break.

Weeping, I struggle to find the right words. "You bastard. I never took you for a coward or thought you'd be so damn gullible you would believe her over me. I guess I never knew you, either." My gaze leaves his eyes, they tell me nothing. I wanted to see fear or hurt or something. Instead, the only thing I see is cold, piercing, lifeless brown eyes.

Not being able to stay quiet any longer, Liam loses it, shouting, "Brax, don't be a dick! Izzy, told you about this guy!"

"Did she? She seems to have left out an important part of the story. The part where she had a daughter. If I knew her, I would have known she had a little girl. What else don't I know?" His words are cunning and void of any emotion as they pierce my heart.

I'm wallowing in hurt and despair, gasping four an ounce of courage. "What in God's name would you have wanted me to say? We were just getting to know each other! She is a part of me buried down deep. In time I would have told you, but not while we were just getting to know one another." Feeling defeated and rejected, I say, "Have you forgotten we have been knee deep in all things Tiffany lately?"

Frustrated, Braxton throws his hands up. "Izzy, she is the mother of my daughter."

Is he really defending her to me? Well, that pretty much says it all. "I see." Rubbing my eyes, I wipe away at my continued tears. I have no fight left in me. Nodding, I say, "It's a good thing she is here with you and you are getting away from me then." I struggle against Liam to get in my car. He is shouting at Braxton, asking if he has lost his fucking mind. Blonde Barbie, known as "Tiffany the bitch," is smiling from ear to ear as she tries to console a conflicted looking Braxton. The awkward way he is standing saddens me. It's not a stance you would typically see. His shoulders are slouched forward, and his arms are drawn back as if protecting himself. Seeing him like this hurts, and for a split second I suspend my anger. His confusion only terrifies me. It terrifies me to a point that I should be angry. He should have believed *me*. He should be pissed off at *her*. Instead, here I am standing here watching Liam defend me.

Turning away, I give Liam a hug after he made me promise to take care of myself. He wants me to call him at the first sign of any trouble. That's not likely to happen, but whatever. He explained he would stop by my place later and I let a chuckle slip out. God, I hope I am long gone before that happens.

I stop and glance one last time over my shoulder as I drive away. Liam and Tiffany are in some standoff, screaming at each other. Braxton is off to the side with his phone in his hand, but his eyes are directed at me. His loose posture and dark stare are breaking my heart. I hold his gaze, wanting to remember every detail of him. It's not his incredibly good looks that I'll remember the most though, it's his killer smile that I will miss every day.

"I love you." I mouth the words before our gaze is broken and I drive away from him for good.

chapter FIFTEEN

I HAVE NO IDEA HOW the hell I made it back to my house. Kara is going to go bat shit crazy when she hears about what happened. Pulling into my driveway, Kara is running down the path.

"Jesus Christ, Izzy! Liam called me and gave me low down of that shit-storm you just left. He is worried sick about you. It seems Brax got his ass handed to him. He told me he got a few good shots in before he had to deal with his bitch of a sister. Witch took off after some phone call. Liam is coming over as soon as he can."

She keeps rattling off, without stopping to take a breath, about how disappointed she is in Brax. I'm standing, frozen to my spot, staring back at her. I'm at a loss for words.

Reaching out, I hug her while looking into her worried eyes for a minute longer. I was going to lose it for sure. "Kara, we need to get the hell out of here. If Dominic is here, well, we need to leave." My throat is sore from all of the pleading and crying and I can't ignore my fear. "He will kill me, or worse, he will torture me, Kara. Either way, I am going to die." Her shaking head in denial turns into hugging me so damn tight, I can't breathe.

"That bastard won't touch you. Liam and I have been talking over the past few days. We have a plan, and it's going to work." I can tell by the strain in her voice she is worried, and she should be. Dominic is not a man to double cross, and that is exactly what I've done.

I'm curious because I had no idea she and Liam were talking about her brother. She hates him as much as I do, but I am still shocked at how involved they are in planning my own escape.

"Come on in the house so we can talk. We don't want to be out in the open any longer than necessary. I don't have a clue where my brother is, and I sure as fuck don't want to find out." She looks around as she hurries me to the front door of my house.

Walking up to the house, I notice a man on a motorcycle around the corner, sitting there observing us. I hold back my scream as my heart is racing, but then I sense something familiar about him. Keeping my eyes trained on him, I slowly stop to get my best friend's attention.

"Kara? Who is the guy on the bike watching us?" Slightly scared and nervous, I point in his direction.

She sighs lowering her voice to a whisper. "Braxton and Liam have some guys watching us, just to make sure. It seems like Liam and his biker buddies are helping Brax with taking care of his girl." I can see her body tense as she calls me Braxton's girl.

"I'm sure he doesn't consider me his girl, any longer. You didn't see the way he looked at me. Tiffany painted a pretty convincing picture, and I got to tell you, I was disgusted with myself when it was all said and done. He believed her over me."

Not agreeing a word I just spoke, she held up her hand. "Hey, that is not what I understand. It seems like Liam got to him and set his ass straight. Brax has his head on straight now. As long as you and I are safe, I don't give a shit. Might sound harsh because I know you love his hot body, but honey our safety is more important and you know it. We can deal with your love fest later. Then I can kick the bitch's ass for bringing all of this shit on us." Her anger and frustration mask the worry lines that stretch across her face.

I let out a loud breath. "I lost him and you're right, I can't deal with all of this right now. I need to watch my back before I am no longer around to watch my back." That thought alone sends shivers down my spine.

Sitting inside, Kara begins telling me her and Liam's plan, and it sucks. They have no clue just how evil Dominic can be. They have never had to outsmart the man like I have.

"This will work, we just need to flush him out and then take him out. Simple." *What?* This plan of theirs not only won't work, it is just plain stupid, not to mention dangerous.

No longer able to sit still, I get up to go pack up my stuff. I know what I need to do, leave this town and run as fast as I can. No clue where, just need to leave.

My phone rings.

Oh, shit. Not now, Braxton!

My stomach rolls and I stop breathing.

What the hell does he want to say to me now?

I'm not going to find out. I can't deal with him yelling at me or worse.

I decline the call and proceed to my room.

It rings once again.

I push the 'Decline Call' button.

It rings yet again!

I push Decline, yet again.

I'm aggravated because this goes on a few more times and just when I am about to shut the damn thing off, it rings again and in a moment of frustration, I answer it.

"HELLO. What the hell do you want, Braxton?"

Silence.

Oh God, I don't have time for this bullshit, and I sure don't need to be yelled at by him. I should be hurt and pissed when it comes to him. Then again, I want nothing more than to hear his voice, a double edge sword.

"Brax..."

"Hello, Izzabella..." The dangerous tone to his voice is like hearing the devil call out your name.

After hearing his voice, I can suddenly hear the sound of my heartbeat beating in my ears. And I drop my phone holding back my scream.

Oh shit, oh shit, oh shit.

My mind is a jumbled mess.

How...Wait... The caller ID showed Braxton's name.

I scramble to pick my phone up, but Kara comes barging in my room with her phone to her ear. She mouths to me she has Liam on the line. I look at my phone in my hand as I start to cry and scream bloody murder.

"Liam, what the fuck is going on?" Showing her frustration as she blows the hair from her face, saying, "No, she dropped her phone and looked like she is about to pass out." She is talking to Liam, but her eyes are dead set on me.

I am mouthing her brother's name in silence, just moving my lips. She understands me as she leans over to follow my gaze to my phone on the floor.

Looking down at the caller ID, she sees Braxton's name is on the screen, and then she understood my silent word of her brother's name. Cocking her head to the side, I can see the moment it registers with her.

"Oh, fuck me," Kara asks deadpan, "Liam, where the hell is Brax?"

Chapter Sixteen

LIAM IS SHOUTING AT BOTH of us. Well, he's not really shouting at us, but the man is beyond furious. Once we'd gathered that Dominic had Braxton's phone, it took no time to realize that none of us has any idea where Braxton is.

Liam is pacing my living room with some men I now know belong to his motorcycle club. I had always known Liam had some association with an MC, but what I had not known, was Braxton was a full member at one time. He still had his cut, but it seemed he was not an active member, (whatever that meant). Maybe the situation with Tiffany and Eve had pulled him away from the MC life. But Liam looks like he is very active in the club and I presently have several members in my living room trying to come up with a plan to find Braxton. 'Once a brother, always a brother' I have been told.

Sitting, wide-eyed and anxiously biting my lower lip, I nervously glance at the badass looking men who are planning a military-style rescue mission. I learned that Liam has eyes all across the town on the look-out for Braxton. A flurry of activity is happening since Liam had just received a call from one of his men, who recently spotted something out of the ordinary at a nearby hotel and storage area. I'm listening, desperate for any news about Braxton, even though there is a possibility he no longer cares about me. Braxton shouldn't be in this mess and he sure as hell does not deserve whatever is happening right now at the hands of Dominic. Dominic has some inches on Braxton, but Braxton has a lot more muscle. It's the way Dominic tortures people that has me terrified, even for a man the size of Braxton.

The thought of him being hurt because of me makes me feel damn near as violent. I'm hypersensitive to any bump or noise around me as I desperately wait for any news. But as my thoughts drift off to the man I've grown to care about, I lose all sense of my surroundings. It's most likely why I don't hear a single word Liam is saying to me. Eventually, he lowers his body until my eyes focus on his. He continually calls out my name until I answer him.

"What?" I whisper.

"We might have located him. It looks like your sick fucker has about four men with him. We are moving out soon."

No compassion in his words, only coldness, a bit of worry and a pinch of disgust. Most likely all directed toward me. I deserve his distaste and even his hatred at this point. I merely nod.

With a determined look, I say, "I'm coming with you."

Liam's head snaps at me with a look that is nothing short of threatening. "Like hell. Until we can figure this shit out you are staying the fuck put! I will have Zeke and Matt stay with you." He directs his eyes at them. Zeke is a tall man who just naturally scares the shit out of me. His bald head sports a bandana; he's wearing a white t-shirt, worn out black jeans with signature black biker boots. His stare is grim and deadly. Matt is shorter than Zeke and in all reality he does not look like he belongs in a biker club. He has such a baby face, it's hard to imagine him being anything but a teddy bear. Matt's longer brown hair lands on his shoulders and his eyes are a bright sparkling blue. As both men survey me and Kara, I can tell babysitting us was not high on their 'to-do' list. Honest to God, Kara seems oblivious to the seriousness of the situation. She's walking around, chatting with all the guys, as if it's some reunion.

Liam's about at the end of his rope, rolling his eyes in response to getting an earful how Matt wants to be a part of the rescue mission, not the babysitting mission. Both men wanted to help and go get Braxton back. Their loyalty was fierce and part of me was happy hearing it. They wanted Braxton safe as much as I do.

Agreeing with them, I interrupt their conversation. "Let them go with you, Liam. Braxton needs everyone he can get to get him home safely. Don't worry about me. If it weren't for me, none of this would be happening." My voice cracks as my ugly tears once again come to life. Guilt can be such a bitch.

Liam discounts my argument by ignoring me and continuing to make their plans. Kara and I resolve ourselves to sitting on the couch and trying to keep our shit together. Just then, a loud crash comes from outside my front door. I jump out of my seat as Kara screams and stands in a protective stance in front of me.

Liam has a gun pointed at the front door while Matt and Travis run straight to the back. Dex and Zeke stay behind to back up Liam if need be. The very idea of Dominic outside of my door has me damn near hyperventilating.

I let out a scream when I hear the front door opening. Just then Braxton comes struggling through my front door, disheveled and bloody. He looks like he went nine rounds and came out on the losing end. He stumbles right into Liam and I run over, desperately trying to comfort him. Not thinking if he would even want to see me, I run and crush him into my arms.

"Braxton. Braxton, oh my God, are you okay?"

After a few seconds: nothing.

"He's not talking, what the fuck? Liam, help." I am trying to hold Braxton up, but soon find myself on the floor with him haphazardly in my lap. He looks gray and lifeless and his breathing seem shallow. I gasp and stifle back the lump in my throat.

"Brax, buddy talk to me," Liam is gently shaking Braxton's shoulders. "Jesus Christ. Brax, speak to me, man." Braxton has yet to respond and his eyes are half closed, looking glossed over. We stretch Braxton out between our two bodies, as we kneel on the floor. Everyone else is hovering around us, quiet as mice.

Little bursts of breath suddenly escape his mouth. And it seems he is struggling to tell us something. Holding my breath, I'm leaning closer so my ear is next to his lips. I'm waiting to hear that he is okay, although he looks anything but okay.

Braxton's focus slowly returns and with a shaky bloody hand, he tries to reach my face. I instantly place my hand over his. The feel of his touch almost stops my heart and instantly comforts my weeping. I ache to feel him, and the mere act of him reaching out to me means everything. I can sense it's taken all of his strength to do this. In my desperate attempt to let him know he means so much to me, I continue to support his hand holding it to my cheek. I know he is my strength, and right now I am his. His brown eyes fully focus on mine now, and I feel my tears stream down my face. I'm seeking the beauty behind all of the bruises and blood that covers his angelic face. Honestly, Braxton's beauty shines through. Blood, bruises, and all.

My eyes actively search for answers. "Baby, are you okay? Braxton, tell me what happened?" My pleas are hard for Braxton to hear because Liam is also questioning him non-stop rather loudly.

He responds with a faint nod of his head and a few rapid blinks of his swollen eyes. His tongue darts out to wet his dry, cracked lips that have two very deep cuts on them. *God, what the hell happened to him?*

Liam's body is rigid, and if he's not on the phone, he is barking orders at the guys here in the house.

Moaning with a hefty sigh, Braxton whispers, "He had a message for me. If I gave you up, he wouldn't lay a finger on me." He stops speaking while holding his left side, wincing in obvious pain.

"He... He did not like my response, so he let me have it. It took all four of them to get the better of me."

Each word's a struggle, each breath painful. It's hard to see him like this. My beautiful, strong Braxton lying beaten like as he is, is just not right. It's seven shades of fucked up, and all my fault. Not being able to stop myself, I lean down and kiss his forehead.

With each tear rolling down my cheeks, I whisper my regrets to him. "I'm so sorry, Braxton. I feel so awful this happened, and it's my fault. Oh God, Braxton, please forgive me?" Rocking him back and forth in my arms, I keep repeating my apologies but they will never be enough.

Liam takes over the conversation, trying to get all of the particulars out of him. Dex called their doctor who takes care of the guys if they get hurt. Little did I know a woman would show up to take my man's clothes off. I was jealous at first, until I see the battered bruises that cover his body. Once I see them, a sick calmness settles over me. I realize what I need to do, I have to find him. I have to end this. I need to see Dominic. It's not going to be easy to get away from Liam and his band of brothers, but I have to.

Braxton is lying down on my couch, all wrapped up and sedated for comfort. Lana told Liam the extent of his injuries; lots of cuts, bruises, a few broken ribs and a hell of a knot on the side of his head. Hopefully, he does not have a concussion.

Seven or eight men are in my house, all sprawled out here and there. Kara and I end up in my room, trying to get some rest so they can figure out what to do next. No one has heard from Dominic. We did happen to find out where they had taken Braxton and how many men Dominic had with him.

Braxton was not able to fully comprehend and explain what the plan was. Liam is hoping tomorrow morning Braxton will feel better to be able to give him more information. Before long my exhaustion takes over, and I drift off.

I wake up to the sound of my phone sometime later. Sitting up, I notice I am alone. Kara is no longer with me. Most likely, she is with Liam. Rubbing my eyes, I try to figure out what number it is. Not recognizing it, I answer it…stupidly.

"Izzabella." Dominic's voice is cold and scary.

My face drains of all its color, I'm lightheaded and nauseous. Tensing up, I know I have to deal with him. One way or another, I need to fix this mess.

With an ache in my heart, the tears well in my eyes. "Dominic. Where the hell are you?" His sarcastic laugh has me playing out worst-case scenarios in my head.

"Are you ready to end this and come home now? It seems that Brax got an idea of what I would do if I did not get you back."

I hate the fact he is talking so smooth and confident. I get chills because I know he has other tricks up his sleeve. He always does.

"Dammit, Dominic. Why did you hurt him? I'm the one you want, not him." I stand with nervous energy.

Cutting me off, he is outraged and lowers his voice, sounding more evil than ever. "That's precisely right; you are what I want. That man, *Brax*, got that message last night. I told him you belong to me and what was going to happen to him if you are not in my arms and back at our GODDAMN HOME!" His shouting proves his frustration and anger are getting the better of him. Normally, Dominic is cool, no matter what. *What is he talking about now?*

"What do you mean, what you would do?" My anger and frustration are getting the better of me.

Very calmly, he asks, "Is he with you now, Izzabella?"

This time when he speaks, it's like a shiver going down my spine and a spike to my heart. The coldness with what he is implying causes me to pause before I answer him. I cry out not able to contain it a minute longer.

"Yes. Why?" It's all I can get out without gasping.

Dominic's laugh is puzzling. "Izzabella, where is his daughter? Once we took him last night, he was with us until he stumbled through your front door. I know he spent the night on your couch, and he is still there. I will ask again, where is his daughter?"

With ice is running through my veins, I jump up and run to the living room. Liam, Dex, and Zeke dash out of their seats as I enter the room with crazed eyes. I notice Braxton is still out cold and don't even react to Kara's questions as I yell over her shoulder to Liam.

"Where the hell is Eve?" The anxiousness in my voice is apparent.

Liam notices me on the phone and puts two and two together. Taking out his phone, he starts pressing numbers. He is pacing the room as his anxiety increases with every ring of his phone.

A heavy sigh escapes his lips. "Tiff, you still got Eve? Listen bitch, I am not playing here. Do. You. Still. Have. Eve?"

I can hear her raising her voice, but have no clue what she is saying. Liam's eyes find mine, nodding his head as if to answer my question.

Satisfied with the fact the Tiffany has Eve, I clench my teeth. How dare he even breathe that sweet girl's name? With a carefully controlled tone I say, "Dominic she is with her mother, why are you even asking me this?" Not having a clue what his game is with Eve.

"Oh yes, Tiffany. Bitch has a mouth on her, but she's not my type at all. She is fake as they come, including her body parts."

I would laugh because I for once agree with him, but this is no laughing matter.

Momentarily pausing, he then continues as if completing his thought. "Back to my point, do you know where Tiffany and the girl are right fucking now, Izzabella?"

He frustrates me so much, I might pull my hair out. "No," I say, sighing deeply, "I don't know where they are. Why are you asking me this, you crazy asshole?"

"Tsk, tsk, tsk Izzabella. You never swore at me, you knew better. A few months with this asshole and all of a sudden, you think it is okay to swear at me? You fucking know better." Gone is his laughter and once again the cold, calculated monster returns.

"What the fuck is going on?" All eyes swing over to the couch. A worn out looking Braxton is trying to hold himself up against the back of the sofa, wincing with pain.

The look of concern on his face knocks out what little breath I had in my lungs. He looks slightly more like himself this morning but still battered and bruised. "Oh Brax." It comes out a muttered sigh and it's all I can get out before clamping my mouth shut with my hand. I want to say more, feel more, but I can't. One minute, I'm speechless as I gaze into his amazingly warm brown eyes. Only seconds later, I remember I have the devil on the phone. Dominic's voice shakes me to my core with panic as I slowly put the phone back to my ear. My eyes slowly return to Braxton's face, and all I can see is bruises. Those bruises and Dominic's voice push me over the edge.

Dominic's voice is full of sarcasm. "Oh, sleeping beauty is waking up, I hear."

Hearing his voice is like needles pricking my spine, and I lose it, snapping, "Shut the hell up, you insensitive prick! You will never hurt anyone I love again! Do you hear me, Dominic?" I'm so tired and beat down when it comes to Dominic. Just call me delusional to think I ever could get free of him. I have lost everything at the hands of this man, but he won't hurt anyone else. Not because of me. It seems I'm talking to myself and the words escape my lips. "I just don't give a shit about me, not anymore."

Dominic is furious and is shouting into the phone. All of his threats aimed at me, only frighten me more knowing what awaits me if I'm in his possession once again. Drowning out his idle threats, I focus on Braxton, and the loving gaze he's giving me instantly calm me. All the traces of conflict that were on his face after his conversation with Tiffany have now disappeared. All I see is my sweet, compassionate Braxton.

Closing his eyes as if savoring the moment, he sweetly smiles. "You called me Brax. Guess we must be friends, huh?"

With every twitch, every breath, and every word he winces in pain. But he still finds it in him to smile, as we recall our conversation about me obsessing over calling him Braxton. Holding out his hand to me, I don't hesitate. I run over to him and kneel down in front of the sofa.

"Oh Braxton, so not the time for jokes," I say laying my head in his lap.

Lowering my gaze, I peer at the voice screaming at me from my phone. Dominic's voice leaves me open-mouthed, but no words escape. As panic grips me, I raise my eyes to look at Braxton's murderous stare. His face looks lethal as he holds out his hand for me to pass him the phone.

I shake my head in disagreement, because this fight is mine and mine alone. I take some breaths to gain some much needed courage. I know I'm failing to do so because tears are welling up in my eyes, yet again.

Hanging my head low against my chest, I surrender my regret and realize I will never let Dominic have his satisfaction when it comes to me. After a long exhale, I close my eyes and say to him. "You can go to hell. I will die before returning to you. Even if it means I blow my goddamn brains out myself. You'll never lay another finger on me."

I've never openly said such sadistic things and hearing myself say them, surprisingly I feel nothing.

When I'm done, I hand my phone over to Braxton. He gives me an agonizing look before a slight smile. The look alone tells me what I need to know. He believes me and he trusts me. Having him believe in me means everything. He is giving me the one thing my family never did: the benefit of the doubt. They handed me over to Dominic without a backward glance. Trust is hard to find in people but he trusts me, a virtual stranger.

Braxton is white knuckling the phone. "Listen to me you piece of shit, where are Tiffany and my daughter? Tiffany, you can have for all I fucking care. My daughter is a whole other story. Give me my goddamn daughter or you will fucking die. You hear what I'm saying?"

I can't hear Dominic's words, only muttered sounds. The whole room is watching Braxton's reactions to the stream of words being thrown at him. His expression is mixed; some serious, some humor, and the rest is; well, I'm not too damn sure.

Liam and Braxton share a look and Braxton nods his head, his way of communicating something. Having no idea what that is about, I just let it go.

We are all watching him and holding our breath as Braxton ends the call. Waiting for what he is going to say, we all gather a little closer. His look is clouded and distant. It's easy to see he is thinking and contemplating. That's what scares me.

"What an asshole." He says, shaking his head.

That's it. That's all he says. I hold out my hand as if saying 'well' and yet nothing.

Looking at the group of men surrounding him one by one, Braxton then drifts his gaze to me. His eyes start to squint as a hint of a smile pulls his lips apart. He pulls me up onto his lap the best he can.

"How the hell you ever got get mixed up with this dick, I will never know. But you will never go back to him again. You hear me, Iz?" He says as he kisses my head.

Holding onto his sweet kiss I have to ask, "What is going on with Tiffany and Eve?"

"Not for you to worry about, just know I got it covered. Fucker won't touch my daughter, now Tiff I couldn't care less. *She's* the reason he is here, not you. I am in the shape I am in because I cared about you and refused to give him what he wants. Which is you, sweetheart."

Closing my eyes, I have to shake my head to disagree. "No, this is all my fault. You will get Eve back, even if I have to take her place. I will go to him if he lets Eve come home unharmed."

"It won't come to that because right about now my daughter is being picked up." He says it like it's no big deal. *What the hell?*

Am I the only one who has no clue what is going on? "Why aren't you going bat shit crazy right now? You are too calm, so what gives?" I say, pulling away from him.

Blowing out a deep breath, he starts to say something, but Liam's phone rings first.

"Yo', give me good news," Liam answers eagerly. "Gotcha'. Thanks, man! Yes, seems all went according to plan." With an arm around Kara's shoulder Liam kisses her head. He nods his head in agreement to whatever was said to him on the other end of the phone. "Yep, my girl knows her brother well. I'll let Brax know, buddy. No, dumbass. He's not moving a muscle, fucker's got broken ribs." He says while looking at Braxton's wrapped body.

Shutting his phone, he grabs Kara and kisses the hell out of her in front of us all.

Squealing out a 'woo-hoo', he sets her down on her feet. "Got my niece back thanks to you, sweet cheeks."

Kara responds with a kiss on Liam's cheek. "Awesome. I'm so relieved because I know Izzy would have traded herself for Eve. That can't happen, she can never go back to my sick brother." She says with such sadness looking right at me. We share a mere smile.

"You all had a plan?" I say with a sigh. "Thank God, I was sweating bullets over here. *Good Lord*, where is Eve now?" I ask.

Braxton interrupts. "Liam I need to get my ass home, so I am there when my baby comes home. I want to try to look somewhat better before she sees me." Braxton says, attempting to get up from the couch. My eyes go wide watching him struggle.

"Here let me help you." The key word is *try* to help him up, because he is taller and outweighs my ass. Smiling, he struggles to stand but takes me with him enveloping me in his arms.

"Iz, give your man a kiss." He takes a deep breath, savoring the moment. "Getting my ass kicked for you hurt likes a bitch, got to be honest." He leans down and I stretch on my tiptoes until our lips meet.

The chemistry is so strong between us once our lips touch, it's like an electric current being unleashed. I put my arms around his neck, pulling him as close as I can. A slight moan escapes when my lips slide against his. I don't ever want to let him go, but there is such uncertainty between us. I finally pull away to break our connection because I need to see his eyes. I need something from them; I need to see that we are going to be okay. In this crazy world, I need some sort of stability.

Like he was reading my mind, Braxton sighs. "Don't worry sweetheart, you're not getting rid me. I know you got questions about that day with Tiffany. I always felt the truth deep down. When she told us she found that fucker I knew I had to tread carefully with her. The fact she went and did such a thing, let me know just how dangerous she really is. Most of what you saw was me speechless, staring at this stranger. This woman is Eve's mother, but at that moment, I had no clue who she was." His eyes lower at the same time my eyes are drawn to his hesitant sigh. "Not much I could do but sit back and listen to this unbelievable run down of your life. The idea she knew more about you than I did pissed me off." His calm words suddenly turn icy as his eyes raise back to mine. "I won't lie, hearing some of that was hard to hear, but I did not mean to intentionally hurt you. What you think you saw, you didn't. I had a lot to process at the moment and I didn't handle it well. I knew I had to hold back and not let my anger take over. That's what she was hoping for. It's what she wanted all along. I wasn't going to give it to her and it killed me to watch the look on your face." Taking my face in his hands, he kisses the tip of my nose.

"Never again, you and I are going to get this worked out. No more Tiffany, no more Dominic. Just you, me, and Eve, tell me you want that, too?" Those dang piercing brown eyes melt me into him.

Closing my eyes, I sob with the fact that's exactly what I want. "More than you will ever know." His lips press against mine and for now, I feel safe.

With a clear of his throat, Liam is eager. "Let's go man, got to clean your ass up before my niece gets an eye full." Cracking his knuckles, Liam exclaims, "I swear to God, if that fucker touches a hair on her head, he will die faster than he thinks."

Both men tell me they will see me later. I nod and watch Braxton hobble out of my front door. Zeke and Matt are to stay behind with Kara and me. Now that Braxton is safe, they seem more willing to stay and help guard us.

Keeping my eye on the men walking down the street to Braxton's house, I turn to look at my best friend. "Kara, what the hell is going to happen next? Dominic is not going to leave, he must have something else planned." I whisper so our bodyguards won't over hear me.

"Damn if I know. Once he figures out we have Eve, he might go crazy. These two guys are no match for my brother. That much I do know."

The lack of confidence in her words have me raising my eyebrows in total agreement with her. "Did Liam say anything to you? He just left with Braxton saying nothing. Something's off." Pulling her hand toward me, I ask, "Are you keeping anything from me?"

"Nope, I'm fresh out of ideas and Liam has not talked to me about anything new. Maybe you're being just a bit paranoid." She says, yanking on my hand so we end up in a hug.

Not ten minutes later, Zeke gets a phone call and informs us we are all going to Braxton's house.

Chapter Seventeen

THE STREET IS PEACEFUL AND DARK AND THE ONLY SOUNDS HEARD ARE OF THE CRICKETS AND NEARBY croaking frogs. At night, they serenade me to sleep. It's serene and most relaxing. The best thing about the 'Evergreen State,' is the overabundant evergreen trees that line the area behind our homes. It's a scene straight out of 'Twilight,' the most beautiful sight ever. I remember taking a hike recently at one of the state parks, the makeshift trail covered in moss led straight to one of the most breathtaking waterfalls I have ever seen. A perfect place to lose yourself in, or hide if you are trying to escape from someone. I found that idea to be ironic.

Slightly laughing to myself, I think *too bad I could not hike Dominic up the trail and drop him over the edge.* A sick thought I know but at the same time, a comforting idea. Not having to look over my shoulders would be a pleasant feeling. It's a feeling I have not had for a very long time.

We are walking behind Zeke and Matt. Not far behind, but enough so we could talk privately. Stopping to tie my shoe, I'm startled by a shooting pain down my spine, as my surroundings suddenly began to spin. The fading scream of Kara was all I heard, as two men subdued her. I caught a glimpse of Matt and Zeke doubled over on the ground as a cloth covered my nose and mouth. With that, my world went dark.

HOLDING MY HEAD, IT'S POUNDING like a jackhammer drilling in my skull, I grimace in pain. Jesus! Slowly opening my eyes, I quickly scan my surroundings but nothing looks familiar. The room is dark, and it resembles a hotel room. Realizing I am under the covers, I am shocked to find I'm only wearing my bra and panties. *WTF!*

Panicking, I sit up and look around the room for my clothes but I see nothing. No purse or phone, and no clothes. Slowly getting out of bed, I rummage around the room, looking in dresser drawers, I'm looking for a phone or even a weapon, anything to help me. The only light at the moment is the moonlight coming in through the window. It's slightly eerie because I have no idea how long I've been here. It's then that I feel arms wrap around me and I freeze!

Just then, he touches my hair and pulls my body to him. His smell, his hands, and his low, menacing voice leave me with a feeling of hopelessness. The way his hands roam my body, I know these hands belong to the one person I fear more than anything. I would rather die than be in this room alone with him. My eyes gripped with fear as Dominic's voice collapses any hope I had left. Here I am, half naked with his hands around my waist. As tears well in my eyes, I wish I were anywhere but here. It's times like these that I slowly close my eyes and silently leave my body.

"My sweet, sweet Izzabella, how I've missed you. Now I know what you are thinking. You are waiting for me to be mad and start yelling at you and are likely waiting for your punishment. You would be wise to remember those things, but..."

Turning inward, withdrawing myself with the way his familiar hands start at my throat and slowly move to caress every inch of my body, I stop breathing. It's vulgar and disgusting. His moans and excitement are as revolting as his erection that is rubbing my backside. I let my tears fall, let my silent screams yell to the moon. I have to be quiet because if I were to vocalize my distaste for him it would end much worse for me. I know because I've made that mistake too many times before. I've learned to swallow my horror and my pain so I can survive on the outside.

Holding my wrists, he spins me around so we are now face to face. Crushing my body against his, he digs his fingers painfully into my hips. Dominic was never one to be gentle, but oh my God, he is pressing so hard I know he will leave bruises, and that is exactly what he intends to do. He wants to leave his mark; it's a reminder of 'who I belong to.' Little does he know, only one man has my heart. Because he is the only man who has ever felt real to me. Braxton Ryles is one of a kind and I'm lucky to have had him in my life, no matter how short.

Dominic threads his hands through my hair as he not so gently winds them around the base of my neck. "You need to sleep for now, I got plans to make. Your Brax and his band of idiots are giving me some problems. Once they got his daughter from under my nose, well, let's just say as long as I got you, an eye for an eye, I guess. He has his daughter, and I have you. A win/win for everyone."

Yeah, his plan to scare me, is working.

"What's the plan? Where is Kara by the way?" I try to stare at the floor so I can escape looking into his death glare. It doesn't work because he takes his finger and tilts my chin toward him.

"Look at me when you want me to answer." His tone and eyes are cold. "Kara, I left in the front yard of that Brax fellow. Mikey roughed her up a bit, to make a statement of course. Now they know I mean business. They have what they wanted and now, so do I. If they are smart, they will leave well enough alone. If they try to find you, well, let's just say, you will pay that price." He takes his hand around the back of my neck and pulls me against him to aggressively put his lips to mine.

Holding my breath, I try to not feel anything, not to put any effort into the rough kiss. The only thing I can think of, is how vile and revolting he feels. I want to gag, but the moment he gets my lower lip in between his teeth, he bites down. I groan and cry, as it not only hurt, but the blood flooding my mouth disgusts me. Wanting nothing more than to vomit, I try to fight. I knew better, but this is just so wrong. I hate every minute his hands and mouth are on me. It's like a death sentence. My struggle and discomfort only excite this sicko. His hands go around my hips as he carries me to the bed, never losing contact, his larger frame traps me under his.

Pulling my legs apart with his knee I suddenly want to leave my body. I don't want this to happen. Sensing my hesitation, he pulls back and looks down at my trembling body. To subdue my arms, he pulls them over my head and holds them with his hands. Crushing his lower body into mine, he grinds his ever so present erection against my panty covered seam. Closing my eyes tight, I beg.

"Please! Please, Dominic. Don't do this. I'm begging you not to do this!" I know it most likely won't matter to him, but I will die trying.

"Ah, what's wrong, Izzabella? Now that you've had someone else, you no longer want me?" His words are surprisingly honest. Not expecting him to seem so human, I keep my eyes closed tight because a leopard does not change its spots.

Giving myself a mental pep talk, I whisper with desperation. "No, I don't want you. Ever again. You hurt me and you wanted to own me, and you have for so long. It took me some time to finally get enough courage to stand up to you, but once you took Willow from me, I stopped caring, so I stood up to you and got the hell away." I say these things to him with confidence because when it came to Dominic I never had much of it. If I did, I usually got punished for it.

With a gentle swipe of his finger, he pushes my hair to the side. "Izzabella, you losing Willow was your entire fault. If I am honest, I want you and her with me. I wanted to be what you wanted me to be, I just couldn't do it. A part of me, a big part of me, likes to hurt you. I get off on it for Christ's sake. I want to cut you so fucking bad right now, I ache for it. A small part of me knows it's wrong and there within lies my problem. My desires outweigh the rational part of me." A look of wonderment crosses his face as he sighs. "You see I have two different sides to me, like two separate people."

The only thing I can do is stare at his confession. Who the hell *is* this guy?

Holding out his right hand, he says, "This represents the good side of me," holding up his left hand, he continues, "this represents my other, less desirable side. You would say the evil side. They go to war, and the most domineering side always wins. The side you don't tend to like."

"Dominic, it sounds like a bi-polar issue to me. They have medicine for that, you know?"

He throws his head back, laughing. "You see? That is why I like you so much. Your sense of humor has always attracted me to you."

"Maybe, I should stop being so funny then," I say arching my eyebrow.

"Now that is also funny, Izzabella," taking a big breath, he ponders a moment. "You were always so sweet and your innocence took my breath away. From the first time I met you, I knew you were going to be mine."

I have to groan, he is more delusional than I thought. "One damn night turned into my fucking nightmare. You took an innocent girl and turned her into some sick obsession. My life ceased to exist the day you took me to your bed."

I can see the confusion on his face as worry lines crease his forehead. The distant look is as if he is lost in his own thoughts. In an instant, his expression changes. The crystal blues are back, and his expression goes from confused to crystal clear, cold and calculated.

He rolls himself, so he is over me again on the bed.

The sharp stab of the knife has me screaming out, the pain is excruciating, to the point I want to pass out. It's been some time since the last mark was placed on my body. Looking down the instant he moves his body, I can see the knife still in my thigh. I try to buck him off of me, but he is too strong. I get one of my legs free and as soon as I do I kick him in the crotch. My bad leg, still having the knife in it, is slightly bent but glued to the bed. The running, red streaks of blood mix with the white sheets. My aggressive kick has transformed Dominic into full fledge manic mode. The sadist has returned with a vengeance.

"I tried not to hurt you. It's you defying me that piss me off." His last word has him pulling the knife out of my thigh and stabs it right in my lower stomach. Son of a mother, this one is deeper and hurts like a bitch.

"STOP."

"STOP."

"STOP."

I cry out my mantra. The stinging and throbbing pain in my leg is one thing, the burning feeling, and the tearing of my flesh has me choking out a gurgling cry. Wincing, my body writhes under the pain coursing through my veins. The idea of him doing this to me again shatters any chance I had that I would make it out unscathed.

Holding my stomach and trying not to move my hurt leg too much, I lay in a pool of my bright red blood. The shock must be setting in because the pain is slowly fading. I can feel my breathing as it begins to slow down, and I want to give into the darkness. Just let it take me over and get me the hell away from this madman. A life without ever seeing Braxton kills me, but this life, a life trapped with Dominic, well that is no life at all. I would rather choose death.

He jumps off me and takes the knife with him, standing, he eyes his handy work and realizes he pushed the knife in my lower stomach too far. It's bleeding too much and doesn't look good. I am light headed and feeling sick. Dear God, just end this. Dying alone is the one thing no one wants. I should be scared shitless right about now, but I'm not, I'm surprisingly calm. Well, as calm as anyone can be with multiple stab wounds and bleeding profusely.

Running out the door, Dominic is calling his trusty patch up doctor. I have had my share of visits from him over the years. His name is Max. In any other situation, I would like Max. His smile is warm, his touch is kind and caring. Over the years, he has gotten to know me, but I have very little knowledge about him. That's the way it's supposed to be. I am not his friend, who the hell knows what the hell I am? Max, being helpful and friendly, has calmed me many times before. But because he works for Dominic, I know I can't trust him.

Before passing out, I swear I can hear Max leaning over me, whispering in my ear.

"Izzy, I will help you, my dear. Please hang on for me. Sleep now and let me work my magic." It's then a cloth is over my nose, and I am once again sent into la-la land.

chapter EIGHTEEN

WAKING UP, MY FOGGY BRAIN is spinning, making me dizzy and nauseous. A faint light shines from the old lamp on the nightstand. It gives off enough of a shadow that I can see the outline of a man in a chair at the end of the bed. Trying to focus my eyes, I'm having trouble making out who he is, exactly. A slight movement of my head has me wincing from the pain, so I try to hold it still in my hands. I know the dizziness must be from the stuff that Max gave me. I could never sit still enough to be stitched up. The idea of it all repulsed me to the point my body would convulse. Max at least thought enough of me to put me out of my temporary suffering, although Dominic was never just a temporary pain. No, he was more of a twenty-four/seven hell sentence.

Just thinking his name has the horror of what happened comes washing back, and it terrifies me. His words, his eyes and his double personality, quickly snap my attention to my stomach and leg. I have a long nightshirt on and panties. Other than the bandages, nothing else. One is covering my lower stomach stretches from hip to hip. Jesus, just how big was the mark he left on me this time?

Moving my leg to the side, I survey the damage. The bandage is small, but the dark color that is oozing through, makes me sick. Laying my head back on the pillow, I control my breathing so I won't throw up. Telling myself over and again, 'I won't throw up, I won't throw up, I won't throw up.'

My tears flow unashamed, I'm scared and alone. As a desperate cry escapes my lips, I realize my cry for help is pointless. As long as I'm with Dominic, I simply cannot be saved. I repeatedly rub my hand and close my eyes, it's the only touch that gives me comfort. When all of a sudden, a warm hand covers mine.

"Hey Izzy, how are you feeling?" He asks with such warmth.

The weariness of his voice lets me know someone does care for me.

My throat is dry as hell, and I'm pissed if I'm honest. "Seriously? You are asking me a question I'm sure you already know the answer to." I say rolling my eyes and wiping my tears away. Oh shit, he's not who I hate right now, but he is the only one next to me I can take my anger out on.

Max wrinkles his forehead, and it's easy to sense he is struggling to find the right words to say to me. "Look Izzy, you have no reason to trust me, but I want to help you. I never liked what Dom has done to you. It sickens me. He would kill me if he knew I was talking to you like this and if he knew just how much I loathe him. I swore after the incident with your brother and Willow, that I had to help you get free from him. I saw the horror, and I felt your cries all the way to my soul. I made a decision. I was going to find a way to help you. I just did not know how until last night."

Looking around the room for any sign of Dominic, I'm hesitant to ask. "How? How are you going to help me, Max?" I keep my voice a whisper so that no other unexpected ears can hear us.

Sighing, Max holds his hand up saying, "I am trying to figure it all out. I have some things I'm working on now. Izzy, that includes finding Willow. I may know who has her."

He tells me the one thing I needed to hear most in the world. More so than telling me I am going to live another day.

"Oh my God! Max, how do you know this?" My eyes grow wide with the possibility. Then reality sets in. "If Dominic ever finds out he…he will kill you. Wh…what about the other members of the Lost Souls?" Seriously, Max was taking an enormous risk for me.

"You let me worry about that. You rest and get yourself better. I know I have to move quickly. Dom wants to get you back home as soon as possible. Seems your guy is causing a lot of grief for Dom. Can't say I don't like it though. Years I fought with myself for allowing him to keep hurting you like he did. Each time I had to patch you up, I cried afterward. No one should have to suffer like that. Then with Willow, I knew one day I would help you and I will."

His warm smile can't disguise the years of guilt that show in his eyes. There is so much pain and sorrow. Another round of tears escapes my eyes, but this time they are happy tears. They are tears of hope!

I am not only surprised by his words, I'm shocked. No one ever crosses Dominic. Ever. If anyone did, they would not live to breathe another day. The only thing I can think to do is pull him into a hug. I am so happy to have someone on my side. Could he really help me? Help me leave Dominic? Help me get my daughter back? I cry at just the thought of spending a day with Willow. Holding her, caring for her the way I should have done all of this time. I wonder if she will ever remember who I am. The time we had was short, but it was the best of my life.

A creak of the door alerts us. "Well, look who's awake." Dominic snaps me back from my happy thoughts. I'm sure he would be able to tell if he could have seen my face. One minute happy and a smile filled with hope. The instant I hear his voice, it disappears, and is replaced with a blank stare void of any emotion. Hatred would be too small an emotion for what I feel for him.

As he crosses the room to my bed, Max immediately smiles and nods his head before leaving the room. On his way out, he reminds Dominic that I need my rest. It seems I lost a lot of blood. Dominic's knife went in a little too far, and that explains why I am in so much pain. Usually, I only have one wound to heal but lucky me, I have two knife wounds to deal with this time. I'm a lucky bitch.

His gaze sends chills down my spine. He is looking at me with a mixture of sadness and concern. Staring back at him, I pull my lips tight lifting my eyebrows as if to convey my less than thrilled attitude. With Dominic, my simple facial expressions tell him more than my words ever could. I can easily insult him with words, but my facial expressions are a subtler way of saying 'fuck off' or better yet 'go to hell, you bastard' with a smile on my face.

"Izzabella, believe it or not, I *am* sorry, I never meant to take it that far. I was upset. You, you left me, and when I got you back, you defied me. It angered me and then I was out of control. Jesus Christ, Izzabella. Why? Why do you make me so fucking mad at you?" Pinching his nose with his fingers, he takes several slow deep breaths.

Dominic has never tried to calm down before, so why now? My brain is telling me to yell, scream or throw the lamp over his head. What good would that do, other than earn me a few more marks on my body? No fucking way. Two is enough to last me a lifetime. The only thing I can do is swallow my anger my hurt, and channel my focus on how I am going to get the hell away from him once and for all.

"Dominic, you took what you wanted from me and when I didn't give it willingly, you punished me. The ugly marks left behind by your blade will always be reminders of the hell I have lived. These marks will always remind me just who you are!" My pained stare is filled with so much misery and suffering, but it's my voice and words that affect him the most.

Dropping his head in shame, he lets out an exasperated sigh. "I know," He admits whispering, "you have every right to hate me, but you have to know I have always cared about you." With a slouch of his shoulders, his eyes stay glued to the floor. "I just have a funny way of showing it."

No Fucking Shit, Asshole.

"Funny way of showing it." I squeal. "You have got to be kidding me. You hurt me. On purpose! You took my child from me. If you even cared an ounce about me, you would have never done that." Finally releasing all of the anger I've held in for so long. "You're sick!" My profound desire to scream all of the things he has wronged me for has given way to my hysterical cries.

His reaction to my tears this time is different, he uses his thumb to wipe them away with gentleness in his touch.

Caressing my cheek with his thumb, he speaks softly. "I am going to fix this. I will make it better. From now on it's going to be you, me, and Willow. The way it should have been all along."

I swear his smile seems genuine. He believes we can be what? A family? A fucking family after all he has done? Oh my God, he is sicker than I thought.

"You cannot be serious. I would never want a family with you. There is no us, how could you ever believe that? Not in a million years will I ever forgive you. You have brought me so much grief and pain. And I have suffered under your hands for so long. I don't even want a life if it means you are in it!" I pull no punches in letting him know this either. A life with him is no life at all, so why would I want to live one? Closing my eyes, I lay my head against the pillow and cry. Standing, his hands tremor with tightly closed fists. His mouth is hanging open, but no words escape.

I have no fight left in me. I'm so done. My heart has been shattered so many times before, but this time, I thought for just one minute, I could be happy. Happy for the first time in so very long.

Braxton and Eve gave me that. They made me happy, they gave me hope.

Even the ups and downs with Tiffany pale in comparison to the hell I faced with Dominic. Not even close. The times spent in Braxton's arms were worth it all. I'd go through hell again if it meant I could spend another night with Braxton. In his arms I felt safe, I felt whole, and I never felt so alive in my life. The pain Dominic caused I mask, because the pain of not seeing Braxton again is what is tearing my motherfucking heart apart.

Clutching the bed sheets in my hands, I hold onto the memory of my last night with Braxton. We were in my bed, Liam and Kara were heavily going at it in the spare room and not too quiet about it, either. I swear it was like we were college roommates, shaking up the night with our boyfriends. Braxton and I laughed about it. We were both carefree, and it felt good to let our hair down and just being us. We never had a lot of time just being us but when we did, I treasured it. Those stolen moments are forever ingrained in my heart. It's what true love should be. He was my soul mate, my best friend, my everything.

Rolling around in bed, our sweat covered bodies glided against one another. Laughing and tickling, he would bite me and I would respond with a lick and a bite of my own. The saltiness and the feel of his warm skin melted under the slickness of my tongue. Flicking his nipple, I trailed my tongue around, biting it gently, only to suck it eagerly. I could feel his body tense and then he would moan with pleasure. The rougher I got, shot waves of passion throughout my body as his rippled with lust.

That was a wild ride as I straddled him like he would straddle his bike. With Braxton sitting up, I anchored my feet to his back as my hands grasp his shoulders. Leaning back, I took him fast and hard, sliding up and down his rock-hard shaft. I bit back the pain with the pleasure, allowing my body to adjust to him. I never had a man the width or length of Braxton. I was intimidated as hell at first because I was afraid there was no way he was going to fit. He put my fears to rest as he gently showed me how I would fit him like a glove. Yep, let's just say it was snug, and I fucking loved every second of it.

Getting closer to my climax, he quickly flipped me on my back. Watching him thrusting in and out of me so hard, I feared I might split in two. It was fucking fantastic. Holding my knees, he spread them wide, plunging in and out harder, and then faster. I swear, I thought I died and gone to heaven! He was perfect.

His brown 'fuck me' eyes seared into mine as they silently beg me for more. There are no words to describe how amazing he makes me feel. Letting my eyes trail down his perfect chest, sans hair, just muscle and sweat, yummy! I can remember every damn detail of that night. It's fresh in my mind and has marked my soul forever.

Seeing his shaft wet with my juices pushed me over the edge, cascading to my own earth shattering climax.

With an animalistic growl, I exclaim. "Oh Braxton! Look at us. Jesus, I never knew it could be this fucking good."

Braxton's manly grunts were synchronized with his every thrust. "Iz, look at the way my dick is wet with your sweet juices. It makes me harder seeing the way we fit together." His words are filled with pure bliss. "Feel it Iz, feel how fuckin' great it is?"

That one night will stay with me till the day I die. Closing my eyes, I'm reliving it as I can almost hear his sexy voice.

Throwing my head back, it's as if a flame had been ignited deep within my core. The spark of a flame catching fire, shooting arrows of lust throughout my writhing body had me positioned in a way that resembles the letter V. Braxton has my legs folded under my knees, holding them to his hips. My hands and dangling feet are the only part of my body touching the mattress. Arched like a twisted pretzel, I never realized I could be so damn flexible. Note to self, this position rocks.

The next thing I know, I'm screaming out his name as I explode. With my eyes tightly closed, I see fireworks.

"Braxton, oh my God!" It's a curdling cry, scream or whatever you want to call it. Every man likes it when a woman screams his name. Well I did not just yell, I fucking pierced my own ears with the decibel of my voice. Never giving a single thought to my roommate next door. Oh no!

Kara knocks on the wall, shouting, "Not funny. Don't make me jealous over there!"

I hear Kara laughing as Liam loudly reminds her who the boss is and shows her she has no need to be jealous when she has him.

Braxton is smirking and rejoicing that I just shouted out to the stars, screaming his name. His smile gradually eases to a look of heated lust. Lowering my legs that no longer have any feeling in them, he positions himself on top me and he kissed the hell out of my already swollen lips. While trembling from the best orgasm of my fucking life, Braxton reached for the rails of my headboard with an iron grip, and slid into me slowly.

I gasp not once, but twice. Squeezing his pecs, my hands slip on the beads of sweat that pepper his chest. I claw at him the instant my insides smolder once again. The electrical current spanning in my chest feels like they are jetting out from my fingers and I know I am about to have an out of body experience.

"Brax. Oh. Oh, sweet fuck. Yes, yes, Braxton." Upon my impending orgasm, I do the only thing I can to help me ground me: I throw my arms above my head, grip the bed rails and hold on tight. Arching my back, I push my body to press against his while takes me to heights I never knew physically possible. My legs feel like jelly, they're shaking so hard. To control them I wrap them around Braxton's lower legs. Anchoring me to him, I'm not sure my body is going to survive another one.

"Izzy, my sweet girl, you feel so amazing. We belong together. Fucking love your tight pussy wrapped around my throbbing cock." His voice is low and gruff. "Iz, Iz, fuck, I'm going to come so hard," he says exploding into a million pieces.

Hot molten lava shoots inside of me, coating my walls as he continues to thrust in and out. He slowly stops pushing and now, I bear his full body weight on top of mine. His massive frame enveloped my smaller petite one, fucking perfect fit!

Before we called it a night, Braxton did take me to new heights yet again. I swear my insides were strung out. My legs would never work properly again, and I thought my vagina fell out somewhere in-between my hoarse voice or when I was drawing blood on Braxton's back with my nails. Doesn't matter. That was a fucking night to remember. Every girl should experience the things I did that night.

Pure Bliss!

chapter NINETEEN

REMEMBERING THAT NIGHT, AND RELIVING those moments of pure ecstasy, allow me to see how content and happy I really was. I read about times like these in my books, but who thinks that shit happens in real life? Well, I didn't. Until Braxton. He has me rethinking the laws of gravity the way my body was floating on cloud nine, not once, but three freaking times. I never knew my body could do that three, or was it four times? Who the hell knows or cares? But like always with Braxton, it just gets better and better.

One minute I remember Braxton and I'm over the moon happy, then my reality here with Dominic shatters my happiness into a dark sadness. I may never see Braxton again. May never feel his touch, or his light-hearted nature. For not knowing him long and sleeping with him only a handful of times, it's amazing how well he knows my body. That man can fine tune my body that blows my ever loving mind.

Simply put, he is my soul mate.

I notice the pills Max left for me on the nightstand with a ginger ale, so I take them. Hopefully, they will knock my ass out. I would rather be knocked out cold than be reminded of where I am and who I am with. Dominic left some time ago, thank goodness for small miracles!

A movement at the end of my bed has Max shifting closer to me.

"You should eat some soup with those, Iz."

Shit how the hell is he always here and I never know it?

"You're like cat or something. So quiet, blending in and I never know you are even here." My voice is light, I can relax with Max. He places my soup on the nightstand. It's steaming hot but I have to admit I'm starving as my stomach rumbles at the sight of it.

"Need some help eating? I can feed you," Max says as he sits down next to me. I should probably be nervous with him so close to me, but after spending more than one night with the man patching me up, I'm not.

"Nah. I can get it, just let it cool." Everything about him is so sweet, the complete opposite from his boss.

I can't help but chuckle. "Dominic could learn some bedside manners from you."

His eyes go wide. "Oh, I would tend to agree with you but better no one hears you say that."

"Your secret is safe with me," I say while placing my hand over his hand that lies on his knee. The gesture is meant to be a way of appreciating all the nice things he has done for me over the years. Mainly stitching me up after his boss has torn me up. But still, he was always nice.

He then hands me a phone from his pocket. "Listen, I just saw Dom leave so you have some time. Take my phone and call Kara or whoever, while you can. He won't ever know, it's the best I can do for now."

I stare at his hand, outstretched to me holding his phone. I am possibly eyeing my chance of escape. Calling Kara, I can make sure she is safe and then she can get the word to Braxton and Liam. My heart races at the thought of hearing Braxton's voice again. I should be more concerned to make sure Kara is all right, but the thought of hearing his angelic voice is making my heart go pitter-patter. I close my eyes at the thought of seeing him again and instantly, tears roll down my face. I can only hope.

"Take it Izzy, you don't have a lot of time. It looked like Dominic was on a mission. Not sure what his plan is, though. Take this time and call him or Kara, I don't care, but do it now." Anxiety is in his words and stretched across his face.

"Okay," I whisper. "Thank you so much, Max." Taking the phone, I nervously try to press numbers. This moment is so monumental, I'm shaking from head to toe.

"Hello? Hello, who's there? Izzy? God, please let this be you." Kara is shouting into the phone. Hearing her voice, I cry with loud sobs. Snot dripping out of my nose-style crying.

"Izzy! Oh my God! Thank God, are you okay? Shit of course you aren't? Why aren't you talking? Izzy, goddammit. Talk to me!"

I hear voices in the background, some noises filter in the receiver before I hear him. My God, my soul mate, my Braxton. I hear a noise and some muffling. Then I hear *him.*

"Izzy! Izzy baby, please talk to me!" His voice is impatient and crazed with anxiety.

I cup my mouth because I am crying so hard. I honestly can't speak. Just hearing the two most important people in my life is wrecking me.

"IZZY!" He shouts into the phone almost breathlessly.

"I'm…I'm here. Oh, Braxton." I say sobbing uncontrollably.

"Baby, it's you. My beautiful angel. I prayed more these past few days than I have my whole fucking life. It took some years off me, Sparkplug." Braxton said breathlessly, as if he's taking his last breath. Hearing my nickname warms my heart and brings out yet another sob.

I'm silent as I thank my lucky stars I can just hear his voice again. Even if it's the last time, it's everything to me. Holding the phone to my forehead I just listen to his voice, marking it to memory so in the dark days ahead, I can recall him saying my name, calling me baby. It's the single most heart-melting thing…to hear him. Second to hearing my child cry the first time, of course.

"Brax, it's so good to hear your voice." A slight chill pricks my spine. "I wasn't sure I would get a chance to hear your voice again. Oh, this hurts so bad."

"Shhh, shhh, listen babe, do you know where you are?" He keeps asking me and my reply is exactly the same each time.

"I have no idea." His sigh tells me he's not satisfied.

"Iz, look out the window and tell me what you see."

The stupid side of me, without thinking, tries to stand up as the pain shoots across my lower stomach. I immediately wince and yelp in pain. Dropping my phone on the bed, I lie back with controlled breaths.

Counting my breaths, I try to relax my body. Braxton is yelling, no, more like shouting down the roof off over the phone. I breathe one big one, one last time and pick up the phone.

"I'm here. I'm here," Slowly panting, I painfully add, "It's okay, but I can't look out the window right now." I leave it at that.

"Why the fuck not? Iz, why can't you look out the motherfucking window for me? Better yet, what the hell just happened to you?" The words come out angry, but I think the anger is more from being scared about me.

"Don't. Don't ask me things you are not prepared to hear the answers to. Just know I can't do it, and before you ask, I'm not okay. I'm hurt and trying my damnedest to stay healthy enough to ask you to do a few things for me."

"What the hell are you saying? What things?" I can tell he must have winced at my request because his voice hitched.

With self-doubt, I am begging on the inside. "Please take care of Kara for me. Take care of…"

"WHAT THE HELL?! No! Izzy, you are not going to talk like that! I'm coming to get you. You hear me, Izzy? DO. YOU. HEAR. ME?" Pausing after each word, his tone is wild.

"Yes. But…but" I can't help but lower my head in shame.

"No but's, honey. Don't you give up hope. Don't give up on me or you." His voice is full of desperation, but it's his plea that touches me most. I cry harder, so hard I can't breathe another word. My lower lip quivers with each whimper that escapes.

The phone is near my ear so I can hear Kara and Braxton shouting. Kara is telling Braxton that if Max was with me it meant only one thing, I'm hurt and he had to patch me up. When those words are aired, I could sense it tore Braxton apart. I could hear his pain and anger as he shouted what he was going to do to Dominic. It should have given me some comfort, but the only thing it did was scare me. The thought of Braxton showing up and confronting Dominic was not a welcome one. My brother did that and look where that got him. Six feet in the ground. All courtesy of me.

As I fall apart listening to my favorite people shouting about me and what they wanted to do to a man who is like the devil, Max takes the phone. I glance at him as he makes a slightly pained expression. He takes the phone and starts to talk.

"Hello, yes, my name is Max. I am trying to help her and if Dom finds out, I am sure as fuck a dead man. Listen, I need to talk to Liam. Get him for me and make it fast." Max is looking out the window. Watching for Dominic to return, I'm sure.

Liam? How the hell does Max know about *Liam?*

"Hey, Liam? I was told to contact you. Well, it seems we have a mutual friend. He put two and two together, so here I am. I wanted to call you as soon as I could." Max paused looking at me with a pained expression on his face and pauses. "No, she is not alright. Yes-yes, but tell him to shut the hell up so we can talk for a minute." Max keeps glancing between me and the window as he holds the curtain.

I can imagine Max is referring to Braxton.

"I will call when I can figure out what our next move is. I need to get to her daughter, somehow." Pausing, Max raises an eyebrow and sighs.

"Yes, that might work. Good idea. Listen, I think he's back so I need to go. Tell him no, he can't talk to her again. It's not safe." Click. Max hit end and deleted the history of the call on his phone.

"Wow, I can see why Dom is so frustrated and upset. Your man is, well, let's just say he's intense." He says with a wild shake of his head.

"That is putting it mildly." I burst out laughing as best I could.

Max leaves the room after making sure I was going to eat some soup before the pain meds send me into sleepy land. I have to admit, the soup was incredible; definitely hit the spot. I drifted off shortly after, to the hushed voices of Max and Dominic.

My last thought, was I sure hope we can trust Max.

He's my last hope.

Chapter Twenty

FOUR DAYS HAVE PASSED AND I feel like the living dead. I developed a fever and Max's fear materialized, I had a massive infection. I heard him arguing with Dominic about getting me stronger antibiotics, what Max was giving me was not strong enough. My illness has given me some damn awful nightmares and even worse hallucinations. Just about an hour ago I thought for sure there was a big ass spider in my room, ready to eat me for lunch. Screaming and hiding under the covers did not help and Dominic hasn't left my side since my last outburst. It seems my mental incompetence brought out his gentle side. If only he knew. He is way, way too late to show this kind of compassion. He did finally agree to send Max to get some stronger meds. Sending Max out to expose him was not something he wanted to do but my death is another something he did not want. The only thing I knew for a fact was I was going to die before he returned with a more potent medicine. Hell, right now, I'd beg death to take me and put me out of my misery.

Being mad with fever and hallucinations is one thing, having Dominic, the nursemaid, was just going to put me over the edge.

Dominic kept ringing out the washcloth and wiping it across my forehead, never looking into my eyes. In fact, he did his best not to. I could tell being this close to me made him uncomfortable. It's times such as these that I can see the kind and caring side of him. Call it wishful thinking, or a moment of temporary insanity but whatever it may be, it has me smiling at the devil. His voice was soft and sweet and he tended to my every need. I need to remind my brain that this is all his fault to begin with.

"Izzabella, you are so dear to me. Do you realize how important you are?" His eyes are shining like diamonds. Dazzling, truly dazzling. With these words, he did, in fact, look into my droopy eyes. Moaning, I close my eyes because it hurts too much to keep them open. I faintly nod and make a hmmm' noise. I'm not sure I actually hear what he is saying, I just agree with whatever he says. His touch is delicate as he strokes the damp hair from my face. It is wet from my fever and the washcloth. Running his fingers down my cheek, he traces my jaw from ear to ear. With my eyes closed, I dream of another man. It's *his* fingers touching my face. It's *his* soft angelic voice soothing me. I let the images of Braxton fill my head and I moan out his name. I couldn't help it.

"Braxton. So nice." I dream of his face and turn my head to lean it into the hand caressing my cheek. It didn't occur to me what I had done until after his name escaped my lips. The moment of clarity came to me and my slip-up came crashing down.

The hand that was sweetly stroking my cheek, stopped moving. His fingers tightened so much, I opened my eyes. "Dominic what are you doing? Leave me alone, I don't feel well."

His face is stone cold. "Don't ever mistake me for him again."

"What are you talking about? Jesus. Paranoid or something?" I realize my mistake, but no way in hell am I going to admit it.

Wiping my head with the cloth, his smile does not match his sadistic tone. "I won't like it if you ever do it again."

I was too tired and too sleepy to give a shit. If I called him by another name well, so be it. I'm spent and have no energy to fight with him. My body knows who it wants, and it's not him.

"As soon as you are well, we are leaving. The sooner," he huffs, "the better. You need to leave this place and you need to leave him. It would be wise for you to realize you will never see him again." His voice is cold and calculated. Yes, now the Dominic I know and hate is back. This side of Dominic I can relate to. The sweet side of him? I have no idea what to think of that guy.

"Max is back, I'll send him in. We're leaving in a few days, better or not. I hate this place and need to get back home. Feel well Izzabella, I have plans for you." He leaves the room with a backward glance.

He will be the death of me, I know it. I can't see how Braxton could ever get me out of this horrible situation. Death just seems an easier escape.

Max enters my room in a hurry. Closing the door, he presses a finger to his lips as to silence me. He sits and takes out three bottles of pills.

I sense the urgency with his fast movements plus, he looks nervous. "Izzy, can you understand me right now?"

With my inability to focus right, I merely nod.

"Listen, I've spoken to Liam and Brax while I was out. We came up with a plan, well I should say Liam and I came up with a plan. Your man is flat out against it, he wants to come in guns blazing. I assured him that his idea was a sure way to get you killed in the process. Dom will take you out before you leave him again."

"What's the plan?" My voice is feeble at best.

Rubbing his hand on his pant leg, Max leans closer to my ear as if to whisper.

"In a nutshell, I'm going to fake your death. I am going to put you in a, let's say a temporary coma. Then I tell Dom you passed away. Then get your body the hell out of here and into the hands of Liam and his brothers. Once you are safe, I will come to wake you up." Staring at me, he pauses for my reaction.

"You're *what*?" My eyes go wide and about bulge out of my head. "How the hell can you put me in a temporary coma, play it off as if I am dead, then turn around and wake me up? What if something goes wrong? What if I don't wake up? Jesus, it feels like I'm already knocking on death's door." My energy is spent, I'm fatigued and I hurt everywhere. Learning of Max's brilliant plan, I'm now panicking with fear.

"When are we doing this?" I don't have the energy to open my eyes and look at him anymore. I might be delusional and sick, not even in the right frame of mind but this idea is beyond wicked.

Sensing Max is moving around quietly, I use my last breaths before I drift off to sleep.

"Wh...when, are, we, doing this?" My words are getting harder to speak. I need sleep, I need to rest.

I feel a pinch in my arm, but I'm too weak to wince or yelp. I can feel his face close up against mine. His places a tender kiss on my forehead. He gets close to my ear and I can feel his breath against it.

"We're doing this right now." That was all he said.

WHAT? My brain heard him but what the hell does it mean?

OH, SHIT. LET ME LIVE THROUGH THIS.

Then the darkness came.

Peace.

Quiet.

Tranquility.

I'm aware my body is being moved but I don't feel any more pain. Voices are getting louder and I'm not sure what the hell is happening. I vaguely recall talking to Max before things got fuzzy. Oh my gosh, whatever Max gave me is definitely working. I haven't felt this at ease in a long time. I have no sadness or sorrow, I just feel...peaceful. God, what a great feeling. I just wish these voices would just stop shouting. Jesus! Let me have a moment of serenity.

chapter TWENTY-ONE

IT'S A BEAUTIFUL, WARM SUMMER day and I'm sitting on a grassy hill overlooking the lake. All the horror of the past few months is now just a distant bump in the road of life. A way to better times and the road that led me to Braxton. Laying my head back, I take in the heat of the sun. The distant laughter of Eve fills my ears. I smile at how at ease I am with her and Braxton in my life. It's like we were meant to be together. The other laugh of a little girl makes me damn right giddy. I can hardly see a tired Braxton as he is chasing them tirelessly on the beach.

"Eve," Braxton huffs out loudly, "Willow, I'm too damn tired to chase you all over the beach. I'll tell you what, you stop running from me and I'll let you bury Iz in the sand." He chuckles as his idea will no doubt have the girls over the moon excited about burying me in the sand. The last time they did, I had sand in places, well, let's just say, places where sand should never hide.

It's the manly grasp of a hand on my shoulder that snaps me out of my peaceful retreat.

"Looks like that did it, now I can sit back and relax," chuckling, he sits down next to me. "All at your expense, the girls sure love to get you under the sand. But I just like to get you cleaned up afterward." Leaning into me, he lightly brushes his lips against mine. The minute his wet lips connect with mine, my animalistic nature takes over and I grasp his neck, pulling him on top of me. As I take ownership of his lips, he moans his approval.

Nipping my lower lip, he smiles, saying, "You're an animal, you know that?"

My throaty laugh is topped off with a fit of giggles. "You love it and you know it. Wouldn't want me any other way, would you, big guy?"

I swear I can feel his heartbeat over mine.

Lips parting, he says, "Oh, don't you know it, babe."

"Momma, time to play with us. We're going to build a sand castle around you. Come on, come on, come on..."

Boy oh boy, she is so excited, my heart melts. Both she and Eve are pulling at me, ready to bury me in the sand. Every time my little girl calls me 'Momma', it brings tears to my eyes. It's something I never thought I would hear.

My moan is shallow, I don't want to show my lack of enthusiasm, it's just I dread getting sand in my shorts again, but I will not disappoint the girls. It's taken us a trip through hell to get here. Let the fun begin.

Just like I thought I would, I had sand in places I never knew possible. Walking into the cold lake to wash myself off, I laugh as I remember Braxton saying he looked forward to cleaning out the sand in my shorts. The four of us ended up splashing and laughing, like the family we'd become.

I look at each of their smiles and I swear, tears form at the sight. Once Willow was found safe, it was pretty easy getting her out of her home, with Max's help. The parents were a couple that barely knew Dominic but were afraid of him, so they did whatever he asked. Max filled Liam in, and both of them delivered Willow safe to me. A part of my heart healed instantly.

My brief moment of happiness came to a screeching halt, though. One minute I am on the beach with my girls and the love of my life and the next, I hear shouting and gunshots.

What the hell?

I can't move. Was I shot? Why can't I move? I start to panic when I can't open my damn eyes. I try to move my head in the direction of the voices and speak but I can't do either.

It's then, that the nightmare that is my life rears its ugly head to destroy the happy moments of my dream. I was never out of this nightmare, never on the beach. Never in the arms of the man I crave, and not being buried in sand by the girls. Wait. Oh, my god! Willow! She was never with us!

It's then I realize I'm still stuck in Hell!

Hell is just like I'd imagine it to be. I'm being jerked around and it feels like being carried over someone's shoulder. It's loud, it's scary, and there is not a damn thing I can do but go along for the ride.

"Liam, get her the fuck out of here! If Dom gets wind she is alive, he will kill us all."

Not needing my eyes to know that voice belongs to Max.

The deep growl that responds is no doubt Liam. "Max, I need to get my guys out and then we can get the hell out of here."

"Arrgghh, Dammit!" Max cries in utter pain. Hissing, he argues with himself about how their master plan was not going according to plan. They had it all laid out, from listening to his rants. I'm both amazed and astonished Max orchestrated this idea. All to get me out. To get me back home.

All, I can hear is the movement of people and a flurry of activity.

"Get in the van, you have to be there to wake Izzy the fuck up man," said an aggravated Liam.

The sounds of gunfire explode nearby and I would have jumped if I had any control over my body but I'm scared stiff. Figuratively and literally. Without eyes, it's amazing what I can pick up with hearing alone. I sense feet shuffling, quiet menacing chatter and loud thuds of items being tossed in the vehicle.

Liam's shouting thunders out. "Brax! Where the hell are you, man!"

His screaming is so loud, my eardrums might have just exploded. The sporadic gunfire and the constant hollering of many men, is not helping my already pounding head, either. I wonder if part of the plan was to have my brain explode, because it just might. Then all of a sudden, things calm down.

"Max, tell me what the hell is going on here?" Dominic's voice is murderous.

Hearing Dominic's voice so close scares me to death. Oh shit, *not good*. I panic. *Can he see me? Will he find out I'm still alive?* Max's grand scheme seemed like an excellent plan. Only I was never given a chance to ponder on it. I was injected with something as soon as the words left Max's lips. Not a nice thing to do and I will point this out to him as soon as I can come back into my body.

"Dom, she's gone. It's only right that Kara gets a say what happens to her now," Max's voice changes from uncertainty to lethal. "*You* did this. *You* killed her. *You* lost your chance of having a say."

I have never heard Max stand up to Dominic before. It's frightening yet finally, someone has the guts to do it. Max has walked away some as their voices have quieted a tad bit. I imagine Max walking away was a way to make sure Dominic is not near my lifeless body. It seems not far enough as Dominic's voice bellows.

"The fuck you say? My sister has nothing to do with this. I *loved* that woman, she should lie in rest where *I* choose."

A hint of remorse is weaved in his words, too bad I don't buy them. It's the thunderous, ominous voice that is vengefully shouting a steady flow of insults directed at Dominic that shakes my world. Hearing Braxton's voice does wonders for my soul but nothing for my nerves. The devil is face to face with my prince, yet again.

"Listen up bastard, that woman is the love of my life. You sick fucker! *You* cut her! *You* hurt her! What part of you being 'the reason she is dead' doesn't register with you?"

Braxton's aggressiveness scares me and I'm terrified Dominic will shoot him. I can only hope someone intervenes.

"Dom, get out of here. Leave it alone and let her have some peace for once. She suffered at your hands and she died at your hands. You took *everything* from her, including your own flesh and blood! At least give her this!"

Max's words are sincere and the way his voice cracks, I'm sure he has tears filling his eyes. It's oddly chilling listening them talk about me as if I am actually dead.

I hear what sounds like a gun being cocked. It may seem that I am dead, but my damn hearing is crystal clear. I hear the gun discharge and then silence. No one is saying a word and no one is moving around. Oh, my god. Someone's been shot, but who?

My mind is working overtime but I'm desperate to hear someone speak. No one does at first.

Then a familiar voice yet startles me. It's a voice I have grown to love over the years, the girl who stood up for me all those years ago. She is standing up for me once again. I gasp in my mind, but I know I make no noise.

Shaken, Kara stutters. "It had to be done. He was never going to let us leave with her body. If not Izzy, it had to be me to end this once and for all. Thank God Liam's guys took out most of Dom's men already. It would have been a bloodbath." She says solemnly.

With the hushed voices, it's easy to pick up the gurgling noise from the person I can only assume is Dominic. His moans and breathing sound labored.

"Why, why would you do this to me?" Dominic says as if he is truly shocking.

With all the voices joining in the drama, it gets harder to understand him. Damn, don't they know I can hear them? With all of this activity going on, it's easy to think I'm dead instead of in a coma.

"Dominic, it's only a matter of time before you take your last breath, I hit you right in the neck." She must have touched him in some way because I heard him hiss.

She leads with a sinister chuckle. "I have a secret for you before you finally die. She's not dead. Izzy is still alive, we put her in a coma so we could fake her death. We played you, *brother*." Her voice turns menacing, as she says, "How does it feel, you sick bastard?"

The shuffling feet and muffled voices descend all around me. Seems like a lot of activity but the low voices make it hard to make out what is happening.

Dominic's voice bellows out. "You bitch, should have taken care of you years ago. I should have taken Izzab..." he suddenly stops speaking. "I had her first, I did things to her that no man can erase. I damaged her, she's damaged goods."

He tries to laugh, but then screams loudly and gurgles as it sounds like he is being strangled or is drowning in his own blood. To say I feel sorry for him would be a lie. He did this to himself. The only regret I may have is that it wasn't me who pulled the trigger. Now Kara will carry this burden around with her for the rest of her life.

"Sorry, you sick piece of shit, you will never say her name again. My woman is never going to be hurt by you again. Just know she is not damaged, she is a precious gem of a woman and I plan on showing her, for the rest of her life, just how special she is. And don't worry about your daughter. I'll be raising her, too. She'll never even know you ever existed. Know that, motherfucker!"

The strong and fierce words Braxton said in my defense are leaving me speechless. How did this happen? How did I find a man so unbelievably strong and loving? If I could, I would curl up and wrap my arms around him, sobbing until the end of time. I want to do just that just show him how much a girl like me could love a guy like him.

The crunching of the gravel is all I hear before I'm being moved again. I can hear voices faintly talking. The conversation is centered around how lucky we were that Dominic only had a few men with him. Otherwise, this plan may not have worked. Suddenly the voices taper off when I feel warm hands. This time, I am cuddled into strong arms. Oh, I know these arms. I don't need to see him realize who he is. The beat of his heart, his fabulous scent, and the overall feeling in his embrace instantly calms me. I wish I could open my eyes to see his face, the face I was not sure I would ever see again. He is here and I can't talk or see him. The comfort of his arms and hands rubbing me is enough. I feel safe, finally.

Heavy breaths fan my face. "Baby, if you can hear me, I'm so sorry. I feel like I failed you. He hurt you, honey and the thought of you having to endure that is fucking killing me. He's gone, honey. Kara shot him and I sped up his demise. He died there knowing I was going to get to keep on loving you. Die knowing you're still alive."

Braxton kisses my head as he whispers in my ear. He cradles my body into his and rocks me sweetly, having no idea I'd heard most of the conversation. I can sense we are not alone and the sounds of bodies rustling and the shutting of doors tell me we must be ready to leave.

"Max, you better be damn ready to get my girl out of this! Let's go, I want my woman back." Braxton's words are intense and anxious.

"Brax," Max sighs, "I won't lie. It's going to be touch and go because she still has a bad infection. I will bring her back but she needs to heal and get this infection under control. I wanted her in the hospital, but Dom would not hear of it."

Braxton interrupts.

"She dies you die, understand?"

There's no mistaking my man's words. I just wish he knew how much Max has done for me. Not just now but over the years, too.

Irritated, Max huffs, agreeing. "Yeah, I understand. Don't worry it's good for you I want the best for her, as well. Wasn't I the one to come up with the idea to get her out? Do you have any idea how much I hated stitching her up after he hurt her for all these years? It's twisted and downright sick."

It's so hard to listen to this.

"Then why did you not help her before?" Braxton asks with more control over his emotions.

Max huffs out a big breath. "I couldn't. I wasn't in a position to do shit." He says, sounding defeated.

Kara tries pleading with Braxton.

"Brax, Max is a good guy. You have no idea what it's like in Dom's home. He's guarded, heavily. Max is like a love sick fool around Izzy. If it wasn't for Dom, I think Max would have snatched her up a long time ago. He has always watched out for her the best he could."

Kara's voice trails off at the same time I feel a cold hand on my shoulder. My girl is once again my champion. It's hard to imagine how she is feeling right now. Close or not, Dominic was her brother and killing him could not have been easy.

"Great, now I have you to contend with?" Braxton says.

"It's true, I care deeply for Izzy but she never shut her mouth about you the entire time. Got on my nerves, too. She only has eyes for you, man. Just hope you realize what a great fucking girl you have."

"Woman, not a girl and I know what a great fucking woman she is. Never knew a woman as strong as my Iz. That 'woman' has been through hell and back, only to be dragged back into it all over again. She will *never* feel that hell again."

I can feel his arms tighten around me. I swear, after listening to them, I would blush if I could. He may not be able to see me smile, but on the inside, I am smiling from ear to ear.

A hand touches my forehead, an ice-cold hand at that.

"Jesus Christ, she's burning up! We need to get her somewhere, fast! I need to get an IV, and these antibiotics started. I can't give her the medication to wake up until I do that!" Max says with a slight hitch in his voice.

Braxton is eager to disagree. "Why can't we wake her up first?" He says astonished and surprised.

It's Max's growl that pauses his response. "The infection could take her life, and *that* has to come first. Her body can't fight the infection *and* wake itself up all at once."

I know Max well enough to know he knows what he is doing. Hopefully, Braxton will leave him to it.

Warm lips scorch my forehead. "Listen here, Iz. Baby, you rest and kick this infection's ass. Then, wake the fuck up to me. You hear me, Iz? You are not dying on me now. Not when I finally got you free from him."

His whisper sends shivers down my spine as my head swims with possibilities. Then, the darkness pulls me back under.

Chapter Twenty-Two

I HAVE NO IDEA HOW much time has passed. With a flutter of my eyelids, I'm waking up and able to recognize I'm in my bedroom. The feel of my warm, fuzzy comforter under my fingertips feels fantastic. My eyes widen as the realization overwhelms me, I made it, I'm alive.

Max's plan worked and I can't help but squeal with delight. My door suddenly squeaks as it slowly opens, sending my heart racing in fear. My instincts tell me to panic but I close my eyes, and concentrating on my breathing. The dip in the bed tells me that someone is sitting next to me and I'm frightened, because Dominic's face is all I can see. I'm not sure how long I'll be looking over my shoulder thinking he is there, waiting for me. It's going to take time… and patience.

A gentle hand moves my hair away from my face. The faintness of the touch and the aroma of cologne clue me into who is sitting next to me, so I lie still so I can absorb his touch and his much needed words.

"Izzy baby, you are a sight for sore eyes," Braxton finally says. "The fever finally broke late last night and Max finally injected the medicine to allow you to wake up. It's all on you now, honey. We are all waiting for you to come back to us."

Braxton then leans in and kisses my lips with a tender peck. The warm feeling of them wakes up parts of my body and I find myself returning to the sweet gesture as I mold my lips to his.

Sensing movement on my part Braxton freezes as I feel his head pull away. I slowly open my eyes and am so shocked, I wince. He looks terrible. The week-old stubble of his beard, is not bad, but his eyes are bloodshot with deep dark circles under them. He looks as bad as I feel.

His breath hitches and he gasps the moment our eyes meet. Instantly his shoulders relax and his face lights up as if he's able to breathe easily for the first time in ages. He begins shouting and my face grimaces with pain. My head hurts like hell but I don't get a chance to say anything because he gently cups my cheeks and kisses me. It's gentle yet filled with so much adoration. It's as if he's talking without words. I feel so much love in this kiss.

With shaky hands, I reach up to touch his face and he quickly covers mine with his own. The emotions contained in our touch speak volumes as we both close our eyes at the same time. When you survive the hell I have, you learn to appreciate these small gestures. A simple smile, a peck on the cheek, the way one feels when a hand gently cups your cheek. Sometimes the best words are not spoken, they are said with the sweetest of touches.

"You came back to me." He breathes out.

My smile comes with a few shaky breaths as I'm weak and finding the strength to speak. "Yeah, who wouldn't come back to her knight and shining armor? You took care of Dominic for me, you came and rescued me." I say struggling.

"How did you know that?" Braxton asks with curiosity.

I catch the sight of Liam at the door and after following my gaze, Braxton shifts to the side, giving me a better view. Gently pushing past them, Max slowly makes his way to my bedside and he looks as if he's aged ten years.

The nod of my head is slight but enough to answer Braxton's question. "I heard it all. I, of course, could not see any of it, but I sure heard it all." My feeble attempt at a laugh falls short. "I was going to come back and haunt you all if I never did wake up."

No longer staying still Kara strides over to me and gently hugs my shoulders. "Hey Izzy, you look like shit, girl." She says laughing.

Everyone laughs but Braxton. He did not find it funny at all. Classic Kara, I loved it.

"I feel as bad as Max and Braxton look. Max looks like he has aged ten years, and Braxton looks like he is a walking zombie." I laugh holding my stomach, which is still quite sore. My sudden yawn is a reminder, of just how exhausted I am.

Max lets out a few swear words motioning with his hands for everyone to leave the room. "She needs rest, and I need to look her over."

Braxton goes to stand but not before grabbing my hand. Max notices this and sighs with exhaustion mixed with aggravation.

"Brax, you need to move away from the bed so I can check her," Max said slightly irritated.

It's easy to sense the tension between them and I can imagine them living under the same roof has been exhausting.

Braxton stands up straighter. "Not leaving her, no fucking way. You can check her out while I hold her hand."

I squeeze his hand, letting him know without words that he needs to cut Max some slack. If it were not for him, I would be dead. With what went down, a hospital visit for me right now is not a good idea. Max is my best hope for a full recovery. Plus, he has been my personal physician for several years. Better Max than a doctor who has a lot of questions about how I got hurt.

"Braxton," I say with a feather-like sigh. "You need some sleep, go home and get some rest. When you come back, I will hopefully be rested and awake." Still holding on tight to his hand, there is so much I want to say to him. Before I drift off to sleep again, I say, "Come here, honey."

Bending down so were nose to nose, I get a better look at his dull brown orbs. It makes me sad as they are not the sparkly ones I've come to expect from him. All the more reason to let him know how much he means to me right this minute.

"I love you," I whisper.

Moaning loudly, Braxton falters to his knees, "Damn girl, I love you too. Must have been while you were sleeping."

Head slightly tilted, his smile matches the sweetness in his eyes. His reference to my favorite movie reminds me of the night we watched it together. While I enjoyed it, Braxton tolerated it at best, reminding me it was a total chick flick. Deep down, I know he liked it as well, he just could not admit it. Being all manly and such.

I admit jokingly. "Damn straight, but I don't want to go to Florence for our honeymoon."

He winks with a shake of his head. "Damn chick flicks." Holding up his finger, he continues saying, "I swear, when you get better, I'll watch anyone you want. First you need to get better because I have plans for you, sweetheart. We can discuss our honeymoon later."

Slightly caught off guard, I blush at the word honeymoon. "Not if you don't get some much-needed rest."

Leaning in to kiss my forehead, he pulls back holding up his hands as if surrendering. "Okay, just coming out of a coma and you're bossy already."

Kara and Liam are cracking up standing at the end of my bed. Max is listening to our conversation looking at his watch and taking my pulse as he holds the hand Braxton is not holding. Kara's laughing breaks up the tension in the room.

"She's back. I don't ever want to see you like that ever again, Missy."

The tears that slide down her face just about break my heart. I realize what happened and for Kara it was liberating, but he was still her brother. She puts on a brave face but I'm not convinced she is okay with killing him.

Before leaving the room, Liam says it's his turn and walks over to me, moving Max out of the way. He knows better than to ask Braxton to move.

Liam takes my cold hand in his. "Glad you're back, Izzy girl. I was close to shooting Brax. *He* was close to being put in a coma until *you* were back in the land of living. The bastard was so hard to control, Max here wanted to lock himself in here with you just to get away from him."

It's so easy to smile and joke with Liam, it's his loving personality. Seeing Kara with a guy like Liam is such an awesome thing. He sacrificed himself, and his brother's to help save me. I'm not sure how to ever repay him for that.

"Liam," I choke up fighting back tears. "Thank you so much. Thank you for helping me." Words will never be enough, but it's a start.

Gripping my hand tighter, Liam's eyes tighten. "Never need to thank me, Izzy girl."

"OUT! All of you need to get out. I need to check her over."

Max is finally shoving everyone out the door, huffing and complaining as he does. I can't help but chuckle to myself. Watching Braxton leave is not a great feeling but as much as I want him near me, the man is looking like walking death. To myself I utter 'Get some rest my sweet, sweet man.' My mind drifts as I watch his backside as he reluctantly walks to the door. I can't help myself; I raise my left eyebrow as I notice how sexy Braxton is.

My exam goes well, and Max talks as he checks each bandage. I wince a few times as I am forced to look at my newest marks. I sigh out a breath, knowing these will be the last from him. He will never touch me again. The reality of knowing this is real and that Dominic is, in fact, gone, brings out a fresh set of tears. Max is giving me a look of pity, but in reality, my tears are out of relief, tears of happiness that I will never have to look over my shoulders ever again. I am finally free.

Max explains it could take over a week to start feeling better and although my wounds are healing nicely, the infection is the primary concern.

I took this private time with Max to grill him about what's been going on since I've been down and out because the aftermath of them killing Dominic worries me. What is going to happen now?

What about Tiffany? I have so many questions, I know Braxton will never tell me the truth because he doesn't want to worry me.

In great detail, Max went on explaining how it all went down. Liam and Max had a plan set in motion after only a few days' time of planning it. Trying to control Braxton was the hardest part.

They found out the client at Braxton's shop with the expensive cars was Dominic, a setup with the help of Tiffany. Dominic wanted eyes on Braxton to see his comings and goings. It was sick, but well executed. He had every detail thought out, Dominic had different plans for how he was going to gain access to me, from what I'm being told. Kara and I walking down the street was his golden opportunity to grab me. For Max, it was easy. Dominic laid out his plans in front of him. The only variable was the how and when he would nab me.

Tiffany is no longer going to cause a problem for me, no other explanations were offered, so I let it go at that. Max explained that Liam had a long talk with his uncle regarding the 'Lost Souls MC' and Dominic Santos. Uncle Marty had been informed all about me and my new connection with Braxton.

After learning of my regrettable history, Liam's uncle was not so keen on Dominic and his connection to the 'MC.' He had no tolerance for violence against women. Uncle Marty also proved most helpful with the disposal of Dominic and the horrific scene at the abandoned old farm house. Off the beaten track, it was perfect and no one heard all of the gunshots and violence that went down that night. His crew went in and handled it all, no blowback on Liam or Braxton, thank god!

His vagueness on the whole Tiffany part does bother me, but I would need to talk to Braxton about it. I'm sure he won't want to talk about her, but that's too damn bad. She is the reason he found me, after all. When Max revealed how dangerous my infection had gotten, it left me speechless.

Max clears his throat with a raised eye. "Brax never left your side. I want to hate him, but that man loves you, Izzy. I guess I missed my chance to steal you away." He says mischievously.

"Pfft. You always got to see me at my worst. I can't believe you don't hate me or something. I want to thank you for taking such good care of me, Max. Seriously, you helped give me my life back."

"It felt good to finally do something right for a change. Helping Dom all of these years was getting more and more difficult. You…You…Ah, I'm just so sorry, Izzy."

I could see the regret wash over his face.

"No, you don't need ever to apologize to me. If it weren't for you, I would not be here. I'm glad you are away from him, too. Now what happens to you? What will you do?" I ask.

Sitting down next to me, he rests his arms on his knees. Looking down at the floor, he takes a moment to think it over.

"I'm…" letting out a sigh, he adds, "I'm going to fucking rest." Max then let out a much-needed laugh.

Looking at me, he smiles tenderly.

"Seriously, I'm not sure. Whatever it is, it is not going to require me to be 'a beck and call' doctor."

With a contented sigh, I shake my head glad to hear it. "Whatever you do, you'll be great." Max gives me a slight smirk and nods.

"Better get some rest, Brax will be in here in no time from his catnap and I'll be here stopping in to check on you."

Max leaves the room, quietly shutting the door behind him. Pulling the covers up higher under my chin, I realize I am in shorts and a loose t-shirt. I have no idea how I got into these clothes or the last time I got cleaned up. My teeth need brushing and from the feel of it, my hair needs a good washing but I'm too tired to do anything. Sleep is calling my name, so I give in and drift off once again.

chapter TWENTY-THREE

"KARA, I CAN SHOWER BY myself. Jesus, quit being a mother hen." I say trying to push her out of my bathroom.

"Oh, Christ Izzy, just be careful. You just got the go-ahead to get up and move around. The bandages are finally off and you are slowly getting back to yourself. Don't overdo it, or Brax will kill *me*. Everyone is under strict orders to make sure you don't move a muscle unless help is around." She says as she rolls her eyes toward the ceiling. Her sarcasm is pretty funny.

I smile big. I can't help it, my man is so possessive. Who wouldn't love to have a big sexy man worry and fret over her?

I blush listening to her continue to harp about Braxton. He has not left my side much since I woke up. If I ever was unsure of his feelings for me, he put them to rest. He touches me regularly and kisses me often. We have yet to have the whole Tiffany talk, but that's a conversation for another day.

I stood my ground when it came to taking a shower by myself. Aching and still somewhat weak, taking my own shower will be liberating for me, knowing I have nothing to run from anymore. With that thought, I graciously walk with my shoulders back and my head held high. Returning to my bedroom in nothing but a towel, my hair is dripping wet, and beads of water glide down my freshly shaved legs. Not the easiest task to accomplish, but I did it; they *so* needed it.

Closing my door, I smile and giggle when I notice a sleeping man in my bed. His large frame takes up most of it. He's wearing a gray long sleeve t-shirt and faded jeans. His hair is longer, and he has yet to shave off the new beard he's wearing. His sharp facial features stand out under his beanie cap. He is totally and utterly sexy. He looks so peaceful, resting like he has no cares in the world. Lately, we haven't had too many quiet moments, so to see him like this is beyond breathtaking.

Leaning against the door, a small moan escapes my lips. I absorb every delectable inch of him, at the same time my desire starts to burn. He has a body I have grown to treasure, a body made for sin. Braxton makes me tremble and shake with those hands, those lips, among his various other body parts. He knows how to tune fine my body; and it sings to him like an instrument only he knows how to play. So much that even when he sleeps, his body still calls out to me. The only thing I want to do is drop my towel. So, I do.

Giving into my desire is easy when it comes to him. All of my vivid dreams as of late have all been about him.

Climbing at the end of the bed, I slowly crawl up his body. Dragging my body over his, I inch up gentle and slow. Straddling his legs, I accidentally grind myself against his belt. Thankfully, my cuts are not touching any part of him when I'm sitting in this position. After gently lifting up his shirt, I lower my face to kiss his stomach. The higher I lift his shirt, the higher I kiss. I notice his stomach retract and roll slightly, looking up I see him smirking trying to contain his laugh. Dammit!

"Hey sparkplug, whatcha' doing?" He says laughing.

"You were supposed to be sleeping. Faker." I give him a pouty look.

Wrapping his hands around me, he mused. "I should stay asleep, damn, this is the way to wake up."

"I missed you, Braxton." And I have. I never thought I would see him again, to be with him like this. My tears sting as they fall.

"Sparkplug no more crying. I'm here."

Braxton's lips brush against mine.

"I was so afraid I was never going to see you again. I...I...I love you so much." I'm not sure words are enough to justify my feelings.

Pondering my words, he noted. "Baby, told you I would get you back. What little faith you have in your man."

"Are you my man?" I pointed out.

"Seriously? Are we back to this again?" He was quick to point out. "You can bet your sweet ass I'm your man. Iz, you are mine, now and forever, no more messing around. I almost lost you and it won't happen a second time."

Those sparkling brown orbs wink at me.

Placing a hand over my heart, I mimic. "Mine." Leaning forward, I gently take his lips and let my kiss do the talking. His tongue traces my bottom lip and is soon exploring my mouth. His assault turns more demanding, and it feels like a tonsil inspection instead of a kiss. I love it, though. In fact, I relish it.

"Shirt Braxton. Lose the shirt, honey." I excitedly fumble with his shirt.

I don't need to tell him twice, he sits up so he can pull it over his head and puts it around me to pull me closer. My chest is rubbing against his and it feels so fucking amazing. My eyes are drawn to something that stands out. It's a design that was not on his body before. What! *Braxton got new ink since I saw him last?*

"What the...? Honey, you got a new tattoo?" I say as I look back at him, astonished.

His look is unsure at best. He seems uneasy as he raises his eyebrows with his lips stretched thin.

"What do you think?" He questions.

I do a double take on the intricate design. It is just under his pec around his heart, and I trace it with my finger. I can see Eve's name but now it connects to a new design. It's beautiful. The outline traces a figure of eight like the infinity symbol, beautiful on its own, but the design doesn't stop there. It flares out into wings that are all black and gray. My eyes travel around the design until they land upon the center of the figure eight. I gasp! In a very elegant script are letters that spell out my name.

"You got my name inked on you." It's not a question because I can apparently read it. *Holy Shit! My man put my name on his chest in ink!*

Braxton whispers as he watches my tears flow down my cheeks. "Iz, please say something, anything," he continues, "why the tears?" Touching my cheeks. "Oh God, Iz, please say something."

"Shhh," I say as I put my finger to his lips. "I freaking love it." I hiccup with my sobs.

Our eyes meet, intently staring into one another. "I love you, Braxton Ryles. You hear me? You are everything to me. You are my special someone." I yearn for this man to the point that I ache. "You own my heart and soul." I marvel saying the words that pretty much sum up my feelings.

He opens his mouth to speak, but hesitates. Without another word, he pulls me down to him and owns my lips. With his hands around my lower back, he grinds his erection into me, and that ignites my own burning need. I am buck naked and getting wetter by the minute. I know he's enjoying this because he keeps whispering how much he does. His face winces as he looks at my newest scars. His eyes draw tight and threaten to tear up.

Oh no. "Don't, Braxton. Just two more marks to add to my list of many ugly ass scars. He's gone, and I need to get used to the fact I have these reminders of him." I give him a half shrug because there is not much else that can be done.

"Baby, someday we will work on covering these up or tattoo around them. We will make them beautiful. I swear to you."

I know he means it and I want to tell him not to worry about it, but I'm forced to look at them every time I am naked. Better yet, Braxton has to see them every time he wants to have sex with me. Can't say that is a turn-on.

"I know, but let's not talk about it now. Today, I want to show you how much I love you. My body may not be perfect, but it is all yours." I say this as I undo his belt and unbutton his jeans. Sliding them down his body, he sits up enough to take them off. He is going commando today, and I don't mind since it is less work for me to do. Smiling at his rock hard erection, I lean into him and lick it from the root to tip. I swirl around the tip like it's my personal ice cream cone, tracing his swelling vein underneath. Each time I do, his body relaxes with shivers. His fingers grip the sheets all the while rocking into my mouth. I happily hollow my cheeks. Nice and slow, twirling his manhood with my tongue, I graze him with my teeth while grabbing his base. My hand and mouth tango with his throbbing hardness.

Sucking harder, my desire surges and each time my hand glides up, I apply even more pressure. His fingers are in my hair, gingerly pulling it a bit tighter. His excitement is a dead giveaway with the intensity of his hold on my hair. The harder he tugs, the louder I respond. I love to pleasure him, to know I am putting that sex crazed expression on his face.

When the first hint of saltiness hits my tongue, I know he's close. Not in my mouth today, I want him to explode inside of me. Leaning forward, I release him with a loud pop. The look on his face is priceless. His heart races, and it's his impending release that has him silently begging.

I smile at his wild expression. "Don't worry love, just getting into a new position. When you come, you do it inside of me. I want to feel you inside of me, Braxton. I need you." I say crawling up his body, his eyes never leaving mine.

Braxton's smile is set off with the twinkle in his eyes. Looking like he is ready to eat me alive, he asks, "Are you sure you're ready?"

"Doesn't matter if I am or not, you're mine." What can I say, I'm desperate at this point.

"Yes, Ma'am." He says with a shake of his head. "No other bitch has me."

"Nice Braxton, calling me a bitch? Should I be honored or pissed?"

"Figure of speech, Sparkplug. Now get your beautiful ass up here on top and ride the wave, baby."

Raising my hips, I pause as the tip of his erection rests at my drenched center. I hover and circle the tip of him never using my hands.

"Sparkplug, will you jump on board before you unman me. It's been awhile, and I'm dying to get up inside that hot body of yours."

Arching my eyebrow, I say, "Shh, don't get bossy. I'm in charge."

"Yes Ma'am, sorry."

Braxton groans out a deep moan when I slowly slide down his shaft. I'm so freaking wet, it feels like a damn slip and slide. We have never used a condom between us. Call me stupid, but at least we talked about it. He told me he was clean, I told him I was the same, and I can't get pregnant so why bother. When a man like Braxton is staring you down, ready to devour your body, the time for small talk is over.

"Oooh baby, you feel so damn good. Iz, your body was made for me." He keeps repeating this over and over again.

I am unable to say much, because the desire to ride him takes over and I let my speed match my need for him. Each up and down motion pull on my stitches, and it's not a great feeling. I try not to think about it because with the first hint of pain on my face, Braxton will stop our lovemaking.

I must have let a slight moan of pain slip from my mouth because he stills his body as his eyes fly open. In that instant, his arms grab mine to stop my body from moving.

"Izzy are you in pain? Goddammit, please tell me you were not hurting yourself?"

"It's okay. Don't stop me, not today." Grabbing his hands, I close my eyes praying. "This is me showing you how much I love you."

"Not if it is hurting you. We can wait to do this and I can make you come without the pain." He says while smiling mischievously.

"Shut it. Lie back and let me fuck you senseless. If I'm in pain, it's all on me." I give him my most bitchy look of 'do not mess with me.' Hopefully, it will work.

Pausing for a moment, he finally lets up on his hold.

"I only agree to this because I'm so damn close that it won't take much. Don't give me that shit eating grin either, Sparkplug, I can still redden your ass for misbehaving."

"You like me misbehaving, plus the idea of you slapping my ass does do some naughty things to me," I say in my sexiest voice.

"You going to talk to me or fuck me?"

"Seven ways to Sunday if I could, right now I settle for yes, honey, I'm going to fuck you really good." If I were one hundred percent healthy, I could get creative in how I take him, but for now I'll settle for a scaled back version.

Taking his hands and intertwining them tightly, I rise slowly and slide back down. Using his hands for support, our eyes never leave one another. My insides are starting to simmer over a smoldering fire. I grind myself all the way down, circling my hips causing enough friction to my clit to light the fuse to my impending release. The fluttering in my stomach gives way to the blazing tingles that line my spine. Arching higher, I push forward aligning our bodies, making sure to hit that sweet spot. I ache to feel over and again.

Doing this a few more times, I scream out as an explosion detonates inside my body. I swear my fingers fused with his, my back arches forward so much I might have fallen over if it wasn't for his hands keeping me planted upright. I don't only scream out his name, I add in more explicit words of the naughty things he makes me feel. The splitting pain I feel is drowned by my moment of pure bliss.

I didn't even realize Braxton hit his orgasm at the same time until I feel his hot lava shooting inside. We are both out of breath, and our hands still fused as one. I lay my head back, panting. He rocked my world. The clearing of a throat alerts me we're not alone.

Still trying to catch my breath, my eyes widen as I turn my head in the direction of the door. Even though Braxton and I have been caught in the act, I'm not the least bit embarrassed. However, Braxton is beet red and has sweat pouring down his chest.

Surprised, I let out a laugh. "Are you blushing, Braxton?"

With one eyebrow lifted, Braxton lets out a chuckle. "Looks like we've got company, Sparkplug."

We both turn back to the wandering eyes of Liam and Kara. We never move or try to cover ourselves. I'm still on top of Braxton with him still inside of me. But my back is to the door, so I'm not overly concerned because they can only see my backside.

"We heard shouting. I'm not sure why we thought we needed to come in here, but we had to make sure. Excellent show, by the way, we got here just in time for the good part. Pretty hot you two," Liam says laughing.

"Glad you enjoyed it so much, now if you excuse us." I turn back to face Braxton and it's then I feel a stabbing pain in my lower stomach.

"Oh, shit." I take my hand out of Braxton's and grab my stomach.

We both look down to the pulled stitches and the slight tinge of blood at my incision.

"Fuck Izzy! I told you." He says, as a look of regret washes over his face.

"I was too worked up to notice," I say, taking a big breath, and holding it to ride out the stabbing feeling. My mind keeps saying it will pass, no biggie.

Just then, Max barges into the room and does a double take at the scene he just walked in on.

Braxton grumbles at Max's not so happy look. "As much as I love to have my girl ride my dick, she went and pulled her stitches out."

"Fuck, you two!" Max says fumingly.

"Yes, that is what happened." I respond with a painful laugh.

Max comes over to look at my stomach.

"Can she at least get off my dick before you start to look? She needs to get some damn underwear on if you're going to be looking down there, buddy."

"Get over yourself, I have seen it all before." Max makes the mistake of admitting this.

"What the hell?" Yeah, not a good thing to say to a very possessive Braxton.

"Long story, just get some clothes, on I will be right back."

Max and the rest leave the room so we can get off of each other and get some clothes on.

Braxton then clears his throat. "Iz, I'm not sure if I should be damn happy I just got laid or pissed off you hurt yourself over it." He is frustrated while getting his jeans back on.

"Be happy, you gave me one hell of a ride," I say as I put on my panties. To be honest, it hurts like hell right now. Shit, maybe not one of my best decisions, but it was such an enjoyable ride.

Max returns and inspects me with gauze and a pair of tweezers.

"Looks like a few stitches popped out. I'll just butterfly them so you won't pop these as well." He looks at me with a mildly pissed expression.

"Honestly Max, can you blame me? I never thought I'd see him again, let alone ravage his body." Raising my shoulders. I say, "I love him."

Max sighs and closes his eyes. "Yeah, we all know. Listen, I'm having some issues trying to find Willow. I had a hold on where she was until they up and left. I'm not sure if Dominic had a hand in it or not."

Chapter Twenty-Four

SITTING AT MY DINING ROOM table are Liam, Kara, Brax, myself, Max, Travis, Dex and lastly, Zeke members of Liam's MC club. Brax's friends and co-workers Alex, Cage, and Brody left earlier. They are running the shop until Braxton decides he is going to go back to work. Honest to God, observing all of these big burly men in one place, was a site.

While they chatted about work, Kara and I sat back just watching them all. Quite amazing I was seated in a room with a handful of these magnificent looking guys, and I'm not talking good looking pretty boys, either. I mean men who are built to look badass, dressed in tight t-shirts and panty-melting jeans that showed off their assets. Liam's crew all wore their cuts over their shirts. Kara was in MC heaven with her mouth wide open as she stared at them from across the room. Priceless!

I admit, I had a hard time deciding who was better looking, my room was wall to wall muscles, tattoos, and crew cuts. But my personal favorite was my hunk of a man who wore his hair slightly longer in the back, causing it to curl around his neck. Sweet Jesus, perfection. Brody and Cage shared their great news with Brax concerning the cars that Dominic brought in as a ruse.

In the end, Braxton got to keep those two very sporty cars to do with as he wished. From what Brody was telling us, Cage and Liam got rid of them and got a pretty penny for them, too. I wasn't listening to everything, I just kept smiling and acting like I was paying attention to what they had to say. Jesus, how the hell can a girl concentrate when all you see is, muscles and tattoos and the faces of men who, with one look alone, could melt your panties off. Who cared at the moment of what they were saying, it was all about the man-candy.

Tonight though, the conversation has shifted from work to finding out as much as we can as to where my daughter could be. It's as if she and the couple she was living with have disappeared. I try not to get too emotionally attached because I have no idea if I will see her again. If I let myself believe I will, it could only shatter my heart once more. I'm too fragile as it is. I will never give up total hope, though.

Small talk has commenced, and the subject we are all avoiding is sitting like an elephant in the room. I know no-one wants to talk about her in front of me, but seriously, dancing around this one topic, they all look nervously around at each other before their eyes shift to me.

"Oh, come on people! Let's just get it all out in the open." Rolling my eyes, I sigh nervously. "What is happening with Tiffany?" I keep my stare between Liam and Braxton, but it's the eye rolling and head shaking from Max and Zeke that catches my attention.

"I'm sick of avoiding this issue, so spill it." I understand some of their apprehensions, at most. What I don't understand is the underlying feeling some things are being kept from me. Braxton has been just a little too uncomfortable whenever we start to mention Tiffany.

"Bitch needs to go the fuck away for good!" Kara says it out as an afterthought, quietly, but we all look in her direction.

It's Liam who clears his throat and says. "My dad, my uncle and I had some serious talks with her. She knows she fucked up," with a shrug of his shoulders, he adds, "she knows how much you mean to Brax. Well, how much you mean to all of us." Liam says as he is talking directly to me.

"Thanks, Liam, but where is she?" I ask almost in a whispering plea.

"Not sure, bitch has gone into hiding. She is no longer allowed to see Eve and she knows it. That is non-negotiable. After the shit... never mind." He says rolling his eyes.

"What?" I'm surprised with the fact Eve is now off limits, but it's the last part of his sentence I am confused over.

It's Braxton that looks a bit nervous, but he speaks up.

"I had a long talk with her when that dick had you. Knew she was behind it, and shit got real. Found out she had no real intentions with our daughter. She wants me, and that's all she really cares about. Made me sick, and I made my decision right then and there. She no longer gets to see her own daughter."

The way his face wrinkles, I can see the pain and anger in his expression. I can only see in my mind the image of a little girl crying for her missing mother.

My eyes connect with him, so I decide to ask, "Oh God, what about Eve?"

"Not going to lie, it was a conversation I would have rather not had. Eve gets it though, that's the sad part. She knows her mother, she picked up on it a long time ago. I think she's a bit relieved and no longer worrying if her momma is coming by or not at all."

"It's never easy to know your mother despises you or just doesn't give a shit. I lived it, I know." Boy did I ever? Going from being loved to, not being loved at all. Disappointment at every turn in their eyes, it took its toll on me and my parents. Being told you're not good enough, or a total screw-up is not only mean, it's wrong to do to any child, no matter their age. My voice trails off, it's a reminder how I felt and still do till this day.

"That's why you are the best thing for Eve and me. She has a mother figure in her life. You."

My eyes shoot to his, as shivers line my spine and goose bumps spread across my arms. Shocked to hear his words, I cover my mouth as tears fill my eyes. Me? How could he think I would be a good mother figure for Eve? I love her, but I'm also all sorts of screwed up. Being a mommy was taken away from me years ago.

"Dominic, you don't need to do this? I beg you not to do this." My whole body started to violently shake at the mere idea he would follow through with his threat to take Willow away from me. I'd been denying him, not to mention threatening to leave him once and for all. Not one to like the word no, or threatened, Dominic is making me pay for every time I had done so.

All of my pleas and tears led into my many failed attempts to beg him to reconsider. I had promised him anything and everything not to take the single most important thing in my life away from me. She was my sole reason for living in this hell hole of a life I created not only for myself but for her. She never asked for any of this. Many a night in the first few months of life I'd questioned, myself wondering if he would ever hurt her. Dominic rarely showed any emotion when it came to Willow. He kept his feelings buried down deep. Even when we found out, he rarely acted like he cared. To be honest, it was more of a distraction for him. My whole pregnancy he kept his distance and his punishments away from me. After she was born...things changed back to the way they were before. Willow was with us but he was always cautious around her.

A few times I did catch the faint hint of a smile that would cross his face as he would watch her sleep. The times when he thought I was not watching him was the only time he showed any emotion towards her. The minute he realized I was watching he would stiffen up and his face would turn ice cold, void of any emotion. I never understood why he acted that way. Why not love his daughter? Was he even capable of love? Yeah, I should already know the answer to that question.

Then, one night we had a huge fight. He was distracted and angry and Willow had been fussy with colic. For the last several weeks she had become extremely fussy in the evenings. For hours it seemed she did nothing but cry and cry. Nothing would console her. Nothing helped. I was spent and near tears myself but Dominic came home and demanded my sole attention. I had been pacing in our room rocking Willow in my arms, doing everything possible to calm her. The louder Willow cried, the louder Dominic raised his voice. The night did not end well. He ended up grabbing his keys and slammed our bedroom door so fiercely, he knocked our picture off of the wall, shattering the glass. The broken glass was reminiscent of my life...broken.

Willow and I ended up in our bed where she had finally drifted off to sleep. I had peace for a few hours until I woke up to find Dominic staring at me with nothing but hatred in his eyes. I knew it then...my day was about to change forever.

Dominic showed me that day exactly how evil he really could be. With little to no explanation, he took Willow from our bed, sleeping so soundly and left with her. Stunned I sat quietly until I realized something was off. He took her that day and I never saw her again. I fell into the deepest and darkest pit of hell from that day on. That day that turned into months. His twisted new game was to torment me...his bargaining chip, Willow. Comply with him and she would return home, deny him and Willow would stay where she was...away from me. He would ask me often 'how much do you want to be a mother again, Izzabella?' Hate was not a strong enough word for what I felt for him. That day moving forward the only thing I did, was plot my escape.

"Braxton, I'm not so sure," I whisper in his ear.

"I am." He says as he kisses the top of my head.

Later that day, we were down at Braxton's house, and I was nervous to see Eve. I had no idea if she would want me around. And I'm not sure how she felt about the new situation with her so called mother. Seeing her the moment our eyes met, I got my answer.

"Izzy!" She hollers as she comes running to me and hugs my waist. I hardly get a chance to walk in the door.

"Hey, beautiful girl," I say and bend slightly holding her against me wincing in slight pain. My incision is healing nicely but any slight bending still hurts.

Eve cries against my shirt holding onto me as tight as she can. I know how she must be feeling. Not having your mother care for you is the hardest thing to accept. I knew when I became a mother myself. I knew what unconditional love meant. I only wish I could give that to Willow.

Eve ended up glued to me all evening. Her grandmother, Emma, Braxton's mom, was a constant in their lives and the only female in Eve's life now. She was an incredible woman and she made me feel comfortable right away. I was surprised to hear Braxton had told her all about me. Emma Ryles is a tall, curvy woman. She's just stunning. Her lovely black hair cascades around her shoulders and her eyes match the ones I have grown to love, they sparkle just like his. She looked a lot like him which made me wonder what he inherited from his father. Braxton doesn't talk much about him. I know he wasn't around a lot, but not sure what that all meant.

"Oh honey, you look too skinny. Brax needs to feed you more." Emma says as she is examining me from, head to toe.

Braxton comes up behind me and wraps his arms around my body. I rest back against him swaying back and forth. As he nuzzles my neck, I lean my head on the side to give him room to nuzzle. Being openly passionate with each other, well, it's awesome.

"Love having you here with me," Braxton whispers in my ear. "Oh Iz, just wait till I get you in my bed for a change. My bed will never seem so inviting as it will be with you in it." Grabbing my hips, he pushes his hardening cock against my backside.

"Hmm, the way you feel against me, its home, Sparkplug." He says with his lips pressed to my neck.

The feel of him pressed against me is one thing, but add in his sexy words, I'm all but putty in his hands.

"I like the sound of that. I'm not going to lie," I whisper, closing my eyes letting my body melt into his. He's right, this feels like home.

Emma loudly announces that dinner is ready. She has this unbelievable spread of cold cut subs, chips, potato salad, vegetables, and even dip. Yum, the sight it all has my stomach grumbling, I'm starving. I admit I am feeling pretty well, all things considered. I'm slowly feeling more like old self. Yesterday, Max informed me that my infection was better. He explained to keep taking my pills and with that he took off earlier today. He was going to try and find out information on Willow's whereabouts. It seems his friendship with Liam has stuck, and Max might decide to join up with his MC. I have to admit, stranger things have happened.

Kara and I fill our plates and sit, relaxing for a change.

"It's weird isn't it?" Waiting to gauge her reaction, I've not had time to ask her how she is dealing with all that had happened. She puts on a brave face but killing your own brother has its consequences, even for my strong-willed friend.

Her face falters with a distant look. "It is what it is. There was no saving him, he was never going to change."

The tears that welled up have me dropping my sandwich and grabbing her in a big hug.

"Shh, I'm so unbelievably sorry, Kara. I made so many mistakes, would-a, could-a, should-a, can't change the past, I suppose."

Kara continues to sob. "The worst of it is my regrets for my niece. Your daughter. Where the hell is she? I just wish I could have done more. More for her, more for you, hell, even more for me." She continually shakes her head, wiping her tears with the back of her hand.

We share the same regrets and guilt, and I find it hard to say the right words to ease her pain. Any mention of Willow about breaks my own heart. I can't go there. I can't think my sweet little girl. She should have been with me. She should have never been taken from me. My throat tightens with each attempt to swallow but my rapid blinking is at least keeping my tears at bay.

Needing to move, I stand and brush my jeans trying to gain some composure. Kara's eyeing me intently. She's trying to read my thoughts. With a shake of my head, I'm trying to tell her, 'not now, can't talk about my daughter.' My feelings are just too raw knowing my only connection to Willow died the instant Dominic did. Now I'm not sure I'll ever see her again. This time for real.

A warm hand suddenly grips my hip and I spin to face Braxton. He notices the bleak expression on my face and instantly he frowns.

Wiping at a tear that escaped my left eye, I try to smile and dismiss my tears with a shake of my head.

"I'm okay. Just, I don't." I huff out, "I don't know." It's all I can say as I'm suddenly hit with the urge to run. I need some space. I need to breathe.

Raising his eyebrow, he asks, "Sparkplug, are you okay?" Of course, that signature eyebrow raise he does likes to give me, instantly calms my nerves.

"I will be in time," with a shrug, I mutter, "maybe." It's the best I can give him right now.

LATER THAT NIGHT, I'M SITTING alone in Braxton's bedroom. He is busy putting Eve to bed, so I took a much needed shower. Realizing I've got no clothes to change into, I open a few dresser drawers looking for a t-shirt to sleep in. I pull one out and instantly smell it. Yes, it smells just like him.

I have to giggle looking in the mirror, his large t-shirt hangs down to my knees. Perfect sleeping shirt, although I'm sure by night's end, I won't need it. Preferably, I'll be naked with a hard body pressed against mine.

Braxton comes strolling in and stops dead in his tracks when he sees me dressed in his shirt. His eyes dart up and down my body. His smile widens and I all of a sudden feel shy. Crossing my legs, I pull the shirt lower. Snickering he shakes his finger at me.

"No. No. No," he says with a shake of his head. "No acting shy, baby. No reason for you and this all this hotness to be shy when it comes to me." Pulling his shirt over his head, he throws it on the floor and takes two giant steps stopping right in front of me.

What sounds like an 'umm' noise escapes his lips as his hands run through my wet hair. "Oh, I do love my girl all wet."

With his hands on my hips, he's pulling me tight against him. The instant friction of his body against mine makes me gasp. Braxton moans lowering his head to lock our lips. No hesitation on his part whatsoever and I accept his invitation.

My body goes limp and I can't help but moan. He makes me weak in the knees, and I begin to sway back and forth losing myself in him.

"Oh, Sweet Jesus. I can never get enough of you. How the hell did I get lucky enough to find you, Braxton?" I slowly pull back and gaze into his big brown eyes. Tonight they sparkle.

I cup his cheeks and gaze into his glorious face. Gazing at this beautiful man, I find it hard to breath. His eyebrows are as dark as his eyes. They entrance me. The line of his jaw is so strong and defined. *Good Lord*, I have never met a man as beautiful as he is. I can't stand it any longer I lean up and kiss each cheek and then guide the tip of my nose to trace and kiss him ever so sweetly. It's soft and sweet and I pour my feelings into each of my kisses. Each time my lips touch his face, he moans and falters into me a little bit more.

My whisper is more like a whimper. "You are so breathtakingly beautiful."

"Mmmm. Not as beautiful as you." He says, keeping his eyes closed.

Within seconds, we are both in bed. Lying on our sides facing each other, he traces his finger along my neck to between my breasts, before settling on my hip. I try not to laugh from his tickle.

"Ticklish are we now?" He asks with a slight giggle of his own.

"Maybe," I say, completely dazed with his lust filled eyes. My burning desire ramps up as the twinkle in his eyes now brimming with raw passion.

Leaning in, he sweetly kisses me. Gently, he strokes my cheek with the pad of his thumb. Wrapping his fingers around the side of my face he is holding my head still while fusing his lips to mine.

Our kiss is sweet and unrushed, unlike most of our other ones. The heat between us feels different. Our lust and need is exposing yet another deeper emotion. Our chemistry is undeniable, our desires for each other are off the charts. But this feels different. This is un-rushed. The fire inside me is smoldering, festering into something greater. I might not live through this, but hell if I don't love every minute of it.

"Baby, I need you so bad. Iz, I need to be so deep inside of you. Oh hell, I fucking love you, Sparkplug." His whispering words float in my mind as his body does all the talking.

I moan and tremble as my desires take control over my body. I reach up, running my fingers through his hair. I tighten my grip positioning myself over him. Braxton lies on his back and is cupping my ass. His fingers dig into my flesh, and I relish the sting of his touch. It heightens my own lustful desires. Rolling my hips, I rock against him to find some much needed relief. The growing ache between my legs is suddenly unbearable to tolerate any longer.

"Oh Braxton," I whisper throwing my head back. "Being with you is the best feeling I have ever had. The thought of never being with you again, I...I can't." My voice cracks and I wince trying to hide my pain.

"Don't even think things like that babe. Let me make love to you. Let me show you how much I truly love you."

Reaching out, he lays a hand on my heart. Seeing him like this, needing me, it's the best feeling in the world.

Sitting up Braxton comes to his knees, pulling me to mirror his stance. We pause only to look at each other. Slowly Braxton slides his hand down my hip and hooks my left leg behind the knee and pulls it over his hip. Trying not to fall back, I hold on tight to his shoulders. Slightly tilted back, he lines himself with my already drenched entrance. Quickly lifting me, his eyes blazing with lust reach out and touch my soul.

The thing, about being able to read people with their eyes alone, has always been an incredible secret of mine, but never as powerful as it is right now. His look is beyond anything I have ever seen before. It's soft but not, it's eager but not, it's so much more.

I can tell Braxton is having trouble keeping his desires under control, he's flaring his nose in sync with his rapid breathing. His chest is rising and retracting so fast the sheen of perspiration beads on his massive chest. The only thing I can think is, I want to lick every inch of this beautiful man.

I lower my gaze to his erection that's just begging to slide into my wet core. I lick my lower lip imagining how wonderful it would be to wrap him around my lips, and I can't help but whimper and moan. When our eyes meet, my mischievous grin gives way as I bite my lower lip.

"Oh, Sparkplug I can see the wheels turning in that head of yours. Can't wait for those plump lips around my dick either, but right now he wants your sweet pussy."

"Who am I to deny him what he wants?" I cheekily answer.

"Watch him as he slides into your pure sweetness baby."

We both look down to his large and eager cock as he slowly comes closer to me where I ache the most. My breath hitches as he starts to slide into me. I am so unbelievably wet he has no issue, pushing in inch by delectable inch. I savor the heat that radiates from him filling me so full.

He feels so incredible; I can't help but roll my eyes as my nails dig into his shoulders, each wave of ecstasy is stronger than the next.

Braxton is holding onto my left leg hooking it around his hip not only to give him leverage but to keep my body still as he slowly thrusts himself in and out of me. Braxton is slow and deliberate as I can't help but moan and grunt in pure unadulterated bliss.

He's taking me higher and closer to what I am craving. His intensity increases and with each push Braxton is becoming more demanding. Worshipping my body, he drives into me circling his hips before retreating and doing it all again increasing his pressure and speed.

Within minutes, he is pushing so hard I stumble back and he comes down with me. He never slips out, he just repositions himself and goes back to his continued thrashing of his hard body into mine. I find it hard to breathe, the only thing I can concentrate on is how incredible he feels.

"Harder. Braxton, give it to me harder. Show me that I'm yours." I have no idea what I am saying as my pleasure is too intense. In fact, I know I'm saying things about every part of his body and what it does to mine.

"Mine, Iz. This. (thrust) Fucking. (thrust) Body. (thrust) Is. (thrust) Mine (final push so hard he detonates)."

"Ooh. Oooh. YES, yes, yes, oh sweet Jesus." It's all I can get out as my world is fucking rocked.

Braxton is breathing so hard, I just realize he came along with me. I must have blacked out, wow. I love it when he explodes and calls out my name and how the hell did I miss it?

"Honey, did I miss something?" I slow my breathing, feeling like some time has lapsed.

With sweat dripping down his face, Braxton wrinkles his forehead. "Excuse me?"

"I swear I must have blacked out because I didn't realize you even came with me. You usually call out my name when you do." I say pushing the wet hair from my forehead trying to gain my wits.

His smile gives way to his light chuckle lying down next to me all stretched out.

"Made my girl blackout? That's excellent shit right there, proves that I am a stud."

I try to smack his sweat covered chest with my hand, but my hand just glides off instead. Some may call it gross, but I love it. He is all sweaty from loving me. Yep, the proud moment makes me giddy.

Cuddling next to him, I lay my head on his wet chest. "Your ego, I swear, sometimes."

"Sparkplug, I'm not going to lie to you when I say it sucks you can't have any more kids. I would love to have my baby inside of you." He says, stroking the back of my head.

I stay silent, no idea what to say honestly. The idea does hurt, but not having my daughter hurts more.

"Baby we are trying to find her, but can I ask you a question?" Brax asks me with some hesitancy.

"Sure," I reply back.

"What happened as to why you can't have any more kids?" I knew he would ask, I just wish I knew more.

"I had a tough time delivering Willow, lost a lot of blood and found out when I woke up that I couldn't have any more children."

That's the truth. The doctor's had to do surgery when my bleeding didn't stop. I was lucky and didn't need a hysterectomy, but surgery was required to stop the bleeding all the same. Not sure what they called it, but it worked so I didn't press for more.

"I'm sorry."

I reply, "Yeah, me too."

chapter TWENTY-FIVE

SAM'S HANDS ARE SHAKING AS he holds his phone out for me. Dragging my eyes from the screen to his face, I gasp covering my mouth, in shock. What is this? Why is he showing this to me? I should be thanking him instead, for showing me what Braxton didn't tell me. Hell, even Liam for that matter. Does this mean Kara could know? I can't imagine she'd hide something like this and she would never outright lie to me. I'm not only repulsed by this, I'm heartbroken.

Slightly shaken, I stumble back on my stool. With my head held low, I'm nervously tapping my thumbs against the bar. Clenching my hands tightly, I have the urge to throw something. Instead, I just concentrate on my thumbs. Shaking my head from side to side, I realize I'm voicing my thoughts out loud. The problem is, I don't give a shit. In my head, out loud, doesn't matter.

Swinging my eyes back up to Sam, I know he's waiting for me to respond. I do what comes naturally.

"Shot of tequila, Sam." It's the only way I'm going to ease the mental picture of a near naked Tiffany. I might need to bleach my eyes.

Slapping his hand on the bar, Sam comes closer to me. Under his breath, he keeps asking himself 'why.' I notice he is running his thumb over his bottom lip, back and forth. I'm sure he is trying to figure out what to say.

I halt his thoughts, with a raise of my hand. "Sam. Don't. Shot, please. Now." He is not moving fast enough.

"Anything for you Izzy, but dammit." Grabbing a bottle of Tequila, he pours two shots. One for me, and I'm guessing one for him. He then grabs two bottles of beers. Opening one, he slides it across the bar.

Raising our shot glasses, we give a silent salute before downing them. Oh, it burns, it burns like hell. It's a welcome feeling though. Taking my cold beer, I swallow quickly, to cool the burn. My eyes tear up with the burn.

Enjoying the coldness of my beer, suddenly it dawns on me. "Sam, how the hell did you get that?" I say, lowering my eyes to his phone.

Sam eyes widen. He's pausing, staring intently at the image that just rocked my world.

"Shit Izzy, I um, well." He says, rubbing his forehead aggressively. "I let myself go down that road with her recently. Upon her passing out in my room, her phone buzzed with a message. I happened to look at it and realized it was from that guy from your past."

He looks pained as he brings up the subject of Dominic. I can tell because his grimace lingers.

Sam points to his phone and says, "I decided to do some snooping while she was passed out. I found some interesting texts she sent to Brax and found her selfies." His face looks like he just drank something sour.

Rubbing his chest, he squeezes one eye shut. "That was one of the pictures I found, and after that, I was so disgusted I left."

I am about to say something when I hear the door to the bar open. In strolls a happy Kara followed in with Liam, and then you guessed it, Braxton. Well, the man of the hour is here. I am choking on my beer in a fit of nerves. I downed this one in record time nodding for Sam to get me another one. And make it quick.

Sam's eyes widen, puzzled. He crosses his arms waiting to see what I'm going to do. He knows I can be a loose cannon when I'm fueled, and right now my fuel indicator is pushing past full. I plaster on my most fakest smile I can, keeping my eyes glued to Sam. The mirror behind the bar allows me to see Braxton walking up behind me smiling from ear to ear. Too bad I'm about to ruin swipe that smile from his face.

"Sam, how are you, buddy?" Braxton casually says as if they are old friends, when, in fact, the opposite is true. They don't like each other on most days. Another disaster thanks to Tiffany aka 'local whore.'

Keeping my eyes in a downward gaze, I play with the label of my beer. Pulling away at the edges, I drop the pieces. Kara skips over and nudges my shoulder with hers. She sits, and orders a round of beers. Sam stands and glares at Braxton a 'less than friendly' grimace. The tension is quickly becoming uncomfortable. No one is saying a word. To say the three of them look puzzled is an understatement.

Kara lets out a snicker. "Not feeling the love in this room, what gives?" She's staring between me then settles her eyes on Sam. I can make out the slight head tilt she gave to Braxton. Responding back, he shakes his head having no clue. He then moves to get a better look at what, no doubt, will be a very icy glare from me. I try to hide my face by fanning my hair to fall forward.

Moving a strand of my hair, he bends lower. "Iz, you okay babe?" He asks me with an oddly cautious tone to his voice. His voice is soft, and his eyes are every bit caring. Shifting his look between everyone in the room, he's questioning everyone with only his look alone. For someone who is guilty, he sure doesn't show it.

The look of concern on his face plays with my mind, and the only thing I want to do is kick him. Hard. If no more, than the reason of me having to see that damn photo.

Not one to bit my tongue, not anymore anyway. I give Sam a slight smirk. "Funny thing you should ask me that." I casually say turning around to face Braxton head on. I'm holding back my urge to slap him. Visions of me throwing my beer bottle at his head, sounds like a good idea. But, I don't. Putting his arm around my shoulder Braxton tries to pull me into a sideways hug. Too bad, I don't go willingly.

A very irritated sigh escapes his lips. "What the hell is wrong, Izzy? Sam, you mind explaining?" Braxton's tone turns ice cold. I happen to turn and glance at his reflection in the mirror finding his glare is menacing, and directed at Sam. Oh Braxton...what have you done?

Sam questions Braxton. "Jesus, how do you do it?" His stance is tense, standing stiff as a board.

Braxton's holding up his hands as if questioning his own sanity. But Sam doesn't pause.

"I mean, you have Izzy. A woman any man would die for, and you just throw it away. For what? A quick lay?"

That does it. With every ticking question and accusation Sam is throwing at Braxton, his face turns red as every facial muscle starts to twitch. Every word Sam is saying, Braxton just stares. He's getting more confused and more irritated by the minute. My mouth is gaping open. I'm stuck staring at Sam with mixed apprehension, because pissing Braxton off is like showing the color red to a bull. The low, menacing growls are then not only coming from Braxton. No, Liam is looking murderous himself.

Seething mad, Braxton grinds his teeth. "What the hell are you talking about, Sam?"

Braxton is standing right up to the bar, then, slams his hand down, spilling his bottle of beer. No one says a word. We are all eerily quiet. I take this moment to stop and stare at the three of them, one at a time. I'm accessing their expressions, watching their movements. Each set of eyes tells me a story. Unfortunately, they tell me everything, I feared they would.

My fear is quickly replaced with anger. "Un-fucking-believable. To think, I could trust you." Throwing my hands up, I shout at all three of them, defeated. "*Seriously*, not one of you could tell me the damn truth?"

They all look at me with wide eyes, their guilt showing on their faces. I'm so mad, but more so, I'm deeply hurt. "All this time, you are all like 'poor Izzy. Feel sorry for Izzy.' Oh my God, all three of you sicken me." Standing up, I push Braxton's chest leaving my hand touching him.

"I came here to tell Sam I am quitting. Of course, he's great about it." Lowering my hand, I drop my eyes to the floor and take a calming breath.

Shaking all images from my head, I bite my lower lip. "He is the only one who has the balls to let me in on the little secret all of you have kept from me." Raising my head, I make sure they see how upset I am. "It's sad. The people who claim to love me the most are the ones always to let me down." Realizing how true my words are, a violent sob escape past my lips.

"Oh my God!" My shaking hand covers my mouth, as the other holds my stomach. Dizziness swirling in my mind, the only echo in the room, is my hurtful cries.

Kara jumps, shouting, 'no-no-no' as she reaches for my shoulders. Shaking them lightly, she exclaims, "Listen to me, I have no idea what Sam told you, but it's not what you think."

Oh, so she knows precisely what I am referring to now.

Snapping my head back, I raise my voice. "What? Are you kidding me?"

It's Braxton who grabs me trying to pull me near him. "Izzy, you need to listen to me right now!" He's clenching his teeth, breathing erratically. Avoiding any eye contact with me, his attention is solely centered on Sam.

Not wanting to witness a bar brawl, Liam is quick to approach Braxton. I'm in a standoff. All sets of eyes are on a confident Sam. He glares right back Braxton, not backing down one bit. Kara for the first time in history is quiet, watching me intently. I can't stand this another minute.

My mouth curls, and I snap. "Oh please. Go ahead Braxton, explain this to me please."

Braxton looks toward the ceiling. "What the fuck?"

He can't deny it. I've got a picture to prove it, so I challenge him. "What. Go on and explain it. I'm waiting." I'm flexing my hands just about to jump out of my damn skin. Do I want to hear this?

It's Liam that shakes his head in obvious denial. "Izzy, none of it is what it appears. I know how much Brax has been beating himself up over this shit." One hand on his hip, he rests the other on Braxton's shoulder.

Oh wow, Liam's confirmation has my chest heaving as a part of me had wished the picture was false. That maybe this nightmare had never happened. Now that knife in my chest just pierced my heart deeper. To dull my pain, I grab the bottle of Tequila, taking a drink. Rejoicing the burn while it slowly slides down my throat, I moan. Burn baby burn.

"I had no idea she did this, Izzy. You have to believe that." Liam's voice is softer this time.

Braxton reaches out as his fingers dig into my shoulder. I recoil with slight discomfort. I know he doesn't mean to be rough. He's not in control right now, and he hates it. Not knowing how I'm going to react has put him on pins and needles. The best way to get to the bottom of this is to show him my proof.

"Okay," grabbing for Sam's phone on the bar, I shove the image at Braxton. "Let me show you the picture I just had to witness."

Holding the image in his hand, he lets out a few swear words. "Jesus Christ."

Yep, that's the answer I got. Raising my eyebrow in disbelief, I slowly look at Kara, and then Liam. All eyes are locked on Braxton. His expression oddly enough, is the same shocked look I had earlier. Only, right now I don't care. I don't question it, because only mine are hurt with his betrayal.

Liam's looking over his shoulder. "Fuck, Brax. She took a fucking picture. Bitch wanted to make sure Izzy saw this." Liam grabs for the phone, and then throws it against the wall, smashing it to pieces.

"Hey Fucker, that was mine!" Sam yells from behind the bar.

Liam shrugs his shoulders, obviously pissed off. "Yeah and I bet you couldn't wait to show Izzy these pictures, huh Sam?"

There's an awkward pause, because Sam stays silent. I'm not sure if Sam told me out of concern for me, or if he wanted to drive a wedge between Braxton and myself. Either way, it just sucks for me.

Clearing her throat, Kara makes sure she has my attention. Snapping her fingers, I do look into her face. "Well, now it's out there. Fucking bitch knew Brax was drunk. She stripped out of her clothes trying to get Brax out of his. Then, the bitch took a selfie?" Kara crosses her arms, nodding her head, before adding, "You know she did it for you to believe that she slept with him, right?" Kara says matter of fact like it's not a big deal.

I'm slightly drunk, but not damn near drunk enough for this to make any sense. In a moment of temporary insanity, I slap my knee, laughing. No idea why, most likely its laugh or cry. And, I really don't want to cry right now. I've cried nonstop over the last few weeks.

Liam and Braxton both appear agitated. Shifting their feet, their faces are red and frowning. Kara just rolls her eyes and takes a drink. It's Sam that looks like he wishes he was anywhere, but here. Thank God the bar is empty besides us. Although this would provide some serious entertainment for the night.

I walk around them all and make my way to the pool tables, in the back room. One, I need some space, and secondly, its play pool, or start throwing bar stools. I want to hit something, maybe I should just haul off and take a swing at Braxton. It might make me feel better, but instead, I pick up the eight ball and roll it down the table. I can sense him before he speaks.

"Play me?" He says with a whisper. "Play with me and talk to me?" As he reaches out for me, I turn away from his touch, walking to the other side of the table. Last thing I need is for him to touch me.

Raising my eyes to meet his, my eyes are cold and detached. "I don't own the bar, do what you want."

"Baby, let me explain. Please hear me out. Just don't interrupt me, okay?"

I nod, but say nothing.

This time he speaks with more confidence, holding up his hand to halt me from saying a word. I glance back to see Kara and Liam. They are quiet, staying near the bar. I'm sure this is intended to give Braxton and me some much-needed privacy. I'm relieved because I'm too tired to talk to all three of them at the same time.

I'm having trouble swallowing, hating to have this conversation with him. I do stop him now. "And what? Listen to you tell me how you wished it never happen. How it was a mistake? How she took advantage of you. Better yet, you don't remember any of it? Does any of this work for you?" My hands are flying about as I speak a mile a minute.

"Exactly," He raises his voice. "It meant nothing. I was drinking to dull the pain of missing you, and she showed up. Then, I drank even more. The next thing I know she's half naked, and my jeans are unbuttoned. Thankfully, Liam came in and ruined her little plan. When I sobered up enough, he explained what he walked in on. I don't want her Iz. You have to believe that." His voice started out seething mad, but ended up remorseful and endearing. A bit of begging, too.

Hearing him say this, I can't help but feel betrayed still. "Fault of your own, or not, she had intentions of taking your clothes off. What would have happened if she had gotten them off? Would you of been able to stop her? The way she smiled in the picture, it was definite 'fuck you moment' all for me." Falling to the floor, I crumble to my knees clenching my fists to my chest. It's too painful as my head can't block that image. First Dominic, now her. God, enough is enough.

Tears stream down my cheeks as my sobs overtake me. Not a moment passes before Braxton cradles me in his lap. Not a second after that Liam and Kara are joining him, on the floor with us.

Kissing my head, Braxton says, "God, baby. Please don't cry. I just got you back. You have no idea what it was like for me, knowing you were being held by *him.* Not knowing what he was doing with you...or to you." His voice cracks.

"Izzy, I'm so sorry," Kara tries to comfort me. Her hand touches my head as she bends to kiss it. "I didn't want to upset you with what she tried to do. She never got what she wanted, so I let it go. Believe me I wanted to kill that bitch. And I will if I ever see her again." Her hand continues to stroke my hair as she keeps telling me how sorry she is.

Liam's voice if full of disappointment. All of his sarcasm and insults are geared toward Tiffany, his sister.

"Izzy, you have to understand, Brax was drunk most days after you went missing. He went off the deep end one night, and I was away trying to get some things worked out with Max. Found out Tiff came over." The beer Liam is holding is now thrown against the wall shattering it. He is voicing his anger towards his brothers for letting this happen at all. Sam jumps up as it took him by surprise.

"You are cleaning that up, dick. No more throwing shit in my bar. Jesus, just get the fuck out will you?" Sam bellows.

Liam sprang to his feet. "Sam, you little prick. This mess is entirely your fault. You started this, so shut the hell up." Liam was all over his shit. Kara was trying to calm all of us down.

Me? I'm just tired of it all. I know Braxton is beating himself up over this, it's all to evident. I may be acting irrational, I know he didn't do anything, but seeing her smiling at the phone. It was like she was smiling just for me. I'm mildly comforted here tight in his lap. Closing my eyes, I want to forget it all. Forget Tiffany, forget Dominic, but I can't seem to want to forget Braxton. I've survived worst. It's finally over, Dominic is gone. I'm free. The only thing is, my heart belongs to Braxton, but is it worth putting up with Tiffany?

"Izzy, look at me honey." Liam kneels down on the floor. I refuse to raise my face to his, I keep it hidden. It's curled to my chest pressed against Braxton. He has me gripped tight, not much room to escape. I'm just too tired and hurt to fight him off.

Liam pauses, before he continues, "If you don't want to look, then just listen, and hear me. Braxton was not doing well. It's not an excuse, it's the truth. Most days he was keyed up and basically worthless. I know when I left that night it was a mistake. He was barely functioning, that is why I thought it was okay not to play babysitter for the time being. I left, and I also found out when I got back from Zeke that Tiffany was here with Brax. I guess my presence was needed. I walked in hearing him murmur to her that it was only you. She didn't take that well. She was even more intent on what she came to do. Pushing more alcohol down his throat, I came in and went crazy. Bitch must have already taken her photo, because I got her the fuck out of there. Lucky, I didn't kick her ass, but I was just more concerned with Brax. He was beyond drunk, more like damn near incoherent." Liam's always so cool, calm and collected. But right now, he is tense and unnerved retelling me what had happened. I have to say, his honesty helps make things more clearly for me to understand.

Pushing myself back, I can't help but look in Braxton's eyes. He's a mess. Tears flowing, his eyes are bloodshot. My usual confident man is not the man in front of me now. I almost feel sorry for him as much as I feel sorry for me. Almost. Without a single doubt, I know he is telling me the truth. I may not like it, but I know he's not entirely to blame either.

I notice the worried expression on Liam's face before I have to ask. "Can you tell me, better yet, can you promise me she is out of my life for good? Is she out of Braxton's life for good? Can you give me that, Liam?" I'm in more control of my emotions, but my voice is still shaky.

Wiping away my tears with his thumb, Liam tells me. "Izzy girl, I know she is out of his life. Yours too. I made it crystal clear to her what would happen if she ever shows her face." His eyes sharpen and his throat groans. The picture in my mind, damn near has me wince.

"Izzy, Brax loves you so much. You have to believe him. Do you honestly think I would let him live? Let alone let him near you, if he weren't?" Kara wags a finger at Braxton. His mild smile quickly dashes.

I let her know that I believe her. I also acknowledge, I think Braxton is telling me the truth. Otherwise he would not be on the damn floor crying with me. It's not his style.

Holding his hand to cup my face, Braxton sighs. "Izzy, I love you so fucking much it hurts. I didn't want to admit it to you. I'm so damn ashamed of it." He lowers his face to mine, eyes deeply settled on mine, he says, "There was no way I was going to hurt you with this shit. I couldn't lose you, not again."

His declaration of love is all I see in his eyes. There is no denying what he feels for me, and how desperately sorry he is. Even though he did nothing wrong, the idea he found himself in this position with her sickens me. Will it always be this way...me feeling insecure when it comes to her?

I need to figure out where to go from here. The more I shake my head back and forth, I can't seem to erase his words and her photo. The harder try to erase the image from my mind, the louder it shouts back. My breathing becomes more erratic. I have the urge to leave. Get out of here and forget Tiffany ever existed. Only with Eve, I can't. I'll never be able to fully escape that bitch.

Pickup up on my anxiety, Braxton shakes. "No. No. No. Izzy do not shake your head at me. You are not leaving. Sweet Jesus, don't even think about leaving me." He's panicking.

His strong arms wrap me in a tight hold. His smell and brute force undo my resolve. Every time. I can't help but cry out louder. No use in pushing him away, I can't move a muscle. He's too strong.

I ramble. "What…what… happens now? I mean, what's next? She keeps coming back, Braxton." I mumble because my face is smashed against his chest. Raising my head, I place my hand on his chest. He is trying to reassure me.

"She took advantage of the situation." His voice is low, sweet even. It's his eyes that move me.

Breaking our silent moment, Liam sighs. "My sister is a piece of work."

"No shit." Braxton chimes in.

"Got that right," Kara says standing back up.

"Liam, have you got any other word on her whereabouts?" Braxton interrupts asking him.

"Fuck no, but don't worry. Now that this charade is out in the open, I can have the guys talk freely. I'll find her ass, don't you worry about that." Liam says trying to find something on his phone.

"Oh God, what a mess. My baby has an evil bitch for a mother." Braxton stumbles and catches the side of the pool table.

"God can't help you now," I say as I walk back to the bar to find my purse and thank Sam for, well I'm not sure what the hell I'm thanking him for.

Sam doesn't even think about it, he says, "Listen Iz, you need anything. Let me know, yeah?" Polite as ever, Sam pulls me in for a hug.

"Thanks for that Sam, but I think you did enough. I'm not mad at you and thanks for letting me work here. I might be back, not sure what I am going to do right now."

"Sparkplug." Braxton hollers walking toward us. "What do you mean you're not sure what you are going to do now? You're coming back to work for me. To be with *me*." His dominant side is showing once again.

Turning back to him, I'm drained of energy. "I'm not sure what I am going to do. You all said your peace. I thank you for being honest, but…"

"Of cou…"

I cut him off.

"But you did not tell me yourself, I had to find out from Sam. That hurts me more than knowing what happened in the first place.

You..." I point at his chest. "You should have told me yourself, right away."

"Iz."

I cut him off again.

"No. You had your say, now I'm telling you, that I don't know right now. I have no idea what I'm going to do." I say it as my tears spill again. I'm an emotional mess. These past weeks have taken their toll on me. I'm not thinking rational at all. Hell, I'm not sure how to feel either.

"Girl, did you not just hear a word I said to you. I *fucking* love you. No matter what the hell happened. You are *my, Iz*."

My body is shaking as I've reached my breaking point. I've got nothing left. I'm exhausted. "I'm no one's. I believe you with what happened. I do. But it doesn't stop the pictures screaming in my head. The fact that she was with you like that makes me sick. Her hands were all over you. What if she had taken all of your clothes off? I can't get that idea out of *my head*. She took my heart in her hands with the idea of shattering it. Her goal was only inches away." My words are almost a plea. The hurt in my voice is easily on display as my body shakes.

With a shake of his head, he raises an eyebrow. "Honey, she didn't take shit."

"Oh, we both know that is not true. She has been involved in every damn thing bad that has happened to me since I moved here." It's all true. "She got us to fight. She led Dominic to me, which led to my kidnapping. Which led me to my near deadly infection, then, she almost fucked you to make sure she destroyed me. I'm tired of fighting *her*, Braxton." I say with my eyes glued to the floor. I'm suddenly hauled into his arms in a crushing hug. Kara is suddenly swearing ready to throw her stool across the room. We all can't help but stare at her.

Her face is read and really angry. "Fuck her, Izzy. You have been through worse, dammit. You do not let her win, you hear me? Grab a hold of your man and show her that he is yours. You get what I'm saying to you?" Kara angry is never a good thing when it is directed at you. She's so animated right now, I bit my cheek. Braxton wants me to go with what she said. Liam just agreed, 'yeah, what she said.'

Braxton whispers in my ear. "Listen to your girl, Izzy. She is right, and you know it. I'm not letting you go, so stop worrying about fighting. You are not alone...lean on me. I'll fight your damn fights girl.

I'll protect you." He tenses for a second, and then says, "I've done a shit job of it so far, but I swear on my life. I'll get it right, Iz."

I pull away from him slightly and look at all three of them. They are all close enough to be in a huddle. Sam and Liam continue to share pleasantries with one another, as Kara's making sure she gets her voice heard.

"Let me ask you something, Braxton? How would you feel if the roles were reversed and you found out Dominic nearly screwed me when I was passed out? Would it be easy to deal with, process it, and simply throw it away?"

I can feel his body tense. His facial expressions turn cold and murderous. He knows exactly what I'm getting at.

"Fuck, I get it okay. I hate it, and there is not a goddamn thing I can do about it. The idea of him with you is the reason I was drinking all the time. It was the only way to numb the pain. Can't you get that, Izzy? It-fucking-killed-me." The only thing he can do is rub the tension from of his face with his hands. Rubbing his forehead mad, like he might rub his skin off.

"I get that we both have been through some serious shit lately. All of it hurts, Braxton." I wrap my hand around his face leaning my forehead against his.

"I know babe. Sparkplug we will get through this. No matter what happens. You hear me. Please, believe I will protect you."

"Brax," I whimper.

Softly, he says, "Yeah, babe."

"You love me right?" It's not a question, just merely a statement.

This makes him slightly chuckle. "Bet your ass, I do."

He pauses, staring into my eyes. "You love me, Iz?"

Oh my sweet Braxton.

Tilting my head to the side, I chuckle. "Someone has too."

For the first time in a while I actually laugh. So hard, he lightly smacks my ass. Yeah, that got my attention.

"Braxton." I yelp, covering my butt with my hand.

Hearing me say this, he moans. "Oh no. You're back to calling me, Braxton."

I give him my most 'are you serious look.' "I like Braxton, you ass." I love this playful side we have with one another. After today, it feels great to play around.

"Yeah, I know." He mutters then kisses my head.

I pause. "Braxton?"

"Yeah babe, you got a question or what?" He laughs holding me to him tightly.

"No question, just an idea." I lean forward gazing into his eyes. I'm about to let it all go. Can I do this? I'm about to find out. "Get me out of here and show me how much you love me. Make me forget that picture. Make me forget this whole nightmare." Lowering my voice to barely a whisper, I lean closer so our noses touch.

Noses still touching, my eyes plead with his big brown eyes. "Show me I'm yours."

"Oh Iz, my pleasure." He then takes my lips in a panty melting kiss. Long, hard and profound.

A low almost painful moan escapes my lips the instant his tongue, lips and hands explore my body. Not caring we are in a room with others. I no longer can hear their conversations anyway.

I do however; hear Liam's loud 'huh.' "Well shit, that was easier than I thought it would go."

Taking a swing with her fist, Kara wipes under her eyes. "Shut up, my girl got hurt again. It's not over though, not by a long shot."

Finally fed up, Sam hollers. "Can you all just please leave my bar? This is a bit too much. For the life of me Brax, she's too good for you." Sam throws the rag he was using to wipe the bar down.

"Yeah, don't I know it, Sam? But, I'll spend my days thanking her for being mine. Just know if I ever find out you pull a stunt like this again, I will fuck you up." The threat in his voice, was real and harsh.

Sam merely rolls his eyes. "Don't pull any stupid shit, and I won't have to."

Okay, time to leave. "Enough." I straighten my mess of hair. "Stay away from your ex Braxton, and he won't have any ammunition to use against you." I only state the obvious holding my hands out in front of me as to say 'well.'

That statement earned me another slap on my ass. Letting out a squeak, we finally leave the bar.

chapter TWENTY-SIX

WE ALL MADE IT BACK to my place and it's quiet. I'm not in the right frame of mind to face Eve at the moment, anyway. I hate her momma even more now. To think she got her greedy little hands on Braxton just pisses me off. Tiffany better hope I never find her. Hell hath no fury like a woman scorned. Yeah, that pretty much sums up how I feel. The next couple of days are going to be hard, but I've survived worse.

Each and every day that followed, was indeed unbearable. I did my best to push any thoughts of Tiffany out of my mind. I just can't seem to forget and it's not only the sick photo, either. It's everything. Braxton tried his best with seducing my mind. As soon as we came home from the bar, he took me hard and fast; then he was slow and seductively sweet. His antics proved most helpful, because she never entered my mind. Braxton knew I was struggling, so he took every chance he could to bare his soul and reassure me. Each word of adoration he spoke, unleashed an endless stream of tears. I believed him, and I believe in him. Lord knows he's dealing with his own feelings. His suffering and many regrets echo with every word and endearing touch. He's more determined to make things right with me. No matter how hard he tried though, he simply can't erase the visuals that flash in my mind. Talk about mental torture.

Yesterday, I received a call from Emma, Braxton's mother. She had learned about the mess with Tiffany, and nearly suffered a heart attack. She was hell bent on talking with me right away. Against

Braxton's argument that she leave well enough alone, she won. Oddly enough, it was her single phone call that eased my mind. She helped me more than anyone else. Not sure if it's her strength, or her extreme love she has for son that impresses me the most. Her obvious distaste for Tiffany is definitely a plus.

For the first five minutes, she went on explaining how no good Tiffany was, as a woman and a mother. Emma's not one to speak ill of another, but Tiffany happened to be Eve's mother, Emma's granddaughter. To her, this was personal.

She explained to me she had a very stern talk with her son in regards to it all. She pointed out to him that he would never find a better woman for him, than me. She caught me off guard with that one. Even after Braxton had filled her in on my past, her thoughts of me never wavered. For the first time in a long time, it felt really good knowing how she feels. It's a wonderful feeling.

When she finally decided to take a breather, she asked me to sit somewhere quiet. Away from the others, so way I could freely talk. Little did I know this woman turned out to be a freaking genius. Who would have known? Just thinking about our conversation brings a smile to my face.

"Izzy, why do you like my son?" Emma had asked softly.

I nervously paused, having this particular conversation with her. Emma intimidates me like no other woman. Swallowing several times, I tried to mutter the courage to tell her. I nervously played with the strands of my hair, ever so thankful this conversation was not in person. It's hard enough on the phone explaining to my man's mother why I like him. Dear Lord, give me strength.

Clearing my throat, I said, "Ah, well. To be honest Emma, the first time I saw him, he stole my breath. I had already met Eve, and fell in love with her almost instantly." The smile and cheerfulness in my voice had me remembering back to the day I met him.

I laughed, recalling some of the colorful conversations I had with Braxton. Biting back a chuckle, I said, "He made me laugh. To be honest, he was a big fat flirt."

Emma's chuckle slowly tapered off. "Do you feel it in your gut when you're around him? That certain feeling that you'd do whatever it took to stay by his side?" She asked very matter of fact.

Hearing her say the words I was surprised they sum up my feelings perfectly.

My voice caught in my throat, saying, "Ah, Emma, how do you know this? I mean the man makes me weak in the knees most of the time. To answer your question, yes. I feel it." I was so in awe of her, I have to hold my phone down just to stare at it wondering if this woman is for real.

"Oh, sweet girl, I know because that is the way his dad made me feel. Just another reason you are perfect for my son." Her idle pause makes me wonder what she was going to say next. "You need to know I am aware of what Tiffany did, and I am truly disgusted by it. Brax was beside himself. He came and we talked for a long while. Mostly it was all about you and how much you mean to him. The moment he saw you, it was lights out for any other woman. Make no mistake the love he has for you, Izzy. The same goes for my granddaughter. You all make a wonderful family. Hopefully, someday your daughter can be a part of the family."

I can't hold back my tears. This woman just took any doubts I had, and blew them out of the water. All the bad memories that involved Tiffany—now seem so insignificant. She just confirmed how much her son loves me, even little Eve. The realization of it all hits me hard. I finally found love. And true love at that. It took me to break, to be able to find the love that was waiting on the other side.

We finished our phone call as I sat outside on my porch, just staring up at the moon. A bright, full moon was on proudly on display. Big bright and beautiful, it lit up the dark street. The slight chill in the air caused me to shiver every so often. July in Washington was nice, but it still had a slight chill to it. My front door squeaked opened, and Kara came walking out. Sitting down next to me, she put her arm around my shoulder, pulling me into a hug.

"Hey sweets, how was Emma? That woman is not one to mess with." Raising her eyebrow, she says laughing.

Letting out a loud chuckle, I nod in agreement. "You got that right."

She's watching my face carefully like she is waiting for me to say something.

Leaning into me, Kara asks, "What did she say to you, you seem quiet?" Hey eyes squint.

Sitting here I take a moment to look around at the evening sky, recalling my conversation with Emma. Contemplating what she said her son felt for me and given the way I feel for him, it's confusing as hell. Should I feel this strongly for a man I hardly know? Is this even the right time to pursue a relationship with anyone this soon? I just don't know. The only thing I do know is I'm in deep when it comes to Braxton.

Turning so my eyes hit hers, I chuckle. "Well, first she vented about hating Tiffany. Then she explained in great detail how much her son loves me. Even little Eve. The kicker, she asked me why I liked her son?"

Kara whistles raising an eye. "Wow, I bet that was a conversation. Did you happen to tell her he gives you incredible orgasms, and the wildest sex you've ever had?" Laughing hard, she bent in half. "Shit, Liam and I have heard you all." She says all the while continuing to chuckle.

I mock a look of mild horror. "No, oh gosh could you imagine?" Talk about mortifying.

"She most likely already knows it, can't fool that lady. Spent a lot of time with her while you were gone. She kept us all sane; her son was another thing though. She saw firsthand how much her son ached for you my dear. That is why we all knew the disaster with Tiffany was just a dog and pony show. He would never intentionally hurt you. That boy is one hundred percent in love with you." She says this pointing a finger at my heart.

My cheeks blush.

"Thanks, Kara for helping me." My smile slowly turns into a grimace, I have to admit. "I want to rip Tiffany's eyeballs out." I laugh, but I'm not joking.

Kara says 'ugh' appearing angry. "Don't worry. Get in line, I get her first."

Crackling her knuckles, there is no mistaking the anger in her voice. I've had something on my mind in regards to Liam, so I had to ask.

"Liam okay with that? By the way, what is going on with you two?" Narrowing my eyes, I ask with the slight curl of my lip.

Her devilish grin spreads wide. "Oh, it's just great sex. He's like sex on a stick." Biting her lip, she's dazed in a dream.

Oh God, really?

"Pfft, please tell me something I don't already know. I can hear you two as well. Remember, thin walls and all." I say laughing so hard I fall into her lap. It feels really good to laugh.

Cupping my shoulder, she sighs. "Oh honey, he makes me laugh. Plus, he keeps me satisfied. It's a win-win."

"Well, I'm happy for you. I'm happy for me, too." Looking from her to the sky above, I think we both are on cloud nine.

Whispering softly, "You did good, Izzy."

Holding back my obvious good fortune for once, I chuckle, "Yeah, he's not so bad is he?"

She does a double-take. "Not so bad, are you kidding me? He is like one hundred percent alpha male sex God. Watch out ladies your panties are going to melt or at least be soaking wet with this man. Jesus, Izzy!"

Okay, wow. I am laughing so hard, I have tears falling down my cheeks. Wiping them away, I admit, "Seriously, I am so screwed."

Giving me a look of 'duh', Kara confirms, "Well, that goes without saying, look at the man."

"No, it's just I'm so completely in love with him. I never knew this kind of love before. Never thought I would find it after everything with Dominic. You know?" Sadness creeps back into my voice. I feel the smack from her hand. Ouch!

"Hey," Kara snaps her fingers at me. "No more sadness. He is G.O.N.E. Never to return. You deserve all the happiness and orgasms a woman can have. Braxton is a man who any woman would love to lick from head to toe. He's yours honey, now enjoy him." Her sideways glance reveals a hint of her Cheshire cat smile.

How can I disagree with her? "Yeah, you're right. Braxton is my own personal Popsicle. I swear I get lost in those eyes of his. I'm a lucky, lucky lady. Don't even get me started on his most favorite body part." A moan emerges from my throat. The mental image of a naked Braxton takes over my every thought. I'm damn near panty melting wet. It makes me realize how bad I have it for him.

She is interrupting my daydream, with her snickering. "Get your mind out of the gutter, or at least share the monumental image you have going on. Not fair not to share with your best friend."

I pucker my lips and blow her a kiss.

"Bitch," she says, jokingly with a roll her eyes.

She can't be serious. "Hey, you got your own piece of eye-candy. I got you your motorcycle man, one with an MC even. You should owe me." I shrug my shoulder into hers.

With a mild click of her tongue, she sighs. "Yeah, yeah I suppose you're right."

She suddenly pauses, a more serious expression appears.

"You know, in your absence we all had some late night talks. I told the guys some things from your past so they could comprehend the hell you were living. It was hard, but Brax needed to hear it. He needed to know no matter what happened, that you didn't want it. You had no choice." Her voice hitches as a loud sob escapes.

Reaching out, I hug her. We spent some time talking about what I did experience. Mostly she cried. Reliving those moments that is better off forgotten. So much had happened. So many things I never thought I would have to feel yet again.

My family is a lost battle, I know. They decided to cut me loose. Granted, they did not know they were being manipulated by Dominic. The cold facts are they washed their hands of me.

During our talk, Braxton and Liam walked out joining us on the porch. Cold beers in our hands, we all try to find some lighter topics to discuss. Braxton has me curled in his lap. Liam is sitting with Kara laying in-between his legs. This is nice.

Clearing his throat, Liam says lightheartedly. "You know Izzy, Emma has non-stop talked about you. She even threatened Brax within an inch of his life. He had to make things right with you." With a slap to Braxton's shoulder, Liam laughed, adding, "Fucking loved every minute of it."

Shrugging off Liam's hand, Braxton grumbled. "Shut it, fucker."

I sigh. "Smart woman."

"I would pay to watch her beat his ass." Kara laughs so hard she chokes on her beer.

Liam can hardly contain his amusement. "Jesus, can't take you anywhere girl." He says, inspecting his legs for any spilled beer.

Slapping his knee, Braxton seizes the moment. "Don't need to take her out, buddy. Strip her naked and have your fun."

"Amen, brother." Liam gleams with a twinkle in his eyes.

They high five one another, having a manly moment. I snuggle in closer to Braxton's chest while Kara shrugs it off before snuggling in-between Liam's legs.

Braxton leans inching closer my ear. "Hey Sparkplug, how's my girl doing?" He pauses to kiss me just under my ear. I embrace his touch. "My mom called me after her talk with you. She's making sure I mind my p's and q's."

"I'm doing okay. Believe it, or not, your mom helped me." I peer over my shoulder to look into his gazing eyes.

He looks slightly confused, tilting his head. "How so?"

I can't help but stroke his cheek. "She told me how much you love me. How miserable you have been. She made me see things in a different light. It's all crystal clear now." My heart spills over as my eyes never leave his, not for one second.

Those big warm, sparkling orbs are gently closing as he brings his face closer with mine. His tongue darts out to lick his lower lip right before they gently press against mine. The softness of his touch restricts my ability to take another breath. I will my eyes to stay open, not daring to miss a second of this precious moment. Like always though, as soon as his lips touch mine, it's all over. I'm internally begging him to strip me bare. It's insane how much I crave the feel of him inside of me.

"Oh, here they go again," Liam clears his throat. Going to stand, he sighs, "I will take this as our cue to leave."

Oh shit. I got so caught up in Braxton, no one else mattered. The only person I saw was him.

"Take care of her, Brax." Kara's soft tone is sweet and endearing.

Walking inside the house Kara is holding Liam's hand. He pauses and winks, looking back over his shoulder before disappearing inside.

"Well," Braxton says jokingly, "we know how to clear a room don't we?"

"Sure do," I laugh so hard I snort. "If this is all it takes, we are golden, honey."

"God, I love it when you call me honey. Never had a woman do that before." His eyes glaze over appearing more serious, more loving. "With you, everything is better. Love you, Iz."

Sweetly caressing my hands with his thumbs, he grips and pulls me. Falling onto him, I squeal as he lays us back on the porch floor. Lying in his arms, it's his most breathtakingly beautiful smile that reaches deep into my soul. It's this single moment that confirms to me, he is the one.

Holding his hand to my heart, I shake with every breath I inhale. "I feel it, you know. Your mom explained it to me. Boy oh boy, was she ever right. I feel you all the way from the top of my head, down to the tip of my toes. I'm hopelessly in love with you, Braxton."

His eyes are warm with love. "Remind me to buy my mom flowers tomorrow. She just saved the girl of my dreams. Never thought of my mom as my ace in my pocket but hey, who am I to complain." Tracing his finger down my cheek, his hot breaths sizzle against my lips. "I fucking love you. You have taken hold of my heart. Iz, you own it now. Don't ever want it back either, it's yours to keep."

Sitting up, I straddle his legs. Wrapping my arms around his shoulders, I pull him closer. I'm kissing him. Starting at one ear to the other and everywhere in between. He groans. His muscles tense, and his erection is now hard as stone. I marvel at the feel of his body.

Playing naughty, I slowly circle my hips. Grinding against him, his hands guide my hips, increasing the friction.

I'm wearing a maxi skirt, so it's pretty easy access. Exactly what I need right now. I fumble with his jeans, using both of my hands to pop his button. Slowly, I unzip him and slide my hand into his boxers. Smooth, hard and absolutely ready for me, I take a hold.

Moaning while I stroke him from root to tip. I caress the bead of pre-come with my thumb, gliding it across his slit. His erratic breathing and sexy moans fill my ears. Rocking his hips into my hand, I'm not sure there is a better feeling than this right now. It's public and naughty.

Braxton reaches under my skirt with each hand running along my thighs, inching very slowly, until they reach the lace of my panties. My moans are not only loud, they are sexy as hell. Between the two of us, I hope the neighbors have their windows closed, because I'm not stopping. From the looks and sounds of it, neither is Braxton.

"Oh baby, you feel so good." His thumbs find their way stroking under the elastic of my panties. "Feel how wet you are? Jesus, you're drenched for me, baby."

His blazing touch feels incredible. I'm barely able to control my breathing, let alone keep my body still. I'm ready for takeoff.

Not able to contain myself. "Hmmm... touch me," I groan. With a rock of my hips, I'm more demanding. "Touch me, Braxton." My body sings as he continues to play it like an instrument. His touch is so soft, like velvet. I continue to keep stroking him. Tracing his protruding vein underneath, it's throbbing with need. Every pulse is making my mouth water. Aching to lick him. Yearning to feel him slide against my tongue. My desire to feel him deep in the back of my throat is undeniable. I hug every delectable inch of him.

With his hands spread wide on my thighs, he uses the tips of his thumbs to caress my swollen bud. Increasing his pressure around my clit, I lift my hips, riding his every sensational touch. It's painstakingly fantastic. Fireworks start to explode behind my closed eyes.

Slowly opening them, I wet my lips in anticipation of devouring his. I remove my hand from between his legs, wrapping my hands around his face. I draw him in closer. With my gaze centered on his mouth, I suck on his lower lip. The moment he enters two fingers inside of me, I increase my hold on his lip. He groans in response.

"Enough, honey. I need you inside of me, like now." Pushing his hands out of my panties, I pull them to the side. Braxton gets what I'm hinting at and slides his jeans down just enough to give me what I want.

As soon as I see he's ready, I climb aboard. In one fast, quick motion, I slide down his shaft. He's long, hard and silky smooth. My wet center is devouring every inch of his cock. My body trembles with each downward motion.

Taking a hold of my hips, Braxton grinds himself deeper inside. My knees are as far apart as they can go; my skirt is pushed up high on my waist. I know my ass has to be hanging out for all to see, but I don't give a damn. My impending orgasm is so damn close, I'm chasing it with all I got.

My fingers dig into his shoulders. I raise my body, so only the tip of his cock remains inside. Pausing for a moment, I slam back home. It honestly has to look like I am doing some squatting exercises. Well, in a way, I guess I am.

"Fuck, Iz," He can barely speak with the way his breath seizes. "You're going to make me come so hard."

That's what I'm talking about. "I need you, Braxton." I'm begging him with every downward thrust, moaning, "Make me feel good."

"Come on Iz, give it to me, baby." Braxton winds his thumbs around to my nub, rubbing it in circles. The juices from our love making are coating his fingers. The minute he strokes me just right, I erupt. Fireworks, bells and even whistles, all go off in my head.

"Ooh fuck. Braxton!" My body arches back. "God, I love you."

"That's right baby. Oh shit." His last deep thrust is so hard; he's like a volcano erupting inside of my womb.

"Oh my." I collapse against his sweat-soaked shirt. "That was something special."

"You got that right, Sparkplug. I swear you're going to be the death of me." Swaying us back and forth, he's still deep inside of me.

"Love you, Braxton."

"Love you more, Iz."

chapter

TWENTY-SEVEN

TODAY IS MY FIRST DAY back at Ryle's Custom Shop. To say I'm overwhelmed is an understatement. The stack of invoices are scattered all over my desk, and the current Parts Order needs to be completed by days end. It's a total mess, but I start to work with a huge smile on my face. I'm back working alongside Braxton. Realization hits knowing a part of the mess on my desk is due to the fact Braxton has not been to work. He was busy tending to me. Many times I urged him to go back to work, but he refused. He told me he would worry the whole time and not get much work done. If he was with me, I'd get my rest and stay out of trouble. Whatever that meant, when he said the word trouble, I rolled my eyes back at him.

Speak of the devil, looking up, he walks into my office. It's like he's a different person, he's smiling and whistling.

"Hey Sparkplug, whatcha' working on?" He lowers his eyes to the stack of papers, and I swear he mumbled 'yikes.'

"Funny man, why don't you sit down and help me with this mess?"

He looks as if I just asked him to try something gross, he snickers holding his hands up. "Oh, I'll take a pass. You are so much better at that stuff. I like to get my hands dirty, not push papers." Giving me a sexy wink, he walks closer and touches my nose with this finger. "That is why I hired you; I get to look at you all day while you push my papers for me. It's a total win-win for me. Beauty and brains…you are the whole package." A day-dream sigh escapes his lips.

Oh he's really good. "Smooth talker, you're pretty happy this morning." It's hard to deny his good spirits. "What gives?"

"Besides you sweetheart, I got news from the doctor's office. All good, I've healed up nicely and all of my blood work looks good. I'm healthy as a horse."

While he is talking to me, I am just admiring the tight black t-shirt he has on. It fits him like a glove. Showing off his biceps and part of the ink on his arms, he's totally a sight to see. Yep, I'm head over heels for this man, and to think he's all mine.

"That's great," I automatically say, dropping the papers I'm holding. "One down and one to go." I'm more than happy Braxton has a clean bill of health. I'm just nervous about getting my all clear. Once I felt better, I had gone to see Braxton's physician for a check-up. We both wanted to make sure my infection was gone and to be honest, I wanted to know I had a clean bill of health as well. My phone suddenly rings. I quickly grab it. "Hello."

"Izzy, this is Pam from Dr. Fields office." Her voice is pleasant.

"Yes, how are you?" I raise my eyebrow, expecting to hear the words 'all is clear.'

"Great. We got the results back from your blood work." She says and pauses.

I'm so excited, I can't help but interrupt her. "Yes, Braxton just told me his good news with his results."

"Yes, he is correct. Is there a time you could come into our office?" Her voice is cautious, a bit unnerving if I'm honest.

I pull my phone away from my ear and look down at it. This was not at all what I was expecting to hear. I wanted what Braxton had received. He's sitting on the edge of my desk looking at an invoice. Hearing my conversation, he tilts his head and uses his hands to say 'what?' I answer with a shrug my shoulder.

Clearing my throat, I quietly reply, "I don't understand."

"We think it's best to go over your results in person. There's nothing for you to worry about." She says in the same sweet voice, only now it's annoying me.

I nervously chuckle. "You may not think so, but why can't you tell me over the phone?" Logical question.

"Dr. Fields would like to talk to you in person. Can you come in around five o'clock?" Not giving anything away, it's not very comforting at all.

Sighing in defeat, I guess I know where I'll be later today. "Um yeah, I can be there. Thanks."

"Bye, Izzy." She says before she disconnects.

"Yeah." I press 'end' and sit back in my chair unsettled.

"What was that all about?" Braxton arches an eye at puzzled.

"Not sure," I say, pulling my hands through my hair. "She wouldn't tell me over the phone. They want me to come in person." I'm not at all thrilled. My good mood has taken a nose dive and I haven't even been back to work for more than an hour.

"Hey."

Getting my attention, he walks around my desk and kneels. Taking my hands in his, he looks at me with such a loving look. "Whatever it is, we'll get through it. Together. Don't borrow trouble, not when there may not be any." Oh Braxton, if only I could.

I'm about to shed a few tears, I can feel them approaching. Swallowing down my nerves, I achingly say, "Easy for you to say, you got a free and clear over the phone. I get, you need to come in so we can talk with you in person bullshit."

Then it hits me all at once.

What the hell? Now my brain is running wild with all sorts of possibilities. Life-threatening diseases to cancer. Whatever it is, it can't be good, otherwise why not tell me on the phone, like Braxton? My last thought is quite chilling. Maybe they want to tell me the bad news in person so they can help pick up the pieces when I fall apart. It's either that or a padded cell.

As if reading my mind, Braxton clears his throat. Not that he needed to, he did it to gain my attention. "Stop it Izzy, stop thinking the worst."

Seriously! "How can I not?"

"Come here." He stands and pulls me with him. Walking us over to the couch he added to my office before I had returned. I imagined he had more naughty things in mind when he bought it, but for now it's a place for me to sit on his lap. He needs to comfort me, and to be honest, I desperately need it.

Laying my head against his chest, I snuggle against his shirt. "What if it's bad, Braxton? What am I going to do?"

Rubbing my back with his hands, he sighs. "Stop it baby. Don't do this, I can't take it to see you sad. We have been through too much to have you taken from me. Stop the nonsense, let's think positive."

I go to say something else, but he squeezes my lips shut with his fingers. Instead, I cry on the inside, all of the emotions I don't want to show on the outside. We take this quiet moment just to look at one another. He leaves his fingers which are keeping my lips from moving, and I take this moment to enjoy being in his arms.

My office door suddenly opens wide as Kara strolls in with Liam. Of course, hand in hand, it's so damn cute. Big bad biker and my sweet best friend, what a sight!

"Why the long faces?" Kara seems surprised looking at Braxton and myself. It's not the fact I'm sitting on his lap; she can read the worry as it radiates off of me.

Liam's expression changes as he arches his eyebrows. "Heard all is good with you man, that should have smiles on both of your faces. What gives?" His eyes dart from Braxton to me.

Both Braxton and I both remain quiet.

"Well," Kara speaks up. "I still want to kick Tiffany's ass. All of this bad shit that has happened is directly tied to that bitch. She's a fucking tornado, comes in destroys anything in her path and leaves a path of destruction."

I could not agree more. "Don't hold back, Kara."

Throwing me a wink, she slugs Liam's arm. "Damn straight."

"Iz needs to go to Dr. Field's office for her results. They want her at five, so we should get some work done." Braxton nods his head at Liam, while he rubs my tense shoulders.

My eyes squeeze shut. "We?" My chest tightens. I know he's going to ask about my reluctance to him going with me.

"You're not going alone." Pointing his finger between us, he seems a bit put off. "We go together, none of this alone shit."

I panic, but give him a too-quick smile. Do I want him to be with me? On one hand yes, of course. But, if it's bad news, I want time to absorb it without him telling me it will be okay a hundred times. If it's bad news, I need to get it delivered to me alone. It's the only way I can take it.

Swallowing hard, my mind is rushing to come up with another plan. "Why don't I take Kara with me, and you can finish some work here. We can come back here right after the appointment." I'm trying to convince him that this is the best possible plan. I don't want to tell him I don't want him there. It's not that I don't want him...I just can't take bad news in front of him.

"Absol..."

I cut him off.

"Hey," I say holding up my hand. "You've been gone for weeks around here. They need you here." I motion towards the garage with my finger. "They are behind, Braxton. You are needed here." He knows that this is the only way I am going to win this argument. Holding my breath, I pray he agrees with me on this.

Wrinkling his face visibly frustrated, I sense he is struggling with the fact that I'm right. Feeling a bit optimistic I lean over kiss his cheek. In his ear I let him know I'll be okay. I promised to call him.

While Braxton's attention is on me, Kara nudges Liam to get him to say something.

"Brax man, the guys are crazy busy. I'll stay and help your ass out. Let the girls go and when they come back, we can close up shop and go eat dinner." Now that sounds like a great plan and with Liam saying it, he might buy it.

"Shit, I don't like it," Braxton replies with what sounds like a growl.

Yes! "Don't be mad. You work with the boys and get all greasy." Knowing how much I know he likes to work with his hands, it will be good for him to work for a change. Playing nurse maid to me was hard on him. He did not like missing work. He's a bit of a workaholic. "It'll be fun for you." Not waiting a moment longer, I give him a loud smack on the lips. This earns a playful slap on the ass in return.

Kara steps over to the couch and puts her arm around me. "We got this girlfriend. Most likely it's just some woman's issue anyway." Holding out her hand to help me up, she says, "She told you not to worry, right?" I assume she is referring to the nurse who called.

I nod.

"No worries then."

THE DRIVE TO THE DOCTOR'S office is very quiet. Pulling into the parking lot, Kara keeps glancing my way. I'm a nervous wreck. The closer we got to the office, the more my stomach starting to churn.

"Izzy, come on." She says with a pat to my hand. "It's going to be okay. I'm here for you."

I keep my stare out the window. Running all sorts of possibilities through my head, all of them have the same common ending, my death. Shit.

"I am going to slap you silly. Stop Izzy, don't do this to yourself." She's got herself all worked up because now she's crying. She wipes away her tears with her fingers. "I can't stand to see you so sad." Taking a deep, pained breath, she whispers. "I'm a little freaked out myself. You've had so much shit to deal with...it's not motherfucking fair."

Reaching my hand over to touch her shoulder I lower mine. "Life's not fair, we both know that." Getting out of the car, I think we both try to find the courage to walk into that damn office. Neither of us are not breaking any speed records getting to the front door.

I nervously chewing my nails nervously while my leg bounces up and down. Sitting here I notice the receptionist keep eyeing me out of the corner of her eye. Her glances are seriously screwing with my mind. I am very aware she knows Braxton since she made a point to have me say 'hi' for her when I see him. Maybe she knows my results and is lining herself up with him as soon as I'm out of the picture. *Oh Jesus, please stop torturing yourself Izzy.*

I feel my phone alert me with an incoming text.

Braxton: I love you...stay strong.

Izzy: Luv U too. No worries.

No need to let him know I'm freaked the fuck out, he already knows it.

Pam walks into the reception area before calling out. "Izzy Parker."

Christ, she knows it's me, why say my last name? I eye Pam, letting out a staggered breath. Okay, let's get this over with. Coming to get my fate, she looks like a happy, busy bee.

I happen to look over my shoulder to Kara, not asking her if she was coming back with me. She stands, not giving me an option. Thank God.

Pam walks us back to Dr. Field's office where we are to sit once again. Now we get to wait longer for my news. Eyeing the office, I notice his many degrees and accolades hanging on the walls. They comfort me some hoping all of these impressive certificates proves he knows what he is doing.

"Stop it, just breathe." Kara keeps saying to me while I continue to bite my nails.

"You're making me regret taking you with me, stop eyeing me. You're starting to freak me out. I'm doing a bang-up job on my own, don't need your help." Sticking my tongue out at her; I love her dearly, but she is making me more anxious. I swear I'm going to throw-up.

Dr. Fields walks in...whistling. I about drop my mouth to the floor. I have no idea what kind of bad news I am going to get, but he is whistling like he is having a great old time.

"Izzy, I'm so glad you could come in as quick as you could." He walks over and sits at his desk opening up a file. Presuming it is mine. Eyeing the page nodding his head, I'm mentally preparing for the worst-case scenarios he is about to tell me. I'm sure of it. Flipping a few more pages, a look of surprise crosses his face as his forehead creases. He then shuts it slowly shifting his eyes till they meet mine.

"How are you feeling, Izzy?" Nothing else! Just how you are feeling?

My throat is so thick I find it impossible to swallow. With a mild throat cough, I stutter, "Fine, but I must admit I'm freaked out right now." I want to shout out 'duh!'

His lower jaw shifts side to side. "Look the only reason I wanted to see you is because something did come back on your blood work. I re-ran them twice to make sure." He looks at me trying to read my mind when his brows drawn up.

I can't take it any longer. "Well, let's just get to it. Am I dying?" I let out a nervous laugh. Kara reaches out taking my hand in hers. She is dead silent, so I know she's freaked.

"Izzy, you're not dying." He confirms with a head nod.

With a staggered sigh. "I'm not?"

"Nope, not today."

My chest lightens and I let out a throaty laugh. "Okay, well what the heck do you need to tell me then?" I'm not dying, so let's have it.

"I was concerned with the fact that you were so adamant about your pregnancy chances when we spoke earlier. With all that has happened with you recently, so when my tests showed that you were indeed pregnant, it threw me off."

I open my mouth and it just stays like that. I know there is no way I could have heard him right. There is no chance of me being pregnant.

Kara scares the hell out of me when she just burst out laughing. Her being overjoyed is an understatement. Most likely she's relieved I'm not sick or dying.

"I love it, yes. Could not have happened to a better person. Izzy, you are going to have Brax's baby. Oh, mother of pearl, that man is going to be on cloud fucking nine when he hears this." Kara looks like she is about to jump out of her chair as her fingers are digging into the arms. Dr. Fields is looking at me with a slight uneasy look, probably because I'm stunned speechless.

"Izzy, say something. Is this a good thing or not a good thing?" Dr. Fields says slowly.

"Um. Happy, of course, just confusing. I was led to believe I could not have any more children. I'm in total shock."

I grab onto Kara's arm in disbelief. Yelping, I damn near slap my cheeks to make sure I'm awake. Was it all a lie? Did Dominic lie to me? How is it possible, because we had unprotected sex plenty of times? How come I never got pregnant again? This is so confusing, I should be overjoyed. Not sitting here shocked trying to figure out my past mess with Dominic.

"I'm so stunned," I breathlessly say, "How far along am I?"

"Great question, your levels are high. I would like to do a quick ultrasound to find out some measurements if that is all right with you? It would be a vaginal ultrasound due to the fact you are most likely early in the pregnancy."

I nodded since my words fail to form. Should I text Braxton? Do I wait? How do I tell him? In my shocked state, I decide to wait.

"Relax Izzy; this will go easier if you relax." I try to relax, but I know Dr. Fields is going to see all of my scars. What will he think? Will he think Braxton gave them to me? Oh God, I hope not. This is the part of my past that will forever follow me.

I undress and put on the gown and lay down on the table. Kara is holding my hand and staring at the screen. The moment I am exposed to him, I freeze. Dr. Fields is now eyeing my lower region which is on full display for him. I can see it in his eyes. I need to say something.

"They are from my past. From a man better off forgotten. I don't need you to think Braxton had anything to do with these." God, this is embarrassing.

"Of course not, Izzy. I have known Brax, all his life. I would say the boy is damn near smitten with you. Is this his baby?"

"Yeah." It's all I can say before this really hits me. I'm pregnant with Braxton's baby. I never thought this was even possible. Holding my hand over my heart, it's filled with hope, and it's filled with grief. Grief for my little girl.

"Oh, honey it's okay." Kara bends down and kisses my forehead.

"You're going to be a momma and Brax is the daddy. Wow that is going to be one great looking kid." Whispering in my ear, she says, "Love you, girl."

Her words sink in. "Oh my God! Kara, how is this even possible? Dominic swore I could not have any more kids, every day it was torture. With him, I never wanted any more. Then with Braxton, I was so upset I couldn't give him any. Now, I'm pregnant with his baby. How can I be so happy and sad at the same time?"

"You're thinking about Willow, honey. It's okay to feel, just feel and don't question it."

Just then, we see my little blip on the screen. Dr. Fields points out that everything looks great, and I am about seven weeks along. I count back the weeks and realize when it most likely happened. It was right before we had our minor break up with the Tiffany fallout. I can almost pinpoint the night it happened. It only makes this that much sweeter. Staring at my little blip on the screen I'm hit with all of my emotions at once. Happy and sad mix together as they fall down my cheeks. My heart swells not only with pride, but with so much hope. Reaching out I touch the screen and trace the bean sized shape. I'm in love, already.

Chapter Twenty-Eight

Leaving the doctor's office, Kara and I drive away in utter shock. I'm still in disbelief, staring at the printout I hold in my trembling hands. I'm afraid to blink or look away for fear it won't be real. I keep telling myself this is indeed really happening. The brochures sitting next to me are all the proof I need to remind me. Braxton and I are going to have a baby. I trace the image of my baby with my finger. But then drop my hand to my belly, lightly caressing it back and forth.

"You better call him, he is waiting you know," Kara said giving me the look. "The man has no patience when it comes to you. Trust me, I have seen it firsthand." She's been on me to call him or text him the minute I found out.

Biting my lip, I hesitantly agree with her. "Yeah, you're right." My fear is I'll fall apart if I hear his voice right now. "I'll text him, but will wait to tell him in person about the baby." Baby? I can't help but smile when I say the word baby. The more I say it, the more I will start to believe it.

"I can't believe it, Kara." Looking over at her the tears fall but I'm smiling big. My eyes gleam and I'm giggling with excitement. "I'm going to have a baby... Braxton's baby." I can't sit still, my feet are now tapping the floor.

Searching in my purse to find my phone, I start to text him, but I'm so damn nervous and excited I can't type correctly. Deep down I know he'll be happy, but a part of me still not one hundred percent sure.

        Izzy: On my way. Luv U

Not a minute later my phone beeps.

        Braxton: Well?

I type laughing.

        Izzy: On my way, be there soon.

Braxton: UR killing me. Honey, what's the news? Just get here fast wait, not too fast. Just hurry.

    Yes, I'm on my way. Hope to hell you're ready for this!
    Pulling up to the shop, Liam walks out the door before we even get a chance to park. Not a second later, Braxton is fast on his heels.
    Kara had said under her breath 'get ready' a few times before we parked the car.
    "Oh shit, here comes trouble. Look at his face! He looks nervous as hell."
    Looking at his tension-filled face my stomach rolls. I might just throw-up, not because of the baby, but because I'm nervous as hell. In a fit of hysterics, I frantically ask, "Shit, how do I tell him? I want it to be special, Kara."
    She is waving her hand in my face as if trying to hush me. "Not a clue, but you're not going to get a chance to think of something, that man is on a mission." She says anxiously undoing her seatbelt.
    "Shit." I'm quickly hiding the brochures in my purse. There is no way I want him being tipped off with those. As I tuck the last one away, my car door flies open. I yelp in surprise as he urgently pulls me out of the car and into a hug.
    "Sparkplug, I love you," he says so sweetly breathing heavily into my ear. Putting me down on my feet, he takes my hands in his pausing to let me know he is serious. "Okay, so out with it."
    Gazing into his eyes, I suddenly struggle to breathe. I'm not sure I can find the right words. Thank my lucky stars I get a few more minutes to come up with an idea because Liam and Kara walk up interrupting the moment. As my eyes leave Braxton, I look over at Kara finding it hard not to laugh. She is beaming with a smile so big, I

have the urge to wipe that off her face. No one notices her though, because three sets of eyes are solely on me. I'm drawing up a blank, shit, this is harder than I thought.

Liam reaches over and puts his hand on Braxton's shoulder for support I presume. Braxton is looking a bit worse for wear as each second passes.

Biting the insides of my cheek, I have a heavy feeling in my stomach. My heart is racing. "Umm. Well, I'm not sure how to explain it." I nervously look from Braxton to the ground, my smile goes stiff. I'm not sure why I'm so nervous, I know deep down he is going to be thrilled. At least that is what I'm hoping for.

"Izzy, you're killing me. Out with it, I can handle anything, just don't make me wait another minute." Braxton looks like he is ready to crawl out of his skin with worry.

With nothing but love and adoration, I lift my eyebrows, suddenly finding some courage.

"Braxton, do you love me?"

He winces a bit shocked at my question I think. "Babe, you know I do."

Sigh. "What if I told you things were going to change for us? That things are going be different. I'm going to change, and be different." Letting my words sink in. He just gazes at me with a 'not a clue' about what I'm talking about.

"Like how," he asks, shaking his head. "Are you sick, Izzy? Oh God, please tell me you're not sick?" His voice cracks.

Holding out my hand to touch his chest, I lean into him. "No honey, I'm not dying. I'm...expanding."

"You're what? What the fuck does that mean?" Braxton reaches out to grab my shoulders but his eyes are directed at Liam for some help.

Pulling out of his tight grip, I pull the sonogram out of my pocket I stuffed in there quickly before he could see it when I got out of the car. My hands tremble with my bundle of nerves as I unfold it.

With his own shaking hands, he keeps adjusting it closer and farther from his face trying to focus on what it could be. I'm bouncing my weight from foot to foot, just waiting for him to smile as the surprise sinks in.

"I don't get it." Scanning the picture, he looks at me with wide eyes. "Is this serious or something?"

Biting my lip, I huff out a sigh. "Or something."

Braxton then falls to his knees; he looks like he is going to cry. I think he gets it, but I'm not sure. Liam about goes down with him, he was still holding onto his shoulder. Kara gasps so loud she is shouting out 'no.'

In a most agonized voice, Braxton winces. "Is it bad Izzy, like some tumor they can take out and you're going to be okay?"

I was totally not thinking this is what he would think. I'm not sure how he could come up with me having a tumor. Kara's laughing so hard I can't help but follow along with her. My poor man has it all wrong. The way Liam is biting back a shit eating grin, it tells me he knows what that sonogram is showing, and it's not a tumor.

Braxton tenses. "Why the hell are you all laughing? My girl is sick."

Bending down next to him, I wrap my arms around his shoulders, and whisper in his ear. "No honey, I'm not sick." Pulling back, I gaze into his warm eyes. "I'm pregnant, Brax." Not sure if the word pregnant, or me calling him Brax that has him clutching his chest.

He continues to study the picture, and then the moment he gets it, he lets his head drop letting out a gasp. Okay, not the reaction I was expecting. Maybe this is bad news for him. A sudden rush of panic washes over me. My skin tingles with the fact he may not be happy at all with this news.

. My shoulders tense. "Braxton."

Slowly his posture relaxes. His warm eyes raise to meet my tear filled ones. The breath I was holding in, instantly deflates.

His eyes dance, searching, wondering. "You're having my baby?" He asks softly.

"Yes, I am."

"I fucking love you." It was all he could say as he stands and pulls me in for a crushing hug.

"I have no clue how this is even possible, but it is," I say.

"Who cares how baby, you got my kid in there and I'm so happy. My dream came true Iz, my dream of having my seed in you. Baby, it's the best damn news." His keeps kissing my head sharing this moment with Liam and Kara. Liam reaches out to hug Braxton before he over excitedly grabs me in a hug and lifts me off the ground.

"Congrats, you two. Izzy girl, this is the best damn news. He was climbing the walls with all sorts of bad shit running through his head." He gives Braxton a good old slap to his back. "You two deserve this news."

I could not agree more, laying my head against my man.

Kara suddenly jumps as if a great idea hits. "Let's go celebrate and eat."

Liam shouts out a 'hell yeah.' "Let's go kids, dinner is on me."

Braxton barks out in a laugh. "My woman is eating for two, whatever she wants." Lifting me up, he carries me in the building hooting and hollering.

We end up eating at a local pizzeria. The three of them all get a cold draft beer while I get a root beer. It's odd the craving you have for a beer when you can't have one. Braxton's eyes follow mine as I stare at the water dripping down his glass of beer.

"Forget it baby," Braxton may be smiling but he's also shaking his head. "No alcohol for you."

I drop my smile. "You're going to enjoy this for nine long months, aren't you?"

Taking a drink, he laughs with a look of superiority. "Bet your ass, I am." Pointing to my flat stomach with his finger, he then claps his hands. "That's my kid in there, and you're my woman." His face takes on a more serious look, "Eve is going to freak, and she will finally have her family." Settling back in his chair, he adds, "She always wanted a brother or sister."

"Yeah, I think she will be the best big sister." The idea of having sweet little Eve as a big sister warms my heart. My face beams. "Let's go spread the good news."

Little did I know, he planned a get together back at his house. His mom and co-workers were there along with a few of Liam's crew. The room was buzzing loudly when Braxton made his big announcement. To say the house erupted in cheers is an understatement. I was hugged, kissed and center of attention. Now we just needed to go and find Eve, we wanted to tell her in private. She was back in her room.

We sat with Eve in her room for some quiet time. I let Braxton take the lead telling his daughter the good news. In minutes, we all were in tears. I swear Eve hugged me so tight I couldn't breathe. She immediately wanted to go and tell everyone she was going to be a big sister. Grandma Emma was getting another grandchild, so she was in seventh heaven.

Eve ran into the living room shouting to everyone what they already knew, but she couldn't care less. We stayed back alone in Eve's room cuddling on her bed. It was nice getting some quiet alone time.

"Can you believe it?" I run my hand down his face to cup his jaw.

"Nope, but I'm not complaining either." Braxton takes my hand touching my ring finger. "Need to put my ring on your finger and make you my wife, Iz."

Cupping my mouth, I gasp, not expecting him to say that. The idea of being his wife is more than I could ever ask for. Just this morning I woke up finding out Braxton is fully healed and healthy. Then I find out I'm having a baby I had no clue I could even have. Now I'm hit with the fact he wants me to be his wife. Wow, this day just keeps getting better and better. Not one to want to wait around, it seems like my life has been one long waiting game. It's time for me to live for a change.

"I want to do it soon Braxton, that way I know your mine forever." I need this, even though I know he's mine. The minute he says his vows, maybe I can then forget all things Tiffany.

"Ah, honey. I'm already yours and you…" he says rubbing his hand across my belly, "are going to have my baby."

"Yes." I fan my face to keep my happy tears at bay. "Huh, Izzy Ryles does have a nice ring to it."

"It sure does babe."

SEVEN LONG MONTHS LATER I am now Mrs. Braxton Ryles. Very much pregnant and am close to giving birth. I feel enormous. No longer being able to see my toes, I waddle like a duck. Most times I love every minute of it. Braxton touches my belly every chance he gets and tells me how much he loves me at least ten times a day. I wanted for nothing. If not Braxton, it was Kara or Liam who made sure I had whatever I needed. Even the guys at work, tended to my every need, it was awesome.

Most days these last few weeks, I spent my time at work with my feet up and had something to nibble on right by my side. I could almost count to the minute when the next person would pop into my office asking me if I needed anything. God, love them all.

These past few months have been both amazing and not so amazing. The bitch known as Tiffany came back into town. She kept repeating it was to make amends, but none of us were fooled. She's always up to something. Good thing for her I was married and pregnant or else I would have taken a swing at her. Liam did his best to keep Kara from kicking her ass. He wanted to keep whatever peace he could.

I kept telling myself I was not going to let her ruin my life; I have a second chance at happiness and she was not going to mess it up. For my own health and the sake of my baby, I happily stayed home as much as possible. However, I did go into work. Bitch was not going to chase me from my job again. I had to promise to let Braxton and Liam handle whatever they needed to do to get Tiffany to leave town, preferably once and for all. I was under the impression, she was gone for good, but I guess I was wrong.

Thankfully, we had just gotten married. It was a small wedding, at the bottom of a cliff. The view was breathtaking. Evergreen Trees lined up all around us for as long as the eye could see. It was peaceful and beautiful, the perfect spot. It was filled with an enormous lot of Harleys, men with MC cuts, and our co-workers. My new family. Eve was our flower girl, dressed all in white with a red bow wrapped around her waist. My dress was the same, even had the same red bow hiding my expanding belly. My dress was sleeveless, and my ever growing cleavage was on full display. I knew my man would love this, and that is how I knew, that was the dress.

Braxton simply wore black jeans and a black button up shirt. His red tie matched my red ribbon. He hated the tie, but I loved it. He did fold up the sleeves to his elbows. This I liked as well, so I could see a hint of his tattoos. My man looked like a dream. What I did not expect were the tears that were streaming down his face when I made it up the long makeshift aisle to meet him with preacher Bob.

"My dream, Iz. You are my dream come true." His words laced with all the love in the world he has for me.

"Oh Braxton, I love you so much," I said in return, cupping his cheek with my hand.

We made up our own vows. Pledging our love, our undying support, and even used the word 'obey' in the end. Yep, it was funny to see him saying in front of his friends and family he was going to obey his woman. All of the guys hollered calling him some not so pleasant things, joking, of course. His cheeks flushed pink.

Biting my lip to contain my laugh, I watched him defend his honor. He had no issues being called names if it meant he had me. I'm not sure what is even wrong with a man saying he is going to 'obey' their woman. I guess with this group, it means something else entirely.

We took a week-long getaway to the mountains. During our honeymoon, I found out Tiffany had shown back up in town. No doubt she knew we were gone on our honeymoon. I wasn't Izzy Ryles for more than a few days when I got hit with her bullshit again. Just when I think we can move on from the past, something creeps up. I came home from my honeymoon not so happy. I was worried about Eve. Braxton had told me Emma was with Eve and she would never hear that her mom has shown back up in town.

Little did Braxton know he was being tested with his newly crowned vows? The vows he pledged to me, he remembered each word as he decided to let Liam handle Tiffany, for the most part. There was little to no contact with Braxton. He promised me he would let Liam deal with her as long as he didn't feel the need to get involved. That could change, I guess.

It was a good thing, the few times I let that wench get to me I started having contractions finding myself nearly bed ridden. The doctor explained to Braxton and myself that I needed to avoid stress as much as possible. Um, yeah, I laughed my butt off. Stress. That's a daily occurrence when Tiffany is in the picture.

I surprised my husband with the news I wanted to officially adopt Eve. I wanted her to know I was her mom now, that she had a mother who loved her. Eve already called me mom. She was such a strong little girl facing what she had with Tiffany. It's now my job to show her the love she deserves. Knowing this, but also knowing that Tiffany would have to live with the fact her daughter is now mine, does satisfy a small part that wants revenge out on her. She has caused so much pain and suffering. She brought Dominic to me. She set up all of that mess. Karma is a bitch.

The day the papers came, we had a party at our house. I moved in with Braxton and Kara and Liam are now renting the house I once rented. They get closer every day; I imagine she will end up being married off soon.

THAT LEADS US TO THE now; I'm sitting in my office at Ryles Custom Shop. Cage and Brody were just checking in on me, it seems they have resolved whatever feelings they had and now really like me. They take any chance they get to sneak into the office and chat with me. I love it. It's all good and fun until Braxton finds them with me in the office. He chases them off to get back to work. His jealous rants are quiet funny to see.

Just now he chased them off for the fifth time today alone. All they were doing was brining me some donuts. My favorite, chocolate with cream filling, yummy.

"Seriously Braxton, I'm like huge. I am not some hot looking bikini babe sitting here. I think you are safe." I'm not only rolling my eyes at his jealous thoughts I find it absurd even.

"Don't care; you're still hot as hell. Belly or not, they need to watch their hands and stop letting their eyes linger on your tits."

I laugh so hard, I wretch in discomfort. "Oh shit, ouch." My hands wrap my hard as stone stomach. Oh shit.

Not at all amused, Braxton glares. "Not funny Iz, quit kidding around."

I wince and double over when the next wave hits. Shit the pain goes all the way down my spine. Holding my stomach, I try to breathe out the pain. Mentally counting just like they taught me in Lamaze class, from years ago.

"Oh shit," he finally realizes I'm seriously hurting. "Are you okay, Sparkplug?"

I hit him with a 'wtf' moment. "No. Do I look like I'm all right?" Counting out loud to five, I scowl. "Honey, it hurts."

Braxton comes over and picks me up in his arms, walking fast through the garage. Cage and Brody stop what they are doing and run over.

Cage shouts. "Shit, what's going on?"

"What the hell do you think? She's in labor; you dick's started this." Braxton shouts rushing us to his truck.

"Us?" They both yell out.

"Stop (huff) it (pant) it's (huff) not (pant) their (huff) faults. I'm using my huff, huff, pant, pant breaths.

The ride to the hospital is a blur. My eyes were shut in pain the whole time, Braxton called the doctor on the way to make sure he would be there. I'm hooked up to all sorts of monitors. The pain is excruciating. Braxton's holding my hand while bouncing his knee a mile a minute. The man is a nervous nelly.

Emma rushes into the room and tells us she has everything under control. She has the girls and we just need to concentrate on bringing her grandbaby into the world.

Yes, I did say girls. About a month ago, Max showed up at our house. He got out of the car and went over to the passenger side and held the hand of a little girl. I knew the instant I looked into her eyes who she was. My heart leaped out of my chest. I ran to her as fast as my pregnant body could take me. She ran to me, by some miracle she felt the need to run into my arms. Max had told her who I was apparently. To my amazement, she was always told about me. I was not around because I simply couldn't. No other explanation, but Willow was just a little girl. She did not require lengthy explanations.

It took about two full days for her to become a fixed part of our lives. Braxton held her and cried himself as he already felt nothing but love for her. Eve was so excited, she would not let any of the guys near Willow. She is now her adopted mother. They are going to be the best of friends, just like me and Kara. Best friends, I can see it now. My new family is so perfect. Willow may have the devil as her birth father, but Braxton will be her true daddy. He will protect her as his own. He had made that promise to Dominic before he died.

Kara got her niece back, and her aunt status is now golden. She spoils Willow to no end. She also adopted Eve, a two for one package. Now my girls have an aunt that spoils them to the moon and back. Eve being Liam's niece and Kara being Willow's aunt, is a pretty unique thing. I swear those two are like an old married couple already. I tease them all the time about having a brood of their own. To that they laugh, they like being the cool aunt and uncle… for now.

Eve is eight years old, and Willow is nearly three. Here we are getting ready to meet our newest member to our growing family. We decided not to know the sex of the baby, we wanted to be surprised. So much of our lives have been a whirlwind for sure, but we wanted this one surprise just for us.

When it was time to push, I wanted to leap off the bed. I was so ready for this to be over.

"Alright Izzy, let's meet our baby. Give me a big push, Sparkplug."

Having been in active labor for hours now, I'm not in the mood for anyone telling me what to do. "I'll Sparkplug you! Why are you smiling like a fool? I'm dying here." I'm in so much pain, and he is sitting here looking all cute. My eyes cut him down and he just laughs it off.

"Nay, you're cute when you're feisty."

I growl while he continues to laugh and snicker. "I'm never going to let you touch me again." I pant, that should do it.

Not buying it one bit, he bites his lip. "Yes, you will. I turn you on."

I open my mouth is mock horror. "Braxton, right now I hate you."

"Yep and in about a half hour when you're looking at our baby, you'll love me again and want more." He looks at the nurse with a look like 'I'm right aren't I' look. She blushes pink, and nods as if to agree with his ass.

Squinting, I growl. "Don't count on it."

"Izzy, push." The doctor and nurse are reminding me to concentrate on my pushing. Bear down and push out your bottom, yeah, yeah, yeah. Just for the love of God, get this kid out of me.

"Ice, Braxton need, ice." I was so tired and hot. I needed something wet and cold. They don't let you drink water, so it's ice chips.

He is hesitant at first. "How about another push, then I'll give you some ice."

"Wow," the nurse blurts out. "Daddy is going to make you work for it. I think she has earned it daddy, give mommy some ice." She gives him a look like give her the damn ice buddy. Okay, I like her again.

I turn my death stare back to daddy. "Yeah, listen to the nurse or you will be ejected buddy."

"Oh Christ, she is feisty. All right mommy, ask nicely?"

"BRAXTON…ICE…NOW."

I got my ice and four pushes later, out came our baby.

"Very good mommy, you have a beautiful baby…boy."

We both cry out. Honestly we thought it was another girl. We have some girl's names picked out, but not too many boys. Of course.

"A boy," I whisper. "Oh Braxton, we have a baby boy."

Wiping his eyes, he smiles and drops his lips to mine for a scorching wet kiss. My tears fall, and I can taste the salt in our kisses. Pulling back Braxton continues to kiss my lips, my cheeks, and even my nose.

"You did it, Sparkplug. Damn, you did really good babe. Look at him Iz, he's perfect." Pink and wet, they laid him on my chest to clean him off.

He weighed in at 7lbs, 8oz and was 21 inches long. He had a head full of dark hair and bright brown eyes like his daddy. We joked the only thing of mine seemed to be his lips and nose.

When he was cleaned up, they put him in his daddy's arms. My big man holding this tiny baby was a sight to see. Looking at them together was precious.

Looking back at my life, it has been filled with such pain and torment. I had lost so much over the years, my family, my innocence, and my confidence. I learned how to live with what I had, living most days in my own thoughts. Finding ways to make it through the day, and more importantly how to avoid the wrath of Dominic was my life. The years of hiding, begging and praying I would not be hurt had taken its toll. It always seemed to end up with Max by my side, stitching me up. Kara fought for years, trying to help me. None of it mattered until I did eventually break.

In the end, I had found my new beginning, my fresh start in a small town in Monroe, Washington. A man by the name of Braxton Ryles stole my heart the moment my eyes found his. He tells me this is the moment he fell head over heels in love with me too. Our time together has been met with grief, loss and a whole lot of stress. In the same amount of time, we found each other. We found our souls and the reason all of the stress and heartache was okay. As long as we had each other in the end, it was all worth it. So much grief, but in the end, it led me here.

"You look sexy with a baby in your arms big guy." I wink at my man holding my new little man.

"Oh yeah, think I can use him as a chick magnet." He softly laughs as he rocks his son. Our son.

"Don't bet on it, he loves his momma too much."

"Yeah, I'm partial to her too. She loves my dumb ass for some reason."

"That she does, indeed."

"What are we going to name him?" I ask.

Pausing a second, he grins. "I like Asher Liam Ryles; Asher after my mom's dad. Liam well that goes without saying."

"I like it. Little Asher." I smile as a few tears escape my eyes.

It has been said that in a moment of insanity, you blurt things out loud. Right now my emotions are running away with me. I want this moment again and again with my man.

"Braxton, I want another one. You were right, I want as many as we can have." My hormones are working double time, and I can't stop crying. Seeing Braxton with Asher is my undoing. This tiny bundle of joy is ours, a part of me and a part of him.

"Not a problem babe. Whenever you're ready, you got it."

"Yes." I smile.

I had it all in a blink of an eye; I went from hell to heaven. My journey was not always sweet and fun, it was the exact opposite. I did my time in hell so I could appreciate my heaven right now in this room. I would spend my life loving Braxton Ryles, loving our little girls and now our little boy. Who knows what the future holds for us, but I am going to enjoy it, every delectable inch of it.

epilogue

LIAM

LIAM RECEIVED THE PHONE CALL a little past two this morning. He found himself a bit confused with his emotions. His father Mick called to let him know his sister was in an accident. Not just a small fender bender, either. It was a head on collision. Gathering his senses, he jumped out of bed and threw on some jeans. Kara stirred in a state of slumber.

"Liam, where are you going?" she said with a yawn.

"Got to go babe, Tiff's been in an accident."

Kara knew better than to add in her comments along the lines of 'who gives a shit' or better yet, 'she got what she deserved.' No, Kara bit her tongue.

"I'm coming with you," jumping out of bed she was fast to put on some jeans and t-shirt.

"On the way, I'll call Brax."

Kara looked at him wide-eyed not quite sure that was a great idea. Tiffany had caused her friend, Izzy, enough grief to last a life time, but she also knew Liam had to do what he felt was right. No matter what, Tiffany was Eve's birth mother.

"Let's head out." He grumbles finding his keys.

On the way to the hospital, Liam had phoned Brax and filled him in on what he knew, which wasn't much. Mick, Liam and Tiffany's father was pretty skim on the details. Liam knew he'd get them once he got to the hospital. Kara kept quiet most of the fifteen-minute drive to the hospital.

Walking into the emergency room waiting area, Liam saw his father sitting there with his head lowered into his hands. A slight ping of anxiety washed over Liam as he feared the worst. Walking with a more determined look on his face, Liam sat next to his father who he had not much of a relationship with to begin with.

"How is she?" Liam asked with a mild gruff tone.

Mick, raised his head to look at his son. Years of regret washed over him. He did not have much of a relationship with either of his children. So much wasted time.

"She's in surgery now. Don't really know much. I'm just sitting here, waiting."

Not five minutes later in walks Brax. You could easily see he was tense. His eyes were stone cold and intense looking. His lips were drawn tight and thin.

Brax gave Liam a nod of his head as he walked over to where Liam, Kara and Mick were sitting.

"What's the news?"

"Not much right now. She's in surgery." Liam responded.

Just then an officer walked up the group of them sitting down.

"I'm Officer Drew Daniels. I've got some questions and would like to go over what happened at the accident."

Officer Daniels had explained what happened at the scene of the accident. Tiffany's blue sedan was traveling down the I-5 South when a car crossed the center line and hit the guard rail, spinning it around to collide with Tiffany's car head on. It looked like Tiffany tried to stop and swerve but there was no escaping it.

Kara reached out and held onto Liam's shaking hand. He was taking it harder than expected.

"What happened to the driver of the other car?" Liam said with controlled anger.

"The person driving that car did not make it. He died at the scene."

"Jesus Christ." Brax held his tongue. He may have his problems with Tiffany but he would never wish this on anyone. Didn't matter how much he hated her for all the problems she caused with Izzy, let alone with Eve.

The police offer sat and asked his questions and they talked an hour. Brax kept looking at his phone.

"Have you called Iz, Brax?" Kara asked hesitantly.

"Not yet. She's been up late with Asher. She was sleeping nicely when I got the call and left to come here. I don't want to wake her, or him for that matter."

The main doors opened to reveal a doctor with his mask around his neck and his cap still on his head. Wiping the tiredness from his eyes, he glanced around the waiting room until his eyes found the group of people he was looking for.

"Family of Tiffany Talbot?"

"Yes." Mick answers as quickly as he stands with the rest of the anxious group.

Doctor Roberts explained Tiffany's many injuries in great detail. He had explained during the surgery she had a setback and she coded twice. Having several broken bones, she had suffered internal bleeding as well. Her heart rate and blood pressure kept dropping and that continues to be his concern. They all listened intently to her injuries but several questions still remained.

Liam's hand shot up. "Wait, what about the baby?"

All eyes shot to him, as three other gasps were easily heard.

"The baby is okay, for now."

Letting out a frustrated sigh, Liam rubbed the back of his neck. He never mentioned it to anyone, he kept this information to himself. It was the real reason Tiffany came back home. Her wild stories never added up, so he thought better than to spread rumors until he could find out the whole story. He knew the minute he mentioned it to Kara, let alone Brax, their world would once again be put in a tail spin.

"What the hell, Liam?" Kara punched him in the arm.

Raising his hands, he stopped her from hitting him again.

"Listen to me, Tiffany had told me some wild stories and to be honest, I had no idea how to deal with it. So I kept it to myself until I could figure it out. Hell, I wasn't even sure it was true. Well, until now that is."

He spent twenty minutes explaining himself and for whatever the reason, he felt like he did the right thing. He had to make sure he had the facts before telling anyone. Fuck, he spent countless hours not sleeping thinking about how in the hell could his sister be dumb enough to get pregnant by Izzy's sick as fuck ex. How in the hell could he tell Izzy let alone Brax or even Kara? Dominic was Kara's brother. This baby was going to bring with it a lot of twisted bullshit.

Liam came up with the most logical plan, a plan that could solve it all. The best thing for everyone was for Tiffany to leave town and never return. No one needed to know about this, Liam was going to get her out of town and then never speak of it again…only know that's not going to happen. Not now.

He knew the days and months to follow were going to be straight up a fucking nightmare. God only knew what destruction Tiffany would leave in her path this time.

Kara

I'LL BE DAMNED. MOVING TO Washington State had been the best thing I've ever done. I needed to keep my girl Izzy safe, but now I have more than one reason to stay. Liam Talbot has me wrapped around his damn finger. The tall handsome biker I'd long for in my fantasies turns out to be a real bad ass who has taken a liking to me too.

We've had some real shitty times so far. I've had to confront my bastard of a brother, Dominic. Fucker came and kidnapped my best friend and once again hurt her like never before. Putting Liam in the middle of that was not fun, but his damn fucked up sister Tiffany did that all on her own. Bitch just had to find my brother. Small fucking world is what it is. Dominic had been in the Lost Souls MC for a long time, and as it turns out, Tiffany and Liam's uncle is in it as well. Not to mention my bad ass biker. These fucking Lost Souls have been a pain in my ass. If I wanted Liam though, I know I have to accept them as a part of my life.

My only option was to make sure Dominic did not leave this state alive. Liam promised he would handle his sister so my Izzy could live in peace now with the love of her life. Brax is a beast of a man, but damn that big ole' teddy bear does love my sweet Izzy. I've never seen a man look at a lady and get so caught up in her. She is the sun in his eyes. I could say the same for her though. She's damn putty in his big ole' hands. They are great when no one is messing with them. Bring the whole Dominic/Tiffany bullshit in the picture that is when things get ugly. Lines blur and old feelings are hard to fight.

It's been a few months since the showdown with my brother. Izzy asks me all the time how I'm doing with it all. I've struggled. I've had my share of nightmares about it all. Shooting your own brother in cold blood is not easy, even if he did deserve it. Better yet, he deserved worse. I keep many of my feelings hidden. Guilt is a bitch. How do I let my best friend know I have some guilt killing my brother even after all he did to destroy her?

"Hey babe. You been outside yet?" Liam eyes me cautiously across the room.

I raise my brows. "Nope. Why?"

"We got another message."

Jesus. What the hell now? This will be the forth not so subtle strange thing to happen to me over the past few weeks. Calling card? Hell, we're not sure and until we are, I refuse to let Liam tell Brax or Izzy one thing about it.

"I'm coming." I set my brush down after trying to tame this wild bed hair I have going on today. I got sidetracked after my shower last night, better yet; I had a 6' 2" hunk of muscle with icy blue eyes attack me after my shower. I never got back to brushing it. I was so tired and worn out, I passed out.

Walking down the hall I notice the front door open ajar. Liam is standing there eyeing the door intently with his arms crossed. It's easy to see how tense he is. His muscles are taut, straining against his white tight t-shirt. My mouth waters and I could easily ogle him all day but the shining metal of something catches my eye. How odd. What the hell?

"What the fuck is that?" I ask as I walk to stand beside him.

"Well," he exclaims with an extended sigh, "what do we make of this? Fuck if I know."

There in our front door is a long serrated hunting knife plunged into the door. If that was not eerie enough, the item that is dangling with it causes me to gasp! His eyes sharply turn to me.

"You know what that is?" He asks and I wish I could lie.

"Unfortunately, I do." I say with a sigh. A sigh of regret—this shit is starting to get to me.

My mind is scrambling trying to piece these subtle mementos together and what they mean. Who are they coming from? Why? All these questions…and no answers. I'm afraid of the damn answers and what they could mean.

I've had my brakes on my car tampered with two weeks ago. That was followed up with slashed tires and broken out back windows. The scariest was the message written in lipstick on my bedroom dresser mirror. I'm always watching! That's all it said. Now I got a knife in my door. With it a personal childhood keepsake. Not just any memory either. Chills run down my spine. Tears threatening to spill over. I have to admit something I never thought I'd have to ever again.

I walk back to the bedroom and find what I'm looking for and return back to Liam who has yet to move muscle. He's deep in thought. Thinking.

"Here."

He holds out his hand and takes the charm from my necklace and reads it.

"Kara?" He questions with a raised eyebrow.

He reads the back of my charm and it dawns on him that the symbol on the front of the charm matches the one that is on the chain attached to my door with this serrated angry looking knife.

"It's a match."

"Yep." I answer.

Slowly, he reaches for the chain attached to the door. "What's this other one going to say when I look at it?"

"Guess."

He holds the charm in his fingers and turns the silver medallion over. His face pales to white and his eyes dart back to mine with worry. And confusion.

"What the fuck?"

"Exactly."

SEALING MY *fate*

BOOK TWO IN THE FATE SERIES

HEIDI LIS

prologue

KARA

April

MY DECISION TO LEAVE CHICAGO both scares and excites me. Living under the microscope of my brother since my best friend, Izzy, up and left without a trace has been nothing short of exhausting.

The constant state of paranoia I've been living with has made it increasingly difficult to play off the façade that she had indeed vanished. I have no choice but to hide the fact that I helped her do it. That little secret is a dangerous one, and comes at a high price if my brother ever figures it out.

I had held onto a glimmer of hope that my brother, Dominic, would eventually move on. Only, it's just that. Hoping and dreaming. Sadly, hopes and dreams are not words I'd usually associate with when it comes to him. With him, words like nightmares and suffering are a better fit. Whenever he showed up, pain always followed.

Earlier tonight, he showed up on my doorstep!

I opened my door slightly, leaving a mere crack to peer through. I made sure to leave the chain in place that secured the door. No way in hell was I welcoming my brother inside. Standing there in his soaking wet trench coat, all courtesy of the torrential downfall, stood a desperate, ominous looking man. The blackness of the sky was matched only by his appearance.

I motion the sign of the cross and say a silent prayer because my flimsy chain is the only obstacle that stands between me and him. Divine intervention is what I need at the moment, but my chained door will have to do.

His goliath eyes centered on my face strikes fear in me. Every prickling sensation it causes unsettles me more. It's plainly obvious he's on the warpath as every sharp breath he takes, his nostrils flare. His tense jaw muscle twitches and if I'm not mistaken, I faintly hear what sounds like the grinding of teeth. I try to remain steady even though I'm terrified.

I slowly raise my trembling hand up the inside of my door to grasp the only thing keeping him on the other side, the chain. I grasp it like it's my lifeline. The ugly truth is this chain could never hold him out if he wanted in, but that's all I have going for me right now.

"Open the door!"

His frightful appearance is one thing, the ominous tone of his demanding voice is enough to send my pulse racing, and the deafening sound of my heartbeat echoes like thunder. Dominic's dominant and aggressive nature is a deadly combination. In a panic, I chance it and look for a place to hide, but my mind is too busy wondering what he's going to do next. I'm sure as hell not welcoming him in, but there is simply no place for me to run and hide.

He's not giving me a second to consider my next move. Instead, he raises his leg and slams his foot against my door. As I feared, it splintered at the hinges providing him easy access. The sheer force of his kick threw me like a rag doll to the floor. Stepping over the split wood, he bypasses me shrugging on the lapels of his coat to shake off the excess rain. He heaves a few sighs, but then turns to confront me with an eerily calm posture. He went from manic to calm in a fraction of a second as my blood turns to ice.

That's not a good sign for me. I'm on the floor immobilized with shock and fear, but then again why am I shocked by him? This is what happens when Dominic does not get what he wants. He turns into the murderous bully I've known him to be.

"Well," *he says surveying my apartment,* "now that I'm inside, shall I have a look around?"

Like I have the choice to say "hell no!" *Instead, I try to sound reasonable.* "Dominic, stop this madness. Just leave. I know nothing, and I have nothing to hide from you." *I'm proud of myself for not cracking under his scrutinizing glare.*

He studies me for a moment as if mulling it over, but then he says, "Tsk-tsk. Not 'til I get what I want. If you would just indulge me by telling me what I want to know, this will be much more pleasant for you... dear sister." He slowly pronounces sister in such a way it casts a new set of chills that go bone deep.

With a conniving look on his face, Dominic glares at me and instantly, my body reacts with uncontrollable shakes. The side of his lip curls, getting the response he had hoped for from me. Afraid and shaking. I'm in no mood to let him continue to torture me, so instead I comply with his wishes. Not by choice, but refusing him will give him what he likes. A challenge. Lifting my hand, my voice cracks, but I give him the go-ahead.

"Knock yourself out. I've got nothing to hide." I pride myself with the fact he won't find a damn thing that will help him locate Izzy. The only thing I have is a phone, and I've taken measures to protect it. I hid it under the floor panels under my bed. I'm thinking there is no way will he think to look there. And for all our sakes, I pray he doesn't.

To stay out of his way I stay put on the floor, but slide up against the wall. All the while he's swiftly moving from room to room. Between his grunts and the noise of my belongings flying overhead, I lower my head, rattled and momentarily freaking out. My insides are in knots, screaming at me to retaliate, but I simply know better. Deep down I knew this day was coming. On some level, I think I tried to prepare myself up for it. I'm just surprised it has taken him this long. He's stopped by before, but this time he's aggressively searching, since he has no other clues to go on. His attempts to find her have left him empty-handed.

When he makes his way down the hall and enters my bedroom, I close my eyes and silently count. The numbers help calm my nerves while my belongings are being tossed around like trash. The loud bangs of my furniture being flipped over infuriate me, but I remain seated. Each loud noise makes me jump and that's the moment angry tears begin to spill over. I'm so nauseated that he's doing this, bile wretches at the base of my throat. I need to direct my anger somewhere, so I slam my fists on the floor beside me until he sets his sights on my most prized possessions. My eyes watch as he edges closer to my bookshelf. It's the single most terrifying moment for me. I can't even take a breath as a part of what makes my life worth living fractures.

Just like the snake he is, when he set his sights on my photo albums, my eyes widen in horror as he does the only thing he knows how to do...destruction. Dominic knows all too well how important my pictures are to me. It's not only my passion, it's who I am. My memories forever ruined all from his fucking temper tantrum. He even went as far as to stop and look at me before he smirked ripping them to shreds, laughing as he did.

I had a decision to make, keep my mouth closed or curse him all to hell. It took every ounce of willpower, but I kept my lips firmly sealed. My silence irritated him so much his face flamed red. I may not be able to beat him, but I sure as hell can deny him what he wants most. A reaction out of me. He had hoped that my pictures would be my Achilles heel to make me talk. Oh, how I love to disappoint him, but look what it cost me?

Years of hard work. Memories forever gone.

Emotionally drained, my body leans forward while my weary eyes stare at the floor in a trance-like state. I'm surrounded by the remains of my busted door and ruined memories, but to survive this, I need my mind to visualize anything other than the disarray that's around me. More times than I can count, I've learned how to shut my mind off to wander to more peaceful places. It's how I've survived him all these years. A much-needed skill when he's in a destructive mood.

Like now!

The sounds of broken glass swiftly pull me back, and as I open my eyes, the crunching sound suddenly stops. Dominic reemerges from my bedroom coming my way. Shattered glass lines the hallway from my bedroom to the living room. While he's grumbling, the first thing I notice is that his hands are empty. I lower my shoulders in relief that my phone is still safely hidden. I'm silently thanking my lucky stars when I'm interrupted by his loud exhale. I risk looking in his eyes and like a bull eyeing the color red, he looks manic. His broad shoulders are heaving, no doubt tired from his excursions but the crazy way his eyes are scrutinizing me, it's terrifying. His lips snarl as he bares his teeth.

"I find nothing?!"

He's tense and edgy with his maddening eyes scanning everywhere. He's making sure he has not missed anything. In my mind, I find a reason to hide a smile, witnessing his failure to find anything does afford me a moment to feel triumphant, but I can't make the mistake of showing it.

"I could have saved you the trouble of making a mess if you would have only listened to me to begin with." I take my time to clearly say each word, but make sure they are filled with contempt and annoyance. I may know better than to get into a shouting match with him, but that doesn't mean I can't find ways to communicate my dissatisfaction.

Dominic reacts swiftly by taking two large steps, and lowers himself to my level. When I deny him my eyes, he places a gloved finger under my chin. Slowly, he raises my head so I'm forced to meet his menacing glare.

"You don't fool me," he snarls. As he adjusts his weight with his feet, he settles with a clearing of his throat. "In fact, a reminder is what you need. So you know what it feels like to double cross me, dear sister."

I start to reply, but he's quick as lightning. Dominic swiftly forms a fist and lands a blow to my ribs. I'm doubled over, gasping to fill my lungs with oxygen. It burns and hurts so bad that my eyes overflow with tears. I cough so violently, my body trembles and shakes. It's taking sheer determination not to break down in front of him. I may cry, but I'd rather die than give him what he wants.

My painful moans are mixed with the strings of saliva that drip from my mouth. As I struggle take in any air, I notice him lowering his face. He takes a gloved hand to pull the hair back from my face.

"Do you have anything to tell me?" he purrs like a lion.

Mentally I'm doing my best to ignore him, but I can't deny his minty breath in my face and the toe-curling pain I feel. My endless stream of tears infuriates me even more. I want to curse him to all damnation, but I fear I might not leave my apartment alive if I do. Instead, I bite my tongue hard enough to taste blood. I can hardly contain my anger anymore so I fist my hands tightly, trying my best to control the rage that's desperate for a release. In a blurry haze, I look at him with nothing but distain in my eyes. I do my best to remain steady even though my voice is far from it.

"I have no clue where SHE IS!" My body straightens like a board as I shout.

A leisurely, but sinister smile emerges before his gloved hands cradle my face. His touch is not welcome, it's a warning. As he wipes my flowing tears with his thumbs, I can taste bile in the back of my throat. His touch not only feels wrong, the texture of his gloves feels like sandpaper against my wet, delicate skin. He leans closer again, resting his lips against my ear. The onslaught of his hot breathing causes me to shudder. Fearful but denying myself of showing it, my eyes close.

"Let me just make sure," he softly whispers. Before his words can resonate, he releases my right cheek. Not wanting to see his face, I kept my eyes closed and without any warning, he lands one more blow. My hand automatically reaches for his fist and as I grip his hand with my trembling fingers, I fear he's finally done it.

I'm afraid he's broken me to the point I won't recover. Not able to hold back any longer I curse him to hell about ten times before he stands, righting his coat. Satisfied with himself, he steps over me and walks out of my door without a backward glance.

I'm left coughing and wincing as each of my breaths burn like fire. As I cry hysterically, I inch my aching body forward until I'm bent over embracing my lower body. Each of my aching tears flows with so much anger and undeniable hurt. Brother or not I make myself a vow, a long overdue promise as I lay here, broken.

I can no longer simply suffer at the hands of my sadistic brother, and I'll spend the rest of my life making sure he never finds Izzy.

After my sobs and tears lessen, I stand up to position my damaged door against the frame. I don't even care that it's not secure. It's obvious my neighbors never heard a damn thing. That, or they didn't want to confront a crazy man. Either way, I'm left to stumble to my room. What's left of my haven resembles the destruction from a tornado. Too damn worn out to care, I wince with every step I take. Judging my steps just right to avoid falling, I make my way to my tossed bed. My flipped mattress is discarded to the floor. Not in the mood to fix it, I crash right where it's lying. I'm exhausted with painful aches and sore muscles. To get somewhat comfortable, I curl into a ball and rest my swollen and weary eyes. I'm incapable of thinking rationally, I'm just too wrecked and shattered right now. Dominic has crushed the last remaining shred of a bond we shared. He's more than proved that I'm nothing to him, so that's it.

There is only one thing left for me to do.

It's time to pack my bags and leave.

I simply need to vanish without a trace just like Izzy had done not so long ago.

I'm left only with my thoughts.

One day my dear brother will have to answer for all his actions.

I can only pray I'm there to witness it.

Chapter One

"New Beginnings"

Kara

June

I LEARNED A LONG TIME ago that life is precious. One, never waste a breathtaking minute of it, and second, never take anything for granted. My motto is simple. With no real guarantee of a tomorrow, live life for today as if it's your last.

If I've learned anything over the last few months, it's just that. The wickedness that stems from my brother is not something easily forgotten. I'm faced with it each day I gaze into Izzy's eyes. For now, she's in a good place. I do, however, fear a part of her is forever damaged. I'm still afraid that Dominic's evil ways will find a crack and seep back into our lives.

Being the sister to Dominic Santos, and living in Chicago was never an easy thing. Most people feared him, and anyone who challenged him ended up beaten or dead. That's the main reason my circle of friends was small. I only hung out with people who have never heard of him. It makes for an awkward conversation, nonetheless, a necessary one. Weird? You bet it is, but effective as well.

With the issues Dominic and I had growing up, things with him did not turn ugly until he had a taste of my friend, Izzy. An innocent overnight sleepover turned out to be the night my friend lost her virginity. To my brother. We laughed about it afterward, but from that point on and for years later, they kept seeing each other.

Once we graduated, Izzy's life ceased to be her own. What should have been the best years of her life, turned out the be the opposite. Our once close friendship became strained at best since I only saw her when Dominic agreed to it. He kept her on a tight leash and unfortunately she was in too deep before she realized Prince Charming was the Devil in disguise. Hell, even I didn't know the true depth of his sick ways. His obsession with her turned sadistic and ugly.

Over time, Izzy slowly opened up to me, choosing every word carefully. The way in which she spoke, I knew she kept the worst parts to herself, but what I did hear was enough to make my blood run cold. To hear her speak with such anguish, crippled my attempt to respond. Overtaken with the fact it was me who introduced them, a tidal wave of guilt flooded my heart. I failed her then and kept failing her, as there was nothing I could do to get her away from him at this point. My parents were far too terrified of Dominic to confront him, and Izzy refused to go to the cops because some of them were friends of his.

Like the old saying goes, it's who you know and who you pay off.

Izzy, eventually had more than enough of him and came up with what she felt was a failsafe plan to escape. With Dominic being the expert of manipulation, she had to plan carefully and do it herself. No one knew him like she did, and she lived with the bastard. I, on the other hand, had dared him a time or two. I even went as far as to stand up to him. Yeah, that never worked out well. In fact, it ended badly, resulting in getting my ass kicked by him. Sister or not, when it came to Izzy, nothing stood in his way.

The day she needed my help in carrying out her plan, was bittersweet for me. Dominic would be watching my every move, so I agreed to stay put and continue living my life like usual. I just needed to pretend that my friend just up and disappeared. I played my part of the distraught friend. The truth was, I was miserable without her sweet face.

Like I knew I would, I had regular visits from him. His main purpose was to pressure me to reveal what, if any, knowledge I had but I stayed firm in my resolve. Over time, I knew he had hoped I would slip up. Trying to stay one step ahead of him, I convinced Izzy not to tell me where she was going. Only to wait, until she settled somewhere. That's the only way to keep honest in saying, 'I had no clue where she went'. He never fully believed that.

I went as far as to stay with mom and dad on occasion. I figured that way, someone could account for my well-being, just in case I came up missing one day. With my brother on the warpath and out of his damn mind, he's unpredictable at best. With a man like my brother, that makes him that much more dangerous.

Dominic's visit left me worried and so crazed out of my mind that I contacted Izzy after he left. Our idea to buy prepaid disposable phones was brilliant. Our limited contact would be untraceable. After I explained his visit, and with no hesitation on her part, she had a ticket waiting for me at the counter of O'Hara Airport that same night. A bit anxious, I spent three hours driving around in circles just to make sure I wasn't followed. Feeling certain I wasn't, I parked my car in long-term parking. With a pat on the roof, I said my good-bye. I'm sure most people don't say good-bye to their car, but knowing I most likely would not return for it anytime soon, I gave the old girl a send-off. In a weird way, it felt like leaving an old friend.

Luckily for me, my work wasn't an issue. Currently, I'm a freelance photographer working with a few Chicago-based independent magazines. The fact I'll be in the Pacific Northwest with the rich breathtaking sights is even better. I can finally break away from tall building landscapes to the great outdoors. An exciting change for me. The only sad part was leaving my parents. Not that we're that close, but they are still my parents. Thankfully, they fully understood and never pressed me for more when I mentioned I'd be leaving town for a while.

My last words, 'I'll call you soon' had been it.

Unsure of what awaited me in Washington State, I felt like a woman without a home. The few late night chats with Izzy had blindsided me with the news of a possible new love interest. After my brother, I swore she would never want another man ever again. But, then a hot man on a Harley will change any hot-blooded woman's mind. Even better, her hot looking neighbor has a best friend, who according to Izzy is, 'hotter than sin'.

Liam Talbot was a man I couldn't wait to meet. Under better circumstances of course, but, man candy can cure any ailment. That, or make one forget about their sick, paranoid brother for a time being. Either way, a win-win for sure.

The night I met this handsome man, I thought I nearly died and gone to heaven.

With many laughs and flowing drinks, I admit I was a bit nervous with clammy hands. When Izzy placed a sweet tap on my shoulder letting me know they had arrived, my heart about jumped out of my chest. Not sure what to do, I froze and pasted on a smile before I turned around.

Checking out Izzy's man, Brax, for the first time nearly had me choking on my beer. Mid-drink, my eyes swallowed this man as he approached our table. I knew it had to be him. The way his eyes lit up like the fourth of July when he looked at Izzy, there was no question. Just when I thought my shaky knees might stop knocking, a man swaggered from behind, and my heart stopped.

Not many things shock me. I've lived through enough bullshit to last me a lifetime, but sometimes the unexpected happens. I mean the feel good kind of unexpected. I'd compare the feeling to a bolt of lightning traveling all the way from the tip of your spine out the end of your tippy toes. Similar to a blaze of energy setting every nerve in your body on fire. An awakening of millions of cells. Yeah, something like that.

That's precisely what happened the minute my dainty eyes landed on a husky-legged, firmly toned man. Did I mention a phenomenal looking man at that? Damn, Izzy never scratched the surface when it came to Liam's hotness.

His sharp eyes had the thickest set of eyelashes I've ever seen on a guy. From where I was standing, they stood out. Oh man, with just one deep stare from him, he spoke to my soul. Sounds corny, but he placed a foothold and damned near pierced it. If you take into account his glacier blue eyes and cupid's bow smile, boy, I was screwed. That hefty combination left my legs buckling and my core aching with a need I've never felt before.

Liam's not only tall, he's bulky and has wildly tousled hair. I'd say a butterscotch-honey color. Butterscotch being one of my favorite candies, now may be my all-time favorite. I swear my ovaries and neglected libido raised their own checkered flag. They knew a winner when they saw one. I couldn't help but let my eyes linger on his ripped, broad shoulders under his shirt. Liam held every bit of my attention.

It wasn't long before every dormant and neglected part of my body slowly started to burn. There was no mistaking the effect he had on me. His sex appeal alone led to a momentary meltdown.

"Sweet. Mother. Mary and Joseph!" I breathlessly whispered at the sight of him.

In the distance, his thick voice carried. "Holy Shit!"

His eyes locked with mine.

My eyes engaged with his.

To describe Liam in one word, it would be *intoxicating*. Standing, at least, six-feet tall, dressed in well-worn jeans and black biker boots, I was a drooling mess. He had these insanely thick curls that draped the back of his neck, and damn, even those are sexy. Enthusiastically, my eyes set off on a journey from his broad shoulders and stopped to feast on his tattooed arms. Tribal designs wrapped his biceps that, at that moment, were brimming against his t-shirt.

Just wow!

I know I'm gawking, so I shift my focus from his arms back to his face. Big mistake, because what I come across is his piercing blue eyes sizing me up, intimately. There is no mistaking the slow arch of his eyes, and, oh boy, a wave of tremors settles between my thighs. The sudden urge to cross my legs was so intense, I did so hoping to cure my strong ache.

Izzy makes the introductions even though it's not necessary. Our eyes locked onto each other the second they crossed paths.

"Charmed to meet you, sweetheart," he said offering his hand. The urge to burst out laughing soared as I was pretty sure no one these days used the word 'charmed' when they met someone. The fact that I was indeed charmed did not go unnoticed.

Studying him, every part of me marveled with his clear open admiration of me.

"Likewise." As the words leave my lips, I can't help but feel the warm glow flow through me.

Drinking in his pleasant profile, it was damn easy to fall victim to his most alluring feature. *His eyes*. They're powerful and demanding in such a way that keeps me from looking away. My eyes refuse to shift their focus. The color of the bluest ocean, his delicate eyes contrast his larger than life image. Every part of him screams big, loud and fearless, but his eyes tell a different story.

While I nervously engaged in small talk, I uncovered a surprise. If you want to call it that, but after hearing him talk, his appearance holds a stark contradiction to the compassionate, sweeter side of him. This blue-eyed, body made for sin man, disguises a sweetness I've never had the pleasure of witnessing before. Men, in my experience, had been lackluster, dull, or eerily possessive. Maybe, just maybe, luck might be on my side this time around.

I was more than ecstatic to discover under his thick layer of handsomeness contains a man with some good ole' southern charm.

Well, I claim him as having good ole' southern charm, but Liam was quick to correct me.

"Oh sweetheart, that's not charm. That's just me being flirty."

Seriously, his sense of humor and easygoing personality had me laughing most of the time. I felt so at ease, I joined in with being a bit 'flirty' myself.

In an attempt to entice him, I arch my neck and flirt with my eyes. When I lean forward, his lower lip retracts behind his teeth. Oh, there was no way to miss that, it only made me want to flirt more.

"Now that's too bad because charm is way sexier than being plain old flirty." Nudging my shoulder in his direction, he releases his lip he was biting.

"Is that so?" He rasps lightly holding me hostage.

The way he's studying me with eyes of blue glass, all captivating and soulful, I knew it in an instant. I realized he was something special.

"So." I manage to say before taking another swig of my beer, aka my confidence builder. The way his eyes consume me, it's like he's drinking in every word. "You see, charm requires using your brain, and doing so proves that you have a certain amount of skill sets." Offering my hand up, I clear my throat, "Flirty is just a bunch of words."

Eyes pulled together, he pauses. "Huh!" Lowering his chin to ponder my less than scientific definition, he graciously nods his head a few times. I'm about to say I'm full of crap and play it off like I'm only messing with him, but instead, he makes a noise to clear his throat. "Wow! I see you have put some thought into this."

I figure it's better to chuckle instead of crawling under the table with embarrassment, so I settle for a light chuckle. "Indeed, I have."

Flirtatiously he winks, then brags, "Well, it's a good thing I got a brain and some amazing skill sets then."

Yep, indeed he had charm in spades!

LIAM

Hours earlier...

"WHAT'S HER STORY ANYWAY?"

I've had this nagging feeling since I heard she's heading our way. I'm not big on surprises, I like things to be planned out. Ever since Kara's name first came up, I've heard all sorts of wild stories.

Brax sighs with a tight-lipped smile with hands in his pockets. "Man, from what I've gathered she's lived under the shell of her asshole brother. She's Izzy's best friend in the world." Lightly stroking his finger along his lip, his hesitation tells me exactly how uneasy he feels. That's not a good sign. "The main thing is she's here, and now we just have to keep them both safe."

I wrestle with my thoughts, but nod my head in agreement, but something tells me shit is going to get serious. And, not in the way he thinks. Both Izzy and Brax have some wild hair that has linked the word 'serious' with my name when it comes to her friend Kara. It's insane.

Not that I'm overly complaining, but to hear them talk, Kara and I are in a committed relationship neither of us knows about or are aware of. Don't get me wrong, I'm all for hooking up and having some easygoing fun, but that's where it stops. Assuming we're going end up in a serious relationship is far-fucking-fetched. The only thing I think of is a ball and chain fastened to my ankle. And that shit does not sit well with me.

This shit needs to be quickly addressed. I've had one, let me say it again, one serious relationship and that ended in a disaster that had me running for the hills. She did a number on me. Since then it's all about me having a good time. No attachments, no expectations, and no commitment. If I live with these three simple rules, it will guarantee that I'm not getting hurt again.

To clear the air and put on the brakes, I wave my hand in Brax's face. "Jesus, you and Izzy have all but tied me to this chick already. Let me add, a chick I've never met, at that! I'm all for helping Izzy girl, you know I am, but you need to slow down, man." I'm so annoyed by even having this conversation that I wipe my hand down my face to try to ward off my anxiety. The exact reason I live with my rules nowadays.

As it is, I'm all worked up, and I do not need this shit. As soon as I said my peace, he throws his head back laughing. Knee slapping kind of laughing. *What the hell is so funny?* My mouth is open, and glare is deadly serious. It does nothing to deter him.

"Yeah buddy, just you wait," he heckles, then tilts his head sideways. He's muttering words I can't make out, and I'm not sure I want to.

That leaves me wondering what the hell am I getting myself into? And, what the fuck does 'just you wait' mean? The answer to that question came the moment my eyes got their first peek at her.

The 'just you wait' comment made perfect sense.

Chapter Two

"Just You Wait"
Liam

Jesus, here I am a grown man but the more I gaze at this woman, my body's acting like a horny teenager. I've had to adjust myself a few times to allow room down south. The second my eyes landed on the table Izzy was occupying, her friend had her back to me, so I surveyed her ass first. And what an ass it was. Long locks flowed across her back with every shift of her body. My eyes drank in the sight of her dark, bouncing curls down to her tight jeans. Jeans which appeared like they were painted on every curve of her body. Damn, she had some serious curves too. Closing my eyes, I all but pray the front of her would match the hotness the back of her teased me with. Like a kid at Christmas, she's my Christmas present I have yet to open.

She's been here settling in, and I've heard how much I'm going to like her. In fact, Brax's exact words to me were, "You are so fucked, brother," I take as meaning she's my type of woman.

With all the constant blabbing about her, I can't help but feel like I already know her. And everything I've heard so far comes with some serious baggage. As I view her in the flesh, I'm not feeling anything remotely close to knowing a damn thing about her. What I am is wound up tight as hell, and I never get anxious, not over a woman.

Her sudden laugh at something slightly shifts her body so I can get a better glimpse of her face. My gaze narrows, seeing nothing but her. It's as if time stands still and my steps come to a halt. She's truly a beauty, and damn, my insides simmer. Glancing around, I get the impression I'm not the only one taken with her beauty. My brows tighten, and a low growl threatens to escape my throat. I'm glaring at every dick that has caught her attention so far. Great, this night is going to end with my fist slamming in some dick's face. Not the evening I had planned, but not something I can just ignore, either

"Are you coming, or what?" Brax barely asks before he hauls off and smacks my shoulder. Appearing a bit pleased with himself, he chuckles, "Fucking told you, man."

Oh yeah, he's just fucking hysterical.

Yeah, yeah whatever. Feeling a bit annoyed that he's right, I shrug off his comment and shift my feet forward casting a warning glare at every dickwad along the way. Yeah, that's right assholes, that woman is with me. Ah damn, did I seriously just think that? Damn Brax. He's got my mind all screwed up.

I take notice of Izzy's gaze as we arrive to their table. She leans forward to whisper something in Kara's ear. A breathtaking smile emerges, and Kara's eyes broaden before they land on my buddy in front of me. Her grin is damn seductive, and my ego suddenly emerges. She's eyeballing Brax, as a giggling Izzy whispers in her ear. The picturesque glow she gives as Brax acknowledges her has her blushing an exquisite shade of red. She's stunning and right then I realize I want that response directed at me instead of him.

Say what you want, but all of my previous rules are long forgotten. The knots in my stomach and nervous energy are not a welcome feeling, but she's a lot to take in. Beautiful for sure, but this woman appears to have a feisty side to her. I can tell by the way she uses her arms and hands when she speaks. She's loud and attention worthy, and she definitely has my undivided attention.

Slowing my advance, I wonder if she normally dresses this way, or if she's dressed to impress. I'm hoping like hell she dressed this sexy just for me. *Damn, there goes my ego again.* Either way, she's damn desirable.

When I finally make it to the table, I step around Brax and settle next to her, making sure to send her a private message with my eyes. It's working because it appears a cat has got her tongue. Her cheeks flush pink, and she's nervously playing with her hair. Her gaze holds my attention until her the aroma of her fragrance distracts me. Ohhh, it's sweet and spicy, just like her. I like it. If that's not enough to tempt me, her perky tits are welcoming. I'm a gentleman, not a pig, but damn they are hard to miss. Her tank top barely covers them up.

To stop from swallowing my tongue, I give her a proper smile and nod my head as Izzy introduces us. Her eyes lock with mine, and mine are all but claiming her. I may not want it, but there's no stopping it from happening. It's happening.

"Charmed to meet you, sweetheart."

"Likewise," she said with a thoughtful smile that curved her mouth.

Nervous fingers find their way to her hair, and she starts twirling it. I assume that's a good sign. I'm not one to miss an opportunity, so I take my time to appreciate her body from head to toe. The lower my eyes drift, she notices and halts my progress by lightly running her pink fingernail across the outline of her chest. Right where her tank delicately touches her skin. I have to say, admiring her little black tank from the front is a whole lot better, considering she has a full chest proudly pushed up on display.

She just keeps getting better and hotter. And now I get a better look at the tattoo covering her right arm, not quite an arm sleeve but close enough. That alone sets her above all in my eyes, I enjoy ink and the fact she does too, well that's something for sure. Damn near biting my lip, my gaze falters as I roam from her frayed jeans to her, oh damn, her tiny feet. Now I'm a perceptive guy, and taking notice of her manicured toes and high-heeled sandals hits me like a ton of bricks. I feel like I've been caught ogling, and she must read my mind because she suddenly turns and wiggles her pink toes at me.

"Wow," I say with a whisper. She's not what I had expected. I wasn't too sure what I did expect, but a hot, sassy woman who had me by the balls without even touching me wasn't it.

My speculative gaze forces my hand to press over my heart like it has suddenly stopped beating. She has no clue what I'm feeling right now. The effect she has on me. A deep growl of satisfaction escapes my lips and she damn near knocks me on my ass when she surprises me with a smack of her lips, like she's blowing me a kiss. She's flirting with me and for once, I'm on the receiving end. Definitely, not what I was expecting.

"Trouble." I breathe out before I realize I've said it out loud.

With a wink, she boasts, "Yeah well, sometimes trouble can be good." She then wraps her pink, glossy lips around her bottle of beer and I for one could not agree with her more. Sometimes trouble is just what we need.

If she only knew the extent of the thoughts running wild in my head, she may think differently. But, goddamn, even her sandals are sexy as hell. I give her one of my panty melting smiles. With a hopeful glint in her eyes, she sips her beer, never breaking the hold she has on me. Appearing ever so alluring and every bit naughty.

Instant chemistry? Fuck yeah.

KARA

HIS LOOKS ALONE BLAZE A pleasurable itch I'm all too eager for him to scratch. And every flirtatious word he says to me, only entices me more. Hell, he's the whole package as far as I'm concerned. With his easy going attitude, my apprehension slowly disappeared as the night went on.

Between my loud and crass mouth mixed in with Liam's playful antics, we undoubtedly stirred up some crazy, off the charts chemistry. It wasn't long 'til neither of us could deny our own desires for one another. The way his eyes lit my insides on fire, I couldn't drink enough to cool me down. Liam's stare captured every sassy remark I made. He devoured every word like a morsel, craving for more.

The uncanny way in which he could easily manipulate some of my deepest desires confused me, but pleased me all the same.

It's been a long time since I've had any form of pleasure that hadn't come from my own devices. For the past year, I've lived with a stalker on the loose. That would keep anyone locked up at home. Tonight, I feel the urge to let loose, and I pray Liam can keep up. Then again, he's brawny enough so I can only hope to keep up with him.

The constant flush of my cheeks did nothing to hide my attraction to him. The way his eyes shamelessly undressed me with nothing more than a warm smile and gentle handshake could only be described as intoxicating. To hell with playing hard to get, my mind's already racing with possibilities while my eyes feasted on his lips. Oh, and what arousing lips they are. All plump and succulent, ready to devour their next meal. Hopefully me, I joke to myself and suddenly feel the need to clear my head.

"I'll be right back."

I excuse myself to go to the ladies' room, I needed a minute to catch my breath and calm my nerves. I never expected to want to jump on him within five minutes of meeting him.

Then again, I never expected his sex appeal to bewitch me, either.

My shaky legs make it to the bathroom as I head straight for the sink. Yes, cold water. That's what I need. Both of my hands grab a hold of the sink while I stare in the mirror.

With a moan, "Oh, wow." I rest my head against the mirror. It's not just that he arouses me, it's that he completely consumes me. How is that possible? We literally just met!

It's insanity at its finest. As I stare at my pale complexion in the mirror, a chuckle of pure giddiness erupts from my throat and echoes in the room. I can't help myself, I feel like I'm back in high school again. Reaching for a paper towel, I wet it to dab the back of my neck. My thick hair is sticking to my skin, but the coolness dampens the prickling heat I'm suddenly feeling. Ahhh, it feels amazing.

Feeling refreshed I leave the wet cloth and close my eyes, letting myself relax when suddenly the door opens. With my eyes still closed and my head tilted back, I whisper to myself, "Get a fucking grip, Kara." It takes me a second to hope whoever walked in did not hear me talking to myself, but I'm sure they did. I wait for a response from whoever just walked in and when I don't hear anything, I slowly open one eye. When I do, I'm greeted with the brightest pair of blue eyes staring intently at me. He's just standing there with a sexy grin on his face.

Oh my God! Yeah, he heard me.

Liam scratches his temple, looking so fucking perfect, while I want to die of embarrassment. "Do you talk to yourself a lot?" He's having trouble holding back his amusement, but he asks me with the world's sexiest smile on his face. Damn. I need another cold cloth or, better yet, a cold shower would work better. I can't form the words, so instead, I shake my head letting him know I usually don't talk to myself. Most days anyway.

With a mild nod himself, he edges closer to stand behind me. His proximity leaves me weak in the knees, so I'm hanging onto the sink with both hands again. Breathing heavily, my eyes lock with his in the mirror. I keep my stance facing forward. Watching him, watching me. His eyes intensify and then very gently his hands reach around my hips. He inches closer. His hard body is barely touching mine, but his hands suddenly tighten their hold. Tilting his head to the side, he watches for my reaction as he presses his hips into mine. His firm fingers and hot, hard body feel so damn great, I'm not able to contain the moan that passes my lips. I'm sure I sound needy and desperate, but it's pointless for me to try and deny it. He's that alluring.

My eyes swing from his to mine, and quickly back to his again. The instant our eyes lock, he slays me with another gorgeous smile. I'm more than tempted to turn around and kiss the living shit out of him, but the good girl in me warns me to act like a lady, instead. Not some sleazy slut ready to strip down in the bar's bathroom. The fact that he followed me in here might be an indication that he's done this before, but bathroom sex is new for me. Since I don't want to be another one of his conquests, I hold back.

I raise my gaze and tilt my head to the side to get a better look at those icy blue eyes of his. "Visit the ladies room often?"

"Nope. Can't say that I do." He takes a glance around the room like he's never seen the inside of the ladies' room before. A slight, 'huh' clears his throat. "This is certainly a first for me. It's nicer than the men's room." Even the slight accent of his deep raspy voice is flirtatious and all kinds of sexy. Either that or I'm in serious need to have sex.

The way his provocative eyes simmer with such heavy intensity, I lose any rational I had left. Not one to deny what he wants, he steadies his hands once again on my hips. Only, this time, he tugs sharply.

A startled but welcomed sigh escapes the instant his hard body touches mine. I can feel his sculpted chest as he sways his body against mine. It's not long before his hardened shaft makes its presence known. Cradling me, the rock of his pelvis feels extraordinary. I'm a whimpering and moaning mess.

Liam swiftly turns me around to cradle my face in both of his hands. The warmth of his hands has my heart fluttering. It's easy for my eyes to get lost in his shapely oceans of blue heaven. There is no other way to describe them.

"Hope you don't mind, but I need to get this out of the way," he says softly but also with a bit of urgency.

Locking his eyes on my lips in a wickedly heavy stare, he inches closer until his lips gently touch mine. The warmth of his breathing ignites every cell in my body. I want him so bad, but I seriously have to question what we are doing. We're in a dirty bar bathroom, but I quickly remind myself, live for today as if it's my last.

Well then, I'll take this opportunity and do just that.

My lips melt into the softness of his. Our moans are both a mixture of desperation and need. The first swipe of his tongue glides across my lower lip before he sinks his teeth into it. The sweet zing of pain and pleasure measure the intensity in which I repay the favor by doing the same to him. Between his desperate groans and my aching moans, we both lose ourselves in each other. His large but gentle hands hold my head at the perfect angle, deepening the kiss. That only increases my need. I anchor my hands around his wrists, finally able to unleash the most powerful kiss I've ever given. I'm not timid, and I'm not shy. I urgently and aggressively take what I want, but Liam is quick to take charge and with his sheer domination, he walks me backward until my body slams against the sink. I'm damn near ready to prop myself up on it when the door pushes open. I was one second away from not giving a shit when they make their presence known.

Two loud gasps interrupt the most insane kiss of my life. Who knew two lips could be that intense? Wow! In my lip-locking-foggy-daze, I get the sense that left up to Liam, he'd be game to give these ladies a show. On the other hand, with my daze able to regain some focus, I flush with embarrassment. My immediate reaction is to touch my aching and most likely bruised lips. The reality that we are in a public bathroom collides with the gaze of the two startled ladies. Liam's a master when it comes to making me forget where we were. He made me forget everything but *him*.

He's not paying much attention to the ladies who are still gawking at us. Instead, his attention is solely on me. Tracing his thumb along my lower lip, he groans. "Damn, better than I imagined. Now, that we got that out of the way, we can head back out to our table. I'm sure a search party may come looking for us if we stay away much longer."

I mumble. "Okay."

We leave the ladies room with nothing but a nod of our heads as Liam takes my hand in his. As we approach our table, Brax and Izzy's expressions are priceless. The double takes from Brax and the jaw-dropping laugh from Izzy left Liam and I snickering. The 'we had just been caught having sex in the bathroom' glares were pretty damn funny. The fact is, I can't say that it wouldn't have happened if we remained alone for much longer. I'd like to think that both of us have more class than that, but when you act like horny teenagers, sometimes you do crazy things you wouldn't normally do.

Hell, since I've met him nothing I feel is rational.

It's anything, but.

Brax shakes his head and chuckles, then reaches over to slap Liam on the shoulder. Liam's head rolls back in a fit of laughter before he sweetly winks at me, and then high five's Brax. While the boys are entertaining one another, I duck my chin, slightly embarrassed and look to Izzy for support. Only I find her eyes darting between the guys with her face red as a tomato. She's barely able to contain her amusement, and I think I've lost my damn mind.

I sulk, "Whatever."

Ignoring the chatty comments, I reach for my drink. Sure enough, Izzy bursts out in a fit of laughter again. I'm so glad I could provide them with such entertainment is all I can think. Feeling a bit sorry for me, Liam reaches over pulls me in for a side hug.

"So tell me a little about yourself?" he asks, and I realize we are now in the question and answer part of the evening. The lingering embarrassment from our bathroom romp is a distant memory, and in its place is the buzz of alcohol. Better known as 'liquid courage'. Without any inhibitions to stop me from telling my sad story, I spill all my baggage starting with the good of course.

"Well, I'm a photographer. A damn good one at that." I am good at what I do, and I'm not afraid to shout it. "Unfortunately, I'm the sister to one sick sadistic bastard, who is hell-bent on finding my best friend and will stop at nothing until he does. If he had to sacrifice me to do it, he wouldn't hesitate or bat-an-eye. Let's see, that leads me to an unknown stalker that has been contacting me for a little over a year now. I have to admit, it's just so strange. He's out there somewhere and I haven't a clue who he is. I'd like to think he's harmless because nothing major has ever happened, but you never can be too sure nowadays I guess." I sober up quickly and realize just how sad my life is. "My life is anything but rainbows and sunshine." I'm about to keep rambling when my eyes leave his hand that is on his bottle of beer to glance at his face. The whole time I talked, I kept my eyes everywhere but on his face.

When I look at him I sensed confusion, but then it simmered to anger. With his jaw firmly set, I notice the thick, pulsating vein in his neck. Thumping firm and erratically. His fun mood has changed, and my big mouth is to blame. I should not have said all that I did. Liam opens his mouth to speak, but I have to intervene. I'm not going to sit here and be pitied by a man who just walked into the Ladies' room to slay me with one hell of a kiss. That might break my heart. If he does, I'll no doubt start crying. I did not tell him all of this just to gain his pity.

I raise my right hand and halt him before he can. Oh boy. His eyes are so comforting. Tears threaten so I prolong an extended sigh to help gain some composure. The last thing he needs is a crying girl on his hands. I hope by me giving him a sincere smile, he'll just let it go and hopefully understand.

To my surprise, he does. He sympathizes, because instead of speaking, he reaches out and holds my hand. Delicately rubbing the top of my knuckles, he makes a point to hold my hand a bit longer than necessary. I'm not sure if it's to comfort me, or to tell me he's sorry, but it doesn't matter the reason. His sincerity and kindness are a welcome change for a girl like me.

Who says chivalry is dead?

More than ready to push all the sad, lingering thoughts from my mind, my eyes shift focus and I jump into Izzy and Brax's current conversation. Unfortunately, the second I do, I wished I hadn't opened my big mouth. I sarcastically roll my eyes to the ceiling when I realize they were candidly speaking about private matters. Certain things I should not be engaging in.

Three sets of surprised eyes land squarely on me and never in my life have I been so embarrassed. What's that make it now? Twice, in one night, or is it three? Oh, who's counting?

"What the hell did I just agree with?" I ask with one eye closed, not sure I'm ready for the answer. Stupid me, I sprang into a private conversation, and now I'm the butt of the joke. Seriously, I jumped right in and agreed with whatever it was Izzy said to her man. With my silly friend, I should have listened a little better before I open my mouth. I blame it on sexy pants who is staring me down with one eye and devouring me with the other.

"Oh really? Do tell, Kara." Brax all but rolls off his stool laughing. He's been chuckling since Liam, and I came back from the restroom together, and he's not quit since. I know my face hurts from laughing so much. With his current fit of laughs, my cheeks flush. To hide my humiliation, I cover my face with my hands, shouting, 'why me?'

"Okay," I surrender and have to know. "So what were you two talking about that I stupidly agreed with?"

Izzy masks her amusement with a sweet little pat on my shoulder. The gesture encourages Brax's returning gaze that resembles, 'really?'

He leans his body my way, beaming with a mischievous grin from ear to ear. I mentally brace myself for whatever he's going to say. "Well, how should I say this? Izzy was about to brag about my…"

Izzy's hand clamps over his mouth. *"Oh, no you don't!"* She shouts so loud, I miss her beer bottle slamming down on the table, but

I sure saw it fly out of the top. Spilled beer, embarrassing moments, and great company guarantee a night with many great laughs.

"Do not listen to him!" she declares. "Brax has his mind in the gutter." Her eyes close to a slit then she lands a solid smack on his back. Lovingly of course. Choking on his beer, he offers me an amused wink.

Enjoying this sideshow, Liam jokes, "When is it not?"

Izzy and I both nod our heads agreeing with that statement.

Brax laughs with a dazzling smile and proposes a toast, "I'll drink to that, brother." That comment earned him a few groans from us ladies.

The bartender Sam, brings us a round of beers and it suddenly dawns on me what tomorrow is and I can't get the words out fast enough. "Are you guys coming over to Izzy's tomorrow night for dinner and the game?" I'm so excited because Izzy and I will be together to watch the hockey playoffs.

"What game?" Brax says in an easygoing manner. "If it includes eating count us in."

His lack of any real excitement makes me realize Izzy has not mentioned her fascination with our Blackhawks. That simply won't do.

I huff and shake my head ashamed at my friend. "Um, well, has Izzy not told you about our obsessions with the Blackhawks? Damn, she makes the same pre-game spread for every game. I'm shocked she hasn't told you about it." Their blank stares have me saying an off comment remark about her moving and forgetting all about our Hawks.

"Christ, my girl moves out here and forgets all about the Hawks. Tazer, would be ashamed." I say clearly disappointed.

Braxton hears a guy's name and gets irritated. Jeez, jealous much?!

Braxton's nose wrinkles before he asks, "Who the hell is Tazer?"

Izzy gives me a 'just really' look before explaining. "Ugh, she is talking about my favorite hockey player. Jonathan Toews, aka Tazer, number 19. Yeah," she confesses, "I'm sort of obsessed with him."

Ha! "Obsessed is putting it mildly, the girl has his jerseys, shirts, socks, hats and let's not forget my favorite… panties." I gladly embarrass my friend proud of her devotion.

"Panties?" Braxton pulls his body in, then slowly releases a deep breath.

"Gotta' like panties." Liam chuckles, before finishing off his beer and slamming it on the table.

"Iz," Braxton, whispers in her ear almost laughing. "Tell me about your Tazer panties."

Her ears are so red, she's so embarrassed. "Good Lord! I only have a few pairs and on game day, well, you know. I do my part so they can win."

This moment is too perfect not to share a story. I reach for Izzy's shoulder. "Oh Shit! Tell them what you told the guy at the sporting goods store that one time! No...better yet, let me."

Not even taking a breath, I don't miss a beat.

"So, we're shopping at this store and sweet little Izzy here, goes up to the sales guy, smiling and looking all innocent as she asks him if they have any Toews panties. Now, this poor kid starts choking and turns all sorts of red because he's embarrassed. So, she decides to play with him some more and tells him she wants him on her ass! I know what she means, she wants 'Toews' on the ass of her panties but by the look on his face, he's totally out of his element. Damn, I wish I took a picture of his face!" I'm laughing so hard I hang on to Liam's shoulder for support. "Imagine if you told him you wanted 'Kane' on your ass instead? We could have played it off as Izzy wanted him to 'cane' her ass. Now, that would have been priceless!"

There is not a dry eye at the table, we are all laughing so hard.

Braxton, snickers under his breath as he says to her, "You are shameless. How about I cane your ass instead?"

Oh shit, this just gets better.

"Well now," she gives him a mischievous grin, "that just won't do since your last name is not Kane, and your first name is not Patrick. But I might consider it, if you can handle the puck like he does."

His throaty growl gives way to his slow smile. "Oh sweetheart, I am going out to buy you some panties that say 'Property of Brax'. How does that sound?"

Izzy is quick to reply, "That might be okay, but on game day? Toews will be on my ass. It's tradition. Can't change it because that would be bad luck."

Liam, in a playful manner gives me sideways hug laughing as if this conversation is the funniest thing he has ever heard. All of a sudden Izzy stops to glare at us and I know I'm in for it.

"Hey, I wouldn't laugh too hard," she says to a laughing Liam, "Kara has "Crawford" on her ass on game days."

Yep, I burst out laughing.

With a hand on Brax's shoulder, Liam chuckled, "We have our hands full with these two. You realize this, right?"

Brax smiles from ear to ear and gazes into Izzy's eyes. "No, shit."

That was how our night went. All of us laughing and having a really great time. Meeting Izzy's new love, Braxton Ryles, has definitely helped my mood. The easy going nature they have is a welcome sight. Their bond seems effortless and seeing my best friend that happy and carefree is worth its weight in gold.

If I could control my overactive libido to cool it a bit, I might be able to ease the constant shade of red from my face. Since meeting Liam, and then becoming acquainted with the power of his lips, I'm a blabbering mess. It's hard for me not to be consumed with him while he stares at me with those eyes of his. Mercy!

I thought I could sneak a peek at him unnoticed, but as my gaze traveled from his chest back to his face, and I damn near choke. Totally not unnoticed. His brazen eyes have been stalking my every move and I'd lie if I said I didn't enjoy it. He catches my eye and hits me with a sweet smile only to top it off with a sexy wink. Talk about sitting in a puddle. I'm fanning my face, forced to have to look away because it suddenly feels like the temperature in the room has risen a mere hundred degrees. Izzy and Brax notice our flirting back and forth but act like they don't notice. When I dare to swing my eyes back to Liam, I can't help but notice he suddenly lowers his center of attention. Following the path of his eyes, my body sizzles in reaction.

When he descends his gaze to my neck, my pulse roars.

The minute they plunge to my chest, my heart zooms.

A needy moan escapes past my throat when I notice Liam suggestively wet his lips. The ache to reciprocate cripples me, because I'd gladly wet those lips of his for him. Once again, as if reading my mind, Liam swiftly raises an eyebrow…releasing a slow, lingering sexy groan.

Dear Lord, kill me now.

Chapter Three

"Ring Tones"

Kara

Leaving the bar, I do a quick glance over my shoulder to find Izzy laughing and shouting the words, "Have fun you two."

Liam is quick to raise his hand over his shoulder to send a wave, then settled himself on his Harley, waiting for me to climb on. It was my decision to either get on or go home with Izzy. Ha! Like it was something I needed to think over. I quickly swung my leg, straddling the big black machine for my first ride ever. I'm officially popping my bike cherry and I must say to cross this off my list of things I must do feels great.

As soon as I wrap my arms around his waist, he gives my hand a gentle squeeze and I'm so excited I squeal with delight. I knew I was in for the ride of my life. I must say nothing could have prepared me for the mind-blowing sensation of having a vibrating beast of a machine between my legs. Talk about stimulating, holy cow! Fully enjoying every rumble of the Harley as it roared to life, my arms tightened and we picked up speed soaring the big open road.

All I could think about was a night between the sheets with Liam as the wind whipped my hair wildly. I've never felt this carefree and eager to push any boundary as long as it ended with a night of wild freaky sex, Liam, and I will never forget. If Liam is half as worked up as I am, it will take a natural disaster to stop us. The sexual tension between us has been brewing all night, and the only words to describe what's going to happen once we unleash our desires will be an earthquake of epic proportions.

I wonder which one of us will give in first? Who knows, but it sure will be fun finding out.

What possibly could go wrong?

Winding our way down a long driveway, it was evident we were not returning home to Izzy's, and I wasn't one bit disappointed. Being alone with him is all I can think about. After that appetizer of a kiss he laid on me, I couldn't wait to be alone with him.

At first, I was puzzled, I thought he lived on the same street as Izzy and Brax, but we are on the outskirts of town where it's nice and quiet. Peaceful. Tall Evergreen trees line the drive concealing a house. It's very serene.

As we ride closer, a small two-story house emerged from the heavy trees. It's hard to imagine anything other than a big log cabin. All macho and masculine. But this house is the polar opposite. It's pale yellow, with white shutters. Aged nicely with character. A very large wrap around porch gives it a homey feel. I'm quite impressed and am loving the bench swing that hangs off to the side.

"Well, what do you think?" Liam comes to a stop and turns his head to see me smiling from ear to ear. Both of us are sitting on the bike while it idles, so I rest my chin against his back.

I'm really at a loss for words. "It's beautiful."

"It's home," he settles with a low sigh.

Liam climbed off the bike, holding out his hand, to lace our fingers. His hand is so much larger than mine, I pause gazing at the stark difference. It's not only the size of his hand that has my attention, but it's also the warmth of his touch. My hands are always so cold, so his warmth feels really nice.

Liam slightly turns when I don't keep pace with him. He notices that my eyes are still focused on our linked hands. "You okay?" His once amused look is quickly replaced with a look of concern.

"Yeah." I bashfully admit, feeling silly as I'm suddenly hit with a wave of nervousness. What? Why now? God, I hate to admit this to him. Not ten minutes ago, I'd been ready to have my way with him. "A bit nervous, I guess."

His eyes widen like he's surprised. "Oh really." Barking out a deep laugh, he challenges, "Where's the feisty girl from an hour ago?"

Great. The last thing I want is to let him down. I know I want him like I need my next drink of water...but the fact that I've not been intimate for a long time starts to mess with my mind. Call it nerves, but I'm a bit gun-shy. This can't be what he was expecting or even wanting. That's why he brought me here. Sex. A night of wild sex. It's what I want as well, I just need a second to calm my nerves. A man like Liam surely can get what he wants, and now is not the time for me to get all timid. Damn it, you only live once, Kara. Pull up your big girl panties and pull it together.

Okay, I just need to breathe. Easy as one, two, three. My little pep talk seemed to help calm my nerves because I suddenly feel a bit more daring. "Oh, she's here trust me. It's just…"

"Hey," he gave a slight tug on my hand. "We don't have to do anything you don't want to, okay?" His eyes not only look sincere and truthful, but his words also melt my heart a bit.

I fake a smile, finding it extremely difficult to think straight around him. "Thanks. Boy, you make it hard not to want you." I tug back on his hand, and he willingly cuddles up to my side.

"Really?" He smiles so wide a dimple forms in his right cheek. "I'm quite adorable, aren't I?"

Oh my God, so damn adorable and hot, I'm putty in his hands, but I'll keep that to myself.

"Well," I jokingly add, "I'll say your ego is big enough."

"Babe," lowering his lips closer to my mine, he whispers, "that's not all that's big."

Oh, he did not!

"Hey, you walked right into that one."

I happily admitted I sure did.

Hand in hand we walk into the house and he steps to the right switching on the lights. The room shines and I'm even more impressed. Damn. I have no idea who decorated his house, but they have one keen eye for what looks good. The main living room is decorated with warm, rustic colors. Light wood moldings with brown leather furniture, it's manly and classy. The neat quality and tidiness suddenly have me a bit uneasy.

"You are a bachelor, right?" Stepping forward, I survey the room. "Or is there a woman hiding somewhere?"

"Ha. No women here. Just me, the way I like it. I don't bring women back to my place very often." He walks around me and heads over to a long island fetching a glass. Turning his body, he holds it up. "Drink?"

"Yes, please." That's exactly what I need.

Lightly chuckling, he fills two glasses of with an amber liquid. I don't ask what it is after he hands it to me, instead, I swallow it in one gulp. If I ever needed to feel confident, it'd be now. I've never had a case of the nerves like I'm having now, it has to be him. He studies me raising his glass and then swallows his drink. Slowly, he lowers his glass but never removes his eyes from mine. My insides are starting to warm up, no doubt from his insanely good looks, but also from the liquid alcohol that is burning a trail down my throat. Yet, it doesn't bother me in the least.

"Liam." I breathlessly whisper as our eyes are intimately locked onto one another.

"Kara." He reciprocates.

That's all we said. Lowering my glass, I place it on the table and step in front of him. My pulse is racing, and I lose all sense of shyness. From the moment I met him, I wanted to be with him like this...the way we are now. Alone.

My lips attack his in a blistering exchange and before long my hands find their way to the back of his neck. His long curls all but beg me to thread my fingers through them. As I firmly grip his soft locks, I pull his head back, taking full advantage of his plump lips. Pure sweetness is all I can taste. A sweetness I could easily become addicted too. My moan is swallowed with his groan and crushing embrace. His hands wrap around my backside and lift my body so I can wrap my legs around his waist. To secure them from slipping, I cross my ankles and we both relish how good this feels.

"Jesus, where have you been?" The mystery in his eyes has me wondering the same thing. It's cliché... but an honest feeling.

"Chicago," I whisper.

He pulls back slightly lifting one eye, and I can't help but chuckle. I thought my answer was pretty funny, even though I knew full well what he meant. I also know humor always helps when you have an overabundance of nervous energy. Like right now.

Liam awkwardly shifts me in his arms all the while having a slight grimace on his face. The source of his distress is clearly evident. The impressive bulge in his jeans tents out enough for me to realize two things. One, my body has a mind of its own grinding against his rock hard erection. The rough seam of his jeans applies the right amount of pressure to my aching center. "Ooooh," a deep groan slips from my lips. The second thing that is blatantly obvious is that he's damn impressive. His ego wasn't lying and honestly, Liam is incredible and larger than life, so why not his cock?

Damn, I'm a lucky, lucky woman.

"Rub against me like that and I won't last, baby."

I'm mesmerized by his lustful eyes and desperate voice. Dear Lord, the way he feels, the only thing I want is more. When it comes to him, I'm greedy and very, very needy. Desperate times calls for desperate measures, and right now, I'm achingly desperate.

"Round one won't count...for either of us," I groan, gliding my teeth along his lower lip. He attempts to say something but groans instead, while I'm lost in this exquisite state of arousal. My panties are drenched and I'm about to orgasm from anticipation alone. I'm not kidding when I say I'm on the brink.

"Might as well give in so we can enjoy the rounds that will follow." I tease with a wink as his face to lights up.

"How many rounds do I have to look forward to?"

To be funny, I tap my finger against my chin like I'm thinking, but then break out with a giggle. "As many as you want."

"Fuck yeah. Now, that's what I want to hear." Time for talking has ended.

I utter the word 'champ' before he silences me. With a loud 'oomph,' my back is pressed up against a cold wall. He quickly raises my hands above my head, locking our fingers. Unable to keep my legs locked, they fall open and slide down until they reach the floor. It's a good thing I'm wearing my favorite sandals with a sizeable heal, because it evens out our height difference just perfectly.

Right now, we line up eyes to eyes and lips to lips.

Liam keeps a firm hold on my hands while his lips skim the side of my neck. The tantalizing heat from his touch feels so good, my eyes roll in the back of my head. To torture me, he traces his soft tongue in a circle behind my ear before his teeth nip at my bare skin. I gasp at the slight zing of pain and hiccup my next wavering breath. Before long, I'm moaning Liam's name like he's the messiah.

"So good...you have no idea how good you feel," I moan with a slight whimper mostly because his body feels so amazing. So much I might just lose my damn mind.

"Babe, look at me." His voice is commanding but not demanding. It's sweet like sugar, and as soon as my eyes meet his, I almost orgasm right then and there. All I see in his eyes is pure lust, and it's speaking to me on a deeper level that I've never experienced before. With a fiendish grin, he smirks, leaning closer to my ear. "Feel me," he groans.

It's not meant as a question either, it's a statement of fact. He manipulates his hard erection by rocking his hips, hoping to tease the ache between my thighs. On every stroke, his speed and intensity increase. He's on the verge of tipping me over the ledge into a sensory overload of pure ecstasy.

"Eyes, Kara. I want to see you fall apart for me."

They drift open to see his intoxicating smile and my hips start to sway to their own rhythm. I raise one leg, securing it around his hip. Liam increases his momentum with vigor, as he places a hand around my waist, to draw me closer into him. On impulse, I wrap my hands around his shoulders and rest my back against the wall deepening his pressure against my pussy. I'm riding this high, relishing every twitch of my legs on the brink of my climax. The pleasure is pure and explosive. Half of my body feels like ice while the other half is on fire. Liam's icy blue eyes invite me into what can only be explained as an alternate universe. Forgetting my own name, I surrender all of myself as every muscle in my body convulses with my gripping orgasm.

"Oh, baby girl." His grin is irresistible and his eyes are devastatingly splendid, reminding me of summer lightening. Totally captivating.

I'm unable to form words, still reeling the effects of my orgasm. Appearing pleased with himself, he lowers his face, and gently kisses the tip of my nose before his lips find mine again. As our lips part, Liam wraps a lock of my hair around his finger. It's a touching sentiment.

"Such beautiful hair," he compliments me before he lands another sizzling kiss. It's divine ecstasy whenever Liam kisses me.

Between each sweet declaration, he whispers with, "Feeling me yet?"

The way he's peppering kisses down my neck to my shoulders, I chuckle once my mind clears from my pleasure fog to focus on his face.

"With your messy hair and bruised lips, I could ask the same thing of you?"

He takes a second to lower his eyes to his proud erection that's on full display just for me. With a slight groan, he guides my hand with his, cupping himself in a firm hold. I can feel his throbbing cock, all hard and inviting. Jesus! I moan with anticipation.

"How's that for proof, baby?"

The sheer size of his proof has my panties dripping wet.

"We need to finish round one for you." I hint then smirk. "By that time, I'll be ready for round two."

Greedy and impatient, I flick his button and unzip his jeans. My hands have a mind of their own. I reach in and am pleasantly surprised gripping the vast size of his cock. Sure, I felt his size grinding against me, but holding it in my hand impresses me even more. The sheer size and width, oh man. One thing is apparent, he's massive—everywhere.

"Oh my God," I say without thinking, "let's hope I can walk out of here tomorrow?" I wish like hell I kept that thought to myself, but I realize I didn't when he chuckles and responds.

"Oh, I hope you can't," he rasped, deep and sensual. "That way I can make you breakfast in bed."

The idea of watching him make me breakfast half naked does sound about damn near perfect.

Not able to hold back any longer, I walk him back until he's against the wall. As quickly as I can, I lower his jeans over his wide hips, to hell with taking his boots off. I'm only interested in a certain part of his body, for now. My hands slide down the sides of his muscular legs, as I lower to the floor. In doing so, I make sure to keep my eyes fully engaged with his. It's much more sensual this way. As I slowly rise, my fingers skim over his body until they cup his face. That's when I lean forward to capture his lips. My tongue traces along the seam of his mouth, as I lower my hands inside the elastic of his boxers. Feeling brave, I sway my hips and lower taking the same journey I did with his jeans. He's completely bare and with nothing between us, my eyes feast on his massively hard cock.

My plan to take my time and pay homage to every inch of his body burns badly, but that will have wait for round two or three. I'm far too needy right now. Instead, my hand strokes his length while the other cups his balls massaging them gently. The dew of his excitement drips, trailing down his impressive length. His bedroom eyes invite me, so I delicately rub his mushroom head.

"Oh, Jesus!" Slips from his lips.

My touch is so sensitive that he thrusts his hips upward. To entice him, I squeeze his cock, leaving Liam sucking for air through his teeth. He exhales with quivering manic gasps. Pleased with his response, I lower my head, holding his stiff cock, and trace my tongue from base to tip. His manly, musky scent envelopes my senses, while my taste buds are flooded with his salty flavor. I welcome his manhood, opening as wide as I can. I'm so in the moment with the idea of pleasuring him, I zone everything else out. Once my lips are fully lubricated with my salvia and his pre-cum, I straighten my spine, hold onto his backside, and prepare to take him in as far as I can.

Not before I give myself a mental pep talk not to gag. I'm in the motion of sliding his head past my lips when his phone lights up and rings. I ignore it because I don't plan on stopping. That is until I feel his leg muscles tense up. With a loud pop, I ease my suction and let him go. My eyes dart to his.

"Shit." He groans with his hands tangled in my hair.

"Don't answer it." I'm not asking, I'm begging, pleading with him not to stop what got we've started here. I'm breathless like I've just ran a mile.

Ring.

Ring.

Ring.

I've never prayed so hard, but I'm praying he ignores whoever is interrupting.

"Dammit! I need to see who it is."

What, no! I lower my head.

Liam bends down and reaches for his phone out of his jean pocket. After he glances at the caller, his face tightens like he's growling. I'm not sure if he's upset we we're interrupted or if it's the caller, but I remain tightlipped with my eyes darting around the room unsure what I should do.

His growl gets louder, "You have to be kidding me." Then answers, "Yeah."

"What are you freaking out about now...?" His back rests against the wall as his eyes shoot to the ceiling.

"Who cares? I sure as hell don't! Listen here, Tiff, do not go anywhere near Brax. I told you this and I won't repeat myself." He's so angry, his demands come across in a low, menacing manner.

As if pushed to the brink, he lowers his chin and grinds his teeth. "Just this once, you get what I'm telling you?"

Gosh, wonder what this once, means?

I watch his annoyed body language, with his hand swatting in the air, but his eyes flash a different emotion. Disbelief, maybe. Worry lines surrounded them as they cast to the floor. I keep silent, just watching, not sure what to say.

Then, he suddenly presses end on his phone and rattles off a string of curse words that would impress a sailor. Blowing out an exasperated sigh, he yanks up his jeans. I lean back, but go to stand, still not saying a word. This once steamy room has a bit of a chill to it now. I wipe away the last of our heated exchange from my lower lip. It appears our night of fun has come to an abrupt end. So, I offer a hint of a smile to mask my disappointment.

"Listen, babe," he starts with, "I have to go and meet with my sister. If it weren't important, I would still have my dick in your mouth, trust me." His humor does draw a chuckle out of me, but the mention of that woman brings out my claws. Her.

I can't help but shake my head seeing red the minute he said her name. I've heard all about his bitch of a sister. The grief she has caused Izzy and Brax is enough to set me off. Unfortunately, I'm not able to control my sarcasm in front of him.

"Tiffany," I exclaim, "the bitch I've heard all about?" I all but spit on the floor before I stop myself. Crap, I know she's his sister.

"Yeah," he snorts with a fixed gaze, "that she is. We're...complicated." He settles with a sigh, then mentions, "I'm keeping my eye on her for Brax and Izzy's sake. She's up to something. I just don't know what yet."

With his explanation, I can't really blame him for having to leave. Just the timing sucks. I'd like to laugh about it, but it's not that funny. Oh, who am I kidding? It's downright hilarious. Give it a day, and I'll be laughing about it.

"Rain check?" He asks with his eyes intently on me.

I shrug one of my shoulders, really wishing for a rewind button. "Oh, yeah sure. You need to go, it's okay." I play it off like it's fine.

"No babe." Stepping closer, so not even an inch stands between us, he tips my chin. "It's far from okay. I was just getting started. Now, I got the worst case of blue balls, and I have to see my sister. Christ, what a mess. Definitely not how I saw this night going down."

I'm about to say, 'me, too' when he places a kiss on my forehead. "Let me take you to Izzy's. I have no idea how long I'll be."

"Ooookay."

We head out and make our way to Izzy's house. As my hair blows wildly, I'm busy coming up with different reasons as to why I'm back so soon. Illness, headache, a house fire, hell anything other than the truth. I can hear it now.

'Hey, why are you home so early?' She'll no doubt ask.

And I'll be forced to come clean. Something along the lines of, 'Oh, well you see while I had Liam's dick in my mouth, his bitch of a sister called and I never got to finish the job.' No way. I'll never be able to say that with a straight face. I'll end up laughing hysterically. No matter what I say, this will be a night I won't forget anytime soon.

THAT NIGHT DID PROVE ONE thing, it was a night I'll likely never forget and not for the reasons I had first thought. That night started a domino effect that would forever shape our lives. Liam's visit with his sister opened the door for the wickedness of my brother to re-enter our lives. In the blink of an eye, Dominic appeared and succeeded with what he had promised to do.

Forty-eight hours of hell led to weeks of living on pins and needles.

My once happy bubble is now a distant memory. All the happiness I felt for the first time in years, came at a price. Call it life, or karma, or even bad luck it doesn't matter the name the results were the same and I didn't have to wait long for the other shoe to drop. Before life came to screeching halt though, Liam and I had some amazing times together. Without interruptions.

Liam, as it turns out is the master in the art of seduction, able to explore the depth of our desires proved just how explosive our sex could be. Clothes ripped to shreds, claw marks and hickeys. Yeah, so many hickeys. My backside had become so acquainted with the walls of his living room, I've left my indentation. I say it's a memory for Liam to recall every day as he passes by it. A daily reminder.

Most nights, we never made it to his bed. Not even close. We had little patience when it came to our passion. The velvety warmth of his lips burned into a fiery possession I fell victim to. He aroused such passion in me that shivers cast by his touch alone. He left me deliriously weak in the knees, craving him and wanting more.

Our lovemaking was rousing and, at times, pleasantly bruising. Liam had an uncanny ability to recognize what I needed and when. He was so delicate when he sensed my vulnerability. Then again, he could turn around and be dominating when I wordlessly ached for a firmer hand.

We fulfilled each other's insane sexual appetites. A magical connection. My willingness to gladly partake in his vigorous adventures only spurred him on more, resulting in him pinning my body down, to play the helpless victim. Damn, those were some of my favorite times hands down. A healthy smack on my ass never felt so good.

Unfortunately, our happy bubble hit a speed bump the night I met Liam's sister. Everything about that night was amazing until all of the oxygen was suddenly sucked out of the bar. I remember Liam and Braxton's happy faces morph into an infuriating rage. God bless Izzy, that girl just rolled her eyes, dismissing her altogether. I, on the other hand, could not dismiss her as easily. Slowly turning around, my eyes landed on the tall blonde. With a scowl on her face and long inch daggers she called nails, she seemed ready to pounce. Directing her hatred at my friend. Not going to happen when I'm around.

Before the night came to an end, I threatened to kick her ass if she caused Izzy any more trouble. A jealous ex is never a good thing. Add in the fact she shares a child with Brax, that is a recipe for *disaster*. Much to my surprise, Liam held no ill will when I threatened the tall blonde. Nope. He actually expressed his desire to watch it happen.

And I could not have adored that man more than at that moment!

The bombshell Tiffany left us with, came at the very end. Her referring to Izzy as Izzabella certainly created a stressful moment. There was only one person who called her that. My *brother*. The possibility that she had somehow contacted my brother was nothing short of haunting. We not only froze, the blood drained from our faces.

Slowly, each domino began to fall over into the next and our lives went from crazy to a living hell. Dominic's mission was to get Izzy back at all costs, and once again the guilt ate at my soul until it transformed into fury. Liam's bitch of a sister set out to cause havoc, and ended up using her family connections to make that happen. As luck would have it for her, it's a small fucking world. Like a one in a million shot lucky. In life, it's all about who you know and who they know. She struck gold. Above all, Tiffany wanted one thing, and she was willing to sacrifice anything to make it happen. Izzy, out of her way. One way or another, dead or alive. It didn't matter to her.

Jealously has a way of making people do insanely unspeakable things all in the name of love. She opened the door for my ill-tempered brother to return, not in the name of love, or jealousy, but with a vengeance.

One of two things can happen when you're living in your own personal hell and are in a new relationship, it will tear you apart like a fucking tornado, or it can bring you closer. The latter happened with Liam and I. Between his sister and my brother reigning hell only joining forces to break our friends apart, Liam and I found common ground. In doing so we shared a bond, as crazy as it sounded. Forced to find a way to live with our own set of issues when it came to our siblings, luckily, we found each other along the way.

Raw, stripped and nowhere to hide, we accepted what we were and what we hoped could be.

A promise for tomorrow, but only if we did it together.

No matter what, and at any cost.

Chapter Four

"Retribution"

Kara

At a farmhouse outside of town...

My fingers tremble as I desperately search my purse for the gun. I fumble a few times until my fingers grip the cold metal. A frightfulness washes over me but it's now or never. My mind wrestles with this concept. Crossing this line would be something I'll never be able to take back. It's a life changing decision. For years I lived in the façade of light, making sure to stay far away from the darkness that happened to be my brother, Dominic. His darkness was pure evil while my light was pure. Opposites.

Keeping my distance is what kept me safe. That's what I believed, anyway. I felt like the more I repeat the same thing, my mind, body, and soul will eventually believe it. My brother and I may be bound by blood, but our souls will never be. I've made that my life's mission.

As hard as it is for me to admit, Dominic wasn't always so bad. At one time he had been my hero, my big brother, and the person I looked up to. For many years, he protected me from any bullies who dared to pick on me at school. He found me a few times crying in quiet corners and that's all it took for him to go into beast-mode, making an example out of the ones who thought it was a good idea to set their sights on me.

Those were the times he stepped up and protected me, and I felt blessed to have a brother like him. I went from being picked on to being envied because I had Dominic for a brother. Needless to say, I appreciated him and took delight in the fact he was a tough guy.

He was admired and feared and anyone who knew I was Dominic's Santos' little sister knew better than to mess with me. Unfortunately, the older he got, the more he evolved into something different. It was like a darkness had settled in his soul, and maybe it had. It's possible he sold his soul to the devil and in return he held power doing the one thing he was always so good at. Instilling fear and inflicting pain.

His personality led him to a job that had been an easy fit for someone like him. He thrived on it, actually. He was called upon by colleagues to collect money when people had not paid off their debts to these acquaintances. Definitely not a job my parents were proud of, but over the years, he grew distant from them as well. He lived in his own little world. The world where he dominated and controlled everything. Our parents often reminded him that where he came from was not the man he had become. I think it was easier for him to live his life with little to no emotion. In doing so, he eliminated anyone who threatened to connect with him on an emotional level. In his line of work, having emotions was the easiest way to get killed. He simply had no time for them.

His task was to inflict pain and suffering as he saw fit, as long as he collected. Years of developing his lethal reputation had fed into his ego, and in turn, increased his own sadistic appetite. He'd become the enforcer.

The day his sights focused on my best friend, Izzy, was the day things changed forever. What started out as an innocent, one-night stand quickly grew into Dominic's unhealthy obsession with her. I'll never be able to fix all the damage my brother has caused. Not only to me, but to her. Her body forever scarred, her life forever changed. My niece is the only bright thing that came out of his obsession with her. Even knowing all the hell we had to deal with, no one felt they could stand up to him. No one dared try.

That's what makes this moment right now so monumental. Do I dare cross over into depths of darkness and become what I despise the most in my brother?

Will I become like him?

Do I even care?

That bastard has done so much damage, inflicted so much pain. For years, it was hard for me to feel anything other than guilt. Feeling guilty, because I was the one to blame. After all, my friendship with Izzy started all of this. I had introduced Dominic to her, and she stayed overnight at our house. Maybe all of my regret and years of feeling guilty will lessen if I take out the threat that still haunts her. Him.

I can do this.

I must do this.

Lord, forgive me for what I'm about to do.

Holding the gun, I aim it higher to my target. Forcing my feet to move forward, I block out the loud voices around me. Dominic is shouting as all the while his back is to me. I steadily keep my focus on him with my gun aimed straight ahead. The rational part of my brain is pleading with me to stop this madness, but my heart had been through enough. It had bled enough over him.

A few tree limbs crack under my feet as I tread over them. Dominic must sense someone is near because he was slowly turning to face me. His eyes widen as his mouth gaped open as if he's shocked to see me. Well, more likely shocked to see me aiming a gun at him. It's only a fraction of a second as his expression morphs into a glare of disgust. His eyes scrutinize me while he's calculating his next move. He's paying close attention to the gun that is wavering in my trembling hand, and to make sure I don't drop the damn thing, I use my other hand to keep my aim steady. With my index finger lightly pressed on the trigger, I ask myself if I can really do this.

His eyes watch my every move, while his head shakes back and forth. It's most maddening, and the deep chuckle he releases is pure evil.

Dominic lowers his chin, raising an eyebrow. "Really?"

It's not really a question he's asking, he's insulting me. Deep down I always knew his arrogance would be his downfall. I just never imagined it would be me who ends his sorry ass, but how fitting. Over the years, he'd preach how light and dark can't survive without the other. Forever laced, like the infinity symbol. One side represents light, and the other represents darkness. When they cross one another, they encompass each other. For one cannot live without the other, and if one shall die, well, it lives on in the other. Right now, that thought is creepy as hell. It's almost a sick joke, but if I need to become dark to end him, so be it. It's a chance I'm willing to take.

"Ironic isn't it?"

I tease as if it's a joke, it's anything but. Judging by the way he's shaking his head and muttering under his breath, he once again underestimates how far I'm willing to go. He has always underestimated me. To taunt him even more, I keep my lips closed but sway the gun side to side as if prompting him for his response. No matter how challenging and unnerving it is to hold a gun to him under his evil glare, I keep my composure and my eye contact.

In a frightening way, he twists his neck to side until it cracks.

"Pathetic is what it is." He ridicules with a prolonged sigh. "I'm not in the mood for this, sister. My Izzabella is gone and finding you here is most troubling to me. It goes to show that this is all your fault. Hell will rain down on you for interfering." His lip curls up on one side at the same time his eyes partially close. Anger emanates from him with every twitch of his body. If he is trying to intimidate me with his threatening glare, he need not bother. My determination to finally stand up to him after all of this time will overcome whatever meaningless gesture or threatening banter he tosses my way.

"Ha," I respond wanting to verbally offend him. Inflicting pain is his world, verbally wounding him will evoke more emotions from him. That's what I aim to do. Any sentiments or feelings will cause way more damage to a man like him. To drive the knife deeper in his broken heart, I reveal the one secret that will devastate him even more.

"More like you're the reason, but no worries, brother." Making sure my obvious distaste for him echoes loud and clear. Only then my expression changes to a lighter, softer face.

"She's not dead like you think. Only put to sleep until we can get her out of here and away from you. Well played plan indeed, brother."

"What did you say?"

Shock is not an emotion I think I've ever seen on his face. Dominic's not one to ever be vulnerable. Recognizing something familiar in my eyes, he reverts back to the evil bastard he is. Yeah, that's the look I need to see. Perfect. Make it easy for me brother. Cold, distant eyes with lips that bare his teeth. When I pull the trigger, I want my gun aimed at this evil bastard I've grown to hate, not the brother I've longed to love. This man before me now is not my brother. With this man, I can happily call on the dark-side to give me strength and courage.

"Checkmate, brother. Have fun in hell."

With that, I squeeze the trigger.

I had moved here to get away from him. Tonight, I made sure he'd never leave here alive. He'll never hurt any of us again. If he would have just let her go, none of this would have happened. If only he would have stayed in Chicago, he'd still be alive. When he took his last breath on this earth, his eyes flashed a moment of regret. Glaring into his soul, a lonely *tear streamed down my face. His final expression as he left this earth, is seared into my mind, forever leaving its mark. His face paled with every wheezing gasp and the whites of his eyes lessened to a shade of gray. While he faces me in his final moments, his face morphed back to the brother I once loved, not the monster he had become. That's the image that haunts me the most.*

When I close my eyes, it's his face I see.
When I cover my ears, it's his voice I hear.
When I'm alone, it's him I still fear.
Is it even possible to be able to see, hear, and fear a dead man?

AT ANY TIME OF DAY, my eyes deceive me when I feel I have seen a glimpse of him among the shadows of others. At night when I'm drifting off to sleep, it's his chilling voice that cries out. That night, I had taken measures to ensure he would forever disappear from our lives, but it seems the only thing that night proved, was dead or alive, Dominic will always continue to haunt me.

I relive that night in my mind, but I still wouldn't change the outcome. I did what had to be done, so why do I continue to feel so much guilt? Why do I find myself crying so much? Why does my heart ache?

Years of abuse have finally come to an end. Izzy could live in peace, and I could hold a small ounce of vindication. I couldn't erase the years of guilt, though. With a weary heart, I'll embrace the ounce of satisfaction that it was my bullet that ended him. It was my bullet that made him bleed. However, the old adage about being careful what you wish for is absolutely true. Sometimes doing the right thing ends up being the one thing that feels wrong.

Liam and I had survived the chaos and hell. We've dealt with meddling sisters, and put an end to an obsessive brother. In the same amount of time, we've gained even more. Willow, Izzy's daughter, is now in her mother's loving arms. The ordeal my brother put them through was sickening. He removed Willow from Izzy, all to prove a point and keep the upper hand. It was nothing but punishment for Izzy not giving into his demands. My adoring niece is a complete angel. I never realized the void I carried when I was without her. Not knowing if we'd ever see her again, it was a welcomed surprise to have her back where she belongs. If there is any drawback, I'd have to say sweet

Willow resembles the Santos side of the family. She looks a lot like my brother. The dark hair, dark eyes and even sharp cherub features. That aside, she has the heart of her mother. Thank God!

Brax's daughter, Eve is Liam's niece and suffers the same fate. She resembles Liam's sister, Tiffany. Tall and blonde.

Our lives are so intertwined, it's a bit mind-boggling. We all sat together one night with Willow in my arms, Eve in Liam's and baby Asher in Izzy's. Asher is Izzy and Brax's new baby. We happily discussed the kids and how our crazy little group is linked in one way or another. By the end of the night and after having a few more drinks, we were in tears laughing until Brax had to open his mouth.

He took it upon himself to question when Liam and I were going to pop out a few little ones, and that pretty much ended the fun. Both Liam and I jumped up and said our good-bye's. Neither one of us is ready for that, we like playing auntie and uncle. We can spoil the kids rotten and then send them home on a sugar high. Izzy assures us that payback will happen when the time is right. To that, we all laugh.

Through all the madness, though, I can say I'm the happiest I've been in a very long time. I wish I could say the same for Liam. Although he appears to be just as happy, there are times he seems withdrawn. Deep down, I fear he's keeping things from me. I wish he'd open up.

Whenever talk of his club comes up, he tenses and changes the subject. I feared my brother's association with the Lost Souls' had more or less complicated matters. I'm smart enough to figure that out, and I can only hope Liam will work things out soon. It's hard enough to try and find sleep without worrying over whatever is bothering him.

Chapter Five

"Nightmares"

Kara

A WAVE OF TREMORS TAKES hold of me at the same time a primal scream escapes past my throat. Gasping for air, I tremble with fear. I'm not aware if my scream or life-like dream woke me up this time. Every damn night I'm being pulled back into the depths of a living hell. It's agony. The erratic beats of my heart are thunderous. My lips tremble, and it's taking everything to fight the shaking and my inconsolable cries. No matter what I do, I can't shake this feeling that he's out there. That he's coming back to settle a score. I know that's not possible, because I killed him. He's dead. His coming back is not possible. So why can't I shake this feeling?

"Babe, you okay?" Liam's sleep induced yawn penetrates the dark room. The sudden click of the bedside lamp lets me know that I've woken him up again. Like every night these days. Wanting to curl up in shame, my first reaction is to check the bedside clock. Closing my eyes momentarily, I don't even need to look, because it's the same time every damn night. Three-fifteen. The significance? I have no fucking clue. The only thing I know without a shadow of a doubt is I'm slowly losing my mind.

"I'm sorry," I sniffle. "Go back to sleep," I say with a faint smile, feeling dreadful that I've disturbed his sleep, yet again. The knot in my belly tightens and twists. All the wishing in the world can't help me escape my dreams.

My only regret is starting out a new relationship with Liam this way. None of what we've been through has been a healthy start to a relationship. I could easily turn it around by asking who and what is normal nowadays?

Lately, I've questioned that.

Liam's relentless in his pursuit to shield me from my demons. After a few heavy sighs, he clears his throat to push his sleepiness aside. He never rolls over and goes back to sleep. Not him. Instead, he gently cradles me against his chest. Keeping his touch light, he traces my back with his fingertips. The beat of his heart thumps in my ear. It's comforting and hypnotic. Unable to fight the fatigue, it's not long before I'm drifting back to sleep. Seeking comfort in his sweet affection is what I crave. Before sleep can find me, though, my mind is determined to make some sense of my continued nightmares. What could they mean? It's insane.

My recurring dream takes me back in time. I'm ten years old again, and Dominic and I are playing hide-and-seek in our backyard. His voice is crystal clear and it's terrifying. Every time I hear it, shivers chill my spine. I compare the sensation to taking a cold shower with icy shards of glass that pierce my skin.

That's what I feel whenever his voice speaks to me.

My brother had a wickedly evil tone. As I got older, his favorite pastime became scaring the hell out of me. One minute he would be cool and we'd have a good time, and the next he'd be so angry it was frightening. He could change at the drop of a dime. As the years passed, my bastard brother took enjoyment in making everyone else uncomfortable. I may have been blind to it at ten, but over the years, I slowly saw his demeanor change. If I had listened to my instincts when I was younger, things could have turned out so differently. The monster that emerged consumed the part of my brother I loved. He was no longer my brother, he transformed into the devil.

"He can't hurt you," Liam softly reminds me, "not anymore."

As sorrow shreds my insides apart, Liam's desperation increases tenfold. His need to fix things is overwhelming, and knowing he can't only fuel his rage. Feeling helpless is like a knife to the heart for a man like him. I wonder what would happen to me if I didn't have Liam. For such a strong woman, I'm not handling this well.

My faint chuckle lets him know I'm not convinced. "Not during the day anyway, but he sure as hell visits me at night. When I'm alone."

"Kara, he's dead." While telling me the facts I already know, his fingers press firmly on my back. I shrug my shoulder and he releases his hold.

Liam sits up and turns me so we are facing each other. His piercing blue eyes appear weary. The dark shadows under his eyes of not getting a full night's sleep in months are starting to take their toll. Guilt swarms me.

His finger raises my chin 'til my eyes rest on his eyes again. "You just need time to work out your guilt or whatever it is you keep blaming yourself for. I would never let anything happen to you. Let that comfort you." Worry lines crease his forehead and without a shadow of a doubt, I know he would protect me with his life.

The problem is, killing my brother had consequences. Even in death, his chaos continues.

Tears stream down my cheeks, and my lips quiver with fear, regret and uncertainty. The failure to find the right words, I do the only thing I can. I shake my head and shrug.

The last thing I hear in my nightmares is what scares me the most. My brother directly tells me, 'you'll be seeing me soon,' then lets out an eerie evil laugh. I'm a prisoner in my own mind.

I don't have an ounce of fight left in me, I'm completely drained. I cringe as I say the words I hate to admit. "Dominic might not be able to hurt me during the day, but he makes sure he visits me every night to make sure I never forget. He'll never leave me in peace."

Liam strongly disagrees. "Baby, we will find a way to stop the nightmares." Lowering his voice to a whisper, he says, "I promise you we will."

It sounds good, but I'm not convinced. His arms wrap around me in a tight hold and I close my eyes in his comfort. I wish to banish all thoughts of my brother with all the damage he's done. I can do this. I keep repeating it several times over and again. If I keep repeating it, maybe I'll start believing it and maybe the nightmares will go away.

Just as I'm about to slip off into slumber, an evil laugh emerges in my sleepy state.

Silly girl, you'll never escape me!

Chapter Six

"Rewind"

Kara

As I dress for the day, I'm hopeful that one day soon, I'll finally be able to break free. To leave the past where it belongs. I admit, it's hard to when Izzy questions me constantly. In her defense, she's like a mother hen making sure I'm okay, but it's no secret that I've struggled since that night. I've had my share of nightmares from doing something I never thought I could ever do. I became what I hated most in my brother. I've become a killer.

It was all too easy at that moment staring at him, but the most haunting part is believing that he wanted me to flip the switch inside me, and pull the trigger. I saw something in his dark eyes, but it wasn't fear. It was something else. In his sick mind, I became him. In his younger years, he always said we shared similar traits. Granted, that was before his split personality. Whatever it was, it's left me to deal with the consequences. Good or bad.

Guilt can be a bitch to live with so to guard my sanity, I hide my torturous feelings the best I can. Anyway, how do I tell my best friend that I feel some guilt for eliminating her biggest threat? He hurt her for so long. How do I look into those doe eyes of hers and regret my actions?

I can't. I can't ever tell her.

Instead, I plant a smile on my face and go about my day. It's far past time I find some work to keep my mind occupied and money in my checking account. Not to mention, I could use a few good distractions. Lord knows, I've had enough bad ones lately.

Movement out of the corner of my eye catches my attention.

"Hey babe, you been outside yet?"

I look over my shoulder to see Liam standing in our bedroom doorway. He's scratching his arm compulsively, appearing uneasy as he does. That puts me on edge right away because witnessing a tense Liam is never a good thing.

"No, why do you ask?"

He frowns, drawing his lips into a tight line. "We got another message."

Jesus, not again!

This will mark the fourth, not so subtle thing to happen over the past few weeks. Calling card? Hell, we're not sure but until we are, I refuse to let Liam tell Brax or Izzy a thing about it. I flat out refuse to disrupt their new found happiness. They're newlyweds, and new parents, to boot; they don't need this craziness, they have plenty to keep them busy. For now, Liam has agreed to keep quiet, but I'd be lying if I said I haven't almost called my best friend to help me deal with the unshakeable set of chills that about knock me to my knees every time we discover one of these so-called messages. It's been tough.

I attempt to brush the tangled mess I call hair, but it's a losing battle, so I give up, drop my brush on the dresser, and turn to face Liam's troubled stare.

"I'm coming."

In an attempt to settle my nerves, I give one last attempt to tame my hair by combing my fingers through my many layers of snarls. As I stare in the mirror at my uncontrolled rat's nest, a not so innocent chuckle escapes, reminding me of the reason behind my tangled mess. There is no denying my morning after sex hair reminds me about last nights' festivities and I'm grinning from ear to ear.

After a stressful day, I enjoyed a relaxing hot shower, only to be pleasantly sidetracked by six-foot-hunk of muscle with icy blue eyes. As I entered our bedroom, dripping wet and in only my towel, an ambush awaited me. Liam leaped from the bed and spent the next hour devouring my body. His heated touches and punishing lips left me happily sated and exhausted.

Now, the morning after, I'm left with hair like Medusa. The easiest thing to do is pull it back in a ponytail. Mission accomplished, so now I'm following a quiet Liam as my hands nervously shake. Liam's not said a word about what kind of message I received this time.

Once I peer around the corner to our living room, I notice that our front door is partly open. I stop moving and watch as Liam walks to the door. He is now standing there, wide legged with his arms crossed. He's staring intently on the front side of the door, just out of my view. Something's wrong because his muscles are taut and straining against his t-shirt. For a split second, I forget everything as I'm am a bit sidetracked with his hotness. It's hard not to when the sun shines on his body.

Shamelessly, my mouth salivates as I ogle him and replay the events of last night. A smile tugs at my lips when my eyes travel to my wrists to see the slight red line from being tied to the bed at Liam's mercy. Subconsciously, I rub my right wrist, until my eyes catch a glimpse of shining metal.

"What the hell is that?" I ask as I walk to stand next to Liam.

"Well," he exclaims with a prolonged sigh, "what do we make of this? Fuck if I know."

There plunged into our front door is a long serrated hunting knife. And if that wasn't eerie enough, the item that is dangling from it sure is. An uneasiness washes over me again as I take a curious step. My eyes quickly do a double take, or was it a triple take? Not sure, but one hundred different emotions hit me all at once.

Liam's eyes widen as they snap to mine.

"You know what this is?" he asks, and I wish I could lie and say not a clue.

But, I can't. Instead, I mumble under my breath.

"Unfortunately, I think I do." I don't know how or why, but it's as if a ghost from the past has come for a visit.

As if watching a slow moving train wreck, my fingertips press against my temples to ease an oncoming migraine. These so-called messages are starting to get to me. My brain hurts trying to piece these messages together and what they could mean. Who are they from? And better yet, why?

All of these questions—and not one plausible answer. I'm honestly afraid of the damn answer. There are too many similarities to my dead brother, and that makes this even more eerie as hell.

I had the brakes on my car tampered with two weeks ago. That thrilling event led to the slash of my tires and a broken out back window. The scariest of them all, besides the long serrated knife in my door, was a message written in lipstick on my bedroom dresser mirror last week.

'I'm watching!'

That's all it said. The intimidating and threatening look of the violent knife leaves me more crazed by the minute. This time, it's more personal with a childhood keepsake attached with it. And not just any keepsake, either. I break out with a shiver as haunting chills run down my spine. I'm forced to remember memories long forgotten and my eyes instantly fill with tears that threaten to spill over. Memories I never thought I'd ever think about again.

Damn him. Even in death, he haunts me.

Without saying a word, I turn to retrieve something I think Liam needs to see. And honestly, I haven't thought about this item in a very long time. Not sure what Liam is going to say, my shoulders sag as my feet slowly shuffle back to our bedroom. I step into the closet and pull back my hanging clothes until I find what I'm looking for. A lone box, all the way in the back. My anxious hands remove the lid and rummage around until I find what I'm looking for. As I hold it in my hand, my stomach rolls and I feel queasy.

"Jesus." I exhale long slow breaths before I return to find Liam in the exact spot. He's not moved a muscle. His eyes are still focused on that damn knife as if, at any minute, he might miraculously find a clue.

Reluctantly, I hold out my hand. "Here."

Liam's eyes leave my face and drop to my hand, to glance at the charm necklace I'm holding tightly in my shaking hand.

"Kara?" With his head to the side, an inquisitive and cautious brow slowly rises. I urge my hand forward almost begging him to take it from me.

With a nod he takes it from my hand while my stomach quivers. He studies it and notices the symbol on the front of mine matches the other charm. A charm that's attached to a long serrated knife hanging on *our* front door.

He hesitates before reaching for the chain on the door. He slowly slides it from the knife and holds it idly between his fingers. As if he's almost afraid to turn it over, he clutches it firmly and questions me. "What's the other side going to say?"

I let his question soak in as I'm drowning in sorrow and a bit of bewilderment. Either way, fear robs me for speaking. Shock doesn't even come close to what I feel right now. I'm too busy trying to understand how this damn necklace found its way here to my door.

"You will never guess." I struggle to say.

He doesn't react. Instead, he clears his throat and turns the charm over. His head flinches back and his eyebrows squish together before he utters, "What the fuck?"

"Exactly." I exclaim.

No one understood my brother's sense of humor, or intellect when he was younger. Silent most of the time, he calculated everything. A deep thinker.

I can't say I have a lot of happy memories when it comes to him. As Dominic got older, I never stopped wishing he'd change his ways. I've seen enough to realize that once evil takes a hold of a person, no amount of mercy or intervention will break the devil within. Dominic became that face of evil.

After living with such god-awful things my brother had done over the years, I had hoped I'd finally find peace the day he left this world. Unfortunately, that's not the case. I feel a sense of something, but it's not peace. It's guilt. And guilt is an emotion that eats at a soul until it consumes every part of it, and no amount of hearing 'you did the right thing' makes it any easier. Even so, if the same situation presented itself again, I can't say that the outcome would have been different.

Over time the guilt, I can learn to live with, because I know things will get easier. I just need my heart to catch up with my brain. Before these damn incidents started happening, I was on the path of doing just that. Lately, though, it feels like I'm stuck in this well of anguish, being forced to suffer for my sin. Compared to Dominic, I never thought I'd sit back and think of *myself* as a sinner.

It's that damn charm!

Well, the charm, combined with my broken windows, and slashed tires that is. I can't help but feel like I'm living a fucking nightmare. Like he's come back from the dead with the sole intent of haunting my ass. I'm even wondering if it's possible that it was *his* message on my mirror? The one that said, 'I'm watching'. Or is it my overactive imagination searching for some common ground, a common link to fit the pieces together? My mind is desperate to make some sense of it all.

Liam's groan draws my attention. "The symbol I can understand. The wording is just *odd*."

I can't deny that so I lower my chin in agreement. There was no way for him to make sense of the wording in their context, he needed to hear the story behind them. We were young when Dominic had our parents buy us matching charm necklaces. The inscriptions were entirely Dominic. Innocent words that held meaning at the time. Only now, the message inscribed is a bit eerie, especially under the current circumstances.

Each of the charms' fronts held a perfect sideways figure eight. The infinity symbol, deep set in sterling silver. It really is quite pretty. Dominic had educated me in the mysterious way that life works. At a young age, his mind was far beyond his years.

There is no boundary that separates life from death. Rather, it's a continuous cycle that evolves but keeps on the same path.

When he first tried to explain his reasons for the inscriptions, it happened after the death of our grandmother. I was very close to her, and the idea she was gone just about killed me. A part of me died with her, but it was Dominic to explain that she continues to live in me. The infinity symbol represents that. I never questioned it because he gave me comfort when I needed it most. The inscription was a product of his intellect; simply a protective, older brother doing something nice for someone who wasn't himself. Yeah, my parents and I were a bit shocked with his gesture. It was probably the only time he did anything out of the generosity of his heart.

As I hear Liam read the words on each charm, I zone out when the word 'demon' passes his lips. That word. His charm. It's all so hauntingly fitting. Eerie for damn sure.

Mine read: May there be an angel to look over you.

His read: Or a demon to protect you.

The million-dollar question is *why* in the hell is *his* charm hanging on my front door?

Liam's eyes roam my trembling body, how I'm still standing I have no clue. He quickly pulls the knife from the door saying a few choice words under his breath. "Don't worry babe, I'll take this to the garage later. No sense in having them in the house."

Little did he know, I was about to ask him to do just that, but he beat me to it. No way in hell do I want that stuff in the house.

With both items in one hand, he uses the other to rub back of his neck as his eyes lower to the floor. He releases a few breaths and I get the feeling he's going to say something I may not want to hear.

"I can't keep this from Brax any longer. I need his help figuring this shit out." His eyes raise up to meet mine. I knew this was coming sooner or later, and I don't blame him for saying it. We've held off mentioning anything, but I have to agree with him at this point. This has gone too far and it's becoming dangerous.

I sob. "I know you do. I just hate it, that's all." Tears threaten, but I do my best to fight them. "I'm so sick of it all. I want it to end. Why can't we just be left alone?"

He quickly frees his hands and wraps me in his loving arms to comfort me. "Babe, your safety comes first. Always." He says it with so much conviction that I instantly feel safe and my anxiety fades.

Afternoon soon spills into evening and Liam and I are ready to tell Brax and Izzy everything. I'm nervous about what kind of reaction I'm going to get from Izzy, I could not eat a thing on my plate. I picked apart my pizza instead. Eagle eye Izzy noticed but is not saying anything. Thank God! Liam is taking charge in explaining things while I sit actively listening to the events that led us to today and the knife in the door. By the look on both of their faces, it's a good thing their kids are at Grandma Ryles house. As soon as Liam stops talking all eyes swing to me.

Brax has a look of concern but Izzy is way past concern, she's pissed. She can't hold back her disbelief. She's shocked and most likely upset with herself for not knowing any of this was happening. That's Izzy for you, so incredibly sweet and caring. Not sure if I mentioned it, but she has a mean streak as well. A real acidic tongue when she's ticked at someone. Right now, it's me.

"What the hell, Kara? You didn't think to let us know this was happening to you? How could you *not* tell us this?"

Yep, she's not happy. She's sitting up straight as a board and is pointing her finger at me like she's scolding me. I understand her anger, but she needs to understand I was only thinking about them when we chose not to keep it to ourselves.

"Izzy…" Liam tries to defend me, but he got a hand shoved in his face. Izzy did not want to hear from him at all. This was personal between two best friends who have survived hell together.

"Izzy, you've both had enough shit to deal with." I struggle to keep from sobbing while making eye contact with both her and Brax.

"You did not need to be bothered with it. Believe me, I wanted to, but I felt it would be better if you didn't know."

Izzy jumps to her feet and hollers, "That's crap, and you know it! I would have been there for you like you were there for me." There, now she's done it. I'm choking back tears as I see her passion when it comes to me. She would save me like I had done for her, without question. That's a powerful thing to have between two friends, rare and uniquely ours.

Brax puts an arm around her waist so she's forced to sit back down. She's sobbing into his chest. "Kara, we stick together and Liam's right, your safety has to come first." He says.

I want to roll my eyes because I hate that we're even having this conversation.

"Any ideas?" I ask as I sit further back in my chair and wipe under my eyes. Maybe if we start talking the hurt look in Izzy's eyes will lessen just a bit, so it doesn't kill me to look into them. Only that doesn't happen. Everybody just looks at one another, not saying a word. I'm not sure what they want me to say, so I hold up a finger to take the lead and play detective.

"Well, Dominic's dead, so that eliminates him." Adding a second finger, I continue, "There is my stalker from Chicago, but he's literally harmless. He only sent innocent love letters. Nothing threatening just persistent, in a stalker way." I wince when I add a third finger, this very real possibility is worrisome. "Maybe someone close to Dominic?" I add, "other than those three, I have nothing." As they nod at me, I take the moment to drift off thinking about anyone close to my brother.

"That's a start," Brax states with a shrug. Liam and Izzy both nod their heads to agree and I suddenly realize they are all agreeing on something I must have zoned out on.

I look at Brax like I've missed something. "What's a start?"

"Chicago," he says matter of fact with a one shoulder shrug.

What? He can't be serious. Then it hits me, I can actually go back to Chicago. With Dominic out of the picture, I don't have to hide anymore. I don't get a minute to think that over because Liam is quick to interrupt.

"Now is not the time for us to be on the road to Chicago. There are some unresolved issues that I've got to settle before we can even think of leaving." He says in frustration then up and stalks into the kitchen. I'm left looking confused as I am clueless to what he is talking about. I swing my eyes to Brax for some answers but he just shrugs his shoulder on his way to the kitchen to join Liam.

"What the hell was that about?" I drop my head to look at Izzy. As her eyes linger on the men in the kitchen, her face shows signs of concern.

"Not sure honey," she sighs and returns her eyes to mine, "but you just have to trust Liam to do the right thing."

I shrug with the thought what else can I do?

With no real answer from Liam, no plans were hatched out, poured over, or even thought out. Liam has been quiet since Brax and Izzy left for home. It's nothing new as he's been this way lately, distracted. His remark about it not being the best time to travel concerns me deeply.

Once again it's another night that I'm left frustrated wondering what's going on with Liam. He's put up a wall that I can't seem to crack. I know I'm not going to get an explanation tonight, so I slip into my nightshirt to get ready for another sleepless night. Liam's already in bed on his side…facing away from me. He's isolating me from his troubles and it's aggravating. Even if it's not his true intentions, the coldness I feel from him hurts. Once again, I'm frustrated and left with more questions than answers. Sleep should be the one thing to look forward to, only now, I hate the idea of falling asleep.

Sometimes my nights are harder to survive than the days.

Chapter Seven

"Relentless Dreams"

Liam

It's the same every night at three-fifteen in the damn morning. She starts tossing and turning, thrashing her arms like she's fighting someone off. It's not long after that she bolts straight up in bed, gasping for her next breath. For the first month I understood it, but it's been months, and it's not getting any better. My woman is suffering, and I have no clue how to help her. So I do what I can—distract her mind, and hold her tight 'til she falls back asleep. Making her feel safe is all I want. For her finally to accept what she's done, and let it go.

I know she's bothered with me not opening up to her and she's right, I have been keeping things from her. Things that keep me up late at night and into the early hours of the morning. Some bad shit is about to happen, and I'm troubled with it. So for now, I can only do what I feel I need to do—just hope I make the right decisions. No price is too high to keep her safe.

The moment Kara aimed a gun and shot her bastard of a brother, I knew it then. No matter how hard we tried, we would not be able to get out of this unscathed. Kara had a score to settle. She made sure it was her, too. I only wish Brax or I had been the one to do it. Shit, we'd sleep like babies if we had because his life isn't the first life we ended.

The issue stems from my ties to the Lost Souls MC and her brother's association. Unfortunately, her brother's arrangement with the Chicago Chapter created a whole other fight that's coming straight for us. If it were just me, I'd be able to live with that. It's them wanting her in exchange that I can't live with. Fuck that, I won't live with. This is the part I've kept from her and for good reason.

Meeting Kara was the best day of my fucking life. My woman's spunky and loud with a wickedly sensual mouth, not to mention she's stunningly gorgeous from head to toe. With long, dark windblown hair, average height, and porcelain skin that's inviting to the touch. Her delicate, hazel eyes only enhance her sexy as hell style. She's not overly flashy, but not simple either. She dresses to match her personality—wild, loud and completely fuckable. All the time and effort she puts into her nails to keep them looking good, you'd be right in assuming she's a bit high maintenance. I may chuckle and shake my head, but I'll happily wear the many scratch marks she'll leave on my back. One thing about Kara, she's feisty when she wants to be and I for one, love every minute of it. My only complaint is the shit storm that has been our lives.

What I wouldn't give for things to be different. From the beginning, we've been fighting something or someone. It doesn't make me desire her any less. In fact, it has me wanting to protect her more, and that's just what I intend to do. But I've got decisions to make so I can figure out who the fuck is stalking Kara, and why. Somehow it's all connected, we just need to figure out *how*. No one is taking her from me, that's a promise I can fucking guarantee.

My uncle's ties to the MC is what started this whole fucking mess to begin with. My sister, Tiffany was handed the information she needed in locating Kara's brother. That's all it took. Talk about a small fucking world, figures he would have ties to the MC himself. Dominic Santos was a twisted man who achieved his status by torturing people. Clients hired him for two reasons: One, he had a great reputation for carrying out his client's wishes. And two, he got shit done quick. I heard that the Chicago chapter hired him so many times, he became an honorary member. That's their business though, not mine. And I don't give a damn, but that's where shit gets complicated. The simple truth is, the club loved his lethal side. It was good for business, and it put fear into anyone who heard about the fucked up shit he did.

It's no wonder that he turned out to be a sadist in his personal life. Shit, it's not like it's that's much of a stretch. Many nights, Brax and I sat and listened in utter disbelief as Kara told the story of how Izzy got hooked up with Dominic and the shit that followed. A total shit story if you ask me. Fucker got what he deserved. Just wish he suffered longer.

Kara proved to be a great help after Dominic kidnapped Izzy because she knew her brother's habits. But stressful days turned into agonizing nights and before long, shit got really bad. I thought we may have to lock Brax up due to his all-out rage which, of course, was completely justified. Having your woman kidnapped is fucked up, but having her taken with the likes of that guy? Shit, she may as well have been a dead woman walking and for all intents and purposes, she was. When he heard that Dominic had his woman, it pushed Brax over the edge. He was out of control and if I wanted to get Izzy back while she was still breathing, I had way better things to do than babysit that fucker.

The history between Izzy and Dominic is nothing short of disturbing. I thought I'd seen it all over the years but hearing the things he did to her, who was the woman he 'loved', was seriously fucked up. Kara's brother, well, he's better off dead.

Dominic Santos' involvement with the 'Lost Souls' was when shit went to a whole new level of complicated. My uncle, Marty, has been a member for most of his adult life. In my early twenties I prospected, earning my cut. Brax was a member for a short time. That is until he hooked up with my sister, Tiffany. They ended up having a kid together. That was when my sister hit a new low and flaked out. She left more than she was around, and that created all sorts of issues. Brax could no longer fulfill his role with the club and take care of his daughter.

Club took a vote and with the overwhelming support of my uncle, he handed in his cut and responsibility to the club. He may not ride, but that doesn't mean he's out of the picture. We still hang out. My uncle was VP back then, and now he is our President. My mother died when I was young and he was her only sibling, so he took it upon himself to make sure my sister and I were taken care of. My father, Mick, was and still is, useless. A town drunk.

The part that's fucked up and keeps me up at night stressing, is the fact my woman is the one who put that sick fuck in the ground. I'm in an impossible position and in the middle of a brewing shitstorm, because more than a few Chicago members are not happy with how things went down. My uncle tried his best to explain all the pain he caused not only Izzy, but his sister as well. *My* Kara. It's enough of an issue that my uncle decided it's best for me to stay away. Let the dust settle. Then, and only then, can I figure out what my future will be. I'm not sure the Club is my future anymore. My heart's not in it like it once was. And I can't help but see the life Brax has made for himself. A life with Izzy. A life I think I might want for Kara and myself. My uncle's not blind, he sees it, and I think he even encourages it. I think in honoring my late mother he's pushing my life in a new direction. A less dangerous one so I can one day create my own family. After all, family was important to my mother and with the mess of the life my sister has created for herself, my uncle is even more determined.

I've been threatened by the Chicago chapter and even heard a few grumblings from *our* men. I withheld information from the club on our mission to rescue Izzy because it was family business, not club business. The problem is the favor I asked my uncle for. I needed help with the clean-up and within hours, the deadly scene at the farmhouse did not exist.

A few favors and markers were used, making it club business. Even if I didn't see it that way. It seems my uncle is dead set on keeping my ass safe and alive. It's possible I may be out of the club and I'm fine with that, as long as they leave Kara out of it. She pulled the trigger on a club member, even if he was just an honorary member, so they want her in return. Yeah, over my dead fucking body.

I even wondered if they are the one's responsible for the shit that's happening with her now. Broken car windows, slashed tires, and a deadly knife, it's not that far of a stretch. It fits their MO, so I need to have a serious talk with Brax, but not anywhere she might hear me.

I refuse to add more stress on her, shit, she's barely hanging on as it is. She likes to act strong in front of people, but I can see right through her. Her eyes don't sparkle like they normally do, and her smile tries to hide her pain.

For now, all I can do is hold my girl in my arms. This is where she belongs, and this is where she'll stay. We'll run if we have to. I'll give my fucking life to make sure she's safe. She did us all a favor when she took that sick bastard out, brother or not. As I lay in bed with her now, her face is sweet as an angel but her night tremors show just how tortured she really is.

Kara's body quakes, as she starts to murmur. "He's.... coming. Please don't let him get me, Liam."

Her mumbling is faint, but I hear it and it cuts me deep. Her soft pleas prove she trusts me enough to protect her though, and not only does my heart swell, it feels pretty fucking great.

The urge to just run is getting stronger every damn day.

But how can you run from your nightmares?

And how do I protect her from them?

Hell, if I know the answer to that.

KARA

AFTER ANOTHER RESTLESS NIGHT, I'M desperately in need of caffeine. Liam's in the kitchen, so I can only hope a cup will be waiting for me. My man makes a wickedly strong brew, and he adds just the right amount of milk and sugar.

God, can he get any more perfect? No doubt about it, I love that man.

"Hey babe, you working today?" Liam walks into the living room with a raised eyebrow. He's holding two cups of coffee and the smile I had just got bigger. My day is starting out good. He's eyeing the bag in my hand, so I hold it up to answer his question. His forehead rises as he breathes out a 'gotcha'.

Once he strolls over to me he pretends like he's going to pass me my cup, but stops and lowers his head so I can kiss those lips of his first. I happily oblige. Taking my cup, I thank him before delighting in the aroma of my freshly brewed cup. After I blow into my cup, I take a generous sip. It's perfect.

In my other hand, I'm holding my camera loosely and put my cup down to make sure I have the right lenses I'm going to need to today. Tanya Harris, from Glendale Magazine, contacted me to take some stunning landscape photos. I'm going to Deception Pass and will hit the trails. I've heard all about the fascinating trails in the heart of tall Evergreen Trees, the perfect backdrop for what I've got in mind. No models required are my favorite three words to hear when I'm working. Trying to please models never really worked for me, so working with nature is right up my alley. I feel my absolute best when I'm working. There's no better way to get out of my head and lately, it's exactly what I need.

"You want to go with me?" I'm hopeful, even though he'll most likely say no.

"I wish," he says, rubbing the back of his neck, his tell when he's nervous about something. "I got some club stuff to handle today."

Ah, yes, club stuff. Whenever the word 'club' leaves his lips these days, he gets tense and uncomfortable all of a sudden. I wish he would just level with me. It's infuriating.

I release a long, slow sigh, "Liam, what's going on? Why won't you open up to me?"

My shoulders sag in total defeat, and I want to yell. I've begged, I've cried, I've shouted...still he remains tight-lipped. His silence irritates me, but I ask again.

"I'm not asking for you tell me club business. I want to know what's going on with you?" Maybe putting it that way may help.

"I...shit. Kara, I can't. No. I *won't* add more shit for you to deal with. You've been through enough."

His voice and body soften. The only time things are tense between us, it's over my dead brother or the club. Remove both of those, and we're the perfect Ken and Barbie.

Well, Ken with tattoos and a killer body. And seriously, Ken never looked that hot when I was playing with Barbie dolls. Back to the task at hand, I clear my childhood thoughts to plead with him. I'm hoping to wear him down enough to finally give in.

Okay, here I go.

"If I'm the problem, you need to tell me." I have my hand outstretched, trying a new strategy to get information out of him.

"Babe." His sigh silences as I cut him off.

"No, Liam." I hate to pull this card, but he leaves me no choice. "Do I need to contact a buddy of Dominic's back home in Chicago? I'm sure they would have no problem telling me anything I need to know." I hold my breath, knowing this will piss him off. I hope enough to get him to spill the beans, but his wide eyes tell me he's not taking the bait. He looks at me like I just slapped him across the face.

"DON'T YOU DARE!" His eyes narrow and he grits his teeth, when he says, "Don't you *ever* call anyone in Chicago, do you hear me? NO ONE associated with him. Ever!"

Okay, I struck a nerve. Never once did I have any desire to call anyone in Dominic's inner circle, I'm not an idiot. I'm sure I'm enemy number one. The one detail I might have overlooked when I decided to sneak up, and end my brother's life. The plan was to get in, get Izzy, and then get the hell out of there. But standing there in the light of the moon, he stood, shouting, projecting his evil. I came with my gun only for our protection, but at that moment...I saw an opportunity.

Killing him was not planned, it happened to be an opportunity to ensure we could all live in peace, so I took it.

With Liam's reaction, it's exactly what I needed to confirm what I'd been thinking all along—he's not upset with me, he's protecting me. I can't help but wonder at what cost?

I drop my guard and plead with him. "What aren't you telling me?" I hate seeing him this way. He has this battle going on, his head and his heart are at battle, but neither are winning. I want to be at his side, supporting him.

He groans as he walks to my side and wraps me in a tight hug. He pulls back and tips my chin to meet his reserved smile. "Don't worry." He then places a kiss on the top of my head and I go limp back in his embrace. "I'll handle it. Just trust me enough to do that, okay?"

It's not that I don't believe him, it's just I've heard this countless times lately from him. It does nothing to settle my nerves or my overactive imagination. I just can't tell him that I'm okay with it.

"Why won't you trust me?" Instead of being grateful for the way he is trying to protect me, I throw it back in his face. I don't mean to, but I need some answers.

Alarmed and clearly caught off guard. Liam winces as if I've wounded him physically.

"Is that what you think? That I don't trust you?"

Shit.

"What else could it be? God, just let me have the truth, Liam."

"How about I'm *protecting you?*! I don't want anything to happen to you. Why can't you see that and just leave it alone?" Turning his back, he starts to storm off. "Let me handle this my way." He throws over his shoulder.

I open and close my mouth twice. My frustration has me scrunching my face and literally biting my tongue. I'm usually not one to back off, but I think raising the white flag might be a good idea. We're getting nowhere.

"Do I have a choice?" I honestly ask, knowing his likely answer.

He turns and lowers his chin, so his eyes gaze into mine. "Not likely, no."

I let my stare linger before I raise my hands. "Okay. Kiss me good-bye then, I need to head out and get some money shots while it's still light out." Figure I might as well drop it. For now.

Liam must agree because his smile returns.

"That, I can do," he smirks delighted that I've given in. After a few wide strides, he seals it with a kiss. Damn frustrating man. I adore him to pieces and he knows it, too. It's why he constantly tells me that he's the perfect man for me. I have to chuckle, because damn straight, he is.

I drive away in my new set of wheels, which is almost an exact replica of the car I left in Chicago. As luck would have it, Liam had a buddy who needed some fast cash, so I got my new Honda at a great price. Good thing it was cheap since my savings is quickly dwindling. As I glance in the rearview camera, Liam is straddling his Harley.

I'm not sure what the rest of the day is going to bring my way, but whatever it is, it's not going to be good. I can feel it. I've had this nagging feeling all morning.

Usually, when I feel this way, things go from bad to worse pretty damn fast.

All the more reason to concentrate on getting my shots taken and then visit Izzy. My idea is to pick Brax's mind for a change. He'll do anything for Izzy. She's my ticket to figuring out what the real story is with Liam, because if anyone knows the truth, it's him. Careful to watch the winding road, I grab my purse from the passenger's seat and search inside feeling for my phone. With my phone on speaker, I press her contact number and give her a friendly head's up.

"Hello." Her tone is cause for alarm.

I'm can hear the strain in her voice. Not an ounce of cheerfulness.

"Oh no, what's wrong?" I almost chuckle when I ask. Never knowing what may come out of her mouth, I mentally brace myself.

"Ugh, where should I start? Asher kept me up all night with Colic, Willow and Eve demand all of my attention, and Brax is pissing me off. How's that? And it's only 9 o'clock in the morning." Wow, she rattles that off without taking a breath.

I can't help but laugh. "Well, you do have your hands full." I kindly remind her. And boy does she ever—a new husband, new baby boy, and two small girls. It's enough to make me crazy, so I'm thankful I have no kids of my own. Spoiling her kids is good enough for me.

"You know? This shit with Liam…" Izzy starts to say and her voice doesn't just trail off, it stops altogether. I pause, waiting for her to finish. When she doesn't, I don't hesitate.

"Liam *what*?"

"Shit, Kara." After a few choice words under her breath, she apologizes. "Honey, I'm sorry…"

I cut her off, because now I'm getting somewhere. "About?"

For five minutes she dances around, making no sense. She's back peddling, and if it wasn't for the fact she's a shit liar, it might not have been so easy to pick up on her lack of skills when it comes to sidetracking.

Well, she can't hide from me in person.

"I'm coming over whenever I finish for the day. Get ready for you and your husband to come clean about Liam. No more bullshit, Izzy. He's holding shit back from me, and I deserve to know what's going on. You know I do."

"What about your nightmares?" She blindsides me.

Okay, I wasn't expecting that question.

"How do you know about those?" I gasp because Liam, it seems, has been having pillow talk with his buddy.

"Who do you think? Brax," she says matter of fact, "Liam tells him everything."

Bingo! "That's what I'm counting on. Be ready to talk." I end my call even more determined to get my answers. If Liam refuses to tell me, I'll get my answers another way.

Slightly over forty-five minutes later, I'm hiking up a trail, snapping pictures of the beautiful forest. The way the sun is just peeking through the towering trees is making my job easier. They are fantastic. I've taken so many great shots, and I can't wait to develop them later. The serenity and complete quietness are so very amazing. The only noise is coming from the streaming water but I have to admit, it's a bit unnerving. I'm completely alone in a forest. Chilling. Never really knowing who could be lurking. I need to remember to bring something I can use as a weapon, because anything could happen to me out here. I'm not exactly intimidating and with my damn luck, a bear or cougar would end up attacking me. Pepper spray would be a good idea. My gun, not so much.

I'm low on the ground, aiming my camera skyward trying to get the perfect sun shot, when I suddenly hear the crackling of sticks. It startles me so much I jump, turning to face in the opposite direction. I do a complete one-eighty, but I don't see anything. I keep still just in case I hear it again. At the moment, the only noise I hear is the thumping of my heart.

After a few seconds, I gather my wits and decide to snap a few more shots when I hear it again. Dammit, it sounds like someone is stepping on fallen tree limbs. That, or an animal. Either way, my heart is pounding as I scan the surroundings very slowly. It's likely the colors of the forest could easily camouflage an animal, so I concentrate the best I can with being scared half shitless. I lower myself to a squat to try and talk myself out of a panic attack, but then I hear the noise again.

Fuck this.

I'm up and dashing in a hurried panic. I've heard it three or four times now, and I don't see a fucking thing. My gut instincts tell me to run like a bat out of hell out of here, and that's exactly what I do.

My camera is around my neck, and my camera bag's slung over my shoulder. I'm hightailing it down the narrow path and almost to my car, when I hear the sudden roar of a motorcycle. It could be totally normal in these neck of the woods, but hearing the pipes roar after I heard strange noises in the woods, I'm not taking any chances. When I notice a family gathering things from their car, I rush and approach them.

"Hi," I say winded. My legs and arms are twitching with adrenaline, but I try to act as calmly as I can. "Have you seen anyone on a motorcycle?"

I ask, but I'm freaking the fuck out. The last thing I need to do is get them worried—they have young children who are staring at me like I'm nuts. I'm not crazy, my mind is just spinning out of control. Was someone watching *me* just now? That's a scary thought. Someone could have easily killed me back there, and no one would be the wiser. Hell, animal attacks are not unheard of around here, either.

The older gentleman eye's his wife and kids. With a nod of his head he explains, and points with his finger, "Yeah, just a few seconds ago. He came from the path and took off like he was in a hurry."

Shit. *He* was on the path. The same path *I* was just running on to get out of there. Yeah, that's not at all worrisome.

I thank them and return to my car, shaken up. As I get the hell out of there, I'm having a conversation with myself…out loud. 'It's nothing. No one was following me'.

My hands are trembling as I try to call Liam.

No answer, just voicemail.

"Shit."

Next, I dial Izzy.

No answer, just voicemail.

"Damn, can't anyone answer their fucking phone?" I scream into my phone before I throw it in the passenger's seat. I turn the volume up on my radio, I'm hoping the music will calm my nerves.

As I drive fifty-five, I'm signing lyrics to *Survival* by my favorite band, Muse. The irony of that particular song, summed up my feelings perfectly. As I get more into the song, I'm singing and thumping my fingers on the steering wheel feeling a bit calmer.

That is until I glance in my rearview mirror.

A motorcycle is a few cars behind. What's more unsettling, is the biker's appearance. He's got a cut on...an MC cut. Of course, I can't make out anything on it, just that he's wearing one. As I lower my foot on the pedal, quickly accelerating, I grip the wheel tighter. When I get nervous like I am now, I often talk out loud to myself.

"Alright, let's see if you are following me or not."

I increase my speed, but keep eyes trained on my rearview mirror. The faster I go, the faster he goes. Not a good sign, so I decide to press my luck and increase my speed even more. A nervous sweat beads my forehead. I'm scared shitless. Thankfully, as I fly around the curve in the road, my eyes see the lights first, a state trooper passes me. His lights turn on immediately as he quickly turns his vehicle around, coming for me. I think this is the first time I've been happy to see a cop chasing me.

This situation could not have turned out any better is the only thought running through my mind. I'm damn excited about getting pulled over and I'll happily take a ticket which is a first for me. Then again, I can try to get out of it and no doubt, the motorcycle will pass us by then. Hopefully, I can get a better look at him then. Damn, that's a good plan.

The police cruiser is behind my car with his lights flashing. I pull over on the shoulder, paying little attention to him. My focus is on the biker as I anxiously coax him to pass us. He's slowing his speed and my eyes about bug out of my head, what the hell is he doing?

"Come on. Come on. Pass me you, idiot." I snap, but not before I hit my steering wheel with my fist.

Totally consumed with the idiot biker that has slowed, I never noticed Trooper Brody Pierce, who is currently tapping on my window with the end of his flashlight. I drag my eyes to his, and by looking at him, I can easily see he's not a happy guy. His stone face shows a no-nonsense expression like I've pissed him off.

Just what I don't need. I lower my window and sheepishly smile hoping to come across friendly, maybe then he'll drop the scowl.

"Do you know the speed limit?" He asks politely, but not overly friendly. I'm a wreck, sweating like crazy. I fear that to him I may appear like a nut or even a drunk. I'm not sure, but now is not the time to flake out. I calmly try to explain things before I'm arrested, or walking the white line to prove my sobriety.

"I think that motorcycle is following me." I blurt out pointing my finger to the slow, approaching bike. Trooper Pierce grabs a hold of his belt and eases back to get a better view of the road. Both of our eyes look back, and that's when I notice the bike is making a U-turn in the opposite direction. *Shit.* To get a better look, I hang my head out the window. I don't see much until he is turned all the way around and heading in the opposite direction. The emblem on the back says 'Lost Souls MC,' the more troubling thing is the big letters that spell, Chicago.

What the hell?

In that moment, it's clear to me that he was the one lurking in the forest, watching me. Jesus, It's not lost on me that he had ample time to do whatever he wanted, and no one would ever know. There are so many places to bury and hide a body in the woods.

"See, look? He's taking off," I shout, and slap my hand on the outside part of my door, "you need to follow him." I'm basically yelling at a State Trooper. By the way he lowers his chin and returns a glaring gaze, I realize I have overstepped the line. He's not buying a word I'm saying, so I explain in greater detail my story.

Ten minutes later, Trooper Pierce hands me back my license, proof of insurance and a hundred and fifty-dollar ticket. "Wow, not cheap is it?" My attempt to be funny fails miserably because he's not even cracking a smile. He hands over my ticket warning me to watch my speed. I want to say, 'yes sir' but I refrain. However, I make sure to let him know he should have gone after the man on the motorcycle. Even after my explanation of what happened back on the trail, he kept on repeating the same thing.

"Ma'am he has not broken any laws. You have."

Fuck, whatever.

I snatch my overly inflated ticket and take a minute to sit and simmer down. As I watch the trooper drive by, I reach for my phone and call Liam. Again, no answer. I then try, Izzy unsuccessfully. When they both don't answer, I try Brax.

"Yo." He answers his phone the same every time, and just having him answer his phone is a relief.

"Hey," I exclaim, "where the hell is everyone? I've called both Liam and Izzy a few times, and no one answers their damn phone."

Brax doesn't say anything right away, and his pause has me more than concerned. The hairs on neck stand.

"Kara, listen to me carefully." The tone in which he uses alarms me. It's not his usual smart, fun-loving tone. Red flags are going up.

"Drive to my place, now!" He commands.

The blood drains from my face. "What's wrong?" I ask, straightening straight as a board. I've got my car in drive, and my foot presses the pedal to the floor. The ticket I just got for speeding is forgotten. Tears fill my eyes as a sense of dread fills my mind and I can't help but feel it's bad news. My bad feeling from earlier was spot on once again.

I may be speaking words to Brax, but I'm unsure of any words that leave my mouth. I'm asking questions left and right, and yet, there is no way I can concentrate on what the answers may be. I'm too panic stricken.

"It's Liam," he sighs, "Jesus, just get here, okay?"

"But...wait a minute..."

That's when his voice lowers, in a dead serious tone, he explains, "I don't have time for this shit right now, so just get here."

"Listen..." I begin to say, but he interrupts.

After exhaling a few groan filled breaths, the next thing I hear is not so much the words, but the way he delivered them.

"He's in bad shape."

Those four words, halt my beating heart.

Chapter Eight

"Consequences"

Liam

40 MINUTES EARLIER...

On my way to the club, I suddenly have an odd sensation to glance over my shoulder. Sure enough, I spot a few bikers lingering back. With a simple adjustment of my mirrors, I keep my eye trained on them. As cars weave in and out, they maintain their distance but hold their position. Fuck. I don't need this shit right now. One, it's too early in the morning and secondly, I'm on my way to the club.

I'm not a man with a lot of patience. I like things controlled, and lately, that's not happening. Just like now, against my better judgment, I pull over when I reach an abandoned parking lot. Not one to mess around, I figure whatever is about to go down, best it happens on the outskirts of town.

I'm only a few miles from the clubhouse and rather than bring this mess to the club's front door and involve others, this is as good a spot as any. After all, this is my situation to settle. Already late for my meeting with my uncle, my no show will at least alert him. I'll deal with his angry ass later. Right now, if these fuckers came for retribution, let's get it over with and move the fuck on.

I've made my feelings known to everyone. I'll happily step away before I give into the demands of the Chicago Chapter. What I find surprising is the new rumors that hint Dominic wasn't as popular with the club as we were led to believe. If true that worked in my favor, but it won't stop the heat coming my way. We live by a certain code. Fuckers wanted me to hand over Kara to them, an eye for an eye, kind of thing. My blood boiled, and I refused. Absolutely, *no* fucking way.

Around here, our club looks after the town and its people. It's a small community, and we like to keep it peaceful. When Dominic came in and forcefully kidnapped Izzy, that shit went against what we stood for. Izzy was a resident, not to mention Brax's woman. She had protection from the club even if she didn't know it.

The Chicago Chapter can demand all they like, they will never get Kara. Even if they killed me, my uncle would never allow it to happen. The position of the club is one thing, but this matter runs deeper than that. It's my family and my girl. I may be enemy number one in a few member's eyes, but fuck if I care. Most of them understand it and know the heat that's on me. Support me or not, they have to follow my uncle's orders.

As long as Kara's not involved, I'm okay.

As I pull into the center of the empty lot, I park my bike. Eager for this showdown, I stand against my bike with my legs wide apart. I appear cool as a cucumber, arms crossed, and shades on. All week, I've noticed the tail they had on me. This cat and mouse game is getting old. They've followed, but they never engaged. It's nothing more than a message to let me know they are there. If they were trying to scare me, they might as well give up. I'm not the duck and hide kind of guy.

As I count the number of them, I'm busy trying to figure out how this little showdown is going to go. I'm accessing my odds, knowing I'm going to take some serious hits, but as long as I get some in as well, I'm okay with it. This was my decision, now it's time to settle it. I can see Kara's beautiful smile and sweet laugh in my mind, that's what I'm protecting. As I switch into kickass mode, I remind myself that these fuckers wanted to hurt my girl. A menacing growl rips past my throat when my phone suddenly beeps.

I don't bother to check my phone's caller ID. I just answer it, "What!"

"We got problems." From the sounds of my uncle, he's not in a great mood. Perfect, as I'm not in much of one either. With the phone to my ear, I kick at the dirt with my boot. Left to glare at the problems that are heading my way. Talk about timing.

"You don't say," I huff as the first biker turns into the lot. "Does it have anything to do with the tail on me for the last few days?" I had no clue if he knew anything about it, but by his slight pause, I'd say he did. I can't stop the snide chuckle that escapes from my throat.

He then, lets out an audible curse. If I had to guess, I'd say he has his phone on speaker because suddenly his voice sounds muffled. It's hard for me to concentrate on what he's saying while not distracting myself from my situation. Suddenly his voice is once again clear.

"My guess is, yes," he replies, "I received news from Chicago that a few of them were in town for a less than friendly visit."

I'm nodding my head as I can validate that claim by counting the men who are pulling in the parking lot. Out of curiosity, I ask, "Who and how many?" If it's more than the men I can count, then I need to make sure Kara is protected. I'm also surveying my odds, never one to lose my cool, though. I'm smart enough to know, winning a fight is not only won with the size of your fists, it's your ability to keep cool in stressful situations.

"Not many from what I've heard. The worst of them is a guy who goes by, Lukas." After clearing his throat, he warns me, "They want a resolution, Liam. They're done waiting to get it."

"I can see that," I calculate my response as the bikers come to a stop. "I'm about to meet them as we speak."

"*Fuck*, where are you?"

BRAX

"HEY, MOTHERFUCKERS. SEEMS TO me that you want to pick a fight with my buddy here, but you needed to bring eight of you for one of him? Not so sure of yourselves, are ya'?"

I'm playing it cool, but make no mistake I have my baseball bat gripped tightly in one hand ready to walk straight into a shit storm. Lucky for me, I'm in a very pissed off mood and walking into this scene only fuels my anger.

Good for me, not so good for them.

The day before, Liam had mentioned he's had a tail on him so I knew I had to keep my eyes peeled because he'd never ask for help, he's too damn stubborn. More like stupid, but I won't argue. What he fails to see is that this mess involves me, too. Liam went out of his way to help get my girl back so there's not a chance I'd let him be on his own, no matter how much he wants it. I agree with him in trying to keep the club from an all-out war, and I know the guys would have his back if push comes to shove. Hell, Marty wouldn't let his nephew get killed.

Either way, shit's not happening with me here.

Liam's been tight-lipped when it comes to Kara over this shit, he thinks keeping her in the dark is what's best for her. I disagree, that damn girl is tougher than most men we know. Growing up with Dominic, she'd have to be. Anyway, if anything happened to Kara, Izzy would have my balls on a platter. Simply put, that's her girl.

It's time to end this shit, once and for all. That evil fucker is dead, and that's a good thing. He caused Izzy more pain and suffering that anyone should have to suffer. My wish is that I had been the one who pulled the trigger. If I have done it, none of this would be happening with Liam and Kara. If these are the men responsible for the things happening to Kara, it's time for that shit to stop as well.

I loosen up with a crack of my neck and roll of my shoulders. Time to kick some ass. Good thing I've got some pent up anger that needs to be released. As it is, Liam's slumped over with these fuckers standing around him in a circle. He's taken some licks, but I know he's hanging in there because he just raised his head to wink at me. That's all I needed to see from him. To let him know it's time to beat some ass like we did back in the day, I return the wink with a shit eating grin.

"What are you going to do about it?"

One stupid fucker eyes me like I repulse him. Yeah, the feeling is mutual asshole. As I get take a better look at him, he has to be joking, because he's lucky if he's one-fifty soaking wet. Shit, Izzy could beat his ass.

"Well fuckers," I spit with a twirl of my bat, "guess you're going to find out." My eyes stay trained on that little prick. He's getting his ass kicked first.

Uncle Marty

"You have two fucking choices to make." I declare.

Two of the members from Chicago came to pay me a less than friendly visit. I've called in favors and I've agreed with letting their men settle the score with my nephew. The way I see it, I've been more than fucking accommodating, and I've had just about enough of their bullshit attitudes.

Liam's choice was to either hand over his girl or take a beating. I may not like it, but that's the way it works in our world. Liam's girl took out a member, like it or not, that has consequences. Hell, that stubborn nephew of mine, he's more pigheaded than I ever was. When I look into his eyes, all I see is my sister. We lost Susan when Liam and Tiffany were young. Mick's a shit father, so I took that role over. I'm no saint and not even a father, but the way I see it, they are more my kids than his.

Makes this shit even more personal.

Forced to deal with these arrogant cocksuckers has my hospitality running real thin. They tied Liam up and did a real number on him. Fuckers even sent me a picture of their location. Just to make sure shit didn't go south, I've had a few of the guys watching their every move since they came to town. No one comes to town without us knowing about it. My leniency only goes so far, so if things got out of hand, our guys would have stepped in and put a stop to it. The way I see it, I was generous not demanding to be present when this shit went down. In return, they need to respect my god damn wishes. They are in my town, after all.

There was no way in hell I'd let them kill my nephew. That was never a fucking option. He's a member of this club, and when that member is family, that's when I had some trouble remaining objective as club president. I had a club to protect first and foremost. It was *his* decision to make. Either give up his girl or give them a piece of him. My job was to honor that decision.

At the moment I'm staring at two of these smugly fuckers laughing to themselves. My eyes narrow and I wonder if they'd still be laughing if they knew just how close they came to finding a bullet in their backs? Fuckers might not be acting so righteous then. To walk in here and disrespect us is not a smart move, life is different here than in Chicago. Our bond runs deep in these neck of the woods, whereas in the city, you don't see such a thing. I'm not sure if it's due to the sheer number of people that live there compared to our little town, or the fact they like to shoot before giving much thought to it.

As I strike a match to light my cigar, I decide to educate them, because they don't appear to be too smart.

"You got what you came for. You didn't get the lady, but you had your turn at my nephew. Now, either you leave peacefully, *or* I put a bullet in your heads."

Oh, now they stop laughing. Fuckers are wise to listen.

The taller gentlemen who is acting like the one in charge has taken offense to me. He's snarling as he eyes me like I was a fucking cockroach. The balls on this fucker may amaze me, but he needs to be put in his place. I make sure when I spit that it just nearly misses his boot. Like a pussy, he jumps back and returns with a snarling glare.

"You're lucky he's still alive for what's happened," he growls, "he got off easy, never forget that old man."

Old man! Call it ignorance or arrogance, but this fucker is just begging for me to shoot him. I rest my hand on my gun at my side, reminding him who started this shit. One more word and I'll have my gun out and pointed right between his eyes.

"Who are you trying to bullshit?" I shout and widen my stance. I'm ready to take this prick to school. "That fucker, the one you idolize was nothing more than a sick bastard, and you know it. I say, we did you all a favor."

"Yeah," he mocks with a one shoulder raise, "maybe that's true."

His lifts his eyes and the way his head bobs from side to side, he's acting like he's got something else to say. Sure enough, his ego must get the better of him, because he smugly brags, "You may want a little head's up. We are not the only ones demanding something. Dominic had friends outside of us. Certain associates. They want answers and they will look into things for themselves."

Fuck, whatever. His cocky demeanor only pisses me off more. Dog or whatever name he goes by fits him, because he needs to be put down like one. The whole time he's yapping his mouth, I've shot him over six times in my mind. The minute he turns his nose up, I realized he's finished with his 'just heads up' banter.

"Consider us warned." I level my eyes on him and his buddy. "Now get the fuck out!"

To avoid any further conversation, the men nod their heads and turn to walk away. Good fucking riddance. Problem finally solved, I throw my cigar down and stomp it out with my boot.

"You got Doc ready?" I shout over my shoulder to Tom, my VP who has been standing nearby. As soon as I heard what was going down with my nephew, I wanted to make sure doc' was prepared.

"Yep, we're ready for him."

Kara

I'M SO FURIOUS AND WORRIED out of my damn mind. What were they thinking? I'm pacing outside in Izzy's driveway, nervously waiting for word from Brax. The damn cicadas are so loud out here, I can't think clearly. My feet keep moving back and forth, as I say a few prayers. I figure we could all use some of those about now. I knew things were bad, but finding out I was what they wanted, that's a bit frightening. I'm not sure what to say about Liam willingly taking one hell of a beating in exchange, that's pure insanity. It also pisses me off.

I want some fucking payback for them hurting him! Dammit!

"Kara." Izzy's soft voice fills my ears. I turn to see her walk down the front steps walking my way. She also looks tense. Both of us have matching worried expressions. Lucky for her, she has the kids as a distraction. Finally getting the kids to bed, she has joined me outside. It's me, her and the damn cicadas.

When I arrived earlier, Izzy filled me in with the news. I guess Brax hightailed it out of here when he suspected Liam may be in some trouble. If it's any consolation, I feel better he was there. The thought of Liam facing those men alone literally makes me sick to my stomach.

Being a mother, Izzy's not able to hold back watching me hurting like I am. She pulls me in for a big hug, but I'm so worked up I'm afraid I'll break down and cry if she hugs me, so I attempt to step back. She's not having any of that, she tightens her hold instead.

"The club did what they had to do from what I understand," she begins to explain, but pauses. "How long does Dominic get to ruin our lives from the grave?"

That wasn't a question I expected from her and quite honestly I wasn't sure how to respond. I wanted to say every damn night, but I don't. Instead, I utter under my breath, "If you only knew." I confess.

"I have nightmares too you know?" Her statement shocks me, and I slip from her embrace. She nods her head and all I can do is shake mine.

Her coming forward and telling me that she has them as well devastates me even more. I had no idea she suffered with them. Of course, why wouldn't she? From the years of abuse she suffered from my brother, I can imagine her memories are all nightmares. My nightmares feel like reminders that will continue to haunt me. All this time instead of worrying about my shit, I should have given more concern to how she's dealing with things. I just imagined her being newly married to Brax now, had vanished all her demons.

"I can only imagine. I'm so sorry." I fight the urge to cry, but my mind quickly switches to worry over Liam. "The waiting is killing me. I want to see him, Izzy. What could be taking so long?"

"I'm not sure," she adds while nervously biting her lower lip. "Let's go inside and wait. Brax will call." She puts her arm around my shoulder and leads us inside.

IT'S A GOOD THING THAT Liam and I have been staying at Izzy's old house on the same street as Brax. Right now, I'm hightailing it down the street. Brax called and said after their doctor worked on Liam at the club, he's returned to our house.

When I reach the porch, Brax walks out looking like he's gone a few rounds himself. I'm so taken in by his appearance, my hands automatically cover my mouth. He's got some cuts and scrapes, and his clothing's torn a bit. At least he's walking and talking, so that's a positive sign.

"Where is he?" I ask out of breath, anxious to get inside. As I reach for the door, he halts my progress from entering the house.

"You need to calm down before you go in there. He's knocked out, doc' gave him some strong meds. He needs to rest."

"Well? How is he? What happened? Why the fuck did he *do this*?" I'm angry and unleashing my worry as my fists pound at Brax's chest. He graciously lets me get it out.

"Slow down, babe," he finally whispers, taking a hold of my hands. "First of all, I got there at the right time. He's had a good ass whooping but nothing is broken, just bloodied and bruised. I want to know where your head is at before you see him?"

Why is he asking me this?

"Seriously, Brax? I'm pissed as *holy hell* this happened," I vent my anger. "He might have few more bruises by the time I'm done with him." Not really, but it makes my point pretty well.

Brax raises an eyebrow and cocks his head. "He did it for you, accept that and leave it at that," he declares. "He needs rest, not more bullshit. I'm not trying to sound heartless sweetheart, I'm only looking out for him."

That does it, the waterworks flow. *I know* he did this for me. He's right, I need to get my head on straight before I see Liam. I can't be an emotional mess.

"Come here," he whispers and pulls me into a hug. "I get it, sweetheart. Just be there for him. A lot of shit needs to get figured out, but for now, it's about him resting."

I nod and dry my tears.

We enter the quiet house and all of a sudden I'm hit with a chilling sensation. I'm nervous knowing a few feet from me, Liam is lying down, beaten. It stops me dead in my tracks. My feet stop working and panicked breaths suddenly feel like the walls are closing in on me. I'm shaking and sweating at the same time as everything in the room blurs in and out of focus.

Great, a panic attack. Brax notices my odd behavior and is quick to help distract me.

"Just how attached are you to Liam's face?" he asks.

My body whips around to face him in utter shock.

"What the hell are you trying to say?" I'm horrified, but Brax breaks out with a smile before he starts laughing.

"Oh, sweetheart, nothing that a few days won't help. I just wanted to get you out of that head of yours. His ugly mug is a bit uglier for the next few days."

"Oh my God, you dick." My heart is about to explode. I'm holding my hand over it as if that's going to help any, and snarl. "You are an ass, you know that, right?" He's biting his lip to control his laughs, and I can't help but join him. Although I won't admit this to him, his sick sense of humor did help me some.

When we walk toward the bedroom, my nerves soar to the point tears fill my eyes. I have no idea what shape he's going to be in when I see him, but I take a deep breath as I enter to find Liam sleeping soundly. Like Brax had mentioned, Liam's beautiful face has taken some hits. One eye is puffy, the other is cut and bruises paint him like a canvas. He's covered up so I'm not sure what's hiding under the blanket. Once again, guilt consumes me. How can it not?

Brax's gentle hand rests on my shoulder and reminds me to be strong.

"He better hope his face doesn't scar because that will piss me off even more. I like his ugly mug, as you put it." I joke and Brax pulls me into a side hug. His warmth and just knowing he was there for Liam, helps me deal with all of these unwelcome emotions. I'm trying not to blame myself, and I think Brax senses that. He nudges my shoulder.

"Yeah, I hear ya' sweetheart. Go ahead and kiss his head, and then let him rest. To keep your ass busy, you can make me some much-needed coffee. That's to repay me for the shots I've taken today. I hate to say it, but I'm a bit sore." He stretches his arms over his head just as I turn to face him.

"Thank you for being there and helping him. I don't know what I'd do if I lost him, Brax. I just don't."

"Don't mention it, he's like a brother to me. He's family. A pain in my ass, but my family all the same."

"KARA, STOP CRYING. I'LL BE fine in a few days." Liam tries to get comfortable while he does his best to stop me from fretting over him. Finally, once he woke up, I lost it. Big time. All my worrying, no sleep and umpteen cups of coffee have me frazzled. Not to mention, I can't stop moving around.

I plead with his swollen, purple face. "Don't hold shit from me again!"

"Don't plan on it, babe. It's over now." Liam winces as he tries to laugh.

"Is it really?" I dare to ask.

He resigns. "For now, it is."

LIAM'S HEALING NICELY, BUT IS getting grumpier as the days go by. It's been a few days and he's been taking it easy, but it's driving him insane. He's not a stay at home and take it easy kind of guy. I, on the other hand, act like mother hen and tend to his every need.

Liam's uncle, Marty, stopped by last night and had a long talk with him. An understanding of sorts was agreed upon by the club. With Liam and his uncle having the best interests of all involved, Liam is stepping away from the club. It's music to my ears since I know Liam envies Brax's lifestyle. Brax goes to work every day at the shop he owns, and returns home every night to his family. Not having any club responsibilities, he is out of the dangerous lifestyle and spends more time at home with his growing family.

Liam handed in his cut and has been given an out to achieve the lifestyle he wants. Plus, an arrangement of such has been reached. It seemed when Brax left the club, he did so with some financial backing from the club. A mutual arrangement.

Liam and I both felt it was the best thing for us. A lot has happened and some members of the club will never let go of it all. As President, Marty needed to make a decision, a decision he could live with being Liam's uncle. Hell, I'm not educated enough to understand how things work within a club. For now, Liam's out and has taken on a partnership with Brax. The plan is to double the output at the repair shop. It's in the best interest of the club, as they have a financial interest in the bottom line. As far as I'm concerned, it's a win for us all.

Peace at last, could it even be possible? I've had no more messages or knives in my door since Liam's ass beating, so it looks like we've made it…finally. We can live like any other normal couple. I, for one, could not be happier…but there are times I can feel Liam's tension. God, I hope he's not hiding other shit from me.

He promised, no more secrets.

Chapter Nine

"Unexpected Call"

Liam

I SIT UNABLE TO FEEL anything other than shock. The phone call I received moments ago has stopped time. My head hangs low while my shoulders ache in response to the gut-wrenching feeling that has no promise of letting up any time soon. The knots low in my stomach tighten their hold as my chest constricts with each breath. There's not much that could shake me, but the freak call from my father has left me shattered. For the first time, I'm fearful I may lose my only sister.

This moment is eerily reminiscent of the little boy who lost his mother all those years ago. I never fully healed after the passing of my mother. The only way for me to deal with the loss was to acknowledge it never happened. I struggled to find a way to get up each day. Finally, I learned to box up the raw emotions that dared to emerge. With a flip of a switch, I found a way to get through each day after that.

Only now with the news that my sister has been in a serious car accident, the only thing I do feel is remorse. The sudden loss that crippled me back then, is what I'm starting to feel now. All my damn bottled up feelings are fighting to finally break loose. The enormity of them and how I might respond if I lose someone else panics me. I'd take an ass beating any day of the week over fighting damn emotions because those motions know where I'm most vulnerable, and they will expose the parts that I've fought like hell to protect.

I've lived with guilt for never allowing myself to fall under the notion that my mother did not go willingly, that she never wanted to leave me, but she had no choice. She developed breast cancer, and that is what took her from this earth. My way of dealing with losing her was to place the blame on her, to blame her for leaving me instead of grieving the way a son should have. To deny myself to heal those wounds back then feels like I let her down.

With my sister, it's more complicated. She's simply not a good person. She's done bad things to good people, people I happen to care about deeply. Simply put, her troubles were brought on by herself. I'm not one to dwell on what led her to be the way she is. Daddy issues, mommy issues, fuck if I know, I was a fucking kid myself.

Right now, my heart is aching for my once little sister. The woman she is now is a different story, and that shit is eating away at me. Fuck.

Tiffany's been anything but a saint. The hell she has caused, and the pain she has inflicted on people I cared about should be enough for me not to give a shit about what happens to her. But the news she may not survive the accident, that's softening the hard feelings I have toward her.

When the words head on crash left my father's lips, I broke out in chills, I can't lie. I've seen the guilt Kara has struggled with over killing her brother, and he fucking deserved it. That bastard was in a league all of his own, and I don't even understand her guilt. She did us all a favor, I just wish I had been the one to do it. Between her brother and my sister, it's a wonder we stand a chance at happiness. Christ.

As I toss the covers back, I rub the sleep from my eyes. I don't want to disturb Kara, so I do a quick glance over my shoulder to see her beautiful face. My sleeping beauty looks peaceful, free from any signs of her hellish nightmares. As quietly as I can, I reach for my jeans discarded on the floor and quickly dress. My thoughts are so preoccupied, I missed Kara stirring behind me. Her slight groan did catch my attention, though. Arms stretching over her head, she's raising an eyebrow curiously.

"Hey," she rasps with a yawn, "where are you going?"

She leans over to check the time on the clock while I bend down to pick up my phone from the nightstand then wipe the tiredness from my face.

"Got to go babe, Tiff's been in an accident." Even if I wanted to say more, I couldn't. I just can't form the words.

Kara stares at me looking a little startled. As her eyes blink rapidly, she opens and closes her mouth a few times, each time without uttering a single sound. She could easily sound off with 'who gives a shit,' but she's not heartless. Shit has me wondering why I'm not saying something along those lines. I guess I'm not heartless either.

I imagine part of the reason for her silence has more to do with her respect for me. Knowing her like I do, she will want to come with me, she'd want to comfort me like I've been doing for her. We are quite the pair. In the short time I've known her, we've managed to live through hell, and bounced back. She also has obliterated the three things I swore I'd never do when it comes to a female. No attachments, no expectations, and no commitment. When it comes to Kara, I not only want to attach myself to her. I'm already in the relationship, and commitment with her. God willing, she's my future. Definitely an unexpected surprise and I think fate has played a hand in all of this.

Right now, I need to figure shit out with my sister. With my shirt on, I grab for my wallet and notice Kara's anxious behavior. Her legs are bouncing nervously, and she's biting her nails. That nasty habit drives me crazy because I love those nails of hers.

"I'm coming with you," she huffs as she jumps out of bed.

She quickly pulls on jeans and a t-shirt and I can't help but grin, she never ceases to amaze me. While gathering her things, she takes a second to reach out and squeeze my hands to comfort me. I've never been more thankful for having her in my life than I am right now. Plus, I'd be lying if I said I'm not enjoying her ass in those jeans as she's darting around as quickly as possible. Damn.

Once I've got my boots on she quickly joins me and grabs her purse. Out the front door, I glance back over my shoulder waiting for her to follow. I lock up and notice the she hasn't said a word, but yet again, neither have I. Old memories force their way into my mind. Better times with my sister.

And suddenly the tightness in my chest creates a heaviness in my heart. My first reaction is to reach for my phone. Over the years whenever my sister pulled a new stunt, my first call was to Brax. I'm not sure it's the best decision since things are different now, but I still feel it's the right thing to do.

"On the way, I'll call Brax to let him know. He should know."

Kara snapped her head so fast it about gave her whiplash. She started to protest but stopped short when she noticed my tight-lipped expression, and the hard edge of my jaw. I'm trying hard but on the verge of losing my shit and I sure as hell don't want to take it out on her, but she needs to let me handle things my way. I'm not in the mood to argue about if I should or should not call him, and I don't want to have a long fucking conversation about it either.

If anyone could understand my feelings right now, it has to be her.

I realize Tiffany's caused Izzy enough grief to last a lifetime, but she has to realize I have to do what I feel is right. Brax never married Tiffany but they did share a beautiful little girl, even if Tiffany no longer holds any responsibility when it came to Eve. She gave that up. Izzy adopted Eve shortly after that.

The triangle we live in even has us scratching our damn heads, not to mention questioning our sanity.

Yes, it was odd. Yes, it was a mess. But, it was also amazingly perfect. A beautiful mess.

My hands fumble with the keys as I open the truck door for her. Before I start to step away, Kara reaches out to put her hand over mine. Even though she stays quiet, she shows she cares and understands with her touch. The gesture is exactly what I need. It proves, Kara understands me like no other woman ever has. She's damn unbelievable that way.

I keep my eyes locked on her hand that's covering my mine, absorbing her warmth before I look back at her sweet face. The sweetest face I've ever known. To hell with the turmoil we face on a daily basis, with her angelic face, she's filling an aching void that has been lost in my heart for years. This is all new to me, but damn with the way she's wormed her way into my heart, it feels like she's been there all along. Christ, now I sound like Brax...damn sorry sap.

I lay my head to rest against the open door and gently sigh, "Let's head out." I know I should be rushing to get to the hospital, but I've never been a fan of being in one. The one and last time I've been in one was when my mother died. The idea to rush there now to await my sisters fate, is more than screwing with my mind.

On the way, I kept my conversation short with Brax, with not a lot of information to give him other than she had been in an accident. Mick, my father, was pretty skim on the details, only that I needed to get to the hospital.

Besides my brief call, the ride has been pretty quiet. My mind's too busy reminding me of the little sister I once loved to the disgraceful woman. Such a waste considering she gave us Eve. That adorable, sweet girl reminds me so much of my sister that it pains me when I look into her eyes. Her mother's eyes.

Before I know it, we're pulling into the parking garage of Valley General Hospital.

Each step is a painful reminder of how I felt walking into this hospital as a kid. This time, I have walls up to make sure I don't break down like I had back then. I'm not sure what I'm walking into, but I'll prepare for the worst anyway. It's the only way I can help keep my shit together, but walking into the entrance all I hear are the words, 'I'm so sorry, she's gone.'

Those were the exact words from the doctor when I lost my mom.

A quick glance over the empty seats in the waiting room, I spot my aging father. His gray hair is slicked back and he's sitting with his head cradled in his hands. I can't stop the twinge of anxiety that grips me with every step I take towards him. He doesn't even sense my presence as I take the seat next to him. Right away it feels like I'm sitting next to a stranger. My father has a strained relationship with Tiff and I and after he lost his wife, my mother, he withdrew from life. Including us, his only children.

"How is she?" I curtly ask keeping my voice steady.

Mick raises his head appearing every bit lost and the picture of a grief stricken father. I've seen this look before, the same lost expression. For my mother and now my sister. I'm not even sure he heard me. The only thing I see when his vacant eyes focus on me is years of regret. I think he suddenly realizes he may lose his daughter and all of the wasted years spent drinking has finally hit home. Hard. His habits to numb the pain over the years can't help him now. For years he acted like he never gave a shit, looking at him now, angers me to the point I have my fists clinched.

I bet we both wish we could get back all of those wasted years. Things might have turned out differently. It's hard for me not to rip into him out of anger to let him know just what kind of worthless father he is, but what's the use? What's done is done and we can't change a damn thing.

If he loses his daughter tonight, I wonder how much guilt he would feel. It's hard not to blame him for her reckless behavior. The way I see it, he has a decision to make here tonight; keep drinking and wallowing, or make sure he takes his fathering duties more seriously. Am I partly to blame for her bad decisions she's made? No, her daddy issues land squarely on his shoulders.

"Um...," clearing his throat, he struggles to explain, "she's in surgery now. I don't really know much else." His eyes lower to his feet, "They told me to sit and wait." He sniffles and wipes away a stray tear. I notice that his eyes have stayed locked on the square tiled floor. I bet he's counted the number of tiles while sitting here, and I'm sure I'll know the count myself before this night is over. Shit, we probably both could use a damn drink.

I introduce Kara to my father but his reception was chilly as best. She played it off as bad timing, but if she only knew this is his actual personality on any given day, she may view him differently. I let it go, it's not like he will be a staple in our life. He hasn't been in mine for years.

It's agonizing with not knowing what to say, or not knowing how long we'll be sitting here. To help pass the time, I rest my hands on my legs, clenching my fists to loosen and to help channel my frustrations. Kara is sitting and rubbing my leg with her hand.

Not five minutes later, in walks a worried and uptight Brax, his scowl sums up my thoughts exactly. His cold stare scans the room until he finds us. The heaviness in his breathing and worrisome expression, I know he has to be sharing my same sentiments. Conflicted.

Brax and I share a similar mindset, we both have seen the good and bad in Tiffany. If not for Eve, the daughter they share, he most likely would not be here right now. To just up and leave his new wife and family says something. My phone call troubled him. Over the years, he'd jump whenever Tiffany got into any trouble, but now, he has a family. Tiffany's the past and the bad blood between them had all been caused by Tiffany, not him. Yet, here he is.

"So what's the news." He flatly asks with no emotion in his voice. It's obvious he was here to get the facts only.

"Not much, she's in surgery now." To ease some tension, I rub the back of my neck. I have a feeling we are going to be here a while.

Kara pats the chair next to her for Brax to sit. She gives him a gentle smile and wraps her hand around his arm. Instantly she snuggles into his shoulder. It's clear he appreciates her kindness, because he reaches out and gives her hand a gentle rub. It's just like her to go out of her way to make everyone feel comforted. That's just the way she is.

Before long, Brax and I took a stroll down memory lane. Recalling the better times, we shared with my sister. It felt so good to crack a few laughs, most of them at his expense. He did go behind my back to get with Tiffany back in the day. It was nice to realize just how many fond memories we had that weren't bad ones. Kara out of the goodness of her heart encouraged us not to give up on her just yet.

"Maybe this will help her turn things around."

Brax and I just nod. Kara though, man, the way this woman surprises me never stops and I fall for her a little bit more each time.

"You know," she exhales, "sometimes things happen to you that encourage you to change the way you live your life, maybe this is one of those times?" With a hold of my hand, she tightened her grip. "Just take one day at a time."

I return with a warm smile. Her words do give me some hope for my sister if she survives. That idea softens my heavy heart. I want to believe it, but the skeptic in me knows that a snake does not change its skin, they only shed it from time to time.

Although shitty timing, and knowing my dad the way I do, you would think I'd be thrilled to introduce Kara to him, but he never talked to her. I baited him a few times to say something, but each time he pretended like he all of sudden lost his hearing.

"Mick, what the hell?" I exclaim. Fucker is pissing me off. I'm about to go off on him when Kara stops me.

"Liam, let it go. Don't push it."

Don't push it, my dad is lucky I don't haul off and smack him. What a dick. In looking over at Brax he makes the motion with his hand to let it go as well.

Finally, the doors slid open, and a police officer stepped in and approached the nurse's station. They spoke for a few minutes before the officer happened to swing his eyes in our direction. Clipboard in hand, he approached us confirming that we are the family of Tiffany Talbot. Satisfied, he proceeded.

"I'm officer Drew Daniels. I have a few questions and would like to go over what happened at the scene of the accident. I'm sure you have some questions of your own?"

As he stood with his clipboard, he flipped a few pages and made additional notes before going into the specifics of the accident. Based on the scene when he arrived, the first responders marked off the area and calculated how the accident occurred. Drivers who witnessed the accident had explained Tiffany's blue sedan was traveling on the I-5 South when a car crossed over the lane and plowed into her vehicle, causing a head-on collision. The tire track markings indicated Tiffany had tried to stop and swerve, but there was no escaping impact.

The words 'no escaping impact' enraged me to the point that bile rose in my throat. Forced to listen to the tragic and carelessness of what happened, I had trouble just sitting in my seat. If not for Kara's cold hand reaching out to grab my fisted hand around my chair in a death grip, I may have cracked the flimsy plastic. My sister never had a chance to prevent the collision. I can't help but lean forward to rest my forearms on my legs as my stomach continues to wretch listening to my old man sob. The details are hard to hear, but as I listen to every word I have my teeth clenched tight. I peer over at Brax who is shaking his head back and forth, cursing under his breath. At that moment, it didn't matter how fucked up my sister was. No one deserves this senseless accident. Even Kara, who has personal grudges against my sister agreed, that this was a tragic accident.

The officer had yet to mention any word, so I asked the burning question. "What happened to the driver of the other car?"

He naturally pauses for a second while his eyes travel to each of us. I have no clue why, maybe he thinks one of us would jump up and hunt him down, who knows. After clearing his throat, he clarifies, "The person driving the vehicle did not survive. He died at the scene."

The words kept repeating themselves in my mind. Died. At. The. Scene.

"Jesus Christ." Brax uttered under his breath in disbelief.

Just a minute ago, I was fucking furious at the man who stupidly caused this accident. The fact he died wasn't what fazed me. I'm fucking angry with the fact Tiffany's in surgery fighting for her life because of him. That doesn't make me heartless, it's just a fact.

It took over thirty minutes for the officer to explain in detail the procedure of things that follow; we sat and listened until the officer excused himself. I took that moment to call my uncle, figuring best to wait until I had more information, or else the waiting room would be overflowing with bikers.

It was nearing four in the morning when Brax and I both had our heads back against the wall, keeping one eye open. Both of our legs crossed at the ankles, with one foot twitching nervously. I hadn't realized it, but Kara pointed it out trying to ease some tension. She swore we were more alike than we even knew. My dad continued to sob, but we all kept quiet, as no one knew what to say. The quietness was eating away at Kara, though. She pondered taking up chain smoking since she already chewed her nails off an hour ago.

"Have you called Izzy, yet?" Kara asked Brax after noticing he had left earlier for a few minutes with his phone in his hand. He shook his head no.

"Not yet. Lately, she's been up late with Asher. She was soundly sleeping when I left, and didn't want to wake her, or him for that matter." He lifted a shoulder and turned his head to face her, "I left a note in case she wakes up and notices I'm gone."

The longer he stayed at the hospital and away from Izzy, the more the guilt shows on his face. He had to know Izzy would understand.

The main doors finally open and in the quiet waiting room, it echoed so loud all of us jumped in our seats. To say we were antsy to hear any news was an understatement. Just then, a doctor emerged with a mask around his neck and a surgeon's cap on his head. Due to the early hour or from the lengthy surgery, he wiped the tiredness from his eyes. He glanced around the waiting room, but it was pretty easy to assume who we were since we were the only ones in the waiting room.

"Family of Tiffany Talbot?" he spoke with a scratchy voice.

"Yes," Mick answered, quickly standing as the rest of us joined.

Doctor Roberts uses his professional sterile voice to explain the list of many injuries Tiffany sustained. When he started throwing out terms like metatarsal and metacarpal, I had no idea what he was saying. I had to stop him right there and ask for simple terms, please.

He obliged. "Bones in her hands and feet."

Once we could understand better with what he was saying, he explained the brute force of the impact on her small body was so severe, the fact she's alive is a miracle. His voice remained steady in explaining she suffered a setback during surgery. She coded not once, but twice.

"Coded?" It wasn't a question, rather just me repeating the shock I felt hearing it. I wasn't alone in shock, either. I think we all gasped.

"Her heart actually stopped beating." He paused to clarify even though we all knew what it meant.

Thankfully, they resuscitated her. He detailed that besides her several broken bones, the surgery was difficult due to her internal bleeding. While they repaired the damage, her heart rate and blood pressure kept dropping. It's still a concern they are monitoring closely. We could do nothing but listen in disbelief and be thankful she's alive despite her injuries.

The helplessness I feel is frustrating the hell out of me. A drink about now would be helpful because I need something to take the edge off. I have a certain secret that's weighing heavily on my shoulders. A few days ago, Tiffany contacted me with some startling and disturbing news. I've kept that shit to myself, but her secret has me questioning what I should do about it. It's nothing new, over the years my sister had me keep secrets and against my better judgment I usually did, but years of keeping my mouth shut only proved disastrous and pointless. Left with no other option, I air her dirty secret.

"Wait," I hesitate regretting what I'm about to reveal. "What about the baby?" I instantly regret that I did not ask him in private, my lack of sleep has impacted my ability to think rationally.

With this little cat out of the bag, I had three sets of eyes staring me like I've lost my mind. I should have known better, so now I close mine and sigh. Shit.

Dr. Roberts contemplated my question with a slight nod, and spoke caution in his soft voice. "At first we had no idea she was pregnant, but our technician did confirm a fetus during her scan. I need to be completely honest, Tiffany has suffered a lot of trauma and we are monitoring her closely. All I can say is for now, she's still pregnant. Time will tell if that will change."

I'm not sure what came over me, but relief was my first reaction. With all the fighting she's doing, she still has her baby. It doesn't matter how I feel about the news or not. I feel a tinge of guilt for not mentioning any news of the baby to anyone. Instead, I kept it to myself as it was the real reason Tiffany suddenly came back home. Her wild stories never added up, so I thought better than to spread any damaging rumors. I figured I'd wait until I could confirm the news for myself. I fucking knew the minute I mentioned the news to Kara, let alone Brax, their worlds would once again be in turmoil.

As the seconds tick away in my mind, I'm reluctant to raise my eyes, and when I do, I face matching angry glares and gasps! My father sits back down in his chair, stunned speechless.

"What the hell, Liam?" Kara snarls and punches me in the arm. Hell, I can't blame her one bit for being upset.

I raise my hand to halt her next swing, though. I drop back in my seat and want to shout that I had everyone's best interest at heart by keeping my mouth shut. I kept the secret to avoid hurting my best friends and my woman.

The fact that this baby exists involves us all, but I'm sure Kara hasn't thought of that scary as shit idea. If she knew that her brother might be the so-called father, that will devastate her. God, this fucking sucks!

I need to make them understand, so I sternly, but calmly explain. "Listen to me, Tiffany told me a wild story and to be honest, I had no idea how to deal with it. So, I kept it to myself until I could figure it the hell out. I didn't even know if it was true. Well, until now, that is." I say with a shoulder shrug and look to gauge their reactions. Brax doesn't say much, but Kara is still shaking her head at me. Mick still has his head down.

I spend the next twenty minutes explaining all that happened and how I came to find out. I left nothing out, even sharing who Tiffany had said who the father was. That bastard Dominic! A significant question that spells *disaster*. Fuck, I've spent countless hours not sleeping and thinking about how in the hell could my sister be dumb enough to get pregnant by Izzy's sick-as-fuck ex? How can I tell Izzy without hurting her? And what about Kara? It affects them all in different way and not one is a good one. Just the fact that this baby exists is going to bring a lot of twisted bullshit with it.

I came up with a logical plan to avoid this disaster at all costs, a plan that could solve it all. The best thing for everyone, including Tiffany, was for her to leave town and never return. No one needed to know a thing about the baby. Shit, I was hell bent on getting her out of town and then never speaking of it again. Only, my best laid plan is not going to happen now.

With the chance that this baby lives, the days and months to follow are sure going to be a straight up fucking mess.

Chapter Ten

"Date Night"

Kara

Seriously, how could he do this? Whenever I think things are going to be normal, the rug gets swept under my feet. All the explaining in the world will not make up for his silence.

"How could you not tell me something as big as that? Jesus, Liam!" Not only am I surprised, but I'm also pissed as hell. The possibility that she could be carrying my brother's child is insane, total ridiculousness.

Liam's stressed out and my continual probing is sounding more like an interrogation. Call it shock or stunned doesn't matter, I can't shut my mind or my mouth off. Both of which do nothing to help Liam's growing agitation. He's sick of explaining himself and as he lowers his hands, he grumbles as he does it.

"I wasn't sure if it was true, Kara, and until I did, I wasn't saying a word. That's all there is to it."

We stand only centimeters from one another, but it feels like miles. Both of us scrutinize one another but this time, we remain quiet. I drop the frown from my face that has been in place since Liam first dropped this bombshell on us at the hospital.

Liam ends up walking out of the room so I'm left with only my thoughts, and that's not a great thing right now. We are both exhausted having had little sleep, but I can't help but think about the fact I've spent the last several hours putting my differences aside for *that* woman. To be the better person, I put my petty differences aside. Now, faced with her baby news I'm not sure what I feel except the stabbing pain above my left eye. A stress migraine is just what I need.

It's just another reason to prove we live in the damn twilight zone. Once again, we're faced with a new set of issues surrounding *Tiffany*. Finally, Liam's bruises are fading, and his ribs are healing just in time to worry over something new.

Beyond exhausted, I walk back to our bedroom to find Liam already in bed but not sleeping, he's waiting for me. I don't hesitate as I climb next to him. He cradles me to his side and when we're like this, shutting out the outside world, it's perfect.

My mind is still trying to wrap itself around the last several hours. I talk it through in my mind, but it's not working so I say it out loud to see if that helps. I'm not necessarily speaking to Liam, I just need to hear myself verbally. I need to see if I can make this make some sense to me.

"If the baby is Dominic's..." I have to stop myself to raise the question, "why did she even sleep with him to begin with? I mean, we are talking about Tiffany..." I cringe when I realize I said that out loud. Oops! "Sorry, let me try this again. Your sister is the baby's mother, my brother is the father...so I'm aunt, you're an uncle, and that leaves...Willow and Eve as its sisters? Jesus, that's fucked up. That leaves baby Asher in the clear. Thank God, someone is."

Okay, I did mention twilight zone. Every single word of that family scenario freaks me the hell out.

"That's why for everyone's sake, I pushed the idea for Tiffany to leave and never come back. If that had happened we would not be having this conversation, and you would not be freaking the hell out over it."

"If that baby does happen to live, no way will Izzy, let alone Brax, will ever let the girls around it. Not that I could blame them, but it's sad in a way."

"Let's just see how things play out. Tiffany has a long road ahead of her, and we're not sure the baby will survive the trauma yet."

I wrap my hands around my head. "It's enough to make my head hurt."

"For now, let's not think about it, we need to get some shut eye."

"Sounds like a plan." I rest my head on his shoulder to get comfy. Sleep sounds superb.

Light fingers trace circles around my temples. "Hey, I got plans for tonight don't forget," he says with a yawn.

I vaguely remember him mentioning it earlier, so it's a good thing he reminded me. Half asleep, I murmur, "Okay." That's the last thing I remember before sleep finds me.

THE PARKING LOT IS EMPTY, but the lights are on inside. It's odd because this place is always busy. Makes me wonder what Liam has planned for our date.

"What are we doing here?" He can't be serious, can he? To find out, I joke with him. "Does our hot date involve bowling?"

I no sooner get the words out, when I'm halted with an iron grip around my waist. With my head back, I look at him to find his eyes sparkling, and him grinning rather mischievously. He's in a better mood and I admit it, so am I.

He smirks, "You'll see." Then he guides me to the door with his hand still around my waist.

Taking out a key from his pocket, he unlocks the door while I'm left to wonder what he has planned. I have to admit though, it's exciting to see him so animated and carefree. I don't see this side of him very often, and it's a damn shame.

"What the hell are you up to?" I chuckle, "and why do you have the keys?"

He stops what he's doing to look at me. "You ask a lot of questions, anyone ever tell you that?" I don't answer, I just flutter my pretty eyes at him.

With the door unlocked, he bends to kiss the tip of my nose. "Patience my dear."

"Alright," I agree, "lead the way."

This place is always busy, no matter what day of the week it is, so I'm busy looking around and wondering if someone is going to pop out of something somewhere.

"Brian, my buddy, owed me a favor."

He divulges this information with a sexy wink and explains that Brian is a family friend, going way back. Before going any further, Liam stops and locks the door behind him. With a twirl, he rubs his hands together like he's warming them up. I'm excited and curious.

"Get ready, sweetheart. We have a date to get started."

I can't deny that his enthusiasm is infectious. A grin a mile-wide spreads across my face.

Liam then flips a few buttons and fiddles with a box behind the counter, to make music play and neon lights shine on each of the twelve lanes. Oh wow, this place is pretty fantastic. I'm about to ask why we are here all alone for a second time, but then I recall his remark about his buddy owing him a favor and let it go. I'll take a date night. Bowling may have been the farthest thing from my mind, but oh well, we are alone and free from interruptions.

"Here's the thing." Liam suddenly holds up one finger. "We're not just bowling," he said with a trace of laughter in his voice.

"We're not?" I ask with an animated yet silky voice. He looks at me with a devilish grin that has my heart hammering in my chest. Something tells me things are going to get naughty before long, because the double meaning behind his gaze was obvious.

"Nope," he said with a quiet emphasis, adding, "you see, this is all about *us* tonight." As he slides up against me, he pulls me to his chest. He's a bit taller than me, so I have to crane my head back to see his face. He lowers his eyes, and sweetly says, "I want to see just how good of a bowler you are."

A knot rises in my throat. Really?

"You're serious?" I ask, maybe my guess of this being anything naughty is way off base.

"You bet, but here's the thing," he says with a rasp of excitement. And once again, I'm hopeful. "It's not a regular bowling game we are playing. This is strip bowling, baby."

"What?" At first I wasn't sure if I heard him right, but the smoldering fire in his eyes incited a fire in the pit my stomach.

"You heard me, sweetheart, start out fully clothed and whoever knocks down the fewest pins, has to lose an article of clothing."

My eyes bug out like he's lost his ever-loving mind, and again, I'm looking for anyone to step out and shout 'gotcha'.

"What if someone *sees* us?" I question the obvious, but I'd be lying if I said the idea wasn't tempting and enticing.

"That's why we're alone, sweetheart, no bystanders to appreciate your sexy ass." His playful and raspy voice echoes while his intense gaze kindles my body.

His suggestive game is super naughty and indecent, but I love it.

I give him a sensual smirk and the sparks I feel have me wanting to applaud the master he is for coming up with this completely crazy idea. "You planned this?" With nothing but a charming grin, I bow, "I have to say, I'm impressed."

With teeth grazing his lower lip, Liam settles with a deep masculine laugh. "Damn straight."

His intense gaze ignites an inferno between my legs and just like that we are in complete unison, connecting sensually. Liam lowers his eyes to land on my parted lips, stimulating the rapid thud of my pulse. His stare so galvanizing, I'm putty in his hands right now.

Totally charged and alive, the anticipation alone was unbearable. I'm lost in this exquisite passion only Liam can bring out in me.

I can definitely chalk this night up to a very unusual, but erotic date. My only wish is to be fully clothed, watching Liam try to bowl while he's buck ass naked. *Hashtag, what a date!*

I'm the first up, and knock down four pins. I celebrate, because I was worried as hell that I'd get a gutter ball, and be forced to strip first. Slowly Liam struts to reach for his ball, all the while intently locking his eyes on mine. As if it's an afterthought, he turns, letting the ball go like he's not even trying. I'm about to shout he's doing it on purpose to get out of his clothes faster but no, that's not what happened. To my amazement, he gets a freaking strike. What in the hell did I agree to? It then dawns on me, I now understand why he invented this naughty little game. He's an excellent bowler!

"What the hell?" I cry, "you didn't even try."

He chuckles and has the biggest shit eating grin on his face, then cocky as ever, stands with a finger pressed to his lips. "Strip, my lady. I say jeans come off first."

I stomp like a child and give another glace around the room making sure no one is around, but then figure 'screw it' and in a huff, discard my jeans. My next attempt is just as dreadful, and my ball ends up a gutter ball. *Dammit!* When Liam mentioned our date night, sexy undergarments came to mind. Only now, I'm regretting that decision of wearing dental floss, better known as my damn black thong. It's normal to bowl with your ass covered, but trying to bowl in only a thong is a bit mortifying. With his eyes glued to my butt cheeks, it does nothing for my confidence. It's a bit chilly bending over to try to line up the damn ball with the pins, and I can't do it without laughing because I know I look ridiculous.

My embarrassment, however, entertains Liam so much, he's whistling with cat calls. I do my best to ignore him while he's admiring my backside. When I release the ball, I close one eye and pray. I momentarily hold my breath while I watch the ball move in slow motion. The rolling ball stays in the center of the lane. With each advancing roll of the ball, I'm jumping up and down. My victory so close I can taste it.

Almost beside myself, I get ready to do a victory dance. Then, at the last minute, it veers to the left. No. No. No. Shit, it ever so slowly rolled into the gutter lane before it could knock down a single pin and Liam gives a standing ovation. All cocky and ever so arrogant, I turn to give him an angry stare. I'm making this way too easy for him, and it's pissing me off.

"This is going to be easier than I thought," he remarked with a sarcastic laugh. To add insult, he brushes his fingertips down his chest, saying, "You may be stark naked while I'm still fully clothed, sweetheart."

Okay, I'm not just pissed, I want revenge on his fucking sexy ass. "Shut the fuck up. Your turn." I use my finger to point toward the lane.

He offers a simple. "Yes, ma'am," before he chuckles and throws the ball. Damn asshat.

From that point on, it pretty can be summed up like this: I suck at bowling and Liam acts like a seasoned pro.

By the fifth frame I'm left in only my bra and thong, while he's shirtless in jeans. It's all about his pleasure and my torture as he seductively disposed of his socks first and then his shirt, leaving me a drooling, wet mess staring at his near nakedness. Just gazing at his chiseled abs is a win in my books. Finally, this game got a little bit more exciting.

Shit, I would have played this better if I had known his strategy all along. It appears he's taken measures by adding articles he defines as clothing. With my luck, he's wearing a few pairs of boxers under his jeans just to make sure I would be the first one naked.

I decide to torment his infuriating but lovely self by turning the tables on him. I take extra time to line up the ball and make sure to lean over longer than necessary. With my ass high and on display, I wiggle it back and forth a few times.

Turnabout is fair play. Plus, the longer I stay in this position, the sooner he'll be up on his feet charging my way. Those naughty thoughts have me all for skipping the rest of the game. It seems strip bowling is a complete turn on. Who knew? A smile forms when I hear him groaning, so I know my plan is working. Just goes to show who's the smarter one. Me.

Sure enough, the next thing I feel is the heat from his bare chest against my back. It's so tantalizing that he easily stokes a gentle but growing fire in my stomach. With my attempt to provoke him, it appears I've lit a fire inside him as well.

"Here," he whispers in my ear, "let me help you line up your next *shot*."

God help me, his words even turn me on.

With his right hand, he glides his fingers down my arm until he covers my hand that is holding the ball. Slowly, and at the same time, his left hand ghosts over my hip before he stretches his hand to cup the right side of my ass, his fingers biting into my bare flesh.

Three things happen simultaneously: I noisily swallow, my eyes roll to the back of my head, and my hand lets go of the ball. Thankfully, it doesn't hit either of our feet, neither of us have any desire to pick it up. Liam's hands snake around to my stomach and gently cup the curve each of my breasts. His touch stimulates my swollen nipples and that aching desire quickly surges to a yearning need. A burning desire to touch him takes over as I raise my arms and curl them behind me to grasp the curls at the back of his neck. Feverishly turned on, Liam sweeps me into his arms and carries us further into the back room that is dimly lit and has two pool tables sitting in the middle.

Not that I hate to play pool, but right now?

"Please tell me we are not playing *pool*," I say with an agonizing plea.

"Not a chance," he whispers low and gruff. "It's more private back here," raising his eyes, he admits, "no windows."

He gently places me on the edge of the pool table before stepping back and giving my nearly naked body a once over. His appreciation and approval of my matching bra and panty resonates with a lustful groan and mischievous grin. My half-lidded eyes drink in the sight of his pecs while I salivate. *Holy fuck he's seriously the hottest man I've ever seen.*

"Out of the thousands of times I've played here, I've never envisioned this happening." His handsome face suddenly sobers and with a troubling frown, his tongue darts between his lips. In that moment I want nothing more than to trace my tongue along his.

When he clears his throat, I snap out of the daydream. "I didn't think this though very well. How the hell did I think we'd make it back home before I needed to be between those thighs and deep inside of you?"

His words *deep inside of me* send a delightful shiver that floods my petal-soft folds. "It would be a shame to let this moment slip away," I moan, and in short order, that mischievous grin of his is once again on full display.

"Lay back, baby." He says while looking at me through hooded eyes.

Oh God, I guess he's not going to let this moment go after all and I'm more than ready.

Little by little, I lay back while slowly spreading my knees apart. Liam's eyes cascade down my body and linger on my most intimate area. I'm flushed but feel desirable all the same. Our eyes briefly connect before Liam responds by guiding my hips to the edge of the table. With a smile on his face, he lines his hard cock up against my drenched center. The sudden pressure against my clit feels so good, I can't help but moan. My vocal response entices his hands to delicately trace the insides of my thighs, inching higher. His thumbs reach the elastic of my panties, and I automatically arch my back off the table. I'm so desperate for relief, one swipe to my swollen clit and that's all it will take. With lust and passion in my mind, I partially close my eyes as my hands automatically guide to my mound, but are hesitant to move any further.

"Oh, baby."

I hear his words, but my eyes drift to a close, giving in to the erotic feel of his touch. His thumbs trace my warm, slick folds, and my hips rise in response, begging for my burst of pleasure. The closer he edges to my aching clit, the anticipation alone feels like pure bliss.

"God you're beautiful," he marvels. I slowly open my lusty eyes to see Liam wet his lower lip as his thumb presses down on my clit. I inhale sharply only to exhale a shuddering breath. My hips gyrate into his hands as waves of ecstasy shatter me like glass. His reaction is reminiscent of a man who has just witnessed the heights of pleasure for the first time. There is just no other way to describe it.

His hands moved to the back of my neck and he raises me enough to kiss me deeply. My arms dangle like noodles, still recovering while his wet lips feel so passionate, they take my breath away.

"So, beautiful," he utters again between kisses.

"So are you." I whisper as his plump lips claim mine again. "Please, I want you to fuck me right here on this table."

His eyes sparkle hearing me plea for him to take me. Both of us are needy and aching for the same thing. I'll have to hand it to him, having sex in a public place definitely heightens the moment. All this added excitement has his face lit up like the Fourth of July because soon I know fireworks will be going off.

"Easy going, or all out, baby? What do you want?"

Yes, now that's what I'm talking about.

"All out. Please, all out." I beg.

Abruptly, my panties are in yanked from my body and my bra is unclasped and tossed to the side. My nakedness draws out sexy groans from him and lips wetting in anticipation. I'm laid out completely bare and under a seductive spell from his icy blue stare. He lowers his head and kisses his way down my stomach, my eyes roll in the back of my head, aching for that first lick of my pussy before he worships my clit. The man has many talents.

"Liam." I pant.

His hands are under my ass, and are lifting my body off of the table as he feasts on me like a man who's been starved. He's not messing around. The grazing sharpness of his teeth pierce my bud and for the second time tonight, I shatter into a million pieces. I'm engulfed with heat that ripples under my skin when a strong rush of desire blazes my entire body. There is simply no disguising my body's reaction to him.

Shivers of delight suddenly consume me when his tongue probes my channel to welcome the warmth of my release. He then slowly lowers my body back to the table, and trails kisses up my stomach until his hard cock is pressing where I desperately ache for him. Two powerful orgasms, and I'm still yearning for more.

Our eyes intently lock as he whispers, "I need you."

Those words echo in my mind, leap in my heart, and make my legs tremble. As if something snaps within him, Liam tenses before he handles me firmly and controlling. All I can think is yes, dominant Liam is damn good. I'm suddenly yanked off the table and briskly flipped around. He flattened the front of my body flat against the table by the force of his hand. Two hands then grasp and arch my hips in a tight grip so he's lined up and probing my entrance. I didn't realize he has already lowered his jeans, but in one swift motion, he's powered himself all the way inside.

It's not gentle or sweet, it's thrusting and thrashing. Just like I asked for.

Each forward motion penetrates my cervix with such commanding precision that it makes the sharp sting of pain deliriously exquisite. His body slamming into mine releases a sweet tempo that is only drowned out by our increasing groans that get louder with each thrust. The sensation of his balls slapping against my soft flesh only enhance my arousal.

"Oh, Jesus! *Liam.*" I exclaim as my body clamps tightly around his impaling cock.

"Fuck," he growls, "clamp down on my dick again."

So I do.

Our bodies move in perfect rhythm. He's sliding back and forth, and every thrust of his hips is met with my tightly clenched walls. My skin is on fire rubbing against the fabric, but I'm not stopping him. To help ease the burn, I'm desperate to find something to hang onto without having him stop his assault, so I suspend my weight on my forearms. This position allows me to push myself backward with every forward thrust he gives.

Oh, my!

In chasing his climax, Liam urgently grabs my shoulders and lifts me so my back is against his chest. He's standing wide legged, fucking me into oblivion. Two more powerful thrusts and he launches his powerful release.

"Jesus. Fuck." He's winded and panting, but he still cradles our sweaty bodies together.

I'm huffing and puffing, I've never experienced anything remotely close to what happened here tonight.

"I'll never look at a pool table the same ever again, you have officially ruined me," I pant, "that and bowling with clothes on will seem kind of damn boring." My mind is completely blown because he's just literally rocked my world.

He gently lowers my body and turns me around to face him. His smile relaxes, but his eyes still sparkle like blue crystal. His eyes search my face seriously and as he moves the wet hair from my face to behind my ear, he yearns.

"Damn girl, I think I'm falling in love with you."

Ohmygod! Ohmygod!

I think I gasped, I'm not sure but my eyes instantly fill with tears. That's the last thing I expected out of his mouth and he's rendered me speechless. Sure, I've thought about it, what girl doesn't, but we've not discussed the L word. Damn, I'm content, blissful, and on cloud fucking nine right now. As he stares at me waiting for a response, all I see is a future with Liam. He's everything I've ever wanted and yet, so much more. For the first time, I'm not scared by allowing myself to love him. Hell, I want him to love me and he just told me he does.

I squeal and jump up to lock my legs around him as Liam quickly tucks both hands under my butt. I squirm while grinning from ear to ear.

"That's okay," I bashfully whisper while looking into his icy blue irises. After planting a sweet kiss to his lips, I admit. "I think I'm already there."

He seems surprised, but then a sweet smile graces his face.

"Really?" He teases with a raised brow.

Oh hell yes, I sure am.

"Without a doubt."

Chapter Eleven

"Love Letters"

Kara

Things were finally good. No, scratch that, things have been great since Liam informed me that he's falling in love with me. Even better, was the news that Tiffany's condition is improving and she's getting stronger. Liam keeps me updated on her condition because I, for obvious reasons, happily stay away from the hospital. She's still pregnant and is currently only speaking to Liam. Whatever. As long as he keeps me in the loop, I'll hold off any judgment or argument. Izzy and Brax, are not taking the news all that well, and I can't blame them.

Today, Izzy and I are baking cookies in her newly remodeled kitchen while the boys are hard at work at Ryles Custom Shop. The change in Liam has been amazing since he started working alongside his best bud. He gets up in a good mood and comes home from a long day the same way. It's such a joy seeing him in such great spirits. What a welcome change. I hear from Izzy that Brax's mood has lifted as well since Liam joined the shop.

With Liam happy and working, life's beginning to resemble some normalcy. Not that we know what that feels like, but all the same, we're happy. I spent the last few weeks taking some of the best shots I've ever had the pleasure of taking. I have a new appreciation for the Pacific Northwest with its great mixture of different landscapes. From the sheer beauty of mountains, to the many hidden waterfalls, to the unlimited number of hiking trails. Take your pick, all of my photos are so realistic, you could almost reach out and touch them.

I am more than excited to sort them out and see what I've got. Now if there were only more time in the day, I'd be able to take on more assignments to collect a few more paychecks. Liam tells me not to worry, but working is good for my mind not to mention my bank account. When it comes down to it, I need to feel like I contribute to our household and not live off him. It's just the way I am.

Today, I'm rewarding myself with a much-needed goof-off day with my favorite family in the world. Izzy seems quiet and not her usual bubbly self, but with her busy life, I'm sure she's just tired with the kids. But I'm still concerned.

"I'm worried about you." I sneak that part into our conversation about baby Asher. Izzy hates it when I worry over her because she feels like most of her life was spent with me worrying over her and for good reason. Things are different now, thank God!

She blissfully ignores my comment, refusing to allow herself to be anything other than supermom. I know her ploy all too well, because I'm the only person who can see through her. This time I clear my throat so she has to acknowledge me. I'm that worried.

"Are you okay?"

"Me?" she mocks as her eyes widen in shock. I maintain my direct stare until she rolls her eyes in return. The spatula she's using to stir the cookie dough is tight in her hand and she has stopped mixing. Not able to ignore me any longer, she exhales and raises an eyebrow as to blow off my question as being ridiculous.

"Yeah, of course," she exclaims. "Never better."

I don't buy it and my face shows it.

"Okay, fine. I'm just tired but I'm really happy for the first time. Things are crazy busy, but I wouldn't change a thing."

She ends her thought with tears in her eyes, but I know those tears are full of love. She wipes at a stray tear and clears her throat before lowering her chin. "Now, fess up about your naked night of bowling," she heckles.

I cough and smack a hand over my heart. I had not expected her to ask me that. What she doesn't know is I intended to fill her in on the juicy details tonight. The flush of my cheeks is not out of embarrassment, but the fact she's heard about it, and not from me.

"How the hell do you know about that? Wait," I gasp, "he didn't!" I'm not asking a question, it's more of an astonished exclamation. Liam's actions only confirm he's just as chatty as chick. Fuck he may be even worse when it comes to him and Brax. Those boys, just can't stop themselves.

Note to self, nothing is sacred when it comes to Liam and Brax.

"Ah...he sure did," she squeals. "And, I have to say, Brax even blushed when he told me. Maybe more like jealous, I'm betting." She quinces her nose and shakes her head, giggling.

"Oh," I mock, "how embarrassing." Great, how can I look Brax in the eye the next time I see him without blushing?

Izzy happily hummed holding back her laughter while I sat and shook my damn head watching her bite her lip. I stick my tongue out at her and that did it, she's bent over laughing hysterically.

"Sure must have been some wild night, I just hope he didn't tell Brian about it."

Shit, I never considered that, but now I'm worried about facing any of Liam's friends now.

Izzy raises her eyes from the mixing bowl after adding a cup of chocolate chips and tries to comfort me with a shoulder shrug and half smile. Shit, talk about anxiety. I sure hope my loose-lipped boyfriend would not include Brian in our activities that night.

Screw it, I need chocolate. Now. Whenever I'm stressed, I eat it by the pound. Good for me, it so happens to be available. I grab a handful of the chocolate delight and pop them into my mouth.

Even the melting morsels can't stop my worrisome mind from imaging every one eventually knowing about our sex filled night at the bowling alley. His friend's place of business. After I pop a few more morsels in my mouth, a disturbing thought crosses my mind.

"Oh, shit!"

In full on panic mode, I freeze. My hand slams on the table, all I can think is the word YouTube.

Izzy jumps and yelps, "What the hell?"

I can't help it, I've got alarming visions floating around in my mind and I'm freaking out. "Brian doesn't have cameras inside the building, does he?" With one eye partially closed, I cringe to wait for her answer. Please no, please no, please no.

"Ha!" her voice rises, "that would be priceless. Totally priceless."

Yeah, she thinks it's funny because it's not her.

"What if it was you and Brax, would it be funny then?" I dare ask, but she just looks at me like I can't be serious.

She wipes her hand on her towel and mocks me by saying, "We would not be crazy enough to get our freak on in a bowling alley. We'll leave it to you two freaks."

"Yeah, so funny," I tease. "When did you become such a comedian?"

"Excuse me, wasn't it you two who had a make-out session in the ladies' room at the bar?"

Well damn, she has me there. But, I can play innocent on both counts.

"Both times," I amusingly point out, "it was Liam's fault. What can I say, he can't resist me."

She just gives me the look.

"Auntie Kara," Eve asks with a tug on my arm. "Play dollies with Willow and me." Her sweet voice and angelic face make her impossible to deny. Liam and I spoil both of them like crazy. I wrap my arm around her shoulder and pull her into a big embrace. She giggles and is so darn cute, I playfully tug on one of her pigtails.

"How about," I ask like I'm mulling it over, "we make some cookies first, then play dolls." Her eyes light up, and mine follow. Her eagerness is damn infectious.

"Okay." She excitedly agrees already shoving up her sleeves.

Baby Asher's intercom suddenly lights up, and boy oh boy, he's not a happy camper. His bellowing is so thunderous, I was afraid something was wrong until Izzy assured me he was okay. Apparently, this was typical behavior for a hungry Asher. Izzy's hands are in the cookie dough, so I jump up to get the noisy little bugger.

"Hey, little man," I say quietly hoping my voice will soothe his wailing, and it did. His cries soften while he's searching for my voice. "What's got you so grumpy? Are you hungry?" His little eyes widen when he sees me and his tiny legs kick a mile a minute. I'd say he's happy because when I pick him up, he squeals with delight. Every time I see him, I'm taken aback, this kid is a Brax mini-me. Without a doubt he is the cutest baby in the world.

He's so active, he's bouncing in my arms as we make our way back to the kitchen. Willow and Eve are pressing the dough on the cookie sheet, and Izzy confirms just how remarkable of a mother she truly is. She's as patient as a saint. When one of the girls gets upset the other one usually follows, but Izzy never loses her cool. She easily turns their frowns into smiles. Right there she gives me hope that I'll be as great of a mom as she is someday. With her it feels effortless, and seeing her this happy after all she's been through brings tears to my eyes.

"Hey mama," I motion to Izzy, "little man is starving."

"Of course he is," she chuckles, "he's just like his daddy. As soon as he wakes up, he wants the boob."

"You did not just say that," I say with a shake of my head because it's not a visual I needed, but laugh all the same.

"Why?" she replies with a playful nudge against my shoulder, "it's the truth."

After she dries her hands, she comes and takes a very excited Asher from my arms. He's squealing and kicking and before she can sit and get her shirt unbuttoned, he has his mouth open. There is no messing around when it comes to feeding time with this one. Just another reason to admire her. I have no clue how she does it all.

My attention is back to the task at hand, I have two sets of eyes watching me. "Alright girls, auntie Kara gets to take over so mommy can feed your brother."

Both girls screech and before you know it, we had four cookie sheets ready for the oven. Clean up took twice as long since the girls chipped in with nothing but good intentions to try and help me, but I never complained. It was fun.

As soon as the kitchen was cleaned and the cookies were cooling, I was off to play dolls with the girls. In the middle of the room we had the Barbie swimming pool, the Corvette Convertible, and the RV all set up. They had dozens of pretty Barbie's, but I got Ken shoved at me. Sure, now I know why they wanted me to play with them.

"Are boys allowed to this party, girls?" I ask, because who wants to play Ken when they have every other Barbie known to man all laid out on the floor? Both of the girls laugh like I just said the funniest thing ever and at the same time, a deep snicker comes from the kitchen.

"Not a chance and tell Ken to take a hike if he knows what's good for him." I hear Brax's deep voice before he appears in the doorway.

"Party pooper." Izzy remarks while burping little Asher in the rocking chair.

"No boys are allowed near Eve or Willow until they are thirty." Brax has a cookie in one hand and a beer in the other but his face is dead serious, making his threat absolutely hilarious.

Good Lord, this family is so awesome. I don't know what I'd do without them. His declaration has me envisioning Brax as his two girls get to dating age. All I can imagine is Brax holding a gun while standing at the door to meet whichever boy is daring enough to ask his baby girls out on a date.

"Oh yeah," I giggle, "let's see how that works out." With a sideways glance, I point to his son who is ignoring all of us while he's nursing. "Little Asher's going to keep busy that's for sure."

"Asher will love having older sisters, won't ya, buddy?" Brax coos at his son before tipping his chin at Liam, who has now settled next to me on the floor.

After taking a sip of his beer, he chuckles, "Can you imagine coming home every night to his sisters' friends all the time? Lucky little man, think of the sleepovers." With Liam's his two cents, he and Brax clink the top of their beers, applauding the fact baby Asher has two older sisters to introduce him to their friends.

The jokes continue and I can sense their jealousy with little Asher's good fortune. Boy will be boys. Izzy and I roll our eyes, smirking as both men continue to boast. Izzy's implying her son will be an angel and will not cause her any gray hairs. Just to burst both of their bubbles, I point out what they are failing to see. One day sweet baby Asher will be a teenage boy with raging hormones.

"You laugh now, but just wait until you find Asher missing from his bed when the sleepovers start happening." I'm fanning my face to help stop the rolling tears of my laughter. Based on the stunned expression on Brax's face, what's funnier is how pale his face is right now.

"Thank you, Kara, for ruining my happy moment. Now I got that idea in the back of my mind, and he's only in diapers." He may be mortified but Izzy and Liam both find it hilarious.

"You're most welcome, big guy." I let him know that's what I'm here for, a dose of reality. With the concerned look on his face, I bet tonight when he's in bed he'll be cursing because he will have three teenagers pretty close in age. I bet those sleepovers will be more than supervised now.

On that note, Izzy takes Asher to get his bath ready, and the girls soon follow. I start an easy dinner so Izzy doesn't have to worry about it, she deserves a break.

I settle on taco's, it's fast and easy. I'm just starting to brown the beef when Liam and Brax join me in the kitchen, they are discussing things about the shop when Liam acts like he just remembered something by raising his finger.

"Babe, I almost forgot, you got a letter in the mail today. I grabbed it when we stopped by the house in case it was important."

He looks at the letter again before holding it out to me. "The postmark says Chicago."

"Oh." I take it from him after I wipe my hands. "Maybe it's from my parents or one of the magazines."

I tear it open and quickly realize it's not from either. The cut out letters glued to the page are familiar, though. I've not received one of these since I left Chicago. None of the previous letters were ever threatening, just an infatuation. For some reason, this one is different. A frightful chill has me quivering when my eyes scan the letter.

Kara,
Tick-Tock. Tick-Tock.
The clock starts.
A flattened tire.
A smashed window.
Your lips a ravishing red.
In a message next to your bed.
I'm close…getting closer.
Watching you…wanting you.
The demon is gone, he can't protect you.
Counting down the days
until I have you.

I'm not sure how long I stared at the letter, or how many times I've read it. I've written this freak off as some silly infatuation since everything he left was harmless. He never left me shit like this! This shit right here? This shit has me fucking terrified!"

"What the fuck?" A fearful whisper leaves my lips.

Liam looks over my shoulder, then snatches the letter from my hands.

"What the fuck does it mean the demon is gone, he can't protect you?"

"No way. No fucking way!" I yell. I can't believe this is happening right now. Things have been going so well…now this!

"The charm…" Liam and I say at the same time.

I explain in detail about the charms to a stunned Brax, followed by Izzy, who joined us again. That led Liam to explaining all that has been happening to me. It baffles me that this last letter mentions *the demon*. The demon has to be Dominic.

The heated conversations going on around me seem like whispers. I pay little attention to them because I'm focused on the fact that this letter found me here. Not only is it bothersome, it's fucking terrifying! Izzy keeps going over the letter.

"Hey Izzy Girl, did you ever hear Dominic get mad or mention anyone in regards to some guy having an obsession with Kara?" Liam's smart enough to think of that possibility.

"No," her voice softens, "I'm sorry."

Great, now she looks like she's going to cry. "It's not your fault, sweetie, you have nothing to be sorry for." I hate that she even has to remember a single day of her life back in Chicago.

"What now?" I say with my shoulders lowered, discouraged.

Brax offers an idea. "I'd say a trip to Chicago, but where do we start to look?"

"Her apartment," Liam sounds off. "Let's find all the letters from this guy and see if we can find something. Anything."

"Sounds like a plan," Brax adds with the nod of his beer bottle as I sit here and listen to them make plans for me without checking with me first.

"I can't go anywhere until I get my shots edited and sent off, I promised a few clients they would have them in the next few days."

"That should work," Brax says while looking over at Izzy for her go ahead. "In the meantime, I'll get things worked out at the shop."

Oh my God, he can't be serious. "You're not leaving Izzy and the kids," I shriek, "what if this sicko is out there? It's obvious he knows where we live, so you can't leave your family unprotected." No way in hell do I want to feel responsible if anything happened. Not that I think it will, but still that's not a good idea until we know more. This new letter is frightening.

"Damn it," Brax exclaims, "you're right."

I understand his need to help us figure this out, but they need to protect their family. Liam and I are capable of doing this alone.

MY EYES ACHE FROM STARING at my computer, I'm going over all of the shots I've taken over the last two weeks. Page after page, they seem to go on forever. I had no idea I'd taken so many. It just goes to show you, I get carried away when I'm in the zone.

In the mix are the fun shots I had taken with Izzy and the kids, they had asked me to get some great family shots for them. While I was at it, I took some shots for our house too. I counted three hundred and twenty-five pictures altogether.

The best and most efficient way for me to organize them is to make a few separate files. One for Izzy, and the others for contracts I need to fulfill. This keeps me organized and it also makes my job easier when it comes to the edits. With a quick drag of the mouse, I can move each shot to its specific folder so one by one, I drag and drop. I'm so deep in the zone, I don't hear Liam sneak up on me.

He rests his chin on the top of my head looking at the computer. "Hey babe, working hard?"

"You know it." I answer without stopping.

He bends and kisses the top of my head while glancing at my photos. A few ooh's and ahh's ring in my ear. "Oh wow, those shots of the kids are amazing. Damn, you're really good."

Of course he walks up when I have shots of Izzy and the kids on the screen. I just explained how far behind I am, and he catches *these* shots on my screen instead of beautiful landscapes. I'm not sure why I worry, because he would never say anything.

"Thanks babe," I say as I bend my head back so I can see his beautiful eyes. "Sit with me. We can scroll through these, and then I can show you some of my shots for the magazines." I know Liam enjoys seeing my professional work, especially when I show him my actual photos in the magazine. His face beams with pride every time I do. It's a pretty cool feeling I have to agree.

As he sits next to me, he points out one of my favorites. "Eve and Willow are so protective of Asher, look at their faces in that one?"

I zone in the one he's talking about and immediately I remember taking that photo. "Oh, I remember that. Izzy ran over this guy's foot with the stroller and when he bent down to look at Asher, the girl's flocked, protecting their little brother. They went so far as to say, "stranger danger" like they were scolding Izzy when she started up a conversation with this complete stranger. It was so funny, I had to snap a picture."

"That's some funny shit," he chuckles and I agree it was definitely that.

"It was."

We continue to scroll through photo after photo when I realize the number of places we've visited lately. Most of the time it was an excuse to get Izzy out of the house, since I usually take her everywhere I go. All it took was a phone call and an hour for her to get the kids ready. Brax is happy she is out of the house, and I enjoy the company. The kids are such a joy to be around.

Each and every shot is just as precious as the one before it. Something suddenly catches my eye so I scroll back to the beginning. First, we had stopped at the Yakima Farmer's Market, then the Petting Zoo, the Aquarium, Pike's Market, and finally the park. That wasn't all in one day, just where we went this last week. I click my mouse and simultaneously I click forward and back. Photo after photo a familiar pattern emerges. What in the hell? What I see is so chilling, I freeze with my fingers on the keyboard. At first I feel like I'm seeing things so before I say a word, I double check again with a forward click of the mouse. My finger taps the mouse faster and faster.

"Babe, what's wrong?" Liam asks as he angles his head to get a better view of what I'm looking at. I'm scanning them so fast because it doesn't take me long to spot out the obvious.

"Look very carefully at these pictures and tell me what you see." I want confirmation I'm not crazy here.

Liam moves closer to the computer and uses the mouse to scroll through the pictures. It's apparent he doesn't see the same thing I do at first, although I'm not sure how he can see a thing with how fast he's scrolling through them. Maybe I've imagined it, but I have no patience so I'm about to point it out to him when he releases the mouse and curses.

"What the fuck?" He asks as he looks at me with wild eyes. "Do you have any idea who the hell he is?"

"No idea," I grumble, and quickly look back at the screen, "never seen him before that day Izzy ran over his foot at the park."

"He's in all of these photos," he frankly says pointing them out individually. One by one, he points to the same guy in all the photos. Each one he's in the back drop, but clearly present. "That means he was everywhere you were," he points out and I shiver at that chilling thought. "I have no clue how you got him in these shots. No matter how fucked up that is, I'm glad you did. Now we have a photo of whoever he is, but now what?" he grumbles while taping the guys' face on the monitor.

I just wonder. "Do you think he's the guy sending the letters?"

"Very well could be," he sighs, "I need to get my hands on those letters from your apartment in Chicago. The more information we have, the better because our situation just got a hell of a lot more serious."

Chapter Twelve

"Home Sweet Home"

Kara

One would think walking into the apartment I've called home for so long would be comforting, but it's not. An eerie calmness blankets the dark walls and it's chilling to look at my ransacked apartment. Visions of what happened the last time I was here still haunt me. It's pretty much in the same shape as I left it, my belongings still scattered throughout the apartment. So much has happened since my last night here that it feels like a lifetime ago.

So many emotions hit me all at once. Mostly good ones, but also not so pleasant one's either. I cover my mouth and hiccup with a soft cry when I spot a photo on the floor of Izzy at graduation. Tears sting my eyes, but this time, they are tears of remembering the better days we once shared. Although, it's impossible not to automatically think of my brother as well. Her past is tied to him, so it's hard not to think of her and *not* think of him. My guilt rears its ugly head and cripples me to the point my knees buckle. All the destruction he's caused in such a short period of time is a hard pill to swallow.

"Babe." Liam tries his best to console me, but understands me enough to let me have this moment.

I realize an emotional breakdown is not going to help me any, so I do what I can to concentrate on other things. For starters, I must remember to thank my dad and my landlord for fixing my front door for me. When I up and left my apartment, I phoned my dad to ask for help with my broken front door. He said without hesitation he would handle it. I'm sure he had a surprise when he saw the condition of my place, but he has yet to mention it to me.

Liam hasn't said much since we've walked into this disaster zone. Most likely, he's either shocked, or is not sure what to say.

The last time I was in this room, my brother was still alive and physically threatening me. The danger I felt from him may be gone, but now we have a new worry, a new threat. At least the chaos of my latest letter has actually eased my three-fifteen a.m. screaming episodes I call nightmares. I'm not sure if it's a great trade off, but Liam and I are resting a little better.

In its place, we spend every waking moment devoted to figuring out who the hell the mystery guy is in the pictures. Brax went ballistic seeing this guy within an arm's reach of his family. It's an unsettling feeling for us all.

"Babe, where are the letters?" Liam asks, I'm sure he's not thrilled seeing my apartment in disarray knowing what happened to me, so better than to focus on that, he'd rather concentrate on the letters. He's made it his mission to see if a possible link between the letters and the mystery man in the photos can be made.

"My nightstand," I say pointing my finger down the hall, "next to my bed. I put them all in there."

Moments later, he returns with a stack of letters in his hand. We sit on the couch and start to read them, beginning with the one on top. An ominous and uncomfortable queasiness takes hold of me as Liam opens the first letter. I've spent so much energy fearing my brother, when all along I had some guy watching me. Just putting that in perspective, is scary as hell.

"Let's hope we find something in these that will help." He scans the first letter whispering every word and as I listen to him reciting every word, I feel incredibly stupid for not taking them as seriously as I should have.

One by one, we read through them. Each time I feel myself tensing. Each letter contains words of admiration, vows of appreciation, and promises of what could be.

"Like I said, they really are tame and non-threatening." Don't ask me why I'm trying to justify and downplay their seriousness because Liam won't buy a word of it.

"I don't know,' he starts with, "there is something fucking creepy about a guy who continues to send the same shit to you." Clearly frustrated, he drops the letter in his lap. Disappointment is all I can see as he rubs his eyes groaning, "I can't believe you didn't report this shit?"

He looks angry and it forces me to further explain. Really, he just needs to understand how I felt at that time.

I tuck a strand of hair behind my ear and do my best to explain. "They never actually scared me, I guess. Listening to you read them just now has me second guessing myself, though."

I rationalize my behavior by convincing myself that I had more pressing matters at the time. For instance, my sadistic brother. Letter boy here seemed harmless enough, so I put them in a drawer and I never thought about them after that. I don't know why I kept them, but reading them now, I see that Liam is right. I should have reported them.

After spending a good amount of time pouring over the letters, we weren't any closer to finding out who mystery guy is. Honestly, we didn't see much of anything other than a sick obsession over me. Damn weirdo.

My empty stomach grumbles, letting us know it's late and time for dinner. Earlier in the day, we made plans to go to my parents for dinner because it's time to have a long overdue talk with them. Plus, I get to introduce Liam. Like a nervous school girl, I'm excited for them to meet him. For once, I feel like we're a normal couple. Imagine that. With the irrational and crazy way our lives have been, this feels nice. The natural progression of things. Meet a nice guy, go on a few dates, and then have him meet the parents. Yep, totally normal.

You never know, maybe talking with my parents about all of this will help me forgive myself. I'm not exactly sure who it will help more, me or them. With the way they had taken the news of Dominic's death, this may be easier than I imagine. They had no real relationship with him. I purposely left out the fact that their son died by my hand. That's more about me, and honestly, I'm not sure they need that information. It would only cause more heartache knowing it was me.

As we pull into the driveway, I park our rental car and give my childhood home a once over. Liam can sense my uneasiness and takes my hand in his.

"You okay?"

I wish I could say yes, but being here I struggle with my emotions.

"Yeah," my voice is shaky as childhood memories flood my mind. "I'm just not sure what I'm going to say to them. How far I'll go to explain things."

"I'm here for you, just go with what you're comfortable with," he sighs and brings my hand to his lips to kiss it. "No pressure, babe."

Okay.

Hand in hand, we make our way to the door when it opens. There in the doorway stand both of my parents with tears glistening in their eyes. Great, now there is no stopping the flood of tears that fall from my eyes. Call it regret, but how the hell do I tell my parents I killed their son? They immediately pull me into their loving arms and in that moment, it's as if they already know what I've done. I could confess all of it right now and for some strange reason I feel that they would completely understand, but I simply can't form those words. It's one thing to free myself from the guilt by telling them, but to actually speak the words out loud is proving too monumental. The fact is, we've all suffered enough and it's about time we live our lives without fear.

"Oh sweetheart, I'm so glad your home. It's time to put things behind us and find a way to move on," my mom says as her voice quivers. "We can't bring your brother back and even if things were different, it wouldn't matter. That's my one true regret, you know. But the failures I feel as a parent are not your failures. Now that you're home, we can find you a new place to live. I've been looking for you…"

I hold my hand up to slow her down because she's talking a mile a damn minute and my head is swimming.

"Take a breath, mom."

She seems over the top, and I've not even considered living here again. Liam has changed that for me. I step back and pull him into a sideways hug.

"Mom, Dad. This is Liam. Liam, these are my parents, Dave and Evelyn Santos."

"Hi, son." My dad welcomes him with a firm handshake. Liam is way taller and broader so my dad calling him son is pretty funny, but not as hilarious as seeing my mother's reaction to him. She's fucking smitten.

"Hello, Liam. It's nice to meet you," she wisps and blushes red, "boy, you are a handsome one, aren't you?"

"Mother." I gawk!

We make our way inside and gather in the kitchen. The delicious smell has my stomach growling in anticipation. My mother is a fantastic cook and an excellent host. She has the table set with piping hot food. It's been way too long since I've tasted one of her many specialties. Tonight it appears it's fried chicken, mashed potatoes and corn. All of it steaming and piping hot.

I, for one, am going to relax for a change and enjoy this meal with peace of mind. It's so nice to sit and share a meal with my parents. Liam so far, seems to be overjoyed to enjoy a meal in peace. This is a new for us. With my plate full, oh damn, the first taste of the chicken tastes so good and moist I moan with every additional bite. The extra butter in the mashed potatoes and the sweetness of the corn, everything tastes incredible. Why is that food tastes so much better when you're not the one cooking it? Whatever the reason, I lick the excess drizzle of melted butter from my lip as I glance over at Liam. He's stopped eating and is currently staring at me with a raised brow.

"What?" I garble with a mouth full of goodness.

He leans over to reach my ear, and whispers, "Keep making those noises and I'm going to have to excuse myself to the bathroom, if you know what I mean."

I cover my mouth, and burst out laughing. Thankfully, my parents are having a conversation of their own. They do, however, pause and watch me, giggling.

"So, what are you going to do now?" my dad asks then inquires, "when are you finally coming home?" My dad has never been to good at being direct, so I know he's fishing to find out how serious things are with Liam. I lower my fork to my plate before I answer.

"Well," I reply with a slight shoulder shrug, "I'm not entirely sure, I haven't made any real plans to be honest." I keep my voice light, not chancing a look at Liam. I'm not sure what he's thinking, so to avoid feeling disappointed, I stare at the corn on my plate.

"Excuse me?" Liam's tone startles me and I can't help but look at him. His surprised look softens to a most alluring smile as he makes his feelings known. "I have a few plans, and that means you have plans too, sweetheart." He assures me with cheeky smile.

I'm so relieved I'm speechless as he reaches over he takes my hand in his. My cheeks flush and I'm about break into a happy dance. I had hoped he would say something to that effect, so when he does, it only confirms how he feels about me and our future.

Liam cuts to the chase once dinner is finished. We came to settle in the front room, and no one is saying a thing. It's like a waiting game to see who will talk first. With the small talk and pleasantries out of the way, it's as if a dark cloud has settled over our heads. I'm not exactly sure where or what our conversation will take us, so it's a little unnerving.

"Dave," Liam directs his attention to my dad and asks, "do you know anything about anyone sending any letters to Kara?"

An uneasy and worrisome expression mars my dad's face as he asks, "What kind of letters, son?"

"If you ask me, I'd say eerie. Not a sound-minded individual, either. If you were to ask Kara, she may say harmless and not give it another thought." Ouch.

My dad leans forward with his forearms on his thighs as he thinks about Liam's comments. It's then he looks up and narrows his eyes as if he's irritated and angry.

"What the hell now? Does this have to do with your brother, as well?" he accuses before lifting his palms. "Do we have him to thank for this? Jesus Christ."

"David, calm yourself." My mother pats dad's leg and turns her attention to me. "Darling, tell me more about these letters."

From start to finish, we discuss them all. From their blank expressions it's pretty obvious they know nothing. I suspected as much, but Liam's not leaving any stone unturned. He wants this shit to end, as all of us do.

"You know," my dad says, "you may want to ride out to Dominic's house. We've been in touch with his attorney and the shocking thing is, his house was paid for and, I know you are not going to like this but, he left it in your name."

"WHAT?" I exclaim.

"I have no idea, it was a total surprise to us too. We have a copy of his will for you, I imagine you want to clean it out while thinking about what you're going to do with it." My dad could have just spoken to me in French, because I feel like I don't have a clue what he is saying. Leave me his house, are they out of their minds!

"I don't want IT. Why the hell would he leave it to me?" I conclude in utter disbelief.

"That's not all." My dad holds up his hands and is looking at me like I better prepare myself.

How can it get any worse? Lord, save me now.

"He left you a letter, it was delivered to us to give to you. In case anything happened to him, we were to get it to you." Again, he's speaking a language I just don't understand. It's not the words, I don't understand the reasoning behind them.

"I don't want *it*." Call it guilt, shame, or anger. It doesn't matter, my shaking body can't distinguish between them right now.

"Yes you do sweetheart, I'll read it if you want, but it may be a smart thing to do." Liam's calming touch and voice reach out and soothe me.

"Whatever," I throw my hands up, "you read it first, and then burn it for all I care. That..." and my tears begin to fall. "That bastard made my life hell, made Izzy's life hell. Why do I want a damn thing from HIM? If he only knew then what I would do to him..." My words are halted by my uncontrolled sobs.

"Hey, don't do this to yourself," Liam whispers in my ear.

LIAM

I REACH OUT AND TAKE the letter from her dad, I have to admit I'm shocked as hell. I never saw this one coming. My gut told me she'd never want to read the damn thing, but if there is any chance that it could have some information pertaining to her stalker, I want to read it. As far as finding out she inherited all of his shit, that one is hard harder to stomach. From all I've gathered, they weren't necessarily close. She feared him and he seemed to go out of his way to make her life hell. Why leave his house to her? Fuck if I know.

Thankfully, we decided to stay the night here at her parents instead of going back to her apartment. To watch her fall apart and flip her shit earlier tonight was hard to see, and I had a hard time calming her back down. It was one thing to for her to learn she had inherited his house but quite another to find out that he left *her* a letter. I fear it may do more harm than good, that's why I want to read it with her. I hope I'm doing the right thing.

Her parents had a hard time in trying to calm her as well, she wanted to shut us all out. Her parents decided it was better to have us read the letter in private, so now she's lying down beside me covering her eyes. I'm holding this letter in my hands and feeling anxious because I'm not sure what I'm about to read.

"Whenever you're ready, read it. We might as well get this over with," I hear her say from under the arm that is still covering her face.

I clear my throat as I unfold the letter. Before I say the first word, I glance at her out of the corner of my eye.

Kara,

There is only one reason for you to be reading this letter, and probably not something either of us wanted. Please humor me and read the letter in full. I realize I'm the last person you want to hear from, but with my death, I hope you will think differently. That idea might seem backwards, but it's just the way it is.

I have to tell you, life is funny in many ways. For instance, it turned me into things I never imagined being. I remember many fond times we had when we were young. I imagine you'd call it the best times of our lives, and I'd tend to agree. Less complicated for sure but the problem is, that wasn't who I truly was. Over the years, life trained the monster that lived within myself. Circumstances and choices I made were solely for the purpose of feeding that part of me, the part that lived in the darkest of places.

It was then, that my soul felt free and the brother you once knew ceased to live. Kara, I'm not a good person and I won't apologize for it. But I do feel something when it comes to you. I'm not one to say I'm sorry for anything I do, but the little boy you once loved regrets ever letting you down. I regret the many times I've put fear in your eyes, and hatred in your heart. I'm only admitting this because if you are reading this, I'm not around to rebuff it.

I am the evil bastard you think I am but always remember, good and evil cannot exist without one another. They keep the balance, just like you and I. Hence, the angel and the demon references from so long ago. I strongly believe this.

That is why I'm leaving you all of my things. You'll figure out what to do with it. After all, mother and father never understood me. You are simply my other being no matter how loud you try to reject that idea.

I need you to understand one important thing. I may be the bastard you hate but remember this, there are far worse people out there. And even though I'm a son of a bitch, I have always watched out for you. Believe me, your feelings are justified but even so, I've made sure to protect you when you didn't even know it. I happily live with the monster that rages inside, but that does not mean anyone else can mess with my sister.

I've made enemies, you'd be smart to remember that. Also keep in mind, evil lurks even in the friendliest of faces. I've never masked mine, but that does not mean others won't. Watch out for yourself, watch out for Izzy, and protect Willow at all costs. I never did because my inner rage wouldn't allow it. My demons demanded blood so there was no room for compassion. With me in hell, I hope you find a bit of peace. I've made my peace a long time ago.

Dominic

Neither of us say a word for some time. That was a hell of a lot to process and I imagine both of us are drawing our own conclusions with his final words.

"How am I supposed to respond to that?" her voice hitches as she shakes her hand in front of her. "How dare he talk to me like that when he had *years* to explain how he really felt. That bastard...how dare he make me feel sorry for him *now*!"

She hits the bed with her two fists and I blow the air from my cheeks wishing like hell I knew how to respond. Hell, I'd even crack a joke to alleviate the hurt I see in her face but I've got nothing. It guts me to see her like this, like she's trying to justify what she had done to her heart. A heart who is focused on remembering her brother as a little boy, not the monster. Son-of-a-bitch. I swear one way or another, I'll make it better for her so she never has to feel this way again. Somehow I'll make it better for her.

I notice she's staring at the ceiling, not moving a damn muscle. She's inside her head and that's not a good thing.

"Babe." I reach for her, but she's too fast.

Like lightning, she reaches for the letter and storms out the door. I'm looking around the room not entirely sure what she's doing, but to give her the space she needs, I stay put.

For now, anyway.

It's fairly quiet so I can hear her speaking softly with her parents. I rub my hand down my face when my phone beeps. Great, someone has left a message.

"Liam...uh it's me, Tiff. Look, I'm not sure what to say here. I'm sorry seems like a good place to start. I want to let you know I'm leaving town, like we discussed before my damn accident. There are too many bad memories around here. Too much has been said and done, for me to try to fix everything. I see that now, and I'm sorry it took me so long to finally figure this shit out. I'm well enough to travel, so I'm leaving tonight and won't be around to say goodbye to you in person. Believe it or not, daddy is coming with me. He wants to help me with the baby and all. Yeah, it's a real shocker. Anyway...take care, big brother. After everything that has happened over the years, just know that I care about you. I'll see you around sometime. Bye."

From reading Kara's letter to my sister's message, the only thing I feel is relief. I think. I don't wish any ill will on my sister, but having her around will do nothing but cause issues. Brax, Izzy and little Eve don't need that shit. I'm torn though, I want to call her back to say goodbye, but it's probably a better idea to just let her go. The triangle I call my life is pretty fucked up because the one thing I know without a doubt is, Eve is better off with Izzy raising her. I love my niece and will make sure she's happy and that will only happen if my sister is not around to interfere. Breaks my heart but it's the truth, Tiffany shattered that relationship. The screwed up part comes with the news of Tiffany's baby. With Dominic said to be the father, that creates a shit storm in itself. I know how much Kara adores her niece, Willow. But this kid brings way too many complicated feelings with it. Enough to make a man drink.

I know, Kara would never want a relationship with that baby because she would never want to hurt Izzy and Willow. She said so herself on more than one occasion. With Dominic and Tiffany as its parents, that poor kid has a double whammy against it from the start.

Tiffany's better off leaving to raise it without any of us around. Maybe that way, the poor kid has a chance. As for Willow and Eve, it's hard to say what they would want. They are too young to make that decision.

My head is pounding just thinking about it. Jesus!

"*Mom*...I don't know how I'm supposed to feel. I hated him. I wanted him dead for so long, and now he leaves this letter that breaks my fucking heart. He lived with two different personalities and we did nothing to help him." I hear Kara say to her mother.

"Darling, don't do this to yourself. Dominic lived the way he wanted, you have to accept that and move on. Torturing yourself over it won't help you. Let it go." Her mother replies.

Shit. I knew it when I read those fucking words, that bastard found a way to continue to torture his sister. The guilt that plagued her for so long was finally starting to ease, but now I'm not sure what the fuck to expect. I can't sit still anymore because the need to comfort my girl is just too strong. So without a second thought, I rush to her.

I hold Kara in my arms as she cries her heart out. I'm doing my best to make sure she knows she has no reason to feel guilty. She never did and she never will again if I can help it. Not anymore, not ever again.

"How can you say that, Liam? He was sick...you read it yourself." Her trembling lip crushes me a little bit more.

"Jesus, Kara," I have to remind her. "He tortured people. He turned Izzy Girl's life into a fucking prison in the middle of Hell. And what about Willow? His own daughter. Don't defend that sick bastard now because deep down, you now I'm right."

Kara's mother tries to reason with her distraught daughter. "Kara, sweetheart, Liam's right. Dominic was smart and even if he was as sick as you're saying, which I highly doubt, he wouldn't have let you help him anyway. You know what I'm saying is true. Don't let him do this to you. Not now, when you've come so far."

She's out of my arms and pacing the room, cursing everything and everyone. The magnitude of her meltdown is from months of hiding her feelings. She's just now unleashing them.

Every *what if* Kara throws out, has me denying them with a head shake. Once she works them out on her own, she'll come to the right conclusion. And that is her brother wouldn't have accepted help even if he thought he had a problem.

At the moment, she's acting on the raw emotions that are at war with her heart. One second she's shouting and the next, she's covering her mouth, holding back a wretched sob. All of the anger, pain, helplessness and all of her other emotions are erupting like a volcano right now. And to make matters worse, every time I attempt to get close to her so I can hold her, she holds her hand up and kindly tells me to back off. She tells me she needs to work through it on her own. I might hate it and disagree, but Kara needs to deal with this once and for all. The sooner the better.

At this point her mother is crying and still trying to console her daughter, who keeps dodging any attempt of physical contact. Dave, her father, is stoic, sitting in the chair with his legs apart and his hands in his lap. I get the faint impression that Kara takes after her dad. Both of them are vocal and animated, but right now it's as if he's waiting for Kara to calm herself so he can approach her.

Sure enough, Kara stops shouting and falls to her knees in a fit of sobs. Just as I start to go to her, her father beats me to it. He's on the floor next to his daughter, holding her and whispering in her ear.

I'm not sure what he's saying, but I won't interrupt him either, they need this closure.

Once and for all.

Chapter Thirteen

"Unexpected Visitor"

Kara

"Are you sure you want to be here?" Liam clicks the car off, turning his head to ask one last time.

"Ummm... not really, but here we are." I stare at the large house that holds no emotional attachment whatsoever. Looking into his eyes I confess, "There is no way I want this house. I'm just going to sell it." I still don't know why he left it to me, but I'm done trying to figure out why.

"You could leave it to your parents," Liam points out and as I mull over that idea, I look at him and nod my head. Leave it to him to find a solution. I wonder what my parents will think of that idea? I make a mental note to talk with them *after* I take a look inside.

"Since we're here, I want to look around and see if I can find anything that will help me understand my brother better. For much of his life, he's been a stranger. Someone I've detested for a long time."

"For good reason," he mumbles before his eyes narrow to give me *the look*. A look that says 'Dominic was insane'.

I can't argue that, but his letter has been eating away at me all the same. He's left me with the real possibility that he was ill and that pulls on my sensitive side. It makes me question that maybe I didn't do enough to see that and did nothing to help him. Was it my place or would he of even let me doesn't matter, my caring side aches all the same. To say I've been a mess, is an understatement.

With my many mood swings in the last twenty-four hours, Liam's been understanding and supportive even though he sees things differently. He's been so awesome because it's hard for me to compartmentalize all of my conflicting emotions. When I was young, I loved my brother. Then as the years went on, I began to despise and loathe him. Then ultimately, I ended up shooting him. But that fucking letter torments me. Maybe I never knew him at all. After all he's done, how can I justify having an ounce of compassion for him?

Now we're standing outside his house. *A house of horrors* is what Izzy and I called it. The fact that the house of horrors now belongs to me is horrifying, but I swallow those negative thoughts as we walk in the door.

All the lights are off except the one inside the door. I take in the dark wood of the foyer. Dark mahogany floors match the dark color trim. A tall staircase off to the side leads upstairs and winds around in a steep curve. Dark walls and darker wall hangings eerily remind me of my brother, dark.

That thought sends a chilling sensation down my body. It has nothing to do with the temperature because it's pretty warm in here. That's odd because no one has been here. No one that I know of anyway.

"Do you think someone's been living here?" I ask.

"Guess we'll find out," Liam mumbles while looking around. He looks over his shoulder and places his hand on my shoulder.

"Hey," he shouts, "*any fuckers* around here?"

I flinch, yelping, "Oh, shit. You scared me." I didn't expect him to shout like that so I press my hand against my chest since I know my heart just leaped out of it.

He flatly points out. "Figured I might as well ask."

Every step I take in this house is unsettling and the dark clouds that gather outside create the eeriest feeling. I twist my fingers together nervously, curling and uncurling them as my breathing becomes shallow. I half anticipate Dominic to step around the corner and start yelling at me.

Both Liam and I wander around the living room, and so far, it's just a dark room. I'm not even sure what the hell we're looking for.

Liam makes a few observations, though.

"Jesus, did anyone ever live here?" He mocks, "Or was it used to take snapshots for magazines?" When his eyes look over at me, I just return a chuckle.

Liam continues to picks up a few knick-knacks and gives them a once over before putting them back down with a shake of his head. He's right about Dominic's house being in order. Nothing was ever out of place, and the house never looked lived in. Dominic was the perfect definition of a neat freak. I, on the other hand, not so much. Not that I'm complaining because being the opposite of my brother feels like a good thing. It gives me hope that I'll never be anything like him.

"Oh, man," Liam sighs, "this flat screen would look great in our living room, babe." Liam's eyes light up and due to the sheer size of it, I can't blame him. It's top of the line and would make watching TV even better. I'd say it's a seventy-inch flat screen. But the idea of having something of Dominic's just doesn't feel right.

"Seriously, think about watching the Blackhawk games on this?" He teases.

Liam plays dirty and uses the one thing he knew would get my attention.

"Ohhh, you knew you'd get me with that, didn't you?" I call him out.

He just smirks, grinning from ear to ear. "Just stating the facts, sweetheart."

"Let's keep looking around." I try to keep him on the task at hand.

An hour later we still haven't found any clues to help us figure out who is sending the letters, or help me understand my brother better, but Liam has all but furnished our house. Every room held a possible item we could take home with us. I love it when he says our house instead of his or mine. My issue is taking some of these things home and to see them every day. It just feels strange.

I pause with a lingering thought, "Maybe I should ask Izzy if she wants anything from here."

Liam snaps his head in my direction so fast, I'm surprised he didn't get whiplash. "Fucking hell, Kara! Do you honestly think Brax will allow *anything* from this house in *their* home?"

"Not that," I say while raising my hands to wave off his notion. "I mean anything she may have left here, that she may want."

"Still, I'd say hell no."

He may think that, but I want to make sure, so I open my purse to reach for my phone and dial her number. I had to hush a grumbling Liam a few times who did not hold back his feelings on me calling her.

"Hey Izzy," I sigh, hoping I'm not making a mistake by calling her. "Listen, I'm at the house. You may think I'm crazy, but do have anything left here that you want? I could grab it while I'm here."

A few things become apparent. I should have just listened to Liam on this one. After she had ranted on for a few agonizing minutes, she encouraged me to burn the house to the ground. Okay, I can't blame her. At least, I asked just in case.

We slowly ended upstairs in the study. The fact Dominic spent most of his time in this particular room only increased my anxiety to be in here. It's hard to put into words what I'm feeling. For some reason he left me all of this and I'm so overwhelmed I stumble to his overly large desk chair and sit down. I rest my trembling hands on the smooth wood. Liam is looking at me oddly, but really my mind is just wondering what kind of business took place in this room? I may have mentioned I wanted to know my brother better, but his seedy lifestyle is something I'd rather not. I'm intimidated just sitting in his chair, let alone thinking about some guy sitting across from the angry glare of Dominic. Yikes.

On that thought I opened a few drawers and close them until the one at the bottom doesn't open. It's locked. Luckily for me, I have a man who can pick any lock when given a challenge.

"Liam, can you help me out?"

In no time at all, Liam had that drawer opened. With the sheer ease it had taken him, I joke he'd missed his calling as a burglar. He even chuckled a few times when he noticed my appreciative grin. With the drawer open, I had no idea what we may find.

"Papers... and a few pictures." I say as I toss the items on the desk one by one. Finally, I take the whole pile and toss it on the desk as Liam took a seat across from me.

"There, now we can both look through them."

"Smart girl," Liam says as he starts to thumb through a few of them.

Most of the papers look like invoices and different agreements of some kind. Some are signed and some are marked confidential. Liam looks at me as I shrug my shoulder, both of us not sure what we are looking at.

I drop a letter I had in my hand, gasping, "What the hell do we do with all of this stuff?" I wasn't only talking about the letters, either.

"Good question. Any papers like these, we box up, you never know who may be wanting them now that Dominic's dead. Since we're not sure what they are, it might be a good idea to stash them away safely until we can sit and study them more."

My Liam, always the sensible and clever one. I'm glad he's thinking, because left up to me, I may have just started a bonfire to watch it all go up in flames.

"Yet another reason why you are so amazing, because I was going to say burn them all. You know, I never gave this much thought, but do you think I'm at risk with him gone? That someone may want to hurt me, knowing he's not around to stop it." God, no matter how insane that sounds it could be a real possibility.

"I wouldn't think so and I sure as hell hope not, but it's definitely a possibility we need to think about." After a second or so, Liam lifts his chin as he holds up one of the letters between his fingers. "These papers of his could be an insurance policy. You never know, we could use these as a bargaining tool."

Not exactly a warm thought, but smart, nonetheless. I find a suitable box we can use and when I reach the pile of pictures, I look over them more carefully as I toss them in the box. Liam must notice something, because he moves so fast that I gasp. His eyes widen as his finger jabs at one of the photos on the desk.

"Anyone look familiar to you?" He questions.

I pick up the photo because at first glance nothing seems familiar. As I take a closer look, I see three gentlemen talking in a park. One of them is my brother, and the guy next to him looks a lot like *Max*. Max who worked for Dominic when he needed to tend to Izzy after my brother went sadistic on her. Frightful memories send shivers down my spine. Those are times I'd rather fucking forget.

"Are you talking about Max?"

"Well, him too, but the other guy is who I was talking about?" he clarifies.

It's hard to see his face clearly since the picture is out of focus. I make an off—cuff joke that the photographer sucked.

"They can't all be as great as you, babe. The question is why take this photo? It's obvious they were being watched."

"Wait...I've seen him. Oh, shit! This is the guy from my pictures. This is the *guy*. What the hell?" I'm about to say the dots are coming together when I damn near climb out of my skin.

A loud crashing noise comes from the hall, causing us both to jump and turn our heads to the doorway.

"What the fuck was that?" I panic, but keep my voice a whisper.

Liam is up on his feet and almost out the door when he turns back and says, "Stay put!"

Oh, to hell with that. As soon as Liam jets around the corner, I jump up and follow, grabbing the fireplace poker along the way. Fuck that, I'm not about to let him go by himself. I make my way to Liam and stay very close behind him. When I grab a hold of his shirt, he turns and looks at me, obviously upset that I followed him. But that's just too damn bad. He frowns and instantly lowers his eyes to see me holding the poker.

His brow furrows. "What are you going to do with that?" He asks in a tense voice.

"Kick ass if I have to," I reply with my chest out. He must find humor in my ability to deliver an ass kicking, because he's biting back a laugh.

He lowers his head and jokes, "Just don't swing at me, babe."

"Ha-ha," I whisper in his ear. We've not heard any other noises but we are still trying to find the source of that crash. We think it came from the kitchen.

Liam peeks around the corner, and I duck down to look around Liam's midsection while I hang onto his belt loop. The man we see sitting at the kitchen table with his back to us seems to be staring out the window, looking at nothing in particular. We glance at one another and shrug our shoulders. Not sure what our next move will be, Liam decides to speak.

"Why don't you stand up, very slowly, and turn around." Liam commands the man.

The man instantly tenses and with his hands up, he stands and slowly turns to face us. I'm gripping my weapon, ready to swing with my legs in a wide stance. I also put some distance between Liam and me so I can use both of my hands to hold the poker in a striking motion. Once our eyes instantly lock with his, a familiar face emerges.

"Max?" We shout at the same time.

"Not who I was expecting," Liam exclaims, "but glad to see a friendly face nonetheless."

All three of us exhale with an audible sigh of relief. I'm not sure who's more in shock right now.

"What the hell are you doing here?" Liam's tone is weary but cautious.

Max doesn't answer Liam's question right away because of the item clutched tightly in my hands preoccupies him. He raises his eyes to mine when a slow smirk parts his lips.

"Kara, you can drop the weapon now." He says, then directs his attention to Liam. "I have to say, I'm surprised to see both of you here, of all places."

"Max," I don't bother to answer him. Instead, I turn it around and ask, "why are you here?" As soon as I ask, he winces and squints his eyes. I can almost hear the wheels turning in his head, and the fact that he has to think about his answer is what troubles me the most.

With an audible breath, he hesitates before speaking. "How long have you been here?" Not only did he not answer my question, he cleverly turned it around to focus on me. Max then looks from Liam to me longer than necessary.

"Not long," I answer while assessing his particular behavior. He is usually so easy going and approachable, but tonight he appears anxious. Maybe he's just as shocked to see us as we are to see him.

I don't know, maybe it's being in this house that is making us all a bit edgy. I drop my scrutinizing look at Max to explain, "I'm looking around the house I newly inherited."

When I said that, his jaw about hit the damn floor.

"You are kidding?" He boasts with a genuine look of shock.

"Nope, I'm afraid not," I say. Now that I've told him my reason, I want to know his. "I'll ask you again Max, why are *you* here?"

"Kara." He starts to say then sets his jaw. I have no idea why he's all tense once again, but his fists are in a tight grip and he seems annoyed by my question.

Liam holds out his arm to make sure I stay put as we both try to figure out why Max is acting so odd. We wait as Max throws his head back to stare at the ceiling, he sighs a few times only to lower his gaze back to mine.

"Kara, you need to get the hell out of here and get back to Washington. It's not safe here for you right now."

Both Liam and I look at each other with matching expressions. What the hell is he talking about?

Chapter Fourteen

"Friend or Foe"

Liam

"Do you have a headache?" Kara stares back at me with her pain-filled eyes half closed. "What gave it away?" She moans.

I grin at her sarcasm, but she's been rubbing her temples since we left Dominic's house.

"Babe," I reach over to rub my hand on her knee. "We will get it figured out."

I try my best to reassure her with words. It's my job to ease her worries, not add to them. I'll cover up my concerns and worry for the both of us. After tonight, I'm not sure what to think. Max showing up at the same time we did does not feel like a coincidence. That's troubling. The only time he seemed genuine was to warn Kara about being here in Chicago. None of what he said or acted made much sense.

Kara studies me, like she's reading my thoughts. It's not like her to let things go, so I'm sure she'll have things to say.

"It's just strange to run into Max at that house. I wonder if he's hiding something."

I want to say I'm not wondering if he is, I know he is, but I'll keep that to myself.

She appears deep in thought, before she continues, "He says he's worried, but he never gave us anything specific as to why. What was even more weird was how quickly he left after receiving that phone call."

"Yeah, I can't argue with that."

She's right. Max's brief explanation that he's been watching the fallout from Dominic's death could be true. When he said some of Dominic's associates felt there could be incriminating evidence at his house poses a serious problem. That was his answer as to why he was at the house to begin with. He said if anyone came to the house snooping around, he'd know their identity. He's right about that, having names would be the first step in finding out if anyone has any plans in harming Kara. It may sound legit to me, but none of it felt genuine. Call me suspicious but until I know otherwise, I'll keep my guard up and my eye on him. If his reasons are legit, I'll owe him for looking out for Kara.

"You know what?" I decide, "I'm putting my faith in what he said." I take her hand and kiss it. "If it keeps you safe, that's all I need to know." Hopefully this will help ease her worries if she knows I'm not obsessing over Max with his odd behavior. I still have my lingering doubts, so he better be telling me the fucking truth.

"But who?" she sighs, "he has to have *some* idea, Liam."

And that right there is the exact reason I'm not fully buying into his story. Max was reluctant to give us a name.

She begins to tap her finger, it's what she does whenever she's nervous. I'm about to call her out on it when she points at me with her index finger.

"Why is it dangerous for me here?"

That question, he did have an explanation for.

"I think what he meant by that was you actually being in that house. If someone did show up looking for something and found you walking around, it could be extremely dangerous."

"Yeah, I guess." She says, finally giving it a rest.

I imagine it's hard for her to think of Max with nothing but good feelings. He's always been there for Izzy and now, all of a sudden, here we're questioning his motives.

"We'll get more information tomorrow but for tonight, let's forget it." I suggest.

You can bet your ass I'll get more answers tomorrow. Besides, I'm sure we were all a bit shocked running into each other, so my bullshit detector may be a little off. Plus, I have no reason to question his motives, after all he did to help us plan Izzy's rescue a few months back.

He was our inside man and did one hell of a job in executing his hair-brained idea to fake Izzy's death so we could get her away from Dominic. It worked like a fucking charm, too. He even stayed longer than necessary so he could monitor her recovery. Not even an overbearing Brax could make him leave. Talk about loyalty and dedication.

After he left, he returned a short time later with Willow in his arms, shocking us all! The bastard, Dominic, had taken her away from Izzy to 'teach her a lesson' and 'keep her in line'.

With all of that, it's hard to think of Max as anything other than a friend. Izzy sees him as more of a savior. Max has proven his loyalty time and time again.

I have this nagging thought that's plaguing me though, and it has everything to do with Dominic's letter to Kara. More specifically the line that said even the friendliest faces mask their real intentions. That doesn't sit well with me, it came across as something really dark and sinister. And since Dominic is the prince of darkness, he would know better than anyone.

I try to push that from my mind and focus on her. "For the rest of the night, let's just concentrate on us."

When I said that, her eyes lit up. When she looks at me like that, I can't deny the power she has over me. My suggestion was meant to take her mind off of our earlier conversation, but the naughty and playful grin she's giving me has me wanting to get her naked. Now.

"We never have enough alone time," she declares.

Her eyes spark a desire deep down in my stomach. "That's for sure, babe. I need to check in with Brax. Then, I'm all yours."

"I'll shower first," She squeals, before jetting from the bed. I'm about to complain about how comfy I was with her in my arms.

She swings her hips suggestively, and that earns her a slap on that pretty ass of hers. My hand stings, but she squeals with delight, and skips to the shower. I'm more than thrilled that we decided to come back to her apartment tonight instead of staying with her parents. I wanted her all to myself and not have to worry about her parents sleeping in the next room. Her parents are cool and all, but I don't think they'd be too happy if they heard us having sex.

The thought of being deep inside my girl has my dick rock hard and standing at attention.

"Shit." I can't help but groan. Even though my dick is aching for my girl, it has to wait so I can make this call first. Lucky for me he answers on the second ring, and like usual, it's his typical one-word greeting.

"Yo."

Just hearing his voice puts me in a good mood. "Hey, buddy, how's it going?"

"Damn, Liam, about fucking time you called. And before you ask, there's nothing going on around here that I can't handle. So, what's new on your end?"

With the way his voice is muffled, he must be holding his hand over the mouthpiece. Listening to his kids in the background has me chuckling. Some things never change, and that's a good thing. Anytime I'm on the phone with him, his kids seem to get louder all of a sudden. We both agree they plan it that way and while I find it humorous, he doesn't. That makes it even funnier.

I can hear him telling the girls that he can't hear Uncle Liam on the other end of the phone. He can hardly get a word in edgewise before one or both of the girls say something back. I'm surprised by his level of patience and how happy the girls get when they find out he's talking to me. That makes my heart skip a beat for sure. Someday, if things work out, I hope to have that with Kara. For now, I'll continue to be Uncle Liam, and spoil his kids.

Things suddenly quiet on his end, then I hear a door closing.

"I give up, I'm on the porch." He says, then mumbles a few words under his breath.

Once I stop laughing, we spend a few minutes talking about my events from earlier. He listens without saying much, until I mention Max.

"Wait a minute," he says, sounding surprised, "Max is there?"

"Yeah, he showed up at that fucker's house. I'm still struggling with the fact her brother left it to her. I just can't wrap my head around that one." When I found a quiet moment, I texted Brax about Dominic's letter to Kara, and he could not believe it either.

"Liam," Brax warns, "something's not right."

His worrisome tone is alarming but I keep my mouth shut, listening to what he has to say. Nothing can ever be fucking easy and straightforward anymore. I curse while he pauses, giving me a minute to vent.

"He showed up here a few days ago."

As soon as he says that, I sit up straight as a board.

"Why the hell did he show up there?" Before he can answer that question, I hit him with another, asking "What did he want?"

Brax tried to respond before I interrupted him, so he waited until he knew I had finished.

"That's the thing. Nothing. He said he just wanted to touch base and see how we're doing considering the circumstances. He was upset that Kara wasn't here, though. I told him you and Kara went back to Chicago. Did he mention that to you?"

"No, he never said a word."

I don't even know what to think. Why would he not tell us about his visit to Brax? I'm more than a little bothered about that. He had plenty of time to say, 'hey, by the way, I stopped in Washington to see you.'

"Well damn, this just gets weirder by the day." My frustrations simmer and settle like a knot in my gut. "He better feel like talking tomorrow, or I will beat it out him."

I sure hope this is all a fucking oversight on his part because Kara doesn't need to add his bullshit on top of everything else she's dealing with.

"Listen, just be careful." He spoke with an almost lecturing tone that felt a bit awkward because usually, it was me saying that to him.

"Yeah," I chuckle, "I hear you, man."

There is no mistaking Brax's sincerity or the seriousness of his words when he said. "Call me if you need me, got it?" his tone of voice said it all.

Not that I think we will need it, I assure him. "I will. Take care yourself."

I'm more than confident we can straighten out this mess with Max tomorrow, we just need to sit down and talk it out. Brax needs to stay put to take care of the shop and watch out for his family because the mystery man in the photos could still be in Washington for all we know.

Before I get a chance to hang up, Brax asks, "Why didn't you say anything to me?"

I don't need to ask him what he meant to know what he's talking about. I don't even need to ask who told him, because there's only one person who would. I know it was my father. Dumbass. Why the hell that man can't keep his big fucking mouth shut, I'll never know.

The fact that we are having this conversation instead of when I'm back home, pisses me off. Now I have to do my best to diffuse any mess my father has stirred up. "She's gone, Brax, that's all that matters." Frustrated, I take a few deep breaths before saying, "I never actually talked to her, she left me a message telling me she and dear old father were leaving town for good. That's all I know, otherwise, I would have told you."

He's sighs and lets out a curse word or two. It's got to be tough, and I feel for him. No matter how he feels about Tiffany, she will always be Eve's birth mother. Having Izzy raising her as her own is the best thing that could have ever happened to Eve. Eve's smart, it's not that she's forgotten about her mother, she just appreciates Izzy taking her place. For the first time in her life, she has someone who acts like a mother should. It tears me up, but I'm also grateful to see my niece so happy.

"It's for the best," he struggles to say because his voice masks the disappointment I know he keeps bottled up.

"You know..." he pauses as his voice cracks.

I can feel the struggle, and it's tearing me up inside. For some reason, he still feels the need to justify his feelings to me. I may be Tiffany's brother, but he has to know how happy I am that they have Izzy.

He settles for a moment, then states what I already know.

"I hate how this all played out, but I can't take any chances with Tiff hurting my family ever again. I never imagined things turning out this way, but Eve's really happy with the family we've created. She has a sister and now a baby brother. Life's the best it's ever been, brother."

"I know that, Brax. You've got one hell of a family and I could not be happier."

"Appreciate that."

I may not need to hear it, but I think he needed to get that off his chest. We both take a second to pause until I'm sidetracked.

Kara strolls in, wrapped in a fluffy white towel. Her hair is dripping wet and I immediately lower my chin leaving my mouth open wide. She not only looks delicious, she smells divine. Sweet peaches and if I'm not mistaken...coconut. Damn. My mind's off to the races, stripping her out of that towel and imagining all the ways I'm going to violate her body. But first, I have to do something.

"I'll call you later." I tell Brax. After I press end, I throw my phone over my shoulder. I must be grinning like an idiot because she raises an eyebrow and returns her own sexy grin. She's not only tempting me, she's torturing me. That little vixen bites her lower lip while lowering her eyes to my cock. The fact she's wet and draped in only a towel, my cock is straining to get free.

Hell yeah, my girl and I are thinking the same naughty things, I'm sure of it.

"Can I ask you a question?" She suddenly asks, but my mind and eyes are staring at her long legs that I imagine wrapped around my waist.

My train of thought is totally stuck on anything sexual. I anticipate hearing a naughty question come from her lips so I lick my lips in preparation and nod my head. Kara has a dirty mind and right now, dirtier the better.

She then throws me for a loop. Out of left field, she asks, "Why didn't you ever tell Brax that Tiffany left town?"

Okay, so that put the brakes on my raging hard on. Of all of the things she could have asked me, that sure as hell wasn't it. She must have heard part of my conversation, and I imagine she's disappointed in me as well. The thing is, one mention of my sister and my raging hard on is deflating quickly.

Argh! I raise my head to the ceiling and ramble, "Well, that was a mood killer. Damn woman!"

I fake cry and sound wounded by lying back, my naughty little game for the moment is ruined. She literally deflated the massive erection I had going on, and I'm quickly trying to figure out how to get it back.

"Okay, let's have a quick chat so we can get back to me having an erection and you coming, hard."

Sounds like a plan to me, just need Kara to agree. She's looking at me sheepishly, so I take her hand and have her sit next to me on the bed. She's rubbing her hands together like she's nervous about something. To calm her down, I take her hand in mine.

I position myself so we are facing one another, but I do not let go of her hand. I'm not good at explaining this serious shit, but she needs to know just how serious I am. I hold her hand firmly, saying, "I have not spoken to my sister directly, she left the message I told you about and that's it. And we have been so preoccupied, I felt it was best to wait and fill Brax in once we got home."

She hesitates for a second then gives me a one-sided smile. "Okay, I was just wondering," she says.

I'm about to kick myself, because instead of taking her in my arms and taking her as she sits beside me in nothing but a towel smelling so fucking good, I'm going to continue our chat. I need my head examined, but I can't get what Brax mentioned about Max out of it. My conscience is bothering me and I feel the need to share it with her.

"Unfortunately," I hesitate, "I found out some information you need to hear."

She looks nervous, and grips her towel more firmly to keep it in place which is the opposite of what I want. I want her to drop it, so I need this conversation to be over in a hurry. I'm trying to get my mind out of the gutter, but it's damn hard. I can feel myself getting hard just looking at her.

Shit. Okay, I need to concentrate on what Brax mentioned about, Max.

"Brax mentioned that our little house crasher was in Washington a few days ago."

She gasps! "Uh-uh, no way."

I nod my head. "He also mentioned that Max was not the least bit thrilled that you were not around. It seems he was hoping to see *you*." I gauge her reaction to that bit of news, but all she does is look at me like I'm crazy. I'm starting to get bothered with the idea he cares a bit too much when it comes to Kara. Based on her reaction just now, it's clear she has no feelings toward him. Which is good...for him. I'd have to gut him for sure then.

"Why didn't Max mention it to us earlier?" she says baffled just like I am. "You would think he'd say, 'oh by the way, I was just in Washington'. Wouldn't you?"

"Great question. One I plan on having him answer tomorrow." I say to ease her mind.

She keeps her eyes on me, but nods in agreement. She doesn't say anything and the minute she shifts her eyes to the floor, I know her mind is racing. I'm not going to let her spend a moment longer all caught up in her head so I distract her.

"Okay," I say with a grin, "now that we got that out of the way...time to get you naked."

Without having to ask her twice, my girl jumps up, faces me and makes a dance out of dropping her white towel. As it pools on the floor, she wiggles her pink painted toes. My eyes slowly travel up her long legs to settle on the swell of her breasts. I swear I've died and gone to heaven because all I see is an angel standing before me. Her smile doesn't reach her eyes, and that's not happening. Not right now.

"Babe, why the sad face? I've got to tell you, standing naked in front of me with a gloomy face is doing a number on my dick." I point downward as her face lightens some, but suddenly her expression changes from a lost expression to needy.

"Please make me forget all of this craziness." Her soft plea cuts straight to my heart and dick. I go to speak, but she leans closer, resting against my knees. "When it's just us, those are the times I feel the best." She is so sincere, so sweet, my eyes threaten to tear up. To make it even harder on me, she's not done being sweet. "You make me feel beautiful, you help me forget and I need that, Liam. I need it now, more than ever."

I'm speechless because I need her just as badly. I reach out and yank her naked body on top of mine and just so she knows I heard her loud and clear, I'll spend the whole night making her forget everything but me.

By the time I'm done, she'll feel like the most beautiful woman in the world because in my eyes, she is. It's an easy task because she is beautiful on the inside and out. Not only is she smart and witty, she'd do anything for the people she cares for. She's already proved that.

"Baby," I whisper as my lips caress her earlobe. To find the perfect angle so her plump lips line up with mine, I run my fingers through her wet hair. With her lips wet and inviting, I trace my tongue along her lower lip to savor her flavorful taste. Always needing more when it comes to her, I draw her lip into my mouth. Her surprised moan spurs me on and I'm eagerly but gently sucking on her moist and warm lip. I know she likes when I do this because her body reacts with tremors and whimpers.

"You are the most amazing woman," I softy say against her lips.

I'm holding back the wisps of hair that fan her face as she's looking at me. As I take in her beauty, her eyes search my face and I know in this moment, I have to open my heart to this beautiful woman. I don't think I've ever been more honest as I am right now. "Your love and compassion are limitless. The day I met you was the best day of my life. And always remember, I'll be the lion that stands behind his lioness. I'll always have your back."

The waterworks open up and her sensual hazel eyes glow with every tear that drops. I'm so caught up in her beauty, I close my eyes and rest my forehead against hers. I can feel every hot breath from her as it fans my face. Her sudden kiss has me responding with my own. The saltiness of her tears flood my senses as I wrap my arms around her.

"Make love to me," she whimpers.

"For you," I sigh with so much love behind the word, "*always.*"

With one last kiss, she sits up and straddles my hips before she wiggles down my thighs. I'm about to ask her what she's doing when she reaches to unzip my jeans. Oh, this won't do. I don't want her to move from where she was, so I lift her hips and guide her sweet ass forward. With her pussy in full view, I'm salivating to have a taste and her eyes widen when she realizes what I have in mind.

Every inch she moves higher up on my chest, she blushes a brighter shade of pink. It's times like these with her that I enjoy the most. To see her turned on and eager to come. I'm ready to devour her.

"Now, that's what I call pretty in pink." My girl is turned on and dripping wet, but I want to take my time, tease her, and really get her worked up.

Kara softly sighs as I continually blow cool breaths against her wet heat while my hands are busy in a lust-arousing exploration of her soft flesh. With my hands as her guide, she rocks her hips in perfect rhythm circling my mouth. Her moans and involuntary tremors are all the convincing I need that she's enjoying this as much as I am. The first sweep of my tongue starts at her warm center and doesn't stop until it lavishes her clit.

She lets out an aching moan. "Oh, yes, baby that's it."

Her soft thighs trap my head and her warmth right where I want it, against my mouth. The current lovemaking of my tongue channeling her core is so fucking hot, I'm about to explode. With her straddling my chest, I struggle with my jeans in an attempt to release my raging hard on. When I raise my hips to help my fumbling hands with the button on my jeans, her body shifts forward. Two things happen in that moment, I got my button undone but with Kara's body suddenly pushed forward, she's riding my face. I'm so hypnotized with her sudden aggressiveness, it's as if she's on an all-out mission get herself off, with my mouth of course. Oh, fuck, this is just too good.

I part the silkiness of her folds while I penetrate her center with my tongue. She's so soft and *wet*. Her taste so unique, I swear I'll never get enough of its exotic essence. I lose my damn mind and feast on her like a caveman. Every lick from my tongue is deliberate, passionate and intense. When I feel like she's on the brink, I pierce her clit with my teeth before I suck her nub in my mouth. It's meant to heighten her pleasure, but I'll be damned, it increases mine as well. I find myself rotating my hips in rhythm, evenly timed with the strokes of my tongue working her over.

"Ahhh. Oh, Liam." She sighs in an all pleasing moment.

That's right baby!

I'm so turned on it's hard to say which one of us is experiencing more pleasure, me, or her. Her groans intensify as I deepen my worship in her channel. Waves of pleasure push her closer to the brink as she clinches and releases a surrendering moan. With her arms back her nails pierce my skin. The pain her nails cause spills over in such a rush, I clench firmly on her clit. The brisk sensation on her bundle of nerves sends her over the edge this time.

She arches her spine and throws her head back withering in sheer pleasure. I get the best view possible in this position. It's like every move she makes as she falls apart is in 3D. She slides her hands across her stomach when the tremors of her climax overtake her. I reach up to brush my thumbs over the swollen buds of her breasts. She's so sensitive that my gentle massage intensifies her orgasm. I notice a bead of sweat roll down between her breasts, I catch it with my finger only to tease her dusty pink nipple. My other hand slides down her taut stomach to her hips. It's then the first wave of her liquid honey trickles from her glistening heat and coats my tongue. Jesus!

We moan in unison when I feel her hand snake behind her as she unzips my jeans. She gives me a wicked grin and in no time her hand fists my cock squeezing it in a firm hold. The feeling of her warm hand squeezing me helps my aching cock. I don't remember a time my cock has ever needed a release this bad.

I continue to worship her sweet body, but am quick to help lower my jeans the best I can with limited coordination. With her still on top of my chest, I'm only able to lower them a few inches, but apparently that's all she needs. She rests back and aggressively, pumps my cock.

"Fuck. Yeah, baby." I groan as my teeth anchor in my lower lip.

"Does that feel good?" She teases with a tight squeeze of my cock.

"Mmmm."

Damn, between her grunting moans and tight fisted grip, I'm lifting my hips, chasing my damn release. She's the only aphrodisiac I'll ever need. Ever. I'm about out of my damn mind, when I feel her legs start to quiver, I know she's climbing. My tongue has been busy building her again, only I hope this time we can come together. I'd rather be inside of her but, goddamn, this just feels too good to stop and change positions.

My face glistens with her essence as I maintain my hip thrust with each pump of her hand. I linger one hand to her lower back to keep her from sliding and soon my other hand drifts lower to cup my aching balls. Kara looks down and smirks when her fingers tease the tip of my dick and I'll be damned it feels so good, I tighten the hold around my balls. I start to feel the familiar tightening of my orgasm and I'm on the verge, so I increase my suction on her clit. She sighs as a hot tide of passion rages through both of us. The intensity of how fucking great this feels can only be described as nirvana. Kara responds by tightening her legs around my head.

Moaning.

Groaning.

Whimpering.

She comes so hard this time she flows like lava and I shoot my come so far, it passed my chest and found its way to her back. I chuckle impressed with my range, as she looks over her shoulder, and returns with an impressive nod of her head.

"Wow, nice shot."

We both break out laughing when she suddenly shivers. I lock my arms around her and slide her down my body to cradle her to my side. As I hold her close, I kiss the top of her head. She looks up and gives me a slight sigh before she kisses my lips. I must say, freshly fucked Kara looks sated and content.

"How's that for loving, baby?" I ask, short of breath, because that was the best damn hand-job I've ever received. I'm not kidding, either. I rub the side of my face still feeling the after effects.

She smirks and shakes her head only to duck her chin in my shoulder.

"That was pretty spectacular." She whispers and then covers her face as if shy all of a sudden. I'm not having any of that, so I push it aside.

"Give me a few minutes," I groan, "because my cock wants what my mouth just had."

I raise my eyebrows, waiting for her response. She pulls back and rolls her eyes.

"Only you would say something like that."

Well, she's right about that. "And you don't?" I challenge her beautiful face, because I know how much she likes my dick.

"Oh hush, of course I want it," she says and cuddles in close, giggling.

And there's that sexy confidence I love so much. Thank you sweetheart.

"Yeah, that's what I thought," I joke but the permanent smile I have on my face is all because of her.

Round two is unhurried and drawn-out. It's not my usual style, but this is as close to fucking perfection as you can get. Tucked nicely between her thighs, I penetrate all the way inside of her. Each thrust is measured but deliberate as her warmth blankets my cock. As I slowly rock out of her body, I slide back in making sure I'm seated fully inside.

Kara is trying her best to entice me to increase my pace. She anchors her legs around me, using any advantage she can use to help speed up my tempo. But what she fails to realize in her sex-crazed state, is I'm stronger than her and I have more self-control. It may be killing me not to give in and pound into her tight pussy, but this right here is lovemaking and it needs to be slow.

My lips brush against hers as I whisper, "I love you, sweetheart."

Then I kiss her all over again.

It seems my comment has touched Kara so much she hiccups with a mouthful of air before tears stream down her face. I continue to gaze into her eyes when her expression suddenly turns serious.

"Liam, I'm so in love with you it hurts."

I swear to God, when she said those words to me my heart leaped out of my chest. I can feel the steady beat of my pulse in my throat and my desire to consumer her takes over.

The slow pace I was trying my hardest to maintain, well, screw that. Kara's words sent my body into hyper-drive. With her body underneath mine, I grab a hold to the iron slats of her headboard to give my thrusts extra support. I breathlessly tell her to 'get ready' and then slam my body into her with as much force as I can. The rails of the headboard act as my anchor.

Kara pulls her knees up allowing me to go deeper with each push. She's riding a pleasure high as I'm blown away with her heat that clenches my cock. Jesus!

My balls tighten and that familiar tingle starts at the bottom of my spine. I refuse to climax without her, though. I change my position, settling back on my knees. I reach and tug her slick body lower my way. Her eyes widen with anticipation when my hands drift over the top of her knees and tilt them back. I'm up on my knees while she's pressed to the mattress elevating that fabulous ass of hers. Once again, I grab the slats of her headboard while she is nicely tucked under my weight. Her body is angled upward while mine is hovering over top. Once again, I grab the slats of her headboard and give her one hell of a crushing ride.

"Harder…Liam…harder!" She yelps, and her encouragement spurs me on.

"Give it to me, sweetheart!"

RIGHT! *Grunt.*

DAMN! *Grunt.*

NOW! *Epic release.*

"Oh…My…God!"

Chapter Fifteen

"Searching for Answers"

Kara

"I can't move a muscle," I joke, "I think you broke me."

I'm draped across his chest, fully sated and feeling well worked over. Not that you'd ever hear me complain, but, Liam was on a mission. He kept true to his word and made me forget my troubles. The word *epic*, and the phrases *earth-shattering*, and *utterly mind-blowing* would best describe our intense lovemaking. But the time we spend afterward just laying together and touching one another, no words could describe this feeling.

With both of us recovering, Liam traces his fingers on my back while I trace the hairs of his chest. His even breathing lulls me until he blows on my face. I open one eye to see his mischievous smirk and can't help but chuckle.

"Make sure you leave me a tip on the nightstand," he laughs.

I should have known something like that was coming from him. It's a wonder, with his ego, that he's able to fit it in my room. Always the jokester and it's one of the things I adore about him. Even in my darkest of moods, he always finds a way to make me laugh. Like now.

With me cradled in his arms, he kisses the top of my head, saying, "Just making sure I keep up my skills, babe. It's all for you."

And with that load of crap, I have to cover my mouth because I'm laughing so hard.

"Always the funny man." I snicker before lowering my gaze to his full lips. It's hard to form any words while staring at his just-fucked face, because he makes me want him all over again, but I manage. His eyes drift to a close, so to get his attention, I tap my finger on his chest.

"I'm all for that," I tease, "If that's what we need to do to keep your skills sharp."

Liam's icy eyes twinkle. "Knew you would see it my way," he boasts, while I quickly get lost in those eyes of his again.

We snuggle, with our bodies half covered with a sheet. I'm on my side, while he's spooning me from behind. Like he always does when were like this, he runs his fingertips up and down my arm. I absolutely love it when he does this.

"Feel good?" He whispers while trailing kisses along my bare shoulder. The minute he nuzzles into the crook of my neck, he tightens his hold, and in no time, I'm drifting off.

"KARA...PSST' WAKE UP."

I faintly hear that a few more times before I open my eyes. In a fog, I'm not sure if I'm awake or still sleeping in a dream.

"Psst', sleepy girl."

Again, I hear a voice. Only this time, it registers with me. It's Dominic's. A cold hand tightens on my shoulder, begging me to turn around, but I can't I'm frozen. Frozen by fear. He is touching me, and it feels so real. I try like hell to convince myself that it's not real, that this is only a nightmare.

He speaks again, and again, I'm terrified with how real he feels.

"I don't have a lot of time, little sister. Turn around."

His voice, this time is a bit more commanding.

I instantly respond. I turn around and gasp as I take in his ghostly appearance. He's pale, literally white as a ghost, but there is a brightness that outlines his silhouette. I'm compelled to reach out and touch him. This is odd, because I'm not afraid of him. All of my other nightmares of him had been dark and haunting. But right now, he's not ominous or threatening. As my hand is about to reach him, he speaks again.

"You need to be careful. Keep your eyes open and go with your feelings. If something doesn't seem right, trust your intuitions."

He's not making any sense, and that causes me to panic. "What are you talking about?" *I reach this time, but he's slowly fading.*

"I've given you all you need, you have to figure the rest out on your own. Keep looking."

Just like that he's fading farther away.

"Dominic," I yell, "what do you mean? You have to tell me...wait don't leave yet."

I break into a sprint to try and catch up.

"Dammit, Dominic. TELL ME WHAT YOU MEANT?"

I shout as loud as I possibly can.

"Hey, babe. Kara, *wake up.*"

Liam's panicked, and is firmly shaking my shoulders when I come out of my dream. I'm drenched in sweat and trembling all over.

I try to speak, but my voice hitches. "Liam, that was so real. Oh, my God." I cover my mouth with my trembling fingers.

Liam's eyes move rapidly over my face, not sure what the hell is going on.

"Babe, another nightmare?" His voice is groggy, yet concerning.

Shamelessly, I nod.

"You've been doing better with those. I thought we were over them," he exhales, "guess not."

"It wasn't like those at all. Tonight, he physically touched my shoulder, forcing me to turn around to face him. I tried to ignore him, but then my body moved on its own." I realize, in telling him about it, it does frighten me.

His forehead creases, no doubt intrigued, asking, "What happened?"

Not really sure that what I'm about to say is going to make any sense, but here I go. "He explained something about him leaving me all I need and that I had to figure the rest out. What, I'm not sure. He told me to trust my instincts, and if something doesn't feel right to go with my gut feeling. It seemed like a warning, but also clues, I guess." I have no fucking clue what to make of it because Dominic's not acted like a caring brother for years.

What the hell, has death stripped every ounce of evil that he had? Or, maybe he had to do a few good deeds to pass the pearly gates to find eternal peace. Whatever that was tonight, it has left me shaken up.

Anyway, I went on to explain how Dominic's body retreated before he fully disappeared, and that the whole time, I never once felt afraid of him. Liam listened and held me tight. And like always, he calmed my body and my mind. I'm not sure of the reason, but Liam looked over at the clock, and sure enough, it read three-fifteen. We both felt that unwelcomed shiver. I wish we could figure out the significance of this time when it comes to my brother and my nightmares but for now, it's a mystery.

"YOU'RE SURE YOU ARE OKAY going over without me?" I hate to do this to him, but I need to meet with my parents.

"Yeah, of course. Do what you need to do with your parents. I'll have a nice chat with Max. By the time you show up, I'll hopefully have the answers we need."

"I promise I won't be long. They want to have a talk about a few things, and I'd like to get it out of the way, too." Boy, oh boy, do I ever. Not that talking with my parents is a bad thing, it could get uncomfortable. I am tired of carrying things on my shoulders. It might feel good to unload my guilt and come clean with how my brother died.

I asked Liam if it'd be okay to drop him off at my brother's house, then come back after my impromptu chat with mom and dad.

As I pull up to the large, multi-story house, we don't notice Max's car in the driveway. It looks like we beat him here.

"That's good, I can look around before he gets here."

Liam makes sure I have my phone on and makes me promise to drive carefully before giving me a kiss. I had to all but offer up my blood, promising to be very diligent with my safety.

I park in my parent's driveway, and turn my head to get a better look at the lone car parked on the side of the street, a few houses back; the darkened windows of the classic black Camaro is not a car you see every day. Its beauty is what first caught my eye. I shut the door of my car and glance back at it one more time, only this time, I notice exhaust coming from behind. It's running. My eyes struggle to see an outline of anyone sitting in the car, but the darkened windows won't allow it.

The chilling sensation causes me to shiver, so I quicken my steps to get inside the house. After I open the front door, I quickly enter and shut it behind me. I rush to the front room, and push the curtain back enough to peer out the window. Suddenly, a tall man in dark clothing is standing a few feet from the car. His hands are in his pockets, and his hoodie hides most of his face. It's difficult to recognize anything since he has his head down.

"Kara," my mom's voice suddenly rings out, "you're home sweetie?"

I turn and motion with my hands for her to join me. "Mom, look out here and tell if you know who this guy is?"

To get a better view, she pulls the curtain back. "Kara, there's no one there." She turns to face me puzzled.

What? I step forward and sure enough, the man is no longer standing there. How is that possible, I had only turned my head for second and now all of a sudden he's gone. All of a sudden we hear the shriek of tires before a black Camaro rushes near the window and when he reaches the window we're looking out of, the car slows. It's obvious whoever is in that car is watching us as we do our best trying to figure out just who this bastard is. This is beyond creepy.

Now that I'm more than slightly panicked, I ask, "Mom, is dad home?" Just like when I was a little girl, if something scared me, I always asked for my dad.

Just then the Camaro suddenly races down the street as we both step away from the window. For a moment we stare into each other's eyes, and both force a smile. I think we are both weirded out some.

My mom breaks our silence by saying, "Your dad is upstairs, I think waiting for you."

I start to walk to the stairs, but stop and turn to face her.

"You okay, mom? You seem anxious?"

"Nothing is wrong, I'm fine."

I want to say bullshit when she starts chatting about coffee and all the things she has to do today, because the more she talks, the more fidgety she becomes. Her arms won't stop moving, and if that isn't enough, she keeps rambling, barely pausing to take a breath. I decide not to walk up the stairs just yet, instead, I watch and listen to my mom ramble.

"I told your dad today that he needed to fix those damn gutters, but he won't listen. I even went as far as to talk to the neighbor boy to see if he would come over and clean them out for me. Someone has got to get it done before the weather changes. You know Dominic..."

The instant she says his name, she stiffens and loses her train of thought. Her back is to me while she's pouring herself a cup of coffee but I can see her trembling arm. Damn it, her arm is shaking so bad she's going to burn her hand on the hot coffee if she's not careful.

"Mom," I stride to take the coffee pot from her hand and turn her to face me. "You need to tell me what's got you so upset. What has happened since the last time we spoke?"

She's looking at me like she's desperate and confused. Those two things are not my mother.

Evelyn Santos is a woman who is never at a loss for words, but right now she's struggling to even form one. I've gone from being frightened to straight out worried and I need her to start talking to me.

"Mom, what is dad doing upstairs?"

No reply.

I ask again.

Not a word, she only nods her chin as her eyes drift to a close. That's it, I turn to take my first step to go upstairs, but my mother reaches out her hand to stop me. She pulls me into a crushing hug and whispers in my ear.

"I'm so sorry."

Not quite the words I expected to hear from her. "What do you mean by that?"

She doesn't answer my question, not really. She just says something that confuses me even more.

"He's been waiting for this day to come."

LIAM

JUST TO STEP INTO THIS house even during the day, gives off some weird vibes. I hope to look around before Max gets here, so I need to make sure no one else is in the house. It's too quiet, so I make my way down the hall, to the study Kara and I were in yesterday. Out of any room in this house, I would think the study would hold the most answers or clues. Shit, I'm not sure what I'm even looking for, but I'll turn this room over just in case.

Yesterday, Kara was sitting at the desk, so I decide to start there. While I sit at the desk, I swivel in the chair and take in the whole room. We barely started looking through the desk before Max showed up unannounced. One drawer one at a time, I'm looking at the papers, pictures, and many different invoices that were left behind, but nothing stands out and grabs my attention. I'm getting frustrated, because I feel like I'm searching for a needle in a haystack and I start questioning myself and my methods when, all of a sudden, I notice something we missed yesterday.

A large bookcase situated on the left side of the room is a replica of the one on the right side of the room, but what catches my eye is the light that appears from behind it. I don't remember seeing it last night. Either we missed it, or someone has been in here. And if so, is that someone still here?

Right now, I'm thankful Kara is not here with me. Who the fuck knows what I'm going to find behind that bookcase. As I stand in front of the opening that separates the wall and bookcase, I take a hold and pull on it slowly. I reach down inside of my boot and grab my knife. I've worn it since we arrived in Chicago. A little piece of mind, I call it.

As I hold my piece of mind firmly in my hand, I take a look and see a staircase that descends to a lower room. A room that has its lights on. I don't hear any noise, so with one last glance over my shoulder, I take the first step, then listen. When I hear nothing, I proceed one step at a time. When I reach step, I feel like I've entered a movie scene.

"What the fuck?"

I'm in a small room, maybe five by ten. There's a small desk with a lamp on in the middle of the room with papers discarded all over it like someone was in a damn hurry looking for something. But my attention is focused elsewhere.

I can't tear my sight away from the massive wall display before me. It resembles what you would find in a detective's office, a police profile of suspects and timelines kind of shit. I count a dozen or so pictures, newspaper cut-outs, handwritten notes, and several red and black highlighted markings. It has my attention, so instead of searching around the side of the room that is dark, I step closer to look at the wall.

I use my finger to trace across from left to right, all the while wondering, "What the hell is all of this?"

I quickly focus on three photos that are centered in the middle of the wall. The fact I recognize the people in two of these only confirms my suspicions that this house does hold clues. The million-dollar question is who the hell is in the third photo, and how does this all fit together?

The middle picture is, without a doubt, a younger Dominic. I recognize him, but his name is also written underneath.

The one on the left is Kara. It's also an older photo, but I'd know that face anywhere. Her name is also written below. Now the third picture, that one stumps me. A guy who appears slightly older, late twenties, early thirties maybe, with the name Vince written below it. I'm already bothered that my girl is on this wall, but what has me even more concerned is who is Vince? And why is he pictured here?

I study the other various pictures, I find one with a teenage boy and a small child. It appears to be the oldest photo on the wall, so I take it down and turn it over.

Written on the back is...*Kara and Vince.*

My eyes stay locked on the handwriting as my fingers tighten their hold on the photo. I sure as hell don't feel like this is some happy photo since it's on this damn wall to begin with. In fact, my blood runs cold thinking it's not. I sure as hell am keeping this one, so I tuck it inside of my jacket. I wonder if Kara even knows who this guy is?

I take five or six breaths when out of the corner of my eye, I see a familiar face and the blood drains from my face. There, pinned to the wall, is a picture of my sister. Why the fuck is a picture of my sister on this goddamn wall? And even more disturbing, is the red circle that is marked around her stomach.

How would anyone know she's pregnant? They wouldn't unless someone has been watching her, like they have been watching all of us. I get so fucking mad I grip my knife before I lunge it in the wall.

"Jesus Christ." The walls are closing in on me as a panic attack hits me, beading my face with sweat. I suddenly find it hard to breathe. I slip down to the floor as my legs give way. I just need a minute to collect myself. With my head resting back against the wall, I look up and again only to have another photo catch my eye. Once again, I'm back to my feet.

This picture clearly shows a younger Dominic with whoever this Vince fellow is. They are standing on a dock near a small cabin in a wooded background. Both have wide smiles like every kid does when they are happy. Under the photo, the faint handwriting gives me the answer I need to into who Vince is and I have say, it's a fucking doozy.

'Brothers even in death'.

Holy Shit!

Well, that explains part of the damn puzzle, but why hasn't Kara ever mentioned another brother, or, her parents for that matter. Dominic never mentioned Vince to her in his letter, either. None of this shit makes sense, it's one thing fucking thing after another. I didn't think anything else could shock me at the moment until I was proven wrong, yet again.

"Your first mistake was coming down here."

From behind me, a sinister sounding voice fills the room. It's deep and unmistaken. I lower my head and curse at myself for not checking that dark room.

"Damn!"

I slowly turn around to see a man shadowed in the darkness. "Who the fuck are you?" I don't bother with pleasantries.

"Oh, I am sure you have some idea now that you have seen the board. My board. The pictures, the names. Pardon me, but I am not in the mood for a walk down memory lane at the moment," he speaks matter of fact and all proper like while slowly appearing from the room. The first thing I notice is that his voice matches his appearance. Not at all what I expected.

Standing before me is a tall and lean man wearing a suit and not one thread out of place, his black hair is dark as the night and is perfectly styled. He even has a solid gold ring around his pinkie along with his gold watch. A stuffy, uptight, kind of guy if you ask me.

Both of us stay silent, assessing one another up.

"Before you open your mouth," he warns me, "let me make myself clear as not to repeat. You need to understand that I am very much interested in what happened to Dominic."

He speaks slowly to articulate each word precisely. Even though everything on the outside shows me he's calm, cool and in control, the way he's continuously turning his pinky ring tells me something else. It tells me he's nervous. Because he's doing it non-stop.

My eyes shift from his finger to his face. "Is that so?" The last thing I want is to appear intimidated by him, so I give him attitude back. I seem to have struck a nerve because he lowers his chin and glares.

"Don't mistake me for anything other than ruthless. Kara took something away from me. That doesn't happen very often to a man like me."

Two things bother me with his comments; One, he knows information he shouldn't, and two, the mention of my girl touches a nerve and instantly I demand to know his intentions. "What do you want with Kara?"

A laugh worthy grin appears on his stoic face. He's enjoying the fact that he's struck a nerve with me, but I sure as hell don't enjoy the fact he is staring at me while he continues to fiddle with his damn ring. I'm standing with my legs apart, and my arms are crossed, with my knife nicely tucked in my hand. I'm all ears.

"My wish is not to harm Kara," he states unwavering, "but I could take something away from her, like *you*!"

That's when he lunges, and before I know It, I'm on my ass. Damn he's quick. I never had a chance to brace myself and I'm pissed at myself for that. It takes a few moments to clear my head, and when

I do, he crosses the room staring back at me with razor thin eyes. He opens his hand and wouldn't you know it, he's holding a knife. *My knife*!

How the hell did he get it from me without me knowing it? I'm not only pissed at myself, I'm fucking furious.

"You see? You are no match for me," he taunts. "If I wanted her dead, she would have died by now. If I want you dead, well, that's just what is going to happen. There is not a lot you can do to stop me. Obviously." He mocks me while he takes the time to straighten his damn suit. Who the fuck is this guy?

I get to my feet, this stuffy suit wearing dick is not just going to decide if he's going to take me out or not. Fast or not, I'm not going down like that. I charge and we lock in a scuffle.

"Leave Kara the hell alone. Does she even know about you?" I manage to say in between dogging his blows and me attempting my own. Fucker is lightning fast on his feet, not that I want to compliment him. He's even fighting in a damn suit. What the fuck?

"Now you are getting personal." He stands back to catch his breath. "You do not have the right to ask me such questions. That is none of your business."

This time, his tone is menacing, like I've struck a nerve. He's on the attack and in our exchange, the tip of my blade inches its way into my side. I screech with the burn caused by him pushing the blade in all the way. My stance weakens as I gasp, and drop to one knee. Vince collects himself, he's checking his arms and suit jacket to see if any of my blood has ruined his precious clothing. I'm bleeding, and he's standing there in a barely wrinkled suit. Prick!

I struggle to exhale a few breaths. I know I have to pull the knife out of my side so with one trembling hand holding the knife, my other presses against my wound. I close my eyes, take a big breath, and count to five. Every slow inch the blade retracts hurts like holy hell. The stinging burn has me rethinking my decision of having it with me. I'm pressing my bloodied hand against my side to slow the bleeding when a noise catches my attention upstairs.

"Liam, you down there?" Max's voice shouts from above.

"Ahhh, yeah, I'm here." I sigh with relief when I know it's him.

I try to sit up some and do my best to slow my breathing. Vince backs out of the room. Right now, my side needs tending too, and the right person to help has just shown up. Call it good luck or I have to have an angel looking out for me because Max can stitch me up. I only hope he has a needle and thread on him.

With Vince retreating into the dark room, I'm about to tell Max when he bolts down the stairs.

"Jesus Christ. What the hell happened to you? And what the fuck is this room?"

All good questions, but he needs to shut up so I can warn him that standing behind him is the man who stabbed me. Max must sense someone because he quickly turns.

"Who the fuck are you?" Max shouts and gets in a stance ready to fight.

"I am none of your concern, *Max*. It looks like your friend may need some medical attention." His eyes settle back to mine.

He called Max by his first name and by the lost expression on Max's face I take it he does not know Vince.

Vince sharply addresses me with a warning. "I will be around. Watching of course. I've got eyes and ears everywhere. You would be wise not to forget that."

Suddenly, he turns and takes the stairs to leave. I'd like to go after him, but I can't move. I'd ask Max too, but I'm afraid Vince is right. I urgently need Max's help.

Max lowers next to me to assess my wound. "Max, have you heard of a guy named Vince before?"

"No. Who is he?" he asks but immediately presses his hand to my side. "Shit, I need to stitch this up." He's gritting his teeth as he takes off his jacket, and uses that to help slow the bleeding. "You know, I'd like to visit with you guys and not have to stitch anyone up for a change."

We both chuckle before he presses harder and I growl in discomfort. To help distract me from my pain, I keep talking.

"Yeah," I blow out in short breaths, "but you'd be bored. That reminds me, I have a few questions that you need to answer."

His eyes linger on mine for an extended minute before he snickers, "Yeah, after I stitch you up. I thought you might have a question or two."

Chapter Sixteen

"Secrets Unfold"

Kara

"Dad, I don't understand." I enter his study to find him pacing back and forth. I'm not sure what has him acting uneasy, but clearly something is. His odd behavior worries me. Softly, I ask, "What's bothering you?"

He lets out a slight chuckle and curses under his breath. It's faint, but I hear it nonetheless. He looks at me with pained eyes and instead of saying anything, I shrug my shoulder, letting him know I'm patiently waiting for an answer. After a few sighs, he offers an explanation.

"I'm just really exhausted from trying to do the right thing." His voice wavers as he gently wipes away a tear. I watch my dad struggle with whatever has him so troubled and I feel helpless. Not sure what else to do, I take a cautious step, but he quickly retreats, nervously cupping his hands together. I've never seen my dad act this way before and the pit in my stomach grows more worrisome.

Twenty minutes later, I finally convince him to follow me downstairs to rejoin my mother. With the three of us in the same room, the tension between my parents is unmistakable. They refuse to even look at one another.

Instead, my mother's plan is to keep herself occupied with work just to avoid having to make any eye contact with my dad. I'm about to say something when I look over at my dad. He, on the other hand, is trying to do the same by looking at his hands like there is something on them. I'm left standing staring at my parents' odd behavior. With every passing second my insecurities grow, but my patience is barely hanging on by a thread.

I step to my dad and place a comforting hand on his shoulder. "Dad, what's going on?"

His eyes briefly close with a cleansing breath. "Kara there is so much to explain and no easy way to make you fully understand." The hint of a quiver in his voice is enough to make my heart to ache. Whatever is going on, it's something that is weighing heavily on both of my parents. Broad lines crease his eyes and around his mouth. I sadly realize in this moment how fast he's aging, only, I don't remember seeing him look this way a few months back.

Just as I'm about to speak of my concern over his health, the front door lunges open. Startled, we all jump to look. A bloodied Max stumbles in with his arm around Liam's shoulder as he helps him inside. It's as if time has slowed. My mouth can't form any words, but my eyes frantically look Liam over from head to toe. Inside the door, he halts his steps and rests his body against the wall. His chest expands, sucking in air like he's having a hard time breathing.

"What the hell?" The sight of so much blood scares me. The side of Liam's shirt is saturated with a dark, crimson color. "Liam, are you okay?" I asked in a panicked voice. Of course he's not, but I have to ask anyway. It's what you naturally ask someone who looks like he does. My hands immediately pat his chest searching for where he's hurt, that's when a faint noise parts his lips and he sucks in a staggered breath. I freeze and instantly pull my hands back, petrified that I've hurt him. He hisses and grabs my hands.

"Let's... just sit down." The noise he's making sounds like something is constricting his lungs, making it hard for him to breathe. I'm sick with worry and taking breaths so shallow, you'd think *I* was the one who was injured.

Max helps Liam to the couch since it's the closest place to have him sit, but my mom is quick to rush over and put a blanket down first. Liam lifts his eyes and voices his appreciation, "Good idea, Evelyn, thank you." Liam sits, wincing a few times as my mother asks my dad to get them both some clean clothing because both of them were in need of them. Max's blood-splattered shirt is nothing compared to Liam's. I'm quick to say he belongs in the hospital, but that was a losing battle. He shoots that idea down because he has Max.

My dad returns with sweatpants and t-shirts for them both. Max expresses his gratitude and excuses himself to change. I have Liam's, and my parents step out of the room to give us some privacy.

"What the hell happened to you?" I ask, carefully removing his shirt. He just shakes his head as my eyes get the first look at the angry looking incision and black stitches. I feel like someone plunges a dagger in my heart. This happened because of me. Tears threaten to spill over, so I bite the inside of my cheek to keep my shit together. "What happened to you?" I ask again. He's still not saying much, but I'm desperate for answers and his silence has me scared, confused, and angry. All three emotions only fuel my anxiety to the point that the tears burn my eyes and spill over. I finish putting on his shirt, and wait for my explanation. I have him lie down so I can take his jeans off next. I've never been so happy for sweat pants, they go on like a breeze. With his bloody clothes in my hand, I stand, still waiting for my explanation. With the daggers I'm throwing at him, Liam finally opens up.

"Babe, let me catch my breath and I'll explain. Just stop worrying, sweetheart."

Oh no, he did not just tell me that!

"Don't." To make sure I don't yell, I clench my teeth as I speak. "Don't tell me not to worry, dammit." Liam must find something comical because he lets out a chuckle but grabs his side quickly.

The others join us in the living room once again. My parents keep to themselves and sit without saying a word. I'm sitting with one leg over the other, glaring between Max and Liam. It's not anger that fuels my glare, it's more fear of the unknown. It's just easier for me to show anger. To ease my nervousness, I clutch my elbows, pressing them to my sides. I'd gladly bite my nails, but they are down to the nub already. That leaves my legs, which right now can't seem to stay still. My mom takes over being the caregiver and host, offering everyone drinks and something to eat. She even thinks to bring Liam some painkillers he so desperately needs, because he's grimacing every time he moves.

He happily takes the pills and tries to get in a comfortable position, so his weight is no longer on the side that is injured. I hate seeing him like this. Soon enough, I'm back biting whichever nail I can find as Liam graciously compliments my mother before he glances at me. "Babe, you should be more like your mom." He assaults me with his damn icy blues, thinking he can get out of hot water with me.

On any other day it would work, but today is not that day.

"Funny." I sneer. "How about you tell me what the fuck happened *to you*?"

"Language." My mother reprimands me with her dainty smile.

I want to yell "Who the hell cares," but Liam pats my knee with his hand. He clears his throat so I will swing my attention from my mother back to him.

"Let me start with this," he says, while pulling out a photo from his jacket that's lying near him and then hands it to me. It's a photo of a teen boy with a little girl in a dress. Nothing appears familiar, so I turn it over. When I do, I have to do a double-take.

"I don't know who this is," I respond while looking at him, slightly confused. He then swings his eyes to my parents who seem curious, themselves.

I inquire as I hold the photo out for my dad. "Do you know who this is?"

His eyes widen with recognition, before a look of anguish and regret emerge. The fleeting gaze he returns to me, clearly admits that he does. My apprehension worsens, but for a minute our eyes stay locked onto one another, and a silent promise filters between us. His eyes find the way to communicate to me that things will be okay and I want to believe him.

The firm hold he has on the photo eases up some to give my mother a chance to see the picture better. Her agile face slowly turns to stone and her stiff posture turns at an angle, facing away from my father. I can't see her face but I don't need to, her body language says it all. After a few agonizing seconds, she slowly turns back around to face my dad. Her expression is filled with hurt and the instant her chin trembles, my dad flinches. Her reaction pains him, and that right there tells me everything I need to know, I'm not going to like his explanation.

My dad coughs a few times before he struggles to take a few breaths. His once firm hold he had on the photo, is now loose, dangling between two fingers. He flips it over and lowers his shoulders. "The young man in the photo is Vince or Vincent, rather." His eyes take a slow deliberate trail until they rest on mine. "You're the little girl."

You're the little girl. Those words repeat in my mind. Okay, is that so bad I want to ask? But as my eyes leave my dad and land on my mom, all I see is turmoil and unrest. Questions are on the tip of my tongue, but I'm unable to form any words.

Liam is quick to comment, though. "I met Vince earlier today, and I sure hope you explain who he is to your daughter before I'm forced to."

I gasp because the guy I'm in the picture with is the same guy who hurt Liam? What in the hell am I missing here? I struggle to make the connection and am real curious as to who this Vince guy is now.

"I'd hate to screw it up as I'm not entirely sure how it all fits, but whatever it is, that information needs to come from you. I have to tell you, I'm sure as hell interested in hearing it for myself." Liam's attention returns to Max, who has been extremely quiet, but right now he's nodding his head too.

As soon as my father begins to speak my mother shoots to her feet as she wipes her nose several times in a tissue. I struggle to maintain my composure as my eyes travel around everyone until they land back on my mom.

"If you all will excuse me." She softly hiccups and dashes out of the room.

"Mom..." I cry out and as I try to stand, Liam is quick to clamp his hand firmly on my thigh. I'm about to smack his hand away when I notice his stare on my dad.

"Kara, sit back and listen to what I have to say," my dad suggests. "Your mom's okay, she just doesn't want to hear this story again."

Based on her reaction, I sure as hell already know that I'm not going to like any of what I'm about to hear, and I certainly don't need any more reminders that our family is one dysfunctional mess. Knots twist in my stomach as I brace myself for the worst while my knuckles turn white with the death grip I have on my shirt. It's easy to figure out that this guy, Vincent, is bad news. He already has two strikes against him in my mind. My mom hates him, and Liam came home in a bloody mess. As far as I'm concerned, he only has one strike left.

"Vincent is my son," my dad softly admits and I'm sure I had heard him wrong. He takes one look at my gaping jaw and continues, "I had an affair very early in our marriage, several years before Dominic was even born. I didn't find out about him until a few years after Dominic was born." He attempts to resume, but I interrupt him. My arm shoots out like a rocket, with a firm hand landing in front of his face.

"You had an affair on mom?!" I shout the words, because they just don't sink in. I always thought my parents had the best marriage because I never saw anything that would cause me to think differently.

Sure, all marriages have issues, but my parents were the exception. Or, so I thought. Even having Dominic as a child, they stayed together.

"We worked it out," he offers the simplest of explanations. "Things turned out for the best. I have always loved your mother, that was never in question. From that one indiscretion, I learned a valuable lesson. One that nearly cost me my marriage. Never have I, or would I, ever do anything like that again. Your mother forgave me and we left it in the past where it belongs."

"Well if that's the case," I say sarcastically, "why am I in a photograph with him?" A feeling of betrayal hits me like a tons of bricks, but the agony written on my dad's face dampens my anger.

"At one time I thought you all could somehow get to know one another, but that never quite worked out." He lowers his gaze back to the photo as his face softens. "This photo was the only time you were ever around Vince." When he raises his eyes this time, he's not looking at me, he's looking at Liam and Max.

"What about Dominic? Did they know about one another?" I had to ask.

"That's a different story." His eyes narrow, tilting his head my way. "For years no," he whispers, "but when Dominic went down the wrong path and took on a lifestyle I never approved of, he found someone who was just like him. Someone he felt understood him. Someone he felt comfortable trusting and for him, that was rare." He didn't have to go on explaining. With him saying how alike Dominic and Vince were, is chilling enough.

"Wow." Both Liam and Max whisper.

"No way," I whisper, fighting to believe him. "When you say 'just alike', exactly how alike are they?" Judging from Liam's bloodstained clothing, I'm assuming more alike than not.

My dad sat up to try and explain this toxic relationship. "They ran in the same circles and worked the same crowds, both of them doing highly illegal things and both just as dangerous. I'm not sure how else to describe it." The simplicity of his explanation leaves me with a hundred and one questions, only I'm not sure I want to know anymore. Unfortunately, there is one plaguing question that I want answered.

"Do you have a relationship with Vince or his mother?" I cringe when I say his mother, because I can't imagine my mother being okay with any of this. Hell, I'm not sure why my mom stayed, knowing what he did. Is that what you do when you're in love? God, could I do the same if Liam did this to me? I better never have to find out.

"Not like you think. Vince reached out to me when he was old enough to understand things. His mother, Violet, no. Obviously, she told him everything for him to find me to begin with, but I've not seen or heard from her. Over the years, I was curious just how close Vince and Dominic could have possibly gotten. So when I heard they had been in touch, your brother advised me to not bother asking about their relationship. He said whatever he and Vince had going on was between them, so I left it at that. I rarely heard from Vince. He has contacted me a handful of times over the years. First, it was to confront me about being his absent father. Other than that, it was purely to get information on Dominic. Your mother had one run in with Vince, and that was enough for her to keep her distance."

Jesus! I don't blame her, but why keep it a secret? It was obvious Dominic knew him.

"Why not tell me? He is as much my brother as Dominic was." Just *thinking* that is enough to make me want to hurl. One sadistic brother is enough, now I find out I have another one. One that appears to be just as dangerous as the other one. That knowledge sends a frightening chill down my spine. Does Vince hate me for what I've done? Surely, he has no idea the hell I lived with... could he?

My dad is vehemently shaking his head as I look up at him. "No!" he answers point blank. "Do not think of him as anything. That's the way he wants it, and that's a good thing, trust me. It had been years, until one day he called me out of the blue wondering if it was true that Dominic had died. Somehow, he found out. You have to remember, Vince embraced Dominic. They had similar tastes and similar goals. They share...," he pauses as a look of confusion or doubt I'm not sure which, flashes across his face before he continues, "let's say they shared the same outlook on life, and lack of empathy when it comes to hurting others. It was Dominic's wishes that Vince stays away from you. That much I do know. It came directly from your brother, himself."

I swear I did not hear him right. This simply can't be true. For one thing, it sure as hell doesn't sound like Dominic.

"What? Why?"

"You would have to get that answer from him, and we all know that isn't going to happen. I have a theory, though. Kara, you don't have a bad bone in your body, thank God!" he chuckles. "Dominic explained it best when it came to your relationship with him. You were the good to his bad. You evened him out—kept the balance was how he explained it. Vince was told he would not gain anything by contacting you, so it was better to leave you alone."

"Had he nothing to gain?" I shout like I've just been insulted. "A sister!" I shout, "That's something to gain."

"Kara," Liam warns, but I dismiss him. Right now, this is between my dad and me. Luckily enough, Max is staying silent, but watching with concern.

"Kara, you can't and mustn't think of him that way... he doesn't think that way about you."

"That's cold," I say with attitude as my dad lowers his chin.

"He has nothing to benefit in regards to the world he lives in, when it comes to you. With Vincent, if he has nothing to gain, you are no use to him. He has no desire to add more people to his close circle. He's a dangerous man, Kara. Runs in the same crowd as Dominic did and it's best you not to get involved with him."

I can feel the tension rolling of his shoulders and I can even appreciate his concern, but lying to me all these years? I'm shocked and shaking my head while his words play out in my mind, before I feel Liam leaning into my shoulder.

He whispers in my ear. "Kara, just be thankful you don't know him. Trust me, you don't want to know him. Ever."

He keeps his voice soft and loving and I appreciate what he's saying. The truth is he's right, only I'm not sure if I want to cry or scream. To be honest, I'm not sure what it is I should be feeling being lied to my whole life?

Soon enough, the mother of migraines is quickly encroaching. My brain is starting to feel like it's slowly being squeezed in a vice. The painful pressure that is building behind my eyes, and the thumping of my pulse beating in my ears is too much. I've reached my limit as the first nauseous roll hits my stomach. Oh no, I fear of what's to come. When I was younger, these symptoms led to a visit to the emergency room. A shot in the hip and day and a half of sleep later was usually what it took to feel better. Yet, I still haven't heard what the hell happened with Liam today. I'm struggling to try and focus on anything, and the way I'm feeling right now, I can only hope to be able to function enough to hear the play by play of events that led to my guy having a knife shoved in his side. But I'm fading fast.

Chapter Seventeen

"Pain"

Liam

"Are you serious?" I'm ten seconds from throwing my phone against the wall. "How the hell did this happen?"

I hold nothing back as I swear this night is one for the records in all things bizarre. My side has ten ugly stitches but thanks to Max, I skipped a grueling hospital visit with endless questions about how a knife ended up in my side to begin with. Then the unbelievable story Kara's dad revealed was seriously nothing short of 'what the fuck?'

On the way to Kara's parents' house, Max and I had a lengthy conversation until I felt somewhat satisfied. Max was upfront about watching out for us, and he swore he had only our best interests at heart. I was relieved because I never wanted to doubt him in the first place.

I am surprised that Max has never heard of anyone named Vincent. All that time around Dominic, and never a word. Not in his presence, anyway. That didn't surprise me because Dominic kept everything under wraps. When Max was around, it was only when Dominic needed him for his doctoring abilities. As a doctor, Max benefitted Dominic greatly, making him valuable and a vital part of Dominic's life. His skills were also extremely vital to Izzy's care. Max treated the bruises Izzy suffered as a result of Dominic's beatings. He also stitched the deeper wounds she suffered when he felt the need to use his knife to punish her for 'being disrespectful'. The fact that Max kept his mouth shut and acted as if he never saw anything was a bonus.

Even some of Dominic's close pals had the special treatment if medical care was needed without having to go to the local ER. Other than that, according to Max, he wasn't around much. I had assumed he was a permanent fixture by listening to Izzy and Kara talk. Being a member of a club, we had our own doctor for the same reasons. No questions, no pointing fingers, and more importantly, no arrests.

After I had given the briefest of explanations of what happened earlier, Kara felt so bad, she needed to rest. I can only imagine what torment my girl's feeling. She likes to bottle up most of her feelings, so I imagine she'll tuck this away deep inside, too. She'll struggle with this, but I won't let her do it alone. We'll figure out what to do next. Unfortunately, it's hard to move forward when we don't know what that prick, Vince, really wants.

Once Kara's mother excused herself to care for her daughter, Max and I carried on a conversation with her father. With it just being us, we could speak freely. With the brutal honesty in which we spoke, I'd like to think we're all on the same page, but a few questions remain.

One being we don't know who the hell the mystery man is in Kara's photos, the ones she took with Izzy and the kids. Secondly, is it possible he is Kara's stalker who's been sending her all of those letters? Our mutual conclusion is Vincent, because he likes playing games for his own sick pleasure. For now, he's the most plausible explanation.

My eyes start to droop in exhaustion. All talked out, I'm finally able to relax. My body's been stressed, stabbed and stitched, all in one day. The stab wound hurts like hell, but the pills I took earlier, lessened the pain some.

I jump when my phone beeps with an incoming call. "Shit," I look at the screen and see it's Brax.

Even though I'm not real excited to relive the events from earlier I know Brax is going to want to know what happened. No sooner than I finish talking, does he jump in with more information about our mysterious photo bomber, and that little piece of information instantly has me wide awake. Max, and Kara's father who has remained quiet all of a sudden sit up straighter in their seats. I pass along to them what I hear from Brax.

"I happen to sneak up on this guy watching my house. I almost shot that fucker's brains out right then and there, swear to God. And I almost did, before common sense took over. I knew we needed to figure out who or what he wanted so I had to spare his miserable life...for the time being, anyway. I may have spared his life, but I had no problem knocking out a few teeth when he was not very forthcoming. It's a good thing I had Cage and Brody from the shop over, or else I may have enjoyed myself a little too much."

Brax pauses, by the way he was breathing heavily, I figured he was trying to control himself. Brax has never been a violent man, but mess with his family, and all bets are off.

"This fucker was outside of my house, watching my wife and kids, Liam! Enough of this bullshit, I want all of this shit over with."

I want to say he's preaching to the choir, but I respectfully keep my mouth shut. I'm more than anxious to hear what he had learned from the guy.

"So," I impatiently ask, "what did you find out?"

"Let me ask you something," he lowers his voice, and with the way he's breathing, I can sense his agitation. "How soon before you are heading back home?"

I wish I could tell him now, but I can't. As soon as possible, that's for damn sure. "As soon as we can," I tell him.

Brax relayed what information he did get out of the mystery man, known as Tyler. Apparently, he's not that much of tough guy, and definitely not a man who's used to getting into fights. He's nothing more than a watchdog. More of a stay behind the scenes kind of guy. He was shocked when he was caught, and being caught by Brax almost made him piss his pants. Any dumbass stupid enough to threaten Brax's family has to have a death wish. Surviving being beaten to a bloody pulp by Dominic, and Izzy barely getting away from him alive has Brax protecting his family like a dog protects his bone. Brax won't hesitate to kill anyone who even looks like they have Izzy and the girls in their sights.

Brax said he had been contacted by an unknown client and was hired over the phone to watch Kara and Izzy, and report all activity to a man he claims he never met. He was hired, other than that, he didn't have much else he could add.

Killing this guy would only further provoke bloodshed... something none of us wanted. If Vincent were his contact guy, that would not bode well for any of us. It's best to play it safe for now.

"After he told me what he was hired to do, I gave him a message to send to his boss, assuming it's that fucker, Vince. I told him if he wants to know something he can come talk himself, but other than that, leave my goddamn family alone."

"I hear you, brother," I say casually, but this burden is weighing on me like a ton of bricks. "Shit, I have no idea what any of this means. He's Kara's brother, so why watch Izzy. If he were interested in anybody, it should be Kara. What's he got planned? What's his fucking end game?" The harder I try to figure him out, I sadly realize it could take me a few life times, and even then I still might not understand. "None of it makes any sense."

"Just keep me posted," Brax responds, "I'm not leaving Iz and the kids. You need to watch your damn back, too. And no more letting anyone stab you with your own fucking knife, hear me?" His slight chuckle may be playful, but the meaning behind his words wasn't.

I exhale with a chuckle suddenly feeling every ache and sore muscle. Exhausted to the point I'm wiped out. I try to laugh at his smart ass comment, but I yawn instead.

"It wasn't the plan, trust me! Anyway, take care of your family."

"Always. Get some rest, and Liam, you do know that includes you, right?" Brax is like my brother and he always makes sure I know it. A smile breaks out across my face, and I tell him how much I appreciate it. Knowing just how close a complete stranger was to them does not feel good. Our goal in life is to guard who we love, so when someone we don't know gets as close to them as Tyler was to Brax's wife and kids, it's a reminder for us to step up our game and pay closer attention to our surroundings.

I press end and exhale with a sigh, taking a second to process the fact that our mystery man now has a name. I turn my attention back to Max, who's lying on the other couch listening intently to my conversation.

"So, who is he?" He questions with a subtle brow raise.

"Tyler," I say returning a questioning look of my own. "We think he works for Vince."

Max is shaking his head as lets out an astonished chuckle. "No shit? Well, things just keep getting more interesting as the day goes on." There is no denying that statement.

"When Brax sets him free, he's going to call Vince." My eyes leave Max to gaze to the floor as I say to no one in particular, "Wonder what happens then?"

Max nods his head. I'm sure thinking about what will happen next. "You know," Max says as he sits up, "maybe this has something to do with the photos on the wall and the cut-outs. Maybe it was Tyler who took the photo of Tiffany, as well? Doesn't explain why it's on the wall with a red fucking circle around her belly, though. We need to go back and look at that wall again, if Vince hasn't trashed it now that we know it's there." He does bring up a few good points.

"Why is it even there to begin with?" I question, "Why was *he* even there? Does any of it make any sense to you?"

"Maybe he was a regular visitor to the house. Could be he was closer to Dominic than we all think," he says relaxing back against the couch, but then suddenly slaps his knees and stares at me wide eyed. "What if he's interested in Tiffany's baby, knowing it's Dominic's?" He squint's his eyes as if he's figured something out, but his look instantly changes. "It makes the most sense, but why not Willow? She's Dominic's." He settles back scratching his head while I ponder what he's said.

"Fuck if I know," I say, still failing to find any logic in Vince's actions. "We could try and figure both of them fuckers out, but with Dominic and Vince being the sadistic psychopaths they are, we wouldn't figure out a goddamn thing. Well, Dominic *was* a sadistic psychopath."

"The more we learn about Vince, the more we see how alike he and Dominic really are. In my opinion, those two fuckers suffer from Borderline Personality Disorder. That could explain Dominic's unpredictable mood swings and uncontrollable rage. Never saw him take any medication, but that doesn't mean he didn't need it. People with BPD often suffer from regulating their emotions, to impulsive and reckless behavior, and last but not least suffer from unstable relationships. Pretty much sums up Dominic, doesn't it?"

I shrug my shoulders, not really giving a shit about him, but it amazes me that both Izzy and Kara still have their sanity after living with him. I just hope they still have it after all this bullshit with Vince is over. Over the past few days, we've uncovered things, and I'm not sure how they all piece together. One thing is for sure, I'm going to get it figured out.

Exhaustion finally overtakes me, so I excuse myself to check in on Kara. Each step I take down the hall is slow as shit as I find her stepping out of the bathroom, looking worse for wear. Her shoulders are sagging, she's dragging her feet and she's looking a little pale. She stops moving as soon as she sees me.

"I'm dying," She groans, but I can't help but think, even with her feeling as bad as she does, she is the prettiest woman I've ever seen. Her beauty is not solely defined by looks either, but her cute, shorty shorts and tank make it hard not to admire her body.

I joke, "Poor baby."

We're are quite the pair. I'm the one who is struggling to walk with each step pulling on my stitches, and she thinks she's dying. If she only knew I'm coming up with ways to kill Vince and hide his body, because every time my wound throbs, I want more and more for him to be in the ground with his brother.

I take this moment to stare at my girl, even feeling as bad as I do, I silently make her a solemn promise to never let anyone hurt her as long as I'm around to stop it. When I reach her, I take her in my arms and plant a kiss on her head and whisper my promise, "Not going to happen, sweetheart. You can't die on me. We've got a full life ahead of us." She mumbles and I know I need to get us to her room. "Let's get you back to bed."

Undressed and in a pair of loose flannel pants, I'm able to get somewhat comfortable. Having Kara tucked safely into my good side feels great, it's where she belongs. I never knew I was missing anything until she stormed into my life. And even with all the chaos, she's been the one bright spot. Just having her in my arms right now is worth all the shit we're going through, and I wouldn't trade her for anything in the world. That being said, I'd like for us to live drama free for the next several years, but I won't be greedy. I know my feisty girl can stir up drama pretty damn fast if she wants to. She deserves to be completely happy and I aim to provide that for her.

Her soft breathing against my chest is nice. I'd enjoy the feeling of her body against mine better if the pain that's stabbing my left eye would ease up. I'm in desperate need to get some rest and with Max on the couch, I hope all the thoughts in my brain will slow down long enough for me to get some sleep. Lord only knows what tomorrow will bring.

If Kara is up for it, I'd like to go back to Dominic's house before shit ends up missing. No matter how crazy that sounds, it may help us connect a few more dots. I suddenly remember the charm that was left in our door. I'm not sure how the hell I could forget it, but Vince is a fit for that one, too. With Vince being at the house, he had access to Dominic's things and was most likely using them to terrorize Kara even more. He admitted he needed for her to suffer the consequences for what she had done.

One thing is for sure, if I'm missing anything, that house may hold the clues. I may be exhausted and in a lot of pain, but I'm really worried about Kara because in her eyes, she did the unthinkable. She never thought she would be able to take a life, but that night she took the only opportunity she had in ending her years of torment.

Vince's explanation that he had no real desire to harm her did appease me some. Although, I don't fully trust him. He tried to end me before Max showed up. But, now what? The fact he is the one with all of the cards is not a position I particularly like. Like in a game of chess, we have to move in response to his moves. We're forced to second guessing everything, but there is only one thing I'm damn sure of.

I will do anything to shield Kara from any harm. That means getting the fuck out of here as soon as we can. There is nothing keeping us here and we'll be a hell of a lot safer away from here.

Maybe I should listen to my damn gut, and get the first flight home. We can figure out the rest there.

I don't like being here on his turf. Just knowing he could pop up anywhere at any time bothers me. At home, I have friends, I have family and I have hiding places so secluded, he'll never find me no matter how hard he tries.

With Kara safe, I can figure out what Vince wants with my sister. Him wanting my sister for anything is a problem for me because he's Dominic's brother, and you know what they say about birds of a feather. Tiffany and I may have our differences, but she's still my sister, and I will go to the end of the fucking earth to protect her. Is it even her that he wants? What if he wants her baby? If it is the baby, how far is he prepared to go to get it?

I have the feeling that I'm not going to like that answer.

Chapter Eighteen

"Dark Rooms"

Kara

"You sure you feel up to this?" Liam asks. He's concerned and I appreciate it, but I'm sick of him asking. It's the fourth time he's asked me since we woke up this morning. I think I should be asking him that same question. He's the one with a side full of angry looking stitches.

"What about you?" I ask and point to his side.

"Babe, you worry too much," his attempt to reassure me earns him a disbelieving glare. "I feel awesome," he says and I'm not sure if he's trying to convince me or him.

Either way, he's full of himself. "Liar," I say as I roll my eyes at him. "But yes, I'm sure. I want to see this room for myself." Upon hearing more about it this morning once my headache subsided, has me intrigued, and now I can't wait to see it for myself.

We enter Dominic's house and are met with complete silence. Liam insisted he walk in first, keeping a tight grip on my hand. I've been given strict orders to stay close to him and not wander off, and I have no problem obeying them. I'm not crazy about the idea of running into my newly found brother. Max is still with us, and it seems he is my other bodyguard while we are here. But I swear, if he touches me again, I might haul off and whack him. He's taking every chance he gets to reach out and 'comfort' me, but he's taking it a bit too far. Even though it's innocent, it feels awkward and wrong. He just better hope Liam doesn't catch him touching me, or else we will have another issue to contend with.

I shrug away from his touch, but in the last few minutes, he's touched my shoulder, held onto my arm, and made a motion to step directly in front of me. I however, step inside only to have Max reach and tug on my elbow. I free my elbow, but not before I give him an icy glare. He instantly pulls back and stares at me like I've offended him. Yeah, whatever.

"Just make sure to keep your eyes open," Max huffs, "I sure as hell don't want a repeat of yesterday."

Well, that goes without saying.

Once inside, Max shut the door and then locks it. The click of the deadbolt has me turning around to eye him oddly.

"You think that will stop him?" I point to the lock.

Max just shrugs his shoulder. "Not likely, but it makes me feel better."

I don't argue, instead I mouth the word, 'whatever'. We cautiously make our way forward, staying close to one another. The only noise heard is the creaking of the hardwood floors as we walk down the long hall to the study. The three of us enter the room, and it's as dark as the rest of the house. Without any hesitation I turn on the light switch and the instant I do, both Max and Liam whip their heads around, glaring at me like I've just committed some major crime.

"What?" I shriek. "There's not enough light in here." I throw my hands up in the air because I don't see the problem.

"Shh." They both respond, and I'm offended by them both, so I stomp my foot like a child having a tantrum.

"Seriously, your shushing' me?"

"Kara, quiet," Max scolds over his shoulder as his eyes scan the room.

"Babe," Liam lowers his voice to almost a whisper, "why alert anyone that we're here?"

"You think he's here, seriously?" I honestly didn't think he would be. My guess is he's long gone, but you never know. Not wanting a repeat from the day before, I change the subject. "Okay, so where is this mystery room located?"

Without saying a word, Liam walks to the larger of the two bookcases that takes up much of the left side of the room. "Dammit." He heavily sighs, striking the wall with his fist. His hands are feeling around the edge of the wood bookcase, but nothing happens. It appears to be sealed shut. Both Max and Liam act on their frustrations by scrutinizing the wall where this apparent secret door is.

"Someone's been here." Liam's voice sounds panicked. Disappointed, he wipes his face with his hand, before he nods his chin at Max. "Help me figure out the trick to open it."

"No problem," Max replies as his hands reach for my shoulders. "Step aside, Kara." Once again, taking the opportunity to touch me. The heat of his hands has me wiggling out of his reach but it doesn't seem to faze him as he rushes by me.

I watched them both run their hands across every square inch of the bookcase, trying to find a way to unlock the hidden passageway. I decide to glance around the room as I walk over to the desk and sit down. As I sit, I have a better vantage point to inspect the whole wall. I start matching up patterns in the wallpaper, that's how determined I am to find a mix-matched pattern that could hold the hidden clue to the door. It's an odd thing feeling, I never knew a hidden passage ever existed. Then again, I can count on two hands the number of times I've been in this room. That's how close I was with Dominic.

Sad, but true.

"Fuck, it has to be here somewhere!" Liam stretches as far he can to reach the top of the wood frame and winces when he pulls his stitches. I scold him to be careful, but he just grumbles and keeps on searching. Best I keep my mouth shut so I don't annoy him. When he's on a mission, there is no stopping him. Even when he's hurting, it seems.

"I'll work on this side, you concentrate on the other," Liam instructs Max between carefully controlled breaths. Max is quick to jump over and start pulling out the books, discarding them to the floor. The only thing is, we don't know if the button is on the bookshelf, or in a book that is on the shelf.

After a few minutes of frantically searching, they find nothing. Only a stack of books piled in a heap on the floor. I want to tell Liam to be careful and not to trip, but decide not to state the obvious. Not that he'd be mad, but he's busy trying to concentrate, plus I know deep down he's worried. He feels that room is the key in finding out the information we strive to obtain. I'm desperate to help as a thought crosses my mind. Taking a chance, I grab my phone from my purse and text the one person who may know something. Izzy.

Me: Hey, would you, by any chance, know of a secret room in Dom's study? If you have, where would Dom most likely keep the switch to unlock it?

A few seconds pass.

Izzy: Wow. A secret room, huh? Weird lol. Check his desk, that would be my first guess. He always made sure to have everything within his reach. Other than that, I haven't a clue.

Perfect!

Me: Thanks, doll. Laters.

Izzy: You better. Pls be careful.

Excited with Izzy's idea that his desk could be the key, I'm tapping my fingers on the top of the desk. I stare at every inch of the top before I push my chair back and run my hands along the underside. The rough underside reveals nothing.

"Shit. It's got to be here somewhere?" Liam stops searching to look over at Max, "Anything?"

"That would be negative," Max quickly replies, stepping back and crossing his arms, clearly frustrated.

I pay little attention to them not saying a word, so I continue to run my hand along every reachable surface. "Damn." Still not finding anything, I open the top drawer and continue to run my hands along the inside walls. Nothing. So, I open the next drawer to do the same. No success, so I move to the next drawer. Last drawer and my hopes are dwindling, but I open it and take out the few papers and a small wooden box that are inside. I don't waste time looking through those because I'm desperate to find a way to get those bookshelves open. I can feel my pulse racing because this feels like a scavenger hunt. I'm mouthing 'please, please, please' until my index finger traces over a small, circular button. Yes!

A tiny button is hidden so well in the pattern of the darkened wood, it will be missed if someone was simply looking for it and not feeling for it.

"Hey, I think I found something." I'm so excited, but I'm also terrified, because I have no idea what I'm about to press. It could be for something entirely different, and that worries me. Screw it, I decide. With my finger on the button, I close my eyes and press down and instantly, a clicking sound echoes in the room. Liam and Max stay where they are, with their eyes focused on me. I open one eye to peek at the bookcase, waiting for something to happen. Just then, the left side of the bookcase slightly dislodges from the wall. Bingo.

Liam offers two thumbs up. "Great job, babe!"

"Beauty and brains." Max chuckles before he realizes Liam has stopped and has given him a less than friendly glare. Max cowers and raises his hands in apology. I chose to ignore him altogether.

"Damn straight." Liam huffs, somewhat appeased with Max's apology.

I step out from behind the desk and am ready to explore when I realize Liam is still glaring at Max and his big mouth. To gain Liam's attention I snap my fingers in front of his face; Liam needs to remain focused and not get sidetracked. He's the jealous type, and I have to admit it is sexy, in a badass kind of way. Truth be told, seeing him bothered turns me on, but right now we have more important things to do.

That will have to wait, 'til later! Anyway, it's ridiculous. We are talking about Max, so Liam has to know he has nothing to worry about. There's not a chance in hell of Max and I ever hooking up. No way, not now, not ever. I'm not saying he's unattractive, in fact he's quite handsome. Only, not my kind of handsome. Where Max has boyish good looks, Liam's sex appeal is on a whole other level. In simpler terms, Max and I have no chemistry whatsoever.

"Move," I say impatiently, "we have more important things to do than you two having a pissing test. You guys can measure your cocks when we're done."

Before Max can take two steps, Liam halts him with a hand on his shoulder. "Careful, dude."

"Right," Max complies with his finger pointing upward. "Got it."

Conflict avoided.

I snicker at them both pointing out the obvious. "Boys, this conversation is ridiculous." As I try to pass by them, I'm stopped with Liam's firm hold on my arm.

"Let Max go first," he warns.

I go to argue it's not necessary, but let it go. Instead, I wave my hand in a sweeping motion offering Max the opportunity of entering the room first as Liam suggested. I follow behind Max and as we take the final step leading into the room, I can't help but think about how this scene right here reminds me something you'd see in a spy movie.

Who the hell has a secret room like this in their house? Besides, my brother, naturally.

I'm standing in the middle of this top secret room and I must say it's eerie and every bit feels like my brother. Cold, strange and secretive. The room is not overly large or fancy. It's lighter than the rest of the house, no dark wood or dark walls. 'Sterile' is the word that comes to my mind as I look around. Sterile, but in disarray at the moment. Besides a desk, two chairs, and a lamp, the room is bare.

"Shit." I hear Max remark and notice he's busy looking at the mess of things dumped on the desk. Not only are there papers scattered all over the desk, but there are more papers littering the floor.

"We're too late," Liam grumbles, standing near a wall that resembles a cork board. Cleary frustrated, he exhales loudly, landing a firm slap of his hand against the wall. Push pins are stuck to the wall but the papers they held in place are gone, except for torn edges of newspapers. There are even smeared words on the wall that look as if someone was trying hard to erase them.

I'm staring, speechless and not sure what to think. Why take the time to put it up and then panic to remove it? We are missing something and I don't have the first clue to what it is. Whoever it was, they were in a hurry and left the place a mess. Even the desk drawers are left open. That tells me someone was in so much of a hurry they did not have time to close them. As I look around the room, my sight is drawn to a dark room off to the side. Damn, now we have a secondary secret room connected to the first secret room. I'm actually starting to wonder what kind of spy my brother could have been.

"What's in that room?" I nod my chin. Both Max and Liam stop what they are doing and look in the direction I mention.

Liam sighs with his hand brushing down his face. "Never made it in there yesterday, but that was where Vince was hiding when I found this room."

I blink at Liam several times not at all amused. Did it occur to either of them, to maybe, I don't know... check this room first? Seriously, my chin hit the floor. Why not tell me this piece of information so we don't make the same mistake as yesterday?

Geesh!

In a huff I take a large step, but Max beats me to it and enters the room first. Damn, he's really pissing me off. He quickly turns on the light switch as we get our first look of nothing, it's not much of a room at all. I'd say it's more of a narrow hallway that leads to what appears to be an outside door. An outside door that's hidden. Of course!

"Well," I sigh understanding things better. "I think we found out how Vince made it into the house unnoticed."

"Looks that way, but now what?" Max questions then turns to look at me, "And, why take the stuff off of the wall?"

That's pretty easy to understand. "There's something he didn't want us to find, but *what*?" My mind is all over the place, but my eyes stay centered down the hall to the small wooden door that leads outside. Something about this hallway keeps nagging at me, but I'm not sure if it's the secret room, the secret entrance, or hell, Vince himself. Better known as my father's best kept secret.

Max is trying to engage me in conversation, but right now I'm too distracted. It doesn't deter him, he keeps talking. Liam is still in the other room, not at all happy to find things missing, because I can hear him cussing.

Max's voice fills the room again in an attempt to gauge me in conversation. "Doesn't answer the question of why all of this is here to begin with."

He's like a broken record, saying the same thing, only I don't have the answer. To investigate further, I might as well find out where this door opens from the outside of the house. I cautiously make my way down the hall, wanting to make sure we're not missing anything else when all of a sudden a cool breeze hits the right side of my face. The idea I've stumbled upon another hidden room stops me in my tracks. When I first stared down the hall, nothing seemed out of the ordinary, but standing here halfway down the hall, it's obvious. There is another secret room, hidden so well I swear my eyes are playing tricks on me.

I turn back to look down the hallway and this time I see Liam, standing with his hand on his neck. He's talking with Max and I wonder if he can see anything from where he's standing, so I ask.

"Liam, stay there, but look this way. Do you see anything different about this wall?" I run my hand along the wall so I can almost pinpoint the place I need him to concentrate on.

He's concentrating and squinting his eyes, but shakes his head. "No, why?"

"Huh." I'm not sure what to say. It's a freaking optical illusion for sure. From his viewpoint part of the wall protrudes out slightly, like plumbing has been dry walled around it. Nothing out of the ordinary. From my vantage point facing the opposite direction, the protruding part is a small opening, only visible from this side. If you look down the hall from where they are standing, all they see is a closed off section of the continuing wall. No opening on that side. Looking more closely, I see that the opening leads to another door. What in the hell, is all I can think?

"What is it?" Liam's not waiting for an answer, he's walking my way with Max close behind.

With my hand extended toward the wall, I'm about to blow their minds. "Another freaking secret room. Jesus, was my brother paranoid or what?" The three of us stand in front of the opening. The neutral colors of the wall and floor conceal things pretty well. The many wall hangings draw your attention, and I'm not sure if that's on purpose to disguise this room, but they have been placed there for a reason. The question is, why showcase them here in a secret hall? I'm thinking that answer is a fairly easy one, they are here for someone.

Liam exhales with a more obvious choice. "Or just weird?"

"Weird works for me." Max says softly while inspecting the hall for any other surprises it may have hidden.

I ignore them both anxious to see what's behind the door only my attempt to proceed is stopped.

Both Max and Liam, shout, "No way," but it's Liam who has a hold of my elbow. I glare at his hand, wanting to shout, 'really?' but instead, I stomp my foot like a petulant child. I'm seriously sick of being told what to do.

Liam shakes his head at me and stands back to get a better look at the secret room. "Shit, there is no way to see this unless you are right in front of it."

"Strange it is." Max says before asking the million-dollar question, "Begs the question once again, why is it here?"

All three of look at one another and shrug our shoulders not having a definite clue.

Max takes the lead and shifts his way through the narrow opening, and pushes the small wooden door open with his foot. Slowly, he walks inside and we follow. Of course, the room is pitch black, and there are no windows. I'm the last to enter and bump into Liam as Max is complaining he can't find the light switch.

We may not be able to see anything, but we can hear. Which is why we freeze when we hear the sound of a round being chambered in a gun.

With a flick of a lighter, a dark shadow materializes before our eyes. Sure enough, there stands a tall man with dark hair and even darker eyes, aiming a gun straight at us.

There was only one other person with hair that dark and eyes even darker, and he's dead. So the man I'm looking at has to be none other than my new found brother, Vince.

Chapter Nineteen

"First Impressions"

Vincent

"YOU JUST COULDN'T LET IT go, could you?"

"Fuck, not you again?" Liam grumbles unable to control his displeasure.

I could be saying the same thing, but I extend my chin in an attempt to let his rudeness roll off my shoulders.

"You just had to come back and snoop where you don't belong." My comment this time is aimed in a different direction. At long last, the time has finally arrived when my sight settles on *her*. Her eyes widen as they connect with mine, and in an instant, I'm hit with familiarity. It's as if I'm staring into Dominic's eyes and an unsettling feeling blasts me like a gust of wind. I'm captivated and totally absorbed until a deep voice breaks my concentration, like a gnat buzzing in my ear.

"And, you do?" Liam challenges me and honestly that's not what irritates me, it's the tone in which he uses that feels like a splinter under my nails. Although hard, I chose to ignore him and not reply, because my concentration is elsewhere.

Scrutinizing.
Studying.
Seeking.
Her.

I hate to admit it, but being in her presence has affected me more than I could have imagined. Scratch that, I'm livid with myself. I just assumed I'd be fueled with anger and disgust with what she had done, but the familiarity in her eyes as she stares back into mine confuses me because I don't feel the rage I should be feeling.

The only thing I have in retaining the upper hand is everything I know about her, and the next to nothing she knows about me. Just the way I like it. Seconds tick away, yet we both continue to stare at one another. While I'm intrigued, I have to wonder what's going on inside that head of hers.

Kara's eyes widen and come together, like she's trying to decide what to think of me. I find it amusing and wonder what degree of fear I'd see in her eyes if she were suddenly made aware of the many plans I had conceived to make her suffer for what she did to Dominic. The many levels of terror I could've easily inflicted on her all the while staying completely unnoticed. Up until yesterday, she had no idea I even existed, but she does now. That changes things, but it's not necessarily a bad thing. Even the best-laid plans need changing now and then, and I do love a challenge.

Lucky for her, that's exactly what happened. My revenge I so desperately felt I needed, is now replaced with optimism, and Kara is the key in making that happen for me. This is the reason why I'm so conflicted with my feelings towards her. I hate to heavily rely on anyone in obtaining what I want, especially when its someone I'm related to in one way or another. That just fucking complicates things worse.

The grief and loss I've felt since Dominic's death has left an irreplaceable void in my life. It saddens me my dear brother wasn't superhuman, after all. His ability to remain unscathed over the years with his reckless behavior, created an ongoing joke between us that he was immortal. Seems meaningless now, but our lifestyles are dangerous. We know the risks, but never did we feel vulnerable. What's ironic, is that part of his life is not what killed him.

Now, I stand tall as my iron-clad stature is cracking. I stare at the one who took him away from me. My superhuman brother is no more. He was taken, far too soon and as I look at her, it's like a part of him is here with me in this room and I miss him even more. The realization he will never return home resurfaces the resentment I feel toward her. Many times I've wondered what our first meeting would be like because I knew one day it would happen, I just never thought it would happen quite like this. The moment I heard voices in the outer room, I shut off the lights. My hope had been they'd eventually just leave, but no such luck.

Of all people to discover my room, it had to be *her*. About to burn my finger with the lighter, I move to the light switch.

As the room fills with light, Kara and I continue to maintain eye contact. Max and Liam automatically take Kara's side. Protecting her. Liam's leaning to one side, no doubt, still sore from our scuffle, and if Max is trying to intimidate me by crossing his arms and widening his stance, he can give it up.

My attention and sight is momentarily studying Max, but after a brief minute, quickly return to her. She's leaning into Liam with her fists tight. No longer in the shadows of the dark, she's getting her first good look at me. If I'm not mistaken with the way she just mouthed, 'wow,' I imagine she sees the familiarity between us. In that moment, I'd give anything to know what she is thinking.

I, on the other hand, have spent a lot of time staring at her face. I've committed her dainty eyes, narrow nose, and her pointed chin to memory. Not to mention, her full head of dark hair. She also has a small mole on her left cheek and a scar under her chin that required stitches after a failed gymnastics trick with Dominic when they were kids.

Yeah, I've studied her and I've also planned out the many ways I would take my vengeance out on her. For now, I'll let those go because at the moment she's speechless, her breathing is shallow, and with the way she's chewing on her bottom lip, she's nervous. While she appears vulnerable and weak, my mind is reminding me just how much I've loathed her while the other part of me is intrigued with her. Christ!

She's wringing her hands and looking at me like she's trying to figure out my end game. For the first time in a very long time, I'm conflicted with my hate and interest I have with her. It's not an emotion I'm used to feeling.

I'm able to pick up on the subtle attempts between Liam and Max. Their sudden eye movements can only mean one thing. They are devising a plan to take my gun, so I need to make sure I stay a step ahead. Liam's quick on his feet, that I remember from yesterday. His shifty eyes are calculating and I almost wish I'd taken care of him yesterday when I had the chance. Right now, I need to stay in charge.

"Now that I can see you all better, why don't you answer a question for me. Why are you here?" I ask with my gun aimed at their tight huddle they have shifted into. There is no quick response so I wait them out. I wait, and to my surprise, Kara speaks first.

"This is my house," Kara says as she stands a little taller but is holding tight onto the bottom of her t-shirt.

She surprises me with her commanding tone. I'll give her that. The mousy girl, who I must say does resemble me in more ways than I'd like, is showing a bit of her backbone. Well, maybe Dominic was wrong about her. She may be more like the two of us than he ever wanted to believe. Go figure, that was probably the mistake that cost him his life.

I won't be making that same fatal mistake, though. That much is certain.

"Funny," I respond, "since I have never seen you here before."

To emphasize my statement, I exclaim. "Ever!"

"Funny," she's quick to retort, "since, I never knew you existed before last night."

Her tone is acidic and sharp. I don't like it and my glare lets her know it.

She rolls her eyes. "Anyway," she resigns, "it doesn't matter. Dominic left the house to me in his will."

The way she says that last part, it leads me to believe that she wanted to shock me with that bit of news. Her eyebrows raise like she's gauging me. And she'd be right. Of all the foolish things he could have done, this would be it. To leave her this house, doesn't make one bit of sense.

"He was a stupid fool," I ramble, "I am sure we could list all of Dominic's downfalls and, my dear, you would be at the top of that list. Would you not agree?"

I leave her with that thought to watch her squirm out of this one. She's silent, and just as Liam goes to speak in her behalf, I raise my voice enough so he doesn't. Without interruption, I keep my conversation flowing with Kara. As she's the key to what I need.

"You are the one responsible for ending his life after all. Though, I must admit, I'm curious for your reasons behind it." As I study her body language, it tells me she's not at all comfortable with this conversation. She's continually shifting her weight between her feet and every so often tilts her neck like it's a nervous habit she does when she's stressed.

Under the scrutiny of my stare, she stands tall, but seems reluctant to share any thoughts. With a slight nod of my chin, I share some of my thoughts on the matter. "Some of *his* decisions—well," I pause with a snide chuckle, "that conversation seems pointless now, doesn't it?" I make the argument with a lip snarl because my anger on Dominic's lack of decision making is pointless!

"What the fuck do you want?" Liam rants.

Why look at him, finally Liam seems to be standing up for his girl, but before I can properly respond I notice Max. His head is forward like he's studying me closely. After I tilt my head to the side, I return the favor by closely studying him. Just like I thought he would, Max shakes his head like he's clearing his thoughts and resumes a more relaxed stance. Now that he's a little less annoying, I answer Liam.

"You will soon enough learn the answer to that question and more." I explain, but with Kara's news about the house, I now have to figure a way to get it from her. This house is part of my plans and she is a stumbling block in getting what I want. It's one thing to push aside my anger I've carried for her, to all of a sudden, needing something from her that means more to me than she'll ever comprehend.

This house.

With the news it's hers now it was like being told my mother had cancer all over again. Like a punch in the gut. I had no clue of his stupid plan because his estate was never a subject we talked about. I have stayed here for the last year because here is where I felt most comfortable. In a lot of ways, this house has been my haven. I would like to think it was also Dominic's haven too because we had so many late nights here just talking, drinking and getting to know each other better as brothers. An oddity for sure, but a positive thing for the both of us.

For years, I lived hating everyone around me. My mother fell ill a few years back and I lost her to cancer. Dominic helped to fill that emptiness; he's all I had left, but now he's gone too and the need to have something that's mine consumes me every waking moment of every day since he's been gone. I have been struggling to find ways to cope, so I hoped being here at the house, around so many familiar things would help, and thankfully it has.

Until now!

Most of my adult life, I have never needed anyone, but as the years went on, things changed and my focus shifted. I wasn't prepared to lose my mother the way I did. I mean it really fucked me up. We were so close, and it took me a long time to get over losing her so unexpectedly. Since then, I chose to only surround myself with people I had a purpose for, and I never got too close. I don't recall how old I was when I reached out to the sperm donor called my father. Fuck, he's not my dad, just a vessel that was used to bring me into this miserable world.

He had a wife, a house with a white picket fence, and two kids. Every fucking thing I spent years wishing I had. Fucking made me ill. They had money and seemed to be living the good life, while my mother and I scrimped and saved for every single penny. That taught me to be very self-sufficient at a young age. It wasn't like wanted to be, but it was the only way to survive. With the streets as my teacher, I grew up real fucking quick, and found every lousy way to make a quick buck. It wasn't long before a gang became my family. Even then, I had to work my way up the food chain. In that way of life, I had to earn everything I got, not a fucking thing was handed to me. And if I fucked up too many times, I knew they'd put a bullet in my head. So, like I said, I had to learn really quickly, until I finally made it to the top of the food chain.

I still work for the Aniello family.

They taught me how to defend myself. Fighting helped, but I was much better at communicating. I could get myself out of any jam with my words instead of my fists. I was a smooth talker and had the ability to process my surroundings in only a minute or so... faster if my life was on the line. The key was keeping them interested and actively engaged in what I was saying until I could figure out how to talk my way out of whatever situation I was in. At the end of the day, it needed to end in my favor.

Most guys use knives, guns, and their fists to get what they want. I simply use my brain and acting abilities to put the fear of whatever God they worshiped in their hearts. Once I did that, I had them. That's not to say I hate violence. No, not at all. When it's necessary, I have no problem drawing first blood.

That's how I met my dear brother, Dominic. I watched him long before I reached out to him. Sperm donor gave me a bit of information, I dug a little deeper on my own. I had no interest in Kara. I had no room in my life for a sobbing, emotionally needy girl. Dominic, was different, he had an association with an MC here in Chicago, and he seemed to have his hands in a lot of pots. His identity and reputation of being a lethal son-of-a-bitch were the reasons our paths crossed. The first time I saw him in action, it was a sight to behold. I only needed to look at him to see how much power he had, and his ability to take care of business without breaking a sweat was impressive. I saw a lot of myself in him that day and I knew then, I had to reach out to him.

Later that night, I started to build my reputation on the streets and being a member of the Aniello Family certainly helped my status. Two brothers started making a name for themselves on the streets of Chicago a few years ago by selling the best product out there and taking out whoever crossed them, no matter the reason. All I have to do is mention their names, and I get instant respect.

Cocaine at one time ruled my life, but I gave it up to make something of myself. My fast talking abilities got me out of some hot water. When Anthony Aniello visited me himself, I knew I was in for it. I had been behind on payments. Instead of inflicting pain, he mentioned that I resembled him during a dark period in his life. He gave me the one thing I never had before…an opportunity…an out, and that night, I gave my loyalty and trust to Marcus and Anthony Aniello.

From that day forward, I had a family to call my own.

I received a phone call late one Friday night and headed to a part of town that housed our storage garages. A seedy part of town, but out of the way of wandering eyes and definitely a place the cops steered clear of. A troubled client of ours was way behind on his payments. Marcus had enough of his bullshit excuses, and wasn't giving him any more time to come up with the money. He called his buddy, Dominic, to collect. At the time, I had no idea it was my brother, Dominic, Marcus was referring to. He referred to him as only one of his buddies.

As far as Marcus and Anthony knew, I had no family. That wasn't necessarily a lie, because at the time, I had yet to meet my brother, better known as The Enforcer. His lethal reputation had been tied to the Lost Souls MC. An outlaw club well known in Chicago. If anyone needed The Enforcer, they knew who to call. But only if lending Dominic out benefitted them in some way. If the Lost Souls wouldn't benefit in some way from lending Dominic out, whoever wanted him needed to find someone else. And if they failed to square up with the Lost Souls, Dominic would be taking them out next. In fact, they encouraged it. They wanted their reputation for being lethal to spread far and wide.

I recall the night I met him with fond memories, and it's a night I will never forget.

When I got to the storage shed, my adrenaline was pumping, I wasn't sure what I was going to find when I walked in. I walked in and saw men standing in a rather large circle taunting and laughing at whatever was under the spotlight in the center. I can only assume it was the tweaker who fell behind in his payments. Poor bastard, he had no idea what he was in store for. I only heard about The Enforcer from the Lost Souls MC and what I heard, was enough to terrify even the toughest man.

As I entered the circle I saw the tweaker, Clint, tied to a chair that was suspended off the floor by a huge chain attached to an overhead beam. I was surprised he wasn't suspended by his hands alone. The Enforcer pacing back and forth in front of him. To look at him, you would think he was a business man instead of a hitman. He had on a dress shirt with the sleeves rolled up to his elbows and a pair of black slacks, but who was I to question what the man wore when he did his job? While he paced, his jaw was tense and his eyes were dark and calculating. They held no emotion and gave nothing away. The chair was another thing that confused me, but I was not about to open my mouth and question his methods. I wasn't trying to be in Clint's place.

Another guy approached and set up a folding table, he then opened a rather large briefcase. Anticipation spiked through my veins and I felt a high no drugs ever gave me. My eyes danced, following his every move, because what I was about to witness, hell, what we all were about to witness, was quite impressive. Everyone wanted to see The Enforcer in action.

The angry looking tools that were lined up neatly in the case shone in the light. Barely able to contain my enthusiasm, I may have winced a time or two gazing at those pain inducing tools. That shit was going to hurt like a motherfucker, I bet Clint wished like hell he had paid his debt on time now. The Enforcer suddenly stopped pacing and walked to the table, eyeing his many tools like he was deciding what to use first. He paused momentarily, swinging his gaze past scanning the crowd and stopped when he reached me. The moment his eyes met mine, an indescribable feeling raced through my veins. He must have felt it as well, because as soon as his eyes traveled in the other direction, they snapped back to mine for another glance. A chilling recognition? I wasn't sure.

With his attention directed elsewhere, he finally spoke. "Marcus, should I give him another chance to miraculously come up with your missing money? Or, can I have my fun now?"

A hostile and yet entertaining chuckle could be heard as Marcus proudly let The Enforcer free. "He's had enough chances, it's time he met my good buddy, Dominic, otherwise known as The Enforcer. After tonight, he can tell everyone what will happen if they fuck with us again. Let tonight be a wake-up call to them all."

Dominic. Surely I had not heard him correctly. I shook my head and had to think about this. I listened and couldn't imagine that this man, was in fact, him. But, looking more closely, it became evident.

The dark hair, dark eyes and rather tall stature, we shared them all. Recalling everything I knew about him I whispered, "Well, I'll be damned." I've not only found a man just as ruthless as me, but my long lost brother. What were the chances? I decided that very night, I'd reach out to him.

"WELL?" SHE ASKS, LOWERING HER gaze to my gun.

I offer a simple, "Yes," while I clear my head of my thoughts. A stroll down memory lane will not do me any good right now. As I gaze into her familiar eyes, it's clear that I don't share that same strong reaction to her that I had with Dominic. I do feel something though. Unfortunately, it's not enough for me to guarantee her safety. Kara took more from me than she could ever give back, but if I can get her to see things my way, that would definitely help in her favor.

If she's smart, there is a way for her to remain unscathed, but it will require her to help me. First things first, I need to get her alone, because there is much to discuss. Before that can happen, I need to deal with her two bodyguards.

"Okay," I force a smile, because I need these two to cooperate. "I need you both to stay in here while I have a little chat with my *sister*." I maintain my smile while their faces look back at me in a state of shock. I'm not sure if it's because I called her my sister or that I want to chat with her alone. Either way, I couldn't give a shit.

Kara groans, "I'm not your sister," then turns and looks over to Liam who is currently staring at me.

"Not fucking likely, asshole." His eyes narrow to slits and his voice is reminiscent of a bulldog about to lose his favorite bone. With that in mind, I can barely hold back my laugh.

He is playing the protective boyfriend by flexing his muscles and once again letting his mouth run away with him. He may be her tall, brooding bodyguard, but what's really eating at him is the fact he is not the one in control. Yeah, asshole you know it and so do I, I'm the only one in control.

"Name calling," I mock and point out the obvious, "I'm the one with the gun. It really is a shame you do not do as your told. I have no problem shooting you both and being done with it, but in doing so, I fear my pending conversation with Kara will not go the way I need it to. So we will try this again. I am going to walk out of this room with Kara. Alone."

Liam is shaking his head like he's not having it while Max tries to convey the message, 'no way' to Kara.

I ignore them. "You both will remain in here and to make sure we're not interrupted I will lock the door from the outside."

Liam curses under his breath, grumbling, "You want to talk with her, you can talk right here."

He has balls, I'll give him that. "I don't think so."

To show them just how serious I am, I raise my gun and aim it at Liam's chest before Kara gasps and shoots her hand up. "Liam, *it's fine*," she says panicked, narrowing her eyes to the size of pebbles and baring her teeth. I do believe threatening Liam is a rather sensitive spot for her, and like I expect, she will convince him to go along with my plan.

"The sooner I get this conversation over, the sooner we can head back home and forget this whole miserable trip," she says with a hand resting on his chest.

I prove my point by aiming my gun at her man. That's a good thing, because fear is a great motivator. Plus, I believe Liam will do just about anything for his woman, even if that means a talk alone with me.

"Listen to your girl, Liam." I nod my chin at Kara to compliment her. "She's the smart one."

"Fuck off."

He's so mad he throws his hand in a huff as Kara urges him to drop it. I almost clap my hands with her performance. I'll say, I'm liking her a bit more and more. That's unfortunate.

"I don't like it." Liam whispers in her ear while giving me his deadly glare.

Just to irritate him further, I stare back with nothing but a smug smile on my face.

"Neither, do I, Kara," Max implies. "If he locks the door, we have no way to reach you." He says with his hand outstretched to her.

I really wish he would just stay out of this, he's been staring at me and typically that would not bother me, but he is most definitely getting under my skin. Call it an intuition.

"It will be fine." Kara replies to both of them.

The nagging feeling or intuition as I call it about Max has not let up, in fact, my gut is telling me that Max is a problem. Naturally, when someone is trouble for me, it usually ends up badly for them. Since, I am not about to change my ways now I look from Kara to Max. Under my intent stare, his eyes go wide like he's wondering what I am going say, but I don't say a word. Instead, I lower the aim of my gun and pull the trigger.

"What the FUCK are you doing?" Kara's horrified voice fills the room.

The sudden rush of adrenaline I feel as I pull the trigger mixed with the smell of gunpowder, is a rush like no other. It's as if time stood still. So much so, I briefly close my eyes and inhale. Upon my exhale, I reopen my eyes.

"Jesus Christ!" Both Liam and Max shout.

Kara is clearly shaken, she drops to her knees to help an agonizing Max, whose fury filled eyes stare back at me. He had not expected that.

I watch Liam and Kara attend to Max who is bent over assessing the hole in his foot. By the way they're acting, you'd think I just fatally shot him instead of his fucking foot. I never intended to kill him, just get him out of my way for a bit. Kara is quick to take off his shoe, while Max has Liam tearing a piece of his sleeve so he can wrap it around his foot to slow the bleeding.

"Oh for fucks' sake!" They act like it's more serious than it really is. "If I wanted you both dead, I would have already done it. Same goes for Kara. I figure this way I have provided both of you with something to do while I have my chat with Kara. Best you get that bleeding stopped as soon as possible." I warn.

Both Liam and Max shoot daggers at me like they want to say, 'fuck you' but neither do. It appears one bullet hole is enough for one night so I keep talking.

"My plans have recently become what's the word, *complicated*. You see, I have bigger things on my mind than you two. Now, if you will excuse us, I need to get moving." I say as I begin to shift towards the door.

"You're a big talker when you have gun, huh?" Liam implied.

His tone alone infuriates me, and I can't control the number of times I've shot him in between his eyes by now. He needs to watch himself because if my plans did not circle around him, I would most likely act on my impulse.

"Seriously?" It seems I need to refresh his ill memory. "It seemed only yesterday, I kicked your ass, took your knife, and stabbed you with it. Do you really think I need my gun?" This stupid fucker is digging his own grave by the minute. Any other day, I may admire his cockiness, but today is not that day. Doesn't bode well for him.

"Enough."

Kara's eyes narrow on mine, and I realize she's doing her part in calming her idiot of a boyfriend and her faithful sidekick Max. Max, who likes to get under my skin, yeah, I know enough about him, but he's never heard of me until recently. He has his own skeletons that I've recently uncovered. That information, I'll keep until I can use it to my advantage. Max could be of some use to me, if he lives to see another day, that is.

Dominic wanted to keep me a secret for reasons known only to him. It worked for me, because the fewer people who knew of me, the better. That did not stop me from learning all I could about all of them. Dominic kept me up to date on everything and in return it helped him by passing the time by talking with me.

The room we're all standing in now and the hidden entry to the house was built just for me. This way, I could enter and leave without anyone in the house knowing I was here to begin with. I've been using this entrance for years and for years I've watched things, learned things, and have grown attached to people...like my brother. When I learned it was Kara that killed him, I couldn't believe it. Then in the most bizarre of ways, new information came to light, like I was presented with a gift. In light of that, I've had a change of heart when it comes to her. She's lucky, it could have been a river of blood. Her blood.

As I shuffle Kara to the door, I point out to Max and Liam, "Both of you need to move to the back of the room while we will excuse ourselves. Don't be foolish, because I will kill you if need be."

I made a point to emphasize that in a low and menacing tone. I've had enough of this back and forth. Once we are outside of the door, I lock it behind me to find Kara backing off to the side, appearing a bit more nervous if her legs shifting their weight from one to the other is any indication. I lower my chin and look at her with raised brows. It appears that out of the reach of her man, she's quite timid.

"Don't get scared now," I say, "in there you were fierce, ready to stand up to me. You disappoint me."

"Oh well, I'm full of disappointments. I'm sure Dominic filled you in." She fires back.

I respond with a brief nod and raise my gun to point it down the hall motioning for her to move that way. "Funny you mention him, because he is what I want to talk to you about." I take a second to warn her. "This can go one of two ways. One, you listen and cooperate. Two, you don't, and you force me to shoot you. I don't have time to waste on tears and bullshit."

She stops walking and turns back to face me. "I won't shed a tear over you, so no worries there."

Her honesty is something to admire for sure.

"In fact, I barely shed a tear for Dominic."

Her brisk comment suddenly stays with me a moment as I think about all I want say to her, but one particular thing weighs heavily on my mind. Something above all, I need to have answered.

I wait until we reach the main room and have a seat before I ask, "Why did you kill him?" This question has been bothering me from the day I found out he was killed. I scrutinize her every expression. I want to see if she squirms or if she even bats an eye for what she had done.

"Does it matter?"

Her back stiffens, and her tone is unwavering. She's not backing down or quivering like I expected her to, but her disrespect toward me is something I will not tolerate. I place my gun on the desk and widen my stare at her.

"Fine," she says throwing up her hands up. "He spent years ruining people's lives. Not only my own, but my best friend, Izzy's. Wait…" she hesitates with an alarming look. "Do you know Izzy?"

She's eager now, wanting something from me. I am not one to divulge anything, but Kara's talking freely, so I don't mind to share a few things.

Definitely a new one for me.

"Of her," I reply, and she relaxes. "I was staying here when she was living here, but she never saw me. I have to say, observing Dominic with her was interesting. He was different around her, and that was not a good thing. She messed with his head. He had no control when it came to her." And that was the truth, Izzy was his kryptonite.

Kara shook her head from side to side, rolling her eyes, and bluntly said, "He was a monster."

Her eyes suddenly glazed over with a somber look before lowering to her feet. As I observe her sincerity and honesty, it strikes a chord. In our line of work, being a monster was considered a good thing. The problem is, she never saw her brother for what he was.

"You say monster, but he wasn't that. Entirely. He was never going to be a nine-to-five, take home to meet the parents' kind of guy. He traveled a different path. We're different," I choke back and clear my throat, "he was different." I'm not sure why I feel the need to explain this to her, but she does have this way of drawing you in.

"Psychotic you mean?" She strikes back, and my eyes shoot up to hers. She didn't understand him at all. I realize now she never will.

"He thought Izzy was his angel. The way I saw it, Izzy was his downfall."

"He died because of how he treated her." She keeps fidgeting with her hands but suddenly stops. "I wanted us to be free of him."

That right there was what I was looking for. Her admission is met with my curious stare. I want to know more.

"Go on," I ask because I want to better understand their dynamic. "Explain that to me?"

I sit back and listen to her every word. She slowly opened up and took me down her memory lane with how she truly felt about him. She went back as far as her childhood where she had some fond memories of him. As she spoke from the heart she appeared less tense, less reserved. Most likely because she had forgotten the gun I had returned to my lap, out of sight. I had always wondered what it would have been like growing up knowing her. Would I be different today? Most likely the answer is, no! It was nice to hear her memories, though. Memories, I never got to share.

Since she's being honest, I ask for her opinion. "Why do you think Dominic never allowed me around you? Why keep me as a secret?"

"Not a clue. Why do you think?" She rapidly responds, not even pausing to consider it.

Huh? I've asked myself this many times, but now I question if he was afraid I would like her. Maybe if things were different, she would like me in return. Would he have felt threatened by that? I wonder if the possibility of her liking me over him was a reason to keep me in the shadows?

With a mild head shake, I can only speculate. "Not a clue."

I spent more time than I anticipated, inquiring more about her. Everything I learned from her, leaves me even more curious about her. My next statement is going to sound harsh, but it's the ugly truth.

"When I found out you had killed him, I was ready to avenge him at all costs. Without even batting an eye, I wanted you to bleed." My eyes narrow but hers falter.

"Not anymore?" She asks quietly but never raises her eyes.

I sigh as it's finally time to fill her in on my plans. I lean forward and rest my arms on the table. "Things have changed, like I said. Some of it may not make sense to you, but you don't need to worry about that. Just know that you need to stay clear of my plans. If you do, I have no reason to harm you or ever interfere in your life."

That's not what she expected me to say, as her eyes are drawn together, I know I have her attention.

"What do you want, then?" Her inquisitive mind is spinning, and this is where she needs to tread carefully.

"I wanted the chance to meet you and have a nice chat and I've enjoyed it more than I thought I would, but there are two things I need from you. That's it."

Her head tilts, like she's thinking what in the world could I possibly want from her. "What are they?" she asks.

"For reasons you don't need to know, I'd very much like this house. You could do the sisterly thing, and sign it over to me." To push this whole family vibe, I say it cheerfully and with a smile, but she's not buying it.

"HA! Absolutely not! And seeing as though you don't view me as your sister, that bullshit won't work."

"Now, that's just semantics." I chuckle and realize it is a delight to spat with her, but we've got other things we need to discuss.

I change my tactics and sit up straighter to see if I can intimidate her. "Leave me this house. This is all I have left of Dominic. Seeing as though I live here and *you don't* ...that should be an easy one."

Hell, I even make it better for her.

"I'm even willing to buy it from you."

Her pause is a good sign, and then she leans back more than likely contemplating my offer. "And, the other?" she inquires.

I'm hesitant with this request because this is where Liam comes into play. "This one will require you to use your persuading skills. When you leave here today, I need you to make sure that man of yours stays clear of his sister. Let her be." I'm mentally counting how long before she reacts, and damn, it didn't take long at all. I didn't even get to five.

"Tiffany?" She gasps as her eyes get as big as saucers.

"The one and only," I admit. "You see, I have plans and those plans are what's keeping you safe. I wasn't kidding when I said I intended to make you suffer, but I have found another way to satisfy my need for retribution. Honestly, for you it's a win-win." If that doesn't convince her, this should help. "No Tiffany around means no more hassle for you or Izzy."

I lay out the pieces, and now the ball is in her court. Will she be smart?

"You want her baby?" she exhales when she figures it out, "Dominic's baby. Why?"

Now she disappoints me.

"Tsk-tsk-tsk. It's not for you to question, or concern yourself with." I make certain she understands. "That's my business."

Her eyes remain steady. "And if Liam or I don't agree?"

"You can agree, or not. That is entirely up to you. My concern is that you stay away and do not interfere. There is a difference. And only one smart move for you to make."

"I'm not sure, he'll agree." She admits with a hint of a whisper. But, she didn't disagree, herself. She thought of Liam's reaction. The way I see it, I have half of the battle won. She pauses but then carries on.

"We've had our differences, but you're dangerous. He won't willingly just stand by and let you hurt her. That's not the type of guy he is." She then places a hand over her heart and raises her voice, "Hell, I can't stand by and let you do that."

"Who said anything about me harming Tiffany," I ask. "Because I sure didn't." I can understand how she may of first thought that, but that is the furthest thing from my mind. Although, anyone who stands in my way, that's a different story.

"You need to think this through." I say as I lower my chin. "Your safety depends on it. That might be enough for him to have a change of heart when it comes to his sister. How important are you to him?" I know she might not like the idea of his sister meaning more to him than she does. She probably never even questioned it, but I'm sure she is now.

"LOOK," I shout with my hand connecting with the table. "It's either I GET what I want or you have to suffer for what you did. It's just that easy!" Just like that my anger has returned with a vengeance. Either Kara suffers for what she did or I get what I want.

Kara stares back at me with a pained gaze, and huffs, "Easy? Maybe for you. What you're asking of me is not easy."

"It is if you want to avoid any harm to come to you." I point out.

"You're a bastard."

"A bastard? Now that's rich coming from a sister who killed her brother." She may wince like my comments pain her, but she'll find no compassion with me. She did after all, just call me a bastard. In the moment, I can't control my inner rage.

"There is ONLY one thing in this whole fucked up mess that will keep me from returning the favor and avenging Dominic. A son. I'm gambling with the idea Tiffany is carrying a son. A son, I could raise as a consolation for the brother you took from me. This way, I'm also taking something from all of you."

Kara sits back in her chair staring at me like she's thinking of what to say. Finally, she does. "Why not have your own?"

Oh, clever girl, you just don't get it. "Not just any son, I want to raise *Dominic's* son. That way, as I grow old, I'll always have a part of him with me." Hell, I've even considered names. Declan. I'll raise him to be wise and he'll learn everything about his true father and just how much I've grown to care for my brother. That's how much I've committed myself to doing the right thing.

I owe Dominic that much.

This is my gift to him.

It's that simple, and Kara is the key to making it all happen. The next several months will reveal how all of our lives play out and what other plans need to be made.

The minute I gave Kara the keys to unlock the room, she ran to get Liam and Max out and I used that time to sneak out. An unexpected call had me rushing out of the house.

Chapter Twenty

"Home At Last"

Kara

I T'S BEEN FIVE GRUELING DAYS, but we're finally back in home in Washington. Five days filled with Liam's grumpy comments and stress about how to handle Vince's plan when it comes to his sister, Tiffany. With tensions running high, the last few days can be summed up in two words, utterly miserable. The aftermath from my face-to-face chat with Vince had been nothing short of a nightmare. I prepared myself for what Liam's reaction would be, but it was worse than I anticipated.

After I gave my play by play of what was said, Liam became enraged. Nothing Max or I said calmed him down. It didn't help any that Vince went and shot Max not even a day after stabbing Liam, so needless to say, we were high on adrenaline and short on patience. With us being emotionally charged it only added gas to the fire. Where Liam saw red when it came to his sister, I was quick reply, what about me?

Not that I was being insensitive when it came to her, I was just pointing out the obvious that she'd made her own bed. Once we made it back to my parent's house, the shouting matches continued, only this time, my parents joined in. All of the yelling created a division, my parents more concerned with my welfare and Liam's need to defend his sister when he felt no one was. The shitty evening came to an end when my mother finally broke down in tears.

By the end of day three, our moods weren't any better, and I was too tired to care about anything. I was more than ready to leave Chicago behind. It no longer felt like the city I'd grown up in and no longer felt like home. Home, to me, was far, far away. My home was near Izzy, my best friend in the whole world. She's the one person, up until Liam, I simply could not live without and I've never needed her more than I did right then. She'd understand and would help me put things into perspective. I feel she's the only person who can truly know how I'm feeling.

The flight back home was unusually quiet. Liam didn't say much, but he held my hand, it was his way of letting me know things would work out. Right now it's not easy, but life never is. We've talked some, but the tension is still there. It's not that I question his feelings for me, I'm more concerned with his new obsession to finding any way to get back at Vince. Not only for stabbing him, but whatever plans he has for Tiffany and her child.

When I freed Liam of that room, it was like letting a lion out of his den. He instantly reached out and pulled me tightly in his arms making sure I was okay. Finally, satisfied that I was, he wanted a play by play account of what Vince said. I began telling him everything as we did a quick, final sweep of the hidden room. None of us wanted to stay there any longer than necessary. Max had wrapped his foot with part of his shirt and found use of a curtain rod from Dominic's study to use as a cane. On our way out, we grabbed the box from the previous day I put aside with miscellaneous things I felt might be somewhat important. Papers, photos, basically anything we felt could hold some value. There was no way I was leaving it behind. The professionally typed and handwritten documents Dominic marked confidential, I definitely wanted. If I ever needed a bargaining tool, I hoped something in this box could be useful.

The non-stop questions from Liam and Max continued throughout the night, and continued into the early morning. They analyzed every word and wore me out with their comments and continued scrutiny. Eventually, I wanted to bang my head against the wall. Their remarks led to more questions that I had no answers for.

In a moment of sheer exhaustion, I made the comment that Vince could have the house, and as long as Tiffany's not in any danger, why not just let it go. Vince said that as long we didn't interfere with his plans, my nightmare was as good as over. That meant we could get back to our lives and finally put all of this hell to rest. In my sleepy state it sounded logical, but the look I received from Liam told me that my comment was not received well. Nope, not at all.

Ever since then, Liam has been uptight and on an all-out mission to find Tiffany, but he's not stopping to think about the danger this could mean for me. And if he has, well, he's not sharing it with me. I'm afraid all he can see is getting his sister away from the lunatic who stabbed him and held him at gunpoint. I fear he's blinded by that damn male ego of his.

I asked my dad to handle selling Dominic's house, I just couldn't deal with it. I don't even care who he sells it to even if that means Vince, I just don't see why it matters. I also told my parents that I was going to split any profits with them. In the beginning, I argued with myself about accepting a dime from the sale, but since then had a change of heart. I figured I'd put the money away for Willow's college fund, but I'll keep that part to myself for now. I figured that Dominic's money needs to be spent actually helping his daughter, the one thing he failed to do when he was alive. Doing this was important to me. If all else failed, I could always tell Izzy that it's money from my parents and not from the sale of his house. Just in case she would have an issue with it. Someday, I'm hoping Izzy lets my parents see Willow. That hasn't happened yet, and with Brax adopting her as his own, it probably won't. Willow is far too young to know that Brax is not her biological father. If it's Izzy wishes to have Willow believe that Brax is her real father, I'll honor that and so will my parents.

These days, today being no different, have only fed into my insecurities. Things are just too quiet. There is only so many times I can hear we're going to be okay to believe it when all I feel is an artic chill between us. It's left my thoughts and emotions all over the place. When he's home and it's really quiet, that's when my insecurities creep in. I'm letting every little thing get to me, and it's slowly starting to drive me crazy.

Tonight, Liam is more agitated than usual because he's not having any luck whatsoever in finding his sister. He's tracking her cell phone and her credit card purchases, yet he can't find anything that could be a clue as to her whereabouts. He has enlisted a buddy who handles these kind of things but so far, nothing. It's like she's vanished. She's either using cash, or someone is helping her. Maybe someone who has an interest in her staying under the radar?

For the past hour, he's been on the phone while I've been forced to sit and listen to him agonize over feeling useless. With each passing day, he becomes more distracted. The growing tension is widening the distance between us. Deep down, I know he doesn't mean to let it happen, but it's just the way it is. He's so hard to read when he's like this and intentional or not, it's driving me crazy. I respond by quietly withdrawing as I listen to him tell whoever he's talking to that he will to stop at nothing to find her. I can't help but feel like his effort to protect me pales in comparison to finding his sister. That leaves a big, gaping hole for me, and I'm not too comfortable with that.

"I've contacted Mick about helping to locate Tiff." Liam says nonchalantly as he walks back into the living room, searching the counter for something. I'm still curled up on the couch and even though he's talking to me, it feels like we're miles apart. Enough so the loneliness I'm feeling makes my heart ache a little more. It's really sad and I can't help but think how did things change so fast?

"Oh, yeah?" I whisper trying hard to stay positive, because even though he's talking to me, it has nothing to do with us.

He reacts like I've offended him and turns to face me. "This concerns him as well, Kara. He's family, too. He's her uncle, and I'm sure knowing that a sick fucker wants her kid is pissing him off just as much." He then grabs his jacket like he's preparing to leave. That's when I snap out of it.

"Liam, have you even stopped and given any thought about what this could mean for me? Do you think he'll come after me if you do find her? Have you even once considered that possibility? Because I've thought about it more times than I'd like to admit!" I'm up from the couch with my arms crossed just waiting for his response will be.

He gives me a pained looked, but quickly shakes his head, firmly saying, "He won't. It's that simple."

That's all he says, and he says it without any emotion at all. Apparently I'm keeping him from something, because he's eyeing his watch instead of paying me any further attention. It pisses me off.

"Really?" I'm more than irritated and annoyed at his lack of care about what happens to me, and it's starting to take its toll. I sarcastically raise my voice, "And you know that for a fact, right?" He has me so pissed I'm begging to get into a shouting match with him, but with the way he's staring at me, he doesn't.

Instead, he lowers his chin and opens his mouth to say something only to close it without saying a word, which does nothing but infuriate me more. His rather easy going regard for my safety is ticking me off, but instead of yelling, I'm balling my fists and literally biting my tongue. I know if I say anything else I'll break down and cry.

When I'm mad, I cry. When I'm sad, I cry. Hell, lately I cry all the damn time and I'm sick of it.

"Listen," he softens his voice, "I need to go. I'm going to see my uncle and the brothers. I'll be home later. Lock up." He stays looking at me for a minute and I know he can see the tears that are threatening to fall. He's fighting on the inside, I see it behind his pained eyes and clenched fists, but he doesn't do anything about it. He grumbles and turns leaving me alone to stand in the living room.

No kiss, no hug...no nothing! Just the door closing behind him.

With it, my heart sinks. The sound of the door closing is the only sound until I wail with a wrenching sob. The pain I saw in his face before he walked out only justifies the strain he's putting himself through. He's created an impossible situation for himself by caring for me, or finding his sister. He wants to do both, I'm just not sure he can successfully.

I'm all for giving him the chance, and have been for days, but it's getting really tough. I've never felt this isolated from him before. I miss his warm embrace and loving touch so much, my chin trembles, and the tears flow with ease. The build-up I've been feeling is now being released. In an act of desperation, I grab a head full of hair in both hands and fall back to the couch let out a cry so violent, it hurts. I've finally found love, and I'm not ready to lose it. As sorrow fills my tears, I have to talk myself down.

As I wipe under my eyes, I heave a few big calming breaths. "You're okay, Kara, so stop with the crying. Liam's worried about his pregnant sister, and she needs him right now. He knows you're okay because you're here with him. Now quit being so damn needy and emotional." I cough to clear my throat, hoping to slow my sobs and tears. And after a few breaths, I try to think of anything that will distract my mind. I try babbling a few more things but, the tears just fall harder. And then I lose it, and repeatedly slam my fists into the couch on either side of me.

Argh!!

I have to remember, this is Liam, and I know Liam well enough to know that what he is thinking has to be logical and rational. It's how he thinks. As long as I'm physically here with him, he'll keep me safe. Anyway, he has repeatedly told me he would never let anything happen to me. I have to put my trust and love in that.

But what if he's wrong?

Staring at the ceiling, I feel as if the walls are caving in on me. I'm half-tempted to fly back to Chicago until things settle. That way,

Liam can focus all his energy on finding Tiffany. I can say I'm just waiting for things to settle, but the truth is, I'll just be running away. It's what I always do when things don't go my way. But my life is on the line, so it's time for me to grow up, trust Liam, and stand up for myself. I just need to believe it! I wish I knew what happened to the confident bitch I used to be.

Besides, if Vince really wants to hurt me, distance won't stop him anyway. So, it looks like I'm a sitting duck, and my fate lies in Liam's hands, who's hell bent on finding and helping his sister, and in the hands of my sadistic brother, Vince, who promises to kill me if he does. How the hell did this happen to me? Oh, right! I sealed my fate the night at that farmhouse. Only now, I hope I can survive it. That night changed my whole being, who I was and who I'm going to be.

A gentle knock at my front door has me up on my feet and rushing to open it. Tears glisten my eyes and my heart swells thinking Liam is on the other side of that door. I've missed his embrace so much, so the idea of Liam wrapping me into his big arms, reminds me just how much I've grown to love him. Maybe after he left, he realized how badly I need him. Both of us are hot-headed, and it's is an issue we each need to work on. I really don't wish his sister any harm, but I want to live too. Surely, he has to see that.

I excitedly open the door, only to have my heart sink and my shoulders sag in disappointment. If my face wasn't a dead giveaway, my body language clearly was.

"Oh, Max, what are you doing here?" It's not that that I'm not happy to see him, I was just wishing for a different man to be there. And anyway, I just saw Max yesterday. He reads my reaction and stumbles back a few steps.

"I...I saw Liam leave," he stutters with a chin nod over his shoulder, "thought you may need a friend." His gentle and sweet smile is hard for me ignore.

"Um, okay. Come in." I can't just send him away, he's a friend. A longtime friend at that.

"I wanted...to talk to you for a second." When he speaks, he drags out his words, like he's unsure of himself. I, one the other hand, read him differently.

"So, you waited until Liam wasn't here for this talk?" It's not a statement, it's a question.

I'm fishing, and the change in his expression lets me know I'm on the right track.

"You would be right," his light chuckle is accompanied by a twinkle in his eyes. "Always the smart one," he chimes in as I turn to walk back inside.

He walks past me using an actual cane today. I stop in the kitchen to fetch us something to drink.

"You're walking better today." My mention of his cane has him chuckling.

"Yeah, the cane helps. It sure isn't sexy though," he says with a shake of his head.

When I enter the living room, I place our drinks on the table and go to sit on the couch across from him. When I sit, his dark eyes travel from my face down my body 'til they rest on the open space next to me. A rush of uneasiness steals my next breath and before I know it, he suddenly stands, and joins me on the couch.

"Ahhh," he lets out a forced chuckle with his hands clasped together. Acting a bit nervous, he leans forward to wipe at his thighs like he's dusting himself off.

I'm not sure what has him acting so weird, but slowly I go to stand only to have him hold out his hand to stop me.

"I've always watched out for you…" he starts to say, but lowers his hands back to his lap. When his eyes reach mine, he exhales with a sigh and it's as if a weight has been lifted. He offers me a sincere smile. "I've always been concerned when it comes to you, so it's hard for me not to say something. Kara, you need to know that I'm genuinely worried when it comes to you." As the word 'you' leaves his lips, his eyes transcend in a dark stare, turning his hazel eyes to dark brown.

"Well," I hesitate. I'm not sure what to say to that, so I go for being polite, "Thank you for your concern for me, Max. But I think Liam does a pretty good job of that." I'm not sure what he's trying to say, but something tells me he cares a bit too much for me and the fact I'm living with another guy. Another guy Max happens to be friends with. Shit. I'm praying like hell this conversation is not headed where I think it's headed.

"He can't." His words come across strong and firm as I wince. "He's blinded with his sister's safety, and that's all he's focused on right now. He's angry Vince got one up on him and, as you know, a man like Liam does not take that lightly. He's so focused on getting Tiffany and her baby to safety, he doesn't realize he's leaving you vulnerable and alone."

I instantly resent him, even though, he's telling the truth. I already know it and I don't want to hear it from him, so my knee-jerk reaction is to defend Liam. God, this sucks!

I attempt to reel in my frustration. "Tiffany is his sister, Max," I remind him like he wasn't aware of that fact.

Max shakes his head, and holds up his finger as if disagreeing with me. "That may be true, Kara, but that's not his real motivation. He wants to get even and one up Vince in return. And I'm afraid it's at your expense." As he expresses his concern, he does it while scooting closer to me. With not feeling comfortable having him this close, I slide so far over, I'm damn near sitting on the arm of the couch.

"Listen," I say, as I put both of my hands in the air between us, hoping to prevent him from getting any closer. "I don't know if what you are saying is true or not. But I'm sure Liam will do what he feels is best. And whenever Liam does something, he always has a reason."

"Are you okay with that?" He questions with a raised eyebrow.

I answer honestly. "I have to be."

Max grumbles. "NO, you most certainly don't. Look. While he spends time finding Tiffany, why don't I take you away somewhere safe until he finds her. Just to make sure you're safe."

What?

I'm staring at him like he's lost his mind, but he's absolutely serious. He's waiting for an answer, but the only thing I can do is chuckle sarcastically.

"You have got to be kidding me."

He must feel like he's pushed me too hard because he's using his hands to calm me down. Either that or back pedal realizing he came on to strong. "I didn't want to freak you out, but you are forcing my hand. Look," he starts, then presses a finger to his lips like there's something he's reluctant to tell me. "I have good information that Vince is on his way here, to your house. Like, tonight, and I need you to get a bag together so we can get out of here. You have little time to waste."

"What are you talking about?" I'm staring at him now like he's gone mad.

"Just don't argue with me, please?" He presses his hands together like he's praying. "For once, do what you're asked to do," he pleads.

Unsure what to do, my foot nervously taps on the floor. I can't up and leave without Liam knowing, but if Max is right, why should I sit here and wait for Vince to get to me. "I have to call Liam." I'm already up and reaching for my phone when Max rushes to my side and tugs on my elbow.

"Call him after we leave. Let's just get you out of this house, and make sure you're safe, first." His sense of urgency frightens me. If he's right, and Vince is on his way, his nervous behavior tonight is completely justified. And if he's wrong, I may end hurting him for making me go through this unnecessarily. I can tell my indecision is irritating him, because while he paces the floor of my front room, he huffs under his breath about us being 'sitting ducks'. Those words hit me hard trailing goosebumps down my arms, so my decision is an easy one to make.

"Oh, all right." I'm going against my better judgment, but if what he is saying is true, I best move my ass. I'm not sure if I'm pissed because he's telling me what to do or the idea that Vince is gunning for me because of Liam's pursuit of his sister. Either way, with every stomp of my foot I'm cursing about messed up sisters and crazy assed brothers. My life's in constant turmoil and my poor bag is only thing I have to take it out on. I yank it from the closet and damn near rip the zipper off.

"Kara, get a move on." Max shouts from the front room.

I grumble as I open my drawers wondering what the fuck I should even pack? How long will I be gone?

Frustrated, I grab a few panties, a couple of t-shirts, jeans and socks. I forgo the make-up, but grab my deodorant and toothbrush. As I do a mental rundown in my mind to figure out if I'm missing anything, Max shouts for me to hurry up once again. I rush, zip my bag and make my way back to the living room. If I forget something, oh well, that's too damn bad. I have to remind myself to stop griping and realize I have nothing to lose and everything to gain. Max is here to help me even though I have no idea where Max got this information, so I make a mental note to ask him after we leave.

LIAM

"So what the fuck are you saying, exactly?"

My uncle sits across the table holding his cigar between his fingers focusing his attention on his curling smoke rings.

"We've been watching that gentleman, very closely." This time when he talks, he sits up with his arms on the table, and his aging eyes appear worried. "In the meantime, I've been busy working with my sources on tracking your sister, and a name popped up, along with the possibility of her whereabouts. But before I had a chance to do anything with it, I received a phone call. The interesting thing is, the guy calling me was the same guy. Call it irony or luck. I don't fucking know, but a Marcus Aniello, from Chicago, tracked me down for a reason." His eyes travel, meeting the gaze of everyone at the table before resting on me once again.

Brax is sitting quietly next to me and Tom, my uncle's VP, is next to him. Both men stay quiet and listen.

I'm an impatient prick at times and right now is one of those times. "And…"

He warns. "You may have another issue than the one you're aware of."

My puzzling glare is met with a blank stare and a raised eyebrow. I have to physically hold onto my chair to keep myself from crawling over this table to slap it out of him. I'm losing it. This cat and mouse question thing my uncle has going on is frustrating me to no end, and he's always been this way. It's in his nature and, like always, it drives me insane.

"Will you just spit it the fuck out? I have a lot of shit on my mind and I'm short on patience."

He ignores my rudeness. "Marcus Aniello, is an interesting fellow who happened to be a close friend of the late Dominic Santos. To make it even more fucking interesting, he works closely with a Vincent Parisi. I'm assuming this name is familiar to you?"

"Vince? You're shitting me," talk about a small fucking world. I know I should have a hundred questions, but right now, I'm is still trying to wrap my head around this bit of information.

"To top it off, it seems he's recently learned of the connection between Dominic and Vincent."

I'm about to open my mouth, but he shuts me down.

"Don't ask me how, those are just the facts as I know them."

"Fucking bizarre," I say under my breath. "Okay, but what does that have to do with what's happening right now?" My mind is scrambling, trying to connect the dots and prepare for what's to come.

"Let's back things up a bit. When you were in Chicago, you and Kara came across a photo that you sent to Brax, remember that?" He questions and I nod, knowing the exact photo he's referring to.

"You wanted to match the guy in that picture to the guy Brax caught spying on his family. Smart move on your part, by the way.

Once Tyler was released by Brax, we decided to tail him. Call it curiosity or not trusting that fucking weasel, but we also ended up having a little chat with him, too. He wasn't overly eager to chat with Brax again, seeing as he pulled a few of his teeth out trying to get him to talk in the first place."

Brax smirked, muttering under this breath. "Wuss."

I can't help but chuckle because I can almost picture my buddy in action. But right now, I'm more focused on what my uncle found out. "What kind of info did you get out of him?"

"After explaining what would happen to him if he didn't come completely clean with us, I decided to show him that picture to see what kind of information we could get out of him."

"Smart thinking." I can't argue with his logic.

"Here's the thing, he mentioned a few details we weren't entirely believing, but we made a note of it. When I was talking with Marcus, he surprisingly, not only backed up what Tyler said, but he went into further details. He had firsthand information, confirming you have someone else you need to watch out for."

"What do you mean? Who?" Like I need another asshole to worry about because I'm at my fucking limit. But I'll do whatever I have to, to make sure my girl is safe. Lately, I've been preoccupied and distant from her. It's not her, I just need time to deal with the shit with my sister and that fucker, Vince. I see red whenever his name is mentioned. I'll make it up to Kara, though. I swear I will. She's safe as long as she's with me.

"Fuck, it never ends." Brax sneers.

My uncle continues after a mild throat clearing. "Marcus shed some light on Dominic. What his feelings were when it came to his sister, your Kara. The main reason Marcus reached out to me at all was to offer us of a peace offering. He gave me something and in return he wants something from us."

Okay, here we go. This is why this meeting was so important, why I rushed out the door leaving Kara. It's about finding my fucking sister as soon as possible. I just never thought doing so could harm the woman I've grown to what, love? Shit, maybe that's why this is so fucking hard? I've never been good at showing any weakness and telling Kara how I'm feeling when it comes to her and my sister, feels like a weakness and something a pussy would do. I've never had such strong feelings over a woman before, and that makes this situation even more fucked. But Kara is not just any woman, she's my woman.

Choosing to protect my sister knowing Vince wants to hurt Kara if I do, is seriously fucking with my head.

"Shit," I say, while emphasizing it with the slam of my fist. "Of course, that fucker wants something. Nothing's ever free, so let's hear it."

He doesn't even stop to take a breath, he just leans forward with his arm on the table, and a finger pointed at my chest. "In return for what I'm going to share with you, he wants you and me to have a conversation with your sister. Together. He knows where she is. He also made it clear that she is not being held hostage, nor is she hurt in any way. He said she's happy and wants us to leave her be."

"Fuck." Of course, he would say that. That's probably Vince forcing her to say those things. The only good thing is that he admits knowing where she is. That's something we can work with.

"Liam, if she is happy as he says, you have to think about letting her be. You can't force her to do something she doesn't want to do." Brax suggests and I stare at him like he's grown two heads. That, or he's lost his mind. Either way, he can't seriously be buying this load of crap.

"He's got her brainwashed. What happens after the baby is born? Then what?" It's hard for me not to snap at him, but he just jumped ship to get in bed with the enemy. I realize he's better off with my sister long gone, and it helps his family if she is. My thing is, I can't just let that fucker have his way.

"We will discuss that with her." My uncle speaks up. "Trust me." His lethal stare lets me know that he has this handled, so I'm all ears for whatever news he gave up.

"What news did he share with you?" I'm prepared to hear it, so far all I'm hearing is bullshit from this guy.

"He has information about Kara." The slight eye gesture he gives me implies that Marcus knows more about my girl than I'd like, but I stay quiet and listen.

Flicking his cigar ashes, he continues. "Most of his knowledge is all the things he's heard from Dominic. He mentioned that he's aware of certain letters being sent to her, he knows exactly who Dominic was keeping away from her, and why."

Well, that's interesting, but old news. We know this already. "Vince, yeah we know."

"Wrong." He's quick to answer and I stare back surprised.

Holding up my hands, I ask, "If not Vince, then who?" To say I'm not skeptical would be a flat out lie.

"Max." I hear the thunder coming from Brax as he smacks his hand on the table, but the mere mention of his name confuses me. No way. He has to be wrong. Not a chance.

"What? No way. He's bullshitting! Max's been the one helping us all this time. Why would it be Max?" I'm pissed because this fucker is giving my uncle false information. It's a waste of our time.

"Liam!" my uncle yells, to get my attention. "I told you I showed him that picture, to see what kind of response we'd get out of him. Well, guess who he pointed out as being his contact person? The person he reports to?" He drops his chin giving me a stern looks and that's all the confirmation I need.

The blood drains from my face and I feel like someone just punched me in the gut. To keep from losing my shit, I stare at my shaking hands in front of me, but my rage curls them into fists. What I need is to take a few deep breaths, but instead, I come unglued.

"Jesus Christ! I'll kill that fucking bastard!" Thinking back to the past few months, I replay our time spent with Max in my mind like a movie in fast-forward. The times Max helped us, all the times he spent with Kara. The more I think back, the more sense things begin to make. His closeness with her, his extra attentiveness, always eager to touch her. Fuck, we thought he was being a friend instead he was living out his fucking fantasy to being with her. In helping us, he had ample opportunities to get close to her. All of it happening under my nose. Holy Shit!

"That. Little. Fucker." Brax's eyes tightened with each word. I think we both felt played for fools. But it's more than that. We trusted him. Just then, a chilling thought entered my mind. Dominic mentioned that the friendliest faces mask their true selves. Jesus Christ!

"Shit. My phone." I reach in my jacket pocket to get my phone just as it beeps with an incoming message.

My adrenaline has my finger shaking, but I press my voicemail to hear her message.

"It's from Kara," I say.

Hey, it's me. Listen, I know things have been stressful between us, and I'm going to make it worse. Max is here. He says Vince is on his way to the house and to make sure we're safe, we should leave. We're on the road now and once we stop, I'll call you to let you know where we are. I...love you, Liam...always.

I press it again.

And again.

And again.

I start to swallow down breaths to keep from shouting, my pulse is racing and I'm dizzy with rage. I drop the phone to the table and ball my hands into the tightest fists that I can. I need to get a grip, and fast, but at the moment all I can think is, "This can't be fucking happening."

"Liam, what's up, man?" Brax reaches out a cautious hand, but stops short of touching me.

I raise my head just as a fury I've never known, sends me in a fit of rage. A new sensation is brewing within. Vengeance. Only one face appears as I close my eyes to welcome my thirst for blood. There's only one person I see. And that person is…Max.

"That motherfucker has her."

chapter

TWENTY-ONE

"Max"

Kara

"Just think about it. You don't have to decide now, but please think it over. For your safety."

"No, Max. Liam would never forgive himself if something happened to me and he sure as hell would not let me just leave without him. I can't go away and not tell him where I am."

Max draws his fingers to pinch his nose, clearly aggravated. "Vince is watching everything. For all we know, he most likely has all of your phones tapped, too. Kara, I've spent years trying to get you to understand and see things the way I do. Years, I've had to keep my distance..."

I gasp. "What?"

"You had no idea, did you?" I took my eyes off the road to plead with her. "All the letters, all of my promises. I wanted nothing more than to be the one to be with you."

"The letters..." Oh, my God! "Max, you sent me all of those letters?"

His knuckles turn white as he grips the hell out of the steering wheel. He's acting odd, like he's fighting with his own demons. Whatever he's thinking, all of a sudden he's accelerating the car. It's dangerous and careless.

"Max...answer me?" I plead.

His jaw locks as he slams his hand on the dashboard. I'm just now realizing that I'm looking at a lunatic who has completely lost it!

Instantly, his mood changes and he says, "I wanted to show you how much you meant to me, but Dominic found out about my little obsession with his little sister, and hit the roof." His face softens as my head is screaming at me, 'did he just say what I think he did?' As if he could read my mind, he nods his head. "He told me to steer clear and stay away from you, or else."

Okay, well I suppose I should be happy with that.

His face suddenly softens as a side smile appears and he seems light-hearted, almost happy. It's as if his mind went somewhere else. I find it hard to swallow, wondering if he's thinking about me. The issue with that is, seeing him in a happy place freaks me the hell out. Unstable is the word I'd use to describe Max right now.

"Instead," he softly confesses, "I secretly sent you letters. I'm not sure if Dominic was aware of it, but if he was, he never said a word. So, I kept sending them. One way or another, I found a way to connect with you. I envisioned you sitting down and reading them. I even signed a few but then erased my name."

I have to look forward to keep from freaking out and jumping out of the damn door. All those letters, all from *Max*!

I'm not sure what to say, but my mind is drifting back to the letters, trying to make sense of them. Did I miss clues that would have led me it to him? The frightening image my mind is stuck on is the movie *Silence of the Lambs*. A fucking bad dream come to life. My life.

"Why? Max, I don't understand. What about...wait, did you send me the threatening letter with the knife and Dominic's charm?" The level of fucked up just hit red.

"You see, now you are just too damn smart for your own good." The way he appears to be enjoying this conversation is making me ill.

"You're a sick bastard."

"Now, let me explain," he quickly lifts his finger. "Vince and I ran into one another at Dom's house late one evening. After the awkward introductions, we had a very long but pleasant conversation. It was odd, considering he knew all about me and I knew zero about him. We had never met before that night, but we quickly found some common ground. We both divulged information to one another and came to a bit of an understanding you could say."

I'm shaking my damn head and listening to this unbelievable story.

"My mistake was helping Liam the day I walked in and found a knife in his side. That wasn't part of the plan, but I stepped up and helped him anyway. That's my instinct Kara, to help people. I'm not one to condone violence, but you should know that by now." He shifts uncomfortably and comments under his breath. "If I had not shown up that day, things would be easier right now. Damn."

Violence! Yeah, that idea sounds good about now. I should unleash some of it on this miserable dick. I'm already thinking of how to get out of this car. If only I could get a message to Liam. How do I do it without raising suspicion with Max, aka, crazy-sick-delusional-idiot-of-a-man? Shouldn't be too hard, he's too busy chatting.

"For Vince, it was a no brainer. I'm his contact on the inside. I relay everything back to Vince, for a price. My price was you. He couldn't ever harm you. He gives me you, and I help him with making sure Tiffany is not found. He has no interest in you, he wants to raise a son. Dominic's son."

"This is so fucked up, Max. You of all people. Why in the hell would you do this?" I raise my voice only to watch his face turn red.

"For YEARS, I've been under the thumb of your bastard of a brother. I owed people and part of my repayment came in rendering my doctoring abilities to your brother when he needed me. I loathed him for the longest time, but then he found out my secret, he knew how obsessed I was with you. I hated him even more after that. He ridiculed me, but he was the biggest hypocrite who ever lived. He could do as he wished to you, but he was the only one who could. But Hell would be the cost if anyone ever bothered you, I didn't understand it at all. I helped Izzy the way I did out of the goodness of my heart, but it was also to screw him over."

He pauses to swipe his hand across his face, then keeps going, "I helped her because of what had happened to her over the years. She's lived through such hell, all because of him. I saved her because she's your best friend and she means something to you. And you mean everything to me. Liam doesn't understand you, and he sure as hell doesn't deserve you."

"Oh, Max." I cry in utter shock.

I can't believe this is happening. Max is nothing but a stalking lunatic who accomplished two things I'll forever be thankful for. Saving Izzy and bringing Willow back to us. After that, it's a straight shot to hell. A twist of fate that leaves a sour taste in my mouth for sure. Even with his admission, I still don't understand.

"Why the threatening letter, Max? Why use his charm against me like you did?"

He mocks. "To scare you and screw with your mind. I wanted to set it up so you would be willing come to me. I'd be the white knight, but my plans never worked out right. Tyler couldn't even do his job right."

The minute he said Tyler, I snapped. This fucker has lied to us all, and if he thinks for one minute I'm not ready to end his sorry ass, he's mistaken. I may be thankful in ways, but his deceit and freaky intentions are sick. I need to end this shit, one way or another because I can't take much more of being in this car with him.

"Are you listening to yourself right now?" My anger bubbles over and before common sense can reach my brain, I lean over and yank on the steering wheel.

Hard.

The car swerves out of control.

MAX

MY HEAD'S POUNDING LIKE MY skull is cracked open. All I wanted to do was take her away. Why can't she see what's right in front of her? *I'm* the right choice. *I* can take care of her. I know what haunts her, and all I want to do is make it better. The pain I feel is excruciating, but I'm not sure what's happened? Every time I try to open my eyes, I can barely focus. Bright flashes of light blind me and everything appears in a fog.

She suddenly coughs. The raspy and wheezing noises concern me, and it takes all of my strength to turn my head her way. My eyes flutter open a few times only to see the image of two Kara's, one appears with a shiny halo. She's smiling and reaches out to touch my arm. I swear, I almost cry out with her endearing touch. This is what I've craved from her for so long. Over her shoulder appears a second image of herself, but this one has a look of revulsion on her face. Her lip snarls when she starts shouting profanities my way and I wince.

"You will not get away with this." She snarls, pointing her finger like a dagger.

"Don't threaten me, baby." I'm not sure if I'm hallucinating or not. I try to focus, but it's challenging. Suddenly, I have both Kara's addressing me. One is sweet, and the other is cynical.

Why am I seeing two of her? I know I can't figure any of this out while cynical Kara keeps shouting. In an attempt to help, I cover my ears but the pain's too much. An unexpected sharpness to the side of my head blinds my already hazy vision and I'm rocking back and forth, cradling my head. Each moan that leaves my lips, slices the pain until it slightly eases. Relief, finally. It's then that I realize she's stopped talking.

I reach for her, but stop as I focus on my hand. It's blood red. But how? Did I hit my head on something or wait...did Kara knock me out?

"Wait." I struggle but then a moment of clarity washes over me. I'm able to focus better and thankfully, I'm no longer seeing two of her. Instead, I see one very distraught Kara. I'm not sure why she's giving me the oddest of expressions. Her face is pale white, and her eyes are wide as if she's in shock. She's disheveled and for the first time, I understand why.

A tree limb has impaled the windshield and the frightening sight unleashes a stabbing pain in my lower abdomen. The pain registers with a punch, and I wince, throwing my head back and struggling to catch a breath. My pulse shallows. Lowering my gaze, I notice a second tree limb coming from the passenger side of the car has impaled itself in my stomach.

"Jesus. How did this happen?" I wheeze.

I know the gravity of our situation, and I can't help but worry more about Kara. I notice her slumped over and it's as if my world is falling apart. To see her lifeless, tears me apart. "Oh no.No.No!" Suddenly my pain doesn't matter, it's all about her. I stretch my left hand over as far as I can to move her blood matted hair from her face. She's breathing, but no longer conscious.

Dear Lord, what have I done?

LIAM

OF ALL OF THE PEOPLE I trusted, it had to be that son-of-a-bitch. Now, I feel like a damn fool. I should have seen it. I always knew he was a touchy feely kind of guy around Kara, but I never thought he sent the letters. My fucking blind eye has cost me dearly because now he has her, and he took her right from under my nose.

Right now, all I want is her in my arms. She's all I ever wanted and I just let things get out of control. I was blinded by a need to punish Vince for what he did to me, but to also ruin his idea of raising a family with my sister's kid. To hell with it. If he wants my sister and her kid, so be it. Sound cruel? You bet, but I'm not the one who spread my legs for a sadistic prick to begin with, she did that all on her own, knowing what kind of man Dominic was. I've spent my life trying to right her wrongs when it came to Eve but things have changed, I have Kara and Eve is content and safe.

I should have let it go like my sister had asked me to. I can't and won't let anything happen to Kara. I know she thinks differently but she's wrong, she's always been my first priority. From the day we came home, I've taken measures to help watch over her to give us another layer of protection. Cody, a buddy of mine is sure to call me soon. He should be following Kara's every move so if she left with Max, he's following them right now. Now, I just have to wait for his call. He won't call until he has a firm destination of where they are.

Kara can't honestly believe I'd let something happen to her, could she?

I know, I haven't been telling her just how much she means to me, but that's just because I've been distracted. How fucking stupid could I have been? She's my entire world, my heart. Things will change and as of right now, things have changed. I'll have that chat with my sister, and if she's good, then that's it. I'll let it go.

First, I need to get my girl back. Have her safe in arms and when I do, the first thing I'll do is tell her how much I love her. Let her know that I can't live in this world if she's not with me.

Then, I'll deal with Max.

Chapter Twenty-Two

"Dazed"

Kara

I'M HAVING AN OUT OF body experience, that's the only answer. For the life of me, I can't figure out why I'm standing in the middle of my street in the dark of night. The night air is cool and it's damn foggy. But here I am, barefoot and in my nightie.

What the hell? Am I awake or dreaming?

The thick layers of fog make it hard to see what's in front of me. The concrete under my feet has to be cold, because every breath that leaves my mouth is visible. What's weird about that is my feet aren't cold. The urge to keep moving is just too strong to deny, so with limited vision due to the rolling fog, I start walking.

"Hello." I rasp. Not sure why I felt the need to say it, but I do and my voice echoes, making me feel more alone than I already am. Looking down at my feet, I can't figure out why I can't stop them from moving forward. I feel like I can't prevent what's going to happen.

Why can't I stop this?

What's happening?

Light appears off in the distance and it seems to be a beacon summoning me. The determination to reach it takes charge of my pace.

"Kara." A faint voice calls out.

It's a whisper, but I hear it.

"Keep coming."

I quicken my pace sprinting down the street. The houses are zipping past, but I'm not getting anywhere. I'm on the same street, still sprinting past the same houses. I push myself to run faster and faster, but I'm still not getting anywhere. I don't understand.

Terrified, I shout out. "I can't get to you. Why can't I get to you?"

"You need to keep trying. Don't give up, you're so close."

I can't keep going.

I'm getting too tired.

I need to rest.

For some reason, I'm able to stop in the middle of the street. Too exhausted to move any farther, my chest is tightening and I struggle to take my next breath. Maybe I can close my eyes and rest. Yeah, rest that's what I need.

"You can't rest. You need to get up."

"Shhh, I'm too tired. Leave me alone." I huff.

I feel arms wrap around me and pick me up, only I can't make out who is carrying me. Whoever has me, it feels like they're running. I summon one eye to open and realize I'm being carried towards a bright light, and an odd, peaceful feeling washes over my body like waves in the ocean. It's not scary at all, it's peaceful and comforting. A faint smile forms as I continue to struggle to focus on the face inches from mine.

Strong, dark eyes glare into mine, somewhat familiar, but I'm just too tired to keep my eyes open. My head falls back as my eyes drift shut.

"Kara, stay with me. You need to hang on."

I'm falling and it feels good. I can hear him, but I have no idea what he's talking about. I suddenly recognize his voice. It makes no sense at all, but when I open my eyes, it's not a man I see. It's a younger version of Dominic.

"How are you here?" I scarcely say the words.

"I don't have time to explain. Just know you are not ready to be here. You have a full life ahead of you. It's simply not your time."

"I don't understand," I sob, "you look different."

"Well," he lightheartedly said, "I couldn't face you as the adult you've grown to hate. I need you to trust me, and to do that, you're seeing me as the younger version of me. The brother you once cared for."

"I...don't..." I'm struggling to form the words, let alone the strength to keep my eyes open. It's just too much, I'm slipping away.

"Not yet, Kara. Stay with me. Please, let me help you."

Just then, my last breath faded into total darkness.
"Again."
"Charging to 400."
"Clear."
"Thump. Thump."
"Pulse?"
"Negative."
"Charge to 400."
"Clear."
"Thump. Thump."
"Pulse?"
"Negative."
"Call it."
"Time of death 3:15."
"You must try it again. NOW!"
"No, we're going to try one more time."
"Charge to 400."
"Charging to 400."
"Clear."
"Thump. Thump."
"Pulse?"
"Beep...Beep...Beep."
"We have a pulse."

Chapter Twenty-Three

"Life Goes On"
Kara

"So you don't recall much of the accident?" Izzy asks.

Even though it's been a month, I still don't recall much of that day. It's like my body is protecting itself from the pain and suffering it endured.

"I can remember things that happened before the accident, and I have slight memories of things that happened after, but the accident itself is a blank."

"And what about your dream?" She asks and the near mention of it makes me chuckle.

"The freaky walk in the dark," I sigh, "yes I do remember that part."

"Maybe it's for the best." She's reluctant to say much because she's not wrapped her head around it all. Max, as it turns out, happens to be the creeper in my life, but he was the saving grace of hers. I've told her time and again to stop torturing herself.

"You're right, but when is life going to feel normal again?"

"Soon," she reminds me. Always the optimist.

From the moment I woke in the hospital, I've not felt the same. Maybe it has to do with the fact, I learned my heart stop beating at the exact time of my repeating nightmares only a few short months ago.

That, or the fact my deceased brother made it his mission to carry me into the light that night.

Did he save my life?

Is he the reason I'm here?

The light that night, could it have been *that* light?

A chilling fact remains, my nightmares all came at 3:15. Who could have ever guessed that would be the time my heart would eventually stop beating. Was it all a warning? A premonition? A question I may never have any answer for.

"Anyway," Izzy points out, "who the hell is normal these days? I've got kids, a husband, and a best friend who is in love with my husband's best friend. Who, I'd like to add, cackle like a couple of old hens. I swear, my life has officially become a circus."

I'm quick to point out the obvious. "You love it and you know it."

Her smile widens. "Bet your ass, I do. Our crazy is normal, remember that."

There is no denying that.

I'd be lying if I said I wasn't concerned about Vince returning and fulfilling his plan to, "make me bleed." It's been a while since anyone has mentioned his name. While I was in the hospital, Liam and his uncle did have that talk with Tiffany and from what I understand, she's happy and content with staying where she is. Chicago. Liam kept his comments short on the matter, and I'm okay with that. As long as he appears satisfied and seems to have let his vendetta go against Vince, I can breathe more easily. Izzy clears her throat and taps my knee with her hand.

"I don't see it," she comments, "I think that was a smoke show. I don't believe he ever intended to harm you. It worked in his favor to act like he wanted to."

Huh? I never thought about it that way and wondered how she came to that conclusion. "What makes you think that?"

Lowering her hands on the table where we are sitting, she clears her throat. "Just thinking about the way Dominic lived his life. If Vince truly wanted to hurt you, he would have done it. I don't think he wanted to. Call it a gut feeling. I don't know."

Wow, she does make a valid point. "I'll go with your reasoning because your way keeps me safely breathing."

SUDDENLY, MY BODY IS BEING shaken. I can hear his voice, but it's muffled. It feels like my body is stuck in a tunnel.

"Kara, wake up!" This time, his robust voice is stern.

I straighten my body while I gasp for my next breath. Just to make sure I'm not dreaming, I feel for the bed around me. I realize I'm wheezing like I just ran a mile with sweat trickling down my face. My hand automatically goes over my heart when I feel strong arms wrap around me.

"Babe, what's going on in that head of yours?"

Liam tightens his hold appearing frantic. Since I've been home from the hospital he's been overly attentive, but also on edge, I swear he's one bad incident short of having a stroke.

"I have no clue," I say to answer his question. To try and slow my racing heart, I suck in big breaths through my nose and exhale through my mouth. "What a strange dream."

Liam grumbles, "More like a freaking nightmare," he suddenly lets out a yawn, "what happened this time?"

What happened this time? Hell, that's a great question!

"It's hard to explain this, but I was running down the same street, a perfect replica to the one I had in the hospital when my heart..." I couldn't even finish the sentence. My reality to how close I came to dying is still hard for me to consider.

"Babe," he whispers as he places kisses to my head, "I don't want you ever to have to think about that ever again."

"I wish I could." I sadly admit.

The fact remains, I can't just forget it. The whole mess with Max at least is over, he didn't survive the accident. He died at the scene. I was unconscious when the paramedics had arrived. Cody, one of Liam's buddies, got to me first and made the call for help. Without him, I would have probably died alongside Max. Thank goodness that didn't happen, because that would not be my ideal way to spend my last moments on earth.

My injuries came in the form of multiple cuts, bruises, and a broken arm. The worst of it came from a splintered tree limb that punctured my side. At the time of the accident, my body was turned facing Max. The doctors said if my body had been facing forward, I could have sustained far worse injuries. My blood loss is what endangered my life. Ironically, that same limb is what killed Max.

Today, I'm feeling better, my bruises are healing and my scar is a reminder that I did survive. I find myself many times a day running my fingers over the rough, raised skin.

"We can tattoo over the scar if you want?"

I know he hates looking at it, but his reaction is different from mine.

"No," I say with confidence, "I won't ever cover it up. It's my reminder to always live for today, and to never, ever give up." Tears fill my eyes and as I look at Liam, his warm face melts my heart.

"You are the strongest woman I've ever met, and I love you more than you can even imagine. When they told us your heart stopped, I collapsed to the floor on my knees," his voice cracks. "I never want to hear those words. It was a good thing Brax was there to lift my ass off of the floor, because when they let me know they got your heart beating again I swear to you, my knees buckled again."

"Oh, Liam." This is the first time I've seen how the accident affected him. There is no misreading the love this man has for me. Good, bad and the ugly parts, too.

I wipe away a few stray tears, while he lets out a slight chuckle. "Izzy, now *that* girl had to be restrained. When she heard those words, she was ready to ram the doors to get to you. I can still hear her cries, they left that much of an impression on me. Not with how loud she was, but the gut wrenching sadness. Those words crushed us all, babe."

"I'm so sorry," I cry out, as streams of tears fall. To know how affected they all were with what happened to me, just shows how much they do love me. I'm so incredibly blessed.

"We love you so much," he whispers.

I nod and lay my head against his chest. "That poor doctor, I can't imagine trying to contain all of you at the same time." I can just picture it in my mind, Brax playing referee between Izzy and Liam. When either of them are determined to do something, they are impossible to control. Poor man.

"Hell, once he said you were still with us, I think he whispered, 'thank God'. There's no way he wanted to face us if you hadn't. Izzy even went as far as to offer her services, she let him know that she'd gladly go back and bitch at your ass until you got sick of listening to her. She commented that would definitely get your heart going."

"I love that crazy woman."

"Babe, she loves you something fierce. By the way, that reminds me, I do believe I owe you some loving."

His eyes wag up and down and I'm all for it.

"Oh, that's a splendid idea. If this is the kind of treatment I can expect..."

"Don't even think about it. Not funny."

I never even had a chance to finish my statement, but he knew what I was talking about anyway. Liam absolutely hates the hospital and each day he visited me, it was written all over his face.

With both of us stripped of our clothes, Liam rests behind me, his body cradling mine. His fingers move the hair from my shoulder, as he kisses along my shoulder.

"So beautiful," he whispers as he nuzzles in the crook of my neck.

While we lay naked, his fingers traced circles on my shoulder, slowly tracing a line down my side. His tender touch and steady breaths are what I live for. Liam's given me the best gift of all, even if he doesn't know it. To be able to love him and to receive his love, all the while being by his side, is a gift in itself. Our journey although fucked up at times, has led us to here, right now. All of the pain, and all the hurt, was all worth it and I'd live it again just to feel this.

The minute Liam lightly traces over the raised skin of my scar, I automatically react by sucking in a breath while my stomach flinches. His light and loving touch caressing the spot that holds such pain with how it happened, creates an endless stream of tears. I'm overly sensitive I know, but I can't stop the mixed emotions I have and he knows it. To help ease my suffering, Liam places measured kisses on my body as he slides down my body closer to my scar on my side.

"Ahhh." I exhale softly.

"I love you," he proclaims, as he continues to kiss every ugly edge that mares my skin.

With big ugly tears, I cry out. "I love you, too." Every emotion I've felt in the last few months comes barreling to the surface. I can no longer deny it, it's time I let it all out. I've tried to contain it, analyze it and bottle it up, but now he's given me the chance to finally release it.

"I'm so sorry," I say over and over. My need to apologize for the mess I basically brought to his front door haunts me, but I've never taken the time to let him know.

"No," he sits up and holds my hands. "You don't get to do that to yourself because none of this is your fault. You didn't ask for it, and you sure didn't bring it on. Sweetheart, never apologize for giving me the best gift I've ever received in my whole life."

I look at him trying to understand what he means, but whatever it is, I'm sure I'll love him even more. "What did you mean by that?"

His face shows how happy he with his smile and sparkling eyes. "You gave me you," he says with nothing but sweet honesty.

Yep, those words open the floodgates. I'm crying harder until he lowers his lips to mine. Soft and sweet, those lips of his dance over mine until his need demands more. His tongue licks my lower lip, nibbling a few times until he's demanding entrance into my mouth. I reach for the back of his neck as I get lost in the best kiss I've ever had. Exquisite.

As he adjusts his body between my legs and nudges them to part wider. My legs automatically fall open to the side. I'm greedy and ready to receive him. The tip of his cock probes my opening and I'm not sure if it's meant to torment me or to let my juices coat him but either way, it feels really damn good. To entice him, I arch my pelvis and wiggle my brows before I wink at him.

"Eager are we?" He smirks.

I almost say that's a dumb question, but instead I respond with, "Yes, most definitely, now fuck me like you want to."

"I'm the one in charge here."

The way his laugh rumbles in his chest turns me on even more.

"I could take over for you if you like?" I offer.

He gives me an exaggerated sigh. "Not a chance, babe. I'm taking my time to love you like you should be loved."

I don't have a chance to respond this time because he's slowly inching his way inside of me. I'm fully absorbed in the sensation of my body as it stretches to accommodate Liam in his slow paced love making.

"Ahhh." I grab a handful of the sheets and arch my neck as he continues his slow assault. Lost in utter bliss, I happily receive all of his pleasure by tightening my muscles to squeeze his cock. He loves it when I do it. In response, Liam's moans intensify as he reaches his hand behind my neck and pulls me toward him, so our lips can meet in a sizzling kiss.

"Oh, fuck me. That's it baby, squeeze my cock." He gasps and starts to rock his hips in perfect rhythm. Each forward thrust is slow and fulfilling. It's not rushed, it's fucking perfection.

I'm climbing and my stomach muscles start to quiver. He's building me higher and higher.

"Look at me, sweetheart." He demands softly and a bit out of breath.

My eyes flutter open.

"I love you so fucking much," he admits, never missing a beat with his feelings when it comes to me. "You own my soul, baby."

Oh my God! This man is shattering every wall I've ever put up. Seriously, could he get any sweeter? Hell no, he's perfect.

"Oh, Liam."

With one forward push, he stops when he's fully seated inside. I can feel his muscles tense as his eyes engage with mine. He takes a moment to study my face before he parts his lips. "Marry me, sweetheart? Say you'll spend the rest of your life with me?"

Those two little words every woman dreams of hearing, just happened to me. A moment so monumental in a girl's life, it's one to never forget. As I grow older, I want to remember what we were doing the minute he proposed. The fact it happened when we were having sex, means I'll have to change my story up to tell it to our future children. I can imagine they'd be grossed out picturing their parents having sex when he popped the question to their mother.

I giggle because that's pretty damn funny, but Liam has no idea what I'm laughing about. He stares at me wondering what the hell is so funny at a time like this. He's waiting for my answer that he already knows will be a big fat yes, but I'm not done absorbing this moment to the fullest.

I lick my lips and lower my eyes past his glistening chest to the junction where our bodies connect. To ogle Liam's toned body as it surrounds my body, is a sight to take in. I could just stare at his chest as it concaves with each heavy breath he takes. My man is one hundred percent sexy and with his proposal, forever mine.

It doesn't mean I won't play with him a bit first.

"On one condition." I finally say to put him out of his misery. I think he was starting to wonder what was taking me so long to answer. I realize this may seem mean, but challenging him knowing full well he'll never forget this moment either, is just too good to pass up.

Liam blinks his eyes several times, as his once loving gaze is replaced with surprise. "Seriously?"

"'Fraid so." I moan with slight agony because Liam picks up his tempo. With every slow withdrawal, he quickly eases back in. I see he's not going to make this easy on me, so I shift my hips in hope to gain some friction where I need it.

Liam chuckles and raises an eyebrow before he slows his speed, withdrawing so only his tip remains.

"Name it, and it's yours," he whispers before shifting his hips sliding all way back inside.

Yes! I'm not sure what I wanted more, his offer of whatever I want, or his body back inside of mine. Either way, he's given me the answer I wanted.

"That's what I was counting on," I moan, unable to hold back my chuckle. I know this little challenge of mine will be one he won't forget.

"Okay, here it is. Fuck me, like I know you want too and if you can get us to climax together, you'll get your answer." This time I lose it laughing. He's looking at me like I've lost my mind.

"That's the strangest way to respond to a proposal, you do realize that, right?"

"Yep, are you complaining or are you going to get busy?" I ask.

"I better get a fucking yes," Liam grumbles but cracks a smile as well.

"You'll get an Oh-My-God-Liam-Yes-Yes-Yes!"

"I fucking love a challenge, sweetheart. Get that yes ready, and don't leave out the Oh-My-God-Liam."

I try to say the words, 'yes, sir'…but Liam's thrusting like a caged beast let loose. My legs are thrown over his shoulders, all the while he holds onto my wrists. He's pounding into me with such force, any lingering soreness from my injuries is well forgotten. I'm in pure-unaltered-passion-loving-toe-curling-ecstasy.

I'll just say that Liam does indeed love a challenge, and he excelled at it in record time. He happily got the answer he wished for, and he also apologized for handling me rougher than he intended to, so he spent the rest of the night making slow but mind blowing love to me.

Later that night I cried for the past, and even cried about the possibilities for our future. On the same night, I said yes to the man of my dreams. Promising to live my life by his side.

I have no idea if I'll ever hear from Vince again, and to be honest, I hope I don't. I do however, hope he finds some happiness and can let go of the past. My fear would be him disrupting our lives once again. I'll always look over my shoulder, but I refuse to live my life in fear ever again.

It would take someone or something to threaten our happy lives, and if that happened, God help them. We've already proven how far we'd go to protect the ones we love.

epilogue

Declan

I'VE HEARD THE STORIES, AND even read the stories, so now it's time for me to continue the story. Call it morbid curiosity, but it's my birthright to know all about my so-called family.

I'm not talking about a stereotypical family, either. Stay at home mother, a hard working father, a few siblings and a dog or two. Not at all, not even white picket fences. That's not the kind of family I'm speaking of.

In my eighteen years, I've lived a good life. Raised by an uncle who has given me more than I most likely deserve. My mother, split years ago. I didn't lose much, shit, she wasn't much of one to begin with. That leads me to my father. He was killed, well murdered actually. I'll even mention who. His sister, my so called aunt, did the ugly deed herself.

How's that for a warm and fuzzy story?

Life hasn't treated me poorly, and I've never wanted for a thing. But, even that can't stop the voices in my head. A minor issue, well *condition* is what my doctors call it. From what I understand, my birth father most likely suffered the same thing. I will never know, because I can't ask him. A slew of names has been thrown at me and written in my lengthy medical files, but at the end of the day, as long as I take my pretty pink pills, I'm a nice enough guy to be around.

Now, if you are around me when I haven't taken them, that's a different story. During my early teenage years, I rebelled and refused to take them. Those are the times, I blacked out and couldn't recall the damage I apparently caused. My uncle, Vince hired a nanny of sorts to make sure I took my meds on time and every day.

A babysitter.

Well, I hate to admit it, but I couldn't take the demons that screamed at me to stop taking them. Now, my uncle is going to have to answer for the pretty blonde dead nanny left in her bedroom.

I tried to warn them, but they didn't want to listen to me then.

But, they are going to have to listen to me now. Her death is on him, that's the way I see it. When I'm off of those damn meds, I can think more clearly and my head's not in a fog. I've packed up all the stories and clippings I've kept about my father, Dominic Santos, because I figure the time for me to meet my long lost relatives is way past due. I've got questions, and I know they have answers. I'll save Kara for last, making sure my anger is justified. My plan is simple, friend them without them knowing who I really am.

My real identity can remain my secret until the time is right to drop the little bombshell. It's going to be one hell of a reunion, if you ask me. I grab my bags, making sure I have all I need, and with my car keys in hand, my mood lightens. I'm whistling my favorite tune as I pass Rachael, my nanny's, door making sure to close it. I'll let my uncle handle that mess, I've got a few days on the road ahead of me.

Willow

"Eve, you have to come with me." She's my older sister and she knows I'm nervous, now all of a sudden she's dragging her feet.

"Willow," she sighs looking down at my hands that are crossed, like I'm praying, "why do I have to come with you to meet some guy you recently just met?" She rolls her eyes, but I just ignore her tantrum.

"You need to check him out for me. You're my wing girl and you are way better at judging people than I am." I screech all ready to beg if I have to.

She taps her foot a few times. "Ask dad, or Uncle Liam. They would *love* to meet him."

Of course she had to bring them into the picture. What a great idea, *not!*

They'd would sit back and intimidate the poor guy making sure he stays away from me.

Argh, she can be so frustrating at times. "Funny, you're hilarious. Let's go before we're late." I shove her ahead of me, but she stops and turns back.

"How did you meet him again?"

For the fifth time, I've already talked with her about the guy I started chatting with from the school's registry. We met on the school's meet new friends chat line. I admit it was odd at first, but this guy seemed nice, different. This will be the first time I get to meet him in person and I'm nervous as hell, my stomach won't stop churning. I spent over two hours getting ready and making sure I look my best. My dark brown hair is fully curled, and my make-up is light. I look pretty. To make a good first impression, I'm in my best jeans that fit me like a glove and a cute t-shirt that's tight, but not overly snug.

I'm a college student, I'm going to dress like one. Eve's older and her tastes run more polished and put together. She'd never be seen leaving the house for a date in jeans and a t-shirt, no way. She'd be all dolled up in some skirt and matching top.

Yuck, not my scene or style.

"Okay, let's go in and meet this one. He'd better not creep me out, or I'm calling dad for backup."

"Dang it Eve, stop making me nervous."

She opens the door to The Shack restaurant. We make our way to the booth in the back, and I get ready to text him like I said I would. Eve orders us two drinks while I pull out my phone and send my text. My nerves made it hard to send, but I finally press send. Now my nerves are churning in my stomach and I look at Eve like I might get sick. I hate dates, I'd rather hang out with friends. This is way too much pressure.

"I wonder what will happen now?" I say taking a big, calming breath, unaware someone was behind me.

"Why hello, Willow." A pleasant voice speaks out.

My eyes go wide in shock as I look at Eve who has a blank expression on her face looking over my shoulder. I turn completely surprised. Damn, that was fast. I just sent him my text.

"Wow," I stammer, "you are fast." I can't help but take in his good looks, boy, he's so handsome I feel like I may be out of my league. Maybe that's what Eve was thinking with her non-expressive gaze a moment ago.

"I was anxiously waiting…for you." He says, then extends his hand to cup my shoulder.

His fingers are warm and firm and I instantly blush because he's so cute. I know it's him because the photo in the chat room matches him perfectly. Thank God! That was my first worry, that he would show up looking nothing like the dark haired guy on my computer. Well, his face is now my screen saver, but he does not need to know that.

He smiles at me but his gaze shifts to my sister, who's not as impressed. She's too busy sizing him up.

"How sweet, don't you think, Eve?" I kick her under the table.

"Yeah, that's not creepy at all," she replies with a raised brow.

"Eve," I warn.

"Eve," his warm voice engages, "I've heard a lot about you."

Oh crap. That won't sit well with her. Sure enough, she shoots daggers at me, and I want to crawl under the table. Eve does not easily warm up to complete strangers. When he said he's heard so much about her, I have to think back to what I've said to him about her. I surely only mentioned the basics. It must be his attempt to butter her up. Hope it works, but I won't hold my breath for fear I'll turn blue first.

"And, I've heard all about you," she snarls with her usual less than friendly attitude. "What's the name again?"

He stares at her for an odd long minute before a smile cracks free. "Declan."

"Got a last name, Declan?"

"Parisi, Declan Parisi."

"Well, Declan Parisi why don't you take a seat."

"I think that's a splendid idea."

CRUEL TWIST OF *fate*

BOOK THREE IN THE FATE SERIES

HEIDI LIS

prologue

I've heard the stories.
I've read the stories too.
Now it's time to continue the story.
For eighteen years, I've lived under the shadow of a man I've never met.
My father, Dominic Santos.
The reason? He died before I was born. Murdered in cold blood.
I'm a fighter by nature, a survivor.
But even that can't stop the voices in my head or the *beast* that lives inside of me.
Fighting is the only thing that keeps me sane,
but fighting alone can't stop what haunts me most.
What haunts me most is realizing that not all monsters live under beds or lurk in the dark.
Monsters are very real and sometimes, they come after you.
They conceal themselves by hiding in plain sight.
They pretend to care, but secretly despise the very air you breathe.
A monster so blinded by hate, can't see his fatal flaw until it's too late.
Not realizing the only thing that can kill a monster... is a *beast*!
My name is Declan Parisi, welcome to my life.

Declan

There is no other feeling like it in the world,
To unleash my rage and exorcise my demons all at the same time.
It's a mind-blowing high that sets me free.
Free to dominate.
Free to defeat.
Free to destroy.
It's the only time I feel alive.

Chapter One

"Where it all began"

AT AN EARLY AGE, I quickly realized I was different from the other kids at school. Never quite understanding why, but while the other kids were laughing in the hallways, I stood alone with a scowl on my face.

Why was it so difficult for me?

A question that continued to haunt me until my early teens, where middle school can be downright brutal. A time when adolescence brings a whole new level of bullshit and every day is an opportunity to take aim at those who dare to be different, when they are just being themselves.

Oh yes, if life is anything, it's full of bullshit lessons that can sting like a motherfucker if you let them. Life handed me a few shitty blows, but it wasn't until then that I realized why I was so different from the others.

Anger.

Do I have anger issues? Fuck yeah, but I like to call it my way of dealing with life's cruel lessons.

I'm a fighter by nature. A survivor. Which is a good thing because trying to create my own identity while being the son of the infamous Dominic Santos has been harder than I could have ever imagined.

The man, the legend, my father.

A ruthless son-of-a-bitch that was feared by just about everyone. I grew up surrounded by a damn ghost whose brutal viciousness helped earn him the nickname, *'the enforcer'* for one thing and one thing only.

My father was the goddamned Grim Reaper, a member of the Lost Souls MC who later joined forces with the Aniello Crime family. The same family I've been around my whole life, since my uncle, Vince Parisi had taken it upon himself to raise me as his own following the death of his half-brother. My uncle has been a part of the Aniello Organization for most of his adult life.

Where my father was the muscle, my uncle's the brains. Turns out he's a bit of a genius with finances. Vince's 'legit' role is the Aniello's accountant and financial advisor. Which is just a snazzy way to say it's his job to maintain two sets of financial records. One legit, and one that's off the record.

Given Vince's closeness to Marcus and my late father's longstanding friendship, it's easy to understand why certain expectations have been set for me. Let's not forget, I'm the spitting image of my old man, only the better version.

We may share the same olive skin, dark hair, penetrating dark eyes, to our bold jawlines and strong Roman noses, but I'm filled out and built like a damn brick house. All in all, a living and breathing reminder for those who knew him well.

The whispers follow me everywhere.

"Wonder if he'll turn out just like his father?"

"He's sure a spitting image of him, it's like that bastard is still alive."

"With his anger issues, the apple sure didn't fall far from the tree."

It's nothing new but being compared to a goddamned ghost every day can start to take its toll. It's not like I can escape it either. My uncle saw fit to raise me in *his* house. Technically, it's my uncles house now but it's filled with many of my father's things, just the way he left them.

Eighteen years ago!

Shit was so crazy my worthless excuse of a mother couldn't take living here for long. One hook-up with Dominic was all it took. They never loved one another from what I heard. That means my existence alone stems from one thing, *a fuck!* Should be no surprise then, when it came to me, she felt zero maternal obligations.

I'm not supposed to know this, but Marcus explained that when the money my uncle had been paying her to stay around suddenly stopped, she packed her shit and took off with little concern how that would affect her six-year-old son. The only thing I remember about her is her platinum blonde hair. *Fucking Pathetic!*

My father may have been the devil, but my mother was the face of pure evil. Tossing me aside like the evening's trash.

My childhood memories have no mother, no father, just an overbearing uncle. If you count Marcus, make that two overbearing uncles. Marcus may not be blood related, but as the old saying goes, when you're family, you're family. So, he's always been Uncle Marcus to me. His brother Anthony not so much. He's more of a loner and pretty much keeps to himself.

Life hasn't treated me too poorly and I've never wanted for a thing, even so, that can't stop the voices in my head. A symptom of my manic-depressive disorder is what the doctors call it and it's likely my father may have suffered from the same fate. Not that it fucking matters, because at the end of the day if I take my pretty pink pills, I'm a nice enough guy to be around.

Which is saying something, because my mood can change on the drop of a dime. If you are unfortunate enough to be around me when I'm off my meds, things are a different story altogether.

A few times I rebelled by simply refusing to take them. Unfortunately, those are the times I blacked out, never remembering the damage I caused.

That was enough for my uncle. He hired a nurse, what I like to call a glorified babysitter to make sure I took my meds and stayed out of trouble.

Yeah, right!

Early years of fighting on the playground, in the bathroom stalls, or even in the classrooms, was leading me down a certain path. A path that family connections certainly helped along the way. With my anger out of control, training became my new outlet.

It was the beginning.

Then... I met her.

Liberty Ross.

Chapter Two

"Not what I expected"

JUNIOR YEAR OF HIGH SCHOOL started out like the rest until a clumsy girl with black glasses walked right into me, immediately dropping her things on the ground. And just like all the other shitty days, this one was particularly bad since my black t-shirt was soaking wet with the Red Bull she was once holding in her hand.

As the other students noticed and began to gather, they were watching on with interest, waiting for a potential train wreck to play out. It ticked me off so much, I kept my mouth shut refusing to give them the show they wanted. They reminded me of salivating dogs, just waiting for me to go off on this girl who didn't get the memo to stay the hell away from me, or out of my path if she saw me coming.

While I was doing my best to air dry my shirt, the girl was busy picking up her belongings. She had yet to say a word, which left me thinking she was most likely close to crying, or too embarrassed to actually say anything at all. Suddenly, she lifted her head at the same time I lowered my gaze to greet her face.

What I had expected to see, I did not. There was no look of shock or embarrassment. No tears. No cowering. None of it. Her damn green eyes were pleasantly striking, but the scowl on her face is what took me by surprise.

This petite girl was not only mad, she was *pissed* off.

I want to laugh, because her angry face was damn cute. Since I was the one with Red Bull all over my shirt, I decide to rile her up. "A bit clumsy, are we?"

She rolled her eyes and I swear I could see steam billow out from her ears as she stood to face me. All five-feet-three of her I'd have to guess. "Bite me you dick, you walked right in front of me."

Ohhh, this girl is feisty. I guess Junior year might not be so bad after all. Unable to help myself, I keep the conversation going all because I couldn't let her walk away from me now. She's way too much fun.

"Really?" I wittingly ask with a one-sided smirk. "It wasn't that you weren't paying attention while holding onto your books and checking your phone in one hand, while holding a Red Bull in the other." She gasps. "Seems to me you weren't watching where *you* were going. Or, did you run into me on purpose?"

Her reaction is priceless.

If looks could kill.

Her lips crunch together tight, like she's ready to unload on me when she suddenly relaxes her face with an eerie calm. Which I had to say, was a bit scary.

"Delusional on both counts, I assure you. Thanks to you, I'm going to be late for my first class."

That explains why I've never seen her before today, she's new. I decide to cut her some slack. With my palms up, I wave the white flag because she's shocked the hell out me and I'm annoyed with the few students that are still standing around. They can't help themselves, they are waiting for me to live up to my asshole reputation, and tear into the new student. Behind her back, I gave them a death glare to move the hell on. They got the message.

"Where are you headed?" I ask as she's looking at her class schedule. "It's the least I can do to guide you in the right direction." I'm extending an olive branch, trying something new to be nice and helpful. In return, all I get is the snarl of her lip. To keep from laughing, I bite the inside of my cheek.

"I know where the hell I'm headed, thank you very much. By the way, thanks again for making me late." As she passes, she utters, *'jackass'*. I'm left shaking my head and chuckling as I continue to watch her storm away and enter the science building. My day just keeps getting better when she enters room 504. Biology.

It's a funny thing, because fourth period I have Biology in room 504. I'm running late myself doing an errand for Mr. Brooks. God, I can't wait to see the look on her face when I walk in the classroom.

Sure enough, after I hand Mr. Brooks the envelope he had me get from the office, my eyes land on her.

"Thank you, Declan," Mr. Brooks says, "you can have a seat by your lab partner, Liberty." His hand extends to the empty seat next to the girl with black glasses and bold green eyes.

Oh, feisty has a unique name. With a shit-eating grin on my face, I wink and take my seat next to my new lab partner for the entire semester.

She seems thrilled to see me. Under her breath, she extends a warm welcome. "You're such a dick. Just my luck that *you* happen to be my lab partner. Wonder if it's too late to switch out of this class?"

I can't contain the chuckle that comes out louder than I intended, and it catches the attention of the other students. That's right fuckers, I have a side other than being a prick. That's the sentiment I convey with my glare. I admit, it's not a side of myself I show very often.

When the looks stop, I lean to my left. "Psst,'" I whisper, "count your lucky stars I am your lab partner, biology happens to be my favorite class. Not to mention, my GPA is a 4.0."

"Cocky and smart," she snips. "How did I ever get so lucky?"

Not what I had expected from her, but nothing she's said has been what I expected. Beauty with a mouth to go with it. How did I get so lucky is what I'm thinking? Then, for whatever reason, who the hell knows, I confess something to her. Well, that's not entirely true. I just want to keep winding her up, because she's sexy as fuck when she's pissed.

I jab her lightly with my elbow. "You didn't actually run into me earlier."

She snaps her head so fast I fear she may have whiplash. "Just what the hell are you saying?"

Yep, she's pissed, and this is guaranteed to piss her off even more. "I noticed you walking around earlier, having a mild meltdown with whomever you were texting. You talk out loud when you text, just to let you know. I just timed my move to be in the exact spot where you would be walking."

She's staring at me with her mouth open wide. "Jesus! Are you *crazy* or a *stalker*?" Her voice sounds outraged, but the slight twitch of her lip conceals a laugh that gives her away.

"You might be onto something with crazy, but stalker? No. Do you know how cute you are when your mad?"

She closes her eyes and shakes her head in disbelief. "Oh my God! My first day at a new school and I just had to meet *you*." I'm not sure if it's a question or a statement so I sit back and wink at her as Mr. Brooks proceeds to instruct the class to open our books. As soon as I open my book, Liberty keeps sighing under her breath while tapping her pencil repeatedly against the desk.

Tap! Tap! Tap! Tap! Tap! Tap!

It's evident the girl can't sit still. This goes on for some time, and I seriously need to let her know that she does not need any extra caffeine, thankfully most of her energy drink spilled on my shirt. When I can't take it any longer, I reach across the table and place my hand over hers to stop that damn annoying tapping noise. I notice her eyes quickly dart to my hand and as she tries to pull it back, I playfully tighten my hold. The coolness of her petite hand surprisingly feels nice against the heat of mine.

She leans forward to look me straight in the eyes, and then gives me the first glimpse of a smile. A breathtaking smile, and the physical contact I initiated seems to be catching up with my brain. I'm not one for close physical contact, never have been. I'm not sure how this happened. I just acted. It was that or throw her pencil across the room.

Now, it was my turn to abruptly pull my hand back, but Liberty is quick. Her other hand gently rests on mine and her light touch feels nice for about one point two seconds. That was when the sharpest fingernail known to man pierces the delicate skin on top of my hand. It may look like a sweet gesture on her part with her hand covering mine, but there is no mistaking her true intention.

"Withdraw the claws, Kittycat." I bite back the sting of discomfort while pretending to pay attention to Mr. Brooks, who is talking endlessly in the front of the class. He's busy running down the timeline for the semester when his eyes happen to land on our unusual hand holding. His brows furrow while he keeps talking as Liberty and I are staring forward with our attention on the whiteboard. Like nothing is going on.

Mr. Brooks interrupts his lesson mid-sentence when everyone's attention shifts our way. "Mr. Parisi can we keep the handholding until after class, please?" Then, lowers his head to peer at me above the rim of his glasses.

"It's not..." I start to refute and then grimace before biting into my lower lip. Liberty is enjoying the fact she's digging her nail in deeper when she promptly answers for me.

"Not a problem, Mr. Brooks. It seems Declan needs a crash course in manners." Pleased with herself, she sends a smirk my way as the class erupts with cautious laughter.

"Hmmm, I see," Mr. Brooks clears his throat, "well, let's keep things cool since this is just the beginning of the semester."

I nod my head as the hushed laughs of the other students start to get louder.

"Keep your paws to yourself, and I won't have to hurt you." Liberty scoffs over her shoulder like she's daring me while I rub the top of my punctured hand.

"Hurt me? Ohhh, now you are just trying to turn me on," I tease back with a slow and seductive smile.

"Pathetic."

If she only knew how true that statement is!

Elliott, a real douche who is sitting at the table next to Liberty, leans her way to say something. I can't hear clearly what he's saying but it still makes me want to punch his face all the same. Her response is classic as she gives me a sideways glance and then sits back in her seat and looks his way.

"Mind your own fucking business. I can make up my mind when it comes to the *dick* sitting next to me."

I know this is about me, Elliott hasn't ever gotten over the time I gave him a busted lip. He mouthed off to me one too many times.

"Mind I ask what that was about?"

"You, of course," she doesn't hesitate. "He was giving me some friendly advice to stay away from you. It seems you are the black plague according to him, then he asked if I knew *who* you were?"

That certainly didn't take long.

The good mood I was in since she spilled her Red Bull over me, and the fun back and forth we've been having has suddenly vanished. Time for reality to sink back in. Even if it was only for a few minutes, I felt what it was like to be normal. Only I'm not.

My sad reality comes creeping back in, placing those stone walls I've built around me back in place.

"He's right," I agree with the bastard, my voice void of any emotion at all. "I'm not a good person to hang around, you'll learn that quick enough."

A few seconds tick by as Liberty slams her fists on the table and looks at me like I just slapped her, never minding she just interrupted the whole class with her outburst. With my attention, along with the rest of the class on her, my hands automatically close into tight fists.

This is exactly why I keep to myself and not bother getting to know anyone. Fucking rumor mill! Yet, here I am! Stupid!

"Wow," she screeches. "I didn't take you to be such a coward. Thought you were different, my bad. Guess I was wrong."

After she apologized to the class, she sat as far away from me as she could. I did not say another word for the rest of the class, but that did not stop Liberty from whispering terms of endearment under her breath. *"Pussy, coward, fraidy-cat, scaredy-cat, chicken, big talker, quitter..."*

That continued until the bell rang at the end of class. I was so fucking angry, not at her, at myself. I was up and out of my seat, but leaned down over the top of the table so our faces were only inches apart.

"I'm none of those things. You don't know anything about me. Elliott Dillard was just trying to save you from the big bad wolf. You should be thanking him instead of trying to piss me the hell off." It was meant to scare her off, but it didn't work.

"Little Red Riding Hood wasn't scared of the big bad wolf, why should I be scared of you?"

Once again, she surprises me. Only this time, it's damn frustrating.

"Fuck, Liberty, I don't know what I was thinking. Just stay away from me." My hands push off the desk and just as I started to walk to the door, the other students parted like the red sea to get out of my way. Just as I was about to turn the corner, she shouted.

"Let's see if you can stay away from me."

Damn that girl!

Chapter Three

"Tortured Souls"

CURVY, MOUTHY AND UTTERLY GORGEOUS, Liberty Ross was quickly becoming a pain in my ass... that I liked more than I should.

She stood out against the norm of all the other girls. A complete opposite of the cliques with preppy handbags and designer clothes. Liberty's style was one that she rocked to perfection. One day she'd show up rocking the goth look, all decked out in black. Then, the next day she'd switch it up wearing some short plaid skirt with long ass stockings that would stop just above her knees. Bright colors, dark colors, mix-match patterns, it didn't matter.

If she liked it, she wore it. That was Liberty Ross, my biology lab partner for the next semester. The girl that was simply impossible to ignore.

Damn, if that girl didn't have me secretly looking forward to seeing what outfit she'd show up in and be rocking for my eyes to feast on. Although, if her outfit didn't stand out, her hair style sure did. She had dark brown roots that gradually changed into the color of the rainbow at the ends of her shoulder length hair. Eyes so piercing green that they seemed to pop against the heavy black she lined them with.

While others looked at her with distaste, I saw the beauty behind her façade. Her appearance so outlandish, so uniquely different, so her. She was a social outcast, just like me.

For years, I thought I was the master of deception, manipulating others just the way I liked them. My plan was simple, it all boiled down to me being an asshole to just about everyone. I liked being by myself, a total loner. None of these people knew me, or ever would.

Imagine my surprise when little Miss Liberty kept defying my attempts to stay away from her. She refused to give up.

Damn girl!

I couldn't tell you the number of times I asked if she had some kind of death wish. She saw straight through my bullshit, and that scared the shit out of me. It also made me admire her even more.

Eventually, she won out.

It was public knowledge I did not socialize much at school, or anywhere else. The handful of friends I have did not attend this school.

This feisty girl completely through me for a loop. Once I let her in and spent time around her, I quickly became addicted, wanting more. The more time I spent with Liberty, the less angry I was. For whatever reason, being around her calmed me in ways nothing ever did before.

I spent more time with her until most of my days were spent with her, or on the phone with her.

That was my first mistake.

Toward the end of Junior year, my bad boy reputation escalated to a new level. My uncle's ties to the Aniello *'crime'* family circulated around school and the rumor mills spread like wild fire. Around the same time, I started to fight at a local college campus and their underground fights they would hold once a month. It quickly became a popular event to attend, so my bad boy reputation now had a level of danger attached to it. All because of the family association.

It all spelled one thing... stay the fuck away from me unless you were looking for trouble.

Libbs, my pet name for Liberty, unfortunately gained a rep for herself and not a good one either. She took some serious heat for just hanging around me but Libbs just ate that shit up. Turning it around on every asshole at our school, telling them where they could shove it, or I'd kick their ass.

Crazy girl made me laugh!

While Libbs wasn't one to share much of her past, I picked up enough that I knew she was dealing with her own set of issues. Where I was angry, she was depressed. We were two peas in a pod and the first time I told her so, she just gazed back at me for the longest of time.

Then she blew me away. *"We are simply two tortured souls who finally found their way home."*

Talk about a moment. I don't know how long I stared into her eyes that slowly filled with tears, but she had stripped me to the bone and touched my soul in a way that left me speechless. She quickly tore down walls I put in place years ago.

Tiffany, my bitch of a mother, abandoning me when I was younger seriously fucked with my head. My dad was dead, so when my mom split I took that shit on, blaming my six-year-old self. I went to sleep each night wondering what I had done wrong to make her not love me enough to stay.

With each passing day, the hurt slowly slipped away. In its place... *anger*. I swore then that I would never trust any female to hurt me again. Why would I? If my own mother, who should love me unconditionally could up and walk out of my life without a backwards glance, why the fuck would I trust any female again?

The female influences in my life, which weren't many, were the women my uncle had around on occasion. He kept them around long enough to fuck 'em before showing them the door. Most of them reminded me of leeches whose goal was to suck as much money as they could get. Sick! You bet I had trust issues when it came to women.

My view of women certainly didn't improve over the years hanging around the Aniello's either. It's common knowledge they were around only when asked. Trinkets, play things, dick warmers, whatever you want to call them, it all meant the same thing.

Don't get me wrong, none of the women were ever mistreated in front of me, but behind closed doors who the hell knows what crazy shit goes on. I've heard stories about some of the crazy fetishes that Anthony was into, which is another reason why I keep my distance from him, but so does everyone else. Marcus tolerates his brother. My uncle Vince has his own thoughts when it comes to Anthony, only he keeps them to himself.

With all of that, it made being around Libbs confusing as hell at first. My dick certainly noticed how gorgeous she was, but my brain worked overtime to suppress any growing urge to fuck her senseless. She wasn't like all those sleazy leeches. She deserved to be treated better than a fuck, she deserved to be loved. Something I'm not capable of.

In no time at all, Libbs became my closest friend and the first female in my life that meant something real to me.

It wasn't long before she had this mystery guy do a real number on her. Of course, she kept most of it from me because she knew I'd kill anyone who would hurt her. With me, Libbs was hard headed and argumentative one minute, then laughing her ass off the next. There was no pretending with us, we just had this special bond. I think we both wanted more but were too damn afraid to admit it. Let alone act on it.

Enter, Jacob Weise.

Around Jacob, she was a different person altogether. Her face would blush in his presence and she'd get so damn tongue-tied around him, it cracked me the hell up. I wondered who the hell this girl was, and what did she do with Libbs.

Slowly, things started to change.

Her face would no longer blush in his presence, and her piercing green eyes lost some of their luster. Other subtle things began to happen as well, like skipping classes and ignoring my phone calls.

Whenever I confronted her, she'd just tell me she was fine. Going as far to say that I should stay out of her personal life. She didn't meddle in mine, so I had no right to meddle in hers. It was like a slap in the face, so I swallowed my simmering anger over the fact she said to stay out of her personal life! I hated it, but I promised not to meddle unless I felt she was in danger. That was my red line. Taking a step back was hell, but this is what she wanted.

That was my second mistake.

A costly mistake that haunts me to this day.

Our Senior year.

Late one Saturday night just before sun went down, I happened to spot Libbs' car parked in a shady part of town where we would hang sometimes. Not the part of town a girl should travel by herself. As I drove closer, the windows in her car appeared foggy. The lights from my truck hit her silhouette as she sat in the driver's seat. From my vantage point, I couldn't tell if anyone was in the car with her.

After months of her distancing herself, I finally decided I had enough. No longer would I put up with her pushing me away. I've done everything she'd asked of me, but I'm fucking done walking around pissed off all the time simply because I was jealous.

That's right... you heard me right. I'm calling Libbs out on her bullshit and finally going to do the right thing. Make that girl mine. *My* Libbs! We've danced around the subject long enough, each of us holding back not wanting to ruin the friendship between us.

That bullshit was ending now!

I pulled in next to her beaten up Honda Civic that had more bumper stickers on the back than paint. She even had a sticker of my name in big white letters on her back window. In red she had the nickname she bestowed on me after watching me fight for the first time. She felt that I needed a badass fighter's name, so she came up with, 'reaper'.

Declan 'Reaper' Parisi.

Right now, my instincts told me something wasn't right. An instant chill ran through my body as the pit of my stomach fell. I shivered with fear even though I'm not the kind of guy who is afraid of much. Only, right now, all I feel is dread and it terrifies me. My heart starts pounding and my pulse is skyrocketing. I'm shouting her name, calling out to her before I can get my truck in park, only to fight with my seatbelt.

"LIBBS. LIBBS. LIBBS." I'm barely able to catch a breath as I kick open the door of my truck. I stumble and make a mad dash to get to her. My fingers are shaking and it takes my brain a second to catch up to understand why her damn door won't open.

Locked!

Goddammit!

Even then, I don't stop trying to open it as flames of anger shoot down my arm. I about rip the damn handle off when I'm out of breath and pressing my hands against the glass of the window. As I try to get a better look at her, I'm having trouble because of the layer of fog that's there. I keep on shouting and then pound harder on the window wishing and hoping to get her to respond and turn her head my way. I desperately want to see those green eyes of hers.

"LIBBS! LIBBS!!! LIBBS!!!!!!" My brain then explodes with fury as each attempt to wake her up fails. It's just another dagger to my heart.

No.No.No. This cannot be happening!

My mind may be paralyzed with fear, but a rush of adrenaline lifts my left fist as I deliver a massive blow to the window. Glass shatters everywhere and it's then I get my first real look at Libbs' pale face. It's like a heavy-weight punch in the gut that leaves me weak in the knees. In one gasp, all the air in my lungs expel.

I don't recall the number of times I muttered her name or kissed her forehead as she weightlessly laid limp in my arms.

So many regrets, so much time wasted, the feeling of guilt consumes me from within. The anguish is beyond-painful and hurts me more than any fists ever could.

Rocking her back and forth in the dark of the deserted parking lot, I glance up at the sky and wonder if there really is a God? Seconds or minutes, I'm not sure how much time passed before my brain kicks in and logic takes over. I take in the scene before me.

Libbs was all alone in the car. No blood. No signs of a struggle. Nothing out of place except for a motor in the back seat that was filling her car with carbon monoxide.

Suicide!

Chapter Four

"Pain & Regrets"

L IBBS COMMITTED FUCKING SUICIDE?
No way!

This wasn't her. Not anymore. She attempted it once, but that was long before we met. Back then, she didn't have me. So, what changed? Were there any signs I missed? Jesus Christ, how could I have let this happen to her?

Things happen in your life that change you forever, this is that moment for me. I never knew my dad, and I can't remember my mom. This is worse. Libbs meant more. With her wrapped in my arms, I couldn't hold onto her tight enough. This is what I was missing all along. To hold her in my arms and kiss those amazing lips of hers.

I failed her, and me.

For the first time in my life tears freely flowed down my face. I'm crying, and I have never cried a day before in my life. Not ever! Not even when my mother left me. No one deserved my tears.

Not until Libbs.

And now the gaping hole in my chest keeps getting wider and more excruciating with each passing second that I breathe, and she doesn't. My life meant something with her in it.

I can't shake the feeling that there is something more here. Someone did this. Someone who knew her history, who knew that this would be accepted as a suicide with no questions asked. Well fuck that! She didn't kill herself and I won't stop until I prove it. I'll gladly defy the devil himself and fuck up whatever fate has taken us to this point. Fucking cruel is what this is. While I sink in the ruins of pain and heartache, it vastly contrasts to Libbs' peaceful face, as if she were fast asleep.

There are no indications of whatever happened here earlier. She shows no signs of pain or trauma, nothing other than a restful sleep. Staring down at her angelic face, I do something that I've imagined doing so many times before. I place the softest of a kiss to her lips moist with my shed tears and make a solemn promise to the best friend I have ever had, ever loved. I may have been too late to save her, but I will not *fail* her. I damn well will figure it out and when I do, I will rain hell on, and punish whoever pushed her into doing something this awful.

The fighter in me vows for revenge.

While my heart pledges to never forget what she meant to me.

With my thoughts lost in the darkest places of my mind, the low rumbling noise from the motor in the back seat of her car finally comes to a stop. The silence is deafening, but just as a flock of birds fly away, a police cruiser pulls into the parking lot with his spot-light shining on us.

None of it feels real. Not the cop. Not the ambulance. Not even when they zip her body inside the black bag and cart her away. I'm just numb.

An hour passes and as I drive home, I pull her cell phone from the pocket of my jacket. Earlier I noticed it lying in the center console of her car and for whatever reason, I grabbed it. I don't know why I did it, I'm just glad I did.

With any luck, I might be able to figure out what was going on with her. I'll start with her contacts and text messages which hopefully hold some clues. The moment something alarming catches my eye, I slam on the brakes of my truck. My mouth goes dry as I stare at the chilling evidence that's right there for me to see, I just can't believe it. My number is on her list of recent calls. I missed a call from her just a few hours ago and my stomach drops as bile retches in the back of my throat.

The days leading up to Libbs' funeral went by in a blur. The days shortly following weren't much better and provided little relief. The more time I had to process things, the worse things got. I went dark... literally and figuratively.

I DIDN'T SLEEP, DIDN'T EAT, and I sure as hell did not go back to school. Vince knew better than to force me, because it would have only ended in a bloodbath if I had. To have look at the everyone's stares and then listen to the rumors and innuendoes would have been a disaster.

To avoid arguing with me when it came to finish my senior year, and graduating on time, he hired a tutor that would work with me on my timetable. Honestly, I couldn't give a fuck if I get my damn high school diploma or not. I had more pressing things to do, school could wait... like forever. That was when my uncle gave me a deadline, making sure I understood that I would be earning that diploma.

Yeah, yeah... whatever!

Most of my time is spent acting like a madman possessed, locked in my bedroom with my stereo blaring. For countless hours at a time, I'm scouring over Libbs' phone, reading every text message and stalking her social media sites. I'm looking for anything and everything.

Luckily, my buddy Dex is one hell of a thief. He lifted her laptop from her house before the cops ever made it there to inform her parents of her accident. I call it an accident, because I sure as fuck know it wasn't a suicide.

On my way home that night, I called Dex in hysterics to explain things I couldn't even comprehend myself. Sometime in the conversation, I mentioned that I had her phone with me, and right then he insisted we needed to get our hands on her computer as well. I never would have thought of that in the moment, but Dex is smart that way. He was able to look at it with a clear head, and he wasn't buying the suicide ruling either.

He may not have known Libbs well, but he liked her, and he knew before I did just how much she meant to me. But, I didn't listen to him. Instead, I did what I always do when it comes to him. I ignore ninety percent of the shit that comes out of his mouth.

It wasn't long before a chilling pattern began to emerge with a recurring and unfamiliar name. The more I combed through her text messages, the more times this name kept showing up. I can't even begin to explain how I feel reading these messages from some strange guy who is basically stalking her. Libbs' responses don't make things any easier on me, it's like she was oblivious to it. The fact that he's like a ghost infuriates me even more. Message after message, the more I read the tighter my chest constricts, until I damn near crush her phone with my bare hands.

My mind is all over the place, and it's then I know what I need to do.

"I need a favor?" I ask my uncle late one evening as he sat at his desk completely engrossed with the papers in front of him. Work, no doubt. There's been this awkward silence between us lately, and it's been going on since Libbs' death.

His eyes slowly rise. "Whatever you need," he says in a low tone, just as his eyes come together. "Always. You know that, Declan."

A brief grin of appreciation is followed with silent moments of an unspoken understanding that passes between us. We've always been close, but for the first time I'm anxious.

After I clear the knot from my throat, I ask, "I need Salvo's help going through a cell phone and possibly a computer."

The implication of what I'm asking has him lifting his right eyebrow, because he knows where I'm going with this. I thought it best to ask him first before Salvo opens his big mouth and rats me out to him later. The guy would do anything for me, but not without my uncle's knowledge first.

"Declan," he exhales with a long sigh, "does this have anything to do with the girl?"

The girl?

The fire in my gut begins to churn but I hold back and bite my tongue. I want nothing more than to lash out at him but losing my cool is not what I want. That would only bring more trouble my way, and right now I don't need any more than I've got.

Vince rubs his brow knowing perfectly well who, then suddenly tosses his glasses on the desk and runs his hands down his face.

"Does it matter?" I manage to spit out with my jaws clinched tight.

"Fuck," he flies out of his chair as his fist slams on the desk. "Yes, it certainly does. Let the police handle it, let them do their job. You are becoming obsessed with this."

He can't be fucking serious. Since when does anyone in the Aniello family let the police handle anything? I'm close enough to family, so the idea that the police will magically come away with any conclusion other than suicide, is ridiculous and naive.

First off, that part of town the cops didn't stray into very often. The fact one just happened to show up when he did was a big fucking shock. There was no way they were going to spend the time or resources to find out what really happened to her when it'd be all too easy for them to write it off like she was some drugged-out teenager who did herself in. One, two, three... just like that. Case closed.

But, I refuse to let that happen. Libbs deserves better and I knew that girl better than just about anyone, which is why I know deep in my bones, something's off. My uncles lack of compassion is seriously starting to piss me off.

I let his comment roll off my shoulders, but just can't let him have the last word. Standing tall with my arms crossed, I challenge his wisdom and set the record straight.

"Since when do *we* let the police handle anything?" I don't wait for his reply. "We don't! We handle it ourselves, so instead of going behind your back, I came to you first. The question is, are you going to help me or not?" Then, I lower my voice. "Just don't make the mistake thinking I'm asking for your permission, because I assure you I'm not. Not on this."

My breathing is harsh and unsteady, and my arms won't stop shaking that's how worked up I am. I have never talked to uncle in a threatening tone before, but I have... now. I think he's just as shocked because his gaze is razor thin, but I don't back down. I stand my ground.

After our mini battle of wills, his shoulders relax before he settles back down in his chair. My composure stays with my eyes in a deadlock with his.

He blinks first.

Eventually, he nods his head and holds out his left hand. "Give me the girl's phone, I'll make sure Salvo gets it done if it's that important to you. And the computer if you have it. I'd do anything for you, you know that. I'm also very concerned this whole ordeal has put you under an enormous amount of stress." This time I nod my head. "You better be watching out for you."

A part of me wanted to ask if that was so hard to agree with, but I know he's worried about me. With good reason, I slowly feel myself losing my grasp on things. "I'll be under a lot *less* stress if Salvo can find something that will help me."

I fill him in on what I've found so far to relate to Salvo. I have the name JC, or it could be initials, J.C.? Who the hell is JC? It's not anyone I can think of, but the weird thing with whoever that is, sent Libbs several coded messages, many on the day she died. None of them make sense to me, but hopefully Salvo can give me more to go on. Like deciphering codes like these, GS2V_XVMG$IZO. He's the best tech guy the Aniello family has. If there is anything to find, he'll find it.

THE DAYS FOLLOWING SEEM LONGER than the day before, leaving me angry, frustrated and emotionally drained. My mood swings are vast and severe, triggering manic episodes that leave a path of destruction wherever I go. My uncle can't hit me over the head to knock my ass out, so the doctor prescribed heavy duty mood stabilizers. If those didn't help, he was instructed to inject me with a tranquilizer that would indeed put my ass out.

The shitty thing about the shots is the severe bouts of depression that follow. Totally fucks with my head and takes days to level out. Vince had seen enough, and Marcus was over the top out of his mind ready to kick my ass himself just to snap me out it.

Like that would work!

That was when my uncle sent me to Nero.

A badass ex-marine, now trainer from hell, who literally kicked my ass on the first day. Vince dropped me off at the door, telling me to get my ass inside the gym because it was time someone straighten me out.

At first, I thought he was bluffing and had finally lost his mind, but he was dead serious. Begrudgingly, I huffed inside the gym. Hard Corps. I found the name peculiar, but given the state of my foul mood, I really couldn't care less. What I saw when I first walked in was a very large and open space that housed state of the art equipment. Whoa!

No one was working out, so I assumed the gym was private. Not a public one, like a Planet Fitness. My eyes were quickly drawn to the different sayings that were plastered all over the gray walls. It dawned on me then, that the name of the gym held a purpose. A significant one.

With sayings like, *Failure is not an option... Pain is only temporary, pride is forever... Nobody ever drowned in sweat... Sweat dries, blood clots, bones heal—suck it up.* To my personal favorite, *Retreat Hell.* Really, it wasn't necessarily the sayings, but the very large Marine logo in the center of the gym.

I should have known it then I was in trouble, but when I turned to face the mountain of a man with a crew cut, black shorts, and shirt with Marine spelled across the front, I stood speechless. Something that doesn't happen very often.

I may have walked in with a chip on my shoulder and guffawed a time or two at what the hell I walked into, but two hours later... I was limping back out and cursing Nero every name in the book with bated breath.

All those slogans on the walls I mentioned when I first walked in, well, he shouted them at me over and over again, making sure I knew those were Marine words to live by.

That night he became my very strict drill Sargent, while I was the angry punk who needed to be taught a lesson by a real life badass.

One who wouldn't be intimated.

One who would strike back ten times as hard.

One who would break me down but teach me to build myself back up.

Those sessions changed my life in ways I never expected them to. Nero's strict training gave me the skill set and the discipline that would later jump start my fighting career. I may have hated Nero Wilkens at one time, but now he has my motherfucking upmost respect. He's also my personal fighting trainer and mentor. I'm the man I am, because of him.

Only today, he's taking way too much enjoyment in punishing me. I'm off my game, my head's just not in it since I'm getting nowhere fast with what happened with Libbs. The weeks keep flying by and still nothing much to go on. It's frustrating the hell out of me.

My knuckles are raw from beating the hell out of the heavy bag. My concentration is all over the place, my timing is off, and Nero has taken me down to the mat about the same number of times he did when I first started to train with him. And it's pissing him off.

Lack of discipline and concentration to a guy like Nero, is simply unacceptable. Even though he knows what I'm going through, it won't excuse things in his eyes. He gets it, even understands why, but showing emotions is not who he is. It's the Marine in him, and that will never change.

Nero also doesn't mince words. He's a straight to the point kind of guy. More times than not, I have to draw my own conclusions as to what he's really trying to tell me with his usual Military metaphors.

Perfect example. "You realize, having all your body parts intact and functioning at the end of the day, beats the alternative."

I'm doubled over, panting due to exertion and damn near exhausted. My body is drenched in blood and sweat, and my brain feels like a bowl of Jell-O. It takes me a minute, but I slowly connect the dots with his latest message of intended motivation.

"Let me guess, more Marine jargon," I say breathlessly, "no matter how tired or broken I feel I am, it's still better than the alternative." The alternative being, *dead*. I just can't say that word.

His face stays firm like stone. "Smart advice is if you ask me, son." Yeah, yeah, yeah. I hear him and all, but I just don't need to hear it today. I catch Dex out of the corner of my eye working with the medicine ball. He trains here with me since he also fights in WCU. Nero has sort of taken him under his wing, only because I asked him to. Dex is a good fighter, definitely a more strategic fighter than me. I think less and hit more, where he hits less and calculates his punches.

Motioning to Dex with my eyes, I alert Nero. "Why don't you go take Dex down a few hundred times and give him some of your good ole' brotherly Marine love." While I found it funny, Nero certainly did not.

Not even a smile. "Nice try, boy, but we're not done yet. Give me a set of squats and lunging jumps, then hit the showers. After that come see me in my office," he commands with a stern look in his eyes, and then turns to walk in the other direction toward his office.

Anyone that knows me, knows I do stupid shit from time to time. It seems like I never learn, and today is no different. Before I can stop my myself, I stupidly talk back because I've been hitting it hard for hours now. "I've got things…"

As the words leave my mouth, Nero's left foot stalls mid step with his back to me, and answers of his shoulder. "Let me clarify." With his left foot on the ground, he turns his head slightly, "After squats, and before lunging jumps, give me five reps with the tire sledge."

It's a good thing he's not looking straight at me, because rolling my eyes at him would earn me another five reps. Without saying anything else, Nero pauses to see if I have any additional comments. *Yeah, right!* When I don't, he doublechecks by asking, "Was there anything else you wanted to say to me?"

"No, Sir."

If I didn't respect his hard ass or know deep down this was just his way of forcing me to work shit out of my head on my own, I would have walked out a long time ago and never brought my ass back. The thing is, Nero knows all about my past, and my many hang-ups. He also personally knows my uncle, Vince. Although, I'm not entirely clear how their paths ever crossed. Nero just gets me. Better yet, he knows how to handle me at my worst.

When Nero is out of ears shot, Dex chuckles from across the room. "What'd you do this time to piss him off?"

"Breathe," I exhale as my leg muscles burn in protest with my first set of squats.

Forty minutes later, my body has been pushed to the limit. There's not one muscle that's not feeling the burn and sore as hell. I'm half limping, half dragging my body to the showers. I stand under the scalding hot water to let the heat and steam work their magic.

By the time I exit the shower, Dex has already come and gone, laughing his ass off that I have to head to Nero's office like I'm still in high school and being sent to the principal's office. I let my middle finger do the talking which only made him laugh harder. Fucker!

Not completely dry, I quickly dress in a fresh pair of shorts and t-shirt before my heavy legs drag my ass to see Nero. All the lights in the gym are still on, but it's empty at this point. As I walk down the narrow hall from the locker room to his office, I hear Nero's loud voice on the phone. From the sounds of it, he's not happy with someone. It's a bit awkward, so I hang back a few feet from the door not sure if I should wait for him to end his call, or simply walk in. Only hanging outside his door feels like I'm eavesdropping, but it seems like a more appropriate and considerate thing to do. I'm sure he has no clue I'm standing just outside his doorway.

I try not to listen, but it's impossible not to.

"When are you going to tell him the truth?"

"That's bullshit and you know it."

"And let me tell you something else, it is my Goddamned business seeing as he is my business."

Well, shit. This is my cue to step away from his door, but I am curious as to who *he* is that he's talking about. Then, I hear a name. My name. That's when I freeze.

"Declan is a smart young man, smarter than you give him credit for. If someone is playing a game with dangerous information that could blow up in your face, you had better be the one to tell him it first. We have a fight coming up and his head is not in the game right now. This shit blows up... You want to fire me? FIRE me, but you better be prepared to take me down if you think I'm going to abandon that boy." WTF?

I've heard more than enough!

I storm in his office. "Who the *fuck* wants to fire you?" My voice commands his immediate attention, but Nero shows no visible sign that my outburst has startled him in the least. Instead, he slowly swivels in his chair and when he sees the fiery look in my eyes, a calculated grin spreads across his usual stone and stoic face.

"Nice to have you back."

Chapter Five

"Monster in the Dark"

*A good sacrifice is one that is not necessarily sound
but leaves your opponent dazed and confused-Rudolph Spielmann
What a perfect quote.
No truer words were ever spoken.
That's precisely what my plans are when it comes to the boy.
I found the perfect sacrificial lamb, and it was a streak of genius.
He doesn't know it, yet, but he took the bait. Hook, line and sinker.
He really made it all too easy for me to find his greatest weakness.*

---

*I've carefully orchestrate each of my moves like a game of chess.
Once the first pawn falls, the rest will soon follow.
And I'll get to sit back and watch it all unfold.
No one will see me coming, but rest assured the fallout will be epic.
After years of waiting.
The time has finally come.
The sweet taste of revenge will be mine.*

Little does Declan know his whole world is about to collapse around him!

Chapter Six

"Discovery"

"Nice to have you back."

That's all Nero says to me.

Christ Almighty! If he won't tell me, I'll pry the damn phone from his fingers, but he beats me to it and hangs up. I get what he's trying to do, but right now is not the best time to poke the beast. Especially when I walk into a conversation that directly relates to me.

"Son, I'm only going to say this once," he walks around to the front of his desk and casually rests against it with his arms folded. "What I say or do on your behalf is my business. You are not to question it, just know I have your back. I'm not the only one worried about you, and that's what that phone call was about. Now, leave it at that. I'm going to give you some time to get the shit that's been eating you alive out of your system. Do what you have to do, but you come back ready to train for our fight next month with Curtis."

Fuck, I hate to hear that pricks name said aloud.

"I know you're hurting, son, but allowing yourself to wallow in pain and suffering will only eat your soul alive."

The muscles in his face twitch as I ignore his every word. All I need is a name. "Who?" I repeat louder this time. I want to know who the fuck he was talking too, but the look on his stone face tells me I'm not going to get it. All I get is more of Nero's military style approach to life. After all, it's his favorite thing to do.

"Have you ever heard this one? Never wrestle with a pig or argue with an idiot."

I kid you not, this is the kind of daily shit Nero comes up with, and every day it leaves me more confused by the minute.

"What the fuck does that have to do with anything?" Again, failing to see his logic, but when he lowers his chin and gives me the look that all but says *which one* of the two of us happens to be arguing, I lower my head in frustration.

"Declan," he eases his tone this time as he studies the deep creases on my tense face. "Just listen to me. You might be surprised one day and realize what I've been saying to you all along is one hundred percent right. It could be soon, it could be years later... but mark my words, one day you'll get it."

After all of that, I may not get a name from him any time soon, but whatever, my choices are limited so I'll start by talking with my uncle the minute I see him this evening.

Then, Nero hits me with this. "Be courteous to everyone, but friendly to no one."

Well, that about sums me up perfectly. He's definitely on a roll tonight... talking in his usual circles. Or, am I missing a bigger message he's trying to send me? Or, is he continuing to talk just to distract me? If that's the case, it's working!

"Always remember this," he cautions with the still of his eyes, "your silence equals consent."

I'm seriously looking at him wondering if I should try to memorize these sayings or write them down because he's going to test me later. They must be for something, because senile he is not.

"Whatever," I give up and throw my hands up in the air, "can we stop all of this now? I'm too damn tired to care right now."

"I'll leave you with this final thought," he says. Oh, thank, God! "That phone call is something that concerns me, not you. Let me figure it out, but I want you to think about something as well. In life, just like in that damn ring, it's a fight. It doesn't matter what you are fighting for in that moment, it's still a battle. To win the battle, you have to be smart, play it smart, and above else, fight smart."

Now that one, I like. Plus, it sounds pretty spot on.

I point to a large plague hanging on the wall behind his desk. "That one is my favorite." I tell him with a smirk as I read the Marine Credo, out loud. "To catch us, you have to be fast. To find us, you have to be smart. To beat us, you have to be kidding."

Nero cracks a slight grin like any proud Marine. "Fucking right!"

While I may still be trying to figure out what he's failing to get through to me, I know without a shadow of a doubt that he has my back. But something is going on and he's trying like hell to distance me from it.

Now that I'm calmed down, I have to ask, "Is all of that your definition of a pep-talk, or just to show me that somewhere in that steel body you have a soft spot for me?"

For the second time tonight, he cracks a smile. A new personal record. "Nah, I'm just too damn mean and stubborn to sit back and watch you hurt like you've been hurting. You need to be more like me." I let a laugh slip out before he continues. "Bottle up whatever shit you need to and don't show any of it to anyone. Ever. Showing emotions is a weakness son, especially in fighting. You're a fighter, the best I've seen in a long time. Plus, I believe in you. Now it's time for you to do just that."

"Yeah, what's that?"

"Fight!"

In theory, it sounded good. Only, the following days and weeks weren't much better. Vince flat out and denied he talked with Nero that night and Salvo wasn't having much luck with Libbs' phone and computer. I slowly kept slipping further into a depression, masking my pain the only way I knew how. By, *fighting*.

The thing is, my appetite for fighting these days was not the same kind Nero had in mind at all. During the day I trained as usual, after I put in a few hours of school with my tutor, Daniel. He's not so bad, gets right to it. And that I like. Our four hours of school work usually takes no more than three, so that gives me an extra hour before I hit the gym.

Then each night I disappear. Feeling helpless is not an emotion I do well with, and with things moving slowly, I had to find a release. Dressed in my usual black hoodie, dark jeans and boots, I left the house on a one-way mission to find the one thing I needed. Street fighting is hostile, violent, and considered the most dangerous form of fighting with its lack of rules and zero regulations. It's the unpredictable danger that I craved. Call it a suicide mission or playing Russian roulette with the stakes being so high, but the dangers were merely a test of my survival skills.

Simply put, I went black.

Libbs' passing has set me on a current path of self-destruction. The only time I felt anything was when I was broken, bloodied and bruised. The adrenaline rush was a high like no other. I was captive to the pain and suffering and my release was to unleash it in ways that was damn frightening for anyone who dared to square off against me. They were my enemy, and each breath they took was one too many.

Many times, I had to be pulled off my opponents after they were lying helpless on the ground. All I wanted to do was punish someone, hell, anyone for that matter. The only thing I could picture in my mind was Libbs dead in my arms. With that fueling my anger, my goal remained in place. Strike first, draw blood and then go in for the kill.

Whatever redeemable quality Libbs saw in me, died along with her in that car. Never again would I let someone get that close to me. The pain is insufferable and more crippling than I can fucking handle. For a fighter, that's saying something.

By the time I made it to bed for the night, the day light hours were already up. I mostly tossed and turned, catching a few hours at that and then dragged my ass to the shower. Each new day, I showed up in the gym with fresh marks from my punishing antics the night before. Everyone saw them, I wasn't fooling anyone even though somewhere in the back of mind I was sure I had.

Tonight, as I slowly crawl into bed, I think I may have pushed my luck too far. It was my fault, I wasn't paying close enough attention when this fucker got a bat handed to him from his buddy. It seems he did not like witnessing me kick his buddie's ass, so he helped him out. I wasn't too worried; his friend couldn't fight worth a damn, but he did land a few good shots to my ribs.

Each shot did it's intended damage, but with each grunt of pain I expelled, it only fueled me on more. Blocking out the pain, I stared him down erupting in a fit of disturbing laughter that left him looking at me like I was damn near crazy. Instead of allowing the pain to cripple me, I stood back and howled with such intensity, the fucker stood motionless. I came at him again, refusing to give up as he shook his head like he couldn't believe I was coming back for more. If he thought a few solid licks to my ribs was enough to stop me, he was sadly mistaken. He dropped the bat just as I got to him and before he knew it, I had him in a solid choke hold. Then, I returned the favor with his own bat, shattering both of his fucking knee caps.

When I returned home, I taped my ribs before coming to bed. Nero is going to kill me if I walk in tomorrow with a broken rib, or two. My left side hurts like hell and with my big fight looming with Curtis coming up with WCU, *Windy City Underground,* it all could be in jeopardy.

I fucked up thinking I was invincible, and if I'm unable to fight due to my own reckless behavior I'll never hear the end of it. If not Nero, Marcus will surely kick my ass. WCU is his baby, but he started this venture with me in mind, without that, I don't think he would have done it. Anthony was against the idea from the beginning, but Marcus had a vision and I was a big part of it.

It's all Marcus can talk about and the buzz he is creating for it is paying off. Just another reason I have to make sure my ass is ready to fight. Plus, when it comes to Curtis Diego, I have some serious motivation. The guy is real fucking scumbag.

Curtis "Dick" Diego, as I refer to him, has a long sordid history with me. Bad blood. I kicked his ass our first fight, and just nearly won the second that's been a controversy of his since. His team believes he won it, but the three judges saw it differently. He even blamed the ref for his loss, spouting off Marcus had paid him off. Which is bullshit. I may be Marcus' golden boy and the best fighter he has, but I don't need him to buy my win's. I earn them. Marcus wouldn't do that anyway, not when his reputation is at stake.

For the last fourteen months, all I've heard is Curtis trashing my name every chance he gets. Marcus is so furious with the little prick for suggesting he has anything to do with the judges scoring the fights, he was close to banning Curtis from ever fighting in WCU again, but I assured him I'd handle it by breaking his neck this time. Marcus gave Curtis and his team one warning that any disrespect against the organization again would end up with him being banned forever.

Just last week, the loudmouth prick had taken things to a new level of low by taking things to a very personal level. That piece of shit can say anything he wants about me, but he crossed the line when he mentioned Libbs by name. He never knew her except when she came to a few of my fights. When he heard a close friend of mine died, Curtis used her death to take pot shots at me.

That's another reason why I've been indulging in street fights. I had to release my aggression, training in the gym wasn't enough. I needed to hurt someone. If his game plan was to fuck with my head, it worked. That's the problem, I'm letting him get to me and making stupid decisions based on it. When it comes to Curtis, I don't need any more motivation to want to kill him.

But, Nero's right, like usual. I need to get my head in the damn game and focus on what needs to be done. That means no more street fights. I need to heal up so I can finish that fucker once and for all.

Early the next morning, I sneak out of the house to avoid seeing my uncle. I'm sore as hell but other than that, my beat-up body is holding up given how much abuse I've put it through lately. While I relied on my bare knuckles and brute strength, I've had knives, broken bottles and baseball bats coming straight for me. What it all boils down to, besides the fact I'm a total badass, is what happens the moment it's just me against them. It's not the muscle, or the weapons that win fights, it's how you use your brain and what kind of mindset you have in the heat of the moment.

Any fight is mental, first and foremost. These past few weeks my mental state has been in a pretty dark place. The more pain I endured, the darker my mind slipped. The next thing I knew, strong arms were pulling me off bloody bodies. One after another.

I knew I wasn't going to be able to sustain that behavior for long, and if I'm going to get my head right now, there is only one place I can do that.

Shortly after Libbs passed, I started writing an open letter to her. It was my way to still feel close to her.

The drive is short and with my notepad in hand, I hike up the hill just as a cool breeze picks up. With the familiar Oak tree just up ahead, a sense of calm eases the butterflies that I always seem to get on my drive to come and see her. Of all the places to bring me a sense of peace, this place certainly shouldn't, but Libbs' here. It's an odd kind of comfort, that's for sure.

After I get comfortable on the neatly mowed grass, I open to my latest passage that I know she'll get a kick out of.

"Today, I went to our favorite hang-out and burger joint, *The Soda Fountain*. Who knew I would look forward to Fifties music and checkerboard vinyl seats," I chuckle because the first time Libbs took me there, I felt like I stepped back into some time warp. Not to mention, my style of music is, Rap. A sharp contrast to Buddy Holly and Jerry Lee Lewis. Listening to Fifties was a bit of a culture shock, but that was Libbs.

"I can't believe you have me hooked on the place now. Even more than that, I order your all-time favorite item, a Banana Chocolate Milk shake. Still not huge fan, but I drink it anyway. Franny misses you like crazy, and it just so happens she renamed your favorite particular milk shake to, *The Liberty.*"

Damn, if that's not the coolest thing. If I had a grandmother, I'd want her to be just like Franny. She and her husband own the burger joint that stands on the corner of 10th and Pine, marking forty years this year. She's awesome and opinionated as they come, and not afraid to let it be known. Sassy as hell, which is most likely why she hit it off with Libbs right away. Franny is in her sixties. She's tiny, curvy and shows no sign of slowing down any time soon. Her white hair is always pulled up in what Libbs explained to me was a bee-hive. Most days she walks around with a pencil behind her ear and is always chewing gum. Joe, her husband is just as boisterous behind the grill, but Franny runs the show.

I went on to explain that Joe and Franny both, created a meal after their favorite adopted son and daughter, meaning me and Libbs. If you walk in there today and order a double cheeseburger with everything, fries and a Chocolate Banana Milk Shake, all you had to order was the, *Liberty-Double Decker.*

I wish I could see Libbs' face hearing that, I bet she'd she be smiling for ear to ear. No doubt, thinking that is cooler than shit. The smile on my face is short lived, as the empty void of missing her creeps back in.

"Ah, hell Libbs, I miss you like crazy thinking it's going to get better, but it doesn't. Salvo is continuing to work hard on finding something for me to go on, and I swear to you I won't stop until I find out what happened. I just need to get my shit together. I have a big fight coming up, but Libbs, I'm so fucked up."

I hate like hell to admit it, but she's the only person who could see through my bullshit anyway.

"I can't get a grip on how angry I get at times, no matter if I take my meds or not. It just consumes me to the point I need to feel physical pain just to make it through the day."

And admitting that feels like I've just hit rock bottom. "God, I need you more than ever, and it scares the hell out of me."

I'm not sure how much time passes, but I don't move or speak another word. I just sit, emotionless except for the phone calls that are blowing up on my phone.

Ignore.

Ignore.

Ignore.

Until... I can no longer press ignore.

A voice calls out. "Hey, Sunshine. Somehow I knew I'd find you here."

I don't need to turn and look who it is. Him coming here to find me feels like an invasion. This place represents my time with Libbs, and that precious time is sacred to me. I can't help but feel the anger swelling deep inside.

"Dex, what the fuck are you doing here?" I realize my tone is more bitter than friendly, but I don't care.

"Well it isn't for your dazzling personality, I can tell you that. But, if I'm being honest I just wanted to see if you're doing okay. If you need anything?"

I've known Dex for more years than I can count, and in those years, he still can't life for shit.

"It's a good thing I consider you my friend or I just might have to hurt you for showing up here."

"There it is," he cautiously chuckles, "that dazzling personality I was talking about. Anyway, you can't hurt me, I'm your only friend."

"Yeah, who needs friends anyway?" I cast a look over my shoulder, then cut right to the chase. "So, who is it this time?" *Like I even need to ask.*

"Who is what?" Dex decides to play stupid and it's not smart on his part to insult my intelligence. I let him understand that with a low and menacing growl from my throat. I honestly don't have any patience for bullshit games.

He insists. "I have no idea what you're talking about."

Sure, he doesn't. Then, why does your voice sound uneasy?

"Vince or Marcus?"

"Well," his voice lingers, "the thing is…"

Three, two, one. "Jesus, Dex just spit it out." I turn around to face him.

"Fuck, Declan," he sighs, and then rubs his forehead. "Okay, it was Anthony."

Anthony? That has my attention. Any other time, Anthony couldn't care less what the hell I was up to.

"What the fuck does he want?"

First of all, Dex is not one who is easily intimidated. He's six-foot-two with muscle to back it up, but we are talking about Anthony here. He makes everyone feel on edge.

"Who knows, but my guess it may have to do with the fact you have a huge fight coming up. Rumor has it, he has some big money on you taking Curtis down. With your daily disappearing acts, people are starting to get nervous."

That's complete bullshit. My best friend in the world suddenly dies and no one can understand that I want to be left the hell alone. Whatever, I couldn't give two fucks about any of it because my attention is suddenly on the cool breeze that floats a familiar fresh aroma in the air. The early morning rain and freshly mowed grass creates a scent Libbs absolutely loved and always talked about.

My troubles with Curtis, or anyone one else for that matter suddenly take a back seat as my thoughts once again drift back to her. I don't think a day will come when I don't associate fresh cut grass with Libbs. Even as intoxicating as it is, it doesn't overshadow that resting under my hand on top of the soft blades of grass, she lies deep below.

All alone.

And, in the dark.

I know all about dark, and none of it is what I want for her.

"It really pisses me off, you know?" I mumble under my breath, momentarily forgetting Dex until his firm hand is on my shoulder.

I automatically tense up, even though this is Dex's way of showing he's here for me. I don't do emotions, especially ones this raw. And one's I'm having trouble coming to terms with.

He smartly removes his hand. "What pisses you off?"

That's a loaded question I could go on answering for days, but what has my blood boiling is the fact my entire hand covers Libbs' tiny nameplate. I find it revolting that's it no bigger than the size of my hand. One, I aim to correct myself. I'll buy her the biggest damn headstone in this cemetery.

"Her parents didn't even buy her a fucking headstone. Just this little plate you can barely see. It's so small people could walk right over it. You can bet your ass, I'll fucking fix that." I growl meaning every damn word.

"Declan, man," Dex struggles with words because he knows the subject of Libbs is like a red-hot button sure to set me off. "I know you're hurting and all, but Anthony might be right. You have a fight coming up, and right now, your head is not in right place."

Excuse me? Dex doesn't even like Anthony, but now he's agreeing with him!

Oh, hell no!!

That has me up on my feet with my fists clenched tight. "You've seen my eyes, right? They are fucking black as midnight. The same color that Libbs is lying in right NOW. Don't tell me my head is not in the right fucking place. I've never been more ready to tear his motherfucking head off."

Now, he's done it. One minute I'm pissed, ready to fight everyone, but then her face pops in my mind and the thought of her lying in the dark, guts me to point I about fall to my knees. I'm a fucking mess but staring at the slab of cement that's no bigger than a damn driveway paver, just infuriates me so much something unexpected happens.

My eyes sting with a world of hurt that overtakes my anger. It's useless to try and stop it, I'm unable to stop the tears filling my eyes. The choking sobs have Dex taking a step back looking perplexed. Pissed off Declan he can handle, emotional mess Declan is unchartered territory. Can't say I blame him. I'm just waiting for to him to ask if I'm on my period. Damn emotions—see this is what happens when you let someone get under your skin.

Dex stands there, blinking a few times, but doesn't leave enough alone. "Your eyes may be black, but your head is definitely not in the right place. Declan, you're a mess. You're obviously hurting. I think it would be best to cancel or postpone the damn fight. Just for now. Give yourself more time."

Grrr! "I'm. Not. Canceling." Fucking hell, the faster I wipe away the tears the faster they continue to fall. The only thing that would make me feel better right now is to get into a goddamned brawl.

"Jesus!" I roar, nearly hyperventilating. "Just say something that will piss me the hell off." My chest burns I'm breathing so fast and irregular, that I'm getting light headed and may just pass the hell out.

The look on Dex's face is one of, *what the hell should I do* as his eyes dance over every inch of my face. After a few uncomfortably seconds, his lips curl in a lopsided grin.

"That, I can do. You see," he starts to ramble, "I've been keeping a secret from you for some time. Always afraid to tell you, but this might be the time to finally clear the air. To just get it off my chest to be free of it once and for all."

Jesus! "Any fucking day now, Dex." I'm bent over with my hands on my knees while I continue to breathe deep, wishing he would just piss me off or take a swing at me. Either would work at this point.

"I slept with Libbs."

I breathe and breathe until... *what the fuck did he just say?*

He says it so fast it takes me a second to process. My mind is seriously screwing with me. I had to have heard him wrong because if he was stupid enough to sleep with Libbs, I'll fucking gut him and not feel bad about doing it. I don't react right away, simply because I can't move. Instead, I tilt my head very slowly to the side as I wait for him to say it again.

Dare him to say it again.

"Declan," he stutters, "did you hear me?"

Oh, I heard alright you motherfucker. My fingers are already starting to twitch.

"I said, I slept with Libbs. It was a while ago and it was after one of your fights. I was scared shitless to say it, but I had to tell you. And I feel so much better for finally getting it off my chest." When he motions with his hand like he's just wiped sweat from his forehead.

In the meantime, I've already killed him ten different ways in my head. The only thing going for Dex, is the fact I know he'd never step over the line like that with me. I'm about to call him out on his bullshit, but if he's daring enough to play me over something like this, I'll make him sweat first.

"You slept with Libbs." I repeat his exact words with a fierce growl as I get in his face eliminating any personal space between us. Just saying those words have me feeling deadly. We are almost nose to nose, and even though we have the same build, I'm ten times more threatening than Dex.

Where I'm dark and dangerous, he's more lukewarm and teddy-bear like.

In a most serious and threatening tone, I slowly say with eyes that narrow into slits like a viper. "My Libbs?" Two words that breathe fire like a flame against the newly scared shitless look of his face.

"I, ah..." he nervously blinks his eyes as his voice lightens, "take it you are pissed?"

"Murderous!"

"Alrighty then," he takes a step back, just out of my reach. "I'm just going to take off since you are looking at me like you might murder me for real."

"Run, Dex," I warn, with an arch of my eye. "Run as fast as you can."

His face turns ghost white. "Shit, I LIED," he admits with his hands out in front of him while he stumbles backwards. "I'm sorry, I lied but you needed to hear something that would snap you out of it. Jesus, I'm about to piss myself." He huffs like he's winded. "Remind me to never get into the ring with you again, like ever!"

He really is a dumbass for pulling a stunt like this.

"Dex, I'm deciding if I should just kill you anyway for even suggesting such a thing. You're a real dick, and a lucky one at that. Lucky for you, I know you better than you know yourself." I remember a time when he said those exact words to me. Right now, I should probably be thanking him for pissing me off like I asked him too, but after that stunt, he'll get no thank you.

He doesn't help matters with the smug grin he gets on his face. "It worked though, didn't it?"

On a scale of one to ten, I'm still hitting close to a hundred. So, it worked, but that's not what brings a mischievous grin to my face.

Dex notices immediately. "Shit. Why are you smiling?" His eyes go wide with worry. "You never smile. What the fuck is going on in that head of yours now?"

He's nervous as he should be, because a brilliant idea just hit me. To see him so nervous, I tip my head back and laugh. Payback is such a bitch.

With a firm slap on his back, I give Dex the good news. "Well, buddy, I just found my sparring partner for the day! Thanks for volunteering."

"Oh, fuck! No, I didn't." He's shaking his head while his face turns a shade of green. And just like that, my mood lightens. The guys at the gym are in for a treat this afternoon.

TWO HOURS LATER, I KNOCKED the piss out of him. Then for kicks, I kept at it. If I was a betting guy, I'd say he will never pull a stunt like that again. I believe the black eye, busted lip and possibly two cracked ribs will make certain of it.

Tonight, Vince and I catch up over dinner. He mentioned that Salvo's been busy and is still looking into Libbs' things. Things are still tense between us but were doing okay. After I excuse myself, I wander into my father's study that I do on occasion. I like to sit in his chair, look at his personal things and wonder what it would be like to have him around. How different things may have been growing up around him.

I'm lost in my thoughts when Vince happens to walk by and notices me sitting at Dominic's old desk. As he quietly leans against the door, he looks lost in his own thoughts when he gets a solemn look to his face. The same look he gets whenever he thinks about his brother.

"I wish you had the chance to know him. I know for a fact he would have been so fucking proud to have had a son. A son who fights, no less." The corners of his mouth lift as we both end up lightly laughing. It brings up something that's always been in the back of my mind.

"Why didn't he have any kids? Or a wife?"

Seems like a logical question until Vince straightens his posture, then pulls his eyes in tight together like the question unsettles him.

"It just wasn't in the cards for him. Your father had to have control in everything he did. His drive, his passion, his view on life, all of it was a pretty amazing thing to be a part of. The short time we knew one another, I was always in awe of him. When I look at you and the man you are growing into, it's like seeing your father reborn all over again. It's truly an amazing thing."

I stay quiet, unsure what to say as Vince nods his head, and then quietly leaves me to my thoughts once again. The one thing that's always been hard for me to understand is how complex my father really was according to the little I know about him. The stories about him paint him one way, but then to live in his house I see a whole other side.

As I get up and walk to the same bookshelf I've been looking at for years, it never seems to amaze me what a huge history buff Dominic was. These books prove it.

On the top shelf, there are books on Napoleon, Hitler, Churchill, Marx, Bolivar to Catherine the Great. Just below that shelf are books about Sir Isaac Newton, Descartes, Galileo to Marco Polo. My father was quite the intellect who had some pretty diverse tastes when it came to reading material.

It's then that I notice something way in the back of the lowest shelf. I've never seen this before. When I stick my hand behind the stack of books, I feel a loose board and then what feels like another book. Barely able to reach it with my fingertips, I stretch my reach to grab ahold of what feels like a ribbon. I inch it forward until I can get a firm hold on it. When I pull it out, I discover what it is.

A journal.

A very nice and dusty journal that has a dark satin ribbon wrapped around it. An unusual rush washes over me like I've been caught stealing as I guiltily look around the room. It's so absurd, I end up laughing at myself.

"Jesus, Declan get a hold of yourself."

With the journal in my hand, I carry it back to the desk and sit down to carefully unravel the knot. The leather is thick and dark brown and has an intricate design on the cover. No doubt, this was an expensive journal and the potential unknown of what's inside creates an excitable nervousness that swirls in my chest.

With the ribbon untied, I blow and then wipe off the many layers of dust that have collected around it. From the looks of it, this book has not been touched in a very long time. Like eighteen years maybe? Oh, shit... the idea this could be my father's journal triples my nervousness as I open to the first page.

The Private Journal of Dominic W Santos

Holy Shit!

The inscription of his name in black, bold lettering, and knowing the insides are filled with *his* thoughts. I'm not sure how to describe how I'm feeling right now.

For the first time in my life, I will get a firsthand account of his life, as he *saw* it. Not the second-hand information I'm used to hearing. All this time, for close to twenty years this journal has sat, untouched and unread.

Slowly, I run my fingers over the worn-out edges and can tell right away he had taken plenty of time to write what's on the inside. Am I ready for this? Ready to get to know the real Dominic Santos, my father, from the only person who knew him best, himself.

Who knows, maybe I'll find some clues as to what really happened to him.

Over the years, Vince and Marcus have been so vague on the matter, leaving me more questions than answers.

Before I delve inside, I decide to take my late-night reading material to my room to get more comfortable. Tonight, I will finally get the chance to get to know the man I've only ever heard legends about.

Chapter Seven

"In His Own Words"

The one place I'm most comfortable besides inside the ring is my bedroom. My sanctuary. It's also the one place I spend most of my time when I'm not at the gym. I have it set up exactly the way I like it. My Mahogany desk sits up against three long rectangular windows that give me the perfect scenic view of the heavily lined trees that line our property. I have a four-pedestal king size bed that sits diagonal in the far corner and faces my most prized position. A sixty-two-inch wall mounted T.V. with Bluetooth surround sound that literally is movie theater quality.

Since this room is where I spend most of my time, I made it the best it can be. I'm not the flashy type, I just know what I like. With the exception of the light-colored gray walls, the rest of my room reflects my true tastes. Deep burgundy and black are about the only colors you will find in here. From black sheets and comforter, to my deep burgundy rug.

When I lay in bed, I'll spend hours looking at my three favorite abstract paintings I have hung across the room. Abstract art defines who I am in a way. Not accurately depicting any one thing, rather left up to your interpretation of what you see and feel. The idea you can create such beauty with the use of shapes and colors, is damn cool. For someone like me, that's the definition of true art.

I decide to take a quick shower and dress in my usual pair of shorts before I get comfortable. I admit I'm jacked and nervous at the same time to dig right in the journal I can't take my eyes off. With a stack of pillows behind my head, I reach for my father's journal from the nightstand. Nervous flitters hit me, because I have no idea what I'm about read. It has the potential to change a lot when it comes to him, and that thought weighs heavily on my mind. Whether it's positive or not, remains to be seen.

From the first page, what stands out at me right away is his elegant handwriting. For a ruthless badass, he writes like a scholar. Very precise script, not the deranged scribblings of madman that I hate to admit, was what I was expecting. It shouldn't be that much of a surprise really given his varied interests in literature, to his obvious intellect that his penmanship wouldn't be anything less than explementary.

What blows my mind and is most intriguing as I hold his journal in my hands, is the fact he wrote these words nearly two decades ago.

With that, I open the book and begin reading.

He mentions aspects of his earlier years, eloquently writing about his parents, Dave and Evelyn Santos. Although he writes highly about them, I get the feeling they weren't particularly close given the way he talks about them using their names instead of, *mom* and *dad*. The little he describes about them is certainly more than I've ever heard about them. Vince has told me very little about my grandparents, and to be honest they've never reached out to me over the years.

When my father mentions he has a *sister,* my mouth hangs open in disbelief. To make sure I read it correctly, I read it again. This little bombshell is quite a surprise and only adds to the mystery of my father's past I know nothing about, the question is why?

Over the next hour, I get lost in learning more about his time with the Lost Souls MC. I've heard of them, but that's it. When he first mentions his best friend by name, Marcus. I instantly know it's Marcus Aniello. That's when things got a bit more interesting. It's pretty clear that Marcus and my father were a lot closer than I ever thought.

I have to say the stories I've been told about my father being brutal were indeed accurate, but to read them in his own words is definitely more spine-chilling. Dominic had no problem going into great length and graphic detail about his creative style he used when he was sent to *muscle-up* on someone, as he put it.

A few times I actually winced at how graphic he was with his words. He even quoted the words the poor bastards would spew at him as he proceeded to torture, and then finally kill them.

His methods of torture were a means to gain information for either, Marcus or Anthony as they often stood by to watch. Once they got the information they needed, Dominic was then given the go ahead to continue with his fun that always ended in death.

All I can say is, *Holy Shit!* Some of the scenes were harder to read than others, and I'm not even the squeamish type. But, damn, for the foreseeable future I don't think I'll be able to get some them out of my head.

What I found surprising, was a possible rift between him and Anthony since I assumed they were friends just like my father was with Marcus. Apparently, that wasn't the case. Some sort of misunderstanding is the only thing he explained. Then, he never mentions it again.

That could have something to do with his obsession he developed for a girl. A name Dominic mentions more and more. Though I have to say, his mood along with his handwriting slowly begin to change so much I can almost feel his erratic behaviors as they take place.

Friday, September 5th -*I couldn't wait to see her today, but I can't show her just how much she affects me. I have feelings for her that are foreign to me, but it doesn't change my view on things because of them. I can't allow it to. She's innocent, almost angelic like, but that won't stop me. I want her. I want to be the one to dirty her up. I'll take her and own her and if anyone ever tries to get in my way of her, I'll skin every inch of skin from their body. Izzabella Parker is mine.*

The one word I would never have associated with him up 'til this point, was vulnerable. Detail after detail, he proudly writes about his tales of torture. Sadistic? There is little doubt, he was as sadistic as they come. A real scary sonofabitch.

The irony for me is how taken he was with this girl. Why her? From what I hear, he had plenty of women, but there was something about Izzy Parker that got to him. For a man so ruthless and self-absorbed to suddenly write about his feelings for her, was odd for sure. She changed him. Only, I'm just not sure for the better.

His next entry is proof of that. His mood was angry, and that clearly comes through even in his handwriting.

Sunday, October 27th- *Izzabella went out again with Kara, and she's late coming home. I knew I should not have allowed her to go. My* sister is poisoning her against me, I can feel it. That simply won't stand. Tonight, oh yes, tonight Izzabella will see just how serious I am when it comes to her. She means the world to me, like the air I breathe. Yet, she has no idea. I shield my insecurities, holding them back. Out of fear she'll run from me. I will have to demonstrate what will happen if she ever tries. It will gut me to do it, but I'll do it anyway. I'll show her just how sadistic and creative I can be. Tonight, I'll share my talents with my love, and my dick is already hard and throbbing just thinking about it.*

I can't close the journal fast enough. I bolt straight up in up bed with my hands in my hair.

"What in the hell was that shit?" I can't finish a single thought because my father wasn't only sadistic, he was borderline psychotic. That was more than a little fucked up and as I try to shake that shit from my mind, I realize now is a good time to take a break. Hell, after that, I need more than a breather, I needed a fucking beer.

Yet, an hour and one beer later, curiosity gets the better of me to pick that damn journal back up.

"Oh, fuck it."

I burn the midnight oil picking up where I left off. I am one hundred percent confident that no one knew the real, Dominic Santos. This journal tells me that this was his safe place to be as raw and honest without the worry of anyone knowing the real story behind the mask he wore. That, I truly believe.

I'm sure he wouldn't want anyone reading his private and personal thoughts, but I can't seem to help myself even though I'm not so sure I want to know more.

Tues, Dec 16th- *The voices are back and loud as ever. I feel out of control with my rage taking me to new heights. I've done more harm than good. I'm living my life as two different people who are different like night and day. It's a battle I have little control of, and in the process, I'm losing the battle to be who I wish I could be. I'm not strong enough to stop the monster who is taking charge, when it's just too easy to give in to him. To let him be the new me.*

Wow! The truth he speaks of creates eerie comparisons between him and I with our shared personalities, and it's damn chilling. However, the light at the end of the tunnel for me, is that there are differences between us as well. *Thank Fucking God!!*

While we both share anger issues and voices in our heads, I know for a fact I would never go as far as he did on occasions. He crossed a line and took joy in physically hurting someone he deeply cared for. To get off on it while doing it sickens me. That's not me. At least, I sure as hell hope not. It's disturbing. Take Libbs for instance, there is not a chance in hell I would have ever hurt her like my father did to Izzy.

This may seem like a ridiculous idea coming from me, but I think I'm mentally stronger than he ever was. Maybe that's partially due to the fact I was properly diagnosed and put on medications to help fight the worst of the damn demons. Even if they don't work all the time. It makes me think I could have helped him if given the chance. It sucks I'll never get the chance to find out.

The things we could have done together. If only.

At times he seems level headed and strong, then he starts rambling like a madman with thoughts all over the place. Which is interesting, because even when his emotions were out of control, he still took the time to write out his regrets. Even when he couldn't find the strength to change them.

Several places in the journal show edges of pages that were torn out, which is odd considering how graphic he details everything else. Why tear them out?

It's not like any of it could be any more damning. Dominic Santos wanted to be the devil, he said so himself. He demanded to be feared by everyone because only then would he gain the respect he so desperately craved. His job required it and his life depended on it.

I will say the brutal honesty in which he spoke during his darker times was when I felt a real connection with him. It made me unbelievably sad and feel sorry for him on a deep and personal level. Like me, my father spent much of his time in pain, silently suffering.

Then, in a goddamned instant, he could turn and become this cold and calculated killer. Going so far as to punish to his beloved *Izzabella,* as he often refers to her, all to prove some arbitrary point. From that time on, he thirsted for the sick pleasure he found in it.

Izzy Parker was my father's kryptonite and the last of his entries stop right before he left for a trip to Washington State to bring his *Izzabella* home after she left him some months before. Sure enough, Marcus' name pops up once again. Now, I have proof he's been holding back on me. Again, the question is why?

It's not every day you get to read the words from a real-life Dr. Jekyll and Mr. Hyde, let alone have it be your own father. Dominic Santos is a twisted tale for sure, but it doesn't matter anymore, he's dead. What can he do from the grave? Plus, I know enough that the world I grew up in, the same world he thrived in, you fill a particular role and that's just what you do. Right or wrong, doesn't matter. It's life or death.

I'm different in that regard. I don't have an official role in the Aniello Organization, other than to fight when I'm scheduled too. Other than that, I live my life. Vince keeps what he does for the Aniello's to himself. It's none of my business and at home, we're like any other normal family if that's even possible.

The reality is, Dominic was a complex man who still confounds me. I'm not naïve or shocked by most of his lifestyle, what I am at odds with is the level of compassion I feel toward him even after reading some of the more fucked-up things about him. I guess, I just understand him better than anyone else could. It's not an excuse for his behavior, it's just an understanding.

As I toss the journal on my bed, the missing torn-out pages scatter to the bed. The pages are creased perfectly in the center and it seems he couldn't discard them after all. I waste little time in reading them.

Then, read them again.

I'm having a hard time with the implications.

As it is, my head is already wrangling with the idea that I somehow could have saved him from himself if given the chance. I admit, it's a stretch, but at the end of the day I'm still his son. What son wouldn't want to help his old man out?

Rationally thinking or not, I was deprived of any opportunity to save him because of *her*, Izzy. The blame starts with her. She was in fact, his downfall. Those are the facts, written in black and white. He left this house to go after her. Somewhere along the way on that trip, he mysteriously dies. Those are the hard-cold facts.

All the years of living in this house, with his things, feeling his presence all around me, he's still somewhat a ghost to me. Even if Izzy had nothing to do with his death, she is the reason he left to go after her. In doing so, he paid with his life.

The bombshell in these missing pages is a real doozy. A cruel secret that somehow my uncle failed to mention to me. Along with the details he shares a sister with my father. Oh, he's got some serious explaining to do.

In my father's own words...

"Izzabella gave birth to our daughter today, Willow."

What the fuck!

I have a sister?

Seriously? A fucking sister! What the hell do I do about this?

I charge my ass down the hall and burst into Vince's private quarters, *without knocking.* Something I don't normally do, but, right now, I couldn't give a shit about his rules. I catch him off guard as he stands in a defensive stance with a gun drawn and aiming between my eyes. He's an accurate shooter, a point he's proven at the gun range a time or two. Still, I don't flinch. Once he realizes there is no immediate danger, he lowers the gun uttering under his breathe, *damn lucky I didn't pull the trigger.*

I let that comment roll off my shoulder when he notices the fire in my eyes. He says nothing, just lowers his eyes to the torn pages gripped tightly in my hands.

"Did you know?" There is no mistaking the accusatory tone in my voice, and he doesn't take it well, but being lied to for my whole life doesn't feel good either.

I repeat. "Did you know?" More demanding this time leaving little doubt that my patience is running thin.

"Son," he uses his calming tone bullshit to try and diffuse the ticking time bomb standing before him. After he places his gun in his desk drawer, he exhales, "You have to give me more before I can answer that question."

Fine, I oblige and take a step closer before tossing the crumpled pieces of paper on his desk. Before he looks down, he gives me a once over and then lets out sigh as he starts to read them over. A look of recognition drains the color from his face. The same kind of look you have when you get caught telling a lie, knowing there is no way to get out of it.

A look that says it all.

Red in the face and with my lips curled in disgust, I call him out on the lie he's been telling me. "So, all this time you knew and said nothing. Why even hide it to begin with?" With frustration getting the better of me, I toss my hands in the air. Only to get angrier with each passing second that he sits there and looks back at me with a blank fucking expression.

It infuriates me. "Why hide the fact I have a FUCKING sister I know nothing about? You told me he had no wife or kids. And, while we're at it, why don't you tell me about the sister you and my father share? Jesus. Christ. Do the lies ever stop with you?" Spit builds at the corners of my mouth as I jab a finger in his face.

The fact he lied to my face just a few hours ago, denying Dominic ever had a wife or any kids is a really a sick fucking joke. The uncompromising look Vince gives me when he raises his eyes from his desk is an ominous look I've seen over the years, just never at me. It's a clear indication he does not like to be challenged. I can tell he's reining in his anger, because his face is bright red and the muscles in his neck are corded. Besides the anger brewing behind his eyes.

Voice strained, he explains, "The things I have done. The things I decided to keep from you were for your own good. You may not believe it, but it's the simple truth. None of the past has anything to do with you, Declan. They want nothing to do with you, or me. Nothing."

Excuse me?

"Wait a minute. *They?* Besides who they are, are you telling me *they* know I exist?"

His eyes lower momentarily. "Yes… well, not exactly. They knew your mother was pregnant with Dominic's child. That's the extent of it." Then, adds, "Might I remind you this was nearly twenty years ago. Shit's been long and buried since then, son."

If that's his idea of an excuse, it's a piss poor one.

"Wow!" I have to tune him out and sit down just to let this shit sink in. "So, *they*," I use finger quotes, "also knew of my mother? Which is interesting in trying to connect the dots. Just what the fuck have you NOT told me?" I ramble without giving any thought to what I'm even saying, I just blurt out the next thing that pops in my head. "Next you are going to tell me, you know exactly why and who killed my father?"

It was meant as an off the cuff remark in the heat of the moment, but the unsettling expression on his face makes my blood run cold. Then, I remember one of Nero's sayings.

"Remember silence is nothing more than an admission of guilt!"

Deep in my bones I've always thought Vince knew more and his silence just confirms it all. It's like someone just punched a hole right through my gut. The chair I'm sitting in starts to shake when I realize it's me and my iron clad grip that's making it do so.

It's one thing to think you've been lied to, but to have it confirmed right in front of your face is an entirely different feeling that rage doesn't even come close to describing it. I need to get the hell out of here before I tear this motherfucking room apart. My feet can't move fast enough as the chair I was in goes flying across the room.

"Declan. Son, wait. Let me explain!"

Not fucking likely.

Nineteen years is long enough to tell me the fucking truth.

Chapter Eight

"Blow Off Steam"

"WOW, WHAT THE FUCK ARE you going to do now?" Dex asks me the one question I've been asking myself for the last few hours. He was more shocked than I was to find out I have a sibling. He finds the whole idea hilarious. The more beer he drinks, the more stupid shit he spouts. My whole reason for being here is to forget, but he's making it impossible.

Neither one of us is twenty-one, but at *The One Eighty Lounge*, that detail means nothing since my *family* owns it. Five years ago, Marcus and Anthony branched out into the oldest and most profitable profession there was. What started out as a seedy strip joint later turned into a classier gentlemen's club.

You won't find any stripper poles or half naked women walking around looking for dollar bills to be slipped into their G-strings. No loud music, hollering, or rowdy crowds. None of that. What you will find are men dressed in suits or casual attire. The atmosphere is laid back with dim lighting around the large oak bar and lounge-style tables.

Thanks to Marcus, all the cocktail waitresses are dressed the same. Black boy shorts, a black and white bustier, black stockings and stilettos. To top it off, they even wear these tiny black bow ties. All his vision and God bless him for it. The ladies are gorgeous.

It's their job to serve the men their drinks and if a deal is struck, there are plenty of private suites upstairs for lap dances, or whatever else is agreed upon.

I got my first blow job in one of the private suites when I was sixteen years old. Vince and Marcus had a business meeting in one of the private suites, so Anthony had Meghan, one of the cocktail waitresses, take me to another suite to show me a good time. Marcus was more than upset with his brother when he found us with my dick in her mouth. As it turned out, Meghan was on duty that night to be his personal arm candy. All to look good for the potential clients he was trying to strike a deal with.

The sight of her on her knees sent him into a rage and the slight smirk on Anthony's face was enough to tell me he did it on purpose. That's Anthony, though. He likes to stir shit up just for kicks. But, in his defense, I don't think any of us knew just how much Marcus liked the full-chested, brunette until he fired her on the spot. Anthony argued she was a waitress for the Club and if his brother had other intentions for her, maybe she shouldn't be 'pussy for hire'.

That ended badly for him. Marcus punched him square in the jaw and told Anthony to mind his own fucking business. Feeling like a real dick, I tried to apologize to Marcus even though I had nothing to do with that little set up, but he wouldn't have it. He got me another beer instead, while uttering something to Vince under his breath. Then, he started to laugh.

When Marcus finally stopped laughing and wiped the tears from his eye, he wrapped his arm around my shoulder. "You should have seen the look on your face," he said with amusement in his eyes. "I have never seen you jump so fast in your life. Here you are, sitting on the couch with your head back and mouth wide open, while Meghan is going to town on your dick... then I open the door and you shot straight up to look at me like, *what the fuck do I do now?* Shit was priceless." Then he got serious. "But, Declan, you are not to blame for the actions of my fucking asshole of a brother. You know him, he likes to stir up trouble where he can, especially with me."

Yeah, that much I knew.

Since that night, Anthony rarely ever comes in here anymore, but I find myself visiting this place often more for the beer than anything else. Vince and Marcus are okay with whatever I do or who I bring with me, but like with every other member of this club, there are rules to abide by.

Dress appropriately.

No fighting.

No getting drunk and causing a scene.

Tip the waitresses... *well.*

And payment is always upfront if you request a private suite with a waitress.

Little do they know I have a few favorites of my own, like Sophia and Gabriella, who are more than eager to meet me outside in my car or truck... *free of charge.* I'm young, good looking, plus, I'm a fighter. What's not to get hot and bothered over? Sophia is a petite, pixie brunette who is extremely hot for how sweet she is. Gabriella is a feisty, dark-haired angel who is flirty and adventurous. It's no wonder this place is a gold mine with ladies like these.

All kidding aside, I tip all the waitresses well for my drinks and they all love me... so it's all good.

Nights like tonight are a bit different because Dex and I are upstairs in one of the larger suites which are mainly reserved for private parties. Tonight, a local DJ we know, Max, has rented the venue for a fund-raising event he has going on. There's a ton of people, good music and plenty of alcohol. When we came here, we had no idea this was going on, but Dex spotted him right away. Now here we are, drinking by ourselves while the rest of the crowd is busy mingling.

"You know what I think?"

No, not really!

"With a name like, Willow, I bet she's hot as hell."

I swear he just won't let this shit go, and the way her name rolls of his tongue with the look on his face like he's fantasizing something highly sexual, creeps me the hell out. The harder I try to block him out by drinking myself stupid, the more he keeps talking.

"Man, I hope she's not a lesbian, or a man-hater in general. That would totally ruin my fantasy of her."

To keep from choking on my mouth full of beer, or spit it all over him, I struggle to swallow before I reach over and smack the back of his head. Hard! There is just not enough beer for me to drown in.

He yelps, *ouch!*

"You deserved it!" I may not know a damn thing about my *so-called* sister I never knew existed until a few hours ago, but that does not mean I'm going to sit here and listen to his crazy shit. It's like she's some new shiny toy he can't be without.

"What the fuck, dude? It's not like you're hard up for attention, you get plenty of pussy." And by plenty, I mean plenty. The guy isn't hurting for female attention at all.

"Oh, come on! Think about it?"

I'd rather not!

When he opens his mouth again, I close my eyes in an attempt to block him out as the idea of knocking his ass out cold, sounds better by the minute.

"If she's anything like you, she's not ugly. Just saying." He literally jabs my shoulder a finger I'm tempted to reach out and break. "But, personality wise? Yeah, that's a total crapshoot when it comes to you, dude."

"Whatever!" Twirling the bottle of beer in my fingers, I take a swig and confirm under my breath. "Never claimed to be a nice guy, Dex."

He laughs. "Well, that's true. But, can you honestly sit here and tell me you are not even a little interested in what she would be like? I mean come on, Declan, seriously? Not even a tiny bit?"

"No." I raise my voice to shut him up.

"Yeah, right!" he dismisses me with a smart-ass look. "We need to definitely find her. For all you know, she could be the woman of my dreams."

Damn. He's ten steps ahead, when I never let on once that was something I would or even want to do. Fucker is jumping the gun just a bit.

"Or your worst nightmare."

He grumbles and gives me a look that all but says I'm a buzzkill. Thanks to Dex, my limit for bullshit for one night has reached an all-time high and the alcohol meant to take my mind off shit isn't helping. Fuck it, if alcohol isn't going to help relax and take my mind of things, I know what will. Getting laid.

With that in mind, I swallow down the last of my beer and give my buddy some parting advice.

"Dex, you're fucked in the head, and you better stay the hell away from her if we ever find her. I mean it, Dex. Fucking hands off, dude."

"Protective of her already?" he teases with his eyes raised and a shit eating grin on his face. "This is a new side of you."

As I stand behind him with a firm hold on both of his shoulders, I lean in and then give him a good hard smack on his back that sends him flying forward.

"Nope, the same old me," I tell him as it's time for me to find some action for the night. I have boatloads of stress I need to work out.

It's been way too long and it's either that or stay and kick Dex's ass. Having my dick down the throat of some girl sounds way better.

Dex knows exactly what I'm looking for when he shouts over his shoulder. "Angie's back there somewhere, if you're looking for her."

He points to the back room of the bar, but that name alone will have me walking in the opposite direction. A definite, no! Been there, done that. Her teeth sure as hell didn't feel good then, plus, I'm not that desperate. I have a better idea in mind.

"Nah, buddy. I'll save her for you." He gives me an appreciative glance as he tips his beer bottle in the air as a way of saying thanks, and inside I'm laughing my ass off. This is what I call true payback.

As I look around the room, I'm gauging my choices when my eyes land on her. Yes, there she is. I saw her walk in earlier and right now she's standing across the room with her back to the wall. She is chatting with some pencil neck wearing khaki pants and a pink shirt. I can't take this guy serious, what man wears pink, anyway?

Not one that is going to stop me from getting what I want, that's for sure. While I pay him no attention, I tilt my head to the side and appreciate Alexa's long, tan legs to her plump cherry lips. Her white skimpy dress is hot, but I'm more drawn to her lips that are straight up pure sinful. Her strawberry blonde hair is shorter than I remember, cut chin length now. The last time I saw her, she had much longer hair, but that's been at least six months ago or more.

No doubt about it, she looks damn fine and must sense me gawking at her, because her bright blue eyes suddenly lock with mine.

As she pretends to listen to what pink shirt is saying, her eyes travel the length of my body with a smile that only gets wider as I approach. On purpose, I cut right in front of pink shirt as Alexa eyes me mischievously.

"Busy tonight?" I comment just as pink shirt clears his throat and stands up straighter giving me a once over like he's going to start shit with me. *Me?* A part of me wishes he would, but I've got one thing on my mind and he's not it. I turn and basically laugh in his face because he has to be joking if he thinks he's going to do anything other than drag his tail between his damn legs to take a fucking hike.

One deadly glare and menacing growl is all it takes. He huffs and turns to walk away, but before he does, I make nice and wave goodbye.

For some reason, he wasn't very receptive.

"That wasn't very nice, Declan," Alexa pouts. "I was looking forward to a quickie with... huh?" Her eyes come together on her perfectly made-up face. "Never did get his name."

Yeah, right?

All she was doing was getting the poor sap to buy her drinks, thinking he was going to get a quick fuck in exchange. It's all a game for girls to act easy just to get some sorry sap willing to keep supplying them with drinks. More times than not, the girls get free drinks and the guy ends up leaving with a major hard-on and a case of blue balls.

I don't play it that way.

Never have.

If I see something I want, playing games is definitely not a part of it. The key is to seduce them, get their juices flowing until they are ready to beg for it. Drinks or no drinks.

To test my theory, I lean into Alexa's side and slowly breathe in her sweet-smelling cologne. With her heels on, she comes up to my chin and as my larger frame consumes her petite one, I reach low and rest my hand on the outside of her leg. With the lightest touch, I slowly trace the tips of my fingers higher until I reach the hem of her white dress. To tease her, I follow the natural curve of her ass that peeks out from under her dress.

The lure of my touch casts shivers down her body as a moan slips from her mouth. When my lips caress her ear, I whisper, "You think jock boy could give you what you really want? A quickie, as you put it?"

My slight groan intensifies into a growl as the feel of her body is making me achingly hard. When my fingers bite into the bare skin of her ass, I unexpectedly yank her body to fall into mine.

"Wouldn't you rather have a wild fuck with a guy who can guarantee you pleasure with more than one orgasm?" I entice her with my lips softly touching the tender skin of her long neck.

Her body falls limp in a puddle of want that has her exactly where I want her. She's putty in my hands at this point.

"Or, am I wrong?" I pull back just to screw with her a bit, but really, I want to hear her say the words. To fucking tell me she wants this as much as I do. I won't force her, but I sure as hell will make it impossible for her to say no.

"Well…" She starts to say as my fingers explore the bare skin under the hem of her dress. "Since it's you that's offering," she achingly whimpers more loudly when the tips of my fingers find the floss of her thong. Her mouth falls open as her head tilts to the side, allowing me to taste the golden skin of her neck that shimmers in the dim light. The sensation is warm and wet, tempting her with the pleasure that's about to come her way.

"You are most definitely not wrong. You, sexy beast."

"Thought so."

Play time is over as my fingers thread in her wavy hair. Then it's an all-out assault on her luscious lips that should come with a warning sign. Damn, it may have only been once, but I could never forget how sweet Alexa tastes. Like cherries. Then it's all I can do not to remember how awesome it feels to have her full lips wrapped around my dick. Fuck, it's been way too long as the edginess from the shit earlier starts to take over.

I'm not nice and I don't take things slow. I'm aggressive and damn near take her right here. My raging hard on has a mind of its own and it wants inside Alexa not really caring who is around for the show, but for what I have in mind, this is not the place.

"Fuck," I tear my lips from her but not before I vigorously suck every last drop of her cherry taste from her lower lip. The sting of discomfort leaves Alexa moaning, telling me how much she likes it as well.

"Not here, let's go." I grab her hand with one thought in my mind, I'm going to fuck the shit out of her. This will mark the first time I've fucked anyone since that shit went down with Libbs. My biggest regret, and most likely the only girl I will ever allow myself to love. This, right here, is different. This is all about fucking.

"Shit, Declan slow down. You're getting lucky so there's no need to hurry."

Who the hell is she kidding!

"The fuck there's not!"

If I use a private suite and not check in with management first, my ass would be in major trouble. That's the cardinal rule, those rooms are for paying members for the girls who are working. First off, Alexa doesn't work here, and I have no patience to go and check if any of the suites are available. Looks like I'm taking this party of two outside.

With a firm grip on her arm, I march toward the exit. Alexa is having a hard time keeping up in her short dress and high heels, and since I'm an impatient dick who's doing his best to control my annoyance with the endless bodies standing around, I do the next best thing. I throw her over my shoulder.

Alexa squeals so loud she pierces my eardrum and gains the attention of those standing nearby. "Damn, cave man." She does her best to cover her exposed ass to everyone with her hand, and to show her just how much of a cave man I can be, I smack that fine ass.

"See ya, man." Dex hollers and waves as we pass him sitting in the exact same spot. When I notice he's talking with all-teeth Angie, I think about warning him about her, but given his shit from earlier, he deserves to find out all on his own.

Good luck with that, buddy!

Once I step out of the elevator with Alexa still over my shoulder, I exit through the back entrance. Alexa slaps my back arguing the whole time in the elevator that I could finally let her down.

My answer. "No! When I put you down, it will be right on my fucking hard cock."

That shut her up!

If I remember right, Alexa loves dirty talk and with her over my shoulder, I slide my left hand up and along the curve of her ass to find the string of her thong drenched. My touch there has Alexa gasping. She's soaking wet, so it takes little effort to slide two of my fingers inside the snug heat of her pussy. Her moans are instantaneous and the cave man in me is delirious when she clinches her muscles around my fingers.

My dick is furiously protesting the treatment my fingers are getting as he wants nothing more than to be balls deep inside of her. It's a real fucking chore to walk straight and not bump into every damn car in the parking lot on the way to my car. I have Alexa moaning and shifting her weight on the edge of my shoulder while I continue plunging my fingers in and out of her, not giving a shit if anyone can see me getting her off like this. Hell, they should be so lucky to see this kind of action.

I have to say, it's a good thing I'm a strong guy or else I would have dropped her by now. The death grip she has on my shirt helps, but damn she's enjoying this so much, her hips can't stop themselves from moving in sync with my fingers. For some reason this damn parking lot seems to have gotten a whole lot bigger, or my patience has finally run out.

Alexa doesn't make it any easier. "Ahhh, God, Declan don't stop."

Her whimpers sound more like a desperate plea and it strokes my ego. I'm just glad my car is parked where it's dimly lit and hidden from any street traffic for what I have in mind. Alexa is so close to exploding, my fingers are pooling in her juices that are now starting to flow down my wrist.

My dick is beyond hard and throbbing by the time we make it to my car. In one swift move, I lower her from my shoulder and lay her flat on the trunk of my car. I'm out of breath, standing before her wildly panting that has little to do with the long walk out here.

Her face is flushed, her lips are parted, and her legs are open wide.

"Fucking beautiful!"

With one aggressive hook of my finger, her thong rips and then my head is between her sinful legs. She throws her head back, exhaling with pure pleasure as the warmth of my mouth eagerly feasts on her wet pussy.

I'm not tasting, I'm savoring and devouring her. Drowning in her like she's the best and last pussy I'll ever have. My tongue is on a fiery pace that shows no signs of letting up when Alexa's pleasure surges into short, wild pants. Determined to keep my mouth where it is, her hands find their way into my short, spikey hair. I continue to punish her with my tongue penetrating deep inside because all I want is for her to fucking explode in my mouth.

"Jesus!" The sensation overload to her clit has her uttering incoherent things and legs trembling so hard, she's squeezing my head. "I don't remember you being like this," she whimpers, "but for the love of God, don't stop. It's good… so good."

Damn, right it's good!

Her bare pussy is glistening when I part her wide and plunge my tongue back inside and fuck her with it. She's sweet and tart, and so damn addictive. When her body tenses and breathing hitches, I know she's on the verge. To push her over the edge, I sink my teeth around her clit and suck until she explodes. Alexa erupts, shouting into the night while grinding her pussy into my mouth to ride out every last drop of pleasure.

It's so fucking hot, that my engines are just getting started. The best remedy for anger is sex, and with the amount of it I have, it's going to take a lot of fucking to cure it, but we're off to a damn good start.

When I glance up, her flushed face and eyes that are wide and glazed over, look down at me. The view is out of this world, her pussy is glistening against the dim light of the full moon in the dark sky. It's still quiet since no one has left the bar, and here I am standing on the fucking edge with my face covered in her juices. The slight breeze that picks up does little to cool me off.

I yank Alexa up by her wrists and easily flip her over so she's kneeling on the trunk of my car this time. With my hands firmly on her hips, I slide her dress up to expose her perfectly round, sweet ass. She's shows no signs of caring who can see us, she eagerly wants more.

With her arousal dripping out of her, the cave man in me craves another taste, but I'm enjoying the view so much I inch her higher on her knees. Jesus, with her ass tilted like this, it's a fucking sight. I rub the cheeks of her ass before spreading her open to expose her drenched pussy and the liquid gold dripping out. My lips are suddenly parched and the only way to quench my thirst is with the sweetness that is purely Alexa.

With the first sweep of my tongue, she yelps and leans forward. "Declan, what the hell has gotten in to you?"

"Complaining?" I lick her glorious center.

"Ahhh, fuck no," she's quick to reply with a gratifying moan.

That's what I thought.

I lick from her clit to her entrance until my throbbing dick can't take it any longer. I make fast work of my jeans to free myself, but first make sure to grab the condoms from my front pocket. Missing the attention of my mouth, Alexa looks over her shoulder and suggestively grinds her hips to entice me to hurry the hell up. Any more enticing, I'll blow my load in my damn hand before I ever get my condom on. When I pull the string of three condoms and toss two of them next to her, she meows like a cat looking at the two unopened condom wrappers.

"Only if you're a good girl."

She playfully pouts, resting rest on her forearms and looks back over her shoulder. "What if I feel like being extra naughty?"

"Well, I'm sure I can come up with something," I tease her with raw heat in my eyes, and a body that feels like it's on fire. "Hope you're ready, because this is going to be hard and fast."

She gives me a wicked grin. "Just give it to me like you want."

My unspent anger and desires surge forward, and I thrust inside of her so hard and fast, I growl with an animalistic need that has me thrusting with energy I had no clue I had. The sharp gasp from Alexa sounds like I knocked the wind out her as she struggles to keep up with me. Her heat envelops my dick like a cocoon when my mind shifts and reminds me why I'm so angry to begin with.

The never-ending lies.

They come crashing down around me and the only thing I can do to deflect them is to fuck them out of my mind. My relentless and vigorous pace with her on her knees and forearms are sure to leaves marks that resemble rug burns. No doubt, she'll bare the marks the same color as my Camaro tomorrow, Cherry Red.

I can't get deep enough or go hard enough to satisfy my angry thirst. My touch is not affectionate, it's demanding as my left-hand finds its way in her hair to give it a hearty pull. My other hand is firmly around her hip as the familiar feeling begins to build low in my balls. When the sudden flame shoots up my spine, my head falls back.

"Fuck. Fuck. FUCKING HELL." A deep-seated growl erupts as I continue until I'm completely spent. All it takes is a flick to her clit and Alexa goes over the edge again. Exhaustion takes over as I topple on top of her. We're both breathing heavy and unable to move.

"Hot damn, that was off the charts." She mutters under my weight but doesn't complain. She shouldn't since she just got fucked better than she's ever been. The night is still young, and I have more aggression to work out.

As she blows a few strands of hair that have fallen over her face, she turns back to ask with a gleam in her eye, "Are you really going to use those other two condoms tonight?"

At first, I'm not sure if she's asking because she's had enough or is hoping for more.

With a hint of smile, I let her know. "Give me a minute or two, and I'll show you."

Her face lights up as her eyes widen. "Really? You can go again that quick?"

I jerk my head back half insulted. "Are you really fucking asking me that? Have the guys you fucked in the past been a one off and that's it?" If that's the case, she's been hanging around the wrong type of guys.

Her face turns red like she's embarrassed, but it's nothing against her. It has more to do with the dickless pricks who can't go more than one time in a night.

"Yeah," she shrugs, "I guess so."

That's just fucking sad and as I slowly get back to my feet, I'm shaking my head. "You've been fucking the wrong guys," I advise her, taking a moment to look at her body that is really a fucking sight to see right now. Her dress is pushed up above her hips, the wide neck is hanging off one shoulder, and her lipstick is smeared from screaming her pleasure against the top of her hands as I took her from behind.

"You're in for a treat tonight," I say with an edge to my voice that puts a smile back on her face. "I'm fucking mad at the world and ready to fuck you into next week. Lucky for you, I have the stamina to back it up."

"Jesus," she has this dreamy look on her face when she sits with her legs over the end of the trunk. "I may just have to keep you," she said in a voice that was damn convincing on her part.

Yeah, that's not happening.

I quickly correct. "For tonight, anyway." And just to make sure there are no misunderstandings, I clarify, "This has nothing to do with anything but a really good fuck! Make no mistake, I'm not looking for more."

"But..." Alexa starts to argue and it's annoying she would think this is anything, but a fuck. The only way to clear that up, is to show her. Once I have the damn condom off and toss it on the ground, I instruct her to get on her stomach with her head in the perfect position.

"Don't get any delusions, Alexa. This is all I fucking need from you."

With that, I ram my cock past her lips and deep in her throat. She's a pro at head and does not disappoint. Her throat widens to accept all of me as I lean forward with my hands resting on each side of her body. The next thing I feel are Alexa's hands as they reach around and grab ahold of my ass to control how deep my cock goes in and out of her mouth.

Her tongue is wicked and as I watch my dick disappear inside her mouth, she surprises the shit out of me as she guides her hand low between my legs and gently applies pressure to the delicate skin just behind my balls. Jesus Christ, it ignites a raw sensation that lets me know I'm going to cum the hardest I've ever had before.

While I'm relentless, Alexa is goddamn amazing.

"Just... a... few... more... FUCK!" Once again, my orgasm rips through me something fierce.

Like the champ she is, Alexa swallows every last drop.

"Feeling better?" she asks while wiping her mouth on the back of her hand.

I'm winded, but crack a smile because after that who wouldn't feel better.

Then, she ruins it.

"You may want to reconsider..." She suggests, which I sharply shut down.

"Don't push it, Alexa."

If I was a normal guy and didn't have trust issues when it came to women, Alexa would be a great girl to have. She's any guy's wet dream. The only problem is I'm not the guy she thinks I am. I'm all for pleasure, just not the headaches.

"Is your pussy ready for more?" I figure if I keep her busy, she'll have less time to talk nonsense.

"Aren't you a little tired and drained for one night?"

"Spread those legs and find out."

I told her I had enough energy to fuck her all night, and her questioning me is like a challenge that gets me hard all over again. Typically, the only time I get this hard so fast is when I'm full blown manic, but I'm not. This is all about proving something and right now, that's punishing Alexa's pussy so she's aching for days.

After I make quick work with the condom, I have her spread-eagle with my arms tucked under her knees. With her dress completely off this time, I'm in total control and get to watch her tits bounce freely.

"Now, you tell me if I'm tired and all drained out?" I harshly snap, and then plunge inside her pussy as it constricts around my intrusion. When I slowly slide my dick all the way out, I quickly thrust back inside until I bottom out and my balls slap against her ass. The timing and rhythm is so perfect I rest my head back to enjoy her warmth when a disturbing image flashes in my mind. An image that overpowers whatever pleasure I was feeling and turns it back into a punishing fuck.

"Get out of my GODDAMN head!" I shout so loud not caring that I do and finish myself off the only way I know how. I grip Alexa by the back of shoulders and raise her body from the car to rest into mine with my dick firmly seated inside.

"Wrap your legs around me and hang the fuck on."

She does without question.

With sheer strength alone, I'm in a half squat with Alexa wrapped tightly around me. I use the strength of my arms around the back of her shoulders to guide my upward thrusts inside of her, grunting like a wild beast.

Hushed voices make their way to the parking lot, but nowhere close to where we are. I don't give a fuck if they were close, the idea of us being watched only spurs me on more. I'll give them a fucking show they'll never forget, and quite possibly will have them having sex in their car all turned on by what they're witnessing.

Alexa mumbles something, constricting my dick like an iron vice. I'd say she's close, and I'm not far behind, so I rear back and thrust inside so hard our bodies slam against my car. We orgasm at the same time. Her high-pitched scream and my intense growl mix in unison as the sounds of clapping around us pick up.

Hiding her body into mine, Alexa looks tuckered out and spent. "I... I... I've had all I can take, Declan." She waves the white flag and it's probably a good thing, because I'm suddenly fucking exhausted.

"Did you fuck your anger away?" She whimpers like she doesn't have an ounce of energy left, lightly chuckling, "I think you fucked me to death."

"Well," I admit, "It wasn't for lack of trying."

Chapter Nine

"Unforgivable"

WHAT A DIFFERENCE A FEW days can make. However, things are still tense with my uncle since the night of our big blowout, and each time he tries to talk with me about it, I only end up getting pissed off all over again and destroy shit. So, for now we called a truce until I feel like I'm able to talk with him about things and not want to rip his head off while doing it.

Days like today are good, I've been spending a few hours a day studying with my tutor Daniel and they are certainly paying off. I passed three of my final exams and am one step closer to earning my diploma. Early. Honestly, it can't come soon enough because I'm over the whole school thing. While earning my diploma is on the top of my uncle's list, it's on the bottom of mine. I've got bigger and better things to occupy my time with, but, come hell or high water I'll get that damn piece of paper, so my uncle can frame the damn thing.

Years from now I'm sure I'll be able to look back and say that diploma was the key to my success. *Like hell!* It's more a waste of time. It's not like I'm going to enroll at some college to earn some bullshit degree. So, again... what difference does it make?

But, whatever!

To make his day, I left the graded tests on Vince's desk so he can be proud of the fact that I am willing to do my best... even if it's more for him than me. Since then, I've spent grueling hours at the gym. I'm sore, tired and ready to call it a night.

When I return home it's late and when I spot two cars parked along by the side of the house, I groan.

"Shit, of all nights."

The last thing I want, or need is company. Even if they are here for Vince. My ass is dragging and all I want is to crawl in bed. Maybe if I'm really quiet I might be able to sneak in unnoticed, but that is wishful thinking.

It doesn't stop me from trying though.

I look and feel like a burglar trying to break in my own house as I carefully turn the knob of the front door and ease my way inside. The sudden arguing coming from the kitchen tells me something is up. Marcus' deep voice is easy to make out. The other voice has more of a gravel to it, so I easily figure out it's Salvo's. Whatever they are discussing, they are not happy about it.

This is a bad sign for two reasons. One, it's too late for them to be over here arguing about anything and two, it means I did something wrong. Shit. What did I do now?

And my day was going so well, too.

Earlier, Nero even commented about my surprisingly good mood lately, then Dex opened his big mouth to explain why. Whatever. Good sex will put anyone in a better mood. Unless you're Dex. He spent that night with all-teeth Angie who ruined any chance of him getting head. Fucking cracked me up.

When the voices from the kitchen suddenly go quiet, I stop in my tracks.

Sure enough, Vince calls. "Declan, can you come in here for a minute."

Damn, there goes sneaking to my room unnoticed. I make my way to the kitchen, just wanting to get this over with.

"Yeah," I exhale, dropping my head. "I'm coming."

I casually enter the kitchen to find three sets of gloomy faces. The tension in the room can be cut with a knife as I take in each of their faces. To make sure I'm not missing something, I look around the room and when nothing seems out of the ordinary, I gingerly ask, "Who died now?"

It was obviously a joke, but the remark does not go over well because each of them winces at the same time. That's when my uncomfortable meter goes into overdrive.

"Please come and sit down for a minute," Marcus asks looking as distressed as I've ever seen him. Resting against the kitchen sink, his hands are in his suit pants pocket, but moving in a nervous fashion.

"O... kay." I reluctantly do as he asks, sitting down while all three of them start to really freak me out. Their eyes never move from me, and it's so unnerving, I blurt out, "Jesus, if this is about my training, I'm working my ass off for this fight if that's what's on your minds."

It's the only thing I can think of as to why they'd be this concerned, but that doesn't make sense either.

"Son," Vince lets out a lingering sigh as joins me at the table. "This has nothing to do with the fight. We just need to fill you in on some information we recently acquired."

When he turns and gives Marcus a slight head nod, a giant lump in my throat forms.

Marcus and Salvo then join us at the table, before Marcus goes on to explain. "As you know Salvo hasn't been finding much on the girl's phone and computer."

The *girl? Not this shit again.*

It's damn irritating and disrespectful to have anyone refer to Libbs as *the girl*.

"Liberty," I sternly correct, "She has a name."

Realizing his mistake of being insensitive, he nods his head. "Of course, I mean no disrespect. On *Liberty's* phone."

That's better.

"Well," I lean forward on the table with my hands folded together. "What's going on?"

The sudden look of uncertainty from Marcus sends up red flags and I'm certainly not liking where any of this is going.

He continues. "I had one of my *contacts*," he emphasizes with his fingers, "a detective friend of mine you could say..."

That's small talk for saying he's a dirty cop on the take, and it's his job to report shit to Marcus. Really, there is little need for him to dance around me. I'm not naïve or stupid when it comes to organized crime and how it works. I'm not seven-years-old anymore.

"Okay," I shrug my shoulders just as my leg starts to bounce under the table. Out of patience, I prompt him, "What did *he* find?" Nervous energy twitches my finger and I can't help but hold my breath, still hanging on to a glimmer of hope that I'm going to finally get the answers that have been plaguing me.

"Declan," Marcus seems reluctant and leans in with his face stone serious. "The news is not good," he admits. "In fact, it's quite disturbing."

That hope I had a moment ago, *gone!*

Everyone stays quiet while my insides burst into flames. Each exhale burns more than the last. If Marcus says it's not good news... it has to be really fucking bad. I swallow loudly and nervously wipe my forehead in preparation for what he's going to say. Only made worse with the way Vince and Salvo are scrutinizing my every move. Honestly, it's freaking me the hell out.

"From the report," Marcus explains under heavy, yet, cautious eyes. "Liberty did not die of carbon monoxide poisoning. Her blood toxicology reports prove that, along with the absence of her organs showing any potential side effects if she had. What that means is that she was dead before she could breathe in any carbon monoxide."

My head tilts to the side while my brain needs a second to let that last part really sink in. The implications of what he's saying, is just impossible for me to grasp. That's when the room starts to spin.

"How is that even possible?" I softly breathe, trying to make any sense when there is none. The harder I try to push it out of my mind, a dark cloud begins to surround me like a blanket. "None of it makes any sense."

With pain behind his eyes, Marcus lowers his voice as if what he's about to say is going to cause him physical pain. "It appears she overdosed on heroine, but the scene was made up to make everyone believe she died from carbon monoxide poisoning instead."

I stare at him giving what he said a lot of thought, but if that's the case, it confirms only one thing.

"Are you suggesting..." I can't even bring myself to say the words out loud.

His nod is telling enough, but he suggests his own version of what happened to her.

"We think she was murdered and the rest was staged. Why, we don't know. That's the issue we are having right now."

"But..." Salvo quickly adds, but one stern look from Marcus, shuts Salvo down fast. The unspoken exchange between Salvo and Vince that follows, stresses me even more.

"Wait... wait...wait a minute." I struggle to get to my feet, shouting louder each time, because this shit is not happening. "But, what? Tell me! Do not lie and keep shit from me like you all have for my entire life." I point at each and every one of them, directly. "Don't fucking lie to me ever again if it concerns me."

Guarded looks pass between them when Marcus slams his fist on the table. "Fuck! We kept things from you for a reason, Declan." Then, he stands. "For your own damn good."

What a fucking joke. If I was seven years old, I might agree with him, but I'm not! I'm an adult and it's about time they treat me like one.

"Yeah, that's what Vince said, but you know what Marcus? It's bullshit and you know it. I swear to God, don't repeat that mistake with me now. Not when it concerns, Libbs."

His left eye starts to twitch as every muscle in his face tightens. I don't remember a time when I've seen Marcus struggle with a decision that weighs on him as heavily as this one. After a few moments pass, with our eyes still heavily engaged, he looks to Vince and then gives Salvo the go ahead with a nod of his chin.

"Tell him, Salvo. If Declan thinks he can handle it, let him prove it. If he doesn't want us to do what *we* think is best for him, then share the shitty news that's only going to *piss him the fuck off.* But," Marcus walks over and makes a final point with his finger pressed into my chest, "before Salvo tells you a thing, you better sit down and just know I'm not going to let any of what you are about to see and hear go unanswered. You hear me? I swear to you…"

The lump in my throat grows as Marcus' face turns ice cold.

"I'm going to find out who the fuck is messing with you, because if they mess with you, they are messing with *me*! And that's a grave fucking mistake to make on their part."

His words are chilling, but to know he has my back gives me the comfort I need. For that, I'm grateful. Right now, I need to hear the news I know I'm not going to fucking like.

Releasing a steady breath, Salvo turns his attention to the phone in his hand. I take a seat.

"About a week ago, her phone started to get a few messages, which is weird because since her death, it's been silent."

It still stings like hell to hear the word death when it comes to Libbs, but I do my best to push it from my mind.

He continues. "They are from a blocked number, and the first message was just a text. The next few are video messages."

There is no mistaking the dread in his voice when he mentions videos. Plural. I don't visually react, but my insides are in hurricane mode. Given the sudden pale look on Salvo's face, it does little to comfort me as he turns to Vince, then back to me.

"You need to be sure you want to see this, Declan. I mean that in the best possible way. Marcus, Vince and I have it under control and we've been going back and forth deciding if we should even tell you at all. You don't need to…"

Vince interrupts with a slight clear of his throat and the longer this is taking is really doing a number on me.

"Declan, I promised you I wouldn't hold things back from you ever again. But, son, you need to think long and hard if this is what you want. We fear you going off in a rage and going *black* for who knows how long, which is not what you need right now. Especially, with the fight coming up. You can wait until after the fight, even. The choice is ultimately yours, we're just trying to protect you."

"There is no choice."

With my jaw clenched tight, I swallow the giant lump in my throat and know there is no going back at this point. My mind is made up.

"Let me see it," I say deadpan, ready to get this over with. Whatever it is, I know it's going to change me forever.

The first text read: The art of deception is a beautiful thing. The first rule: Never fully believe what your eyes first tell you.

Cryptic is my first thought, odd is the second, as my gaze slowly raises to Salvo who is sitting across from me. The puzzling thing is whoever sent this, knows we have her phone. That stunning realization makes me almost hate myself for what I'm going to do next. Press the little triangle that will play the video.

A prickling sensation runs down my spine as my forehead breaks out with sweat. To say I'm a little fucking tense and anxious is an understatement while I stretch my neck from side to side, similar to what I do to prepare myself before a fight. Only, something tells me nothing could ever prepare me for what I'm about to witness.

The video starts off shaky as if the person recording is walking. The shot is aimed down, and the only noise comes from the rustling of leaves as they walk over them. Whoever it is, they're clever enough not to show their shoes in the shot. It appears to be late in the day given the lack of daylight when in the distance a young woman appears to be sitting at a picnic table with her head down like she's crying. The closer the camera gets, the better I can see the woman and that's when a strangled growl erupts at the same time my fist slams on the table. I can't fucking breathe. My lungs seize as the intense hold

I have on her phone nearly crushes it. I try to speak, but the knot in my throat cuts it off. It's an impossible struggle and as much as I hate to be fucking watching this, I find myself lifting it closer to my face to make sure I don't miss a damn thing.

Like, any hidden clues.

To see Libbs so distraught and crying infuriates me, but so help me God, the look on her face when she looks up at the person holding the camera takes my anger to an all-time high. She seems scared to death and it brings out a dark and dangerous growl to erupt from deep in my chest. Her delicate eyes go wide with fear and her face turns ghostly white.

My response is immediate.

"Who the *FUCK* is this asshole?" I explode with such force the table moves a foot at least while my eyes remain deadlocked on the screen, praying like hell I get just one chance to see this motherfucker's face. Just one time is all I need to burn his face to memory.

Salvo attempts to answer in a disparaging voice. "Declan, I've watched the videos over and over again. We never get a look at his face, but the park could be the one on Fuller Ave given the arch of the gate that's over Liberty's shoulder."

I somehow missed that, but when I look more closely, he's right. It's the only park I know that has that kind of gate, and it pisses me off even more.

"She'd never go there alone." I argue because Libbs knew how unsafe that part of town was. She'd never just be sitting there alone... *unless she was waiting for someone.*

No way! My head won't stop shaking from side to side. "Something is wrong here, it just doesn't make any sense." Since I started watching this, I can't help but have this nagging feeling that just won't let up.

That's when my eye catches something new. "Wait... what the hell was that?" Before anyone can respond, I hit rewind.

"He's showing her pictures that are hard to make out, but the last one is of *you*." The distain in Marcus' words leaves a sinking feeling.

Me?

Puzzled and just to make sure I heard him right, I look up just in time to see the snarl of his lip begin to quiver. Once again, the nagging feeling has me rewinding the video, so I can watch it back in slow-motion this time just as my uncle utters something under his breath.

It's hard to see the photos on the picnic table with any clarity, but Libbs starts to cry harder when he puts the last photo in front of her. The jackass zooms in, so I can easily see it's a picture of me and her. One, someone took without us realizing it. That shit does not settle well with me, either. Who the fuck would be watching us to snap some random picture? It just doesn't make any sense at all.

"I don't..."

"Son," Vince lays a firm but shaky hand over mine. With eyes full of concern, he strongly urges me this time. "Maybe it's best not to watch anymore."

I'm not sure what he could be hinting at, but there's not a chance in hell I'm stopping now.

"I don't have a choice."

"Yes," he urges again, "you do."

"No," I look him dead in the eye, stone faced, "I fucking don't." I just pray I'm not making a mistake.

When the next video starts to play, right away it's more graphic and a hell of a lot more sinister than the first. Holy shit! Just sitting back and watching this is harder than I thought it would be, knowing what happened to her. When I think I've seen the worst, I'm proven wrong on the worst possible level.

Libbs starts to fiercely shake her head to something we can't hear, and then starts to struggle as two men flank her side and proceed to roll up one sleeve.

That makes three now.

Three men who are going to pay.

My vision goes blurry.

No! No! No! No!

"Fucking Hell!!"

An explosion in my head bursts as my heart screams out in wild protest at what I'm seeing. The phone in my hand begins to shake as my entire body convulses. I'm so enraged and disgusted, I can't sit still. Vince, who is sitting next to me, reaches over to lay his hand on my arm to offer me comfort when there is none to have.

What I see next... there are no words for.

One of the guys tightens a band around her arm and I know what's next without watching. The heroin found in her system, this is how it got there. My outburst sends the chair flying across the room as bile climbs to the back of my throat. I barely make it to the sink in time before I violently throw up.

"JESUS. FUCKING.CHRIST." I roar with my head hung low. I'm heaving and breaking out in a cold sweat as my body continues to shake uncontrollably. Each time I heave, more tears stream down my face. My gut reaction is to tear this fucking room apart, but it's spinning so damn hard that my knees give out as I buckle and hit the floor.

I can't think straight. I sure as hell can't see straight and I find it impossible to move. Time just stands still. And for the next few moments, I cease to exist.

Until the pain returns.

My chest gets so incredibly tight that it's hard to catch my next breath. Am I having a heart attack? Oh, God every gasp of air feels like fire blazing an agonizing trail through my lungs. The only thing I can do is lean forward, so I'm doubled over on my hands, wheezing to force the air into my lungs. I can't tell if I'm crying or groaning because everything hurts so motherfucking bad I just want it to end.

Three sets of shoes appear in front of me and as I struggle to lift my head, their extremely worried and furious faces are all I see. None of them have a clue how to help me. They've never seen me like this. Hell, no one has.

"They fucking killed her, didn't they?" My voice is unfamiliar as the vile truth leaves my lips. It comes from a place of unbridled hurt, anger and so much damn sorrow. I can't stomach to watch any more, but I still need the confirmation. When no one answers, I roar. "DIDN'T THEY?" My mouth is wide open, and my breathing is so labored, a trail of saliva hits the floor. Jesus, I'm a fucking mess.

Marcus and Vince finally approach me, not able to take looking at me like this any longer. I raise my hand as a warning for them to stay the hell back. The last thing I need is to be touched. What I need, is to hear the rest.

Marcus stops right where he is, just out of arms reach from me. "Yes. After they injected her, it seems they took her to her car to set up the scene with the motor in the back seat to make it look like a suicide due to carbon monoxide poisoning."

"The video is from that night?"

I suspected it as much, but knowing those were her last moments on earth just destroys me even more. To know Libbs spent her last moments scared and crying before being murdered by those three men is incomprehensible to me. She knew she was going to die and there wasn't a damn thing she could do to prevent it. The fucked-up part, if I had to pick out one, is the asshole who taped it all as it happened. There's a special place in hell for him and I plan on sending him there. Personally.

Knowing how much his answer is going hurt me, Marcus confirmed what I already suspected to be true.

"How the fuck did they know I'd be the one to find her that night? I drove there by pure chance."

Vince shares his opinion. "We don't know if they planned on you finding her or not. It could be completely coincidental it happened that way."

It takes some time, but once I'm able to breathe easier, I sit back on my knees, and then slowly get to my feet. The splash of cold water is just what I need as I close my eyes and do my best to control my raging thoughts. This time when Vince reaches out and lays a hand on my shoulder, I don't push him away. I accept the gesture and turn to let him know how grateful I am that he's here for me. I extend the same look to Marcus and Salvo and am taken back by the tears I see in Marcus' eyes. It's so unlike him to ever show any real emotion.

"What about the guys who..." I struggle to say the words, "who held her down while that sick fuck stuck her arm with that damn poison? Any idea who they are? Because they sealed their fates and I'm not talking about jail time either."

Judging from the look on Marcus' face, I'd say he's in total agreement.

"Not yet, but I assure you I have men on it. Eventually, I will find out who they are. And when I do, I will make fucking sure they pay dearly for what they have done to you and to her. I know how much Liberty meant to you, Declan. They made a big fucking mistake by making this personal. Why they have involved you in all of this, I'm not sure. But, the fact they had pictures of you and then to go and kill an innocent girl... grave mistake!"

Out of nowhere, I ask a question I never thought I would. "How do you think my dad would have handled this if he were still alive?"

It takes Salvo less than a second to reply.

"Dominic would torch hell itself and make damn sure those fuckers suffered until they begged for him to end their lives. Then, he'd just keep it up making damn sure everyone knew not to mess with *his son* ever again."

My thoughts exactly!

"He'd make sure everyone knew not to mess with his son ever again!"

That thought replays in my mind like a recording, only it's not. It's the voices in my head reminding me just who my father was, and what it means for me as his son. I may not have met him, but that does not mean I can't learn a thing or two from him. Who knows, maybe I am more like him than I realize. It's then the voices imprison me with three key thoughts: *discipline, patience and determination.*

Oh, yeah, these fuckers are going to pay!

It's what he stood for and what I need to aspire too. Closing my eyes, I can feel some change taking place. I don't fight it, I give into. What's the worst that could happen? I highly doubt shit could get any worse for me at this point.

All I know is after I open my eyes, every raw emotion I was engulfed in is suddenly soothed by a new sense of self-possession. The rather composed and sinister laugh that erupts from deep down inside is like an out of body experience. I don't even have to look in a mirror to know that my eyes are black as coal and frigid as hell.

Feeling three sets of eyes burning a hole in my head, I raise my gaze to theirs... with an allusive grin that turns sadistic in nature. I'm met with what can only be described as apprehension and unease.

My eyes shift back to her phone on the table. I find that it's paused on her horrific face just moments before she took her last breath. *Did she know?* Fuck, of course, she did.

My thoughts come out as ramblings, but I never raise my voice. "Hell would be too easy a place to send them for what they did. There is *not* a chance in hell of that happening. What I have in mind for them will make Hell seem like a stroll in the fucking park."

The dead silence in the room is no doubt in reaction to my eerie and bizarre sense of self-control. With baffled faces looking my way, I'm sure they are just waiting for me to go bat shit crazy. Lashing out is what I do best. But, make no mistake. What I'm feeling goes way beyond anger. It's on the other side of the world kind of beyond anger.

The only difference, I'm able to separate my emotions for the first time in my life. It allows me to resist every urge to destroy everything in this house, one board at a time.

In the back of my mind, a voice sounds off. *"There is a time and place for anger. Revenge is never reckless or sloppy. You use it, channel it and when it's time... you fucking unleash it!"*

That's it... the key to surviving this. Remain as detached as humanly possible until I find out who they are. And when I do... God Almighty won't be able to save them then. No one will.

To make sure that happens, I directly my next comment to Marcus. "Make sure *I* am the one who gets to do it."

His eyes narrow as if asking me if I'm sure? My answer back comes in the form of a deep snarl.

"That's the only way," I growl and then point a finger at my chest. "To keep the beast under control and in check. If someone dares takes that chance away from me, I'll fucking take everyone down with me." It's not a threat, it's a promise!

This is the first time I've ever taken this tone with Marcus but given the circumstances, it's justified. They may be looking at me with shocked faces, but I know the line I'm about to cross, and I know there will be no going back. I don't give a damn. To be able to live with myself, it has to be done.

I turn to grab a water from the fridge since my throat is dry as hell and decide to call it a night. Without a single word, I leave the three of them where they sit, speechless

"What the fuck was that?" The shock in Salvo's voice comes through even though he tries to keep it at a minimum. "That shit was *not* Declan, and it was scary as fuck. Did you see the look on his face?"

"We need to watch him," Vince urges in a voice full of concern. "That shit right there was nothing short of—"

"Dominic!" Marcus answers with a shallow sigh, but also with a hint of amazement.

Briefly closing my eyes, my breathing slows at the memory of my father. When I open them again, I do so with a dark and sinister smile to my face.

Chapter Ten

"A Monster Plan"

The video's been sent.
He's seen it by now and I can only imagine the guilt, the hate, and the helplessness he must be feeling.
Oh, the joy it brings.
And no one will ever trace it back to me.
To have seen his face.... priceless!

With him spiraling on the edge
It's almost time for the start of phase two of my plan.

The photos.
Some old. Some new.
All meant to send him spiraling over the edge.

I heard he found Dominic's journal, and I can only imagine what kind of fucked up shit that was to read.
If the boy thinks the things kept from him about his past were bad, just wait 'til he sees the surprise I have in store for him.

His perfect little world is about to crumble down around him.
It's about damn time.
For twenty years, I've lived with what's been done to me.
Now, it's time I return the favor.
Sealing the envelope, I flip it over and write...

Declan Parisi
Personal & Confidential.

Chapter Eleven

"A Game Changer"

I train.
    I eat.
I sleep.
Then, I do it all over again.
It leaves me with little time to study, but I still find a way to get it done. These past few days leading up to the fight of my life, have been long and exhausting. But, it's finally here.
The buzz in the arena is electric, but with the help of Ludacris and Eminem rapping in my ear, I easily block it out. The music keeps me focused and energized for what should be one hell of a showdown. The biggest of my amateur career so far. Also, the one I'm most looking forward to considering it's against the one guy I despise the most, Curtis Diego.
Over the last few days, things have escalated with all the pre-fight trash talk that's getting more personal and uglier by the day. On a positive note, all the buzz has skyrocketed the bets being placed. Vince has been busier than usual keeping a watchful eye on the bet tallies, while Marcus and Anthony continue to promote what's turned into the most anticipated fight in *Windy City Underground* since its inception a few years ago.
The growth in *WCU* has been steady and becoming more and more popular over time. Prior to *WCU*, the majority revenue for the

Aniello organization was in sports betting. Over the last few years, since the creation of *WCU*, their revenue has tripled.

It's taken on a beast of its own and I'd be lying if I said that hasn't added some extra pressure to make sure I perform at my best. My career is just starting to really take off, thanks to the numerous scrappy fights I've previously been involved in.

I've taken my share of beatings a time or two, but I've beaten the hell out of way more. The only record that means anything is my undefeated status within *WCU*. I sure as hell don't plan on that changing any time soon, including the fight tonight.

It's no wonder with all of the distractions lately, that this week has been an increasingly difficult one for me. Nero, already a pretty intense guy to begin with, has dialed up his intensity by a hundred percent in an attempt to keep me focused on the one thing that means everything, the fight.

To do that, I need to push everything else out of my mind. Like videotapes, journals and the need for revenge. Tonight, my focus has to be solely on Curtis and it shouldn't be too hard, given the bad blood between us.

As each day drew closer to the fight, my mood shifted to match the color of my eyes, dark.

Since that dreadful night in the kitchen, something changed inside of me. That's the only way to explain it. I'm angrier than ever, but my ability to channel and control it like I have, is something I've never been able to do before. Who knows, maybe the reference Marcus made about me acting like my father has some truth to it. If anyone could channel their fucking anger, it was him. The difference, he knew exactly how to relieve it.

Vince told me he made a call to Rachel to stop by soon just to check in with me. It seems my so-called babysitter will be making house calls again to make sure I'm taking my meds and not spiraling out of control. It should piss me off but a part of me misses her... well parts of her anyway.

I'll just lie to her like I've lied to everyone else when it comes to my meds. With my new super power of self-control, it's been easy to play off that I've been taking them when I haven't at all. I need to be real fucking angry for this fight.

Which makes having Dex and Kingston at my side even more vital. They are in my corner whenever I fight. One, it doesn't take much to set me off, so they flank my sides to deflect any potential issues that may arise. Secondly, they both are fighters and the only friends I trust.

Their expertise is invaluable to me when we're either training or having them in my corner during the fight. Dex is far more comfortable fighting on his feet, but Kingston is king shit when it comes to taking the fight to the mat. Both are great fighters with their own style of fighting. When it comes to the three of us, we have a pack. It's not about just one of us. It's about the three of us as a unit.

As much as they have my back, I have theirs. The three of us are hell on wheels and a reckon to deal with. Our opponents may only be fighting one of us inside the ring, but it may as well be the three of us because the other two are outside the ring and busy shouting instructions throughout the fight. Not to mention, all the prep work we do in the gym prior to the fight.

That's not to say we don't have egos, because each of us sure as hell does. We're cocky and arrogant fighters, but we don't let that come between the work that needs to be done to prepare for our fights. That's what makes us different. Dex and I have known each other longer, but Kingston came along about a year ago and just seemed like a natural fit. We made a pact to stick together and help one another out. So far, it's worked out well.

In our trio, Dex's fighting style is *the art of eight limbs*. Muay Thai, is a style of MMA fighting that concentrates on the eight points of contact using punches, knees, elbows, and kicks. Kingston is all Jiu-Jitsu and damn impressive with his ground fighting. His ability to subdue opponents with different choke holds comes in handy if his opponent is larger than his five-foot-ten, one hundred, seventy-pound frame. Then, there's me, a classic southpaw heavy striker who feels most comfortable leading with my right fist and foot since I'm left handed. I like to ground to pound, but I've got a wicked knee strike to counter my punches.

Between the three of us, we bring a lot to the table to help one another out for whatever style of fighter we face.

With the growing popularity of Windy City Underground, the Aniello's knew they would have to conceal the location from authorities, so they purposely built it under one of their own large and outdated gyms. A lot of planning was put into a location that would not draw any unwarranted attention to what really happens here. Situated on the south side of Chicago, Pete's Gym looks like a rundown, over-sized gym.

With a secret, hidden entrance, the lower level of the gym houses a monstrous area that surrounds the octagon. The space is big enough to hold several hundred people, but for those who don't like rowdy crowds, off-site betting is an option via a special internet connection that broadcasts the fights to a few select locations. Also owned by the Aniello family.

What can I say, fighting for the Aniello's does have its perks... but it doesn't guarantee us automatic wins either. The refs and judges are licensed and sanctioned, meaning they are legit when it comes to scoring every fight in *WCU*. They have reputations and it's their names on the bottom line. Professionals who will not be bought or pressured to call a fight that's not won on the fighter's merit alone. That's the way it should be. I certainly don't need family connections to win fights for me. That's not who Dex, Kingston and I are. The only way this works is for us to win, lose or draw on our own.

Until it's time to head downstairs to the arena, I hang upstairs where it's less chaotic in a separate locker room that Dex, Kingston and I share. Our opponents are sent to wait downstairs in the locker room where it's loud and chaotic.

Yes, it's strategy and we'll gladly use it so our advantage. When it's time, there's a separate stairwell that takes us downstairs, so we walk out of the lower room just like any other fighter.

The closer it gets to the start of the fight, the more anxious I feel, making it even more important for me to be away from the noise. When there are that many people confined in a small space who are out to see bloodshed, it can be a huge distraction to contend with. Those last few minutes before a fight are important. I need that time to go from training-mode Declan, to beast-mode Declan.

With my hands wrapped, I'm dressed in my customary black fighting shorts, sitting on the bench and keeping loose with the help of music. I sway to the beat, roll one shoulder at a time, making sure to stretch my neck just as Dex suddenly walks in.

"Hey, man it's almost time. Let's go over a few things."

Dex bends down in front of me and lines his face with mine, making sure I listen to him even though my headphones are still on. I lift one of the earphones from my ear so I can do just that.

"Listen, Curtis has been training hard on his take downs and floor techniques. Watch out for his leg kicks and don't get caught in a sweep. He takes you down, we got problems." The idea that fucker is going to take me down is an insult. "He knows how lethal you are with your hands, so he's going to avoid them at all costs."

To put his mind at ease, I assure him. "Nero and I have been working hard to make sure I keep the fight on our feet as much as possible. But, if he takes me down," I snarl just saying the words. "Kingston's been a real help in that area."

Not fully convinced, Dex shakes his head, talking under his breath.

"Dex, I got this. Trust me. I want this fucker to bleed." Boy, isn't that the truth. With his remarks about Libbs, that alone makes me want to break his fucking face.

Nodding his head, he sighs and then slaps my shoulder. "I know you do, man. Just be sure to keep that thick head of yours in the game and don't let him get under your skin so you lose focus. He's going to try to knock you off your game, be ready for it."

He's right, but I don't think there is anything Curtis could say or do that would change just how bad I want to knock his head clean off his shoulders.

Suddenly, the doors to the locker room open as Vince and Marcus walk in currently in a heated conversation. Vince looks stressed as he shows Marcus something from the stack of papers he has in his hands. Marcus places a deliberate hand on his hip while cursing under his breath at Vince low enough I can't make out what he said.

Vince doesn't take kindly to it, and shouts back. "I don't have a fucking clue what's going on!"

Marcus maintains his glare, then rubs his forehead. "This shit doesn't make any sense, why now with under an hour to go?"

Curious, I lift my chin in their direction. "What's going on?"

Marcus responds but doesn't look my way. "Nothing."

"Yeah, it's look like nothing. Spill it." I get to my feet, taking off my headphones.

Somewhat apprehensive, Vince sidesteps Marcus. "In the last hour, ten thousand dollars' worth of bets have been placed. The odds just switched big time."

Dex and Kingston who have now joined us, react. "That's great. What's the issue?"

Marcus grumbles, "On Curtis." Then punches the closest locker.

My jaw hit the floor. "What?"

Dex can't believe it. "You're shitting me?"

Marcus turns to give him an icy glare while you can almost see the wheels turning in his head. "We've never had this kind of shift so close to the start of the fight, and never had this amount go against one of our fighters. I know you and Curtis have bad blood, but this is something different all together. The amount is too high, to be incidental."

"It doesn't matter," I argue with the obvious, "they're going to lose it… and you're going to keep it in return."

Both Dex and Kingston nod their heads.

"Keep that confidence, Declan. Right on, man." Kingston is the only one looking at Vince and Marcus like they are Debbie Downers and with the way he turns his gaze on me, I can tell he's a bit wary that this is not the type of news I should be hearing before a fight. "Let Declan get ready, you two do whatever you need to do," he says shooing them away, "but do it away from here."

With the shared look between them, I'd say they completely agree.

"Nero gets wind you two are in here talking this shit, he's going to go ballistic." Dex clues them in as he ushers them with his hands to get out of here. It's a bit too late, the news is starting to sink in when Nero walks through the double doors with his usual no-bullshit attitude. He immediately looks sternly at Vince and Marcus.

"Well, it's not like you two to be in here before a fight. What's going on?"

Nero is one observant son-of-a-bitch and is quick to assess the expression on Dex and Kingston's faces and then Marcus and Vince's before his eyes finally scrutinize my face and tense body language. And react, he does. "Doesn't matter, you two OUT!" He all but pushes them out the door as they willingly go.

When it comes to me and fighting, Nero gets the say all. Even to them.

The minute the doors close, Nero turns to face the three of us. "Finally!" He clasps his hands and looks around as if looking for something. "Dex, Kingston come with me for a minute and leave Declan to his music. He looks like he needs a few moments to himself."

He gives me a nod of his chin because Nero knows me better than anyone, and knew I needed a moment. He also gave me a stern look that meant to clear my fucking head from whatever happened a few moments ago. I'm sure he's grilling Dex and Kingston outside the door right now.

I take advantage of the moment and place my headphones back on. The calm before the storm is the way I see it as I return to the bench and rest against the lockers. With the music blaring once again, I momentarily close my eyes and concentrate on my breathing.

Who cares if anyone bet a large amount of money on Curtis, it doesn't mean anything. Since when do I involve myself with odds and betting, *never*! Vince handles my finances. And it's not like I've ever wanted or needed a damn thing. I'm pretty sure my bank account has more than the usual twenty-year-old has so as long as I go out and win, who really gives a shit.

After a few more breaths, I open my eyes and immediately something catches my attention. A yellow envelope is lying on the floor just inside the door, like someone slid it underneath. I'm sure I didn't see it there when Vince and Marcus left, or when Nero and the guys walked out.

There is hand writing on the top that I can't make out from here, so I get up to get a closer look. Staring right back at me in big and bold letters, *my name*. An ill-feeling rocks the pit of my stomach.

Under my name, it reads personal and confidential.

What in the hell?

I can't help but get a bad feeling as I cautiously pick it up like it might bite me before taking it with me to sit back down. Tapping the envelope against my hand, my eyes glance up at the clock on the wall to see the fight is only twenty-nine minutes away. Before I can overthink things too much, I tear the envelope open and peer inside.

Photos.

I quickly flip over the tops to count them.

One… two… three… four… five.

Five in total, and all enlarged to the size of a sheet of paper. Every nerve cell in my body tells me whatever these are cannot be good. Before I commit to look at them, my eyes drift shut as my left leg starts to shake wildly. My mind automatically shifts back to the last time I had to look at something and that sure as hell did not end well. The lump in my throat feels like it's nearly cutting off my ability to breathe.

If these photos are from the same person, it's not fucking wise for me to look at them right before the fight. Only, I can't stop myself.

Here goes nothing!

One glance at the first photo is all it takes to damn near knock the wind out of me.

"Oh. Fucking Hell. No!"

———

MY PLAN TONIGHT WAS SIMPLE. *Destroy Curtis.*
Now as I enter the ring, I have only one thing on my mind.
The photos!
It changes everything. A real game changer.

I need to make a decision, and fast given the fight is about to start. Those were the instructions left for me to discover on the back of the photos. One could call it blackmail, but it's more of a give and take. Just how badly do I want what he is offering me.

My head is all fucked up, and my jaw's been clenched tight since I discovered that damn envelope. The heavy stare Curtis is giving me across the ring is like an iron fist around my neck. Suffocating me from within. I feel like a caged animal, with my surrounds closing in around me.

Every heavy breath I take, my chest thrusts forward as I frantically pace back and forth with my shoulders square. I'm staring at Curtis who is only a few feet from me, with nothing but pure disgust in my eyes. When he smirks back, my vision goes white.

Months of waiting for this night has felt like a lifetime. And each day, I've played out every scenario in my mind a million times over. All ending the same way, a KO!

Now, everything has changed.

Everything, except my hatred of Curtis Diego. My intense rage for him has only intensified with time to the point I want to tear him from limb to limb. It makes the contents of the envelope even more devastating, and the choice I made back in the locker room. That much more difficult to defend.

The steady chants from the crowd are getting more deafening with the anticipation of blood shed only moments away.

Am I doing the right thing, plagues my mind as I glance over my shoulder at Nero, Dex and Kingston one last time. All three of their eyes are heavily engaged on me. From the moment, they returned to the locker room, they could sense something was wrong. By then, I had the envelope and its contents tucked away in my locker.

I gave very little away while my mind was pre-occupied with the mysterious envelope. During the last minute-instructions from Nero, my jaws remained clenched as I never once looked him in the eye. It's not unusual behavior for me for me to remain quiet, but to not face him eye to eye, definitely is. I'm sure that's why none of them are a hundred percent certain nothing is going on with me.

Out of the corner of my eye, Curtis nonchalantly gestures with his finger to the other side of the room. My eyes follow his finger over the heads of jumping and screaming fans, but nothing catches my eye at first. Then, out of nowhere, a man steps into my view with his back against the wall. He crosses his arms and nods at me with a shit eating grin on his face.

Up until twenty-nine minutes ago, he was an unfamiliar face. Now, his face is branded to memory. Every deep crease in his forehead, to the deep vertical scar on his left cheek, to the white scar on his upper lip. My vision goes blurry with rage and it takes every ounce of self-control I have not to rush over and take a pound of his flesh. A disrespectful laugh distinguishes itself from the loud chants in the crowd as my eyes draw to the source. Curtis. I'll deal with that fucker soon enough, and the second I turned my attention away, it was enough time for the bastard against the wall to disappear.

A dangerous game has been set into motion and as Curtis continues to laugh, a violent growl ecapes past my throat. The only reason that guy showed up here, at this exact moment, is nothing short of a reminder of the contents of the envelope. A not so subtle gesture of this sick and twisted game I've been pulled into for reasons unbeknownst to me. It enrages me past the breaking point.

If they want to play, so be it.

Game on, motherfucker!

Come and get me!!

Chapter Twelve

"The Fight"

WHATEVER SANITY I HAD LEFT, checked out the minute we approach one another in the middle of the ring. Standing toe to toe, we're sizing one another up when the ref asks us to touch hands.

Like Hell!

Before the start of the fight, the ref stands back to ask if we're ready while Curtis and I are locked in a frenzied glare. Without breaking eye contact, we both nod our heads just waiting for the magic words.

Then.

"Let's get it on!" The ref instructs as chaos begins.

I charge first as Curtis is slow to meet me in the center of the ring. My fists are raised and in position as I waste little time. My swing is swift and heavy, but a tad late. Curtis quickly ducks as my fist whiffs past his face.

Dammit.

He's quick, but I'm relentless. I keep swinging while he dodges and dances on his feet. The fucker is faster than the last time we fought. Then again, my head is so fucked up my timing is off. I'm running on pure rage, not strategy. And it feeds his ego.

"You ready to fight, pussy?" He taunts me with a smirk, playing up to his fans.

Dex is shouting for me not to fall for his bullshit and concentrate on my punches. Curtis waves him off and keeps going.

"Come on big boy, whatcha' got for me?"

His smug smirk is the only thing I see and the best way to shut him up is to knock his teeth in. As we trade jabs and dance around, I'm eyeing that chin of his... waiting for the perfect time to nail him with my left uppercut. Only his big mouth is hard to ignore.

"You're all talk, you, pussy wannabe."

And it's getting even harder.

I lose focus just in time for him to connect with a leg sweep that sends me to the mat. Instead of charging me while I'm down, he stands back to mouth off some more.

"Stand up and take it from a real man. I'll gladly rip you apart!"

This time he taunts and disrespects me by framing his hands around his dick to give his fans a show. Standing back up, I've heard just about enough. When he's about to smart off again, I close the gap between us and deliver a blow so powerful, it connects with his jaw that sends his head swinging to the side. He stumbles and looks back at me with eyes full of shock. That's right fucker, I wink at him with my own smirk. He clearly wasn't expecting that, and he'd do best to remember to watch it when he mouths off to me. I can only take so much of him pushing all my buttons.

I hold back, cautious of not unloading on his ass and its killing me. That damn envelope. For a fighter there is no worse scenario than the one I'm facing right now. I compare it to trying to fight with one hand tied behind my back.

Almost an impossibility!

But, those were the instructions.

Go the distance.

Throw the fight.

All for a price.

To add insult, I'm to lose all three rounds in a convincing fashion. Meaning, I have to let Curtis kick my ass without really striking back, at the same time, make a show out it. It's the ultimate humiliation in every possible way for a guy like me.

The fight here tonight is not the fight the fans came to watch. It's the fight with myself to restrain my every instinct to end this fucker once and for all.

The terms were non-negotiable and spelled out in the contents of envelope. All meant to punish and entice me at the same time. A tic for tac. Blackmail. The link between the envelope and the video of Libbs proves that whatever charade this is, it's long from being over.

When I figure out who is behind this, I'll end him along with the fuckers in that video. Until then, my best bet is to play along and get the information I need. It all starts with letting Curtis deliver punch after punch, taunting me between each swing.

"You ain't shit, pretty boy! I'm gonna fuck that face up so good you won't look so pretty anymore."

"The ladies won't like it once I rearrange that face of yours!"

I'm counting in my head, drowning out his voice, but when I get close enough and wrap him up, I make sure to deliver a message of my own. "Keep talking fuck face, I'll remember every word." Then, before I toss his ass aside, I deliver a solemn promise. "I'm going to find out who is behind this shit, and after I kill them, *I'm coming for you*! So, keep right on talking shit."

It's not even a question in my mind, Curtis sealed his fate when he pointed out the asshole before the fight. Judging by how wide his eyes are right now, it's all the confirmation I need. He's a part of this and it doesn't matter how much or how little. His day will come.

Curtis seems more than bothered with my comments and is quickly looking into the crowd like he's looking for someone specific. Could I actually get lucky enough to see who is behind all of this? A rush of excitement hits me for the first time since this nightmare of a fight started. Only, Curtis quickly turns back and lands a shot to my temple with an arrogant smirk on his face. He's laughing as disappointment sets in because I never had a chance to see who he was looking for. It sets me off with the sudden urge to wrap my hands around his thick neck and squeeze until Curtis turns blue. The cold realization that I could actually pull off throwing this fight is creeping doubts in my mind.

I'm delivering punches and kicks, and taking more shots than I should be. And it really is pissing me off. My chances of following through with this all comes down to what's been promised to me if I do throw this fight.

The stakes are high, the payoff even higher.

Curtis keeps playing up to the crowd enjoying a fight he already knows the outcome too. He flaunts his ego because he knows my hands are literally tied by my own accord, and he's loving every minute of it. It is infuriating, but to sell this shit show I dodge some of his swings, only to be slow enough to get nailed a few times to take the brunt of his punishments.

A few of them sting like a sonofabitch, and each time he lands a good one, Kingston and Dex are shouting at me like crazy, taking out their aggression by rattling the cage of the octagon. I can't stomach it to look over at their faces and the one voice I haven't heard at all, is the bluster of Nero's voice. That tells me plenty. He's always been able to read me like a book, including when I'm not trying my best. Like now!

I endure hit after hit and do so with each photo forefront in my mind. That's the only way this fucker is going to remain on his feet for all three rounds. I remind myself of what I'm getting in return, and when Liberty's face flashes in my mind… it makes it all worth it. Ten times over.

This is for her!

The moment I opened the envelope, everything changed. Not only for tonight, but for the foreseeable future. I hate the word blackmail, but that's what it is. All wrapped up in a nice package, all meant to piss me the hell off. It certainly did that!

But, this blackmail comes with temptation?

In exchange for throwing the fight, I would receive valuable information. The kind of information I'd just about do anything for. If it were only me, the decision would have been easy, but this decision also affects those around me. I have people who have put time and money into me and this fight. Banking on me to win and I hate to consider the money Marcus and Anthony stand to lose, but I have no real choice.

They knew what to entice me with, something I wouldn't walk away from.

The first photo told me a lot about whoever is behind all of this. Whoever it is, is well connected and informed. Not only about me, but my father as well.

Imagine my shock when the first photo I look at is my father on his knees in front of a woman holding a gun to his head. A woman with long dark hair, who appears so shaken up she's holding the gun with two hands. Dominic seems to be mocking her judging by the smirk on his face in mid-laughter. '*Who am I*' was written by the woman's face with a large white question mark.

The next photo is a man with Liberty. The same guy Curtis pointed to before the start of the fight. The one standing against the wall. That's the reason I wanted to tear that fuckers head off, and still intend to do. Whoever he is, his days are numbered.

In the picture, he's sitting in the front seat of her car, passenger side. She's sitting in the exact position I found her in that horrible night. If I had to guess, it was taken the same night, only earlier. Maybe even right before I found her, and that dreadful thought hit me like a ton of bricks. Had someone been watching us that night when I found her?

That disturbing thought is just as sick as the fucker in the car with her. His vulgar disrespect for her is mind-numbing but doing so knowing she was no longer alive... that just makes me murderous. Above his smug grin was another big white question mark stating, "Who am I?" with, "what are you willing to do to find out these answers and so much more? I have them all!"

It certainly seemed that way to me.

The other photo was kind of a mystery. Two girls, and if I had to guess, around my age. Early twenties or so. One has dark hair, the other is blonde. Both attractive and walking along a rocky beach. I've never seen these two girls before in my life and have no clue who they could be. According to the writing on this picture, these girls are a piece of the puzzle. Whatever the hell that is supposed to mean.

With all of this shit going on in my head while trying to pull off a convincing loss on purpose is harder than I thought it would be. Half of the time, my head and instincts are waging a war. My head is all about the photos and my instincts are wanting to tear into Curtis. Lucky for me, Curtis takes advantage and sneaks up on me to get some good licks in. It's actually helping me get my own assed kicked.

The first round goes to Curtis. No surprise. I'm just thinking, I got this. Two more to go!

Round two goes pretty much the same as round one. My core fans are getting restless with my lackluster performance while Curtis ramps up his taunting. He's now directing his hits to my corner as the bell signals the end of the second round.

"If you guys need a real fighter to train with, give me a call. Your boy is fucking pathetic."

By this time, I'm winded and feeling dejected, so I don't bother to comment back. Any other time, I'd tear his ass up. My unwillingness to say a word only enrages Dex to the point he spits on the ground and gets into a shouting match like he's ready to take this fight over for me.

"Oh, yeah," Dex shouts. "My boy has kicked your ass TWICE, motherfucker. He's more of a fighter than you'll ever be."

Just not tonight is all I can think with my head low. The licks I'm letting Curtis get in on me are starting to hit me hard. It's not all an act anymore. My body has taken some serious damaging shots.

"What the FUCK are you doing OUT THERE! Get your head out of your ass and fight this sonofabitch!" Kingston is chewing in one ear while Dex and Curtis continue their back and forth pissing match.

Nero lowers in front of me and has Kingston pour ice cold water over my neck and shoulders. Shaking the access off, I open my eyes to find Nero's angry face inches from mine.

He mixes no words. "You have no defense. Your hands are too low. Your strikes are too slow. You have no fight in you, and I know for a fact you are *throwing* this fucking fight. Why? I sure as hell have no clue. That's all on you son, but don't expect me to stand by and watch this shit show continue."

It's tearing me up to let him down like this. More than that, I'm disrespecting him and what he stands for. As a former Marine, to give up in anything is simply inconceivable. With me not giving him one word in my defense, it tells Nero all he needs. One of his favorite sayings comes to mind, 'silence is nothing more than an admission of guilt'.

He utters a few more choice words, then straightens up and quietly exits the octagon. Dex and Kingston are going nuts wondering what the hell is going on and cursing under their breath. Curtis doesn't let this golden opportunity go to waste either, he's all over it continuing to run his mouth.

"You are so pathetic your trainer is even walking out on you. L.O.S.E.R!!"

I can't imagine a night ever getting any worse than this, and my body is reeling in the effects. From across the ring, I raise my gaze to Curtis and silently let him know with my look that one day soon his time will come. It may not be tonight, but it will happen. And when it does, I'll take my time pounding every inch of his body until he's beaten within an inch of his life. He may win the fight, but he's not the better fighter. Not by a long shot.

I've done my part and made the fight convincing so far, but I also made sure to get a few good shots in there just to remind him of what's coming his way. Only worse. I need to make sure he doesn't forget my little effort tonight is all for show. He's not getting me at my best. Each hit he delivers, is returned with a death glare all meant to remind him I'll be back. Mark my words and count the days. It's only a matter of time.

At the end of round two, I feel more confident that I can do this. I've come this far, what's one more round? It should be the easiest if anything and it can't come soon enough.

Curtis starts round three with kicks to my mid-section, strikes to my kidneys and jabs to my face. He wants to hurt me, bad. Most likely scared of what's to come his way, and in my mind, I tally each hit he lands and promise to return the favor, tenfold.

Curtis gets crafty and lands a solid hit to my jaw that instantly buckles my knees before I drop. He takes full advantage like a pit bull in heat this time and comes around my back to stretch his arm under my chin in a choke hold that he hopes to submit me with. My hands immediately go up to help ease the tight hold he has that's cutting off my air supply. Before I can do anything else, Curtis forces my body backwards as he does his best to maintain his hold over me.

Kingston is shouting instructions at me to get out of it. I know what to do, it's just hard to get any oxygen to make it happen. Like I anticipated, Curtis has left his right-side unprotected and it's the perfect place to strike with my elbow. Just as I make my move with my elbow, Curtis stupidly grumbles in my ear instead of chocking me out with a submission.

"Too bad about your girl. I heard she had a sweet tasting pussy. Just my luck, I didn't get a taste for myself. Tell me, just how good it was?"

That's all it took.

I see Motherfucking RED!

My chest is heaving, and my mouth is wide open as I struggle for every breath. Fueled only with a fury of anger to the likes I've never felt before, I suddenly feel revived. My body is shaking all over as Curtis finds himself struggling to maintain his hold. Each pant of air expands my chest and after I take the biggest breath I can, I lean as far forward, taking Curtis with me. His body is stretched and while his mind is busy on keeping his arms around my neck, that's when I pull my elbow back and ram it into his unprotected side. Repeatedly.

He has no option but to loosen his hold. Twisting my body like a madman, I jump to escape. When I'm free, I light his ass up like a crazed animal who's suddenly been let loose. I'm punching, kneeing and jabbing every inch of his body I can connect with and it's a freeing feeling like none other. Curtis is finally feeling just how brutal I can be and he's nothing but a damn fifthly liar who needs to be taught a lesson.

Nothing else matters. It's an all-out war.

The voices in my head guide me. "Show NO MERCY! NO MERCY! NO MERCY!"

The crowd is suddenly on their feet erupting in cheers as I deliver a barrage of body shots to a stunned Curtis who has had the tables turned on him. He's trying his best to wrap me up because at the moment he has no defense. His hands are low, he's winded and every attempt to block my shots, fails. Hell, I may be winded, but I'm fucking determined.

Curtis is bloodied and spent, slowing down by the minute.

This is the fight everyone paid to see.

Barely standing on shaky legs, I get my first look the damage I've caused. His lower lip has a nasty split down the middle and his left eye has a deep laceration that is allowing a steady stream of blood to run in his eye. The ref is quick to stop all action, so a doctor can check him out. He's a damn bloody mess, but I'm nowhere close to being done with him.

"Declan! No Mercy!"

My lips repeat those words as I block everyone else out. It's only me and him as I wait on my side of the ring for the doctors to tend to his eye. As we wait for the ref to continue the fight, my deadly glare never leaves his. My focus is laser sharp, my body is tense, and my head is shifting side to side. The last thing I can do is stand still, all I want is to fight. Dex and Kingston take the opportunity to blast instructions at me, but all I hear is white noise.

My sights, my thoughts, and the voices in my head are all shouting the same thing.

Pummel Curtis Diego to a bloody pulp.

When I'm like this, he's no match for me. Not even close. The beast inside can only be contained for so long, and when the ref gives the okay to resume the fight. I charge.

Curtis strikes first but swings wide and misses. I've waited to get my arms around that neck of his, and now's my chance. I advance with my elbow around his neck and position my hold. Then, I restrict his air flow. The harder I squeeze, the more satisfying it is. A feral growl escapes past my throat as he struggles.

When he manages to choke the words, it feels like a bolt of lightning to my spine.

"The deal!"

What the fuck is he talking about? The deal?

Then, it hits me.

The contents of the envelope.

All crashes down around me.

"Do you want to know the answers to these questions and so much more? What would you do to get them?"

Jesus Christ!

What the fuck am I doing?

Momentarily paralyzed, each breath feels like sharp razor blades slicing into my soul. I instantly drop my hold on Curtis and stumble to one knee. The haunting realization that I was seconds away from ruining everything, courses through my veins. Earlier this evening, I was handed both a blessing and a curse.

What would I do to find out who killed Libbs? Anything! That's the blessing. The fallout will be my curse.

Down on one knee, Curtis struggles to catch a breath but comes at me seeing his best shot to end the fight. I glance up just in time to see his knee connect with my chin, and it's all over. My head violently snaps back and the next thing I know I'm flat on my back.

Dazed.

Stunned.

Motionless.

An eruption of boos and cheers ensue.

Dex is shouting the move was illegal since I was defenseless and down on one knee. Curtis and his camp are arguing against it, saying he was aiming for my body not my chin. The ref is quick to rush over to assess me as my body feels weightless, like I'm floating.

That's when my mind reverts back to the worst of those damn haunting photos.

The fourth picture was of three men. Each of them has the same tattoo, a half-moon shape on the top side of their left thumbs. Surprisingly, it was visible for me to quickly identify. I noticed the same tattoos on the men in the videos, the ones who held her down and shot her with drugs. At the time, I kept that bit of information to myself. I have no idea if Marcus, Salvo or Vince had noticed that or not. It was the only concrete thing I had to connect the men who ultimately were responsible that fatal night.

To be able to somewhat see their faces hit me with a crippling rage. Slightly out of focus, it was like they were mocking me by laughing in the picture like they just heard the best joke of their pathetic lives. A feral anger raced in my veins looking at them celebrating while Liberty lies cold and underground in a wooden box.

Unlike in the video's, the picture shows the three of them standing close together in someone's office or home. If I had to guess,

I'd say it's a living room because of the couch in the middle of the room. A dark red wall stands behind them with a gold framed painting that matched the curtains. I took note of everything. They appear to be sharing a drink and like the rest of the photos, the same white question mark is present. *"Do you want to know who these men are? If so, what are you willing to sacrifice to find out?"*

Whoever sent this, saved the best for last. The one that would almost guarantee I would do anything. The last photo answered one question I had earlier. Someone was indeed watching me that night and had proof of it. I felt violated and sickened beyond reason as a single tear ran down my cheek being pulled back to that night once again.

In my arms, I was holding Libbs in that parking lot before the police showed up. I appear to be leaning down and whispering something in her ear. And I don't even have to guess what I was saying. I remember it word for word.

"You once told me our tortured souls had finally found home in each other, but sweetheart you are finally home where there is no more pain, no more suffering. Just don't you dare forget me, because I'll be seeing you again one day. Then, I'll kick your ass for leaving me alone in this shitty world. I should have told you this, and I'll regret it for the rest of my life. I love you Libbs, and I just wish like hell I told you while you were alive. It could have changed everything for us!"

My last promise. *"I won't rest until I find out what happened to you. When I do, someone will pay!"*

To have to go back to that night and live it all over again was fucking torture. I would have agreed to anything at that point. Throwing a fight was nothing. Not when in return it gave me those fuckers heads on a silver platter.

Once I laid the five photos out on the bench and took a closer look, small arrows appeared in the corners which led me to turn them all over. When I did, it was only a matter of lining them up.

The written instructions were cleverly done in some movie style Hollywood fashion, or an episode of CSI. The cryptic instructions were simple. To find my answers, I had to do what they wanted.

Blackmail in its purest!

The next thing I know, a strong and putrid smell burns my nose. Right away, I know it's smelling salts. Shit, that only means one thing. As my sense come too, muffled voices become clear and louder. It takes me a second or two, but that's all it took to be reminded once again the bullshit that was my life. It smacks me right in the face.

With Dex on one side, and Kingston on the other, it feels like forever to wait for the final verdict of the fight. Damn, I'll raise the white flag to just end it.

Declare Curtis the winner and let me get the hell out of here.

I'll have to swallow the bile in the back of my throat as the ref raises Curtis' arm in the air declaring him the victor, but that's my price to guarantee I get what I desperately deserve and earned.

As we all wait, I replay the fight in my head. I had it all in check until the third round when Curtis ran his big mouth and pushed me too far by crossing the line. Stupid fucker! A grave mistake on his part, one that could have been devastating. It was a fucking miracle I was able to rein my shit back in so Curtis could get his KO. The only way that dick was going to beat me was by me throwing it, so he had better enjoy it while he can.

I won't lie, to have to hear his name called as the winner will be the worst feeling in the world. What I need right now, is sleep… for a straight week.

I must have a dazed look on my face because Kingston hits me with smelling salts once again, causing my head to jerk back. I hit him with a *what the fuck* look while he instantly raises his shoulders.

"Oops! Sorry, man. Just making sure you're with us."

I grumble.

Dex finds it funny as he leans down to get me to stand up, looking for Kingston to help on his side. Kingston eyes him and then throws the smelling salts before he reaches down to help me to my feet. Smart man. Once upright, I survey the damage. My damn head is throbbing, my knuckles are raw and bloodied, but it's my ribs that feel the worst.

The entire arena is in chaos as we all… wait!

Finally, the announcer takes to the microphone in the middle of the ring as a rancid taste hits the back of my throat. I hate to lose any fight, but don't regret the decision I made. It's just the thought of losing to Curtis fuck-face Diego. Of all the opponents for tonight's fight, it had to be the one guy I hate the most.

The announcer sounds off. "Ladies and Gentlemen, we have a decision. Due to the illegal kick to the head to a downed opponent, Curtis Diego has been disqualified! Therefore, your winner is Declan 'Reaper' Parisi."

As a flush of adrenaline disorients me, three things happen simultaneously.

My mouth falls open.

My right-hand clutches at my chest.

And my knees give out.

While Dex and Kingston are congratulating me by slapping my back, the crowd erupts in cheers. All it does is drives a dagger deep in my chest.

I'm breathless, forced to accept the undeniable truth while my brain is actively doing its best to deny it.

Oh, Jesus, no!

I can't WIN the fight!!

Chapter Thirteen

"Betrayal"

Not only did I let that fucker kick my ass, he then turned around and fucked me over again by doing something so stupid, so unnecessary, it goes to show how inept of a fighter Curtis really is.

This is *his* fault.
It cost me *everything*!
Now, I'll get nothing.
No names.
No answers.
Nothing, but a banged-up body.
Fuck that!

It's been said when you have nothing left to lose, it's the time you become the most dangerous. I could not agree more with that statement than I do right now.

The hellhole in the pit of my stomach grows with each staggering breath I take. I feel like I'm burning from the inside out with only one thing on my find. Find Curtis Diego!

Once the decision was announced, he high-tailed it out of the ring followed by his team. As I rush out of the cage my jaws are locked tight, and my eyes are set in a cold, hard squint. I resemble a caged animal that's just escaped, but even that doesn't deter the fans from congratulating me as I pass them by. Our expressions could not be more opposite.

No one knows just how dark my thoughts have been since I watched that damn video. It changed me. Slowly turning into an obsession. Three assholes who consume my days and plague my nightmares. Up to now, I've kept my shit together with the sole purpose of knowing one day I'll get my revenge. Payback for Libbs.

Tonight, I was one step closer to that goal… only to have it ripped away. The promise of the identities of those three men was like dangling a carrot in front of my face until it was all I could taste. The only thing left now, is the nasty, bitter aftertaste of betrayal.

I'm out for blood and nothing short of having my hands stained in theirs will satisfy me. One way or another, I will find them all. Every last one of them who have done me wrong. Not forgetting the one who calls himself, *monster*. The mastermind behind it all.

It's a good thing I'm not afraid of the dark, or the boogie man for that matter, because my days of allowing him to pull my strings are done. I'm drawing a line in the sand. I'll take the little information I have and figure the rest out on my own. It may take me longer, but I have all the time in the world. Unlike them.

Which brings me back to now. Before I can think about the rest, I first need to find Curtis. If he thought he could just up and disappear, he's fucking crazier than I thought. I can only imagine the hot water he's in screwing up the well laid out plans of his boss. What a complete idiot. It certainly explains the ton of dough that was bet on Curtis prior to the start of the fight. With the unexpected outcome of the fight, I hope there is something left of Curtis for me to get my hands on. I'll save his ass for last, right now, all I need from him are answers.

When I reach the door his locker room, I barge inside. "CURTIS, you bastard!" The echo of my boisterous voice bounces off the walls of the small room as my eyes taken in the sight before me.

"Where the fuck are you?" The room is empty and in total disarray like someone left in a damn hurry. Towels and empty water bottles are tossed to the floor, locker doors are left open and benches are pushed aside like several people rushed out the door all at once.

"Arrrrrrgh!" I can't believe it! Minutes. I missed him by a matter of minutes and it pisses me off so much I send the nearest bench across the room with one swift kick.

Dammit!

Refusing to give up now, I haul my ass down the long hall that leads to the back alley in hopes of catching him before he does leave the premises. It's a long shot, but worth it especially if I do catch him. Although, any hope I had quickly diminished when I find the alleyway dark and quiet. No sign of Curtis, his team, or any cars whatsoever. The piece of shit just vanished knowing I'd come looking for him.

Left with nothing but a mindfuck of emotions swirling in my head, the last thing I want is to go back inside. Yet, as much as I hate the idea of facing anyone, I need to collect my things. The envelope and its contents are in my bag, hanging in my locker room.

Opening the door, I keep my head low with a grimace on my face and head back inside. Trolling down the hallway, I avert looking in the eyes of the fans who shout *congrats* as I pass them by. The last thing I feel like is celebrating. The second, having to explain to them why I'm not.

When I enter the locker room, it's quiet so I quickly gather my things without taking the time to shower or change my clothes. I simply pull on my black Hoodie and pull the hood as low as I can to conceal my face. Surprisingly enough, I make it to my car without incident.

A moment later, I fishtail it out of the parking-lot agitated while trying to get a handle on the hellish events from the earlier. When ear-piercing music fails to help relax me, I inhale a few times, blowing the air from my cheeks on each exhale. I do this a few times, but it proves useless as well. That's when a barrage of *what if's* and *what happens now* take over my thoughts like a cancer. The timing for a mom and pop convenience store that appear up ahead could not have come at a better time.

I immediately pull over and once inside, I grab the first bottle of liquor I find on the shelf. It doesn't matter what it is, as long as it's alcohol. The fact I've gone a few rounds and look like hell, it's not a shock when the elderly woman behind the counter looks at me half scared like I may rob her. It's not surprising that she didn't bother to card me, like it would have mattered if she had. My fake ID is spot on.

After paying, the gray-haired woman looks back at me nervously, acting like she wants to say something. She decides against it, and hands me my brown paper bag instead, but not before her slightly droopy eyes express the idea she hopes my night will get better.

This can only help, is the look I leave her with as I twist open the bottle before I hit the door.

The moment the amber colored liquid hits my lips, it burns a trail down my throat to my stomach. With little food to absorb the liquid, the warmth starts to spread in seconds. I usually don't eat much before a fight and may very well be kicking myself later for drinking on an empty stomach. Right now, I just don't give a damn.

With alcohol clouding my judgement, my mind is all over the place trying to figure out what my plans are going to be. Between the video and photos, I don't have a ton to go on, but it's more than I had yesterday. A definite plus, but with the nagging feeling that things are going to be crazy around here over the next few days, I decide it might be best for me to skip town for a bit. It will give me time to think and heal. The last thing I need right now is more distractions.

If my phone is any indication, distractions are all I'm going to have. It's been blowing up since I left the gym. No surprises, I've missed calls from Vince, Marcus and Dex. The other number is a bit of surprise, even though it shouldn't be at all. It has more to do with Vince, than her. Of course, I'm talking about Nurse Rachel. The twelve missed calls I've had in the span of twenty minutes makes me want to throw my phone out the window. The last thing I want to do is talk... to anyone.

The drive home is uneventful, considering the bottle between my legs is reaching the half empty mark. Somehow, I made it home in one piece, convincing myself that I'm barely even buzzed. Although, when I step out of my car and am hit with the brisk breeze, my extremities begin to tingle. It becomes apparent very quickly just how buzzed I am.

I know I don't have a lot time, so I decide to put the bottle away for later while I take a cold shower to clear my head and sober me up. Fresh from the shower, I dress quickly and waste little time to collect my things and pack when I hear the slam of a car door.

"Shit."

I thought I'd have more time and as I peek outside my window to see the blue Honda parked next to the garage, my entire body tenses. Jesus! Of all nights to suddenly show up. This has Vince written all over it. It's just like him to send the pretty blonde who has had plenty of experience taking care of me when I've been at my worst.

Who knows what Nero could have said to him once he left the ring tonight. Either way, Vince is smart and I'm sure she was his first call.

Rachel showing up though, only complicates things further. While she technically has a room here at the house, it's been vacant for quite some time. When Vince hired her, the job came with a room, so she had a place to rest and could keep an eye on me at the same time. It came in handy on the nights she had to sedate me because my behaviors got so out of control.

When all other attempts fail, their last resort was to knock my ass out cold.

These days, her room remains unoccupied because she has no reason to use it. I'm a different person now compared to back then. The downside, I miss seeing her pretty face. Among other parts of her, but that's not what I should be thinking about right now.

It's just that when it comes to Rachel, aka, my so-called *'babysitter'* there are a few things to know. Her job was to watch over me and deal with my shitty mood swings, take me to doctor appointments, and most importantly make sure I took my medications. Basically, all the crap a personal home health care worker would do and more.

The more, was to keep my ass out of trouble. Hell, she was paid, and paid well for her services. Did I give her a run for her money, hell yes? I was an out of control dick, angry at the world.

Still am, most days!

Rachel never complained though. I respect her for that but would never tell her that to her face. Once the medications started to work and my behaviors turned around, her services weren't needed nearly as much. These days I feel older than my years and would like to think wiser, but that's up for debate depending on who you ask on any given day.

Given the amount of stress I've been under lately, it's more than fucking bizarre I've been able to remain as calm as I have considering the shit storm that's been brewing. It shocks the hell out of me that I've been able to channel my anger into more of a ticking time bomb, waiting for the exact moment to implode.

What's even more surprising, I'm doing it all medication free. This is the longest I've gone without taking them, and no one seems the wiser. The best way to describe how I'm feeling is eerily despondent from any crippling emotion whatsoever. It makes me wonder if this is what my father felt at certain times throughout his life. Dominic, by all accounts, was the master of controlling his rage until it was time to unleash it. Maybe Salvo was onto something the night he compared my odd behavior with my late fathers. In that moment, I felt a real sense of pride. A feeling I've rarely ever felt before.

What I can say with certainty is without Rachel's help during the hardest of times in my life, I'm not sure I'd be here today. It's scary, but truthful. At the point her visits dwindled to a quick check in with me, Rachel had already fallen under my charm. I could say she took advantage of me in my weaker moments, but that'd be a flat-out, bullshit of a lie.

A high-strung guy like me needs to blow off steam from time to time and if it wasn't with one of the waitresses at The One Eighty Club, Rachel was my go to girl.

As far I know, my uncle remains clueless still to this day. But, what did he expect by hiring a sexy blonde to be my caregiver. She's a bombshell, with a rockin' body. Tall and curvy in all the right places. With an amazing ass, and perky, full tits. If you look at her from the side, Rachel has this tiny waist shows off her perfectly round ass. Girl's got it going on.

Shit cracks me up when I think of her as my personal nurse, because it reminds me of some old porno flicks Dex and I used to watch. In fact, we watched them so many times, the tape wore out. I can still picture it in my mind though, Rachel enters my room in a white, skimpy nursing outfit. Which she never wore even when I begged her to. But in my perverted mind that's what she'd be wearing on her knees in front of me. Looking up at me with nothing but sin in her eyes.

Without looking, I know she's standing outside my door watching me, and the last thing on my mind is roleplaying some old porno flick. The only hiccup in that plan is I've been drinking and she's only an arm length away. It's either a disaster in the making, or at best, a distraction.

Since, I don't need either at the moment, my mission of destroying my room in the process of speed packing, is still on. The best thing for me is to be long gone before Vince returns home and wants to talk. God forbid, Marcus shows up with him.

That shit is not helpful to focus on, I need to remain on the task at hand. Ignoring Rachel's stare, I continue to pull things from my closet and rush to pile them on my bed, next to my bag. I'm moving so fast, I begin to sweat all over again. It's not like I need much in the way of clothes and whatever I don't have, I can buy. Who knows how long I'll be gone anyway.

Every cell in my body is hyper-aware of Rachel's quiet presence as she stands in my doorway. Figuring I can't ignore her much longer, I turn and give her a stern look that says I'm not interested in a social visit. It's a look she's used to seeing from me, and just like then, she seems to be unaffected. Back then, all she had to do was batt her pretty eyes and I'd eventually cave in.

Just, not tonight!

Rachel knows the drill, it's a gamble whenever she walks in just which Declan she would be facing. The manageable, or the unmanageable, asshole. She's a smart girl, she'll figure it out. I'd pretty much guarantee it judging by the unforgiving scowl on my face.

Yet, she doesn't take the hint, she ignores it altogether.

"Declan," she replies in a tender and endearing voice, "are you alright?"

Shit, I almost forgot how sweet Rachel's voice is, but on cue my dick remembers and betrays me by growing hard. It remembers what that sweet mouth of hers can do, and all I can think, is *really?* This is not the time for this shit!

My scowl matches my intent. "You need to leave!" My tone alone she should have her walking in the other direction.

Rachel just stands there with her head off to the side, and sighs. "Come, on, Declan."

Her refusal to leave is annoying, but not enough to keep me from turning back around to continue to pack. Until I feel her sneak up behind me and gently rest a hand on my shoulder. It's not a welcome touch. With a swift jerk of my shoulder, I deject her attempt to comfort me and angrily begin to jam my clothes in my bag.

My jaw starts to twitch as the sweet scent of her cologne fills my room. Her presence is delaying me and making things ten times as hard. By hard, I mean the growing ache between my legs that is begging for attention.

Should be no surprise since I fought earlier tonight. Any other fight night by now, I'd typically be spending time lost between some chick's legs instead of being moody and pissed off, and packing.

The struggle is real since Rachel has been that chick on many occasions. The natural urge to satisfy my dick's need is reaching what little self-control I have left in me. Earlier tonight I wasn't in control of things, and look where that got me?

It only fuels my drive to take it all back... starting with her.

Thoughts of packing are pushed aside for more pressing matters.

Rachel has two choices. Either one works, but the latter involves her lips wrapped around my thick shaft. Right about now, that sounds way better than having her leave. The choice is hers, and time is ticking. I'm so worked up it won't take me long anyway.

With a lazy grin, I abruptly reach out and grab her wrists, pulling her body flush against mine. Her face immediately lights up reacting to my jet-black, lust-crazed eyes. The last thing Rachel does is give me any indication she wants to leave. Her lips part as the heat of desire flickers in her honey colored eyes.

The leftover testosterone from the fight earlier, suddenly overtakes all of my senses. I act like I have all the time in the world, forgetting about getting the hell out of here. With her body pressed against mine, I'm fixated on her heavy breathing and the noises she gives with each loud exhale. The sweet scent of her perfume is a like a knockout punch. I have never needed to come so fucking much in my life as I do right now. With the tips of my fingers wrapped around her wrists, I can feel her pulse take off.

"Are you going to leave?" The slight roughness of my voice is out of desperate need as my eyes linger on her full lips. Lips that happen to be the cure for my dying ache.

Rachel's eyes dance over my face. "No, I'm not leaving," she says before teasing me by gliding her tongue to wet her lower lip. "I'm here for *you*."

I believe every word that she's being genuine, but that doesn't stop a distrustful smirk that slowly emerges on my face. As much as my ego wants to think she's purely here for me, I don't trust that easily. Especially these days.

After a quiet moment, Rachel unfortunately only confirms my suspicion. "Vince called concerned and wanted me to come check on you."

My grin slips into a disgruntle frown that has me swallowing the bitter taste left in my mouth.

A growl emerges once again. "Is that the only reason you're here? For my uncle?"

Rachel's cheeks heat up, because the professional line between us was crossed long ago. With my arms suddenly crossed, my eyes narrow as she nervously starts to twist at the ends of her sweater.

"No, I'm not here because he asked me too," she swallows loudly. "I'm here because I want to be here. For you, Declan."

My face is stone cold, but my dick is standing up to applause. Rachel's eyes lower to zero in on the obvious and her eyes immediately turn feisty. Big, bold and daring at the same time she gets this wicked grin on her face. It sends a warmth throughout my body that I'm not able to resist one moment longer.

When I take a predatory step forward, Rachel lightly chuckles, taking a step back. It's like a game of cat and mouse. We continue this until her back bumps into the wall, having me snicker with a *tsk'ing* noise letting her know I got her right where I want her. Standing barely an inch apart, her rapid breathing swells the cups of her breasts to burst under her Navy-Blue V-neck sweater. With her cleavage on full display.

It's fucking glorious!

My hands tangle in her hair as I aggressively take her lips with mine. She melts into my body, taking all I have to give. Rachel is just what the doctor ordered, and she knows better than anyone what I need. Turning raw power into passion, and then ultimately satisfaction.

She slides her hands up my chest before giving me a hefty shove back. Her show of control barely moves me an inch, but it's enough to notice her red and swollen lips. A darkness sets in her eyes before she moves lightning fast. Grabbing a hold of my shirt with both hands, she pulls me back in for more.

Crazy woman likes it as rough as I do. When her hands snake around the back of my neck, she tucks them under the collar of my shirt. Her cool touch against the heat of my skin feels incredible when ten razor sharp daggers, slice into my back. The rush of endorphins creates an overpowering high, I fucking savor.

My back is consumed in this stinging blaze that shortly thereafter, turns into a pleasurable burn. It's a pain like non-other. A pain that sets me free. All of the anguish, the suffering and the anger I've been imprisoned with for so long, suddenly doesn't feel as crippling.

I can finally breathe.

A moment when the voices return.

For as long as I can remember, I've been plagued with voices that torment me with dark thoughts. Only, to turn around and seduce me with the single promise to end all my suffering. All I have to do is listen and give into them.

Is it pleasure, you seek?

Fuck yeah! Right now, it's all about my pleasure.

Wouldn't you rather feel like this all the time? To be in control of your emotions, instead of being a prisoner, strapped with them?

No doubt about that. Yes!

Then, it's time. All you have to do is deny any emotion that makes you feel vulnerable. If you can't feel it, it can't hurt you!

Exactly how the fuck do I do that?

It's been in you all along, you just need to switch your feelings off. Close your eyes, feel the change take place. When you open them, it will be done! Remember, emotions are for weak-minded people. Not the strong!

It's hard to argue with voices in your head because if you talk out loud people will think your insane. Who knows, maybe I am. Before I can close my eyes or speak out loud though, Rachel does the one thing that pushes me over the edge. She sinks her claws into my back once again, this time deep enough to draw blood. My back wretches as I absorb the pain that naturally closes my eyes.

I'm no masochist, but my racing heart due to the sudden surge with adrenaline is a new kind of high.

It sets off a change.

Like a flip of a switch.

Chapter Fourteen

"No Turning Back"

The feeling is surreal. I envision myself standing in the middle of the ocean watching the tide carry out the last of the pain in my heart along with it. A burden finally set-free.

With each passing second, the after effects lift me until I feel ten-feet tall, growing broader and bolder. It's both, euphoric and exhilarating, and it leaves me feeling nearly indestructible.

It's a change that has me wondering if Rachel can sense any of it but since she's busy grinding her hot pussy against my hard thigh, I doubt it. Her hot little hands are touching any part of my bare skin they can reach. It's damn hypnotic to watch her use my body to get herself off.

Every pleasurable moan that leaves her lips, stroke my ultraistic ego that wants more than anything to exercise my will over her.

"You came for my cock, didn't you, Rachel?"

My brash talk turns the apple of her cheeks bright red as excitable shivers cast down her arms.

"Oh, yes." She softly sighs, raising her eyes to mine.

With minimal space between us, I slide my hands down the curves of her body until they come to rest under the globes her ass. In one swift movement, I haul her to my chest, then aggressively pin her body against the wall. Rachel automatically wraps her legs around my waist, anchoring her pussy to align with my steel length.

The lack of tenderness is a turn on for me and judging from her wide-eyes and erratic breathing that sounds more like a wild panting, I'd say she's plenty turned on as well. The only emotion I see on her face is desire. She's so needy right now, I could do whatever I want. The best part... she'd let me.

Just to play with her, I grumble next to her ear. "You're such a little whore, just begging to be fucked."

Like I expected, Rachel doesn't deny it. Her teeth sink into her lower lip as she shamelessly grins. I can't help but chuckle, because this damn girl is putty in my hands and it leaves me with one thought. More.

I lower my hand over her pussy and roughly rub the seam of her jeans directly over her clit. The welcome friction sends Rachel's head back, exhaling in a pleasure-seeking sigh. If the inferno of heat against my hand is any indication, Rachel is soaking wet ready for my hard cock to fuck her into oblivion. Impatient as hell, I jam one hand down the front of her jeans and easily slide my fingers under the elastic of her panties. Hot damn! Rachel does not disappoint. She's deliciously bare and sopping wet.

"Fuck, yes!"

With my fingers coated in her warm juices, I lightly stroke over her clit.

"Yeeessss!"

As my fingers slide down her slit and tease her opening, Rachel's breathing hitches with anticipation. Timing my move perfectly, I sink my teeth into the tender skin behind her ear at the same time my fingers abruptly probe up inside her warm pussy.

The mixture of pleasure and pain has Rachel erupting in wild whimpers that echoes throughout my bedroom. The slick flow of her juices lubricates my probing fingers as they penetrate in and out of her. Chasing her climax, Rachel starts to slide sideways. To keep her upright and where I want her, I secure my thigh between her legs, preventing her from escaping. With one hand playing with her pussy, my other hand tangles in her hair and tilts her head to the side closest to my mouth.

"You're so wet for me, aren't you? *Nurse Rachel!*"

I sensually tease her, knowing she'll go crazy for it. Sure enough, she blushes with a smile like she's embarrassed by it.

"You like it when I call you that, don't you? It turns you on."

If Rachel likes one thing, it's to role play.

"Yes," she whimpers, clinging onto my shirt. "I shouldn't... but I do."

Fuck that! She's an adult. I'm an adult. With only three years age difference between us, she can pretend and act all righteous, but there is no denying that sex is written all over face. Not to mention, she's currently gushing all over my fingers.

Ignoring her last remark, I reply slightly miffed. "You, fucking love what I do to you."

There's no denying that. Rachel's body remembers the things I can do to make her feel alive. Besides, there has never been anything nice and sweet between us. It's always been raw and gritty. What can I say? Rachel like's it rough.

To prove my point, my fingers penetrate deeper and faster while Rachel is closer to climaxing. She feels damn good, squeezing my fingers, but when I feel her breathing change, like she's on the brink. I recall her shitty comment and deny her any pleasure by removing my hand from her pants, with an arrogant smirk.

A frustrated Rachel, clings to my body whimpering, knowing her climax was that close. Her displeasure only satisfies me. Instead of ticking me off with her bullshit by saying she *shouldn't* like or want what's happening between us, she could be coming right now. Since she did tick me off, she *shouldn't* mind waiting a bit longer for that much needed release.

"That was mean."

Her cheeks are rosy red while she sounds a bit out of breath. When she looks up at me and pins me with a look of desperation, I laugh.

"So needy."

This time, I tease her by running the tip of my nose along her jawline and when I reach the dip in her chin, I raise my lips to lightly brush over the top of hers. Her eyes widen, like she's expecting me to deepen the kiss, but I have other plans.

I lift my middle finger that was deep inside her pussy and part my lips as her tangy taste floods my taste buds. Releasing a low and savoring moan, like she's the best thing I've ever tasted. Rachel's eyes remain transfixed on my finger as her mouth falls open with a whimpered response.

What kind of gentlemen would I be if I didn't share? I offer her a finger still glistening wet with her juices. "Taste how sweet you are?"

Rachel willingly complies by wrapping her hot lips around my finger. Jesus, the warmth of her mouth sends a shot of desire straight to my raging length. My hips jerk forward seeking friction against her lower stomach, while her mouth wraps around my finger like a glove. Her devotion to my finger is so intense, it nearly brings me to my knees.

Foreplay is over!

I urge her to her knees. "Do the same to my cock."

As Rachel drops her to knees, her lips part in a wicked grin, and whatever air that was left in my lungs, expels the second she gets busy freeing my cock from my jeans. Nine inches of smooth, hard muscle then probes between her plush lips, finding nirvana inside her warm mouth.

Rachel fists the base of my cock in one hand as her tongue swirls the head like she's teasing me the way I teased her earlier. Only, I'm not having any of that.

I jerk my hips forward, making my cock disappear inside her mouth. Clearly, that gets her attention. "Take me deep and make me come down that throat of yours."

With that, she starts sucking like a dream, making it way too easy for me to get her to do what I want. When I want it. That should fucking thrill me that she's working my cock like a pro, but it doesn't satisfy me for long. The urge to be in total control is just too powerful.

To take charge, I wrap both of my hands are around her head and start to fuck her mouth. I'm controlling the pace, and tempo when she starts to resist me by gagging. It's damn irritating, because Rachel is not allowing her throat to adjust to my size.

"Relax your throat!" I urge her with my jaws set and mid-thrusting. Rachel tries by breathing through her nose but fails. To help her, I slide a hand down the side of her face to massage her neck and guide her head further back. That should do the trick. It's worked before.

Do I let up? No.

I keep feeding her my cock, going as far back as I can, but the last thing I want is for her to throw up all over my junk. What I want, is for her to relax her mouth long enough to satisfy me. She's done this plenty of times before, she's just not concentrating enough. Her mind is not about satisfying me, and that pisses me off.

Rachel came here tonight knowing full well what would happen if she did. Besides, the word no has yet to come from her pretty little mouth. The way her cheeks hollow out with the perfect amount of suction is the tipping point for me to ease up on how far I thrust inside her mouth. The sensation of her moans as they vibrate against my dick is fuck amazing.

She's definitely hit the spot that's going to send me over the edge as the familiar build up starts to spread. With my head back and eyes closed, I'm set to explode when I feel a shift in Rachel's body. The wicked thought she's touching her pussy is definitely the kind of action I do not want miss. In my mind, I'm envisioning blowing my load while watching her stroke her clit. When I glance down, I see I'm way off base.

Rachel is not touching her pussy at all. She's discreetly reaching behind her and pulling something out of her back pocket. The crazy thing, she's not missing a beat sucking me off.

What the hell?

My balls freeze up, but Rachel has yet to realize I'm watching her. When her hand slowly comes around to the front, I'm fucking shocked to see what she is holding in her hand. A fully loaded syringe.

It dawns on me what she's really up too. This lying, manipulative bitch came here to distract me enough, so she could inject me with a tranquilizer to knock my ass out.

Anger rocks me as the pit in my stomach explodes with such fury, I jolt back to free my cock from her mouth. Bitch doesn't deserve my cock. Rachel is so startled, she jerks her head up to witness the wrath in my eyes. My lips pull back, baring my teeth as I erupt with the back of my hand connecting with the side of her face.

"What the *fuck* do you think you're going to do with that?" I explode with such anger my face feels inferno red, which happens to be the color of her burning cheek.

Rachel just stares back at me dumbstruck, rubbing her cheek. I expect her to cry or at the very least act sorry for her bullshit actions, but she does neither.

"Vince wanted me to help you," she argues under her breath while my eyes stare at the nasty needle. Even my nightmares know what's on the other side once the contents freely flow in my veins.

"After tonight, he said you couldn't be trusted on your own. He hoped by sedating you, that you would sleep off whatever it is going on inside your head." She may sound sincere, but her face shows no signs of it. "We just want to help you, Declan."

Help me?

Is this some fucking joke?

Whatever bullshit Vince thinks he knows, he doesn't. None of them do. What they all fail to realize is just how far I would go to deal with the fucking devil himself to get the answers I need. Which makes Rachel's excuse laughable. If she thinks I'm buying into her innocent look, and her well thought out words, she's seriously mistaken. She should know better than anyone to lie to my face when I know if someone is trying to bullshit me. Plus, none of it matches the honest look behind her eyes. I can't put my finger on it yet, but something is off with her.

As I hastily zip my jeans, Rachel starts to scramble.

"Declan, please?" She reaches out to me which is not a good idea on her part.

"Please, WHAT?" I take a step back trying to wrap my head around the fact the one person sent to help me is nothing but a manipulative and lying...

"Bitch, tell me something?" I demand with pure venom behind my voice. "Did Vince tell you to suck my cock first or do it after you knocked me the hell out?"

Her reaction is priceless!

Rachel gasps and looks at me utterly repulsed, which is exactly what I wanted to see.

Fear. Shock. Worry.

I see her in a whole new light, and it disgusts me.

An angry outburst explodes in my mind.

She's no better than every other person who has ever let you down, or flat out lied to you! Haven't you had enough betrayal from the ones who claim to want what's best for you? It's time to show them what happens when they do!

The voice urges me.

The only one person you can count on, is YOU.

It becomes crystal clear to me, this is how my father felt for most of his life. He wrote it all down, explaining the only person he could rely on was himself. With the voices in his head, guiding him. I know what I need to do. Channel him.

Closing my eyes, the answer is immediate.

Make her FUCKING PAY for her deceit.

Opening my eyes, a chilling sensation takes place. When I look at Rachel, I lower my chin and expose a deep snarl that lifts the corner of my lip. Her eyes say it all. She's frightened.

It's a good look on her. So, I decide to keep it there as long as possible. When I take a step in her direction, Rachel instantly cowers against the wall. Unsure of what's to come.

Physical pain is something I know well. And would be the quickest way to make her pay. That's not going to happen. What I want is for her to suffer. To feel every bit of what her betrayal has done to me. Ten times over.

Standing over her with contempt in my eyes, I lower to my knees so there is barely an inch between us. Eye to eye, Rachel swallows loudly as her shallow breaths mix with the heaviness of mine.

"Tell me something?" I ask with a venomous smirk, ready to strike. "Did you have to drop to your knees and suck Vince? All the while wishing it was me instead?"

It's something I've never considered, until right now. And the vision of her on her knees for my uncle makes me sick. What an absolute whore. "All this time I thought he was clueless, but damn, he's been experiencing the goods just like I was."

The contempt she sees in my eyes overshadows the look of disgust in hers when she reaches up and connects with my jaw. The slap is loud enough it vibrates throughout my entire room. I throw my head back, laughing. The physical sting is nothing but foreplay to me.

Teach this lying bitch a lesson!

That's the plan.

"Do you know what the opposite of hurt is, Rachel?"

Her eyes immediately fall to the cheek she just slapped, before looking back at me with an uneasy expression on her face. Low enough that I can barely hear, she answers, "Anger."

I always knew she was a smart girl, but does she know just how angry I really am?

"That's right." I breathe, and then lean in close with my eyes centered on her lying mouth. "Now, tell me who feels better ramming their cock down your throat, you… fucking… whore? Mine or his?"

Judging from the way Rachel jerks her head from mine, I believe that one stung just a bit.

"That's cruel, and low even for you."

That's not low, it's laughable. And I'm just getting started.

"Low, for me! Really? Weren't you the one sucking my cock getting ready to fucking stick me with a needle when I wasn't looking?"

She looks back at me speechless.

"I know it's a bitch to hear the fucking truth, Rachel. But, that shit was low, even for you."

I definitely struck a chord. Her face just explodes. "You," she shrieks, "are a son of a bitch!"

While that is true, it's not up for debate. A conversation for another day, possibly. Right now, we have bigger issues than dredging up old scars about my deadbeat, bitch of mother.

For instance, why Rachel is glaring at me with unusually wide eyes and pupils that continue to jerk back and forth. It reminds me of what an old saying about crazy eyes. Avoid them at all costs because they belong to a crazy person.

Sure enough, Rachel goes certifiable.

She lunges forward, picks up the needle from the floor and lets out a blood curdling scream. Aiming for my torso, Rachel doesn't seem to care where the hell it connects, just that it does. It happens lightning fast, but the bitch knows I fight for a living. The first instinct when feeling threatened is to deflect, then, defend.

I dodge her advance with my forearm out as it connects with her mid-section. Her body is sent spiraling back until she lands with a heavy thud. The syringe drops from her hand as Rachel turns into the exorcist right in front of my eyes. I wait to see if her head will revolve all the way and to see if she will spew green shit across the room.

"You really are pathetic!" She screeches with an unfamiliar menacing undertone to her voice as she scrambles on the floor reaching for the syringe. Instead of rushing over to kick the damn thing out of her hand like I should, I'm looking at her like she's got a few screws loose somewhere.

The Rachel on the floor losing it, is not the Rachel I know. And she definitely wouldn't be looking back at me wildly with savage eyes holding the damn syringe like it's some prized trophy. Before she does anything she will most definitely regret, I give her one chance to save herself. Even though she doesn't deserve it.

"Bitch, I'm not playing with you. I will hurt you if you don't leave my fucking house right now."

Rachel shrugs my warning off with snide chuckle and delivers a blow of her own. "This bitch is going to knock your ass out. Besides," her voice lowers yet again, "if it were up to me, I would have permanently dealt with you a long time ago."

The look on her face, says it all, *gotcha!*

With the hairs on the back of neck standing at attention, my fists instantly curl. "What the fuck are you talking about?"

"It's just a matter of time, Declan." Rachel warns me with an ominous twinkle in her eyes. Then, turns psycho and charges at me again.

Bitch is fast, but not as quick as me.

I have my hand wrapped around her throat before she can make any contact with my body. Her momentum is no match against my iron grasp. My hold is so tight, I can feel the steady beats of her racing pulse. I don't hesitate, I drive her body straight back into the wall with enough force the wall shakes. This time, when she drops the damn syringe, I kick is across the room. Out of her reach.

There is not a muscle in my body that is not shaking with anger. I literally have to fight the urge not to crush her wind pipe.

"*Tell me* what the fuck you are talking about? Or, so, help me, *God* I will snap your fucking neck like a toothpick."

While Rachel struggles to suck in air, her face starts to turn a reddish purple. Clawing at her throat, she scratches the shit out of arms in the process. She only has one option so it's no surprise she nods her head.

I maintain my tight hold just to make sure she sees the seriousness behind my eyes. Once I ease my hand from around her neck, she stumbles to the floor with a hand around her throat. She wheezes for some much needed air.

"Start talking!" I demand as the voice returns.

Teach this BITCH a lesson. She's goading you, making fun of YOU. This is the time to send a message. Show this lying whore what happens when someone crosses you! Show her NOW!

Jesus Christ!

I have to shut the voices out, so I can concentrate on Rachel who is bent over holding up a hand like she needs a minute. The last thing I am feeling is patient. My body is in pre-fight mode. My fists are clenched, and my body is twitching ready to explode. She better start talking soon before I decide to give in the voices. Then, it will be too late. The only way to stop from tearing into her, is to give her a minute. Looking at her only enrages me, so I turn around taking a minute for myself.

Stupid mistake on my part.

Rachel is like a coiled snake, timing her strike. Somehow, the bitch moved so fast and quietly that I didn't realize a damn thing until a sudden pinch in my lower calf startles me enough that I jump back. It's a damn good thing I have fast reflexes because before she can inject the poison in my leg, the back of my hand connects with her other cheek and sends her head flying back. Now she'll have matching marks on both cheeks. I yank the needle from my leg, hoping like hell none of that shit has entered my bloodstream.

If Rachel thought she had seen me at my worst, she has no clue what she's about to encounter.

"WHAT THE FUCK IS WRONG WITH YOU?" I advance so fast, she backs up wiping the blood from her split lip on the back of her hand. The fucked-up part, she's laughing.

"Who the fuck, are you?" I come to realize in that moment, Rachel is not at all who she claims to be.

She continues to laugh like something is really fucking funny. "You have no idea the plans *he* has in store for you."

He?

The plot thickens.

"*Who?*"

Acting like she doesn't hear me, she continues to laugh.

"Who, GODAMMIT?" That certainly got her attention.

As her laugh dies down, she hums. "I'll let you in on a little secret? It's not Vince I've been sucking off all this time, it's the man set out to destroy *you*. Working for Vince was my cover." Grinning victoriously, she tilts her head to the side. "All meant to get to *you*."

All I see is red!

In a flash, I have my hand securely around her neck and lift her from the floor until her legs dangle below.

The mix of blood and adrenaline has my head pounding when the thunderous voice returns.

KILL THIS BITCH!

END HER NOW!!

My nostrils flare with each heavy breath. With renewed determination, I start to squeeze the life out of this lying bitch once and for all. After all, she played me, and my uncle, but something she said bothers me.

"Get to me?" I snarl in her face as salvia spits from my mouth. "Why?"

"Because you have to suffer... like I had to." She struggles but manages to answer in a raspy voice. "Like he's had to suffer. One day, it was always meant to come back on you. You must pay for what your fath..."

I cut off her remaining air supply.

"What the *fuck* are you talking about?"

With small, squealed gasps, she says, "You don't see it now, but... you will. He'll make sure of it. After all... *(gasp)* he got... to *(gasp)* your sweet Liberty... *(gasp)* didn't he?"

There's a fine line when it comes to me. Rachel just crossed that line.

I speak the last words she will ever hear. "I don't need you to tell me who *he* is. I'll find out on my fucking own. He made a grave mistake by sending you here, thinking I'd let you walk free once I found out. He *thought wrong!*" I seethe with fury. "Maybe it's time I send him *a fucking message!!*"

"Wait... wait!" Rachel struggles with the strain of my hand against her vocal chords, but still manages to speak hoarsely.

The last thing I want is to hear anything else she has to say, but for some insane reason, I listen. Even though it's a real struggle. With an intense pounding in my ears, I have no doubt she speaks the truth. What she says clouds my vision and momentarily leaves me in a near catatonic state. Rachel takes full advantage to pull one last desperate stunt. From the tip of her boot, she pulls out a knife and exerts just enough energy to stab it in my left shoulder blade. If she was hoping like hell I'd drop her ass to the floor, she's mistaken.

The last thing I feel is pain. Her twisted story hits me like a bolt of lightning. Setting off violent tremors that start low in my body and gradually work their way upwards to the hand I have around her skinny neck. Her pulse speeds up as she looks at me for the first time with terror behind her eyes.

I never flinch.

While Rachel took pleasure in taunting me with what *his* plans are, my outrage is nothing short of declaring an all-out war.

The goddamned knife sticking out my shoulder makes me want to wipe the fucking smirk from her face. With my face directly in front of hers, my fingers tighten around her neck, pressing, closing. My eyes burn with emptiness and rage knowing her lungs are burning in pain, desperate for the air I deny. Her face turns a sickening color as she struggles to wiggle free.

Do I feel like a monster?

No. I don't.

Rachel knew what was going to happen to her the minute she admitted it was *her* who brought Liberty into this mess. Not to mention, revealing *his* future plans.

This is payback.

She has to pay!

No longer ignoring the voices, the edge of my vision goes dark as I unleash the fury from deep inside.

In her own words, Rachel found the ultimate way to get to me. Then, she told *him*. The truth hurts more than any lie could. It hits me in ways that would turn any saint into a hardened criminal.

With my free hand, I yank the knife from my shoulder and strike with five quick and repetitive slashes. All to her midsection. Erupting, "That's for Liberty, you fucking bitch!!" With the blade in place, I slowly twist it as the fight begins to leave her body.

Rachel's long, skinny fingers furiously claw at my arms until they fall limp at her sides. Eyes still open, I draw a small amount of comfort that the last thing the cunt saw, was me!

My entire body erupts and violently shakes from the massive rush of adrenaline. When I peer down at my crimson stained hand.

Her haunting last words only prove this shit isn't over... not by a long shot.

Reality comes crashing down around me. The room begins to spin as my ability to breathe stops. Forced to ease my hold around Rachel's neck, I toss her lifeless body aside.

Polarized with just what happened, I'm unable to hold back any longer. Falling to my knees, my head falls back as every ounce of aggression spills out in a bellowing outburst. Until I drop in sheer exhaustion.

"FUUUUCCCKKK!!!"

They say when one is close to dying they confess their sins. All Rachel did was taunt me with things yet to come.

"Jesus. Fucking. Christ." I pace the floor with blood-stained hands in my hair. My eyes zero in on Rachel, then, drift to the syringe lying near the open door. It gives me a moment to reflect before the fire in my chest returns.

Shit just went to a whole new level.

I was to play by *his rules*... and I did!

Those rules have changed!

Chapter Fifteen

"Set Back"

*T*HERE ARE CERTAIN THINGS *I tolerate. Incompetence isn't one of them.*

Yet, here I sit, in the dim light of my office facing the fact I foolishly put my confidence and money in an incompetent, fucking idiot.

A mistake I won't make twice.

When I made the decision to make my move, I did so thoughtfully and with careful planning. I knew once this started there was no going back. I willingly took that risk knowing full well what will happen if my name is linked back to any of it. That's my level of commitment because after years of harboring bad blood, my need for retribution was something I could no longer deny. From there, things just fell into place.

The faint double knock at the door alerts me that Dio has arrived.

"Boss."

My right-hand man enters with a curt nod of his head. Following behind is an anxiety filled Curtis, who looks like he'd rather be anywhere but here.

He should be.

Immediately sensing the tension in the room, he moves forward like he's sinking in quick sand while avoiding any direct eye contact with me.

Not a wise a move on his part.

Dio jumps in with a helpful nudge to his back as Curtis stumbles forward. My silence has him looking around the room like he's expecting to be jumped at any moment. It's completely unnecessary on his part, unless he pisses me off even more than he already has. If that's the case, the baseball bat in my lower drawer is within reach.

When Curtis seems reluctant to sit down, Dio forcibly plants his ass in one of the chairs directly across from my desk. Even though Curtis is a big guy, Dio handles him with ease. Quite simply, Dio is a force not to reckon with. Towering over Curtis by several inches, his bald head, dark glasses and black suit only adds to his intimidation factor. Dio is a man of few words, but full of action.

With Curtis firmly in his seat, he appears even more skittish when Dio comes to stand directly behind him. Arms crossed. Looking like he might piss himself, a fretful Curtis slowly turns back around pale as a fucking ghost. His hesitancy to look me in the eye proves to me he's not the fierce fighter he claims.

He's nothing but an opportunistic street thug who fucked me over tonight. Killing him now might make me feel better short term and as funny as it's going to sound. Losing ten large on him tonight might be the only thing that keeps him alive. I sure as fuck did not get where I am today without using every opportunity to gain leverage over people. Ten large is a hell of a lot of leverage to use at my disposal. He may prove to be useful to me in the future.

Right now, what I need from him is to answer for his actions earlier tonight. And to do it without me killing him in the process. Given his intelligence level, there is no guarantee he's walking out of here still breathing.

Composed with a straight face, I lean forward to get a good read of his eyes. "Do you have any idea how much time and effort I put into my plans?"

A simple yes, or no, will do.

Only Curtis doesn't seem eager to give me either. He's busy shifting uncomfortably in his seat and uttering shit under his breath. His lack of discipline with his actions earlier tonight and his current disrespect for me has me all but reaching for the baseball bat that's hidden in my lower drawer.

"Just what the fuck were you thinking?" *My fists slam down on my desk.*

Curtis jerks in his seat.

"I...I..." he stutters as sweat begins to break out across forehead. Knees bouncing wildly, he clears his throat and avoids my intense and disapproving glare by lowering the rim of his cap.

"Are you trying to insult me? If so, I'll fucking kill you right now." That gets his attention.

His head snaps up as he fumbles over his own tongue. "Why would you think... no, of course not."

"Remove your hat and look me in the face like a fucking man." Forgoing the bat in my lower drawer, I reach for my gun in the top drawer instead.

His fucking hat is off as he wipes the perspiration on his forehead with his arm. Eyes on me, I lay the gun on the desk and pick up what's left of my scotch. I have never needed a drink so bad in my fucking life. Swirling the amber liquid a few times, I swallow it down in one shot before hurling the glass across the room. The glass shatters everywhere.

Curtis jumps out of his seat but is quickly forced to stay put with the help of Dio's hands firmly placed on his shoulders.

The irony of the shattered glass is not lost on me. It's oddly reminiscent of what happened to my plans tonight.

With a slow, disapproving shake of my head, my expression turns to stone. "I was watching you out there tonight. Strutting your shit, taunting the boy like you were the superior fighter."

Curtis takes offense to my comment and presses his hand against his chest. "I am the better fighter," he scoffs.

"Really?" I lift one eye about to educate his ass on a thing or two since he's blinded by his own ignorance. "Let me tell you something, you, fucking, ignorant idiot. I handed you a guaranteed win and you still LOST THE FIGHT." Enraged to the point I feel like I'm suffocating, I loosen the tie around my neck. "Tell me something Curtis, do you consider me a fucking idiot?"

I watch the look of terror wash over his face.

"What?" he gasps with his back straight as a board. "No, never." He defends himself by adamantly shaking his head back and forth. When he reads the look on my face, he corrects his mistake. "No, sir."

Fucking right.

"Then answer me this, what do you think I should do since you fucked up my plans and lost me a hell of a lot of money tonight. Money, I bet on you?" I ask the question not giving a damn with what he has to say in return. I want to watch him squirm in his seat with endless possibilities of what I could do to him. To see his fear.

And fear is all I see as he scrambles to respond. "Why not just take Declan out if you hate the guy so much?"

He fails to own up to his failure by deflecting it all back to the boy.

With my arms on my desk, I lean forward. "You really aren't very intelligent, are you?" *I ask with an ingenuine laugh from deep in my throat.* "Have you always been like this or have you been hit one too many times in the head?" *The rise in my voice matches my fuming temper.* "If I wanted him dead, I would have done it years ago. That's not the purpose behind any of this." *I motion with my hand in the air before spitefully glaring into his widening eyes.* "And if you ever question me again, I'll put a fucking bullet between your eyes. My motives are not a concern of yours. What you should be more concerned with, is how you are going to work off the ten grand you owe me."

Mouth going slack, Curtis stills. "What do you have in mind?"

"For now, nothing. Dio has the arrangements for you to lay low until I contact you. Is that understood? No screwing up again."

"I understand, sir. I'll do whatever you need me to do." *Curtis exhales as if he was holding his breath as his whole-body sags in relief. His life has been spared. Little does he know he still needs to pay for his fuck-up. That's not negotiable. To let him walk out of here with no repercussions is something I cannot let stand.*

Curtis never saw it coming.

For the last few minutes, I've had a firm grasp on the bat as it rests on my lap. Just as Curtis stands thinking he was going to start a mini vacation while laying low, Dio grabs his wrist and forces his hand on my desk. The strike is hard and fast. And it sends him to his knees.

"Jesus CHRIST."

"Close enough, you fucking imbecile. That was for disobeying and not following my plan. Don't ever do it again. Next time, I'll break every bone in your fucking body starting with your feet.

"Dio get this low life piece of shit out of my office and make sure he gets out of sight and stays there." *Earlier, I gave Dio the information with very strict instructions on where to take Curtis for the foreseeable future. An out of the way cabin, I rented months ago. He needs to be out of the public eye so no one can find him, especially Declan."*

"Yes, boss. I'll take care of it. No worries." *Dio answers with authority, dragging Curtis and his bad hand clutched to his chest.*

The relief I felt moments ago is short lived. With the bat still firmly in my hand I unleash my frustrations in an angry outburst, smashing everything in sight. All night I've kept myself in check and played my part, not daring to show the real anger swelling inside. The longer I have to keep up this charade, the harder this is going to be. By the time I stop, I'm out of breath as I take in the damage I've caused. Damn. My office resembles a demolition zone. None of it affects me much until I see my favorite desk lamp that cost me a small fortune, smashed to pieces.

Stepping over debris, I sink in my chair that somehow survived with only minor damage to the arms. As I turn and face the windows, I fumble with my tie before tossing it on the floor.

Just beyond the densely wooded area that lines the backside of the property, is Vince and Declan's home. I can't help but wonder what the boy will do now that he has the photos in his possession. Declan's unpredictable behavior does pose some concerns. I need to think fast and set things in motion earlier than I planned to.

Which reminds me to look at the time. By now, I should have heard something from Rachel. My long time secret weapon. Without her inside information, none of this could have worked as well as it has. Even though I encouraged her to get into a physical relationship with him, I fucking despised the idea of him ejaculating inside her pussy. I had to come to terms that a fuck here and there and the occasional blow-job was worth it for her to gain his trust and collect valuable information I could use against him.

After tonight, I feared the boy might run, but was relieved to find out Vince had already phoned her. Of course, he was worried about Declan, so he asked her to check in with him. That shit fit perfectly into my plans.

Given the time that has passed, Rachel should have injected Declan by now sending his ass for a two or three day sleeping coma. Enough time for me to plan out my next move. However, I can't be complacent when it comes to him. If there is one thing I know, it's a desperate man is a dangerous man.

That is something I know a thing or two about. Makes me wonder out of the two of us, who is more desperate?

When the phone rings, I assume it's Rachel telling me it's done. Only, it's not her name that shows up on the Caller ID.

Fuck, what could he want at this hour?

It's not what he says.

It's how he says it.

"We have a big fucking problem..."

Chapter Sixteen

"Road Trip"

NOT BEING ABLE TO TURN back is no longer just an empty threat, it's my reality and it's just as fucking brutal as the sight before me. A motionless Rachel, lying face down in a pool of her own blood.

Do I regret it?

No, and for one simple reason. If it wasn't for Rachel, Liberty would still be alive today. That evil bitch found the one thing that meant everything to me and gave her to *him* because she knew it would destroy me.

Even though my uncle couldn't have known her true intentions, it was ultimately his decision to hire her. So, right or wrong, I put some of the blame squarely on his shoulders. It's the reason I left him a not so subtle message on the wall in her room, in her blood. Next to her lifeless body, I scattered copies of each photo I received earlier tonight. Above her head, the words read, *Lying whore deserved what she got*. That should get his attention when he gets home.

After I had a moment to cool off and clean up, I grabbed the rest of my things.

The only way I'm going to catch this son of a bitch is to be one step ahead of him. Thanks to Rachel and her big mouth, she gave me a chance to do just that.

I paid close attention to every word she rasped in between whimpered breaths. Rachel met her fate, and in doing so, helped free me from feeling powerless. Instead of being the hunted, I will now become the hunter!

I can't imagine *he* would ever think Rachel would run her mouth to me about him or his plans, but damn, at the off chance *his* woman could be that fucker's downfall... now that's karma.

I stayed stoic as she told me about his plans to go after Willow, Dominic and Izzy's daughter, and my half-sister. I have no idea why, since I've never met the girl, but who knows what that crazy fucker is thinking. The way I see it, I get the opportunity to meet my long-lost relatives.

Rachel all but confirmed my suspicions about Kara, my father's sister. I'll wait to meet with her last. After all, she was the one who pulled the trigger and murdered him.

I can keep my true identity a secret until it's time to drop that little bomb. It's hard to say what I'll most look forward to, catching that son of a bitch or coming face to face with *them*. Either way, it's going to be one hell of a reunion.

BAGS IN HAND, I LOCK the door behind me as I step outside to the night's cool breeze. What I see next stops me in my tracks.

A casual-looking Dex is leaning against his car like he has no care in the world, eyes to the sky like he's stargazing. He has no clue the shit-show he would have walked into if he went inside my house instead. As if he saw me from the corner of his eye, Dex swings his head my way and frowns before muttering something under his breath.

"What are you doing here, Dex?"

Like I said something funny, the corners of his mouth lifts into a sly smile when his eyes lower to my bags. "Well, it seems I know you better than you know yourself."

I have no idea what that means, but the slow arch of his left eyebrow makes me self-conscious. Thinking about the bloody scene in my room, I swiftly give myself a once over. That's when I see a streak of blood on the inside of my left wrist. Considering how much of it there was, I'm amazed that's all I see.

After I moved Rachel to her room, I stripped down and showered determined to rid myself of that bitch once and for all. It's not like I could leave the house covered in blood and not be noticed. As discreetly as possible, I wipe my wrist on the side of my dark jeans, playing it off as an itch.

Hopefully Dex didn't catch it. Though I'm not entirely sure, since he's suddenly shaking his head and making an irritating *'tsking'* noise with his mouth. It fucking annoys me and instantly has my blood boiling to the point I can no longer hold back the chaos in my head. An unrelenting consequence of being off my meds and one that is not easy to regain control of. When it comes my meds, I have a real love/hate for how they make me feel. It's times like these when my emotions run so high that I start to second guess everything. Who wouldn't after a night like I had. My nerves are fucking shot and I'm not sure how much more I can take in one night.

I cop an attitude and lash out at my best friend. "Just what the fuck is that supposed to mean, Dex, *you know me better than myself?*"

He casually points to the bags in my hand. "First tell me where you are off to in such a hurry?"

With a heavy roll of my eyes, I snidely comment, "I don't have time for thirty questions Dex, and I sure as hell don't have to explain myself to you." I march past him on my way to my car that happens to be parked next to his. With a pop of the trunk, I talk under my breath. "I wasn't aware I needed to check in with you. Besides, what I'm doing has nothing to do with you."

"Wow," he counters back in a tone that is condescending. "That's how you're going to play it, huh?"

My eyes meet his in a cold stare. "Dex, I'm just saying none of this is *your* business. I need to get out of town for a few days, that's all. I'm not trying to be a dick, so stop pissing me off. I got a lot of shit on my mind."

He faces me like he's at the end of his rope. He thrusts his hands in the air and accuses me of being a royal dick when all he is trying to do is be a friend. "God," he loses it, kicking up dirt with his shoes like a child having a tantrum, "you are such a pain in the ass sometimes."

I toss the last of my bags in the trunk and turn to argue with a six-foot man-child, nose to nose. "What the fuck do you want from me?"

My fists are drawn tight and my breathing is sporadic when the first wave of exhaustion finally hits. This day has been both physically and emotionally draining, and that's not counting the stress I've been living with leading up to tonight. I'm spent, thoroughly frustrated and fucking angry.

My attempt to slam the trunk is stopped by an equally frustrated Dex and his overpowering hands. He gets in my face, as angry as I've ever seen him.

"How about the truth, Declan? Just what the fuck happened with you tonight? It sure as hell wasn't a fight. Not on your part anyway!"

Jesus! So this is what has him so upset? The fucking fight feels like it happened days ago, considering all the other shit that's happened since. Now is just not the time to talk.

"I got beat," I exclaim with a I don't really give a shit attitude that stands against everything I stand for. With the idea he'll buy it. "Simple as that."

Dex huffs and deliberately throws his palms down. "Fuck that!" he heckles, "That's bullshit, and you know it! You're ten times the fighter Curtis is! Just tell me the truth and let me help you. Why is that so goddamn hard?"

The more he presses, the harder this becomes. I'm stubborn as hell, and him pushing is only going to make things worse. As it is, my teeth are grinding against one another. I've wasted enough time.

"I need time! Just let it be, Dex. Do not push me on this, not when I'm this close to losing my shit with you. After tonight... that's not a good idea."

His head rests back as he grumbles at the sky above. The minute he lowers his face again, he spots the blue Honda parked next to the garage. Dex looks over at me with a knowing grin on his face. He knows full well who that car belongs to and the sordid relationship I had with her.

Shit.

"Huh." He whistles with a shake of his head and looks as if he's painting a visual image in his head. "I see Rachel is here. Tell me, did she help you relieve any stress? Because if she did, it sure as hell didn't help your mood any."

The moment he mentions her name, it's like dousing myself in kerosene and lighting it on fire. I ignore the pain of biting my tongue as the taste of rusty metal flows freely in my mouth. A vision of her lifeless body fills my mind as the echo of voices rejoice in her demise.

"When I left her," I point over my shoulder, toward my bedroom window, "she was a bloody mess."

"Bloody mess, huh?" He eyeballs me completely caught off guard like he's trying to make sense of my comment. "Kinky... I guess."

Couldn't be any farther from the truth. "Nothing kinky about it," I scowl, "She's dead."

The shock on his face searches for clarity in mine. "She's... what?"

I suddenly regret saying a word, but there is no taking it back now. "Just remember, you asked for this."

He lowers his chin and sighs. *Give me a break!*

Fine. "I nearly choked the fucking life out her. Then, just to make sure the lying cunt didn't breathe a second longer, I stabbed her. Multiple times."

His eyes snap wide open. "You stabbed her?"

"With the knife she stabbed me with first." I say as I point to my shoulder where she stabbed me. The raw and edgy tone in my voice is one I barely recognize.

I see the struggle on his face, trying to determine if I'm bullshitting him or not. He stares at me, shaking his head like he's waiting for me to say *gotcha* or something like that. No such luck. This is as real as it gets.

"Let me get this straight," he slowly rephrases, "she stabbed you... then, you *killed* her? As in she's not breathing kind of killed?"

"One and the same." Then, the bombshell. "Libbs is dead because of her, Dex. She fucking deserved worse."

"What the hell are you talking about?"

Dex really liked Libbs, so the shock is going to hit him almost as hard as it did me. Almost.

After ten minutes of going back and forth, I finally give in because every minute we stand here talking puts me at a greater risk of running into Vince. I gotta get the fuck out of here before he comes home.

"I have to go, Dex, and right now, I just need to be alone. I'll call you when I get to a hotel."

He looks at me like I'm crazy. "Fuck that! You're not just going to drop some information like that on me and think I'm going to wait for a fucking phone call. You really have lost your mind if you believe that shit!"

"Fine! Get in the fucking car, and remember, you asked for this."

Dex reaches into his car and grabs a very full duffel bag.

"Wha..."

"What can I say?" he smiles all smug like, "I told I knew you better than you know yourself. I came prepared just in case you tried to skip town for a few days. And I couldn't let you do that without sharing the information I have for you."

Starting the car, I give him a curious look as a satisfied grin spreads on his face. As soon as we hit the highway, heading west, I recount every gruesome detail. Some of things he knew, most he did not. I don't get to say much at one time, because Dex keeps interrupting me with, *no fucking way* or *holy shit.*

It's not long before both of our phones start blowing up as the real *holy shit* moment happens. Vince finally made it home.

Dex shifts in his seat uncomfortably. "I wonder what he's going to say about all of this?"

"It doesn't matter at this point," I try to ease the level of concern I heard in his voice. "Anyway, I have some hard questions Vince needs to answer. Starting with how he found Rachel to begin with. It's an important clue as to who she's really working with. Then, while he's at it, he can fucking explain everything he knows about Kara Santos."

When I first got home tonight, I made a beeline for Vince's office. With him not at home, it was the perfect time to act on a feeling I had since I saw the woman in the photo holding a gun to my father's head.

For years I knew Vince was holding back certain things from me, and my father's journal proves it. To keep something as big as Dominic having a sister from me tells me something just as big is the reason *why*. Vince had to have something hidden somewhere, I was sure of it. After his office turned up nothing, I went into his bedroom to search for a damn needle in a haystack. Everywhere I looked turned up nothing. Just as I was ready to quit looking, I stumbled upon a box hidden in one of his dresser drawers.

A box filled with pictures.

One of them caught my eye right away. Given his distinct profile, I knew it had to be my father, Dominic, back in his teens. It was like looking at a picture of me present day, that's how sure I was that it was him. He was standing with an arm around a younger girl. Their resemblance was uncanny. The same olive skin, charcoal hair, and eyes so penetrating they feel like they can reach into your soul with one look. Enough similarities that the young girl in this photo was the same older woman holding a gun to Dominic's head in the other picture I now possess. If I needed any further confirmation, the names Dominic and Kara Santos were scribbled on the back.

If not for Dominic's journal, I'm not sure I would ever know that Kara Santos even exists. Now that I do, it certainly complicates things. She's my aunt. My uncle, Vince's, half-sister. And the person who shot and killed her own brother.

What pisses me off the most, is it took some fucking psycho to send me a random photo for me to uncover the mystery *who* murdered my father nearly twenty years ago. Whoever sent those to me knows how badly I want to find out the truth, no matter how ugly that truth may be.

Who knew just how fucked-up the truth could be though? It's some cruel twist of fate to be killed by your own flesh and blood. And it only proves one thing. Committing murder seems to run in my family. Damn, if that's not a chilling thought!

"It's not the same thing, Declan." Dex quickly points out, disagreeing with me on one issue. "You had no intention of killing Rachel, until she went all crazy on your ass. I'd call that more self-defense than out right murder. Besides, self-defense is lawfully reasonable and not a capital offense if proven in a court of law."

He sounds just like a Law and Order rerun and it's weirdly amusing to hear it from big bad Dex.

"If you say so." The last thing I need to worry about is the law. Covering shit up like this is nothing new when it comes to the Aniello family. Given the circumstances, Vince and Marcus will personally see to it that it's handled quickly and quietly.

Dex finally asks me the one thing I've been asking myself since we left the house, exactly what are my plans?

"I'm not sure I have a solid plan at this point. I'm so fucking tired right now, I could pull over and fall asleep in a matter of minutes."

A glimmer of hope shines in Dex's face.

"Not on your life." The thought of him driving my car is scary enough to keep my ass awake until we do pull over for the night. "I've rode with you before, it's not pretty."

"You suck!" He gruffly replies, disappointed that he won't be driving my Camaro any time soon. Instead, he turns his attention to my radio and before he can find the XM channel I know he's going to look for, I give him his only warning for our entire trip.

"You put on the Eighties or some crap like that, I'll drop you off right here on the side of the road. I hear that crap enough at the gym." Dex has the worst taste possible when it comes to music. It's like he's stuck in some time warp back in the year 1982. For some reason, he's obsessed with a generation he's not even remotely close with age wise.

He takes offense and answers with the same old line. "Eighties are the best, you are just in denial." To make it worse, he's doing some awful dance moves by swinging his head and snapping his fingers.

Jesus! Just when I think he's lost his damn mind, he shocks me again. "You ever listen to Hair Nation?"

I kid you not, he even says it with a straight face. "I have no clue what that is, nor do I want to know. Dude, just put on heavy metal or Rap."

He cusses, *all right,* before scrolling through the channels one at a time. Each channel sounding worse than the one before. I swear he's doing this on purpose to drive me insane. Losing patience, I slam my hand on the steering wheel. "Dex, just hit any of the pre-sets."

"Oh, chill the hell out and loosen up," he protests. "By the end of this trip I'll have you listening to the Eighties. Mark my words."

"Not a chance in hell!"

"Whatever!" He ignores me as *Green Lights* by NF begins to play. I take over the controls and crank up the radio making sure to glare at Dex. *Now that's music*!

Able to relax with music worth listening to, we say very little while we pass mile marker after mile marker. Even though I'm tired, it's more important to put as many miles between us and home as possible.

It doesn't take long for us to start the one conversation that's been on both of our minds. I pull into the next rest stop to take a break, making sure to grab the envelope from my bag in the trunk. I made sure to make a number of copies, because you never know when you're going to need them. I toss it to Dex before we make it back on the Interstate.

After he looks at each one, he drops the pictures in his lap and scratches the top of his head.

"Jesus, Declan, this shit is messed up."

I give him a side-ways glance. "Yeah, it is. And it's only going to get worse."

"Well, that depends on how you look at it," he suggests with an odd smirk that I'm almost afraid to ask. "I have some information for you. Over the last few weeks, Kingston and I have been doing some digging ourselves, wanting to help any way we could. He's damn handy with computers. If fighting doesn't work out for him, he'll make one hell of a private eye... or a criminal."

"What'd he find?"

Without saying anything, Dex reaches in the backseat to pull a folder from his bag. An empty feeling settles in my stomach when I eye the folder he's holding. I have no clue what information he has, and the unknown has me wrapping my hands tightly around the steering wheel.

Dex is on the edge of his seat with eyes full of excitement. "Okay... here we go."

Then, his mouth is off to the races rambling with tidbits of information so damn fast, I have a hard time keeping up with what he's saying.

All I hear is, '*Kingston did this... found this... but went back and searched....*'

"Hold up! Can you slow your ass down, Sherlock?" My brain is on cruise control, while I try to rub the fatigue from my eyes. "I'm tired as fuck and listening to you is like trying to contain the energizer bunny."

Dex can't control his excitement and doesn't take my interruption well. He's annoyed and rolling his eyes at me. "Can you please focus for a few more minutes, this shit is about to get good. If it would help, I could use sign language? I learned it from watching infomercials late one weekend."

I look at him with pity behind my eyes, because I can almost picture him doing this. "Dex, you really need to get a life."

"What? Like you have any room to talk," he sighs and says something under his breath about people living in glass houses.

Jesus, it's like pulling teeth with him. "Any day now, Dex."

"Fine. We found a Willow Ryles living in Washington State who is twenty-four years old. She is currently enrolled in an extended art program at a local college in Bothell, Washington." Raising a clever eyebrow, he smirks, "She's the artsy-type."

A weird sensation settles in my chest while Dex continues to obsess over a girl he's never met. The more he says about her, the more real she seems. She's not just a name in a journal anymore and for some reason, it rattles me.

"Wait, Ryles? Why not Santos?" It only makes sense that her name should be Santos seeing she is Dominic Santos' daughter.

"Why is your last name Parisi instead of Santos?" Dex turns it around until it oddly makes more sense. "It's possible that it could be the same kind of thing."

It's possible. In my case, I happen to know why Vince choose his last name for me instead of Dominic's.

Vince was raised by a single mother and was given her last name, Parisi. It wasn't until he met Dominic that he began to resent not having the name Santos since they shared the same father. After I was born, Vince struggled with the idea but ultimately decided to give me his last name. I think growing up without a father figure bothered him more than he let on. I also think he did it to honor his late mother.

Unfortunately, Dominic's legacy died along with him. It's kind of fucked up if you ask me. Neither of his kids, Willow or myself, will carry on the Santos name. The legendary enforcer who was larger than life now feels like an urban legend... a forgotten part of the past with no real connection to the present.

When I hear Dex suddenly mention Izzy Parker's name, my ears perk up and he once again has my full attention.

"Izzy Parker is married, going by Izzy Parker-Ryles now. Her husband, Braxton Ryles, is the owner of Ryles Custom shop and was, at one time, was a member of the Lost Souls MC. The interesting thing is a guy that works with him, Liam Talbott, was also once a member of the same MC. And wait 'til you hear this... he has a wife. Kara Santos-Talbott."

What are the fucking chances?

"It's just too much of a fucking coincidence that it's the same MC my father had an association with."

Growing up, I heard Marcus mention the Lost Souls MC a time or two. Besides being an outlaw club, I don't know shit about them. I never gave them a second thought until I read Dominic's journal. Even then, he said very little about their dealings.

This new information is a lot to take in, but I try while weaving through cars and flirting with the speed limit. The interior of the car lights up as my phone starts blowing up again. Each time, I hit ignore. And, each time, Dex says I should just pick it up and face the music.

We both know they won't give up until they hear from me, but my mind is focused on more important things right now. Things back home can wait.

"Dex, focus here." I talk over the continual beeping he seems preoccupied with.

"Let me try and understand something," I say louder than I normally would. "I get the whole Willow *Ryles*. Obviously, she has Izzy's husband's last name. It doesn't take a genius to figure that one out, but I wonder if Willow has any idea who her *real* father is? Has she been raised to think that Braxton is her real dad?"

"Who cares? What does that have to do with anything?" He asks with a blank stare on his face, missing the obvious.

"You serious? For starters, because it's a bullshit lie." I get that I have no proof of what Willow knows or not, but the thing I hate more than anything is being fucking lied to. It makes me sick to think the same kind of bullshit happened to her, being lied to for all these years.

Which brings me to the biggest, most scandalous secret that's been kept secret from me.

"So, Kara Santos is now Kara Talbott?" That name is like a double punch in the gut that leaves a nasty, bitter aftertaste in my mouth. As much as it pains me to say it, the truth brings with it a new level of hurt.

"We know the bitch shot him in cold blood, but that's not all. Is it just another big coincidence that my bitch of a mother's last name is also Talbott? That I can remember her telling me she had a brother? And she was from Washington State?"

There's not much else I can honestly say I remember about her, other than her platinum blonde hair.

A low *hmmm'* escapes past my throat. "The dots are slowly coming together."

Then it hits me...

A conversation. The chilling memory hits me hard as I unintentionally weave out of the center lane. Thankfully no other cars were coming, but Dex shouts out with his hands planted on the dashboard anyway.

Like living a nightmare, I vividly remember the night I first found out about Willow. After reading Dominic's journal, I confronted Vince. The harder I pressed, the more he continued to shut me down. Then, he specifically told me that none of *them* want a thing to do with me. Which means, they all knew back then Tiffany was pregnant with Dominic's kid.

I pull off on the side of the road and slam on the brakes.

No. No. No. It can't be...

I reach over to the scattered photo's on Dex's lap and toss them around until I find the one I'm looking for. The picture of two girls that was in the damn envelope. The same one with the odd message that these two girls are a part of the puzzle that leads back to me. The girl with dark brown hair has to be Willow. I take a closer look at the girl with blonde hair who was a mystery up until now. Suddenly it becomes clear and the realization leaves me speechless. Hands trembling, my breaths come hard and fast. The blonde-haired girl, a shade so platinum. *Oh, hell no!*

I swallow the lump in my throat and practically trip over my tongue trying to get the words out of my mouth. "Dex, did you come across any other names associated with Willow, Izzy or Kara?

Anything that could explain who the girl with blonde hair is with Willow?" I close my eyes and hope I'm wrong.

"We did, actually. It seems Willow has a sister. Her name is Eve Ryles."

My eyes shoot wide open. "Ryles? Not Talbott, are you sure?" Damn, that's not what I was expecting him to say, but that doesn't make sense... unless.

"*Holy shit!*" I say in one exasperated breath.

"Holy shit, what?" Dex looks at me and then at the picture, wondering what he's missed.

"Ryles... Braxton Ryles," I shout at Dex. "Jesus, in Dominic's journal he talked about a woman who contacted him. That's how he found out where Izzy was before he left for Washington State to bring her back home. He said the woman found him because she felt Izzy was coming between her man and *little girl*. Holy fuck, Dex. Eve Ryles," my voice hitches at the same time my eyes are literally popping out of their socket. Holding the picture up, I tap my finger on the blonde girl's face. "This girl, Eve, is Tiffany and Braxton's daughter. Who else could it be?"

"That would make Eve," he lowers his voice, "*your half-sister?*" Dex is shaking his head, throwing out all sorts of cuss words, connecting the dots. "But Willow is also your half-sister," he says with an astounded look on his face.

"That's what the message meant on the photo, they both are a piece of the puzzle that connects back to me." Wiping a hand down my face, my head falls back against the seat. "Guess we figured that one out on our fucking own, Sherlock."

Mouth still open, Dex rubs the back of his neck staring at the road ahead. "Do you feel like we've entered the twilight zone? Because I sure as hell do!"

I do the only thing I can, laugh, because my life feels like it's been one giant episode of the twilight zone lately. The inside of the car goes silent for a moment until Dex starts to get text message after text message. As he quickly reads them, his face drains of all color. Then, he starts to freak the fuck out.

"Ahhh... Declan, you need to answer your damn phone because they are now endangering my life if you don't. Apparently, Marcus, Vince and Anthony are at your house, pissed the fuck off and losing patience."

It sounds like a stunt they would pull, and their attempt to threaten Dex is juvenile. With a roll of my eyes, I pull back on the highway wanting nothing more than to put more miles between us. The way I see it, I'm the one who deserves to be pissed the fuck off. With all the shit I learned tonight, I'm not sure what or who pisses me off more.

"Ahhh, Declan."

"Dammit, Dex, I told you not to come with me. That's on you. Let them threaten you all they want. I'll talk to them when I'm fucking ready. I'm sure by now they've found the copies of the photos I left, or maybe they found Rachel. Either way, I don't give a fuck!"

"*Or* Rachel?" Dex shouts, nearly jumping out of his seat. "I'm sure it *all* has to do with Rachel?"

With my jaw tight, I declare for a final time. "They can fucking wait!"

I should have known Dex wouldn't take having his life threatened well, they're making him think he's in more danger than he actually is. It's only a ploy. I want to tell him not to worry about it, but he turns to look out the window.

I don't realize what he's doing until it's too late.

A familiar voice erupts in anger.

Chapter Seventeen

"Revelations"

"**WHAT THE FUCK, DECLAN?** YOU had better have a *goddamned* good reason why I have a *dead* fucking body in my house!"

Damn it all to hell!

I wildly swing my eyes at Dex to find him holding his phone. Anger swells as my eyes raise to his. "*What the fuck did you do?*"

His face stills as the tension between us builds.

Once again, the roar of Vince's voice cracks like thunder. "*Answer me!*"

My silence just pisses him off more, but I can't help it. My body just reacts. His voice is like a trigger to the rage inside and it feels like I'm in a chokehold. I can't breathe, and it seems like the lines on the road are blurring. I have to get my shit together. I start taking long, slow breaths so I can deal with the situation fucking Dex put me in.

It's not that I'm shocked by how mad Vince is. Hell, I expected him to be. From the moment he walked into that bloody scene at home, he had to face just how far out of control things have spiraled.

I know once he hears all the twisted shit that happened, he'll calm down and understand. My family lives and breathes by one motto. *An eye for an eye.* It's all I've heard growing up. If someone hits you hard, you hit them back ten times harder.

That's what I did!

I'm just too damn drained to have that conversation tonight. Which is why Dex going behind my back and calling him fucking pisses me off. This situation is what I wanted to fucking avoid until I had time to sleep and get my head straight. It's not every day you find out your nurse is nothing more than a lying whore sent to spy on you by the man hell-bent on taking you down. Rachel got what was coming to her. She made her bed and thanks to me, she'll sleep in it. For eternity!

It fucking infuriates me that I let it happen right under my nose. She played me and as much as I loathe that bitch for her part in all of this, it doesn't even come close to the hate I have for the *man* behind it, whoever he is. He can take his fucking vendetta, or whatever the fuck this is and shove it up his ass! I can't wait until he finds out it was *me* who left his bitch to bleed out all over my bedroom floor.

If tonight's revelations have taught me anything, it's renewed my vow that no one is going to stand in my way. *He* may have been the one to start this, but I will be the one to end it. I'll fucking die before I ever let him get to that close to me again. I'd even die each day all over again, just to fuck-up his plans. To make his life a living hell. All I have to do is picture Libbs' pale face and hear her desperate screams to give me the motivation I need, to remind me how evil he is, and what he's taken from me.

"*Why* aren't you *answering me?*" Vince shouts again, losing what little patience he has left.

This time, my reaction is different. The near-deafening level of his voice creates an explosion in my head. Pain shoots down my spine as my muscles begin to spasm. Dex freaks out and tries to grab the wheel, but quickly backs the fuck off when he sees me glaring at him. He slides over far as he can with the palm of his hands in the air. It gives me the perfect view of his phone that highlights Vince's name. Bile rises to the back of my throat. I'm tempted to throat punch Dex just to teach his ass a lesson. To fucking respect what the hell I tell him, and to never ever go behind my back again.

He looks scared shitless, having to sit in the middle of the shit-storm he created. It's his own fault, he made the call. When Dex mouths an apology, I ignore it will a roll of my eyes. Right now, he can shove his apology up his ass. It's too late to say, *oops, I'm sorry*. I still have an outraged uncle to deal with.

After a few deep breaths, I swallow back my anger and attempt to calmly say, "What I need right now…" is all I get out before heated voices on the phone go from a low chatter to a vicious shouting match.

Marcus and Anthony are so loud and angry at one another that Vince joins in the shouting, saying he can't hear a damn thing I say.

The chaos around me only intensifies. Once again, I glare at Dex, "*Look what the fuck you started!*"

Without mincing words, I snarl. "Give me the fucking phone, you idiot!"

Dex hands it over like he's glad to give it up.

I shout into the phone. "Listen! I'm not apologizing for a damn thing, and I'm not in the fucking mood to play twenty questions with you tonight. Give me some breathing room and I'll call you when I'm ready to hash it out." I grit my teeth, annoyed that they're still battling on like it's World War III. "Under the circumstances, I think all *three* of you can understand where the fuck I'm coming from, so give me what I *ask* for."

If anyone understands how I'm feeling, it's them. I can't count how many times I have witnessed all three of them brooding and pissed off after shit went south. It's just a given to let that person have some time before they all meet up to hash things out.

Before Vince can respond, I end the call.

"Declan..." Dex cautiously mutters.

"Don't!" I snap, not wanting to hear a single word from his mouth.

It's not even three seconds later. The phone in my hand lights up with Vince calling *again*. *Jesus H. Christ!* Since I obviously didn't get my point across the first time, I'll just have to make sure I do this time.

With an iron grip, I slam the phone against the steering wheel. One. Two. Three times. Each blow shatters more of the glass as tiny shards slice my hand. On the fourth try, Dex tries to intervene by reaching over to save what's left of his phone, but I'll be damned if he thinks he's getting it back.

Over my dead body! I jerk it out of his reach, letting out a gnarly noise from the base of my throat. I'm not sure who pisses me off more right now, Vince or Dex, but I have a solution for both. I roll down my window and chuck his phone out into the darkness. My satisfaction comes from the noise it makes as it hits the pavement.

Dex reaches for it, but he's too slow. "What the fuck, Declan? That was *my* phone!" His voice in full out panic mode.

"It sure the fuck was, and I won't be missing any sleep over it! Maybe next time you'll think before pissing me off and make a phone call to *my* family. Jesus, Dex!" I don't bother to ask him what he was thinking because it's clear that he wasn't.

He shakes his head in disgust. "You're a fucking idiot!"

"I've been called worse."

He goes from being mad to suddenly looking ill. "You have no idea how much I need my phone."

Feeling no remorse, I watch the mile markers pass us by as I stretch my aching body. "You should have thought of that before you went behind my back."

The following few minutes are in silence and it's the fucking best. It gives me time to chill out, and let go of any leftover anger. If he had only shut his phone off like I did mine, none of that shit would have happened. No pissed off phone call, no threatening of anyone's life, and Dex would still have a phone. Serves his ass right.

He has his head in his hands, taking deep breaths. That's when he blurts out, "That's how she communicates with me."

When he raises his eyes, he finds me watching him out of the corner of my eye.

"You're kidding, right? You can't be this upset over some booty call, Dex." My mouth slacks open as I swat his shoulder. "You're not that desperate... are you?"

Judging by the worry lines on his face, I guess I have my answer. It's not like Dex is an ugly fucker. Most chicks find him to be the whole package. Besides being in great physical shape, he's into chick flicks. That's his MO, and it gets him laid all the time. For him to be like this? Damn, I can't hold back. I'm laughing my ass off. Here I was wanting to strangle him a few minutes ago. Now, all I feel is, *bad!*

"Do I at least know her, because she must be damn good for you to be acting so *weird*." I'm no genius, but if she's that good why doesn't Dex have her number memorized? It doesn't add up, and in the back of my mind I wonder what else he's hiding.

"You wouldn't understand!" He eventually says in a low far away voice.

"You're right about that. I will never understand chicks, and I don't want to." Dex is all the proof I need. Yet, curiosity is eating away at me. I'd rather be grilling him, than having to deal with my own shit anyway.

I know for a fact he hasn't mentioned anyone new lately. That means I already know her. I start ticking off names in my head and get stuck on one. Oh, hell No! Please don't tell me Dex is upset over all-teeth Angie? No, fucking way! My dick hurts just thinking about her.

"Just tell me it's not." I scrunch up my face like I'm in pain. It's hard to forget, no matter how hard I try. When I get ready to just yell out her name, he looks over with a guilty-as-sin look all over his face.

"You're not going to like this, but if you hear me out, you'll see I was only trying to help."

The words, *only trying to help* are an instant red flag. His body language confirms I'm not going to like it. His body is tense and his back is straight as a board. Immediately, I ease off the gas and pull the car to the shoulder of the road. After slamming it into park, I lower my head and close my eyes. The tension coming from him makes it hard to watch.

With my voice dipping dangerously low, I ask, "Dex, what the fuck have you done now?"

At first, he tries to deflect my question with one of his own by asking what I'm going to do about back home. More exact, what am I going to do about Vince. Telling me that they won't simply wait around for me to call.

He's stalling, and it's not a great idea when he has me on edge. My patience is at an all-time low.

"Dex, deflecting is only going to make matters worse. Stop the *bullshit* and tell me what the *fuck* you've done."

He looks me straight in the eye, silently begging me to understand. "Alright, along with the things we found, Kingston and I found a way for *you* to introduce yourself to Willow."

Not exactly what I expected him to say. Talk about out of left fucking field. It has me scratching my head, but it also stirs up something else. A disturbing feeling I'm not very comfortable with.

"It's not as bad as you think." He says it like he expects me to just believe that just because he said it. Then, comes the bombshell that changes everything. "We actually set it up like you're new to town and looking to make a friend."

Hold up one motherfucking minute!!

Smoke must be barreling out of my ears because Dex reacts like I'm on fire.

"Declan, this is perfect, given your recent situation. Think about it." He tries to convince me but fails, miserably.

"I'll tell you what *I'm fucking thinking*!" I shout with my fists inches from his face.

"Just stop a minute!" Dex raises his voice as determined as I've ever seen him. "I've just given you the perfect way to watch out for her if that sick bastard tries to get her. The timing couldn't be more perfect." Then, he blurts out without thinking. "You should be thanking me."

There is no way he just said that to me.

"Well, not right now, obviously, given your foul mood. But later, you'll see it's a good plan." His biggest problem is he doesn't know when to shut the hell up.

Dex has the balls to say I should thank him! For what, invading into my personal life? Finding out information is one thing I have no objections with, but to actually go behind my back and make decisions for me without talking to me like Dex has is fucked-up and wrong!

He mistakes my sudden silence as a good sign. Which couldn't be any further from the truth.

He boasts. "I'm a genius for coming up with the idea, but Kingston? Man, he's a damn genius behind the computer. I had no idea he knew how to do all that crafty shit. Makes me wish I knew him when I was still in school."

"How could you do something like this without talking with me first? This is *my life*, Dex. Not yours!" I erupt with my heart hammering, and my breathing ragged.

"You're right, it is," he tosses his hands in the air. "We're also your friends who want nothing more than to help you."

Grabbing a fistful of his papers still on his lap, I fling them in his face. "How does *this* help me?"

The look in his eyes tells me he's not backing down. He grabs ahold of one of the papers that landed squarely on his chest. "Well, if you would just look at it!"

He shoves it under my nose, as I swat it with the back of my hand.

"Get that out of my face."

"Fine, then allow me. It's says in black and white that Willow attends Cornish College for the Arts. Now, look here." He points lower on the page where it shows information about a student's profile. I assume it must be hers, but looking at it closer, I see I'm way off. It's a fake profile. Mine.

"Yes, it's a picture of you," his voice tries to remain strong, but wavers just a bit. "As of three weeks ago, you are enrolled as an out of state transfer student at Cornish College."

That's does it!

I reach over and grab him by his shirt, so we're nose to nose.

"You had no right to do that. Up until tonight, I hadn't decided when I was going to contact her, *if ever*. From the start though, you've had this infatuation with her. Is this about me, Dex, or your obsession? Because from where I'm sitting right now, I'm not so sure. From the night I told you about Willow, you haven't stopped talking about her."

"You're tripping," he struggles to pull his head back against my tight grip on his shirt.

"Am I really?" I snort. "Are you so blind you can't see the obvious in front of your face? Why this jacked plan of yours will never work? From the top of my head, I can list ten different reasons. Number one, I don't have an artistic bone in my body."

Instead of arguing back, Dex frees himself from my stronghold and straightens out his shirt. Deep down, I know he would do anything to prove me wrong. So, when he gets a cocky grin on his face, my eyes go razor sharp.

"So far it's working. I've been chatting with *your* sister for a week now... as *you*."

I don't blink.

I don't swallow.

And I sure as hell don't breathe.

Dex, on the other hand, talks like he's proud of himself. Calling it fate that it all worked out the way it has.

"Our way in was through the school's online chat. A place to meet others at the college. Lucky for you, Willow has an active profile. Naturally, we had to use your profile picture so when you meet her in person, she doesn't freak the fuck out. Think about this way, the ice has already broken. And, she already thinks you're nice and funny."

Nice and funny!!

Two words that don't even come close to describing me. Dex, maybe, but certainly not me. Not only has he stepped over the line by injecting himself in my personal shit without my knowledge, he's lying his ass off at the same time. Talking to *my* fucking sister!!

He's crossed so far over the fucking line, all I see is red!

Then, I listen to the voices that shout in my head.

The minute my right fist connects with his jaw... it's lights out!!

He never saw it coming.

Chapter Eighteen

"Strike A Nerve"

"YOU FUCKING COLD COCKED ME!" Dex's mood hasn't lightened any. From the time he woke up to the moment we pulled into the Holiday Inn for the night, he's been bitching because I knocked his ass out.

"You deserved it, and don't say you didn't," I said as we step into the elevator. What did you honestly think I would do when you told me? Motherfucker, you know how I feel about deceit and betrayal."

Double checking our room number, I press button for the second floor.

With his back against the wall, Dex calls me out. "What's got you so uptight anyway? This can work. At least my way you can keep a closer eye on her without her calling the cops and accusing you of being some stalker. It's just a way to meet her, you don't have to keep the lie going once you tell her who you really are."

I turn and glare at him. "This exact conversation ended with my fist in your face earlier, you'd be wise to remember that."

We don't we see eye to eye, and the way I see it. I'm the only one that counts in this situation.

"You can't stay angry at the world forever, Declan. Just like you need to be able to recognize when you need help and ask for it. At the fight, you should have told us then. You can't do all of this on your own and it's crazy to think that you can."

When the elevator doors open, I step out with one thought. "Maybe, but it sure would be a hell of a lot easier."

"Easier?" Dex shouts from behind me, refusing to drop it. "You are so full of shit. You're just too pig-headed and used to bottling all of your shit up so damn tight you don't know how to ask for help. You see it as a weakness but if you would pull your head out of your ass for a minute, you'd see how much easier things could be with a little help."

Inserting the key to open the door to room two forty-four, I sarcastically remark over my shoulder. "Is that your professional opinion, Dr. Phil?"

He flips me off which makes me laugh. "You know what? Being your friend is not only a pain in the ass, it literally fucking hurts sometimes." Following me in the room, he rubs the purple bruise that's just starting to show on his jaw. In a huff, he throws his bags on one of the double beds and stands with his hands low on his hips.

"I wasn't going to say this, but you're not leaving me much choice. I admit, it was shitty to go behind your back like I did. I should have just collected the information and given it to you to decide what you wanted to do with it. And I would have, if it weren't for…" he stops and turns his back to me like he's struggling for words.

"Weren't for what?" I ask.

Dex stays like that for a minute longer, then drops his shoulders before he turns back around. When he does, his eyes look full of conflict. "You aren't the only one hurting in all of this," he admits with a slight waver to his voice like he's hurting. "The way that bastard just discarded *Liberty* like a piece of trash. Fuck it," he shudders, "you know what, it doesn't even matter how I felt, because it pales in comparison to the way it fucking destroyed you. It's still destroying you. You're out of control, Declan." Then, just to prove his point, he hits me a low blow. "Just look at what happened with Rachel?"

It strikes a nerve!

"Watch it, Dex!" My eyes darken as my voice dips low.

His face turns red as he harshly responds. "Are you being serious right now? Your reaction right now, just proves my point. I want to prevent what happened to Liberty from ever happening to you again. Whether it be Willow or Eve. Hell, I don't know. What I *do* know is you *can't* go through that shit again. You won't come back from it."

"How can you be so sure I can now?" I challenge him since he seems to have all the answers.

"Because I'm going to help in any way I can to fucking stop him. Even if that means pissing you the fuck off in the process." His eyes flash a gentle but firm warning as one corner of his mouth twists upward.

My skin literally feels like it's on fire. The prick that I am turns around without responding to a word my best friend said in search of the bottle of booze I stashed in my bag. The truth is I don't know what to say to him, so I cop out by saying nothing. With the bottle in my hand, I storm off to the bathroom and lock the door.

A minute after that, the door to our room slams shut.

I stand in front of the mirror and take a hard look at myself. A face I hardly recognize stares back at me. "You look like shit!" I utter to myself, raising the bottle to my mouth to drown in my sorrows. I'm a selfish prick, and too damn stubborn to tell my best fucking friend in the world that I get it. That's he's one hundred percent right. I'm a self-absorbed bastard who would rather stay angry than face what really cuts me deep. I'm not kidding when I say I'm done being fucking vulnerable.

Turning the shower to scalding hot, I stand under the water with my head hung low. With one hand on the wall, the other one holds the bottle to my lips. I finish the last drop of alcohol in record time. It's not nearly enough, but I don't even realize it slips out of hand until I notice the flow of red blood as it goes down the drain.

Worn-out, and too tired to give a damn that my feet are bleeding from stepping on glass, I dress in a pair of shorts and stumble out of the bathroom before collapsing on the bed. With Dex nowhere in sight and a head splitting migraine coming on strong, I'm out before I know it.

THE FOLLOWING DAY ISN'T MUCH better. I feel like shit. There's not a muscle in my body that isn't stiff or screaming out in excruciating pain. My head's in a fog so I know I've been out for a while. I had no idea it would be fifteen hours to be exact. I slept most of the day away. At first, I'm not sure where I am, until I hear Dex and his hushed voice in mid-conversation as he starts to laugh.

It takes me a few more minutes to finally keep my eyes open. When I sit up, I see the television is on, but the volume is turned down. The curtains are drawn, and the only light in the room is coming from the bathroom. Dex is lying on his bed with his back to me, quietly talking on the phone. The empty pizza boxes and soda cans sprawled on the table suddenly makes my stomach growl with hunger pains.

"I can't wait to meet to you either."

That is so Dex, and it cracks me up because he is one smooth operator. I think little of it, until our conversation from last night comes rushing back like a bad dream.

Willow. His disaster plan. *That's how she communicates with me. I've been talking to her as you.*

A plan sprung on me last-minute after the worst day of my life. I was angry, hell, I was furious to hear he had been talking to her. Fuck it, the damage is done. It doesn't matter what I think or what I say at this point, it's already happening. Just what the hell do I do now?

The moment I yawn and stretch my aching muscles, Dex suddenly turns. Panic flashes over his face as his eyes look down at the phone in his hand.

"Hey, listen, Willow, my buddy Dex just got here so I need to go. I'll talk to you soon. Sure, you bet. Yep, laters."

Unfuckingbelieveable!

He's *still* talking with her as me, but then uses me as him as an excuse to get off the phone! He didn't learn shit the first time I knocked his ass out! I stare at him with a blank stare, because I have no words. Looks like I'll have to knock his ass out again to show him just how fucking serious I was about him going behind my back.

Dex tosses the phone in his hand on the bed next to him when I notice it's my phone. He lays flat on his back and looks at the ceiling. Exhaling deeply.

"Listen, I know you're still pissed at me and I get it, but I need you to think about why this plan makes the best sense. If you go in guns blazing, spouting about who you are, what do you think is going to happen? Brax, and Liam are going to kick your ass and send you packing. Let's say by chance, you suddenly go off about some lunatic that may or may not be gunning for Willow, do you honestly think they are going to believe a word you say? Hell no!

"The only way this works is for you to get to know her, and for her get to know you. That way you can get a feel for the family. From there, we can figure things out. If you truly want answers about the past like you say you do, this is the only way you're going to get them. I can't imagine Izzy or Kara will easily just rehash the past with you. I'm sorry, Declan, but you are the enemy here. You represent the worst of their past. Who knows how they will react when they meet you face to face."

It's obvious he's put a lot of thought into this and I can't argue with most of what he has to say. I just hate to waste time playing games knowing I have a lunatic to watch out for. One who has killed before to get what he wants. And I have no reason to believe he won't do it again. He's going to have an axe to grind with me after what I did to Rachel.

I may not be able to control him, but I can keep Willow from being used as bait or caught in the crosshairs. I don't know her, and hell, I may not even like her, but she's as much a part of Dominic as I am. That makes her vulnerable and puts her in danger.

Something Vince said to me years ago suddenly made more sense to me now than it did when he first said it.

Declan, always remember this; Money can't buy happiness or forgiveness. Just like it can't buy redemption or salvation. It can't guarantee you time or protect you from the evil in the world. However, the one thing money can buy is power and power is everything.

I decide to look at things from a different perspective to see if I can figure out something that can help give us the upper hand. I try to get inside the mindset of that motherfucker.

"Here's the thing," I glance over at Dex and rub my chin, starting with the obvious. "This fucker knows everything about me. He knows how angry and unpredictable I can be. What if that's what he's counting on? Like he's orchestrating these things to happen to put me in situations he knows I won't react well to. Otherwise, why send me the photos?"

Then, it dawns on me. "That's it. He wants me to lose my shit. He's counting on it." I feel optimistic for the first time, until my brows slowly come together. "The question is why?"

"Easy," Dex answers with a shrug of his shoulders. "If you lose your head, you lose focus. If your focus is off him, he can continue on as he sees fit."

He's right. Up to now, all I've done is play right into his fucking hands. "Motherfucker!" I extend my reach for the bedside lamp before I send it across the room to shatter against the wall.

Staring at the mess on the floor, Dex lets out an uneasy groan. "I get that this is super bad timing on my part, but we have another issue to deal with."

The way he says we, suggests it's more me.

"Yeah, well I hit my limit of issues the minute we hit the highway." If this issue is anything like the last one he sprung one me, I swear I won't be responsible for his wellbeing.

"What the hell are you talking about now?" I lean over on my side to face him with fingers twitching.

Dex pauses and looks at me under the heavy hood of his eyes. "Since you were dead to the world for the last fifteen hours, your phone kept lighting up like the Fourth of July. Let's just say the content of those messages prompted me to reply. Immediately!"

I cover my head with a pillow and groan. Not this again.

"What did he want now?"

"Well, here's the thing," he explains, clearly uncomfortable. "Since you were dead to the world, *I* had to fill Vince and Marcus in on everything that's been going on with you. And I mean *everything*," his voice slowly trailing off, "they left me no choice."

Since that is absolute the last thing I expected Dex to say, it takes a few seconds to let *everything,* sink in. My face turns to stone as I whip the pillow straight at his head.

"Are you out of your fucking mind? Did it ever occur to you shit that personal should have only come from me? ME! It was between me and *my* family."

He cowers slightly at my menacing scowl, but still defends his actions. "I don't know what you want me to say or what you think I could have done differently given the situation I was in?"

"Did it ever occur to you to *lie*? Or tell them they had to wait for me to wake up so I could tell them directly? Jesus, Dex, you have no problem lying any other time. But when it really fucking counts you have to be Mother Theresa!" I'm so pissed, the pounding in my head intensifies until it's almost too painful to remain still. I have to move around before I really do some damage. The shitty expression on his face only infuriates me more. "Did you not learn a goddamn thing last night about what happens when you do *shit* you shouldn't?"

Before I know it, he blows up and is on his feet. "Lie! That's your answer?"

I know I didn't stutter, so the cold and hard expression on my face stays the same.

Dex chokes, "Oh my God, you are serious! You would have me to lie to *your* family? Are you *insane*?"

I heard one word, *insane!*

I jump to my feet, ignoring the aches and pain and bruised ribs from the fight the night before. Even though my body is in recovery mode, my mind is ready to kick Dex's ass. I'm unsteady on my feet and most likely dehydrated, but I'm ready to go. That's how fucking *insane* I am.

Dex raises an eye at me and dismisses me with a wave of his hand. "Sit down before you hurt yourself even more out of sheer stupidity. *Damn idiot.*"

Not happening. He's pushed me too far this time.

I advance and jab a finger so hard against his chest, he slightly stumbles backward. "You should have *fucking* told them you don't know shit!" The strain in my voice cracks.

Face red as hell, Dex just snaps and flies into action. His chest is out ready to push back at me just as hard. He shoves me back so hard I easily lose my balance, which is something that doesn't happen often. My flexibility and timing are shit, so I have no chance of recovery. My lower back is stiff and unwilling to bend while the muscles in my legs are rock hard and lifeless. The only thing that saves my ass from nailing the floor is my outstretched arm that lands on the edge of the bed. It softens the blow, but now I'm bent backwards in an awkward position.

The fighter in Dex sees his opening and takes it. With a scowl on his face, he pins me in place with the strength of his upper body. Breathing heavy, he looks down at me with wild eyes. His face is beet red like he's ready to combust, a reaction I relate with very well.

He uses this power position to his advantage and shouts in my face, so enraged his entire body shakes as spit from his mouth lands everywhere.

"You're out of your *goddamned* mind if you think I'm going to lie to *Marcus fucking Aniello* when he and your uncle are breathing down my fucking neck to give them information. They assumed since I was with you, that *I fucking* knew everything. Which *I do*!!"

"Get the *fuck* out of my face!"

Dex makes the mistake of throwing throw his head and laughing, pushing every button he can. Then taunts me by saying, "What are you going to do about it?"

Feeling a rush of adrenaline pump in my veins, I respond with a cynical grin. "You're about to find out." His mistake, thinking I'd back down. He knows how much I love a challenge. This shit right now is no different.

I catch him completely off guard as I wrap my arms around his legs to do a classic double-leg takedown. Just like that, I take control, though every move hurts like a bitch. Pain can be a beautiful motivator.

More than pissed, Dex fights back and struggles to get free. The more he fights, the more aggressive I get until I'm finally able to straddle him and pin his wrists to the floor.

"My turn," I snarl in his face this time releasing the mounting stress over the last few days. "You know what your problem is, Dex? You can't keep your fucking mouth shut! *I told* you not to go behind my back. You said it yourself, Marcus and Vince *assumed* you knew something, not that you did. There's a big fucking difference. My *personal* shit is *off limits!*"

Every ounce of intensity in my voice is returned with the heat in his eyes.

"It was your fucking family!" He shouts at the top of his voice wildly thrusting his body in quick side-to-side motions. Holy shit. A searing pain blazes up my left side so intense my back bows, forcing my hands to release the hold I had on his wrists.

He sees his opening and clocks me with an elbow square in the jaw. It sends me flying off his body to land on my bad side. Payback from last night, I'm sure.

He kneels next to me while I wince in pain. "Listen for a one goddamned minute instead of being so absorbed in your own fucking head. Have you once considered what your family is going through? No, I bet you haven't. So while you curl up like a girl holding onto your sore as shit ribs and bruised *ego,* listen to what I have to say and get it through that thick skull of yours."

Like I want to hear a word he has to say. "Fuck off, Dex!"

He ignores my comment. "Vince is beside himself and Marcus is ready to burn the city to look for whoever is doing this to you. Hell, even Anthony is up in arms ready to start a war. And what about me, you ask?"

"Hey," I stop him right there. "I didn't invite you to come along. You just climbed in my car, that's on you. Bitch all you want, but you're the one who wanted to come along."

He throws his hands in the air and grumbles, "Jesus. H. Christ, you pain in the ass. I'm here having to put up with your moody ass while you have your feelings hurt over me doing my best to calm your family down. Do you know how hard that was? *Do you*? Yes, you should have been the one to explain, but you couldn't."

"I was asleep, not dead."

"You weren't just asleep! Your body literally shut down... for fifteen hours! Do you get that?"

The only thing I get is how I wish like hell my body would do it again.

"I suggest you stop now, before your mouth gets you in any more trouble."

"Is that supposed to scare me?" He laughs, then lowers his head in a cocky swagger like he's challenging me. "Are you going to teach me a lesson? If that's what it takes for you to stop with your petty bullshit, well, let's get to it then." He motions with his arms. "Come and teach me a lesson. The sooner you get this out of your system, the sooner we can get on to more serious things."

"Like what, me kicking your ass?"

"No," he smugly replies, "me, kicking yours!"

As soon as we get to our feet he advances like a bull and takes the first of many swings. I dodge them, but barely. After he misses on the next swing, I wrap him up again at his midsection, using my weight as an advantage. Not only do I have a good twenty to thirty pounds on Dex, I bench press a hell of a lot more than he does.

If I keep a low hold on him, it will be difficult for him to use any knee strikes. The last thing I need is more hits to the ribs. I'm sucking in air as it is with my mouth open, but I do whatever it takes to block out the intense pain.

Dex is relentless and fierce as he tries to free my hold around his waist by trying to slide his hands between his body and my arms. Unable to break my hold, he delivers blows with his elbows where ever he can connect.

I can't keep this up for long. With my fighting skills seriously impaired, I think of the next best thing and drive my heel on top of his foot. Like I expected, Dex lifts his foot from the ground for just a second. When he does, I drive his body straight back as we land on the edge of his bed. Our weight hits it just right as it rolls straight into the wall with a loud thud.

The jolt loosens my hold and Dex is so damn fast, he dodges my attempt to grab a hold of his hands. I see it coming but am too slow to react in time. Dex rears his leg back and connects his foot with my sore ribs. It sends me flying back once more in excruciating pain.

I land on the floor in the space between the beds and roll on my side, groaning, "You prick." It hurts so fucking bad a nasty taste settles in the back of my throat. I spit the taste out on the floor and glare back. "Did you aim for my ribs on purpose? Dick move, just to let you know." I move my hand covering my left side only to see the purple bruise left from Curtis that now has a red footprint next to it.

Winded, Dex stands with his hands on his hips and laughs. "Nah, I guess I just got lucky. Are you finished with your tantrum? Did you get it out of your system, or do you need me to actually break a few of your ribs first?"

His cocky attitude is hilarious, but then again, I may be delirious from the pain at this point. "Dex. Dex. Dex. I like your confidence, but you are wrong." I struggle to get to my knees once again, then stand.

He tilts his head to the side, looking amused. "Oh, yeah. Why's that?"

"I haven't gotten it all out of my system." I lower my body in a fighter's stance and stretch my neck from side to side, keeping every ounce of pain from showing on my face.

"You're a crazy fucker!" He complains, but reluctantly gets in the same position.

"I already know that. Just like I know you're not going to break my ribs so don't threaten me with that shit. And Dex, I'm not going to stop until you say you are done going behind my fucking back and doing stupid shit to piss me off!"

"We're going to be here a while then."

He lowers his guard just enough I take my shot. I reach out with my hands around his head and pull it down at the same time my knee connects with his chest.

He drops to one knee and tries to catch his breath. He's wheezing and holding a hand over his sternum. He has yet to say a word, but his body language says he's ready to wave the white flag. All I need are words. I'm not sure how much gas I have left in the tank for much more.

Just when I think he's going to say them, he lunges forward and takes one hell of a swing at my face. A wild grunt erupts from his throat as his knuckles connect with my mouth and split my lip wide open. Blood pours from my mouth.

Dex backs away breathing heavy but looks on satisfied. "Now, I'm done. As far as your damn apology, I said it earlier if you would have bothered to listen."

My mouth hurts so bad, it feels like he may have knocked out a few teeth. I reach up just to make sure my teeth are there.

"Jesus. I fucking hate you!" I spit the blood filling my mouth on the floor as I look for a shirt or something to hold against my mouth to stop the bleeding.

"Yeah, well, feeling's mutual so, here." He throws me a towel he got from the bathroom.

We're both still breathing heavy and if he's anything like the way I am, his feelings are just as raw. My head is fucked up with everything going on. I'm pissed at the world, tired as fuck and hurting everywhere. I need time to cool down and there is no way I'm going to be able to do it with him in the room.

I glower at him with a fixed glare while he stands with his hands on his knees. "*Get out*, Dex. I don't care where you go just get the fuck out for a while."

He goes to argue when my phone beeps with an incoming message.

"*Ignore it.*" I stop him from taking one step to look for the damn thing. The room is in disarray and somewhere in the mess of the bed pushed against the wall with the covers on the floor, is my phone.

It beeps again.

And again.

Dex can't help himself but throw the covers around to search until he finds it.

"Just take it and get the hell out. I'm sure whoever it is, wants to talk with you since you are so fucking popular these days!"

"Declan…"

"*Out!!*"

He turns to grab his wallet and shoves it with my phone in his pocket. Just as he turns to leave the phone beeps again. It's a good thing he's taking it with him because it wouldn't survive another second left alone with me.

After the door slams shut, I get up and drag my ass to the bathroom to look at the damage to my lip. Damn, the right side of my upper lip is split wide open. It's angry-looking, red, and nasty and needs a few stitches, but there is no fucking way I'm going to the hospital. Once I get the bleeding to stop, I'll call down to the front desk and see if they have a sewing kit. Wouldn't be the first time I used a needle and thread on myself, and it won't be the last.

I wet the towel and wince as the pressure against my mouth stings. Too tired to move, I slide down the wall and sit on the cold floor. Eyes closed, I maybe get five minutes if I'm lucky before hell breaks loose again.

The room to our door blasts open, banging into the wall. My first thought is Vince and Marcus have caught up with us. Instead, I hear the loud and unsettling voice of hyped up Dex.

"DECLAN. Get your ass out here now. You have to see this!"

Chapter Nineteen

"Video"

"WHAT THE HELL IS IT now?" I storm from the bathroom with a piercing scowl, still holding the washcloth to my swollen lip. To say I'm more than a little pissed at him right now would be an understatement, but one look at his face and it no longer matters.

The expressions in his hard eyes were compelling, urgent and disconcerting. Eyes that drape me with a black chill and turns my blood ice-cold.

His voice wavers, "I... I don't know what this is. I watched the first few seconds and then got my ass back here to show you."

Dex shoves the phone right in front of my face, not realizing it's so close I can't see a damn thing. I snatch it away from him to see what's so damn important and what I find are three video messages, all sent from the same unknown number. All sent in the last few minutes.

A warning voice whispers in my head as alarm bells sound like some sixth sense. Haunting flashbacks from the last video that was sent to me to watch invade my thoughts. With it the stab of guilt that's buried deep. Memories too painful to talk about but will haunt me for the rest of my life.

I immediately break out in a cold sweat, wrestling with the decision to press play or not, like I have a choice. The timing of this messes with my head because it's hard for me to imagine that these videos are purely coincidental and not part of a perfectly timed strategic move.

My stomach knots with a sickening sense of déjà-vu as I slowly raise my eyes to meet the dark and cautious stare from Dex. Then, I press play.

The video starts off jumpy, but when it comes into focus, the sight before me is both alarming and disturbing. My fingers crush the phone in my hand without me even realizing it.

Whoever is filming the video is doing it from the front seat of a car, with the volume muted. The sky is pitch black, but the two-story brick house with black shutters and well-maintained yard is lit up with help of property lights. There are several interior lights on, like someone is inside the house.

Suddenly, the camera zooms in on a second story window when a dark shadow walks from behind the curtain. It's impossible to make out who the person is since all I can see is a dark shadow as it moves around the room. A second figure appears, and the two shadows are now quickly moving from one end to the room the other. As the shot widens, it stays centered on that second story window for about ten more seconds before the video abruptly ends.

"Holy shit, Declan. That's..."

I confirm his suspicions with a hostile gaze. "I know," I growl with a low pitch to my voice. "Did you happen to see anything that lets us know when this was taped?"

Disappointment flashes in his eyes before he lowers them to the floor with a shake of his head.

"This fucker is taunting me." Since I don't know when this was recorded, I can't rule out that one of the dark shadows is me. If it is, that means someone has been watching me from my own damn house.

That realization has Dex shifting uncomfortably. "There is only one way to get this shot of your room, and it's from the back of the house. Whoever took this had to be parked in the back of the house and the only way to get there is to drive all the way down your long driveway. That's more than fucking gutsy."

It's true, our driveway is over a mile long. It's not the kind of driveway someone pulls into by accident and then just turns around. If you drive up to our house, you do it on purpose.

"Maybe," I consider all possibilities. "Unless it's Rachel. She wouldn't raise any suspicion if she was sitting in our driveway."

Dex lifts his brows as if to agree. "Yeah, could be. I guess we'll know more when we see what's on the other videos." Then, he anxiously coughs. "Look, about earlier…"

I put my hand out to stop him there. Right now, that's not in the forefront of my mind. Not when I have this to deal with. My fight with Dex is bullshit compared to the other shit that's going on in my life.

With my finger hovering over the triangle of the second video, I heavily sigh, then press *play* again. The only thing I hear is the beat of my own heart as it loudly thumps in my ears while Dex and I stay glued to the screen of my phone as the second video starts to play. A low growl escapes my throat as my body temperature rises. Straight away, I'm so alarmed that the hair on the back of my neck stands straight up.

"This fucker is straight up crazy!" He's taping shit from *inside* my house. Even if we figure out this is Rachel's doing, the shit is still whacked.

This time, the video starts off shaky as someone is doing their best to hide it from inside the bookshelf in our main living room, just off the kitchen. There is no volume in this video either. It's uneventful in the first few seconds, until Vince storms in the room. He has a deep scowl on his face as he pours himself a drink, then pours a second one. When he finishes, he picks them both up and sticks his hand out when Marcus enters the room. He swipes the glass from Vince and downs it in one big gulp.

We don't need volume to know they are both mad as hell. Their body language says it loud and clear. It looks like a heated conversation ensues, because they are both shouting and pointing fingers at one another.

"Damn, I really wish we could hear what the hell they're saying." Dex complains over my shoulder when something catches his eye. "Wait, did you see that?"

"See what?" The only thing I see Marcus in an angry rant.

Dex grumbles. "Great, you missed it." He hastily reaches for my phone as I jerk it out of his reach.

"Stop, I'm watching it."

Refusing to let it go, he urges me. "Just rewind it and see for yourself."

Fine. I make a show out of it by holding the phone up to his face and then swipe my finger to rewind the video by twenty seconds or so. It starts playing when Vince hands Marcus his drink and I concentrate on every little thing that happens after.

"Wait for it... there," Dex points with his finger, "right there. Did you see it?"

I'm not sure because the moment he shouted in my ear, it broke my concentration. One again, I rewind by ten seconds and watch it again more closely. At one point, Marcus points his finger away from where Vince is standing.

"See that, right there. It looks like he's shouting at someone else."

Huh? "If so, I wonder who?"

"I have an idea, and if I'm right, that means this video was taken *last night*!"

"Last night?" My head snaps to his. If that's the case, there is no way Rachel is the one taping these videos. Which means. "This fucker was in my house last night!"

That doesn't sit well with me, and it takes everything in me to just clamp my jaws tight to watch the rest of the rest of the video. The last twenty seconds are much of the same while Marcus and Vince continue to shout. That's when Anthony walks in the room with something in his hand. It looks like my pictures... the pictures I left for Vince. The only way I know is because each of those photos were blown up. Even from my angle, I can see the top photo as he passes by the camera.

"Holy shit, he's holding onto the pictures I left for Vince... last night."

Marcus takes the pictures from Anthony and points to one of them as he shouts something in his face. Anthony reacts by blowing up at his brother before he turns and does the same thing to Vince, like Vince had said something to him to set him off. Vince reaches over and grabs the photos from Marcus before throwing them across the room.

"Damn! Wonder what the hell are they arguing about?"

"Who knows," Dex replies, "but shit sure was intense."

As the video ends, we pause and look at one another.

Holding my breath, I press *play* on the final video. "Here goes nothing."

The screen is black and then it switches to a shocking scene that leaves Dex gasping while covering his mouth with his hand.

"Jesus Christ." This asshole is standing in my room, showing the bloody scene of the struggle that took place earlier. Wiping a hand down my face, I exhale with a burst of air making sure to miss my lip that's now swollen like a balloon. Thankfully the bleeding has stopped though.

"Damn, that's sick!" Dex chokes like he's visibly shaken, and it irritates the hell out of me.

"Don't fucking watch if you can't stomach it," I angrily spat, because I'll be damned if he's going to make me out to be the villain in this clusterfuck. He doesn't say a word back, nor does he turn away.

The camera shot then travels down the hall and I know where he's heading. Rachel's room. The door slowly opens as the phone jumps around due to the shaking hand of the person holding it. Rachel's body is on the bed, just as I left her. The camera slightly turns and when it swings back to her, there is something that wasn't there when I left. A single white rose rests on her chest.

Dex leans in closer, then looks at me with his mouth wide open. "Did you leave that?"

"What? Hell no!"

"Oh shit," he replies under his breath and rests a hand on my shoulder. "That can't be good."

What it is, I'm not sure, but while Dex has his mind on the meaning of the flower, I watch as the shot moves on the message I wrote on the wall in her blood. That's when the phone really starts to shake like his hands are twitching in rage.

"Whoever this is, I don't think they like you calling her a lying whore."

"Like I give a fuck!" I irritatingly shrug his hand from my shoulder, knowing what I have to do next. "I need to call Vince."

"Before you do that," Dex lets out an uncomfortable cough. "I need to fill you in on my conversation with Vince and Marcus first."

I lower my head to my chest like I don't have enough bullshit running through my head already, but when I turn and see the grim look on his face, I concede.

"Fine, but before we get into that, go downstairs and see if you can get a hold on a needle and some thread. I can't call Vince and be on the phone for who knows how long with my lip bleeding all over the place. And, since you've been stuffing your face, grab me a few pizzas. I'm fucking starving."

He stands there looking at me when he lowers his chin. "Does this mean I'm forgiven for earlier?"

"Hell no," I scoff. "And Dex, I'm warning you, don't ever pull shit like that again."

An understanding passes between us as he lets it go with a slight nod of his head.

"Dammit Dex!"

"Quit your bitching and hold still," he jabs me with the needle again like it's payback. "I only got one more stitch and I'm done." He looks like he's way too much fun. His shit-eating grin proves it.

I grumble, "You suck as a nurse." That comment got me a painful lift of my lip as he tugged on the thread harder then he needed to.

"Better get used to it since you killed the last one. Looks like your stuck with me."

I growl with a roll of my eyes, letting him know he's not funny. If he'd just get it done I'd be fine, but he's going extra slow, making it hurt more than it should.

When Dex came back with a bag full of shit, the smell of piping hot pizza was the only thing I wanted. My lip could fucking wait until the stabbing pain in my stomach was fed. Two large pizzas, a liter of Pepsi, and a few Advil later, I agreed to let Dex stitch me up. What the hell was I thinking?

"Sit your ass still!"

"Fuck! Just get it done already! But I'm telling you now, you better not screw it up and leave a nasty looking scar."

"Yeah, yeah yeah," he breathes through his teeth. "Shut the fuck up. Every time you talk, it messes me up and pulls on the stitches."

Whatever!

"Okay, so wait 'til you hear this shit." Dex goes on to tell me about his very candid conversation with Vince when I was knocked the fuck out.

"After I tried to wake your ass up several times, Vince had enough and told me to start talking. Marcus and Anthony were both there at the time and things got so heated between them, Vince had to step in and break them up. The argument started when Anthony challenged Marcus and Vince on their stance that whoever is behind this made a *fatal* mistake when he revealed sensitive information to you they never intended for you to find out.

"From there, shit got even crazier when Anthony started taking your side about deserving to know the truth. All of it. He blames them for this whole mess and how it's all gone down. Convinced that if they had told you everything from the beginning, there would be nothing to expose. That's when Marcus lost it."

Damn!

Anthony on my side, agreeing with me and not them? It's strange, but crazier things have happened. The *holy shit* moment for me is Anthony saying his brother and my uncle are to blame for this mess. I can guarantee Vince and Marcus were fucking furious to hear that. It's a good thing Anthony is fast on his feet, because he's not a fighter. Marcus, however, is explosive. I've seen him knock out many teeth and break several jaws with one swing over the years. My uncle Vince, is more guarded and tends to keep things to himself, but he can dish out one hell of a beating if need be.

It's a wonder Anthony made it out of the house walking on his own two legs.

"I've never seen your uncle that pissed off," Dex mentions, concentrating on his handy work. Then, slowly looks down at me. "Do you think he'll turn up here?" The thought of Vince showing up makes him no unnerved, it causes him to give a hearty tug on the thread, lifting my lip with it.

"Damn, take it easy," I hiss through my teeth, finding out just how difficult it is to talk and not move my lips too much. "I have no idea, but when push comes to shove, he can be a scary motherfucker." That's what I tried to say anyway, but most of it came out like a mumbled mess.

Dex heard me just fine, if the anxious expression on his face is anything to go by. He cautions, "He wants blood for whoever is behind this. They flipped out and were livid over the contents of the envelope finding out you were pressured into taking a dive on the fight with Curtis. To top it off, I about pissed myself knowing I had to be the one to explain the situation with Rachel to none other than your uncle and *Marcus fucking Aniello*. That took years off my life, dude. From that point on, shit went to a whole new level of crazy. Before they ended the call, they told me to keep your ass here until they called back."

By the look on his face, Dex is still a bit freaked out. To me, they're family, but to him, they are people never to fucking cross.

"Did they?" I ask.

He looks down like I'm ridiculous just as he ties the last knot. "Hell yes, five times."

"Fuck. Then sending these three videos to Vince should *really* make their day," I remark as I do just that.

As if on cue, my phone rings!

MY TALK WITH VINCE WAS long overdue and uncomfortable. We talked and shouted, but then we came together to try and make sense of things. He is as determined as I am and is in close contact with Marcus, who has feelers all over the city to find out who the three men are in the photographs I left. Much to his disapproval though, I ignored his plea to come home so we could re-group. I'm not going home until I finish what I set out to do.

That was three days ago.

Since then, Dex and I finally made it to the quaint little town of Monroe, Washington. Population, eighteen thousand and thirty miles north from the hustle of Seattle. We found the perfect place to stay along route 2. The Fairground Inn, a low-key motel that sits on the outskirt of town and is easily accessible. Not what you would consider a five-star resort, but we're not here on vacation.

Once Vince got it through his thick head that I wasn't coming home until I finished this, he's made it a point to constantly check in with me. It's a pain the ass, but it keeps him off my back.

In the meantime, Marcus is continuing to work things on his end. With the copies of the photos I left, he and Salvo both are working their sources double time. Salvo even thinks he's picked up a few clues from the prints themselves, but nothing concrete that he's willing to share just yet. If they can somehow identify any of the three men and find them, we can figure out who is behind it all.

Vince has a real issue with Dex and his big plan. The last thing he wants is me to be anywhere near any of my long-lost relatives. His exact words, *"It will be opening a can of worms and it will not end well."*

For some reason, he seems to think that their rejection of me will somehow hurt me on a deeper level than I'm willing to admit. I had to assure him that all I want from them are answers, not start a family bond.

Finding himself on the losing end of the argument, he finally began to open up about Kara and the few times he interacted with her over the years. It was the first time I ever felt that he was being completely honest with me.

Though he did make a point to say that he does not, nor will he ever, regret his decision not to tell me that she was the one who killed my father. He stands by his decision; *the truth would have only hurt you further!*

When it came to my half siblings, Willow and Eve, Vince didn't know much about them. Marcus knows more when it comes to Kara,

Izzy, and Willow because he was the closet with Dominic during those times. Their friendship spanned over many years.

Marcus was there, listening for most of the conversation until he took part in it himself. The feeling I got from Marcus is one of guilt and regret. I could hear how raw it still is for him all these years later.

He almost came with Dominic to Washington State to get Izzy, but at the last minute changed his plans. In his mind, if he would have come along, my father may still be alive today. It's a guilt he carries with him every day. He got choked up when he admitted he feels like he has somehow let me down.

It was tough to hear, but I needed to hear all of it.

Especially when it came to the harder conversation.

For her part in killing Dominic, a deal was struck to save Kara's life in return. The Chicago chapter of the Lost Souls MC wanted retribution and took it out in blood by kicking the shit out of Liam Talbott, even though he was a member himself. All because he refused to hand over his woman.

Then Marcus got to the part of the story where my unexpected arrival came into play. Things got interesting very fast and new plans were immediately set in motion.

It was Vince who made the deal for me with Kara even though my mother, Tiffany, despised Izzy and Kara both. The last thing Liam wanted was his sister, *my mother* to be mixed up with Vince at all. It was bad enough she got knocked up by Dominic who, by all accounts, was the devil himself.

It didn't matter what his sister wanted, Liam was going to make sure his sister got out of the mess she found herself in. After Vince convinced Tiffany to come back to Chicago with him to have the baby, Vince went to Kara, knowing she was the best bet when it came to Liam.

If Liam agreed to leave his sister in peace to have me in Chicago with Vince, then Vince and Marcus both would simply walk away with no more bloodshed. Kara could live without any further retribution for what she had done.

For Vince, all that mattered was me. He wanted to make sure I was born and cared for by those who knew my father best. By those who cared about him and would make damn sure I knew how important my father was to them.

That was nearly twenty years ago!

Deals were made, and everyone seemed to get what they wanted.

Except for one.

Me.

Shit was cleaned up, covered up, and all but forgotten.

Only...

What about what I want?

Did any of them ever consider that?

Don't I count?

Obviously not!

Well, that's just too damn bad. If Libbs' death has taught me anything, it's that life is too short.

If they thought, they could just sweep my father's death under the rug and get away with it forever, they thought fucking wrong! I never made a deal with anyone and I won't be told what to do now. This is my life and I deserve to have my questions answered.

Who ever said my life was going to be easy, anyway? It all comes down to one thing. To be able to move on with my life, I have a few demons to confront first.

And it starts... now!

Chapter Twenty

"First Meetings"

"**A**RE YOU READY FOR THIS?" Dex said.

The skepticism in his voice has me rolling my eyes.

With an unnatural groan, I reply, "What do you think, asswipe?" *I still can't believe I let him talk me into this.*

Ever since Dex announced this little set up for me to meet Willow, it has been weighing heavily on my mind. And it has only been made worse by the fact she's bringing her sister, *my* sister, Eve, with her.

How the hell am I going to be able to sit there knowing who they are, when they have no clue who the hell I really am? It's bad enough Willow thinks I'm some art student enrolling at her school. What's worse, I have to play it off like I've been the one she's been talking with for the past few weeks.

The odds of me pulling this off without a hitch is zero! I'm trying to keep an open mind, but as I pull into The Shack, a restaurant we agreed to meet at, I'm having second thoughts.

"Are you sure this is the place she picked?" I ask Dex, slightly confused. From the look of it, this is the last place I'd expect to find college students hanging out. The overly sized lodge is outdated and looks like nothing has changed since it opened. Judging by the décor, the rugged woodsy, log cabin vibe with overgrowing moss everywhere, this place has been here a long while.

I mutter under my breath. "I should have just brought you along with me."

Dex laughs at my misery. "You got this. I prepped you with all the important shit anyway. Plus, you listened to the recordings of our conversations, that I will add was another genius move on my part. You'll be fine."

It's true, he taped a few conversations for me to listen to, but he insisted he stay back at the motel just in case she accidentally recognized his voice over mine. Lucky for us, we both have gravelly voices so similar, people mistake us for one another all the time. It's another reason why he thought his plan could work. He's also digging the new phone I got him once we got to town, since I did throw his out the window. I bought it on one condition, he is not allowed to give his new number to my uncle until we get back to Chicago. The less interference the better.

"Did she mention what kind of car she drives?" I think to ask because what someone drives say a lot about them. It's true. Take my cherry red Camaro for instance. It's hot and fast, just like me!

"Nah, man. No clue."

"That's probably a good thing since the choices are four-door sedans and minivans." It's kind of funny, but what's not is this shitty gravel pit they call a parking lot. It has more potholes than not, and no specific areas marked for parking.

Fuck that, I head for the back where there is small patch of grass next to a bunch of trees. Back here I should avoid door dings and layers of dust from idiots driving in and out of this dust bowl of a parking lot. If I don't bottom my car out first. It pisses me off and I haven't even walked in the door yet.

This is crazy! The more I look around, the more I'm sure I'm in the wrong place. "Dex, are you sure this is the place because I find it hard to believe this is where Willow picked to meet? It's the sort of place old people hang out at." I subtly say into my earpiece. The last thing I need is for someone to think I'm talking to myself. Then again, I might fit right in.

He laughs like it's some inside joke I'm missing. "Jesus, Declan we're not in Chicago. This is the Northwest. Everything is different here, if you hadn't noticed."

"You're a fucking barrel of laughs." I huff under my breath. "Anything else you want tell me? If so, hurry the fuck up so I can get this shit the fuck over with."

He stops chuckling long enough to take a breath. "Quit your bitching, just chat with her and find out if anything weird is going on with her lately."

"Besides me?"

"Oh, GOD!" He yells into the phone. "You're impossible to deal with sometimes. Make some shit up about a rumor you heard about some guy stalking girls in the area. Ask her if she's noticed anything out of the ordinary? I don't know, just go with the flow and see how it plays out."

"Yeah, I guess. I'll call ya soon."

"Hey, before you hang up. Remember I've played it off with her that I'm not feeling well so I disguised my voice some just in case she happens to say anything about our voices not quite matching up."

Ugh! "Remind me again why I'm doing this? Like this isn't going to be hard enough, I need to play off I have a slight cold as well? Anything else I need to fake?"

Leave it to Dex to be the voice of reason. "Think of the bigger picture here. Keep Willow safe and catch the psycho."

Just then, a red car pulls into the parking lot with two females. "Shit, it's too late to back now anyway." The red, two door Toyota parks next to the side of the building. "Two girls just pulled in a red Toyota."

"Showtime." Dex says excitedly as the pit in my stomach drops.

I end the call, ready to get this shit show over with.

WILLOW

Twenty Minutes Earlier ...

"EVE, YOU HAVE TO COME with me." My older sister knows I'm nervous. Now, all of a sudden, she's dragging her feet.

"Willow," she sighs, looking down at my hands that are folded like I'm praying, "why do I have to come and have lunch with some guy you just met?" She rolls her eyes, but I ignore her.

"You need to check him out for me. You're my wing girl and you are way better at judging people than I am." I'm prepared to beg if need be.

She taps her foot a few times. "Ask Dad or Uncle Liam. They would love to meet him."

Of course, she had to bring them into the picture. What a great idea. Not!

Argh! She can be so frustrating at times. "Funny. You're hilarious. Let's go before we're late." I shove her ahead of me, but she stops and turns back.

"How did you find him again?"

I've already talked with Eve about the guy I started chatting with from the school's registry. We met on the school's meet new friends chat line. I admit it was odd at first, but this guy seemed nice, different. This will be the first time I get to meet him in person. I'm nervous as hell and my stomach won't stop churning. I spent over two hours getting ready making sure I look my best. My dark brown hair is fully curled, and my makeup is light. I look pretty. To make a good first impression, I'm in my best jeans that fit me like a glove and a cute t-shirt that's tight, but not overly snug.

I'm a college student, I'm going to dress like one. Eve's older so her tastes are more polished. She'd never be seen leaving the house for a date in jeans and a t-shirt. She'd be all dolled up in some skirt and matching top.

Yuck, not my scene or style.

"Okay, let's go and meet this one. He'd better not creep me out or I'm calling Dad for backup."

"Dang it, Eve, stop making me nervous."

When we arrive, she opens the door to The Shack. It's mid-day so it's not busy like it normally is for dinner. Forgoing the tables in the center of the room, we make our way to a booth in the back. Once we take a seat, Eve orders us drinks while I pull out my phone and send him a text like I said I would. The butterflies are at top speed in my stomach and I feel like I might get sick. The pressure is way too much.

"I wonder what will happen now?" I say taking a big, calming breath, unaware someone was behind me.

"Why hello, Willow." A low and pleasant voice speaks out.

My eyes go wide in shock as I look at Eve who has a blank expression on her face looking over my shoulder. I turn, completely surprised.

"Wow," I stammer. "You are fast," I ramble, taking in his good looks. Boy, he's so handsome, I feel like I may be out of my league. Maybe that's what Eve was thinking with her non-expressive gaze a moment ago.

"I was waiting...for you." He says, then extends his hand to cup my shoulder.

His fingers are warm and firm. I instantly blush because he's so cute. I know it's him because the photo in the chat matches him perfectly. Thank God! That was my first worry, that he would show up looking nothing like the dark-haired guy on my computer. Well, his face is now my screen saver, but he does *not* need to know that.

He smiles at me as his gaze shifts to my sister, who's not as impressed. She's too busy sizing him up.

"How sweet. Don't you think, Eve?" I kick her under the table.

"Yeah, that's not creepy at all," she replies with a raised brow.

"Eve," I warn.

"Eve," his warm voice engages, "I've heard a lot about you."

Oh crap. That won't sit well with her. Sure enough, she shoots daggers at me and I want to crawl under the table. Eve does not easily warm up to people. When he said he's heard so much about her, I have to think back to what I've said to him about her. Surely I only mentioned the basics. It must be his attempt to butter her up or something. Hope it works, but I won't hold my breath for fear I'll turn blue first.

"And I've heard about you," she snarls with her usual less than friendly attitude. "What's the name again?"

He stares at her for a long, awkward minute before a smile cracks free. "Declan."

"Got a last name, Declan?"

"Parisi. Declan Parisi."

"Well, Declan Parisi, why don't you take a seat."

"I think that's a splendid idea."

Declan

What the fuck was I thinking?

Splendid idea? *Not even fucking close! And who the fuck even says splendid anymore?*

Right off the bat, I can tell two things. One, Willow looks so damn young and naïve, which means she's likely way too trusting, and that's not good. It just makes it easier for the psycho who has her in his sights to get to her and makes it harder for me to stop him.

While Eve, on the other hand, appears not to trust anyone. She's given me one hell of an attitude since I walked up. Prim and proper, dressed well, not a hair out of place. Right now, her arms are crossed, and her head is slightly tilted to the side. Her eagle eyes are watching my every move, scrutinizing me.

Is she shitting me right now? It's almost laughable because if this is her way to intimidate or to try and get a read on me, she can knock herself out! She'll get neither.

After I take a seat in the booth across from them, the waitress comes and takes my drink order. The entire time, I can feel Eve's heavy stare and instantly something clicks. The irony is a bit strange, but it seems like Eve and I may have something in common after all. Makes me wonder if good ol' mom has burned her in the past too.

Even so, it doesn't stop my hands from curling into fists under the table. Bitchy women make my blood boil. Usually I avoid them at all costs, but this is different. I get the feeling no matter *who* showed up today to meet Willow, the hardhearted bitch in Eve would be giving them the same despising look she's giving me now. I wonder if this is more than just looking out for her little sister.

If I had to guess, I'd say little sister gets way more attention from the opposite sex than she does. Is Eve jealous of Willow? I'd bet money on it.

I can just add this to the level of already bizarre shit that's happened so far on this trip. This morning, when I was looking at the photo of them that was inside the envelope, I had this idea what they would be like. Only, sitting across from them now, I see I couldn't have been more wrong. They seem as different as night and day.

The awkward tension is broken when Willow's phone rings.

"Sorry, I need to take this really quickly, it's my mom," She says with a flush to her cheeks, like she's embarrassed her mother is checking up on her.

To keep from making some dick comment that would only embarrass her more, I utter, "No worries, take your time. We all know how mothers can be."

Boy, do we. Just saying it leaves a nasty taste in mouth as I shift my gaze from Willow to Eve. My hope is to get a reaction out of her but, like I expected, she never flinches. Her face is still as stone. Looks like Willow is the lucky one with a mother who gives a shit enough to call.

Talk about confronting demons. Desperate times call for desperate measures.

There is no love loss for my bitch of a mother. Eve giving off the vibe she's nothing but a cold-hearted bitch isn't that surprising to me, considering we share the same mother. Shit's not entirely her fault.

Major Bitch Syndrome just runs in her genes, and unfortunately for Eve, she inherited our mother's looks and personality.

By the grace of God, Willow seems to be the complete opposite and it's the only reason I'm still here. There's something about her that intrigues me. I can't figure what it is, but her eyes are a dead ringer to mine. From the photo's I've seen of our father, there is no mistaking where we get our looks from.

It blows my fucking mind to sit here between these two. One represents the worst part of me, while the other makes me want to know more. Jesus, the information I could unload on them right now would rock their worlds.

This whole situation feels like an acid trip gone bad.

After Willow ends her call, she bashfully looks at me and blushes again, then hides her face behind her dark hair.

Heat rises from the pit of my stomach. I don't think I've heard all the conversations Dex and Willow have had because nothing in Willow's chestnut eyes and thick lashes suggests she sees me as just a friend. I'm going to kill Dex and his 'charming personality.' If he led her on, intentionally or not, because of his obsession with her, I'll gut him like a fucking fish. There is no way around it, I'm going to hell for this and I'll be sure to take Dex with me.

I need to fix this now, before it gets out of hand. I can't have her thinking there is anything remotely romantic between us. God, I can hardly look at her and not see my own dark eyes staring back at me. The only difference is hers are warm. Not hard and cold like mine.

It takes the sound of Eve clearing her throat to break our stare. Though, I'm not sure what's worse. It takes real effort to look at her because her damn platinum hair is enough of a reminder of our 'mother' that it makes my stomach roll.

I'm half tempted to blurt out if she's heard from mommy dearest lately. Like I would give a shit either way, but still. I wonder, was Eve a burden to her like I was, or was it just me that she didn't give a fuck about?

Her eyes shoot daggers at me. "What's with the messed-up face?"

"Eve," Willow blurts out like she's totally appalled at her older sister, "please just stop."

"What," Eve snips back playing the part of the bitchy older sister, "it's a reasonable question. Got any anger issues, Declan we need to be made aware of?"

"EVE!" Willow looks so upset, I'm not sure if she wants to deck her sister or cry.

Either way, it's official. I've entered the motherfucking twilight zone and it will be a damn miracle if I don't fuck this up by saying something I shouldn't. But damn, I'd like to give Eve a taste of her own fucking medicine.

"It's okay, Willow," I lose the snarl of my lip to show Willow that Eve's comments don't affect me. "I fight every now and then to make money. I'm not ashamed of what I do."

Willow forces a smile before turning her attention to Eve. "That's how he pays for school, Eve. I told you this."

I did? I mean Dex did? Shit, he didn't tell me that.

To switch the subject real fucking fast, I mentally start ticking off the all things Dex told me about Willow until one sticks. Her passion for art. Shit, Dex has drilled that into my head enough that I shouldn't screw this up.

Ignoring Eve altogether, I turn my attention to Willow. "So, tell me again, why Da Vinci? What is it that you find most fascinating?"

I know her answer before she gives it, but the instant expression on her face surprises me. Her eyes light up and her mega-watt smile beams against the rush of color in her cheeks.

After she tucks a strand of her hair behind her ear, she bashfully chuckles, then looks up. "He was a genius, a true pioneer when it comes to the beauty of art. I love to study his work. He once said, *'Painting is poetry that is seen rather than felt, and poetry is painting that is felt rather than seen.'* I mean, what's not to like?"

Eve scoffs. "Besides the fact he's been dead for centuries?" Her rude comment is followed with a snippy roll of her eyes before she goes back to picking at her perfectly manicured hands. Damn. If I didn't know any better I'd say Eve is a bit bitter, or her true colors are showing. Her comment hit Willow where she wanted it to. Willow recoils and looks down with a dejected look that instantly sets me off. What a bitch move. When I look at Eve this time, I have a different view of her.

Well, come on, dear sister, let's see how you stack up against me.

I lean across the table and wait until Eve is forced to look at me in the eyes. "I get that I'm not a blonde, but what does *that* have to do with anything she just said?" I cut her down for sounding utterly ridiculous and decide I'm going to teach her what it feels like to belittled in front of others. Thank you, Dex, for the art history lesson. I'm about to teach the ice princess a thing or two.

I hold her spiteful gaze as she throws me another dirty look. Then, I give one back, talking directly to her. "Art is timeless. A concept based on one's own interpretation and expression, but the philosophy is the same. Art is the study of pure beauty and taste. If appreciated correctly, it should move you and evoke feelings you may not even know you have. Only shallow, narrowminded people would find that useless and a waste of time."

Her expression hardens and just as she opens her mouth to respond, both of their phones go off at the same time. A brief exchange happens between them before they look down at their phones. Red flags go up as both of their bodies go straight as a board.

What the hell now?

"Is something wrong?" I look between them to see if I can gauge anything, but the only thing they do is silently communicate with one another with their eyes.

Eve speaks first, "Ah, we have to go. Now!" She abruptly jumps up and stares at me before she motions for Willow to follow her.

"Yeah, sorry about this." Willow lightly whispers, refusing to look at me at all. "Something just came up."

Whispering to one another, Eve puts her arm around Willow's shoulder and narrowly glances back one more time before they head straight for the door.

That was fucking strange! I think to myself as a chill runs down my spine. Before the door closes, Willow takes one last look over her shoulder. When our eyes connect, she immediately lowers them with a shake of her head as they rush to their car.

Something is very wrong, and my gut feeling tells me it's *him!*

The question is how!

"Can I get you anything else?" The waitress approaches the booth with her pen and paper while looking over her shoulder for the two girls who were sitting here just a moment ago.

"No, I hate to drink alone."

She gives me a confused look, asking, "Well, where did the girls..."

I cut her off. "Gone."

She has no idea what to say, so she just turns and walks off.

I have my phone out and begin to text Dex when an incoming message pops up with an unknown number.

Unknown: Are you enjoying your lunch?

Bastard! My eyes shoot up and look over my shoulder at every table in the restaurant that have customers sitting at them. Three women and a guy who are pushing eighty. I think I can scratch him out as my psycho.

Fuck it. I text back.

Me: I was until you interrupted it! That was you wasn't it?

Unknown: Smart boy.

Boy my ass!

Me: This isn't fair you know. You know my name, why not tell me yours? Unless you're afraid, that is.

Let's see how he responds to that.

Unknown: What? And spoil all the fun? No, I don't think so. This is my game, my rules. Remember that.

Me: Game? Is that what you call killing Liberty, a game?

In the meantime, I shoot Dex a text.

Me: Dex, we have a big problem. He's here and texting me!! Willow and Eve left in a hurry. On my way back!

When this comes in.

Unknown: I underestimated you. Clearly, that can't happen again. And just so you know, you will pay for what you did to Rachel. Maybe Willow can make up for it.

Motherfucker!

Me: Leave her out of this, you don't want her. You want ME! Come and get me you pansy-ass motherfucker! Let's settle whatever the fuck you want face-to-face!

Unknown: Be careful what you wish for, boy!

Boy? I'm going to show that piece of shit just how much of a fucking boy I am!!

I toss a few dollars on the table and head outside to call Dex. He picks the worst time possible NOT to answer his phone. When I get to my car, I drop my keys trying to press the unlock button on my remote. That's when I hear a strange noise coming from the thick trees behind the area where I parked. With the phone still to my ear, I bend over just as Dex finally answers.

"Damn, it's about time you picked…"

That's when it happens.

I never saw it coming.

Everything just goes black!

Chapter Twenty-One

"The Time has come"

*P**LANS ARE IN MOTION.*
Everything is going like clockwork, but I fear my time is running out. Things are starting to heat up and my actions are starting to raise a few eyebrows. It won't be long before they figure it out, so I need to finish this.

I watch from the window as my men work toward getting things set up for my unsuspecting guests this evening. After all this time and all this work, tonight it all comes to a head. Tonight, I finish it.

My phone beeps with the message that the boy is inside the restaurant with Willow and Eve, but I think his lunch plans are in about to be interrupted any minute now. I'm sure my text to Izzy will cut that little reunion short.

While I wait, I light my cigar and watch the smoke rings rise in the air until they dissipate. Just then, Dio's voice comes over the walkie-talkie sitting on my desk.

"Boss, the girls just left the restaurant."
Excellent.
It's time.
I text the boy.

Unknown: Are you enjoying your lunch?

Declan: I was until you interrupted it! That was you wasn't it?

He's clever. Just not clever enough.

Unknown: Smart boy.

Declan: This isn't fair you know. You know my name, why not tell me yours? Unless you're afraid, that is.

If he only knew. Soon enough he will. While I text with the boy, I need to have to Dio ready, so I grab the walkie-talkie.
"The boy should be leaving the restaurant at any minute. Be alert. Be ready. Get it done!"
"Copy that."
Good. Good.
Then, the boy sends me this!

Declan: Leave her out of this, you don't want her. You want ME! Come and get me you pansy-ass motherfucker! Let's settle whatever the fuck you want face-to-face!

On second thought.
"And, Dio, make it hurt!"
With that, I send my last text.

Unknown: Be careful what you wish for, boy!

Tossing the phone on my desk, I sit back and roll my cigar in my fingers before I take a puff. With my head back, I let out, one, two, three smoke rings of smoke and watch them float in the air above me. With painful images filling my mind, my lip quivers before turning into a sadistic grin as a low menacing laugh echoes throughout the room.

Chapter Twenty-Two

Dex

"Yo Declan, you there?" Even though cell reception around here sucks, my gut tells me something is off. When I hear a harsh groan followed with a loud thud, that's when the hairs on the back of my neck stand up and my stomach hits the floor.

"Hey!" I shout into the phone, freaking the hell out. "Declan, you there? Come on, man, *answer* me!"

The silence is deafening.

Fuck! Fuck! Fuck!

What I wouldn't give for this to be just another one of Declan's stupid pranks, but my gut tells me otherwise. This is no practical joke, it's very real. And real fucking serious.

"What a dumb ass," I gripe to myself and call his phone again. It's easier to be pissed at him than face the worst. The fact that his phone rings is a good sign, but it's short lived. With each unanswered ring, my apprehension grows as the call goes straight to his god-awful voicemail.

'Who are you, what do you want, why do I care? Just leave a message! Beep!'

Yeah, I'd like to leave him a message alright, but I'd rather he just answer the phone. No matter how many times I call, nothing changes. I'm sent to that same damn voicemail that I despise, but I call it a few more times just to hear his egotistical voice.

I'm in way over my head. I knew the danger, but I really didn't think it would come to this. When I think of Declan, I think of him as being invincible. Indestructible. That's what makes this so fucking hard to believe. Vince is going to kill me if anything happens to Declan and it makes me wonder if this was the plan that fucking madman had along. To get Declan away from Chicago and away from his family, so he can take his shot? If that's the case, we walked right into that trap.

Dammit, Vince tried to warn us, told us to come back home until they could figure this shit out, but Declan's one stubborn prick who hates being told what to do. Vince even threatened my ass and told me to keep an eye on Declan once he finally realized Declan wasn't coming home just yet. His instructions to me were clear... don't let things get out of control and don't let Declan take any unnecessary risks.

Which is laughable since we we're talking about Declan. The one who is always out of control and thrives on taking unnecessary risks. I didn't argue though. I value my life, so I kept my big mouth shut. Since pissing Vince off would be like playing Russian roulette. No, thank you!

The thing is, I'm a no-win situation. If something has happened to Declan, there's no telling what that sick fuck will do to him. I have no choice, Declan will just have to beat my ass later for breaking my promise. I'm calling his uncle.

As I start to dial his number, I break out in a sweat. One ring leads to two, then three.

Come on. Pick the hell up!

Finally. "Vince Parisi." His gruff voice is short and hostile.

Shit, this isn't good, and I'm about make it worse.

"Hey Vince," I manage to say before my throat seizes up with the regret of what I'm about to tell him. It doesn't help that he intimidates the hell out of me. I'm not sure if he knows it me, because he has yet to say word which makes this phone call ten-thousand times worse.

"It's me, Dex," I say into complete silence.

Eventually, Vince puts me out of my misery and grumbles into the phone. "This is *not* a good a time, Dex."

"Is it ever?" I foolishly blurt out feeling the pressure while I pace in the same small area of our motel room. "I'm calling to let you know Declan got a text from that asshole a short time ago. He's here."

With an iron fist, Vince roars, "WHAT?"

I don't get a chance to repeat myself because Vince is already barking orders at someone else.

"Marcus! Get in here and bring Anthony with you!" He roars like a mighty lion, so loud, I have to hold the phone away from my ear.

Oh shit, that's just fucking great. Marcus and Anthony are there. I instantly feel nauseous as the blood drains from my face, knowing, yet again, I have to be the one to spill the bad news. This shit has got to stop happening to me.

I decide to give myself a mental pep talk this time around. The best way to do it is just say what I have to say, and not overthink a goddamn thing. My best friend could be in serious trouble and needs help from his family, and we're hundreds of miles away from home. Sounds good to me, now to just say it to them.

I hear Vince telling them about Declan getting a text message as they continue into their own side conversation. It's nerve-wracking to the point I feel ready to explode. Raising my voice, I interrupt them just to get it out. "Listen, I think we have a bigger problem on our hands."

They immediately stop talking as the phone goes eerily silent. "What are you saying?"

I swallow one last time, getting my nerve up with my eyes closed tight and the phone smashed to my ear. Shit is about to hit the fan. "Ah, well, I'm not one hundred percent sure, but it seems that Declan may be missing?"

Talk about excruciating. The last part just rushes out of my mouth as I hold my breath and brace myself for impact. I start to wonder if our call got disconnected, because it is dead silent. Just as I look to check the connection, Vince erupts with hurricane strength force ready to destroy anything in his path while Marcus is barking orders to someone in the background.

"Dex, you better explain to me what the fuck you mean by 'may be missing,' because I gave you strict orders to *watch out for him*." Then, he really rips into me. "I knew this plan of yours was reckless. You better get your ass out there and find him right motherfucking, *now*! We'll see what we can do from here, but this shit stops now. Be prepared to see me real fucking soon." The last thing I hear is this, "Marcus, I'm going to *kill*..."

Click!

What the hell was that?

Going to kill?

Who?

Me? Marcus? Somebody else?

Sonofabitch! I let my frustration get the better of me as I hurl my phone across the room. "Goddammit!" Lucky for me it didn't break, but it also did little to help calm my nerves. With my fingers locked on top of my head, I pace back and forth in our tiny motel room feeling like the walls are closing in on me. There is no way in hell I can sit still to try and figure out what to do next.

The way I see it, I have two options; one, get my ass to The Shack to see if Declan's car is still there. He typically carries a second set of keys with him whenever he travels, so I'm hoping I can find an extra set in one of his bags. It makes sense to start there.

The second is a bit trickier, but I may not have a choice considering what little I have to go on. A text message and disconnected call isn't much. I need more, and I need it now. Time is definitely not on my side and any detail, no matter how insignificant, could be the one thing I need to figure out what happened with Declan.

Talking with the person who saw him last just makes sense even though that has the potential to blow up in my face. I'll have to expose the lie and explain who Declan really is and why we're really here. It's a risk, but it's a chance I'm willing to take.

Hopefully Willow will understand we only did this to protect her.

THE GOOD NEWS IS I found the extra set of keys to Declan's car. With keys in hand, I haul ass and run from the Fairfield Inn to The Shack, not paying any attention to the dreary sky I've become accustomed to. Since we've been here, I have yet to see the sun actually shine. It's all doom and gloom day after day. I can't wait to get home to Chicago where the sun shines a hell of a lot more than here.

Just my luck, it starts to pour before I make it a block from the motel. I do my best to ignore the chill in the air and pull the hood of my sweatshirt up before picking up my pace. By the time I run the mile to the parking lot of The Shack, I'm soaking wet and winded.

Right away, I spot Declan's Camaro and a weird sensation hits me. I'm not sure if it's good or bad that his car is still here, but a different kind of chill runs down my spine.

I count about twenty cars in the parking lot, but none of them are parked near Declan's car. He parked it all the way in the back. I'm cautious as I approach his car, taking a second to look around and see if anything seems out of place. One pull on a door handle, I find the car still locked and I'm thankful I have the extra set. Since nothing seems out of the ordinary on the inside of the car, I walk around and stop once I notice drag marks on that the ground run from the driver's side and lead into the heavy brush just behind. Due to the rain, the ground is slightly muddy, but it helps make the few set of footprints that are there stand out even more.

A sickening feeling sinks in my gut as I lean down to inspect what is most definitely drag marks. A shiny keyring catches my eye under the car, Declan's. There is no reason for them to be here unless they were accidentally kicked there in some sort of scuffle. I add them to the spare set in my pocket and follow the drag mark that lead into a heavy brush behind the car. On the other side is a big, open field, and that's where the drag marks suddenly stop.

"Fuck!" Goddamned dead end. Frustrated and with nothing to go on, I kick the ground and mumble under my breath, "Declan where the hell are you?"

A voice comes out of nowhere.

"Hey, whatcha' doin' back here? This is private property." The unfriendly voice of a woman startles me just as I turn around.

At first, I'm too stunned to speak. It's not every day I get yelled at by some middle-aged woman wearing an apron and carrying a broom like a weapon. I keep from laughing and put my hands out in front of me to show her I mean her no harm. Then I calmly explain, "I'm looking for my friend. I had no idea this was private property."

She stares at me for a moment, then makes a *huh* noise from her throat like she's trying to decide if I'm telling her the truth. "Is that your car?" She inquires with a nod of her head in the direction of Declan's car. "'Cause it sure looked like you were aiming to break into it? You sure you aren't a robber or somethin'?"

"*Me?*" I look at her like she's crazy, not considering how it could have looked to anyone watching me. I argue, "No, I'm not a thief. That's his car. I told you, I'm looking for my friend, that's all."

Her eyes lower to my wet clothing. "Why you are running with your hood up like some robber then?"

I glance up at the dreary sky. "I hate to point it out you, but it's raining."

"Yeah," she shrugs her shoulders, "so what."

I forget that she lives with this weather every day. Right now, she's arguing with me in the rain like it's no big deal. Frustrated, I pull my hood down and then reach for the keys from my jeans pocket before I jingle them in front of her face. "I have keys, I'm no robber."

That seems to satisfy her. "You never can be sure nowadays, can ya?"

I lightly chuckle, "Guess not, but can I ask you something?" I figure if this nosy lady is so interested in what I'm doing, maybe she saw something earlier. "Do you work or live around here?"

She nods her head. "My husband and I run The Shack and live up there on the hill."

The same property I happen to be standing on. Just by chance, I ask, "Did you happen to see anything earlier, I'm afraid something may have happened to my friend who was in your restaurant just a few hours ago."

She raises her chin and narrowly gazes at me. "I might have seen something, not sure it's much of anything though. Why don't we get out the rain, I'll get you a cup of coffee and tell you what I saw."

I sigh with a bit of relief and grin that she no longer is eyeing me like a criminal. "That would be great, but I'm in kind of a hurry to find him."

She pauses and raises a questioning eye. "Is he in trouble?"

I inwardly cringe. The word 'trouble' doesn't begin to cover it. "Could be," I truthfully answer deeply troubled by what that could mean.

She reads the somber look of my face, then gives me a reassuring smile. "Well, let's hope you find him then. By the way, I'm Joanie. Joanie Sutton. Roger and I have owned this place going on thirty years now."

"No shit?" I say thinking nothing of it when she stops and jerks her head back like I've somehow insulted her.

"Show some respect. I swear, your generation is nothing but foul-mouthed heathens."

I laugh but try to cover it up by clearing my throat. "Yes ma'am. I'm sorry, I meant no disrespect. I'm Dex." I introduce myself, inwardly laughing this time. Who the hell would have thought the word *shit* would be so offensive these days?

Once we get inside, she guides me take a seat at the long line of stools that are right off the kitchen area. She shakes off the rain and kindly treats me.

"I'll get you a warm cup of coffee and a piece of cherry pie. It's fresh, I made it this morning."

The last thing I want is to be rude, but time is ticking. With a smile on my face, I comment with a bit of urgency behind my voice.

"Thank you, that'd be great, but I really just need to hear what you have to say." Then, I remind her once again. "I don't have a lot of time."

One hand drops low on her hip as she puts down the broom she was wielding as a weapon. Then, she scolds me. "You can't help your friend soaking wet and hungry. I'll just be a minute. Maybe Roger or one of the girls saw something, let me ask around. Our daughter, Piper, was working earlier, maybe she saw something. I'll call up to the house to see if she's there. Now, sit tight and do as your told."

It's useless for me to argue with Joanie, and I can't help but instantly like her. I graciously nod and chuckle and wait like the lady said.

A sudden buzz in jeans pocket lets me know I have a message and I can't get to it fast enough, hoping it's from Declan. As I stand and get my phone from my front pocket, I read the very direct and short message that feels more like death sentence.

Vince: We're on our way!!!

"Oh, fuck!" That was fast, and all I know is I better have some damn answers by the time they get here.

"Now what I'd say about your language?" Joanie speaks up and slaps my hand as she slides a piece of cherry pie with a steaming cup of coffee out in front of me.

I mouth the word *sorry* at her scowling face and try to swallow the sudden lump that's stuck my throat knowing what's coming this way. As I take a sip of coffee, I hope like hell Joanie has information for me, otherwise I'm making that uncomfortable call to Willow sooner than I hoped. I don't think this day can get any worse.

Just as Joanie takes a seat next to me, the front door of the restaurant opens and in walks two guys. She automatically turns and greets them just as I take another sip of coffee. Caffeine is the last thing I need. My legs can't stop bouncing as it is. I'm so amped up and stressed out, I'm one shock away from having a heart attack.

"Right on time, boys," Joanie says in a friendly voice to them. "Why don't you sit down here while I go and see if Roger has your dinners boxed up? You two can sit with this young man, he thinks his friend is missing."

I wince, because the last thing I need is to draw any unwanted attention and complicate a situation that's already way too complicated. *Hurry up Joanie, get their food and send them on their way.*

Just as the two bulky men take seat on the stools next to me, Joanie strides up to one of them with her arm around his broad shoulders. Smiling proudly, she introduces them to me just as I take another sip of hot coffee.

"This here, is Braxton Ryles, and that there is Liam Talbott. They know this town better than anyone. If your friend is missing, these two can help. They're good people."

Coffee spews from my mouth and lands on my cherry pie.

Holy shit!

I was dead wrong; my day just got a whole lot worse.

Chapter Twenty-Three

Dex

WHAT ARE THE ODDS?
Of all people to walk in here, it just had to be them. Talk about awkward. The situation playing out in front of me is downright crazy. Like the fact I'm wet and cold, but still breaking out in a sweat at the same time.

Brax turns to face me, looking restless, while Liam looks on over his shoulder. "When's the last time you've seen or talked to your friend?"

His question feels more like an interrogation where I'm the low life criminal and he's the badass detective, intimidating me with the way his body is crouched forward with one arm resting on the table and the other on the back of the stool.

"Uhhh," I stammer before I swallow loudly and shift uncomfortably in my seat. Instead of answering him straight on, I look his way out of the corner of my eye. This is insane. If the guy only knew who *he* was referring to, this conversation would be entirely different. I focus on anything but him. The intensity on his face alone makes this conversation even more of a struggle. I know I have to say something, so I keep it simple and lowkey.

"It's been a few hours, but when it comes to him anything is possible." I downplay things on purpose to create some doubt in their minds, even though I have none in mine.

Liam reads between the lines and draws his own conclusion. He chuckles, "He a dick or what?"

"*Well*," I snort, laugh and choke at the same time. "It's funny you put it like that."

"Yep, a total dick," he snidely remarks with a chin nod. "I get it."

He doesn't know the half of it. When Brax's phone goes off, it vibrates on the table in front of him as he reaches to answer it. Perfect timing if you ask me. If he's preoccupied, he won't be asking me questions. Now if Joanie would hurry her ass up with their food, they could leave, and I'd be set.

Brax's body immediately goes stiff. Something tells me this call is bad news. Once again, those damn chills run down my spine and I get that sinking feeling in the pit of my gut. Liam switches his eagle eyes from me to Brax, and the vibe coming from them right now only confirms my earlier suspicions about them. If Declan were ever at odds with them and it came to blows, things would not end well for him. These two look like they spend the same amount of time in the gym as Declan and I do.

Here's what the conversation from his end sounds like.

"Hey babe, what's up?"

"Izzy, slow down... what did you just say? Willow? He said what?"

"Do not let that man inside our home until I get there. You hear me? Babe calm down. Nothing is going to happen to anyone."

"Tell Asher to grab a damn bat and use it if he has to."

"On my way, babe."

Holy shit. The more I hear, the worse it gets.

"Joanie," Brax lets out a full-throated shout so loud, everyone in the restaurant is now looking this way. "Make it quick, I have to get home."

Liam quickly stands and gruffly demands, "What the hell is going on?"

What the hell is right?

Every nerve cell in my body is on high alert. My knees are bouncing, my hands are shaking, and I feel like I'm in the eye of a storm. Some shit is going down and the timing is in no way coincidental. First, Declan goes missing, now someone just *happens* to go to Brax and Izzy's house and is stirring up trouble.

This shit is coming to a head at the worst possible time. Instead of dreading that Vince and Marcus are on their way here, I wish they were already here.

Brax explains things to Liam about what's going on and I get quite an earful. "Some jackass is at the house saying Willow is in danger. He's spouting all sorts of crazy shit that has Izzy all upset. She tried to reach Willow on her cell but, so far, she's not answering."

Liam goes into full protective mode. Deep-toned and threatening, "Danger from who?"

"Don't know. Just said the fucker is from *Chicago* if that tells you anything."

I don't miss the implication of what Brax really meant when he said, 'Chicago' and by the look on Liam's face, he doesn't either. Any ties they have to Chicago all lead back to one person. Dominic.

The tension is off the charts.

"Fucking hell!" Liam roars in an angry outburst and slams his fist on the table. "I better call Kara. The last thing I need is to have any of this shit bleed over onto her. She's battled those fucking demons for so long, and this is not the news she needs right now. She's pregnant."

Brax reassures him with a hand on his shoulder and a commanding voice. "No need, Izzy already texted her. She's on her way over to the house. We'll get this shit settled once we get home, just like we did before."

The dire tone in his voice is chilling and when Liam doesn't reply, I look up in time to see a silent understanding pass between them.

"Joanie!" Brax shouts again. This time, Joanie comes rushing from the back with a box full of brown paper bags.

"Sorry, I was hurrying as fast as I could." She hands Brax the box full of food. "Everything is here and more. Now go and get yourselves home safe and sound."

Brax slides some bills on the table, then looks down at me. "Sorry to hear about your friend, I hope you find him soon. I have issues of my own to deal with right now or else I'd stay and see what I could do to help."

"Oh," I breathe with a shake of my head, half elated, half freaked out. "It's not a problem, I completely understand. It sounds like you're needed at home." I realize I'm rambling, so I just shut the hell up.

Brax extends a tight smile, then thanks Joanie before he and Liam rush out the front door. When Joanie escapes to the back once again, I slide a few bucks on the table and get up to leave. I act on a wild and incredibly stupid hunch.

I sneak out the door like I'm undercover and run low to ground, making sure to weave my way around parked cars to give me cover.

Just as I make it to Declan's car, Brax and Liam race out of the parking lot together in a black Ford truck.

As I rev the engine, I mutter under my breath. "This is the craziest and stupidest thing I've ever done." However, it's the only way to know who is at Brax's house.

Instead of getting into all of this by calling Vince, I text.

Me: Following up on a lead. Text you soon with details.

He responds immediately.

Vince: FIND HIM!

Fuck! "I'm trying!" I scream into the phone before tossing it aside.

This feels so weird right now. Declan has never let me drive his car no matter how many times I've tried. I've dreamt of driving this car and now that I am, I'm driving this beast of a machine like I'm driving Miss Daisy while Brax is driving like a bat out of hell.

I hit the gas and enjoy the roar of the engine. It's a guy thing, but there is nothing better than feeling the purr of an engine at your control. That's when I see Brax veer off the road about a mile ahead onto what looks like a damn gravel road. Great, Declan will kill me for sure if I shit up and damage his car. I don't think in terms of *if* we find Declan, it's *when* we find Declan.

I make my turn on Fawles Road making sure to keep some distance between us and not follow too closely. I don't get too far when I find myself in a bit of trouble. The gravel road is now a thick layer of mud due to all the rain and I manage to hit every pothole. It slows me way down while the truck continues to fly with ease. I manage to make it a few more feet before the road deteriorates to the point I get stuck and lose sight of the truck.

Nofuckingway!

This is not happening right now. My fists slam down on the wheel in a rage. I can't believe I came this far only to have it end like this! How the hell am I going to explain myself to Vince or Marcus? *Yeah, I was on my way to find out who may be behind all of this but couldn't because I got the car stuck in the mud. Oh, well, we'll get him next time!*

Hell no, I'd rather face a firing squad. *Get it together, Dex!* I breathe out to ease the tension and run a jerky hand through my hair.

There is no way in hell I'm making that call. Even if I have to get out and walk all night to find a house with a damn black truck parked outside, I refuse to give up.

When I put the car in reverse, something catches my attention out of the corner of my eye. A yellow sticky note is lying on the passenger's side floor. I stretch my fingers and lean over to grab a hold of it. When I look at my own handwritten note, I start to laugh.

The only way this note found its way to the floor had to be when Declan flung my papers in my face while we were arguing the other night. At the time it pissed me the hell off but right now, I'm happy as hell to see a note that just happens to have Brax and Izzy's home address on it. Not to waste a single minute, I enter it into the car's GPS. Damn motherfucking right! I got it!

No more than a mile or so on the right-hand side of the street. Feeling a bit more opportunistic than I did a few moments ago, I ease the car into drive and then reverse. It takes a few tries and a few Hail Mary's to free my back tires from the mud hole they sunk into.

It may come as a bit of a shock, but the rain, once again, picks up so heavy I can hardly see in front of me.

Oh, come the fuck on already!

I swear I can't catch a break. If I don't get off this road soon, I'll be stuck here for god knows how long. Screw that!

I hit the gas and my wheels spin, I put the car in reverse with the same results. Finally, after a few more forward and backward motions, I break free. I step on the gas harder than I intend and mud flies everywhere, even covering the windows.

If nothing else, the mud will help camouflage the cherry red color of the Camaro to match the same old, dreary, gray sky. If I get stuck again though, it won't really matter. To play it safe, I keep the car on the right side of the road to avoid the many sinking potholes. With nightfall fast approaching, I turn my lights on as I creep down the road with virtually no visibility.

No one with a half a brain would travel on this road in these conditions. Now, the only idiot on the road is me. The feeling is desolate and one of isolation. It dawns on me, if I suddenly went missing for any reason, no one would ever find me. That's not a comforting thought. Not with what I'm doing and *who* I'm following.

Before long, I roll up to find a black Ford truck and four other vehicles parked outside a large cabin style home. Every light is on in the house and, from the looks of it, a lot of activity is going on inside.

I drive past the house to find an open field with thick patches of brush and trees. It's the perfect place to hide the car from the road. Not to mention, it's dark as hell.

Once out of the car, I zip my hoodie and start to trek back in the pouring rain to get a good look inside that house. Just over the hill, the house comes into view. My clothes are completely drenched for the second time today. It will be a miracle if I don't end up with pneumonia. Even though I'm bone-shaking cold, I advance on the house like a ninja. I duck and hide behind one car only and advance to the next. That's when I start to hear the raised voices of what sounds like a heated conversation.

By the time I slide against the side of the house, there's not a part of my body that's not nervously shaking. It has nothing to do with how cold and wet I am, either.

To get a look at where the commotion is coming from, I have to make my way to the large set of bay windows that bow out from the front of the house. Unfortunately, it's a bit of an obstacle course to get there. Thick bushes and oversized rocks are not the most ideal for a guy my size to maneuver around to sneak up on anyone, let alone a house full of people yelling at one another.

Despite that, I crawl on my hands and knees and weave through the wet bark, rocks, and bushes. My hands are cold and cut to shit, but I feel pretty goddamn good that I made it this far without being chased or shot at.

Unfortunately, my good fortune is short lived. I don't get a chance to look inside the window because the sudden scream of a girl inside scares the shit out of me. My first instinct is to run inside, but that's not even a possibility. Fear twists my insides just as my heart leaps into my throat.

It startles me so much I freeze where I am on my hands and knees and don't hear the front door slam open until it's almost too late. I panic and faceplant in the bushes and muddy ground under the big-ass window.

Before my face hits the mud, I bite my tongue to stop from shouting out in utter pain. I never noticed the fucking sharp things on the bush before I nosedived into it. If that doesn't teach my ass a lesson, I don't know what will.

Talk about being petrified, I can't breathe or move a damn muscle when I barely see someone running by. My heart almost beats out of my chest because I have no idea if I've been caught or not. The sound of a car door slamming lets me know that I haven't. For now, I'm safe.

Still reeling from the close call, I'm able to lift my head enough to breathe and sneak a peek around. It's then the sound of heavy steps bolt through the front door when my face once again hits the mud. Fuck! I gotta stop doing that shit. I have mud in my mouth!

The next thing I hear is a devastated cry from Brax as his heavy footsteps thud past me. Once again, I remain unnoticed in the muddy bushes.

"WILLOW," Brax frantically shouts with a heaviness in his voice. "Don't go! Give us a chance to explain!"

I hear what sounds like hands slapping against the glass when the engine of a car roars to life. I look up just in time to see Willow crying behind the wheel as she guns the car in reverse. Brax runs as fast as he can, but it's too late. "WILLOW!"

The sheer agony in his voice is beyond inconsolable and cuts me deep. It's not the kind of pain I'm used to. Physical pain is deliberate and short-lived but the pain in his voice, that's something else entirely. I've heard it once before. The night Declan lost Liberty. His screams were just as gut-wrenching as Brax's just now.

Whatever went on inside that house had to be big. A part of me is relieved to find her safe. Obviously hurting, but otherwise safe. The other part is a bit harder to explain.

In the time spent pretending to be Declan while on the phone with her, I got to know Willow on a personal level. Then to see her in person for the first time while she's crying her heart out, all I wanted to do was reach out to her. To console her when that's the last thing I should want to do.

Careful not to make any noise, I watch Brax out of the corner of my eye. He's standing in the driveway with his head low and hands resting on his hips. His chest expands while he quietly sobs. I don't care who you are, it's impossible not to feel something when you see a big guy like him so visibly broken.

It appears like he's trying to get his emotions in check. He throws his head back and exhales deeply a few times. When he lowers his head, his face turns stone cold and murderous as he storms back to the house.

The shouting takes on whole level before the door even closes.

"You better have a goddamned good reason for coming here and fucking with my family! If *anything* happens to Willow I'm holding you the fuck responsible. Start talking."

Damn, I'm up on my feet and looking in the window to see Brax holding a man against the wall. Brax and his wide shoulders block my view from seeing the man's face.

"Listen," I hear the man yell back. "We don't have time to play games here. He's come here to get revenge. How the hell was I supposed to know you never told the girl the truth?"

Oh, fuck!

That pissed Brax off to the point he picks him up by the front of his suit jacket and slams him against the wall. "That's none of your business, she *my* daughter, motherfucker!"

That's when a hulk of a man in a dark suit rushes up behind Brax. Before he can do a damn thing, Liam pulls out a gun and aims it at his head.

Jesus H. Christ! Knowing I might witness an actual murder with my own eyes is terrifying, but I can't look away.

The guy Brax has pinned to the wall says something to his guy as he slowly backs away from Brax like he was told to do. Once he does, Liam lowers his gun and does the same.

A petite woman with brown hair walks up next to Brax looking ready to burst into flames. Her face is bright red, as she nervously continues to run a hand through her long hair.

The scene before me looks like a fucking standoff. There's Brax, Liam and who I assume are Izzy and Kara on one side. Then, the mystery man against the wall and dark suit who has his back to me at the moment.

The woman I assume is Izzy, has her finger pointed in the face of the man her husband has pinned to the wall in a death grip.

She screams. "Brax is the only father Willow's ever known! That's the way we wanted it! Who gave you the right to come to my home and tell my daughter otherwise motherfucker?" Then, she reaches out and slaps him right across the face. "Now, get the *fuck* out of my house!"

From outside the window, I'm silently cheering her on. What a total badass.

That's when the man pinned to the wall comes unglued. "He's come to get *her*. Don't you see what I'm telling you? Declan has finally learned about *all* of you."

Declan? The minute I hear the guy say Declan's name, it's like a punch to the gut. A chilling thought runs through me. *What the fuck?*

"For years," the man's hoarse voice changes as he erupts into anger, Brax tightens his hold by leaning his body into the much smaller man.

The guy continues to shout in Brax's face. "He's wanted the truth about what really happened to his father. *He* finally does. Now, he's here and he's a danger to everyone. The boy killed before he came here. That's how serious this is for all of you."

I listen on in bewilderment, too damned stunned to breathe. Not only is this bastard twisting the truth, he's making Declan out to be the monster *he* really is.

There is something else at work here and it's a hell of a lot more sinister than any of us could have imagined.

Nothing could have prepared me for what happens next.

A chill of black silence suddenly fills the room inside.

"Oh, my God!" Izzy is the first to speak as she looks over at Brax. A trembling hand covers her mouth.

Brax looks like a volcano on the verge of erupting. Fear. Anger. Determination. That and more flashes across his face.

Eventually, he drops his hold on the man and backs away to take Izzy in his arms. As the face of the real monster comes into view my knees go weak.

Straightening his jacket, he continues to spin his story. "Take your pick. Izzy, Willow, Kara... he's come for all of you. He wants answers, but mostly he wants revenge."

The eruption from Brax finally comes.

"I don't give a *fuck* what he wants, he's not getting a motherfucking thing from my family. If he's really gunning for them, he'll have to go through me first."

"I'm trying to prevent any of it from happening. That's why I'm here, to finally end..." He abruptly stops with his hands twisted in front of him. His slip of control was enough to raise suspicion.

Brax backs away. "What's in it for you?"

This motherfucker is a dead man. Something this big can only to explained by catching him on video, my word alone won't work. Not with something this big. Somewhere between elation that I caught him and fear that I will end up dead if sees me hit me like a ton of bricks. My hands are shaking so bad, I'm having trouble getting my phone from my front jean pocket.

Okay, okay, okay. Once I get it free, I raise it up to record the evidence I need. Evidence that will bring relief to some, and destruction to others.

Who knows if any audio will record? I'm having a hard time hearing them now since the shouting has lowered. The fact that *Anthony* is standing in Brax and Izzy's living room speaks for itself. What I heard him say, that's the damning part.

The recording starts just as all eyes are on Anthony. When I zoom in on his face, I almost piss myself. His head shifts slightly so his line of sight lands squarely on the window where I'm standing. SHIT!

Thinking I've been caught, I duck my head but keep the phone recording from the lower corner and watch the screen to see if I need to run like hell or not. It's eerie. He doesn't say a thing or moves a muscle. Anthony just stares out the window like he's looking right at me.

After a minute or two, he explains without emotion. "Let's just say a little bit of redemption. Declan is disturbed and needs help. He's much like Dominic in that respect. He needs to be stopped just like his father was before it's too late. Vince is blind to it all and my brother Marcus likes what he sees in him. He's Marcus' golden boy in Windy City Underground. When he looks at Declan, all he sees is a younger version of Dominic. *That's my problem.*"

All eyes in the room stay on Anthony.

"Seems to me you have an axe to grind." Brax's comment gets a reaction. Not with words, but a growl.

"Jesus! Does it matter?" Izzy's face turns white as a ghost as she stands motionless. "I thought we were done with all this twenty years ago."

The woman I assume is Kara walks over to Izzy and places an arm around her shoulder. "I buried my ghosts that night."

Anthony walks across the room and stops behind Kara. Over her shoulder, he comments. "Some ghosts don't stay buried."

I zoom the shot on his cold and wickedly eerie smirk.

Smile you, sonofabitch, I got you!

Timing is once again not on my side.

My phone suddenly rings. Loudly. A stupid move on my part. I set the volume on high while I was recording. With wet, cold, muddy fingers, I try to put it on silent but drop it instead. It falls under the window and after I pick it up, I hit my head on the edge of the window.

I'm sure they all heard a noise coming from the window, so I run as fast as I can along the side of the house and make a beeline behind the garage, toward the car.

I hear the front door slam open and someone shout, "Who's there?"

I don't slow down. I don't stop. I stay low and never look back. When my phone rings again. I answer it on the run.

"Hey," I huff winded and determined to keep my voice low.

"Dex, it's Vince."

How is it that this guy always calls at the worse possible times?

"Vince, you won't believe who I just saw." In a rush, I glance back over my shoulder to see if I'm being chased just in time to trip over a log I never saw. Umph! I stumble and fall in a bunch of tall grass. The landing sends my phone flying.

"Shit," I whisper-shout, gasping in pain and crawl to the phone. "Vince, you still there?"

"Dex, what the fuck is going on?"

Wincing, I wrap my hand around the ankle I just twisted. "Fuck, I thought I was being chased when I tripped. I think I twisted my damn ankle." Once again making sure to keep my voice to a minimum.

Impatient, Vince lashes out into the phone. "Chased? Why the fuck are you being chased?"

"That's what I'm trying to tell you," I whisper in a frantic tone while I try to stand to put the least amount of weight on my bad ankle. I'm not that far from the car, but one step later, I'm back on the ground in pain. I hiss through the discomfort, "Just listen and don't ask any questions when I tell you this. I was spying outside Brax and Izzy's house and *Anthony* is inside telling them this is all Declan's fault. He told them Declan is the one out to hurt Willow and wants revenge for Dominic." Then, I brace for it.

"MOTHERFUCKER!" Vince roars so loud I hold the phone to my shirt to conceal the noise. "Look, we already figured out Anthony is the one behind it. I'll explain when we land. Are you alright? Are you somewhere safe?"

Safe? I'm about to say 'not likely' when I hear the snapping of twigs like someone is running my way.

"Fuck! I think they're coming this way?" I whisper in the phone and hide as low as I can, hoping the tall grass hides me. There is no way I can outrun anyone if forced to. "Don't say a word!" I quietly let him know and lower the phone to hide any light or noise that could give me away.

Suddenly, I hear voices.

"Dio," Anthony calls out, "you see anything over there?"

"No, Boss. Nothing."

By the sounds of their voices, they are almost on top of me. I don't dare breathe until movement out of the corner of my eye catches my attention. Off to the left of me I see Anthony run up to the hulk of the guy he calls Dio. My nerves tense immediately.

I can easily hear the annoyance in Anthony's voice amid the croaking frogs in the wet land I happen to be hiding in.

"Listen, while we have a moment alone, tell me, did they grab the girl?"

Dio confirms, "They got her. The plan worked perfectly."

"Good, good," Anthony responds with a sickening chuckle I'd like to strangle him with. "Looks like Curtis may have redeemed himself after all. We now have the boy and the girl."

His comment is followed by an awkward pause while every ounce of blood drains from my face. *We have the boy!*

"Sir, didn't Curtis explain?"

"Explain what?" Anthony growls back.

"They don't have *him*. Something went wrong during the pick-up."

Oh, thank fuck.

"No," he erupts, "this is the first I'm hearing of this. Then where the hell is he, Dio?"

"No one knows, sir." Dio responds in military style, seemingly unphased with how irritate his boss is.

"Do I need to remind you my plan does not work without him? Find him. NOW!"

Dio has the phone to his ear as they take off in the opposite direction. Resting my head on the ground, I exhale heavily and put the phone back to my ear.

"Please tell me you heard that?"

Vince chillingly responds, "We heard it all! The question is, if they don't have Declan then who the fuck does?"

Chapter Twenty-Four

"A Dream"
Declan

DAMN, I MUST HAVE LEFT my window open again last night. It's cold as hell in here, but the last thing I want to do is to get out of bed to close it. Especially when all my lazy ass needs to do is pull the covers up over my head. There's only one problem, the signal my brain is sending to my arms to reach down and grab the covers is somehow not getting through.

Normally, I wouldn't consider it a big deal and forget about it until I either wake up or get so cold I have to get up and shut the window.

Out of nowhere, I hear the voice of a female and not a good one, either. A voice so high-pitched and loud it sounds like she's standing next to me with a bullhorn up to her mouth. The ungodly noise is so piercing it gives me one hell of a migraine.

"Hey," the voice hollers once again, "you need to wake the fuck up!"

Wake up? Who the fuck is this chick kidding? The only thing I need to do is to figure out a way to silence the siren she calls a fucking voice. A voice that should come with a label that says, "Warning. Hazardous to your fucking ears."

Something tells me the pounding in my head is more than just her annoying voice though. I'm either suffering from one of the worst hangovers ever, or I have been beaten within an inch of my life. I got aches and pains all over, but the worst of it is in my head.

The fucked-up part? I don't remember a damn thing. Including *her*.

To make matters worse, when I try to shout back that I am fucking awake, my lips don't move. The only thing I can think is that my mind is playing tricks on me because when I go to open my eyes. They don't open.

What the fuck?

My body won't do a damn thing I want it to. Am I even alive?

Lucky for me, I don't have to wait long to find out.

I'm suddenly drenched with ice-cold water. Not a drinking glass worth either. It's more like a bucket. I'm soaking wet and the shock jolts my body to life. I'm suddenly awake with eyes wide open while I gasp for air.

"Fucking hell!"

I wheeze, feeling like I'm deprived of oxygen, only to shy away from the brightness of the room. If I thought the ice water was bad, it's nothing compared to the way my eyes react to the light in the room. The pain is indescribable. Using my hands as shields, I close my eyes to ease the pain. It does nothing but create tears. Tears that feel like hot lava leaking from my eyes.

As if things couldn't get any worse!

"Well, look at that!" She squeals as if surprised. "You're alive after all."

Debatable!

Given how awful I feel, I'm not so easily convinced. I'm soaked to the bone and shivering so damn bad my teeth are chattering. My legs are stiff and I'm sure I can't wiggle my toes. It's a chore to raise my head enough to reply to the blur of a girl standing in front of me.

I croak, "Another shock like that and I won't be. Now, if you could just shut the fuck up long enough for me to think, I may figure out just who the hell you are. While you're standing there staring at me, maybe get me a blanket or two? Unless you are indeed trying to kill me." I can't be too safe and until I can wrap my head around just what the fuck is going on, she's enemy number one.

She lets out a wild gasp. "Wait, *what*? No. Of course not."

Her six-word reply says it all. No! She certainly cannot keep her mouth shut for longer than a minute.

"I'll go and fetch you some blankets. And I'm sorry, the water was really cold but, in my defense, I didn't mean to dump the whole bucket on you."

While she rambles and reminds me of that awful memory, I close my eyes and try to clear my head. Shit's foggy and it's hell to focus on anything while a mini jackhammer is going to town in my head. I have no clue where I am or who the girl is.

When I look down, all I see is a cold and damp *cement* floor.

My head shoots up so fast a strong wave of nausea about knocks me back down. Dazed and confused, I panic. "Where the fuck am I?" I yell louder than I should, and I instantly pay for it. Trying to hold my head still, I take in the unfamiliar surroundings. None of it makes any sense. I have no memory of being in this room.

My anxiety level skyrockets.

In a mad rush, I make the big mistake of moving my head too fast when the room starts to spin out of control. Nothing I do seems to stop it or slow it down. That's when things take a turn for the worse. It's impossible to swallow back the vomit in the back of my throat any longer.

"Hey, *hey*. Oh, shit!"

She freaks out and rushes over to me just in time to watch me heave, only to cringe at the sound and eventually start to dry heave herself. By the time it stops, I'm worn the fuck out.

"Jesus," she sighs and hovers over me, "I leave you for two minutes to get you a blanket and look what happens. I'm no nurse, but I'd say you have a concussion. It's not that surprising considering the shape you were in when I found you. While you were out, I looked up how to treat a concussion and the first it said is not to let the person..."

"Fall asleep," I roughly reply. "Yeah, I know all about concussions."

"You've had a few, huh?" she asks with pity in her voice.

I feel like death and she wants to have a conversation. If that's the case, there is only one conversation to be had.

"Who the fuck are you?" I groan with each word feeling weaker by the minute. "What happened to me?" I mumble, "I don't remember a thing."

My words are nothing more than faint whispers when refreshing cool hands wipe away the beads of sweat on my forehead. I'm cold as hell but sick enough to sweat. I feel like the walking dead even though I can't even get to my feet to walk. What the fuck kind of irony is that?

"Shhh." The girl softly says in my ear just as my eyes close.

I can't stop it from happening even though I'm doing everything I can to fight it. She has yet to tell me a damn thing. As I wage a war on the inside, the warmth of a blanket has me surrendering to the sweet call of sleep.

That's when I faintly hear. "My name is Piper. Don't worry, I won't let anything else happen to you. Those men who did this will never find you here so just rest for now. I'll tell you everything when you wake up."

That's when everything fades to black.

IT'S DARK OUT WHEN I open my eyes. My body is warm and I'm finally able to feel my toes. That's the good news. The bad, everything else feels like hell. My head is pounding, and I feel like I could throw up again at any minute.

"Hey, sleepyhead."

Her voice is soft this time and it comforts me, which makes me feel terrible. The last voice that gave me comfort like this was Libbs and I feel like I'm dishonoring her memory by taking comfort in this voice. The girl I know as Piper, because it's the last thing she said to me before I passed out, is sitting next to me with a cloth on my forehead and a book in her lap. The issue I had with my vision earlier is gone and I'm able to focus on her face for the first time. She's no longer the girl with a loud voice and blurry face. Now that I'm able to get a good look at her, I know I've never seen her before. Piper is a girl I would remember if I had.

Not even the jackhammer in my head or the urge to throw up again could stop me from noticing her sun-kissed hair, her bright, hazel eyes or the patch of freckles on her nose. It's just way too easy for me to get lost in her looks.

And there lies the problem.

Red flags go up everywhere since I have yet to figure out what she has to do with *any* of this. What's her game? It's the only way I see it because that's all my life has been lately. One fucking game after another. None of them have been good either.

I continue to stare at her and wonder. *Just who are you, Piper?*

I scrutinize every little detail. From the way the tip of her nose curves up to the scar above her right ear that's barely hidden in her hairline She knows I'm watching her, too. Her breathing picks up as her eyes wildly look around until she abruptly gets up and walks across the room. It's a good thing she propped a bunch of pillows behind my head because this way I don't have to move my head to keep my eyes focused on her. The last thing I need to do is move my head and get the room spinning again.

I take everything in, thinking something in here will trigger a memory.

"Why are you staring at me like that?" She asks while she nervously starts fidgeting with the ends of her sweatshirt that's two sizes too big.

"Like what, *Piper*?"

She seems shocked that I used her name because her mouth falls open as her eyes go wide. "You remember me telling you that? I wasn't sure if you heard any of what I said." She giggles, and her cheeks turn bright red. "It's a good thing I didn't say everything that was running through my mind then. Lordy, that would make this," she motions with her fingers between us, "uncomfortable for the both of us."

Even though it hurts like hell to do it, I chuckle along with her. I should be grilling her, but I can't resist. Now that I get a good look at her, I'm surprised by how tiny she is. With the voice I heard when I first woke up, I expected to see someone other than a petite girl who can't be more than five-foot two, if I had to guess. Hell, I'd wager to bet that little miss Piper has a killer body under her baggie-ass clothes.

The longer I stare at her, the more nervous she gets, but it has to be this way until I know I can trust her. She has yet to explain any fucking thing and it's past time she does.

When I open my mouth to ask her a question, she interrupts me first.

"At least you didn't die, that's one thing I have that going for me." Her voice is soft, but I can the stress in her words. "I mean if you could have seen you last night, you would be thinking the same thing. Trust me."

"*Can* I... trust you?" I lay it out there because it doesn't take a genius to figure out this girl is no threat. Thank fuck, because I'm in no condition to fight anybody right now. But the question still needs to be answered.

"Where am I?"

"This," Piper explains with her arms stretched wide and a tremor of a smile, "would be my home."

I one thing I know... my eyes don't lie.

My face tightens into a scowl. "This is not going to work if you start off by lying to me, Piper. This is not a *home*," I harshly point. "It's a barn, with straw." How do I know? There are bales of it everywhere.

I couldn't believe what I was seeing but kept my mouth shut. I wanted to see what kind of explanation I would get. Either way, it's not like I can just get up and leave.

Piper glares me like she's cussing me out in her head when she defiantly lifts her chin. "First of all," her voice hardens as her hands ball into fists. "I'm *not* lying to you, *Declan Parisi*."

Now I'm pissed.

I know I never told her my name so how the fuck does she know it.

Unless...

No! Not her too!

Dark thoughts fill my mind and it happens so fast, I don't realize it until it's too late. I'm not the one with the cynical laugh.

They are.

Well, well, well. Now we're getting somewhere. And it's about fucking time. Okay, little miss Piper, let's get this shit started.

I continue to wait in silence with my jaw set so tight I can feel the twitch of my muscle in my cheek.

She breaks the stare and turns away. "This *barn*, as you put it, is on my parent's property. The upper loft happens to be my bedroom." Then she turns back and points with her finger, "The reason you are on the floor is because I couldn't lug your heavy ass up the stairs by myself." She's so riled up she shoves the sleeves of her sweatshirt up only to have them fall back down.

Fine. "Explain how you know my name. And just *where* is this barn, exactly?"

She huffs, "The last place you were yesterday when two goons came and roughed your ass up pretty good before trying to stuff you in the back of their van. Lucky for you, I noticed two men sniffing around that clearly had no business doing so. Some people just stick out like a sore thumb, ya' know what I mean?"

It's clear from the shitty look on her face that she includes me in her sarcastic jab. Like I give a fuck. I have more serious shit to deal with. The fact that I was *roughed up,* as she put it, by two men I don't remember is a real fucking problem. Frustration doesn't even begin to describe what I feel right now. The look on my face tells her it's time for her to start talking right goddamn now, the restless chatter going on in my head right now is only going to get louder. And if that happens, it's not going to end well for her.

"Tell me everything and don't leave anything out. Start by telling me what happened after I left The Shack yesterday." I figure it'd be the best place to start since it's the last thing I do remember.

Once I contain the chatter in my head and drop the scowl from my face, Piper loses the annoyed look on her face.

"Okay. You already know my name is Piper. My folks run the restaurant where most days I work in the kitchen. Just over the dish sink is a window that happens to face the parking lot."

Now we're getting somewhere.

"Before you showed up, I saw two guys snooping around the place like they are casing the joint or something. I didn't want to upset my mom or dad, so I kept it to myself and watched them until they drove off in a van. About ten minutes later, I see a fancy red Camaro pull in and park in the area those guys were looking around. It was a pretty weird coincidence since no one really ever parks that far back."

"Jesus." I close my eyes, pissed at myself for being so unprepared. "By any chance did you get a good look at them? Anything that could help me figure out who they might be."

I can see the disappoint on her face as she shakes her head.

"No, they were too far away for me to tell anything besides being tall, skinny and having dark hair. It wasn't until I stumbled upon you that I may have heard a few things."

"Like?"

"Ummm, look," Piper hesitates with an uncomfortable look on her face. "Are you sure you want to hear everything right now? I could skip over the worst parts and just tell you what I know about them? Even though it isn't a whole lot."

Not a chance.

My response is immediate. "No, I want to know everything. Don't leave anything out."

"Okay. At the time I had no idea who you were. I overheard one of them say the name Declan a few times. It wasn't until I looked in your wallet that I knew it was you. You need to understand, I wasn't sure you were even alive at that point. You weren't moving at all."

I won't lie. Some of what she said is hard to hear. The other gives me an odd sense of relief. It means she didn't know who I was before she found me. It also means, she has no part in any of it.

"To hear you talk, I must look pretty fucked-up. How bad can it be? I know it can't be pretty, but I'm a fighter for Christ's sake. I'm used to this kind of shit. Obviously not what happened to me kind of shit, but you get the drift."

Her mouth hangs open. "*You... you're a fighter?*"

"That's what I said. Why are you really so surprised?"

"Oh, god this is not going to come out right," she admits in a breathy tone. "It's just that... you're obviously not that good. Maybe you need to find a new profession."

What the fuck?

I take immediate offense. "I happen to be a damn good fighter. You're just seeing the after- effects of the equivalent of three fights in a just a few days' times. I had a big fight the night I left Chicago to come here only to get in a blow out with my buddy in our hotel room the following night. Then I was jumped by two thugs last night. That's a whole lot of fighting in a short period of time, even for the best fighters. Under the circumstances, I'd say I'm holding up pretty damn well."

I can't believe I'm defending myself to this chick and getting pissed off while doing it. It's not like my head isn't already pounding like a motherfucker.

"Geesh, take it easy why don't ya'? No need to get defensive. It makes no difference to me if you can fight worth a damn or not. It does answer a few questions for me though."

"How reassuring," I roll my eyes. "Do share."

"It just makes sense why your face looks like it does and it also backs up my concussion theory. Your poor brain must feel like mush right now."

This is so not helpful. "Concussion or not, I need to get out here and meet up with my buddy, then call my uncle. They have to be going crazy about now."

I lean forward and get to my knees, but when I try and stand on one leg the room sways to the right. I about topple over when Piper runs at me at full speed from across the room just in time before my face hits the floor.

"Okay, big guy, that's enough. You need to rest and get some food in you. Not to mention get off the cold hard ground. You rolled over in your sleep and there was no way I could move you back on the makeshift bed I had for you."

Straw and blankets, that's been my bed. I might as well be a damned animal. If I could only eat the straw I'd be set. Damn, I am hungry.

"Food would be good. And Advil. God don't forget that. Oh, and my phone. Do you have it?"

She shakes her head. "No, I never saw it. Unfortunately, I don't have one either. Let me get you some food from the restaurant first and then we can figure out what to do next. I could always call someone for you from the restaurant if you want."

"Okay. Just be careful, who knows if those guys are back looking for me."

Piper grins and salutes me with her fingers. "I will, but I highly doubt they'd still be around here looking for you now."

"Why do you think that?"

"Well, duh! Do criminals ever return to the scene of the crime? I mean we're a hundred yards or so from the restaurant on my parents' property. Which is gated. Plus, after I moved in here, my uncle Jack set up cameras around the property for my security. If anyone comes sneaking around here, I will know it."

"*Okay!*" I'm not sure what else to say. I'm still having a hard time believing I met a girl who has her room in a barn.

She runs up the stairs to grab her purse and is off a hurry. "Okay, so sit tight and I'll be back with food and Advil. I'll also grab the first aid kit to clean up the cuts on your face."

"You seem awfully concerned about my face," I ask considering this is twice she's mentioned it.

"After seeing your license and looking at you now, yes. Trust me, while you were out I was staring at it getting an idea how you really look. And I definitely have to say you are way prettier without all of those nasty cuts and bruises all over your face."

"I'm glad you think so." I try not to laugh as I watch her try not to insult me. We exchange a light laugh and it reminds me what life was like before all this started. Being around Piper is easy and the fact she doesn't know me, or my situation is fucking perfect. Finally, I can just let my guard down. *One night... I just need one night.*

Piper is checking for something in her purse when an alarm suddenly goes off.

"Shit, someone's here."

Chapter Twenty-Five

"Discovery"

P ATIENCE IS ONE THING I have very little of, even on my good days. In high stress situations like this one, that impatience quadruples.

"Piper?" I cup my hands around mouth and shout in a frantic whisper. Piper ran upstairs to the loft to check the monitor for who or what triggered the alarm.

When she doesn't answer as quickly as I like, I get antsy and shout her name again. A little louder this time.

"Piper, what do you see?"

Finally, she responds. "Shhh, quiet. I got two guys around back."

Shit, that's all I needed to hear. I'll be damned if I'm going to be an easy target if it is the same pricks from yesterday. Even though my head is heavy and I'm feeling a bit woozy, I still manage to get to my feet and slowly walk across the room to the wooden stairs that lead to the loft.

"What's going on now?" I shout up the stairs feeling more on edge with each passing second. As tension mixes with uncertainty, a rush of adrenaline courses through my body. My heart rate speeds up at an alarming rate. With my back to the wall, I keep my eyes centered on the only way inside. The big overhead doors. I don't know who may come through them, I just know I'm in no shape to go toe-to-toe with anyone. But I will defend myself and Piper.

The first thing I do is look for anything I could use as a weapon. A shiny pitchfork in the corner catches my eye, as well as lot of other things. This is no ordinary *barn*. At least not the kind I'm used to seeing back home in Illinois. It's surprisingly clean and reminds me more of a finished outbuilding. One that happens to be filled with bales of hay and an overhead loft. The only comparison to a barn I can find is the cement floor.

Even though I can't see much of the loft from down here, it looks like it runs the length of the entire building. Which makes it one hell of a bedroom. No wonder she likes it so much.

A heavy thud from upstairs quickly gets my attention as my eyes follow the pattern of her footsteps as they travel down the length of the room and back.

What the hell is she doing?

The next thing I know, Piper bolts down the stairs nearly plowing right into me.

She jumps and freaks out when she sees me up on my feet. "What the hell? You scared the shit out of me," she cries out with a hand over her chest. "We have to hide you… *now!*" Panic flashes on her face as she grabs my arm and rushes me through a doorway into a separate room. It reminds me of a miniature stable with its sliding door. I look at her with a curious eye, wondering what her intentions are. All I see are stacks of hay, but *where the hell are the animals*?

"Are there any animals in here that could jump out at any moment?"

She ignores my comment with a roll of her eyes. "Never mind that. Just listen to me," Piper is in full control mode and calling the shots like I should trust everything she says. Strangely enough, I do. "We don't have time to get you outside, so you have to hide in here. Get down so I can hide you in the hay."

I look at the ground and then back at her. "Are you crazy? I'm not letting you cover me up with hay. I'll stay in here, but I'm not hiding on the ground like an animal."

She gets right in my face. "Shhh, we don't have time to go back and forth. We haven't had any animals in here for months. The hay is clean… well, mostly, I think."

"Mostly?" I stare at her wide-eyed and astounded. "You… you're insane! How can you sleep in here with *animals*?"

Piper gives me a look that tells me she's going to get even with me for that comment.

"Being around animals is a hell of a lot better than dealing with *people* who don't listen! Now sit your ass down and shut the hell up before those idiots come through the door."

I don't go down willingly so Piper pushes my ass down.

"Easy," I protest her manhandling of me, but do so with a sly smirk. "Concussion remember?"

Piper's face scrunches together as she lets out a growl. "Are you always this aggravating? Just… be a good boy and don't make any more noise."

She scolds me with her finger like I'm a bad child. If she thinks she's going to have the last word with a comment like that, she best think again. The 'good boy' in me jokingly flips her off.

Her mouth drops open. "Hey, I saw that. Is that the kind of thanks I get for saving your ass… *again*? Just stay here and let me handle this."

That's when we hear a loud bang coming from the large oversized door.

"Hello, anyone inside?" A deep, masculine voice shouts from just outside the door.

Just from the tone of his voice, I can tell he's nothing but trouble. My body's natural defenses are on high alert and respond whenever I feel a threatened. My breathing lowers to a slow and steady pace as every muscle in my body hardens.

What the fuck am I doing in here when I should be the one out there handling this. There is no way I can stay in here if things get ugly. Concussion or not.

The next thing I hear is the squeaking of a door opening. It sucks because I can't see a goddamn thing that's going on out there, so I have to prepare for anything.

Except the loud shriek from Piper.

"Shit, you scared me half to death. I didn't hear anyone with my earbuds in. I wear them when I clean up in here. Is there something I can help you with? You lost or something?"

Damn, here I am with my heart is beating out of my chest, while little miss Piper is chill under pressure. Impressive!

"We're looking for a guy," the guy with the deep voice asks Piper and knowing she is out there with him really gets my blood going. "You wouldn't have happened to see anyone hanging around, would ya' sweetheart? You'd remember him if you had. His face is all messed up, and he'd most likely be walking with a limp."

"Wow, I gotta say that doesn't sound like any guy I want to run into. Thankfully, I have not. As you can see, I've been busy in here."

Then, the jackass has the balls to ask.

"Mind if we look around? I would hate to have you accidentally stumble upon him while you are *cleaning*. A small girl like yourself could get hurt."

I can't contain the growl that slips past my throat. I swear that fucker better not lay one finger on her.

If Piper is scared, she sure doesn't show it. She laughs back at him. "I've got a big pitchfork. Plus, I don't scare that easily. So, to answer your question, no, you may not search the barn. I don't know who you two are? I'm going to have to ask you to leave now."

She specifically said 'two' and if I didn't know better, I'd say it's her way of letting me know that they are the two guys from yesterday.

That's when the second male speaks up. "We're wasting our time here. He's long gone by now. Let's go."

An odd prickling sensation rushes over me because his voice sounds so fucking familiar.

He continues, "I'll leave my number. If anyone shows up, you give this number a call. You should be careful, he's dangerous."

"Absolutely," Piper willingly plays along. "I'll give you a call right away. Though, I don't know who I'm calling. There's no name here."

He chuckles. "Curtis."

Motherfucker!

Sirens go off in my mind. I swear I'm going to kill that bastard with my bare hands. Unable to stay in here any longer, I slide my back against the wall go to look around the corner to get a good at that sonofabitch. Only, Piper crashes into me at the same time. She catches me so off guard, I stumble backwards but recover with my arms tightly wrapped around her.

The fearless girl from a moment ago is gone. It's as if Piper is releasing the fear she's been so courageously hiding. With her body pressed into mine, I can feel her heart thumping wildly. With her in my arms like this, it makes me realize just how fragile she is underneath that tough exterior of hers.

I do my best to soothe her. "Hey, it's okay. They're gone now." I calmly say to her even though I'm pissed as hell that they scared her like this. With my arms protectively around her, Piper responds by clinging on to me tighter. "Piper, I won't let anything happen to you. Like you said, you saved my ass twice."

Like I hoped, she softly laughs, but it doesn't last long. "It was them, Declan. At one point, I was so sure they recognized me, but I'm not so sure if they did or not."

"You didn't sound scared at all," I admit. "Actually, I was pretty impressed." Piper's definitely badass.

"Shut up!" She shies away from me and swats at my chest with her hand. "We need to get you out of here, they may show back up."

I nod because she's right. "I should get back to my motel out on Highway 2 and connect with my buddy Dex. The Fairground Inn, you know it?"

"Yeah, sure I do. You need to eat though, and we still need to find a way to get you there."

It seems besides not having a phone, Piper doesn't have a car either. How that's even possible these days, I have no idea.

"Just get me to a phone. I'm sure Dex has my car by now. He can come and get me."

Piper acts like she's listening, but frowns. "Do you think you can walk?"

"Yeah, why? What do you have in mind?"

"If we walk down the hill to The Shack. I can get us something to eat and you can use the phone while we're there."

"Let's do it."

DOWN THE HILL WAS MORE like the length of a few football fields. It wasn't easy, I nearly tripped several times over branches and am sure I twisted my ankle in a hole. It was insanely dark, but the cool breeze did help clear my head. When Piper said it was a little bit of a walk, she wasn't kidding. I don't know how the hell she got me up there to begin with, but I did hear her say she dragged me part of the way.

Once we made it to The Shack, Piper snuck us in through the delivery door that led to the pantry next to the kitchen. I was to sit tight and wait while she went to see if the coast was clear. A short time later, she returned with two paper bags and a set of keys.

"Dad's truck." She jingles them in her hand.

I follow her to the black Chevy pick-up parked next to the building. "We're good. I got us food, a first aid kit with Advil, and my mom's cell phone."

"That's great. Did you see anyone suspicious?"

"No, not at all. Let me give you this though." When I watch Piper slide her hand inside her shirt, my mouth goes dry. By the time I shut down the dirty thoughts floating in my mind, Piper pulls out a cell phone. *Okay.* Not what I was expecting and an instant guilt slams into me for admiring Piper when Libbs is fucking dead.

She doesn't think much of it until her eyes meet mine. Then, she blushes. "My hands were full carrying the bags, it was just easier to put it in my bra."

I free my thoughts with a shake of my head. "Hey, no judgement on my part. Feel free to touch... wait, forget I said that." I sigh feeling like it's just got really hot in here when I take the phone from her hands. "Thanks."

She softly replies, "You're welcome."

It takes me a moment to push the thoughts of Piper touching things out of my mind before I can call Dex.

It takes four unanswered rings for my mind to switch gears. *Dammit, Dex answer your damn phone!*

I end the call and dial it again.

Still, no answer.

"Christ."

"What, he's not answering?"

"No." I exhale with head down. It's been hours with no contact with Dex. Who knows what kind of shit he's been up to. Since he didn't answer, I know who I need to call next. I just don't feel like getting the third degree right now.

"Shit. Shit. Shit."

"Jesus," Piper jumps in her seat. "What now?"

I grumble, rubbing the building tension from the back of neck. "I have to call my uncle."

She shrugs her shoulders and looks at me strangely. "Is that a bad thing?"

"It depends," I chuckle. "You don't know my uncle."

She smiles at my smirk as she opens a bag and pops a French fry in her mouth. The smell of greasy food has me in a food trance.

"Here," she passes me the bag, but not before teasing me with it. "Eat first, then call your uncle."

That offer was just too good to pass up.

We pull up at the motel just as we finish eating. A quick scan of parking lot for my car comes up empty. Since it wasn't parked where I left it at the restaurant, I know Dex found my spare keys and is most likely is driving it. Smart on his part. I just wish I knew where the hell he was now.

Piper pulls into a spot and puts the truck in park. Things between us up to now have been fairly easy going considering. Right now, though, the silence is bordering on uncomfortable.

I rub my hands along the top of my jeans and turn to face her. "I can stop at the front desk and get a key to the room. You can take off, I don't want you mixed up in this more than you already are. It's dangerous and you've stuck your neck out enough for me."

Piper has this look on her face before she bursts out laughing. "You can't say it, can ya?"

I stare clueless. "Say what?"

"That I saved your ass, *twice.*" She then raises her hand waiting on me to give her a high five. What do I do? Give her the high five. If there is one thing I can say about Piper, it's that she has a weird sense of humor.

I give her a lopsided smirk because her care-free smile is that infectious. I also point out, "You also fed and drove me here."

Her smile broadens, "That's just how awesome of a person I am."

Before her ego gets any bigger, I reel it back in. "Yes, but let's not forget you almost gave me a heart attack and hyperthermia by pouring cold as hell water on me after I slept on a cold cement floor."

Her face falls flat before she pouts. "Way to go. What a way to ruin my moment. Anyway, a girl's gotta have fun sometimes."

"Is that what you call…" I abruptly switch gears when a pair of headlights pull into the parking lot behind us. To make sure we're not seen, I immediately duck and pull Piper down with me.

"Are you getting even with me or trying get fresh?" she giggles.

"Neither, just be quiet and stay down. I'm trying to see who pulled in just now." I quickly realize that my arm is resting over the top of Piper's back, so I slowly move it to the side and lean up over top of her to look out the window instead.

"They can't hear you, ya know. No need to whisper," she struggles to talk with the weight of my body on hers.

Unfortunately, I don't hear much of what she has to say because something else has caught my attention. "What the fuck?" I could not make any sense of what was playing out in front of me.

"What's going on now?" Piper quickly responds, struggling to get herself up so she can see for herself.

"Over there under the tree by the sidewalk," I direct her with a nod of my head.

"Good thing you said sidewalk, because there are trees everywhere. Oh, wait a minute. Is that? No way!" she turns to face me with a look of disbelief.

"Yep," I confirm with a deep-seated growl. "That's Curtis."

She mouths, *no way*! "What's he doing here? Does he know you're staying here?"

"No. I have no idea why he's here." I answer with my eyes glued on Curtis when Piper notices something else.

"Who are the other men that are walking his way?"

Shit, I didn't see them but now that I have, I almost wish I didn't. "Something's not right. No way Curtis should be here… and definitely not with Marcus and Vince."

I don't know what the fuck happened over the last twenty-four hours, but this shit just got a whole lot more fucked.

I can feel Piper's eyes on me when she asks, "Who are they?" I can only imagine the ideas running through her head, but I bet none of them come close to the truth. "My uncles."

Her mouth falls open. "No! But wait a second, didn't you tell me you hated that Curtis guy? I know for a fact he was one of the guys who beat the shit out of you and just happens to be the same guy who was at the barn not that long ago. Now he's here with your uncles? Why?"

That's the million-dollar question, one I have no answer for. But I know where to get it. "Stay quiet for a minute, I'm going to make a call and I don't want them to know I'm here watching them."

Piper points over her shoulder and gets an excited look on her face. Then uses her fingers to pretend to zip her mouth closed before throwing away the key. I just stare at her and shake my head. I have never met a girl like her before.

It takes me a minute to remember Vince's number from memory. If I had my phone with me I would just click on his name, but unfortunately, my phone is still unaccounted for. After I hit call, I watch Vince as he pulls a phone from his jacket.

"Vince Parisi," he gruffly answers.

It takes a lot of restraint to keep my voice as even as possible, like I can simply erase from my mind what I see in front me. "Vince, it's me."

"Declan?" his voice rises as he looks over at Marcus. "Where are you? We've been looking all over for you? Are you safe, son?"

No thanks to the fucker standing next to you.

My voice dips low, "I'm safe now. Ran into a bit of trouble though. Two men jumped me yesterday and kicked my ass. I woke up safe, thanks to... *someone.*" I keep Piper's name out of it, but I look long and hard into her big, brown eyes. Her cheeks blush as a slow smile emerges.

"Where are you?" Vince demands with an unusual edge to his voice before he rests his head back looking to the sky.

I'm not sure what to make of it or, the fact Marcus seems to be in a heated back and forth with Curtis. Until I know what's up, I'm not telling anyone where I am.

"Safe, that's all I can tell you for now. I will tell you something though, I'm not sure how or why, but I recognized one of the men from last night." I drop the bomb just in time to watch it explode. "It was Curtis."

"Curtis?" Vince erupts, then steps in front of him. "As in Curtis *Diego?*"

I watch the drama play out before I confirm with a malicious smile on my face. "Yes!"

"Hold on," Vince growls into the phone as I watch him lower it against his chest. Then, with this free hand, he swings and lands a massive blow to the right side of Curtis' face.

"Oh, damn! Did you see that?" Unable to hold back, Piper squeals before she clamps a hand over her mouth.

Nothing makes me happier than to see that bastard spill blood, but I got to admit, "Vince has one hell of a swing."

"Declan, you still there?" Vince has the phone to his ear once again while he shakes the sting from his hand.

"Yep, still here." I'm damn tempted to tell him he still has it going on when Marcus impatiently yanks the phone from Vince.

"Declan, we need to know where you are? No more games. It's far too dangerous for you to be on your own right now. Things are not safe, and we need to talk. I have a lot to tell you."

You don't say!

"Should we start with *Curtis?*"

Marcus looks curiously at the phone then whips his head around to scan the parking lot. Piper and I once again slide back down to remain out of sight.

"Are you here right now? Obviously, you can see us. Are you in your room?"

I'm about sick of him questioning me to death when I have some of my own. Anger pours out of me as the nasty taste of betrayal once again raises its ugly head. "That fucker blindsided me last night with another guy and gave me one hell of a beat down. I'll ask you one more time, why is *he* with you and Vince?" I can't hold back my rage or control how hard my body starts to shake in response. I do, however, feel tiny cold hands wrap around my face.

"Breathe," she softly whispers, "just breathe."

I close my eyes and welcome the way my body responds to her calming voice. I only wish to feel this calm once I open my eyes. Especially when all I can hear is Marcus throwing threats around. Surprisingly, it's not directed at me. I look up to see Marcus standing right in front of Curtis this time. Way too close for comfort, well, for Curtis anyway.

Marcus drops his voice so low that it can only mean one thing. Trouble. Staring Curtis down, he talks directly to me. "If Curtis here wants to live to see another day, he will do what he's told. Right now, that means he is double crossing the man he's working for to report to *me*. Only he failed to mention one critical detail. His involvement in what happened to you. A costly mistake he'll pay dearly for, I assure you!"

He tosses the phone to Vince, yelling, "Find out where he is. I need to teach Curtis which Aniello brother not to fuck over."

I'm so excited to watch Curtis get his ass handed him that my fists twitch and jerk with every swing Marcus unloads. That I let what he said go over my head.

Vince is in my ear once again. "Declan stop this bullshit and tell us where you are. You can't be handling this too well on your own. Look, I have your meds with me."

I stop him right there because Piper heard him and is now looking at me with an odd expression as she mouths the word, *meds*?

Time to change the subject. "Do you know where Dex is?" He has to know. There is no doubt Dex has been in touch with him. When Vince pauses longer than necessary, the hairs on the back of my neck stand up.

He finally admits, "He's following Anthony."

"Anthony?" Okay, this is some strange shit. Why would Dex be following him? Then my mind connects the dots with the comment from Marcus. Heat burns in the pit of my stomach. "Why is he following Anthony? And what exactly did Marcus mean when said he needed to teach Curtis which Aniello brother not to fuck over?" The answer is right in front of my face and I need to hear the motherfucking words to believe it's true.

Vince literally turns my world upside down.

"Because Anthony is the one who is behind it all. We put the clues together once Marcus found one of the punks in the video. Anthony's been evading us, but when Dex called and said you went missing after receiving a text, we knew exactly where to find him. We're here to end this shit and take you home."

I let his words sink in.

"I let you down and I'm sorry for that. Just come to us. I don't want you alone, we can all sit down and figure things out together."

Somehow, I keep my shit together on the outside, even though I'm fucking furious on the inside. I can't explain it, maybe it has to do with Piper being this close to me. Either that, or I'm in shock.

When I hear the phone beep with an incoming call, I look down at the number. For once, Dex has impeccable timing. He could not have called me at a more perfect time. If Dex is watching Anthony, I need to get to Dex. Where I find Dex, I find Anthony!

A man I once trusted.

A man I grew up with.

A man I considered family.

He's the same motherfucker with his hands all over the dagger in my back!

I'm going to tear that motherfucker apart. The fact that he's an Aniello and Marcus' brother means nothing to me. He crossed the fucking line and no one can save his sorry ass now. The fiery pits of hell have been opened up as far as I'm concerned, and it unleashes one hell of roar that erupts inside my head. Not so long ago, I made a vow to Libbs. A vow I fully intend to make good on.

I don't mince my words with Vince as I end the call. "No one ends this but me!"

When I connect the call with Dex, I all but threaten him. "Where the fuck are you?"

He stutters, "Declan, is that you man? I'm returning the call I missed a few minutes ago. Whose phone are you calling me from? You know what, who gives a shit. Goddamn, I have been so fucking worried about you. Vince and Marcus…"

"I already know," I snap. "I'm watching them now. Did you know Curtis is here with them?"

He exhales with a loud groan. "There's a lot you don't know. A hell of a lot."

"Like *Anthony*?" I can't even say his name without envisioning violence.

"How the fuck did you find that out? Better yet, what happened to you?"

"I'm coming to you, but no one needs to know that." By *no one*, Dex knows exactly who I'm referring to. "I know you're following Anthony, tell me where."

"Dude, I have your car. How are you going to get to me if you want to keep it from Vince?"

I look into Piper's wide eyes who is taking in every word of my conversation. Every so often I catch her poking her head up to watch the drama unfold in front of her. The entire time she's been rubbing her hand along my forearm like it's her way of keeping me as calm as possible. I can only imagine what she must be thinking. But no matter how bad those thoughts may be, I can guarantee the truth is a hell of a lot worse.

She's different than most girls. Instead of shying away from the danger she unintentionally finds herself smack dab in the middle of, she does the opposite and seems to thrive on it like some adrenaline junkie.

Which explains a lot.

It's hard to look the other way, especially when she looks at me with such intensity. Like now, as the calm in her eyes capture the fury in mine, nothing else seems to exist. Even with the crazy shit going on around us, I feel an unspoken bond form between us.

Thrown off guard, I shake my head, getting my mind focused on the matter at hand. With no emotion at all, I answer his question, "I'm with Piper."

Dex quickly shouts, "Who the fuck is Piper?"

chapter

TWENTY-SIX

"Showdown"

I CONDENSE THE EVENTS OF the last twenty-four hours into the span of a couple of minutes. Dex is still somewhere between shock and disbelief, but eventually gives up his location where he is staking out an old farm house, watching Anthony's every move. That was thirty minutes ago.

Right now, Piper and I are traveling on State Route 92 heading toward Granite Falls. An area of nothing but woods that's a perfect hiding place for a rat like Anthony.

The voices in my head roar like angry thunderclouds the closer we get to our destination. Piper's been mostly quiet but navigates Dex's directions with ease while I sit back, silently brooding. The trees out here are so fucking thick, I can't put into words how different it feels compared to the noisy streets of Chicago.

Piper slows down as we approach a street too damn dark to read the name of.

She softly says, "This should be Portage Ave." And she's right, it is.

We wind our way around the bend when I tell her, "Pull over and kill the lights." According to Dex, Anthony is holed up in an old farmhouse just up the road. I don't see my car or Dex anywhere, but I don't feel like going any farther until I know exactly how far it is to that farmhouse.

With the lights off, we're surrounded by darkness. It should give us the advantage of sneaking up to the house without being seen.

"Wow, look at that," Piper comments with her finger over my left shoulder. When I look over and take a quick glance, my reaction is completely different than hers.

"It's eerie as fuck." I tell her just as a thick layer of fog travels from the trees and surrounds the truck, limiting our visibility even more.

"Oh, it is not," she argues back as she leans forward to look out all around us. "It's completely rad!"

I watch her strangely just waiting for her to say she's also into horror movies as I dial Dex to let him know we're here. He picks up on the second ring.

"Yo, man. We're here, where you at?" Seems like a stupid question since I can't see two feet in front of the truck now. It's not a good thing, especially if somebody wants to sneak up on us.

He replies like his concentration is elsewhere. "This fucking fog is making it impossible to see shit, but I've got movement going on up here." The anxiousness in his voice is impossible to miss but his voice suddenly turns angry and some kind of interference keeps me from hearing what he's saying.

"Dex," I raise my voice, "I can't hear you, you're breaking up pretty bad." Then, a string of words come across clear as a bell and I can't believe what I'm hearing. The words are few, but they're enough to make my skin crawl and blood boil. "*What?* Are you kidding me? How the fuck did that happen, Dex?"

I snap at him like it's somehow his fault when my fist slams on the dashboard. Piper lets out a yelp, but I can't help my angry outburst. What he said catches me off guard and changes everything. My plan to go in and snap Anthony's neck just got a lot harder.

The one fucking thing I wanted to avoid has happened.

"Where is she now?" I try to control my anger long enough to think. "How many men do you see?" I think fast as my mind comes up with the most painful possibilities to end these fuckers. I'm so over this shit! What he tells me next royally pisses me off.

"You fucking wait for me, got it? So help me God, Dex, if I hear one more excuse from you I'm going to… I don't give a fuck that you called Vince, you stay right the fuck there until I get to you. And keep your fucking eyes on her!"

"Sonofabitch!" I lean forward and hang my head, trying to control my erratic breathing. I have one hand on the door ready to

715

open it when Piper nearly jumps out of her seat with a hand on her chest.

"What the hell is going on?"

With my eyes closed, all I see is Anthony's face as the voices repeat his name in my mind. *Anthony. Anthony. Anthony.*

The feel of her hand on my arm breaks the spell.

I pant each word. "That motherfucker is going to die. I'm going to make sure…" I suddenly stop my rant realizing Piper shouldn't be here or around any of this shit any longer. I contain my scowl long enough to look over and see the mixed emotions in her eyes. In a flat and most serious tone, I explain what needs to happen. "You need to leave. I don't want you anywhere near here. Do you understand?"

She challenges me with a roll of her eyes. "Stop telling me to go and just tell me what's going on?"

"I'm trying my damnedest to be nice here and not be a dick, but don't push me on this. Just go!"

"No. Not 'til you tell me what you're about to do. Because from the sound of it, it's something only an idiot would consider doing."

Goddamn stubborn woman! I fucking knew I should have kept my mouth shut instead of answering many of her questions on the ride out here. Each of my answers was a condensed version of the truth because the truth is far worse than the books she likes to read.

"For the last time, Piper, just leave! Trust me when I say you don't want to be anywhere near here. Now go!" I open the door and jump from the truck, zipping up my hoodie as I disappear in the thick mist to go find Dex.

I jog along the side of the road in total fog when I hear the truck start up and take off in the opposite direction. It gives me a small ounce of relief that Piper won't be caught in any crosshairs or watch me do something she thinks would be unforgiveable.

I trek a mile or so when the fog lifts just enough for me to see lights of a farmhouse and lights coming from inside a barn. I know I'm close, now I just need to find Dex. From what he said, he's hiding out in the field across the road, behind a bunch of trees.

A big part of me doesn't want Dex involved in this any more than he is. If this shit gets out of hand, and it probably will, I don't want him to get hurt. That's why I make a last-minute change to the plan. I crouch low and run my ass to the side of the big, red barn and slowly make my way around to the front. One of the doors is cracked open, so I can hear voices inside talking over one another in a heated conversation. I can hear three or four different voices, but who knows if there any more people inside.

One voice stands out from the rest. Willow. Her scared and helpless pleas gut me. "Why are you doing this? What do you want from me?" Listening to her automatically makes me wonder if Libbs asked the same questions before that fucker murdered her. He's going to fucking die!

I rest my head against the barn to control the rage that's building inside, and it takes all I have to not storm inside. Suddenly, a man comes outside and passes right by without noticing me. He heads for one of the black SUVs and grabs what looks like a bag or something. I don't sit and watch, I react.

I sneak up behind him as he rustles through a bag, grabbing duck-tape and a rope. I don't have to wonder who he plans on using that on, so jump him from behind and snap his neck, watching him fall to the ground. If I had an ounce of remorse for what I just did, it disappears when I look at his face. I recognize him right away. Mikey Anderson. One of Anthony's guys.

Call it vindication or revenge, it doesn't matter to me anymore. I want one person and I'll take down as many as I need to get to Anthony. I see the keys in truck along with weapons and other useful tools.

Fuck it. I throw logic out the window and get in the truck, ready to start it up and drive it straight into the barn when a hand reaches in the open window and grabs me.

"Look who came to join the party. The guest of honor. Anthony will be most pleased."

Fucking Dio! A giant who just happens to be Anthony's right-hand man who currently has his big ass hand wrapped around my throat while the other holds a 9mm in my face.

"Go ahead," I struggle against his iron grip to gasp for air. "Pull the trigger you pussy. I dare you!"

"And miss the fun... I don't think so. Boss has plans for you, painful ones too. It didn't have to be this way," he preaches in a condescending voice, "but you fucked up when you killed his woman. All bets are off now. He's out for blood."

"That makes two of us, and all bets were off the minute he murdered Liberty! That cunt Rachel, fucking deserved to die. I had fun watching her blood flow as I stabbed her repeatedly. Made sure she suffered a lot worse than Libbs, too."

Dio's face instantly hardens as the vein in his forehead protrudes. He's pissed and yanks me from the front seat of the SUV and shoves me to the ground, putting his foot on my back. He grabs the rope and gets busy tying my hands together behind me before lifting me to my knees.

"Get up!" Dio orders me, wrenching my shoulder harder than necessary. But then again, I don't make it easy either. "I said let's go," he growls and presses the barrel of the gun against my temple, like that's somehow going to make me cooperate with him.

I mockingly laugh knowing full well he's not going to pull the trigger and keep his boss from getting his prize.

"Where is that motherfucking boss of yours anyway? In the barn picking on a poor defenseless woman?" I turn and briefly catch his eyes. "Now that you have me, you can let her go."

I highly doubt they will, but it's worth a shot for her sake.

"Shut the fuck up and keep moving." He shoves me ahead of him as I hear a thud followed by a grunting noise.

My body tenses as I glance over my shoulder just in time to see Dio drop to his knees and slump forward. Unaware of what's happening, I quickly turn. Behind him in the thick fog emerges the silhouette of small person swinging a baseball bat.

"Miss me yet?" There standing all proud is Piper who is twirling the bat in one hand while the other is low on her hip. A smirk full of attitude. "Looks like you may need my help after all."

To say I'm speechless is an understatement. Before I even get a chance to say a word, Dex rushes through the fog with a frantic look on his face. He looks around just to make sure no one else is going to jump out as he rushes us to cover, behind the SUV. Breathing heavy like he was running, he can't seem to pull his eyes from Piper who is still holding the bat like it's her new best friend. I turn around and shove my hands in front of him so he can untie me.

"This one belongs to you I take it?" He grumbles in my ear obviously upset I went off on my own like I demanded he not do. "Are you out of your mind? What the fuck kind of stupid ass stunt was that? Go and get yourself caught, is that your big plan?"

Oh, for fucks sake! "No, my plan was to drive this SUV into the barn and then do whatever it takes to find Anthony."

"Nice. What about Willow, you, dumbass? Or is getting her killed not a big deal anymore?"

"She shouldn't even be here," I snap at him, then yell at Piper. "Neither should you. That stunt of yours was incredibly stupid. Brave, but stupid."

Her face enflames before she scowls back and points her finger right back at me. "Saved your ass though, didn't I? How many times does that make it now? Oh yeah, three!"

Dex looks at the two us like, *really*? Then, snidely remarks. "That one's still up in the air. Vince and Marcus should be here any minute and I guarantee there is no saving him from them."

"That means I don't have much time. Dex, get Piper out of here. I'm going in."

"No! Goddammit Declan," he raises his voice slightly, but I'm already ten steps ahead aiming to sneak in the barn.

It's quiet. Too quiet. I look back one last time, but the fog makes it hard to see if Dex and Piper are still near the SUV or if have taken off like I asked. Doubtful, but I don't have time to watch out for them and get to Anthony before Marcus shows up.

A loud noise startles me, but it's not coming from the barn, it's coming from the farmhouse that's about forty feet from where I am. I don't hesitate, I sneak in the small opening of the barn door, making sure not to move it so it doesn't make any noise.

I see Willow slumped over and tied to a chair and my stomach drops. No one else seems to be around so I run over and drop to my knees in front of her.

"Hey. Hey Willow," I urgently whisper and cup her face to see if I can get her to respond. Her hair is wet and warm and when I pull my hands back, my right hand is covered in her blood. My breath catches in my chest.

"No, no, no, no. Shit, no! Willow, come on, wake up for me," I gently try and rouse her by holding her head up and moving the hair away from her face. Her face is pale, but she is breathing. "Thank fuck. Come on Willow, wake up for me. We don't have a lot of time."

She starts to stir and groans words I can't make any sense of. I make quick work on the ropes around her ankles first. It seemed like a good idea until the warm flow of vomit runs down my back.

She coughs and continues to gag as I keep working on the knot, trying not to think about her blowing chunks on me.

"What the hell," she moans until she's wakes enough to realize what's going on.

"Declan, what the fuck are you doing here? What's this all about and why are they after me? That man came to my house and told me some guy named Dominic was my father and the things he said about you... oh, Jesus! I'm so confused."

"I know, and I don't have a lot of time to explain everything to you right now Willow, but he's right about one thing. Dominic Santos is the name of your real dad, he was my father too. I never had a chance to meet him either. As for the rest of what Anthony said about me, it's not true. I'm not here to hurt you. I came to stop him from hurting you, to get some answers I have about the night our father was killed and to end that sonofabitch for everything he has ruined in my life."

"Did... did you just say Santos?"

I see the wheels in her head working.

"That's for another time to explain. Right now, let's get you out of here." She's white as a ghost and looks ready to pass out when I finally free her legs.

"Hurry before he comes back, he's creepy as hell."

"Don't worry," I try to ease the worry in her eyes without letting how angry I am scare her, "I won't let him hurt you. Not like he did to Lib..." I choke up, not sure where that came from but stopped short enough of saying her name. Her memory is never far off, though.

"I don't know what he did to you, but I'm sorry that it happened. Hopefully we get out of here and can talk. Oh my God... NOOOOO!"

As I lean over to work on the rope behind her back, that's the last thing I hear. The gunshot is deafening and from that point on everything happens in slow motion. Willow's face is one of shock and horror as she continues to shout words that comes across as muffled screams.

I start to get lightheaded and the air in the room feels like it's evaporating. I stumble for a moment and look down into her eyes.

"Declan, can you hear me? Declan... no, god, no!"

As I fall to my knees, I hear her yell, "Dad, what have you done?!"

Chapter Twenty-Seven

"Black Out"

One minute I'm struggling to catch a breath, and the next I'm physically thrown to the ground and held there by the sole of a thick, black boot pressing down on my chest.

"Liam make sure he doesn't fucking move." A deep voice instructs the man who is standing over me with a scowl and a lethal glare in his eyes.

"I don't think that's going to be a problem. Declan isn't going to give us any trouble, now are you?" The brazen look in his eyes is more of a warning. Or is it a dare? If I had any doubts as to which, he makes his point by lifting the heel of his boot to taunt me with it hovering directly over the dark red spot of my shirt.

"Fuck... *you*!" I spit.

His smiles and leans forward. "Wrong answer, asshole," he lets his comment linger before he twists the sole of his boot into my open wound. A blazing heat rips through my shoulder and inflicts the worst kind of hell I've ever known.

"*Fuuuuucccckkkkkk!*" My body shudders in excruciating pain just as Willow's desperate screams fill the room.

"Dad, Liam, *stop it.* You're hurting him. He was trying to help me. Stop! Stop!"

I'm sucking in air between my gritted teeth, inconsolable and writhing on the floor, but the last thing I'm ever going to do is ask for mercy from this motherfucker. With my shoulder and arm basically useless and given the fact I'm banged the hell up, I know my chances to overpower Liam aren't that great.

Out of the corner of my eye, I see Willow leap from her chair once she's freed. Her face winces when she gets a look at the angry welts the ropes left around her wrists, but quickly looks up when she hears another of my grueling moans. Without questioning herself, she tries to rush my way when a strong arm reaches out to stop her.

"I don't think so," Brax stops her in her tracks as he throws the rope he freed Willow from over to Liam. Instructing him, "Tie him up."

"No," Willow raises her voice in protest. "You can't do that. He was freeing me when you two showed up and shot him."

Brax violently shakes his head not having it. "I don't care, I don't trust the sonofabitch. I say leave him here for the others to figure this shit out. I'm taking you the fuck home right now."

"No, he was saving me, did you not just hear me?"

"Willow, you need to trust us on this. These people are bad news and we need to get you the fuck out of here while we can." Liam warns Willow as he rolls me over and brings me upright to my knees.

"Trust?" She hollers back, "Why should I listen to either one of you when all you've done is lie to me? At least Declan told me the truth about who my *real* father is!"

He fumbles and tries to tie my hands behind my back when I swallow back the pain I'm in to lift my head. "You're one to fucking talk, or does that only apply to, Kara?" Aim and fire. I zing him where I know it counts. They say the truth always hurts the most.

His face tightens as his shock instantly changes into rage. Muscles start to twitch in his taut cheek as I momentarily rejoice that my comment was a direct hit. One that earns me one hell of backhand that sends my head whipping sideways. The first thing I see are stars, but I smile anyway before leaning forward to spit blood at his feet.

"Keep your fucking mouth shut." I get a stern warning from both men, but it's too late. The damage's been done. Willow quietly steps back and looks between her dad and Liam, before settling her eyes back on me.

"What the hell am I missing here?" She's not questioning them, she's looking directly at me.

Like I knew they would, they both hold tight forcing my hand. "Trustworthy men like yourselves," I taunt, "why keep lying through your fucking teeth. Why not spill the rest of the family secret?"

"I said shut the *fuck up!*" Brax advances and knees me in the face, which sends me flying back. It couldn't have worked any better. Since my hands weren't tied they easily slip from the ropes, allowing me to break my fall.

On shaky legs, I go to stand only to hear a gun cock behind me. Then, I hear *his* voice.

"This is quite entertaining, but I have unwanted guests coming and little time to spare." Anthony enters the barn while listening on for the last few minutes. He's not alone, but it fucking thrills me to know that he's down at least two men I can attest for. Three in total come in with him that are packing heavy heat. Make it four if you count the fucker behind me.

Guns are aimed at everyone, but the only one Anthony seems most interested in is me.

"Boys look who we have here, it's the guest of honor. I knew if given the right incentive you'd come crawling to me. It's pathetic, but who am I to complain," he sighs as he walks around me doing what he does best. Hear himself talk. "A tough guy, yet, so vulnerable. That's your downfall and will be what finally takes you out. What a fucking waste. I have no clue what my brother see's in you. I suppose it doesn't matter, because I have you both now."

Red in the face, Brax steps forward until a gun is pressed to his temple. "*What the fuck are you doing?*" He shouts at Anthony, looking like he's ready to explode. "You tipped us off that *he* was here holding Willow. And now you come in and point a fucking gun at us?"

Anthony stares back with a blank face, then erupts in laughter. "You're quick, I'll give you that. You're just not that smart. When I was at your house, you ate up every line of bullshit I fed you. Not because you believed it, but because you couldn't stand the idea of Declan ever coming within an inch of your precious family."

"You got that fucking right," Brax growls, not backing down an inch. "That now includes you."

Anthony shakes his head finding that even funnier. "Threatening me isn't going to help you. Now, if you'll excuse me I would like a chat with the boy… and the girl." Anthony then motions for his thugs to tie up Brax and Liam to a beam in the corner of the barn, well out of his way.

When he walks over to me, I'm barely standing and clutching my shoulder, but I know I only get one shot to do this right. Everything boils down to this one moment.

"I'm going to fucking kill you, Anthony, for everything you've done. And I swear to God, I'm going to make it hurt 'til you take your last breath."

Sizing up the shape I'm in, Anthony raises a cocky eyebrow, feeling confident to be this close to me without feeling threated at all. "Always the tough guy," he gets right in my face and threatens, "I'd like to see you try, really, but I have a little story to tell you and Willow. A story you might want to hear."

"I don't want a fucking thing from you except tear you from limb to limb." I match the intensity in his dark, soulless eyes, making damn sure he sees the rage that's still alive somewhere in my broken body. That I have enough left in me to make good on my threat. Fucker knows I won't back down, now he's about to learn that I won't break.

Anthony regards me for a moment before he motions with his fingers, getting two of his guys to surround me. So disappointing, what a pussy.

"You think guns are going to scare me? That fucker," I say, nodding my head toward Brax, "shot me and I'm still standing."

Irritation flares in Anthony's eyes. "Just barely, but let's get back to the point. You want something from me. You want to know *why*? Why *Liberty*, why *you*, why your *father* was murdered in cold blood? So many unanswered questions, that only I have the answers too. Isn't that why you're here? To find out the answers that have long haunted you?

"Hmmm? *Come on, Declan! Don't fucking tell me you haven't longed to be in the same room with me?* No more games. Just the honest fucking truth before I *end* your miserable life. The question is what to do with dear Willow? I had no real intentions with her, but the minute you killed Rachel, those intentions changed."

Brax goes insane, pulling on the ropes that restrain him and Liam. "Don't you fucking touch a hair on her motherfucking head!"

Curtis 'fucking' Diego happens to rush into the barn at the same time and he heads straight over to Anthony. My gaze on him narrows wondering what the hell he's up to now.

Anthony just glares at him. "Where the fuck have you been? And why the hell are you bleeding?"

Curtis glances over at me to see if I'm going to keep my mouth shut that I saw him earlier with Marcus and Vince. Speaking of, where are Marcus and Vince? If Curtis is here, that means they are nearby.

"I had a few *issues* to clear up, that's all," Curtis answers with a sour look on his face and then bends down to whisper something in Anthony's ear.

In the corner, Brax is hot at it cursing at the guy standing guard over him and Liam while Anthony quietly argues with something Curtis said in his ear.

The commotion gets under Anthony's skin. "Would someone shut them the hell up." No sooner did the words leave his mouth someone knocks Liam out with a single hit to the back of the head with the end of a gun.

Without thinking of her own personal safety, Willow runs and jumps on the back of the guy as he gets ready to land a blow to back of Brax's head. It does little good as he just shrugs her off with ease.

The scene terrifies Willow who can't watch and lowers her head with her hands over her ears. She closes her eyes tight while willing herself to be anywhere but here.

I open my mouth, but no words come out. My body is locked with rage as my eyes negatively shift from Anthony to Curtis. He's the wild card in this right now and I want his ass almost as much as I want Anthony's.

"What, no comment, Declan?" Anthony taunts. "Impressive, but let's see what happens when I tell you a story. One that starts with your father and ends with you. It's only fitting the story ends in the exact spot your father was gunned down nearly twenty years ago. Bet you didn't know that, did you? Don't believe me? Just look around. If you had taken any time at all to look closely at the photo I sent you, the one right before Kara shot him, you might recognize the farmhouse or the barn in the background.

"Do you know why this is place is still here? Why Dominic chose to bring Izzy here after he kidnapped her all those years ago? No? Well, I'll tell you anyway. It's property owned and leased by associates of the Aniello organization. Convenient, wouldn't you say?"

"Seems like a fucking waste to me," I criticize his plan because I know it get under his skin. "So, this is your master plan? To get me here just to kill me? Seems like a lot to go through when you could have easily done it in Chicago, and it still doesn't explain why you want Willow. What does she have to do with any of this? Let her go, I'm the one you really want."

"That's true. I didn't intend to kill you at first, but the moment you killed Rachel, you have no idea how you changed fate in that one moment. Mine, yours, Rachel's, and even dear Willow's." Anthony's looks down as his face tries to hide his pain. When he looks up, he looks over at me with a faraway gaze and a soft sigh. "I loved her, you know? Rachel."

I didn't, but even if I had it wouldn't have changed the outcome. I'd still do it all over again.

"You see, I had this big proposal all planned out. White roses, red roses, and room full of candles and light music playing in the background. She would have said yes, and when the time was right we would have eloped on a private beach somewhere in the Mediterranean. That's how much I loved and looked forward to a life with her, but that all changed," he pauses as his eyes grow cold. "Because of you. My plan started to fall apart the closer she got with you. I couldn't just stand by and let that happen. Actions needed to be taken. That's why this all started in the first place."

If anyone is to blame, it's him. He's the one who sent her to Vince to get hired in the first place. Let's see how much he likes this. "Rachel, the fine piece of ass that she was. Can't imagine how it was for you to love her like you say you do, just to get inside of her, knowing I was already there. Damn, that just had to kill you. Did you ever wonder if she moaned more for me than you? Did she call out my name when you couldn't fuck her like I could?"

Motherfucker looks like he's ready to explode but stops short of doing a damn thing. He's too busy with his fists to his face like he's somehow trying to block out the image of his woman bent over for me.

"You're such a fucking pussy, Anthony. Explains why Rachel kept coming back, she didn't want another pussy, she wanted a man to pound that tight pussy of hers. No wonder Marcus liked Dominic more than you."

And right there, I have my answer.

"Holy shit, that's it, isn't it? Why you hated my old man so much? He wasn't a pussy like you. He was lethal motherfucker who pegged you for what you were back then. You were jealous of him. Dominic replaced you in Marcus's eyes, right? Relied more and more on him because he got shit done and built an untouchable reputation in the process. He got the respect you felt you deserved, but never got. And you hated him for it.

"It all makes sense now. The older I got, more and more chatter followed me around. How much I looked like him, acted like him. No wonder you hated the idea of Windy City Underground at first. Marcus was paying more attention to me and the better I got in the ring, the more you despised me for it. You're the one who is fucking pathetic and my old man pegged you for what you were, didn't he? He wasn't like you. Only a real man stands and fights for what he wants, not like you. You stand back and send in your woman to do the dirty work for you."

He erupts. "You *killed* Rachel."

How dare he throw that in my face.

"YEAH, MOTHERFUCKER, I DID!! BECAUSE OF HER, YOU MURDERED LIBERTY!"

"That's where you're wrong!" he seethes through gritted teeth, pacing in front of me. "You might as well have been the one to inject the lethal dose of heroine to that girl's arm. I may be many things, but blind isn't one of them. I saw the change in Rachel. Fucking made me sick. She denied it, boy did she ever, but I saw right through her. She started spending more nights with you, saying it was to get more information for me. She became distant, and that's when I knew."

He pauses for a moment like he's collecting his thoughts with a distant look in his eyes. Before he turns to face me with a look of pure evil. "Figured since you were taking Rachel away from me, I was going to take something away from you. Tell me, was fucking Rachel worth the life of that girl of yours?"

Everything just goes red. Anthony's right, the time for games is over. No more playing, no more words. I explode and unleash everything that's left in me. I simply open my mind and free my rage.

I feel no pain.

I hear no sounds.

And the only one I see is Anthony.

I knew then I'd most likely die in that barn, full of bullet holes, but I made my peace with that, knowing I'd be okay with it as long as I took Anthony out with me. The vow I made to Libbs means more to me than my own life.

The next few minutes are a blur...

My head tilts back as the beast from within erupts a guttural moan that lets everyone know that he has arrived.

Anthony scurries and grabs a gun from one of his guys and points it at me. But by the time he can pull the trigger, I have him by his neck and lift him so his feet dangle above the floor.

The commotion around me doesn't deter me and when Anthony gasps calling for his men to shoot me, I squeeze tighter until I see the whites of his eyes turn blood red.

Yes! That's what I want. I want this motherfucker to bleed, but I need it to hurt!

I throw him to into two of his men and knock them down with him. When I turn to face the others, I see that Curtis has one knocked out and is in a struggle with the other. One of the men that went down with Anthony goes to stand, then charges at me without the aid of his gun that must have gotten knocked out of his hand. I crack my neck and hunch down with my arms out ready to take his ass down. Before he can reach me though, a shot rings out as the man charging my way falls to knees. Parts of his head explodes and sprays my face as a gush of blood pours from his mouth. As his limp body falls forward, the menacing scowl of Vince appears out of the darkness holding a smoking gun.

"*Vince, stop him. You have to stop him.*" *Anthony calls out to Vince who hasn't taken his eyes off me.*

I don't pause for a second, I stomp over to Anthony as he tries to crawl away, choking and gasping for air.

I land a debilitating blow with my boot to his lower back and land another until I hear the sound of his spine break. His agonizing cries are like music to my ears.

"*Sound familiar, motherfucker? That's the same kind of cries Liberty made when you videotaped her death for me to see. I hear that cry every damn night before I go to sleep. I swore to myself the last noise you were ever going to make was that same scream.*"

I roll him over because the last face he's going to see before he dies is mine. Tears stream down his face as saliva flies from his open mouth. Yet, I feel nothing. My job isn't done. I step closer and rest my boot on his throat, but don't apply pressure.

"*Show me your fear! Show me the same fucking fear I saw in her eyes before she died. GIVE ME YOUR FEAR!!*"

He refuses, so I slowly apply pressure until he realizes he's about to take his last breath. It's then that he shows me what I want to see.

Chapter Twenty-Eight

"Confronting Demons"

I GROAN AND STRETCH THE ache in my shoulder as I attempt to open my eyes from under heavy lids. The first thing I see is unfamiliar floral wallpaper and the bed I'm lying in. I shake the grogginess from my head only to discover I'm shirtless with a tightly bandaged shoulder.

The door slowly squeaks open as Vince sneaks in, unaware that I'm awake. When he sees me staring back at him, it's as if a giant weight has been lifted. His face visibly lightens as he sighs with relief.

"It's good to see you awake, even though I'm surprised that you are. How are you feeling?"

When I speak, my voice is thick and hoarse, like I have a frog in my throat. "Dazed I guess, everything seems a bit foggy right now." A thought that would normally worry me but given the fact that Vince is not ripping into me, I'm not. Even though he's watching me extra careful.

"That's understandable," he reassures me with a calming voice. "You were pretty much out of your mind when we walked in." Suddenly, his vibe changes. His shoulders get tense as the creases around his eyes deepen. "From the look of things, we got there just in the nick of time."

I frown finding his comment a bit strange. "Why do you say that?"

He eyes me cautiously, then asks, "What exactly do you remember?"

"Ahhh, let's see," I recall the events as I best remember, "Anthony and his men had us at gunpoint and then ..." I pause as I recall a distinct scream.

"Wait, what happened with Willow?" I struggle to sit up in bed as the memories start to come back to me. "Is she okay?"

Vince already has his hands up as he walks next to the bed. "Calm down, everyone is fine." He urges me to take a few breaths, then questions, "Tell me what you last remember about Anthony specifically?"

His asking me this does little to calm me down. "Other than wanting to kill the sonofabitch, not much."

When Vince's eyes trail to the floor, I know something is off and it instantly pisses me off. "I did, didn't I? Kill him?"

Rather than stand uncomfortably, Vince exhales and sits down on the edge of the bed. Then he tells me what really happened.

"I know you wanted to be the one to kill Anthony for everything he did, and no one faults you for that, son." I know he's being totally sincere because that's the only time he calls me 'son.' 'Nephew' just doesn't seem right since he's the only father-figure I've ever known.

He continues, "Having said that, Marcus and I knew that you *couldn't* be the one to do it. Who you were in that moment is not who you really are, no matter how much you believe it to be true. Rage and revenge can do awful things to anyone. Living with the consequences, even worse."

"Wait, what the hell are you trying to say to me?"

This time, he turns to face me with eyes determined and a voice full of contempt. "I'm saying that Anthony is taken care of and disposed of. That's all you need to know. He's long gone and paid the ultimate price for all of his wrong doings."

I'm speechless and can't believe what I'm hearing. Then again, I'm not *totally* shocked. But I'd be lying if I said I didn't feel cheated. "Who did it then?" I demand.

He gives me a warning look. "Declan..."

"'Declan' my ass! I fucking asked *who*, Vince? I deserve to know!"

He doesn't want to say, but eventually he does. "Marcus. He knew that he had to be the one, because there was no way he was going to let you live your life carrying that burden or dealing with the consequences. Anthony was *his* brother, *his* responsibility, and

Dominic was his best friend. Taking out a man like Anthony has consequences. Do you understand what I'm saying to you?"

Unfortunately I do, I just don't give a damn.

"What you need to understand, Declan, is you and I are the only family Marcus has. And family protects one another. What Anthony did was unforgivable to Marcus, and seeing as he was his brother, Marcus knew what he had to do. No questions and no regrets."

"That wasn't the deal though, and you know it. I vividly remember telling you both that whoever was behind this was mine."

"Yes, you did, and Marcus is seeing to it that you will still get your opportunity to make things right. He has something for you when we get home to Chicago."

I have no clue what he's talking about. "Like what?"

"The guys in the video, he has two of them now and is closing in on the third. He swears nothing will happen to them until you get back. In the meantime, Marcus is having them followed. They aren't going anywhere."

I know full well what that means. They are likely strung up by their arms in one of the old warehouses Marcus likes to use when he is going to dispose of someone. "Where is Marcus now? Why isn't he here?"

Vince's face looks pained as he admits, "He left shortly after he did what he came here to do. He said he needed to be by himself for a few days before he goes back to Chicago to deal with any potential fallout."

"Is anybody really going to miss that asshole?" I utter under my breath, then bring up the elephant in the room since he has yet to say a word about him. "What's the deal with Curtis?"

Vince shakes his head. "That's enough questions for now, you need to rest. There will be plenty of time for that later. Nero has all of us on strict instructions to let you rest stress-free until you are healthy enough to travel."

The first thing I think is holy shit, Nero is here, the second has me laughing. "Are you sure he was talking about me when he said that?"

"Yeah, I know. I raised an eyebrow when he said that too, but in his defense, it took him some time to stitch you up and make note all of your injuries. Fucker was cursing the whole time and almost took Dex out when he found out about the fight that broke out between you two. You were lucky you were out for all of that. Which reminds me, how's your head feeling?"

"Why," I ask with a sense of humor, "am I dying or something?"

"Humor me," Vince exhales with a fake smile plastered on his face.

"Besides feeling like it's a bowling ball centered on my shoulders," I remark, "surprisingly quiet."

His laugh should have alerted me. "I had Nero mix in your medication with any pain meds he gives you. I knew you stopped taking them and from the scene we walked in on, it was the only call to make. You were out of control."

I scowl at him, but it's not for the reasons he may think. I don't like anyone doing shit to me that I don't approve of, but right now I really don't give a shit. I smirk, "No wonder I'm so mellow."

"You need to be for what I have to tell you," he comments with tension around his eyes. "You have some visitors that have been waiting to talk with you. Against my better wishes, I might add."

I raise a questioning brow. "Since when do you do anything you don't want to do? That's very un-Vince of you."

"I'm here with you, that's the difference. Izzy, Kara and Willow are here. They know you have questions and are willing to talk with you. One more thing, we have a pipsqueak of girl we can't seem to get rid of. Driving Dex crazy is one reason to like her, but she's determined not to leave until she sees you."

I smile knowing it can only be one person. "Piper?"

"Yes. We have a nickname for her. Bulldog. For not knowing you long, she's quite protective over you." Then, he uncharacteristically chuckles. "Even with me."

"That's either impressive, or you're losing your tough guy image." He silently laughs and rolls his eyes.

"Funny, but on a more serious note, I had a long talk with her about everything and I let her know how much I appreciated all that she did for you. I'm not sure you'd still be alive if not for her help."

"Oh Christ," I groan and shake my damn head. "How much did you offer to pay her?" I can see it in his eyes.

"Now that is none of your business." He gets up to leave but stops when he gets to the door. "I'll send them in, but the door stays open. I'll be close by if you need anything. And just so you know, Piper tore up my check. She thought I was paying her for only doing the right thing. She was quite insulted. Strange cat, that one," he sighs under his breath and leaves.

I've known Vince my whole life and no matter what he wants me to think, I know he likes her. Which is strange and scary at the same time. A knock on the door reveals a grumpy Nero as he stumbles in. He tries to hide the relief on his face with his usual frown, but I can see through him as he gets busy taking my vitals.

"I didn't know you were a nursemaid as well as a trainer?" I lighten the mood and joke with him, but, as usual, Nero gets the last laugh when he applies just the right amount of pressure to my shoulder.

Damn! The only thing I can do is grit my teeth and grimace through the pain.

"I can't have my best fighter going off and getting himself killed, now can I? That would leave me with Dex and Kingston," he says with a not-on-your-life kind of scowl, "there's no way in hell I was having that." He says matter of fact as he jots things down in a notebook-like journal that was lying on a dresser.

"Is that your way of telling me you like me?" I jokingly remind him. "The, 'daily pain in your ass' as you so eloquently put it?"

His hand stops writing as he shrugs his shoulders. "Not everyone gets me like you do, what can I say. Now, let's get serious for a minute. I want you to listen very closely to what I have to say. If at any time you start to get upset when they come in, you let me know and everyone leaves. Got it? I'm not having you get upset, you've been through more than enough."

"Yes, sir!" I salute him with my fingers just as he adds a clear liquid to the I.V. in my arm. If I didn't know better, I'd say this is his way of making sure I obey his orders to remain calm. Smart man!

He pauses to do a double take. "I like this new, agreeable side of you, but," his face grows serious, "you're lucky to be alive and not filled with bullet holes right now. What you need to realize is the past is the past. Have this talk, get it all out, ask your questions. Then, it's done. Period. We only look to the future from here on out. That involves me owning your ass and getting you ready to get back inside the ring. I have your next fight on paper, all we need to do is put in the date."

My mouth falls open. "Are you insane? I'm not ready... oh, who am I kidding. Who will I be fighting?"

Nero grins like a motherfucker. "I'm surprised you even have to ask. Curtis. Marcus knew you'd want a rematch. He's making sure you get that chance."

That right there just proves how much Marcus gets me, and it gets my blood pumping. Talk about motivation. My chance to get back at Curtis will ensure one fast as hell recovery.

"Training starts the minute you give me the green light."

His face lights up as he rubs his hands together. "Now that's what I like to hear."

THE ROOM IS EERILY QUIET and uncomfortable as Izzy walks in the room, alone. My eyes drop to the familiar book she has in her hands. Dominic's journal. There is only one way for her to have it. Dex must have given it to her to read over.

She eyes me cautiously as she stands a few feet from the bed. "I hope you don't mind, but I wanted to talk with you alone before Willow came in. I'm sure you have some questions that would be hard for Willow to hear given the circumstances."

Right away she impresses me. "It's weird to have you here in front of me. In my head, I had everything planned out what I would say to you. I feel like I know so much about you when, in reality, I only know you through Dominic's eyes."

"That's true and I have to tell you, it wasn't easy to read most of what's in this journal. It's true you don't know me, only what you've read and what little Marcus or Vince may have told you. I can't imagine what you must be thinking. But I have to admit, it's hard to look at you, because all I see is *him*. You look so much like him it's scary, but I get the feeling your nothing like him."

"Even after everything that went down, and the things I have done, you still feel that way about me? That I'm not some monster? I find that hard to believe. Your husband shot me, after all."

She winces. "I know, and I'd like to apologize for that. But he was only protecting his daughter. Before you say anything, let me finish. When I look at you, I see a young man who's confused and angry. A young man who suffered a terrible tragedy that wasn't his fault. You didn't have to come here and help Willow, but you did. She told me you tried to free her... I guess what I'm trying to say is I see that you care, and I see how devoted you are to the friend you lost. How you live your life is up to you, Declan. But you are not him. Trust me, that's a good thing."

The whole time she spoke, I had one question I wanted her to answer. "Why did she do it?"

Izzy looks on and sighs before she sets the journal down on the bed next to me. "Kara will tell you herself, but she was terrified of Dominic, and with good reason given how violent he'd become with her. Not to mention all the awful things he did to me. She knew he'd eventually kill me, so it was either him or me."

"In the journal he talks about how much he cared for you and Willow. He went as far as to call it love for someone like him."

There is little she can do to hide the pain behind her eyes.

"I read that part, and it was incredibly difficult because he sure didn't show it. At first but over the years, not at all." Even though I see and feel her pain, I find myself in a unique position having read Dominic's journal. I want to ask her something I'm sure won't be easy, but I've never been able to let it go. "He mentioned it was easier for him to give into the voices instead of feeling powerless. His feelings for you were something he never could get a grasp on, why do you think that is?"

Her face turns emotionless as her voice drops. "I have no answer for that."

I don't buy that, not for a minute. "You know what I find sad? That he felt it was so much easier for him to become this altered version of himself who wouldn't let him love anything other than his power. That it had to be one or the other."

She sees something in my face, and it prompts her to ask, "Do you think you have similar issues? I'm not trying to judge but before I let Willow walk in here, I'd like to know the answer."

I find no reason to lie or feel angry that she asked such a personal question, even though I am surprised by it. "I do hear voices but if you're worried I'm going to turn into raging lunatic any time soon, rest assured, Nero has enough medication pumped into me to sedate a horse I'm guessing. Though you should know I've lived with them long enough that I have some control over them, where I feel Dominic never did."

"Some advice," she offers with a tenderness in her eyes, like a mother talking to a child. "Keep taking them, Declan. If not for yourself, then for whoever comes into your life. Do it for her and for the life you'd like to have. Don't suffer the same fate as him. Be stronger than he ever was."

Fucking hell, if I ever had any doubts what Dominic saw in Izzy, I don't anymore. It's too bad he couldn't change, something tells me she's one hell of a woman.

"You look tired, so let me grab Kara. We're on strict orders not to overdo things with you. It was important for me to personally thank you for what you did and were willing to do for Willow. I don't know how Willow feels because she's closed herself off, but don't hurt her. I came here willingly and with an open mind. Don't make me regret it."

The lines are drawn and with little to misunderstand, Izzy doesn't pull any punches. Gotta' hand it to her, I respect that.

Not ten seconds later, voices get testy in the other room as I hear Dex raising his voice. Worst case scenarios run through my mind, especially if Vince and Brax are in the same room together. That's when a bundle of energy known as Piper bursts in the room.

"Dude, I swear to God you have nine lives or something. Does this sort of thing happen often with you or what? I've known you for all of thirty hours and most of that time has been with you lying on your back, either shot or beat up." The whole time she talks, her hands are moving as fast as her mouth like she's either jacked up on caffeine, or in some sort of shock. Who could blame her, the girl's been exposed to some serious shit in the last few days.

She is a sight for sore eyes though. "I can't believe you're here but," I can't believe I'm going to say this, "I'm happy that you are. And that you're safe. Even though you don't listen for shit." Twice. I asked her to leave twice, and both times, she didn't listen to a word I said.

She bobs her head like she hears me, but once again, doesn't really listen. "Yes, well, someone had to make sure Nero was taking good care of you. Plus, I was still pissed at you for making me leave with Dex. If we had been with you, maybe you wouldn't have been shot. Did you ever think about that?"

When it comes to Piper, being honest just comes easy for me. "For what I was going to do, I didn't want you to see me like that. I don't know what I would have done if you got hurt because of me. I couldn't take that risk because you've risked so much for me."

"As you can see, I'm fine. You're alive, so all is good. Now," she points over her shoulder toward the door, "if we can just get through tonight." Then, whispers, "I swear, Vince is ready to shoot everyone out there and Nero is standing guard like he's your personal bodyguard, ready to attack anyone who even looks at you wrong. Though Dex and Willow seem to be hitting it off okay."

What? "Keep him away from her, he's had this thing for her from the time I found out I had a sister."

Piper then overhears something in the other room and is busy using her hands to hush me. "Shh, listen to what's going on out there. I'm staying in here where it's safe."

"That boy is no good, just like his old man. Makes me sick just to think of him in the same room with Willow."

Willow is heard shouting back. "That's funny since he and I share the same father."

"No! You may share the same DNA, but that motherfucker was never a part of your life. And he sure as hell was never a father to you."

"He wasn't one to Declan either! How can you hate him so much when you don't even know him?"

"I don't need to get to know him!"

Izzy's voice is easily heard over Vince, who is demanding that Brax either shut the fuck up or leave. "Everyone needs to take a step back and cool off here. Brax, Willow wanted to come and talk with Declan and no matter how you and I feel about it, she's an adult and is free to make her own choices. If you can't take it, go home. I'll be there shortly."

"The fuck I am! I'm not leaving you and Willow here alone."

That's when Vince finally snaps. "Then respect what the hell I say, because my willingness to let you step one foot in this house is about more than I can stomach, seeing as you shot Declan. You're lucky I don't return the favor."

"FYI," Piper enthusiastically fingers as quotes, "someone else is going to get shot before this night is over. That's all I'm saying." Which is funny, since I've known her all she's done is talk.

Like she's going to be hanging out with me for a while, she's gets comfy lying on the opposite end of the bed with her legs stretched out facing me.

"Are you..." I started to say when Willow walks in the room. Following on her heels is Dex, looking like he has shit to get off his chest. His face is red, and his eyes have yet to leave Willow. What I did not expect was the argument from the other room to flow into mine. It's clear Brax has an issue with Dex when it comes to Willow.

"Jesus, Dad! Are you following us in here, too? I'm just a little sick of you judging Declan when you don't even know him. He didn't come to harm any of us. The only thing he does want, is answers about his father. *Our* father. Don't crucify him when you don't know the fucked-up shit he's lived through."

I'd be lying if I said I wasn't speechless.

Just then, Nero and Vince barge in the room and flank each side of the bed like I'm completely defenseless. Piper sits up as well creating a barrier between them and me. Fuck, they all act like I'm incapable and helpless.

Brax ignores everything and everybody as he angrily shouts back, like I'm not even in the same room as him. "He killed a woman for Christ's sakes. Why should I trust a Goddamned thing he says, or you, for that matter?" he scowls at Dex. "You've just admitted to lying to my daughter for weeks now."

Dex rolls his eyes and decides to talk to Willow instead. "Willow, I want you to know that everything I did was for all the right reasons, even though it may not look like it. I don't want you to leave here tonight without you knowing the biggest reason behind it all. I was hoping you didn't know the truth about who your real father was. Hell, I was banking on it. Hoping that once you found out that you would want to get to know Declan. Because maybe, just maybe, you could turn out to be the one person in his life he could completely relate with.

"You don't know him, but every time he steps into the ring it's like he's fighting a damn ghost. The ghost of who everyone expects him to be, given who his father was. While he's angry and stubborn as hell, he's not a bad person. And he's definitely not the monster Anthony portrayed him to be. While Dominic Santos may be the worst kind of evil to some ... you need to understand that to Declan and the family he grew up around, he meant something entirely different.

"Dex," I say with a deep growl, warning him to shut his mouth. "That's enough!" But he just goes on as if I didn't say anything.

"Declan's furious because he's been lied to his whole life. He never knew what really happened to his father. Imagine how he felt when he found out his father's own sister was the one who killed him? Then find out he has two sisters he never knew existed."

"He still killed a woman," Brax interjects refusing to be ignored. He says with nothing but contempt as his eyes swing to me, looking like he wishes he had a gun in hands right now. Little does he know, I'm more than sure that Vince has one on him as he stands guard next to my side.

Refusing to shut his mouth, Dex carries on ignoring Vince's subtle throat clearings. He's determined to get shit off his chest one way or another.

"No, it doesn't but before you crucify him, you should know that bitch lied to him. She's the reason the only person Declan ever truly felt something for was brutally murdered, just to fuck him over. That fucker sent him a videotape of her murder for him to watch." Then he throws a punch no one saw coming. "Plus, if we're really talking about killing someone, Kara did so herself. I'm mean if we're comparing notes here."

"I don't buy a word you say," Brax contends, going as far to say, "That boy is nothing but a lowlife version of his..."

That's when Vince has heard just about enough. He steps forward with livid scowl as his hand reaches inside his suit jacket.

Willow's gasp catches his attention and as he sees the horror flash over her innocent face, he stands down. Restraint is not something he shows often, but Vince does, and it surprises even me.

He threatens Brax instead. "I wouldn't finish that sentence if I were you. Get out while the girl talks with Declan. You can go peacefully, or I will make you. The choice is yours, but personally I..."

"That won't be necessary," Izzy steps forward to yank on his arm as he looks at Willow.

"I'll be outside waiting on you." And just when he gets to the door and we all take a breather, he stops to look over his shoulder. "As far as I'm concerned, you can all fuck off. The sooner you get back to Chicago, the better. Don't expect me to sit back and thank you for shit. Not when all you did was come here and disrupt our happy lives."

Then he looks directly at me, "Don't forget, this happened because of you. Think about that, boy!"

"Dad, you need to chill the hell out. God, enough already. Mom, please... for me."

It wasn't easy, but Brax went with Izzy, followed by an itchy-fingered Vince. Nero stands guard at the door shaking his head, cursing under his breath about how this is not the time to be upsetting me when I should be resting. With Dex, Willow and Piper in my room, Kara walks in very slowly as she eyes me cautiously.

"Willow, do you think you could let us talk alone first. I promise not to be long, and maybe send your mom back in if you wouldn't mind."

"Oh, okay. I guess I could do that." Willow looks half frightened but is not alone as Dex volunteers to walk out with her.

Piper is the last to leave, and asks me, "Are you sure? I can sit in the corner."

I motion for her to go. Who the hell knows the direction this conversation is going to go. On her way out, Piper mumbles something about getting Vince. It barely registers with me because my attention is centered on the one woman who ruined my life before I was ever born.

Kara breaks the silence between us first. "It pains me to be here, and to look at you is even harder than I thought it would be. You look so much like Dominic, it's downright scary."

"I could say the same for you. Looking at you in person is harder than I thought it would be, as well. Although, it doesn't change what you did."

She swallows loudly and appears more anxious. "I'm sorry for things that were kept from you, but I'm not sorry for what I did. I did what I had to do to survive, that is something I think even you can understand."

Survival? Yes, I understand that all too well. Sympathy for killing my father? No. The question I have to ask myself is: am I willing to listen with an open mind?

That's when Vince and Izzy rush in, getting a feel in the room before Vince wisely closes the door behind him.

Everyone is silent, but all eyes are on me as I sit up in bed and take a minute to gather my thoughts. It seems the conversation I had rehearsed in my mind for months now has suddenly escaped me. As I look from Izzy to Kara and then to Vince, one thing sticks out at me.

"Four different lives connected by one common thread, Dominic Santos. How does it feel," I ask visibly shaken by the emotions hitting me all at once now that we're all in the same room together? "Having to face not only one black sheep of the family," I point at Vince, "but two now, counting myself? Must be hard for you."

Kara eyes linger for a moment before lowering to the floor. "Look, I don't have a problem with you, or Vince for that matter, as long as we don't have anything to do with one another. That life, the life Dominic led, I want no part of. Not then, not now. Like I said, I have no problem with you and I want it to remain that way. This shit happened a long time ago and now I'm pregnant with my first child and I can't be all stressed-out. But this shit is stressing me the hell out. I just wanted to say my peace and I hope you can somehow find yours."

"Peace?" The shock in my voice registers somewhere between disgust and disbelief. "That's an odd choice of words. Have you lived in peace for the last twenty years, knowing you killed your brother?"

Her eyes widen. "Hell no. You have no idea the hell I've lived with knowing what I did. At one time he was my fun-loving brother, then he became this..." her mouth twists trying to find the word.

"Monster? Is that what you were going to say?"

She stares at me straight in the eye, and answers, "Yes."

Man, she is a piece of work and as I give a side glance at Vince, he looks just as disgusted. He looks like he wants to say something, but I shake my head at him, letting him know not to get involved.

"You see, this is the part I just can't get past, *Auntie Kara*." I glare at her, lowering my voice, "Those voices your brother had, well, I have them too. So would you just gun me down and go on living like it's no big deal? Saying, 'well, it had to be done'?"

"Look, I didn't say…"

"THE HELL YOU DIDN'T!"

Vince steps forward as I am slow to get out of bed. I hold my hand up capable of getting out of the damn bed myself. I grab Dominic's journal and turn to Kara.

"Did you know he talked about you? Quite fondly, actually, a number of times in here. So much so I thought, hell, I might actually like getting to know her. Fucking ironic. You say he turned into this monster, and I'm not saying he didn't in your eyes. What I have a real issue with is here you are blaming him for being a monster, when the monster inside of you did something just as evil. Shit, look at Vince. Look at me. It seems all the Santos' have a bit of a monster inside of them, wouldn't you say?"

Kara starts to weep as Izzy takes her in her arms. "I don't know what you want me to say, I've said what I came to say. I have nothing else for you."

"Really? So that's it? You did what you had to do and fuck everyone else? Dominic was a brother, a friend, and a father to Willow and me. You say you changed your lives for the better, but what about us? What about how we feel? Or do we not count?"

Kara wipes away her tears, lightly sobbing, "You two are both better off not knowing that sick bastard. You just have to believe me, but really, there is nothing else I can say or do that will ever give you the satisfaction you think you deserve. Nothing I say or do will bring him back."

She's right, nothing will ever bring him back, but she's wrong about one thing. There is something she can say that will give me satisfaction. Something I want to hear from her lips. When I hand my father's journal to Kara, she is reluctant to take it from my hands. "Take it," I strongly urge with eyes that dictate she has no other choice. "Take it and open to the page that is bent in half." I've had this page marked for a while. Not sure why, but in this moment, I know.

Kara takes the journal from me and opens it to the page, but the tears streaming down her cheeks make it difficult for her to focus. She prompts Izzy to take the journal from her hands.

"Let me read it for you," Izzy reaches out to comfort her friend but that's not happening.

"No! I want *her* to read the words. Out loud."

Izzy protests, "Declan, this isn't helping anyone." She looks on with deep compassion in her eyes and if she's hoping that's going to work on me, it won't. Not about this.

"You sure about that? Kara talks about him like he was a fucking soulless monster who deserved what he got. I'm sure that's what she tells herself just so she can sleep better at night."

My accusation is met with a gasp as Kara's eyes overflow with tears. Periodically she glances up at the ceiling to fight them back but quickly swipes them away as they fall. I can see the spark of anger behind her dark eyes and take comfort in knowing I put it there. She should feel at least a tenth of the anger I've lived with for so long.

I take a moment to look at Vince, then Izzy. "What I want is for Kara to know exactly how I *see* him. The father I never got to meet, because of *her*. What better way for her to know how I feel than to read the words from his own handwriting." Then, I stare in her eyes, "*Read it!*"

Vince, who has remained quiet, acts like he may say something but I cut him with a pointed look that says, *back the fuck off*. This is my moment and I deserve to have it.

Kara somberly reads the words I have memorized. "Nothing in life is forever. I've lived with the good and the bad. I'm sure my life will end with regrets. A man like me doesn't live a life like I do and not have a few things that will haunt them to their dying day. One of my biggest regrets will be Kara. Having a little sister is a big responsibility. One I took seriously until the day she betrayed me and helped Izzabella leave. That was something I simply cannot forgive her for. If I've ever done anything right by her, I hope she realizes that in my cold, dark heart she has a place that will always beat for her. Deep down she's always known the truth about me. I inscribed them in our matching charm bracelets when our grandmother died.

The figure eight symbolizing; *There is no boundary that separates life from death. Rather, it's a continuous cycle that evolves but keeps on the same path.*

Her charm read; *May there be an angel to look after you.*

Mine; *Or a demon to protect you.*"

Kara wipes a stray tear from her cheek and she breaks down with a trembling hand over her shoulder.

"Oh, my god! I totally remember this day like it was yesterday. I opened them up and can remember how perfect they were at the time. There is something else that you wouldn't know, but," she tells me a gentle clearing of her throat, "I almost died after things went down with Dominic because of a guy named Max, who kidnapped me. I remember it was so dark out, but I kept running down a street toward a voice. His voice. After what I did to him, he was still guiding me back to the light, telling me it wasn't my time yet." She faces me with tears full of regret and sorrow as I listen without any judgement.

"I hated him," her voice wavers, "but I also loved him. That's makes me sound crazy, right? How could I love someone who hurt my best friend like he did? I'm sorry, Declan, but my brother was a monster who had to be stopped. I did it, but I have to live with that burden. It came with a price. I have to face my niece every day knowing what I did, but I also know what I did was in her best interest. You may not believe it, but I did what was best for you, too. Vince," she eyes him and lightly laughs, "is complicated."

Vince and Izzy both chuckle as Kara breaks free from her tears and stands a bit taller. "We've only talked a handful of times over the years, but in my heart, I know you will be a better human being because you had Vince as a father figure, and not Dominic."

I think about my father's comment with the infinity symbol and there not being a separation from the living and the dead. That we all live on in some continuous cycle, and after listening to Kara and Izzy, I feel content on some level. I'm not as angry as I was, but that could have more to do with the fallout with Anthony. Who knows, maybe I'm just tired of it all.

"For what it's worth," Vince says to Kara and Izzy, "I think this went better than even I expected it to. What I think is important here is that Declan gets some closure, so he can put this chapter behind him. It's hard for him to understand how we can put it behind us, but we've had twenty years of healing. He hasn't. I don't expect you to embrace him into your lives, but to hate him for no other reason that he's Dom's son is not right either. You must take into consideration how Willow feels now. She is just as much a victim as Declan in all of this."

Speaking of Willow, she saunters in the room with tears in her eyes. It's obvious she's been outside the door and overheard parts of our conversation.

"No one said we hated him, Vince," Kara sniffles as Izzy walks over and takes Willow in a comforting hug.

"Is there anything else you want to ask us?" Izzy turns to ask me as I begin to feel wobblily on my feet. Damn pain meds are kicking in now.

I shake my head, not sure what else there is to say at this point. If there was, I'm sure I can draw my own conclusions. There is nothing Kara or Izzy can say that will ever satisfy the emptiness in my soul from not getting to a chance to get to know my father, but what I can say is the short talk I had with them puts my mind more at ease.

After Izzy, Kara and Vince leave the room, Willow stands, lightly swaying on her feet, and wipes away a few of her own tears as she tries to find the words to an impossible situation she finds herself smack in the middle of.

Breathlessly she says to me, "I don't really know what I want to say other than thank you and I'm sorry for my..." she stops herself short of saying something that has come easy for her until today.

"You can say it, Willow," I try to assure the confusion I see on her face.

"I know, it's just that he's the only dad I've ever known and now to find something like this, I feel like I don't know who I am anymore."

"Look," I say with one hundred percent confidence, "you're the same person you were yesterday and the day before that. Once we leave, you can go back to be that same person and put this all behind you. I won't come back, and I won't bother you or Eve ever again."

Willow stops short of snorting, as she wipes her nose on the back of her hand, "Yeah, she can be a bit much. It's so weird that she's your sister too."

"Does she ever talk with..."

"Tiffany," Willow's face lights up as she blows out a giant puff of air. "Ahhh, heck no. We haven't heard from her in years. I did ask if Eve if she wanted to come and talk with you, but she refused. Personally, I think it's best not to push it."

"Oh, God no. Trust me, that's more than alright, I had my fill of her at The Shack. I don't think we would ever get along. Just saying."

"No, I suppose not." she dips her chin to her chest, then shyly looks up. "Looks like we have more in common than you and her." She says it like she's proud of it.

"I agree with you on that, and Willow, can I just say something? I've been listening to conversations on an off, just don't be too mad at Dex. He really was only trying to help, in his own way." Why I feel the need to defend him, who the hell knows, but I feel for the guy. Especially since he's standing outside my door, looking like a lost puppy. What the hell am I even saying? Damn pain meds.

Willow chews on the inside of her cheek and blushes. "I won't, but I better go. My dad is pretty upset, and mom will only be able to contain him for so long. I really just wanted to say thanks."

I nod my head as the fight to keep my eyes open starts to fail. Willow walks out but sticks her head in the door at the last minute.

"Do you mind if I call you sometime, maybe? I don't know, to just talk about... *him*. It may seem stupid, I'm sorry. Just forget I said anything."

"It's okay, Willow. I don't mind at all, actually. I think it might help us both, who knows."

"Really?" she gets this big smile on her face.

"Yes, you have Dex's number, obviously. He'll text you my number."

"Okay, that's good. Really, really good." She squeaks and turns to leave.

I have a total of two minutes of complete peace and silence before I hear Dex's voice and have to open my eyes.

"Shit, that went better than I expected," Dex exhales, flopping on the bed.

"Yeah, I agree," Piper adds, shaking her head and flops down on the other side, so I'm sandwiched between the two of them. "I was waiting for someone else to get shot."

I bow my head and yawn, "Don't sound so disappointed."

They both laugh when Nero and Vince come walking back in the room, cracking the whip.

"Alright, everyone, *out*! Declan needs to rest so we can get the hell out of here and back home to Chicago."

By the look on Vince's face, from what I can see through the tired slits of my eyes, I'd say that could be as early as tomorrow. For the first time in a long time, I drift off to sleep and think of my dad without all the anger that usually comes along with it. I go to sleep with a peace of mind that I've never quite felt before.

Chapter Twenty-Nine

"A Bloody Vow"

"Where the hell are we going?" Not that I don't trust Marcus, I just don't understand why he, Vince and Salvo are driving me to the middle of nowhere at dusk. There's not a house or business around for miles, just open fields. I was going to comment on how smooth the ride was in his new Cadillac SUV but then he turned down the dirt road from hell. He weaves the vehicle from one side of the road to the other to miss the big potholes, but even the little ones are giving my shoulder hell.

We've been back in Chicago for exactly two weeks and Marcus has avoided me until today. He's been checking in with Vince every day to see how I'm doing but wasn't quite ready to talk to me face to face. I guess this drive is supposed to clear the air between us.

I'm sitting in the front with Marcus while Vince and Salvo are in the back. I figure at any time now he's going to say something, but his stone-cold face hasn't changed in the last thirty minutes that we've been driving. Suddenly, Marcus hangs a left turn onto another dirt road and drives along a large stretch of property that has a six-foot chain-linked fence around the perimeter. About a mile down we approach a giant warehouse and the only way in is by a security guard stationed at the entrance.

As we approach the gate, a gray-haired man wearing a security guard uniform steps out from his Jeep that's parked off to the side. He steps around the gate and walks up to our vehicle with a face that is all business. Marcus rolls down his window when the security guard lowers his head and looks inside our vehicle before nodding his head at Marcus. "Good evening, Mr. Aniello."

"Evening, Tom, any issues this evening?"

"No, sir." Tom casually shifts his eyes my way. "Everything is ready as you requested."

"Excellent." Marcus then smiles for the first time since we've left the house.

After we pass through the gate, the security guard closes it behind us and returns to his Jeep. The closer we get to the old warehouse, the more I get a feel for what's going on. Although, I'm not sure why no one has said anything to me yet.

Marcus drives us around the back of the deteriorating building when I peer over at him. "Love what you've done with the place." There are more broken windows than not, but the graffiti that covers the concrete wall is a nice touch.

Marcus doesn't seem to mind because he smiles at me like he's proud of the place. "That's the thing, no one pays attention to a run-down shithole in the middle of nowhere. When I make a promise, I deliver. Inside are the three men responsible for killing your friend. We're here to finish this once and for all. It's your call, your show. We're here to help if you want, but if not, we're here only to observe."

I stare at him, wondering why the hell they are just dropping this on me now. A little notice would have been nice so I could be prepared. "Christ. We're doing this right now?" I ask for confirmation while my heart feels like it's pounding out of my chest.

"If you're ready," he says as he looks over his shoulder at Salvo and Vince who have their doors open ready to step out.

A cynical inner voice cuts through my thoughts. "I will be," I say with a tight expression as the weight of this day can finally be let go. The long-awaited day of reckoning I've dreamt of for those three fuckers is finally here. As I step from the vehicle and approach the building, a slow mercurial smile emerges.

Marcus and Salvo led the way inside as Vince and I walk in behind. My first impression, the inside is just as shitty and rundown as the outside. The opening and slamming of the heavy steel door scares about a dozen pigeons. They scatter around the room, kicking up a decade worth of dust and pigeon feathers.

"Jesus." The shit flying in the air is so thick, I cover my mouth and nose with one hand to keep from inhaling any of it, while fanning my face with the other to keep from getting in my eyes. I notice Vince doing the same thing but Marcus picks up pace as we follow when two men emerge from an entryway.

They nod their heads at Marcus, shielding their mouths from the shit flying in the air. As he walks past them, he gives them the good news. "Not to worry, boys, you won't be here much longer. Declan is finally here to finish it."

"Yes sir," the taller of the two answers as they both look over at me like it's the best news they've heard in a long time. Can't say I blame them, I can't imagine being holed up in this dark and dirty shithole all day long.

I've had a deep gnawing in the pit of my stomach since walking in here. Heavy breathing does little to calm my nerves, but when I walk inside the room and look up, everything changes.

A mix of fucking emotions hit me from every direction. Anger, rage, sadness and fury to name a few. And to Marcus' point, no amount of preparation would have helped me when I finally come face to face with the monsters who took so much from me. In the last few weeks, I've worked on taking care of myself, getting myself in a good place. Physically and mentally. For this moment right now, I need to throw it all away. Turn my back on everything I've been working so hard at and dig deep into the darkest parts of my soul.

The room is quiet as all eyes turn back on me. I stand back with my feet planted apart, my chest thrust forward and my chin low on my chest. I've played this scenario out in my head so many times. What I would do in this moment, knowing what they did and the joy they took in doing it. It's a total mindfuck as flashback after flashback of Libbs replays in mind until I'm breathing heavy and visibly shaking.

My sight is laser sharp and dialed in on the sight before me, nothing else. The only thing I hear is the erratic thumping of my own heartbeat in my ears. In the center of the large room are sheets of plastic that hang from the rafters. As the winds pick up and howl against the broken-out windows, the sheets of plastic start to sway. More sheets line the floors under the chairs that the three men are securely tied to.

Each one is zip-tied with their hands behind their backs and feet strapped to the legs of the chairs. All three are gagged with duct tape securely around their heads. Beaten and dirty, these fuckers are nothing more than a motley crew of scumbags who look like the only they care about is their next fix. Makes me fucking sick to know these lowlife motherfuckers had their hands on Libbs, let alone knowing their faces are the last thing she ever saw. The moment we walked in, all three of them looked over with eyes that said it all. They know we came as the judge, the jury and the executioner. It's not hard to figure out who the executioner is since I'm loosening up and cracking my knuckles.

That's when one of the scumbags decides it's a good idea to start screaming and thrash around in his chair. Literally choking on his own words, he chuckles nastily while giving me a look of distain. White-hot anger shot out of me like a bolt of lightning as shock yielded to fury. I lit his ass up until his face was barely recognizable.

In a blink of an eye, my hands are stained red and my fingers are oozing in thick, sticky red blood. Scumbags head lolls from side to side as his half-swollen eyes wildly stray around the room. His screams are muffled as a mixture of blood and sweat stain his white shirt.

"Can't hear a word you're saying motherfucker." My nostrils flare with fury right in his face when I notice a table off to the side.

With Vince and Salvo standing off to the side, Marcus informs me with a trace of laughter in his voice. "We thought you might find those useful."

"I see a few I like." I grin with approval and reach for the pipe wrench first to get a feel for it. Small and heavy, definitely something that can do a lot of damage, for sure.

"What do you think?" I ask the same fucker whose face is beaten to a pulp. With one-eye swollen nearly shut, and his nose busted clearly broken, he's one ugly motherfucker. His eyes are wide and he's shaking his head back and forth. The longer I stare at him, the worse he looks.

"Pipe wrench, screwdriver, hammer?" I rattle those off one at a time and pick them up just to add an element of visual torture. He screams and hollers until the rag in his mouth is saturated, saliva leaking from the sides of his mouth. There's so much, he starts to choke on it. Out of desperation, he starts mumbling shit at Vince, Marcus and Salvo.

"Hey, dumb fuck," I kick at his leg. "They're not here to save you, they came to watch. Since I can't understand a word you say, I'll just pick this one right here." I run my fingers over the pipe wrench and look up to in time to see the terror in his eyes.

When I raise it up, he goes nuts. Screaming like a banshee and thrashing in his chair, doing anything he can to move it, like he has a chance to get out of this. The only way these fuckers are leaving this room, are in body bags.

Wrench in hand, I step over to him, switching it from hand to hand just to watch him squirm. Bastard knows what's coming and he knows I'm going to fucking enjoy doing it. I waste no time. With one crushing blow, I take out his right knee.

Each pathetic whimper and agonizing scream from him urges me on more as adrenaline makes my blood soar through my veins. I continue to punish him without taking a break between each solid strike of the hardened steel. I aim for his left knee next before striking each elbow. My goal is to inflict as much pain as possible while the other two watch on in horror.

With a swift kick to the leg of the chair, the asshole goes down on his side. I land a heavy blow to each ankle, making sure to demolish them before going for his wrists. This motherfucker is screaming like a stuck pig and by the time I stand back to view my handiwork, I'm winded. His ass is in pain but I block out his screams and the noise coming from the other two as they continue to watch, feeling completely helpless. Now they know how Libbs felt that night. Helpless.

I think of her as I stare at the piece of shit as his own tears run down his cheeks. I think about how much she suffered at the hands of these three cocksuckers. Broken bones and dislocated joints is just not enough to erase her scared look from my memory. These fuckers need to suffer more. A hell of a lot more.

The blows continue as I smash each leg, but I don't stop there. I walk around and lean down to stare at him, make sure my face is the last fucking thing he ever sees.

"Fuck you!" I toss the pipe in the air and catch it with an iron grip before smashing it against the side of his jaw. *Crack!* Blood seeps from the corners of his mouth as I stagger above him and drop the pipe on the ground next to his head. One more blow ought to do it, but for that I want something else from the table. Something heavier. I pick up the sledgehammer, but let it drop the ground with a heavy thud before dragging it over next to his head.

He's barely conscious at this point so I take the time to look over at the other two. One is already in tears and pissed himself, while the other is playing tough without an ounce of terror in his eyes. Oooh, I'll save that motherfucker for last. We'll see if he's as tough after he watches me torture these two fucks.

With my eyes locked on tough guy, I lift the sledge hammer with my good arm, since my left is still healing. I use all my strength to deliver one final blow to his temple. Blood and chunks of his brain spray my face, some even landing on his friends. His body convulses for the last time before going still.

Panting and breathing heavy, I drop the handle the sledgehammer and bend forward with my hands on my knees.

"Declan...," Marcus calls from behind as Vince and Salvo talk among themselves.

"No!" I glance his way with a shake my head, letting him know I got this. He holds his hands up and eases back, eventually putting his hands in this pants pockets. Salvo bends forward and looks over at Marcus.

"If that was him getting warmed up. Shit, we may need to back the hell up."

All three of them are standing off to the side watching the darkest parts of me play out in front of them. The sadistic side of Marcus seems to enjoy every bloody minute, adding in his own style of commentary while Salvo doubles over laughing and biting into his knuckles reacting to the sight before him. Vince has a different expression on his face and even though Marcus is encouraging him to relax, telling him this is the outlet I need, he just can't bring himself to do it.

His face is filled apprehension and worry. I hold Vince's long stare long enough to let him see that it's still me in charge. That I'm not spinning out of control. This isn't about me. This is justice for Libbs and I have to deliver it myself. Then, and only then, will I be okay.

This time when I walk over to the table, I pick up a syringe filled with a dark blue liquid. With it in my hand, I hold it up and turn to Marcus.

His face lights up with one devious smirk. "Lethal and extremely painful. Injecting it slowly will prolong his life but will also drag out his agony. Before full cardiac arrest, his brain will most likely hemorrhage if every organ in his body doesn't shut down first. Like I said, lethal and painful."

Sounds good to me. With that, I turn to face my next victim as I run my hand over his bald head. "You heard him. If I inject it slowly it will prolong your life, but you'll suffer a greater death. I didn't give your friend a choice, would you like one?" This dumb fuck has no idea what choice I'm giving him, but he's nodding his head like he's holding out for a glimmer of hope that he can somehow still get out of this with his life.

"Don't get too excited," I say, watching the small glimmer of hope in his eyes extinguish. "You're still going to die a painful death."

He lets loose a string of jumbled words in a panic before he utters a single word. "Noooooo."

I glare into the irises of his eyes and wonder how many times Libbs said the exact same word that night? With her in the forefront of my mind, I snarl my demand, "The girl, what was her name?"

Baldy's eyes scrunch together as he shakes his head like he has no idea who I'm talking about.

"Lying to me is only going to make it worse on you. No worries though, I have something in mind to help jog your memory." I hold up the syringe in front of him and look at him like I'm staring all the way down to his soul.

"Do not fuck with me," I give him his only warning. "Answer my question or I swear to God, I'm going to make this a hell of a lot worse on you."

Then, just to make sure the fucker on my right with the permanent scowl and scar down the right side of his face is still paying attention, I warn his ass. "The less he cooperates, the worse it's going to be on you." Like that matters, I remember his ass. He was the one at the fight.

His scowl deepens as he utters around his gag what sounds like, *fuck you.*

He's feisty, I'll give him that. I'll have to be extra creative with him. Just to piss him off more, I wink. "No, I don't think I will, but I have some items that are going to fuck you as soon as I'm done choking the life out your buddy here. Keep watching, I'm sure you'll enjoy this."

Still keeping up the tough guy act, he growls and the best I can make out, threatens me. Bastard is just begging for me reach out and snap his skinny neck. It pisses me off more than I already am so when I turn back to attention back to baldly, I angrily rip the tape from his face.

"Give me her name?" I demand more urgent this time and losing patience with this asshole quickly.

"Fuuuuucckkkkk yyouuuuuuuuu." The cracked-out fucker shouts, then has the balls to spit in my face, bragging, "She cried like a bitch, begging for her life. Calling out your name, *Declan, Declan.* Like you're some fucking white knight coming to save her."

"SHUT YOUR FUCKING MOUTH!" I backhand him so hard his mouth falls to the side. That's when something shiny catches my eye. Gold teeth. Now I know I saw some pliers on that table. While I'm at it, I grab the pliers, a screwdriver, something interesting that looks extra painful and something to keep his mouth open. Improvising, I take a second screwdriver and use the hammer to break off the plastic handle. With that propped between his back teeth, it will force his mouth to stay open.

"Hey Salvo," I holler across the room, "what's gold going for these days?"

When I look over my shoulder, he's looking between Vince and Marcus before he turns to face me. "How the hell should I know?"

Salvo may be a bit slow at what's about to happen, but Marcus isn't. He lowers his head, snickering to Vince. "This should certainly be entertaining."

I'm not looking to entertain anyone. The only thing I care about is inflicting as much pain as I can before they take their last breath.

I grab the handle of the screwdriver I broke off from my pocket. "Open wide motherfucker." Only, he's not having it. He seals his lip tight fighting back tooth and nail. "Open your fucking mouth."

When he refuses a second time, like I knew he would, I grab the other screw driver I put in my back pocket and jam it all the way through his knee, down to the handle. He thrashes and throws his head back, screaming bloody murder. While his mouth is wide open, I shove the plastic screwdriver handle between his back teeth, forcing it stay open. He continues to fight me, but it's of little use at this point.

I shout over his screaming. "I was only going for the gold ones, but you made me ask you twice." With a violent jerk of his head, I open the pliers and reach for a molar in the back. "This is the way this is going to go down. For each tooth I pull, I'm going to tell you one amazing fact about the girl you killed. From the looks of it, you're going to learn quite a few things about her."

The more he struggles, the tighter my choke hold gets. "Her name," I shout, "was Liberty Ross!" Then, with every ounce of strength I have, I twist back and forth, harder each time until the damn tooth pops from its socket. He erupts in violent screams and thrashes and even though everything inside of me tells me to end him, I simply refuse to make it easy.

I ramp up the pain. For each tooth I extract, I inject a small amount of the lethal and painful liquid into his arm just like they did to Libbs. His reaction is immediate as his body spasms in a grotesque way. In his ear I whisper, "I'm going to stand by and get off just like you did when you killed the only girl I ever loved. A totally innocent girl who did not deserve it, but you, you fucking deserve everything you're getting."

When his body retreats like he can't take any more and his eyes start to roll in the back of his head, I slap his cheeks. "Hey, none of that shit. No passing out."

With the second tooth, I tell him her favorite color. "Black." *Yank!*

The third, her favorite food. "Hamburgers and banana-chocolate Milkshakes." *Yank!*

"Her favorite perfume? Daisy." *Yank!*

"Her favorite band? Muse." *Yank!*

"Her favorite Hockey Team? Black Hawks." *Yank!*

"Skirts or jeans? Skirts." *Yank!*

"Plaid or stripes? Neither. She liked paisley." *Yank!*

Once I get started, I can't stop. I list off twenty-eight facts in total until his mouth is nothing more than empty holes and a bloody mess. The more he sucks in air through his mouth, the more he chokes on his own blood.

Holding the last tooth, I realize my mistake. "Dammit," I curse myself adding one more to the pile of teeth at his feet. "I got so carried away, I forgot your shot." I'm not sure he can hear me or even cares at this point. Shock has set in and he's losing his battle to stay conscious. To make up for it, I inject the rest of the syringe and watch his body barely respond. I know my time is running out with him and even though it wrecks me to fucking shreds, I say the last two things I'll ever say to this motherfucker.

"My nickname for her was Libbs." I can't help but get teary eyed and this last one doesn't come willingly. It chokes me up. "Do you want to know what her greatest fear was?" I ask just as his eyes go white. "*To be alone.*"

He's gone within seconds. His lifeless body sags forward covered in blood. I take a moment to collect my thoughts before I walk over to the table for a last time.

The first thing I say to him, "You're the one who smiled and took a selfie next to her dead body, *right?*"

He doesn't answer or flinch.

"You're the one who injected her with the lethal dose of heroine as well, am I *right?*"

Again, he doesn't answer, but his breathing picks up as beads of sweat roll down his face.

"I don't need you to answer, I can just check your hand for a tattoo. Let's see if I'm right." I walk around him and sure enough, I see the edge of the crescent moon tattoo that has haunted me ever since I saw it in the video.

"Didn't think I'd remember, huh? Too bad for you, I have a great memory."

Then I retrieve the one item I've been most looking forward to using. A pair of heavy-duty handheld gardening shears that're perfect for what I have in mind.

"Ohhh, fuck. That shit is going to hurt," Salvo erupts in laughter as Vince tells me to speed this along. I think he's seen more than he's comfortable with. Marcus on the other hand, nods his head, intently watching.

I don't waste any more breath on this fucker. It's all action.

One by one, I snip each of his fingers off and watch the blood drip from his body until his chair is surrounded in a pool of blood. Removing his shoes, I do the same to his toes. By now, he's stopped all thrashing and screaming as his head hangs low. I grab a hold of his thick brown hair and yank his head back to find him unconscious.

"It's the ones who always act the toughest that end up being the biggest pussies. His buddies stayed conscious longer than he did." I turn away, disgusted, knowing he's still very much alive.

"It's only a matter of time, he'll eventually bleed out," Marcus interrupts my thoughts like he's reading my mind.

"As much as I like the idea of rats eating him, I can't walk out of here knowing he's still alive. Justice won't be served until he takes his last breath." Marcus nods his head and places his hands on his hips exposing his semi-automatic tucked safely inside his jacket. With that, I turn as my mind flashes with the horrific image of Libbs' lifeless face and that's all it takes for me to walk over and retrieve Marcus' gun before I end that miserable fucks life.

I LEFT THAT NIGHT WITH a peace of mind knowing I can finally put it all behind me. Marcus and I had our talk with the promise to never mention it again, or dwell on the things we can't change. A few days later, I went to Libbs' gravesite to let her know she could finally rest in peace. That I kept my vow and saw things through to the end and made sure each of them dearly paid for what they did to her. Even though nothing will ever be enough to bring her back, I let her know once again just how sorry I am that it happened in the first place. No amount of rights will ever correct the wrong that was done to her, but I can live knowing it was me who served out the only justice I saw fit.

I'd like to think that one day I'll see her again, even though I'm not a spiritual guy by any means. I imagine she'll be spending that time thinking up ways to get even with me about one thing or another. With her spitfire personality, I can only imagine how traumatic it will be and I can't wait to find out. Until then, I'll continue to live my life to the fullest because that is exactly what she would want me to do.

As I went to bed late that night on the verge of drifting off to sleep, a strange thing happened that I can't explain. Hell, I don't know, maybe I was asleep. Maybe it was all a dream, even though it felt damn real. Out of nowhere, a soft breeze swept through my open window with a familiar scent I'd recognize almost anywhere. *Daisy*, Libbs favorite perfume. Then, like a whisper in the night, I hear a faint *thank you* in my ear before it vanishes just as quickly as it came.

IT'S BEEN EXACTLY A HUNDRED and eighty-two days since we left Washington and I've used every one of those days to heal myself physically and emotionally. In that same of time, I've been training non-stop with one thing on my mind. My rematch with Curtis. October 15th has been circled on my calendar in a red Sharpie since I got the date from Nero. That's two weeks from today.

Since coming home, Dex refuses to leave my side and pretty much hangs out with me twenty-four seven. Thankfully, once I was given the green light from Nero to start training, I spend most of time at the gym, with Dex never too far away. When I'm not at the gym, Dex ends up hanging out with me at the house like he's afraid to let me out of his sight. I'm sure Vince and Marcus have something to do with this, but nothing they'd admit to. As much as I gripe and complain about Dex being a pain the ass, it does help having him around. I'll never admit it though.

Life is slowly returning to normal around here, as normal as our lives can be anyway. Once the shock of Anthony's sudden heart attack was made public by Marcus, the condolences started coming in. Few know what really happened, and Marcus is hellbent on keeping it that way. After all, he has a business to run and relationships to maintain with people who worked directly under Anthony. No matter how hard he tries though, the rumors still swirl around the timing of it all. I was told to distance myself from any gossip and to let Marcus and Vince deal with it. They didn't need to tell me twice.

There is one surprise that's come out of this.

Piper.

Without me knowing, Vince bought Piper a new iPhone X before we left Washington. Since she tore up his check, it was his way to repay her for the kindness she showed me. But I think there might be something more to it since the first thing she did after she got it was blackmail me with the damn thing. She said I owed her for saving my ass on more than one occasion. All I had to do to repay her is answer when she calls, which I may have smiled at. Then she said, if she ever decides to call my stubborn ass. Her words, not mine. Though she's not far off the mark. I never expected to hear from her again but four nights later, she called.

I answered.

That one phone call became frequent phone calls. Now we talk almost daily. Sometimes twice a day, once in the morning and then late that night. I'm not used to this shit. I never knew a girl could talk as much as Piper. Then again, I never had any interest in having a conversation with a girl that didn't end with me between her legs.

Maybe that's why this thing between us just works. The miles between us have forced us into a long-distance friendship. And It wasn't long before I started looking forward to our talks, me asking what kind of shit she got into that day while she asked how my training's going. The girl is doing a number on me and the fact she lives across the damn country doesn't help. Our conversations were light and easygoing but one day, Piper decided to play dirty and take us from the confines of the friendzone into the X-rated zone. Now I'm either going to bed with a raging hard-on or waking up with one with thoughts of her doing something indecent on my mind.

Under that sweet exterior is a vixen hellbent on making sure I don't forget her. Like that's even possible. Not when her new favorite past time includes torturing me with a highly sexual game of Would You Rather. If she keeps this up, I'll be taking a road trip very, very soon and pay the little vixen a personal visit.

Not long after that, Willow reached out to me to see how I was doing. She got up the courage to ask me what I really know about Dominic. Shocked the shit out of me that she was even interested in finding out more about him, considering the strong feelings her family has when it comes to him.

The conversation didn't last long though. Eve came in the room, making it impossible for Willow to talk and hide the fact she was talking to me. From the sounds of it, Willow feels isolated in wanting to know more things about him, but her family shuts it down by saying, *'you're better off not knowing a thing about that man.'* Not even taking Willow's feelings into consideration. It's fucking sad.

I'm the only person she feels she can confide in, besides Dex. They seem to be hit it off from what I can tell. It's great but fucking awkward at the same time. I talk to both of them and lately, it's impossible for either one of them not to ask what the other one is saying about them. I told them both do not ask me shit like that. I'm not some chick playing this she-said-he-said shit. No way. It's hilarious though. According to Willow they talk a few times a week on average. Dex makes it sound like they talk as much as Piper and I talk. I still don't like it, but at least Willow has another person she can talk to without judgement or being put down.

I was happy to hear that Piper and Willow started hanging out together and are becoming good friends. Surprisingly, they're the same age. They're both twenty-four which was a shock because I would have never pegged Piper for being older than eighteen and even that's a stretch. I had a fucking field day with calling her a cradle robber since she has a few years on me. It pissed her off, like I knew it would. But she gets even by sending me funny baby memes all damn day.

When my phone chimes with a text, Dex and I both look at one another. A grimace on my face and a shit-eating grin on his.

"What she'd send this time?" he asks with a chuckle, lying on the couch opposite me.

"I'm too tired to look," I yawn, rubbing the tiredness from my eyes. "If Nero doesn't to kill me first, Piper will with those fucking crying baby videos and shit she's constantly sending. It's starting to freak me the fuck out."

He huffs, "It's your own goddamn fault. You started it."

I groan, "Don't remind me."

"That reminds me," his voice turns serious as he turns on his side with his arm tucked under his head. "What's the deal with Izzy and Brax being total dicks to Willow? She just wants to know about her real dad. I don't get it. You hate the guy, fine, but damn he fathered the girl which means she has every right to ask all the questions she wants."

I haven't seen him this worked up in weeks. "Like you need to ask."

"Yeah, stupid question to ask you. I just feel for the girl, you know?"

I roll my eyes because Dex makes no secret of how he feels when it comes to her. The fact that she's my sister, which still takes some getting used to, makes it even more awkward. "Yeah, Dex, I know how you feel, which is why we should change the subject." If my words don't work, my glare should.

He shrugs me off, mumbling under his breath, "I'm just saying."

I need to put a stop to his doom and gloom attitude. "Dex, quit worrying about it. I've already talked to her about Dominic and told her some things. Hell, I even extended her an invitation to come here anytime she wants if she wants to know more."

The look on his face tells me he did not know that bit of information.

"I'm not that much of a dick, Dex."

"It's not that, I'm just surprised. That's so unlike you... wait a minute. Did you extend the invitation for Willow, or in the hopes she brings a certain half-pint friend with her?"

"I like to look at it as a win-win for us both. Can you blame me?"

"You're such an ass, Declan." He grumbles, shaking his damn head at me when he knows, if given the chance, he'd do the exact same thing.

"Ass? If Willow does come here, you get to see her. Did you think of that?"

The smirk on his face vanishes like he suddenly realizes it's his chance to see her as well. "Damn, you're right. Scratch what I said, you're a damn genius."

"I know."

"Willow said Piper wants to come see you fight sometime. Do you think that means...,"

I don't want to deflate the hopeful look in his eyes, I just don't think it's in the cards. "Nah, I doubt it. It's too soon, and Piper hasn't mentioned anything about it."

"It's a damn shame. Nero has whipped your ass into the best shape you've ever been in. I didn't think it was possible but you're a lot fucking scarier now. Fucking Curtis is in for a world of hurt."

It's true, I'm leaner than I've ever been and the extra work in the weight room has definitely paid off. I feel stronger than I ever have.

"I've never trained harder and I really didn't need any extra motivation for this one. Curtis doesn't know what's waiting for him."

I look and see a familiar face on Dex. One I've seen a million times before.

"Just make sure you don't let him get inside your head and don't get inside your own damn head with all the crazy shit from the last fight. All that shit is water under the bridge." He pauses, then asks, "right?"

Water under the bridge? I don't think so.

"Shut the fuck up with that shit, would ya? Worry less about me and more about your late-night chats with Willow?" He glares at me, hating that she tells me shit about him whenever we happen to talk.

"That's none of your business."

"It is if she tells me shit. I can't help it, I am her brother."

"Don't fucking remind me."

"Fact, brother. I can't help it."

"You sure let that come out of your mouth like your somehow proud of that. I think you secretly like having a sibling?"

"Since she and Piper have become friends, I can't really escape her, now can I?

"Bullshit, you like it that you have a sister. Now, Eve on the other hand."

"Oh, God no. Do not go there." While Willow and I have this whatever the hell you want to call it. Eve and I do not. Which is fine with me.

"What's crazy is you and Piper. I didn't think I'd ever see you this close with anyone again. It's nice. I want things to work out."

"You want it to work out, so you and Willow can work out."

Dex does little to hide his grin. "Doesn't hurt."

Looking at the time and sick of listening to my stomach growl, I sit up and stretch deciding it's time to eat. "Enough of this girly talk, let's go grab a burger before we have to head to the gym."

"Nero's going to have your ass for that, you know." Dex warns me like the mother hen he has become as of late.

I glare at the little narc. "Not if you don't tell him."

"Ha," he laughs, "that fucker can smell an onion ring on you a mile away. How are you going to hide a greasy-ass burger?"

As I pass by the couch on my way to the kitchen, I sarcastically say with a smirk. "I'll shower and brush my teeth. Now get your ass to my car or I'll leave you behind."

Dex suddenly changes his tune, when he sees I'm dead serious. "Damn, I'm not missing a burger. For my silence, you're buying."

Like that's anything new. I grab my keys and wallet from the kitchen counter and head toward the front door while Dex gets his shoes on. Checking the time on my phone, I open the front door and walk smack dab into someone standing at my door.

"What the hell?" Jesus, I step back, pissed that I damn near dropped my phone. It bobbles in my hand, but I retrieve it before it hits the concrete. Standing upright, I'm ready to rip into whoever the hell is lingering there when I look up and spot who it is. My mouth drops open, but no words come out.

"Surprise!"

"Double surprise!!"

Surprise? Shock is more like it. That's why it takes me a second or two to convince myself I'm not imagining it. There's not one, but two unexpected surprises at my door. With bags. The first thing that runs through my mind is I won't be needing to take that road trip after all. After my phone calls with Piper, it's hard to look at the little minx without wanting to throw her over my shoulder and take her upstairs. Her flirty little eyes and flushed cheeks aren't helping matters either. And if that isn't enough, her little white romper leaves little to imagination.

I can't pull my eyes away from her, so I shout to Dex over my shoulder. "Yo Dex, you may want to hurry up and come see this." He'd never believe me even if I tell him Willow was at the door too.

"Dex is here?" Willow screeches and giggles like a girl with a crush. A big crush, and it's enough to pull my attention from Piper and make me lose my appetite. Willow quickly fixes her hair with her hands and then tugs on Piper's arm and chuckles. Her cheeks are flushed and that's when something clicks. A sweet thought until it turns into a very disturbing one.

What if this is Willow's first crush? It seems impossible since she's twenty-four, but it's possible. Jesus H Christ, what if she's never? I can't even fucking say it, let alone think it. If that's the case, Dex better keep his fucking hands and dick to himself, or I swear to God, I'll fucking kill him.

It's enough to make me lightheaded and nauseous and I stumble back against the door, ignoring the fact I have yet to greet them. Piper lets me off the hook asking me, "Glad to see me?" The heat in her cheeks blossom.

"Definitely, just surprised. Obviously," I laugh at myself considering how stupid I must look right now.

Piper lightly chuckles, "I don't know, I think you look really good when your face isn't all bruised up and your lips aren't swollen like balloons."

Damn girl doesn't sugarcoat shit.

"You and that mouth of yours." I reach over to stroke the side of her cheek and wonder if I affect her in person like I do in our late-night phone calls. I'm hoping to test the theory that long-distance friendships could indeed turn into something more.

Sure enough, Piper doesn't disappoint. She inhales sharply and briefly closes her eyes as she leans into my touch. When her eyes open and connect with mine again, the chemistry that's been building between us on the phone, intensifies until it damn near erupts.

"Willow, holy shit, you're here. Like really here." Dex can't believe it either and rushes past me in a hurry. She leaps into his arms as he picks up and whirls her around in a big hug.

On his way to get to Willow, he bumps me into Piper, which I use to my advantage. I overplay it and stumble into her with my arms tightly around her to prevent us both of falling. Fuck it, I tighten my hold and her tiny body melts into me like she was made to fit there. The strong beat of her heart against my chest feels like music.

Throwing daggers at Dex, I whisper in Piper's ear. "I can't believe you are really here. Does this mean you're here for the fight?"

She snuggles into my chest with a sigh of content. "I almost can't believe we're here either, but we both wanted to see you fight and it gives Willow some time to talk with you. Plus, she wants to check out Art Colleges here in Chicago."

I had no idea she was even considering something permanent and honestly, it's not a horrible idea.

Until Piper says, "It was Dex's idea, actually."

"What?" I raise my voice and pull back from Piper, glaring at Dex who is looking straight at me.

Willow explains, using her hand to break my stare at Dex so I can look at her. "I wanted to get to know you more and what better way than to attend college here at the same time?"

"I hate to point out the obvious, but Izzy and Brax are never going to allow that. I'm not sure how you pulled off coming here at all to watch my fight. Do I need to worry that Brax is going to jump out of the bushes to shoot me again but dead this time?" I say it as a joke, I'm fucking serious.

"They're not happy I'm here, but I told them I'm just coming for two weeks and then I'm coming home. They have no idea you're fighting or that I'm considering moving here. Either way, I'm an adult. I can do what I want."

"Where are you going to stay for the next two weeks?" I look down at her bags and hold my breath waiting hoping like hell she doesn't say what I think she's going to say.

"I, well, we were hoping...."

"Willow can stay at my place." Dex jumps at the opportunity and her face lights up but she chews nervously on her bottom lip. My earlier assumption plays out in front of me like a nightmare. Whether it's true or not, I'm not going to make it easy for them two to be alone together. I send Dex a death glare that says we need to have a very serious talk.

"NO!" I put an end to that discussion. "Willow and Piper can both stay here, we have more than enough rooms. I'm sure Vince won't mind." Like hell, but he won't have much a choice since they are already here. "It will just take a bit of getting used to for everyone."

"Vince likes me," Piper says playfully. "He'll be fine with it. Plus, I can keep an eye on you while I'm here. He will definitely be okay with that."

"Oh, that's just great," Dex throws a hand over his head, sulking. "While you're busy with Piper, what's Willow supposed to do? If she stayed with me, I'm just saying that might be better... for her."

Nice try, Dex. "Zip it, lover boy," I warn. "When you want to see Willow, and if Willow wants to see you, then you can come over here. Damn, Dex, you practically live here already."

"Fine," he spits, checking his watch. "If you want to grab that burger, we better get to it. You have two hours before you have to be back at the gym. And once Nero finds out you have two houseguests this close to the fight, he's going to flip his shit."

"Let me handle Nero and Vince." Then I tell the girls, "If you want, you can put your bags in the foyer. We can work out the sleeping arrangements later. We were just going out to get something to eat if you care to join us. I'm starving." They both nod their heads and place their bags inside while Dex stands there laughing under his breath.

"This is not going to go over well."

Boy, don't I know it. Who knows if Brax and Izzy even know that Willow is in Chicago. And Vince, the last thing Brax warned him about was to keep me far away from Willow or else he'd come looking for me to finish the job he started. In my defense, Willow came to me not the other way around. This is the type of distraction I don't need right before a fight, but it's hard to argue that point when a cute-as-hell girl runs up and hooks her hand around my arm.

Dex watches on with a snarky smirk as he leans over and whispers in my ear, "Yeah, buddy, you're fucked!" Then slaps me on the back and winks at Piper before catching up to Willow, who is grabbing something out of her car.

"I'm going to be, unlike you." I mumble so low even Piper didn't hear it.

Once we pile into my car, I shoot Vince a quick text, in case he comes home to a strange car in the driveway with Washington plates and bags in the foyer.

> **Me:** Heads up. We have guests staying at the house for the next two weeks.
>
> **Vince:** Funny you should say that. Just received a nasty phone call from Kara. We NEED TO TALK!!!

I decide then is a good time to just switch my phone off.

Chapter Thirty

"Moving On"

Lunch was great until we got back to find Vince anxiously waiting in the kitchen. He didn't even wait until we were alone to rip into me.

"What the hell are you thinking?" Pacing back and forth in the kitchen, Vince pinches the bridge of his nose with his fingers like he has one of his nasty migraines. Although his tone is low, it's still commanding.

"What?" I argue to Vince but keep a watchful eye on Willow and Piper who freeze where they are. "We have plenty of room and Willow wants to know more about Dominic. What better place to do that than here. It's just for two weeks, that's it."

"Wrong." He raises his voice with his finger pointed at me this time, then turns to face Willow's scared, pale face. He doesn't even flinch. "They have no idea you're here, they think you two are off camping in the damn mountains. They called me instead on some wild hunch. I know you don't know me very well, but I don't take it well when someone accuses me of lying after I denied having any knowledge of your whereabouts."

Willow backs into Dex as I step in front of Vince.

"Back off, Vince. Don't treat her that way." I get that he's pissed but this is not the way to handle this. Instead, I calmly urge him to take a step back and cool off. I should have known that wouldn't work with Vince. He just shifts his anger toward me.

"Don't be naïve, Declan. Those people hate you and would like nothing more than to come here and stir shit up. I won't stand for it. Not when you're getting your life on track and you have a fight to concentrate on. Listen," he backs away with his head tilted up before he directs his attention back to Willow. "While I may not have any issues with you, Willow. That doesn't mean I don't when it comes to your family. I'll do whatever it takes to prevent any issues showing up on our doorstep. Understand?"

"I understand," she says in a voice that's barely a whisper. "I'll call mom and tell her the truth. I don't want to cause any problems, they just won't share much with me about *him* and I'm sick of it. I'm not a child anymore they can lie to. I'm an adult."

I look at Vince, remembering not too long ago I said the exact same words to him. He briefly looks my way before turning back to Willow. I can almost see a soft spot in his eyes as he sympathizes with what she says.

"Listen, you want to be treated like an adult, fine, I'll treat you as one. But do not come into my home lying about your whereabouts. I don't care if you stay here, but you have to fix this with them. We kept our end of the deal, you came to us but that doesn't mean I'll stand by if this blows up in your face either."

The tone of his voice once again turns threatening. "Jesus, Vince, I think she gets it."

"No, he's right Declan," Willow steps forward with a genuine look of concern. "I didn't think things through like I should have and I'm sorry. I'll give my mom a call right now."

Judging by the look on her face, I'd say it's the last thing she wants to do but knew she'd have to do it at some point. When she sits down at the kitchen table and starts to tap her phone, Dex, Piper and I all look at one another not sure what to say.

Vince doesn't have that issue and starts by encouraging her. "I think that's a good idea. Best to get things squared away now, because Declan needs to get back to the gym soon. The last thing I need is a moody ex-Marine pestering me wondering why he's late."

Dex laughs under his breath as Vince turns to leave the kitchen but stops and turns around. "If things work out and you do get to stay, Willow, I have some things of Dominic's you may want to see." Then almost awkwardly, his eyes linger between Willow and I. "I must admit having you both here in this house is quite something even my brother would be at a loss of words with. With how crazy things were at that farmhouse, I didn't realize 'til tonight just how much you both resemble my brother."

Before he gets too choked up, he smiles and nods before leaving. I hate to admit, what he said got to me, so I can only imagine what it did to Willow. Sure enough, we all look at Willow at the same time just as her eyes gloss over. She stands with her phone in the air as she fights back the tears that threaten to spill over. "I'll just go outside to make the call."

"Do you want me to come?" Piper quietly asks, but Willow shakes her head before quietly walking out the door.

"Damn, Declan, do you think I should go out there in case she needs some moral support?" Dex turns, bouncing on his heels and ducks to look out the window so he can keep an eye on Willow without her knowing it.

"No, let her handle it. If she couldn't she never would have made the trip to begin with. She's stronger than we think." I can see it in her, even if her family doesn't. All it does is aggravate me to the point I realize this bullshit is going cause me to be late. Maybe the timing of their trip isn't such a good idea after all, seeing as the few hours they've been here, I'm uptight as shit and distracted from what I need to be doing.

"I'm going to go shower and get ready or I'm going to be late. You guys can hang in here or in the living room, just make yourselves at home or whatever." While Dex is busy watching Willow out the window, Piper is carefully watching me as she waves with a faint smile. I feel bad, but there is nothing I can do but return her smile.

By the time I'm done showering and leave the house, Willow is still on the phone but sitting in her car now and looks to be crying. She doesn't even look up when I drive away.

By the time I made it to the gym, Nero had my ass for being fifteen minutes late. Tardiness to him is like an insult that shows one's lack of discipline. He made me pay for it to ensure I get the message even though I'm rarely late, if ever, but I have a sneaking suspicion Vince called him prior to my arrival.

Two and a half hours later, I hit the showers trying to ease the ache in my muscles but I'm also anxious to get my ass home at the same time. After I change Nero waits in the hallway with his back against the wall.

"Good workout, son. Get a good night's rest and be here a half hour early tomorrow morning. From here on out to the fight, no late nights, no extra stress and no distractions. You hear me?"

"Loud and clear." I salute him wanting nothing more than to tell him to lay off my ass but think better of it as I walk by because his eyes are burning a hole in the back of my head. If Nero thinks I'm distracted in any way, it's going to be nothing but hell for me 'til the fight.

In retrospect, hell would have been a vacation compared to what I endured, but the night before the fight all I can say is I'm more than ready.

I'M ANXIOUS ALL THE WAY home and feel more at ease when I see Willow's car is still here. As I walk into the kitchen I can't believe my eyes. Willow, Dex and Piper are sitting at the table laughing... with Vince and Marcus.

"What the hell?"

"Oh, there he is now. Bet Nero had your ass for being late, didn't he?" Marcus laughs with the rest of them as I continue to stare at them wondering what the hell changed in the last few hours.

"Mind explaining to me what's going on here?"

"What's it look like?" Vince grins with his hands folded behind his head, like he's relaxed. "We're sharing stories with Willow. That's why she came, is it not?"

"Well, yeah, but when I left Willow was in her car crying. Now she's laughing. Mind filling me on what happened in-between?"

The minute I ask, all eyes suddenly shift to Willow.

Her face heats up as she leans her arms on the table but leans toward Dex who is seated to her left. Her voice is soft, "I'll spare you the long story, for the short version. Mom has agreed to let me stay for a few days. If I keep in contact with her, she won't tell dad where I am." She cautiously waits for me to reply.

"Just like that?" I question, finding that hard to believe.

"Well, no," she lightly chuckles and points over at Vince. "She made me put Vince on the phone and she also wanted to talk with Marcus."

That's just... *what?* Strange.

Marcus scoots his chair back to explain so he doesn't have to look over his shoulder. "You need to remember that I knew Izzy way back in the day. Even then, she knew once I gave my word on something it was as good as gold. I never go back when I give my word, this you know."

I nod already knowing that to be true.

"Having said that," he lowers his tone, "she wanted my word that nothing would happen to Willow and Piper while they are here. It was just as much of a surprise to me I assure you, but there is something else that you don't know. Something Willow needs to tell you that might make a bit more sense."

Willow's face heats up with the attention squarely back on her. Dex reaches over and grabs her hands for support while Piper rests a hand on her shoulder encouraging her with a nod of her chin. As Marcus and Vince watch on, they utter something back and forth between themselves.

"What's going on?" It's obvious I'm the only one left in the dark and it doesn't settle well with me.

"Declan, why don't you sit down and let Willow explain. Come relax while I'll grab you a sub from fridge since I'm sure you're hungry. We all ate earlier." Vince stands and offers me his chair next to Marcus, but at the last minute I put my hand on his shoulder and walk by.

"Not that I don't want to sit next to you, but this girl is way better looking." I grin at Piper who pats the chair next to her with a beaming smile.

Marcus slaps a hand over his chest. "You wound me but who can blame you. Not only is she better looking, she smells good."

Piper fans herself and leans her head to the side so I can bend down to check out her new perfume, but I still glare at Marcus who finds my scowling humorous. He utters, *interesting* under his breath and turns his head to Vince who hides his own smirk the best he can when he slides me a sandwich across the table.

"Hi," Piper softly whispers leaning into my side as I gently rub the top of her hand that's resting on my arm.

With the rest of the table quiet, Willow sits up in her chair and proceeds to pick at her nails. Her voice relatively low like she's nervous, "Declan, I haven't been completely honest with you about my intentions for coming here. Wanting to know more about Dominic was only half the reason."

"Okay." My appetite suddenly takes a nosedive and after I return my sub to the plate, I push it forward on the table when I notice all eyes are on me. "Why are you all staring at me? What's going on?"

"Nothing's going on, just listen and relax, man." Dex sits with his arms crossed, nudging Willow to continue.

"I don't know why this is so hard for me, but I kind of find you intimidating," she timidly admits, "What I mean to say, is, I want to get to know more about you but I was afraid you would tell me no. At the farmhouse I got the distinct impression that you're a private person who doesn't let a lot of people in your life."

I don't know why I find that so hard to believe, but I do. "Why would you want to get to know me?"

"Declan," Piper and Dex say in unison, while Vince and Marcus just shake their heads.

Willow speaks up looking over at Vince as he nods for her to continue. "Why wouldn't I, you're my brother. Listen, I know some things about our father from my mom, and most of them are downright terrifying. Then I look at you, and I see the good in you."

Her eyes start to tear up as my comfort level dips. Piper wipes a stray tear from her cheek as Willow continues, "You came to save me, so I don't know, I feel if I can get to know you better than maybe I'll be able to feel better about myself knowing who my real father is... well, who he was. Does that make any sense to you?"

More so than she could ever know.

"First of all, Willow you are your own person, as am I. Plus, Dominic was a complex person and did things I don't agree with, but he lived with his own demons in a world that's completely different from yours."

She lightly scowls. "Why is it a bad thing to want to get to know you? From the few times we've talked on the phone, I've gotten to know you some and I want to know more. Anyway, Piper thinks you're pretty cool."

"Piper, you're going to take her word for it? The girl who ignores danger and when all common sense tells her to run, she doesn't. This Piper?" I say with my finger pointed at a grinning Piper who seems awfully proud of her careless actions.

Dex finds it funny, chuckling, "Seems to me she's just as stubborn as you are."

I shoot him a warning glare. "Shut it, not helping any."

"Oh, hush," Piper reaches over with a hand over my mouth. "If you recall, I saved your butt, three times. Now stop thinking so negatively about yourself and get to know your sister, would ya? I happen to think she's pretty cool as well. You're both more alike than you know." She raises her shoulders and winks at us both.

"That settles it then." Marcus claps his hands like it's a done deal, and I quickly realize it doesn't matter what I think.

"Don't worry, Willow," Vince reassures her, "just give him a chance to let it sink in, he's doesn't trust easily."

Jesus, I am in the room.

Before I can say a thing, Willow leans forward. "Declan if you don't want me here, I'll go. I won't force you, but I've done a lot of thinking about all of this. Whether you want to admit it or not, you saved me that night at the farmhouse. You didn't have to, but you did. If not for you, I may have never found out that Brax wasn't my real dad. I'm a firm believer that things happen for a reason, and believe it or not, I think in some crazy way fate brought us together."

Fate?

Vince and Marcus turn to one another and shrug their shoulders.

Vince mutters, "I like that."

"I do too," Marcus settles back in his chair and exchanges a look with us both. "It doesn't matter what either of you think about your father," he says. "Who he was or what kind of person he was. When I look at the both of you sitting here at the same table, I see the best of my best friend and whatever roll you play in each other's lives is your choice. Think about that before you make any hasty decisions. That's all I say."

After those words of wisdom how can I say no?

For the next few days, Willow and I did spend time together one on one getting to know each other a little better. When I wasn't at the gym, the four of us spent time watching movies, playing games and just hanging around the house. Trying to find alone time with Piper was difficult, because Marcus gave Izzy his word the girls would bunk together, and he would see that personal boundaries would be followed. Damn cock blocker. I've gone to bed each night with a raging hard on only to find satisfaction from my hand knowing Piper is just down the hall in shorts and a tank top.

Tonight, after I returned from training, Willow and I sat in Dominic's office on the floor next to the book case. Her questions tonight were more personal and sensitive so Dex and Piper decided to watch a movie, so we could talk in private.

I could tell all evening that something was bothering her.

"Declan, can I ask you something personal?"

Her long face dips behind her hair as she nervously chews on her lower lip. I immediately tense up, having no clue where this is going, but I'm already uncomfortable. Feeling trapped with no way out, I nod my head.

She then asks me the one thing that never crossed my mind. "Is it true about the voices? That you have them, like *he* did?"

I sit with my head against the books and exhale all the air in my lungs at once. I'm surprised, but not entirely shocked either. With her face still partially hidden behind her hair I can tell she's embarrassed to ask. Which is the opposite way I want her to feel. If I have them, why not her? Since I don't know that to be true, I chose my words carefully.

"Yeah, it's true. Although, I didn't realize you knew anything about that." Then, I lower my face to hers as the pit in my stomach grows because I know how bad they can be, and I'd hate to think she suffers with them as well, but I still ask, "Do you have them?"

She doesn't answer right away, but when she looks up at me like she's fighting back years of tears, it guts me. Chicks and crying is so not my thing. For this though, I can't stop myself from putting my arm around her shoulder and pulling her into a hug. I can feel her hands tighten around my shirt as she begins sobbing uncontrollably.

"Hey, let me tell you something," I say with a low and comforting tone as I tighten my hold around her trembling body. "For a long time, we didn't know what was causing my erratic behavior and mood swings, but Vince had finally had enough and had me properly diagnosed. Over time, I did learn to control them the best I could. But now I'm in a good place, finally able to put things behind me. I'm not the same pissed-off, angry prick that I once was." She half laughs, half snorts which is funny, but I still have something to tell her that might make her feel better. "You don't have to tell me, just know it's not a death sentence and there is help. You just keep looking until you find what works for you, then do it."

In a real shaky but honest voice, she admits, "It scares me sometimes."

Part of the battle is admitting it, which takes a hell of a lot of guts. Remembering some of my lowest times and the vow to never revisit them, I honestly tell her, "Yeah, me too."

"Oh, right, I don't think anything could scare you. Have you seen yourself lately?" She pulls out of the hug and wipes her eyes looking at me like I'm lying to her. That I somehow don't get scared from time to time.

"You might be surprised. We all have our demons, Willow."

"Yeah, I suppose," she sighs with her arms crossed over her knees and her head to the side looking off in the distance like her mind is a million miles away.

"Is that the reason why you wanted to talk with me?"

Her eyes gloss over as they swing back on me. "Not the only reason, but yes. I'm sorry."

"Why? I'm not. I'm here to help if you want it."

"Thanks. It's getting late and someone has a big fight tomorrow night. Just a heads up, Piper *may* have had a few shirts made up."

I grumble, "Do I even want to know?"

"No, but you'll find out soon enough when you see us cheering you on in the crowd."

"Now, I'm officially scared."

She chuckles, "Ha. Ha." Then, stands up to go get Piper before heading upstairs. "Good talk. Night, little brother."

Now that's funny as shit. "Little?" I criticize. "Compared to you I'm a giant. Good to bed."

After Willow left the room, I sat there for a few extra minutes like I've done so many nights before, thinking of everything, but coming up with nothing. It's quiet, almost peaceful and that's definitely a first for me.

DEX AND I ARRIVED AT Windy City Underground about two hours before the fight. Nero is on edge like usual, barking out orders while Marcus and Vince keep a watchful eye to make sure no yellow envelopes slide under the door this time. They aren't taking any chances.

"Is he here yet?" I ask Dex if Curtis and his team have arrived because it'd be just like him to pull some bullshit stunt and do a no-show.

"Yep, all good. He got here about ten minutes ago. Cocky as usual, saying all sorts of bullshit. I suppose that's a good thing. How are you holding up?" He eyes me cautiously as he finishes taping up my knuckles.

"Good, ready to go beat that pricks ass."

"That's what I like to hear," he says just as the doors swing wide open.

Kingston walks in carrying a few extra rolls of tape and checks over the pail that holds the items any fighter may need during a fight like bottles of water, smelling salts, Vaseline and plenty of gauze. He nods his chin, humming to some song as he walks by us to grab a few more items from Nero's locker.

When Dex is all finished he grabs my headphones and cranks up my pre-fight playlist before placing them over my ears. It's my routine. I simply close my eyes, concentrate on taking long breaths and rest back against the lockers getting myself psyched up.

When Nero taps my shoulder, I open my eyes and read his lips, "It's go time."

Yes, it is. Time to put all the training and bullshit from the last fight behind me and remember every ounce of blood, sweat and pain it took to get me here. I push everything out of my mind as I leave the locker room and the moment my eyes land on Curtis, I feel the change as it happens.

With my game face on, a rush of adrenaline spikes my pulse as a surge of blood flows to my extremities. The rush gives me a raw sense of strength that ripples throughout my body while my hands curl into iron fists. My lips draw back exposing my teeth and my chest rises with every short, rapid burst of air. I seek one thing and one thing only. The fight. Where my desire ignites into vengeance and the need to hurt and see blood is just too strong to deny.

My transformation to the Reaper is complete.

I'm tapped in and focused on Curtis like I have tunnel vision. I don't hear my introduction as I enter the arena or the roar of the fans. I block it all out and enter the ring, never taking my eyes off him. He stretches with his arms over his head and paces back and forth in front of his team, nodding at whatever bullshit they're telling him. Then laughs and smirks at me like he honestly thinks he has a chance of beating me.

Fucker is delusional. Yesterday, I cornered Marcus and asked him a question I never thought I would, but I just had to make sure. Windy City Underground is his baby and he takes it very seriously, so when I asked him if he paid Curtis to take a dive, you would have thought I committed a mortal sin. He not only got pissed but shoved me back against the wall making sure this conversation stayed between us.

"You of all people should know that answer to that. The fact that you even *thought* to ask me that pisses me the fuck off. Listen to me carefully because I'll only say this once," it was like he was breathing fire in my face, "I'd do almost anything for you, you know this, but in this fucking arena, your wins and losses are all on you. I won't ever do anything that could tarnish WCU's reputation or my own. Got it?"

"Got it, I just had to make sure."

"Good, now go get your ass in the gym. Declan, you mean the world the me and I'd never disrespect you as a fighter. The only way to be great at anything is fail from time to time. Learn from it so it never happens again."

It was uncomfortable to ask, but necessary all the same.

Speaking of Marcus, when I look up and catch his eye as he stands in his usual corner office in the upper deck, his eyes pass over mine before coming back and raising his glass. I don't see Willow and Piper up there with him though. It was decided they would watch upstairs with him to avoid getting sucked into the craziness down below. But before the start of the fight, I look over my shoulder and find Piper and Willow in the stands sitting with Jimmy, one of Marcus' guys.

What the fuck are they doing down here? The last thing I need is to worry about some jackass bothering them, so I quickly look at Dex and point to them with a look on my face that says, 'what the fuck.' But that fucker just winks at me. What the hell is he thinking?

When I quickly turn back and look at Piper, she proudly shows me the matching shirts her and Willow are wearing. A black shirt that reads, Declan 'Reaper' Parisi then turns around and shows me the back which reads, 'Reaper's Girl,' while the back of Willow's reads, 'Reapers Big Sis.'

I wink at her and Willow with a lopsided smile before turning my attention back to Curtis. He notices the exchange and given the smug look on his face, I'd say he read the back of her shirt too. My mood darkens as I tune everything else out. I glare at him with a murderous look when he winks and blows me a kiss, trying to get inside my head.

When I don't respond, he makes a motion with his hands and shouts he's going to break me. Fucker talks to much, that's his problem and if this is an attempt to get under my skin, it won't work. He can run that mouth of his all of he wants, one good hit from me should take care of it.

Dex and Kingston are both yelling at me to ignore him, but that ain't gonna happen. The referee calls us to the center of the ring to give us our pre-fight instructions when he tells us to touch gloves, we both us refuse.

Before Curtis returns to his side to wait for the fight to begin, he taunts me. "Hot new pussy, Declan? You may want to send her my way tonight since you won't be able do anything but suck your food through a straw. I'll take my time with her, make sure to show her a good time."

Fucker doesn't get it yet, but he will. I've got a world of hurt in store for him, new moves Kingston and I have been practicing for some time. He can talk all he wants, all it does it make me want to hurt him more.

Each second is longer than the one before as Curtis and I are standing in our fighter's stance just waiting to hear the magic words that will start the fight.

Finally, the ref lowers his hand, saying those four magic words. "Let's get it on!"

Like two bulls charging at one another, we meet in the middle of the ring. Curtis immediately drops, wanting to take my legs out and take the fight directly to the mat. He's a wrestler by nature and knows it's his best way to beat me.

Normally, I would do whatever to keep the fight on our feet where I'm stronger and free to land my best blows. To his surprise, I don't back up and try to get free of his hold on my legs. I'm more than ready to fight him where he feels the strongest, because I know it won't be enough to beat me.

I want him at his best, so I can beat the shit out him. I want him to know he gave me his best and still lost.

I'm stronger and quicker than he remembers so when I drop in front of him, I shoot for his back and hyperextend his right arm above his head and bend it back in an armlock. I secure my hand over my wrist and tighten the hold until I hear him grunt in pain. Fucking music to my ears.

He struggles to clear the hold and I ease up on my pressure wanting to prevent that fucker from tapping out and end this too quick. Back on our feet, he jabs with a left that I easily duck but he lands a right that rings my bell.

The loud oooh's from the crowd erupt but I easily recover. He comes at me again with a series of jabs and leg kicks but landing none. He's slow and his timing is way off. He shrugs off each miss clearly letting his frustrations get the better of him.

He leaps forward and locks his arms around my midsection from behind leaning all his weight forward. He cleverly tightens his hold as he hooks one leg around mine using his weight to take me down on one knee. I widen my stance making it more difficult for him while Nero shouts in one ear, and Dex and Kingston in the other. That's when Curtis plows ahead and drives me into the fence.

I can feel his hold slip and when I get a hand around his wrist I hook it behind his back and maneuver my leg to take him down. From the side guard position, with his feet facing me, I securely wrap both of my legs around one of his and secure it behind my back with my arm to hyperextend his knee. The farther I stretch my body back, it pushes his knee to the point of breaking it.

Curtis screams out in pain, but I maintain my hold until I see out of the corner of my eye his hand lift up like he might tap out, and just when I release my hold the bell sounds for the end of the first round.

The second round starts with a series of punishing blows that send Curtis to the mat, dazed and winded. I don't attack, I wait for him to get to his knees so I can continue beating his ass to a pulp. As he stands on wobbly legs and sucking in air, I see so many openings that would end this fight in a hurry, but I'm just not ready to do that yet.

This time as I advance, I get a hold of his arm and twist it back and then drive him to the mat, so he lands on his shoulder. The sweet sound of pain comes in two forms; Curtis screaming and the popping sound of a dislocated shoulder.

The ref temporarily stops the fight so a man from Curtis' team could come out and pop it back into place. After asking Curtis if he's able to continue to fight, I'm right back at it. Punishing him with leg sweeps and jabs until I feel the time is right. With my legs in perfect place I land a perfect upper cut that sent Curtis' head back and his mouth piece flying from his mouth. He was out cold before he hit the mat.

Lights out, motherfucker!

I stand back and watch the ref look him over before declaring the fight was officially over.

While the ref raised my hand in the air, the announcer declared, "With two minutes left in the 2nd round, your winner by KO, Declan 'Reaper' Parisi."

The eruption from the crowd rocks the place as Nero, Dex and Kingston rush inside the cage. Among the frenzy of congrats and high fives, it's a mad house as I make my way to the locker room. I'm on a mission with only one person on my mind. Once I step inside, I spot Piper and Willow across the room chatting. Once she sees me enter her face lights up and I swear it's one of the prettiest smiles I've ever seen. She squeals and runs across the room jumping into my outstretched arms.

"Oh, my God. That was insane. You were amazing."

I don't hesitate, I crush my lips to hers and kiss her like I've wanted to since I left Washington. I've been patient and respectful of her personal boundaries, but I can only take so much. This kiss is raw and savage. I'd like nothing more than take her to the shower room and strip her naked. Since that's impossible, this will have to do.

"Damn straight, he's amazing." Dex ruins the moment as he rushes up and gives us both a giant bear hug.

The locker room got loud real fast once Marcus, Vince and Nero came strolling in laughing, hollering and slapping one another on the back, while Kingston and Willow ran around spraying everyone with champagne.

With the celebration well under way, I take a step back to reflect and take in the scene before me. In that moment, I couldn't help but think back to my conversation with Willow recently. At the time I discounted it, but I don't know, maybe she has a point.

"Remember when I told you that I think everything happens for a reason?" I nod vaguely remembering that conversation, when Willow says, "This right here, me and you, it's fate."

Fate?

"Yep, don't tell me you don't believe in fate. Let me put it this way. Our pasts are tragic in one way or another, and it took an even worse tragedy for our paths to cross and for us to meet. Personally, I'd like to think out of all that pain and really fucked-up shit, you and I are the good that came out of it. That's why we need to stick together. And if that's not enough for you, I've got one better." Her eyes squint mischievously with a wicked grin on her face.

"Oh, do tell." Jesus, I can't wait to hear this.

"If not for me," she says with a twinkle in her eyes, "you never would have met Piper."

"Ahhh, Piper," I lower my head and chuckle. Gotta hand it to her, she's good.

"Yes, Piper," she giggles and nudges my shoulder. "The girl you can't stop checking out whenever she's around. The girl you talk to every day. The girl..."

I lean in the opposite direction, raising my damn brows. "Okay, I get the point. You're nuts, you know that?"

"Yeah, well, they tell me it runs in the family."

Ha. Ha. Ha.

"Willow, I hate to burst you're bubble, but I've always thought of fate as nothing more than one of life's cruel lessons." Out of the corner *of my eye, I see her smile fade.* "I guess I never bought into the fairytales like girls do when it comes to fate."

She studies my face with her brows pulled together and an arm over my shoulder. "Huh, guess I'll just have to change your mind on that then."

And something tells me that she will.

About the Author

HEIDI GREW UP IN THE Midwest, but currently resides with her husband and four children in the Pacific Northwest. Heidi most enjoys spending time outdoors with her family. Between raising her children and obsessing over her favorite reads, she has let the storyteller within herself come to life.

With the love and support of her family, she is following her dream while teaching her children how important it is to follow theirs. She prides herself in believing anything is possible, the first step is believing in yourself.

Heidi's passionate and loving style in which she lives her lives her life comes through in her writing. Her heart has led her down the genre path of a contemporary and suspense romance writer, but she has plans to extend her vision into other genres as well.

Follow the Author:

www.heidilisbooks.com
AMAZON: https://amzn.to/2x746jC
FACEBOOK: https://bit.ly/2s6q0On
TWITTER: https://bit.ly/2GL1g3C
BOOKBUB: https://bit.ly/2KL5Lxg